Witches & Warlocks

Witches & Warlocks

TALES OF BLACK MAGIC, OLD & NEW

Selected by Marvin Kaye

BARNES
&NOBLE
BOOKS
NEW YORK

This edition published by Barnes & Noble, Inc.,
by arrangement with Doubleday Direct

1993 Barnes & Noble Books

ISBN 1-56619-253-6

Printed and bound in the United States of America

M 9 8 7 6 5 4 3

BVG

Acknowledgments

"The Witch" from *Passions and Other Stories* by Isaac Bashevis Singer, translated by Joseph Singer, copyright © 1970, 1973, 1974, 1975 by Isaac Bashevis Singer. Reprinted by permission of Farrar, Straus and Giroux, Inc.

"Moment of Truth" copyright © 1989 by Gerry Levinson. All rights reserved. Printed by permission of the author.

"Fat Chance" copyright © 1988 by Thomas D. Sadler. Reprinted from *Beyond Science Fiction and Fantasy.*

"The Traveler" copyright © 1945; renewed 1973 by Ray Bradbury. Reprinted by permission of Don Congdon Associates, Inc.

"Wizard Crystal" copyright © 1973 by Manus Pinkwater. Reprinted by permission of the author.

"Perfidious Amber" by Tanith Lee first appeared in *Swords of Darkness V,* copyright © 1979 by Andrew J. Offut. Reprinted by permission of the author.

"The Curse of the Wandering Gypsy" copyright © 1989 by Patricia Mullen. All rights reserved. Printed by permission of the author.

"Sanguinarius" copyright © 1967 by Ray Russell. Used by permission of the author.

"Vasilisa and the Witch," English adaptation copyright © 1989 by Marvin Kaye. All rights reserved.

"The Mirror" copyright © 1989 by Margaret Mayo McGlynn. All rights reserved. Printed by permission of the author.

"The Tiger's Eye" copyright © 1962 by the Estate of L. Frank Baum. Reprinted by permission of Robert A. Baum.

"A Smell of Sulphur" copyright © 1981 by Marvin Kaye. All rights reserved.

"The Chaney Legacy" copyright © 1986 by TZ Publications. Reprinted by permission of the author.

"Seeing Them" copyright © 1989 by Phantasm Press. Reprinted by arrangement with the author. First published in *The Horror Show.*

"Doll-Baby" copyright © 1989 by C. H. Sherman. All rights reserved. Printed by permission of the author.

"The Party Animal" copyright © 1989 by Alvin Vogel. All rights reserved. Printed by permission of the author.

"The Up-to-Date Sorcerer" copyright © 1958 by Mercury Press, Inc. Reprinted by permission of the author.

Contents

CONTENTS

Introduction

"Power, alas! naught but misery brings!"
—Thomas Haynes Bayly

"Power, like a desolating pestilence
Pollutes whate'er it touches . . ."
—Percy Bysshe Shelley

Despite these addenda to the familiar dictum that power tends to corrupt and absolute power corrupts absolutely, a dark fascination and drive toward power exist within the human psyche, from the tyrant who bullies an enslaved populace down to those benevolent dictators who rule families and/or corporations in real life and on TV and in films. To study the leadership dynamic of a political party or even a social club is to perceive in varying degree the subtly manipulative character of all power structures. Even that hallowed (and comparatively modern) institution, romantic love, is so fraught with status games as to warrant an entire subcategory of self-help literature that purports to guide us through the tangled ploys of interpersonal domination.

It is therefore reasonable to conclude that practitioners of black magic—adepts, cabalists, conjurers, enchanters, mages, magicians, shamans, sorcerers, warlocks, witch doctors, witches, and wizards—seek to understand and control esoteric knowledge in order to shape their own and their neighbors' destinies. But though their motivation may be essentially the same, the character of those who pursue such arcane paths differs greatly. The priest-magician stood close to the control center of early societies, but by the Middle Ages those skilled in conjuration and divination were more apt to be outcast Gypsies, one or two of whom might rise to the precarious eminence of a Cagliostro or Doctor Faustus (who appears twice in these pages): rebel spirits riskily pursuing their careers at variance to church and state. But the majority of historical (as opposed to literary) witches and warlocks are more apt to be low-status folk with a poignant need to identify with the strength of the horned god, whether in his simpler, anthropomorphic guise or his latter decadent persona, the Devil. Thus, the bourgeois sorcerers described in these pages by W. B. Yeats bring to mind Friedrich Nietzsche's observation that it is only the weak who need to display their alleged puissance. The concept of the Nietzschean *Uebermensch* is generally misunderstood: the "over-man" was conceived as a beneficent leader possessed of such inner strength that he could afford to be *ethically* superior. Had Nietzsche lived, he surely would have regarded Hitler as the supreme *under*man, steeped as he was in cruelty and, not at all coincidentally, astrology, which promised him the power to shape future events. (How depressing that a madman's obsession should be shared by the wife of an American president.)

The price of slaking one's thirst for power is traditionally dear. At best, it is a great drain of vital energy, at worst it allegedly demands the soul's allegiance to Hell . . . and yet the world never wants for witches. A behavioral system that promotes a sense of community and makes its members feel important will always attract participants. (For further discussion, see Appendix I, "The Two Witchcrafts.")

The stories in this anthology are primarily concerned with supernatural power and those who wield it. Though some benevolent mages leaven the mix, and in at least two tales—Robert Bloch's "The Chaney Legacy" and John Tunney's "Light-Headed"—the apparatus of black magic (in theatrical parlance, the props) dominates the action, most of the forty-one entertainments that follow are concerned with malevolent practitioners of the black arts. And if after that you crave more unholy delights, consult Appendix III for a list of other recommended books and films about witches, warlocks, and the rest of their Halloweeny set.

—MARVIN KAYE
New York City, 1988

Witches & Warlocks

The Witch

ISAAC BASHEVIS SINGER

Witches and warlocks are generally associated with Christianity and paganism, but ISAAC BASHEVIS SINGER, *a former resident of Warsaw now living in New York City, is the author of a body of Nobel Prize–winning fiction steeped in the occult traditions of Chasidism, a mystic branch of Polish Judaism that has produced many fine examples of supernatural literature. Singer's work includes such acclaimed works as* The Family Moskat, The Magician of Lublin, The Spinoza of Market Street, *and the following passionate tale of love, guilt, and dark magic.*

"In a culture of pure egotism, how can you call anyone an egotist?" Mark Meitels half thought, half mumbled. But Lena's self-love virtually bedazzled one. Even her own mother spoke of it. All of Mark's friends maintained that Lena was capable of loving only herself. A doctor had once labeled her a narcissist.

Yes, he, Mark Meitels, had made a fatal mistake. But at least he didn't have to fear that Lena would fall in love with someone else.

Now Lena had just finished breakfast. The maid, Stasia, had made up the bedroom, and Lena lay down on the sofa in the living room—a small woman with black hair worn in a high pompadour, black eyes, and high cheekbones. At thirty-seven she still looked like a girl, exactly as she had when he first met her.

Lena refused to have children. She told Mark on frequent occasions that she hadn't the slightest urge to get pregnant and go into labor just so that another brat could wander in the world. It never occurred to her to take a job and help Mark earn a living. Even in bed, she constantly worried him not to disarrange her hairdo, not to wrinkle or tear her silk nightgown. He kissed her tiny mouth but she rarely kissed back.

Now, in her flowered kimono and slippers with pompons, she looked Japanese. Everything about her had remained petite, smooth, and delicate. She reminded Mark of the china dolls sometimes seen in antique-store windows.

"Lena, I'm going."

"Eh? Well, all right."

He bent down to kiss her forehead. Although it was still early in the day, her lips were already heavily rouged. Her fingernails were long, pointed, freshly manicured. She had eaten her breakfast exactly as the doctor had prescribed it for her—an egg, a single slice of bread, and a cup of black coffee. Lena weighed herself several times daily, and if she had gained a quarter of a pound, she promptly took measures to lose it again. She passed the day reading fashion magazines, visiting dressmakers, milliners, and Stanislaw the hairdresser. Occasionally she strolled down Marshalkowska Street window-shopping. She was always on the lookout for bargains and coveted all kinds of trinkets—Mark never understood why—an ivory-inlaid music box that played "Good Morning!", countless strings of imitation pearls in all shades and colors, exotic earrings, bracelets, and chains that could be worn only to a masquerade.

Mark Meitels had long faced the realization that Lena was still a child but without any childish joy—a pampered, angry little girl, ready to pout if something interfered with her whims. "An error, a fatal error," Mark Meitels grunted to himself for the hundredth time. But to divorce such a creature would be impossible. She would get sick and her mother would raise hell. One way or another, he had grown accustomed to her caprices. The apartment was always spotless. Stasia feared Lena and gave in to all her wishes. The floor always gleamed and every stick of furniture was dusted and polished daily. Without lifting a finger herself, Lena ran an exacting household. Fortunately, Stasia was a healthy wench and good-natured besides. She labored from six-thirty in the morning until late into the night and took off only a few hours every other Sunday to go to church or possibly to meet some boy friend.

Mark Meitels was a tall man in his early forties, a teacher of mathematics and physics at a private girls' Gymnasium. He couldn't have existed if he didn't hold down a second job—writing textbooks that were used in the Polish schools and received laudatory reviews in pedagogic journals. Mark Meitels had been an officer in Pilsudski's Legion and had won a medal for heroism in the 1920 Polish-Bolshevik war. He was one of those rare individuals who excel at whatever they undertake. He knew languages, played the piano, rode horseback, and had the reputation of being one of the best teachers in Warsaw. His pupils were infatuated with him, but he avoided all indiscretions. Something of the military lingered in his erect carriage and his entire conduct. He spoke sparingly and to the point. He was courteous toward the school authorities and the students. His chief virtue lay in the fact that he could explain an algebraic formula or geometric theorem to girls who had no aptitude for mathematics. He received frequent offers from other Gymnasium principals but he stayed at the school where he had begun his teaching career.

Now, before leaving the house, Mark Meitels checked himself in the hall mirror. The overcoat hung smoothly on his erect figure, the tie was straight, the derby fit perfectly. Mark Meitels had a long face and nose, full lips, a narrow chin, and big black eyes beneath dark brows. His gaze expressed a sense of discipline and the gravity of one who knows exactly how to behave, and who possessed sufficient inner strength to remain consistent. His friends, male and female, all of whom were in the teaching profession, spoke of him with admiration. Mark Meitels practiced what he preached, kept his temper, avoided all intrigue and lander. After a drink at a party he might become somewhat ironical, but even then he behaved with dignity.

But his failure in marriage was indisputable. True, his mother-in-law was rich and in due course he would inherit her wealth, but for now she was in vigorous health, and stingy besides. The situation in Poland in the early 1930's was such that you couldn't plan too far ahead.

Mark Meitels could easily have had affairs on the side, but as far as anyone could tell, he remained faithful to his wife. It was apparent to everyone that Lena could offer him neither spiritual nor physical satisfaction. In a moment of weakness he had even confided this to an intimate, and the "secret" soon spread. To dissipate his energies, Mark Meitels took long walks. In the summers he swam in the Vistula, and before retiring for the night he lifted weights and gave himself cold rubs. This led to quarrels with Lena, who complained that he wet the bathroom floor and messed up the study.

Actually, Lena wasn't merely his direct opposite but a deadly opponent. If he praised a book, she immediately found fault with it. If a play pleased him, she forced him to leave the theater before the second act. Lena hated mathematics, physics, and everything connected with science. She read the popular novels of Dekobra and Marguerite. She liked sentimental dramas and tragedies. In her thin little voice she sang the hits from the musical *Qui pro Quo* and other revues. She often ordered Stasia to prepare dishes that Mark couldn't stand—bouillons to be sipped out of tiny cups, cakes soggy with cream, too-sweet cocoa. Mark was always hungry after dinner. On his long evening walks across the Praga Bridge as far as Pelcowizna or past Mokotów on the way to Wilanów, he would buy a loaf of pumpernickel or a bag of apples.

Lena's self-love was especially evident in the bedroom. She forbade him to come near her for days preceding and following her period. She didn't like conversation in bed and clamped his mouth shut when he said something she considered unaesthetic. Before going to sleep she spent an hour in front of her mirror conducting various experiments with her hair and anointing, smearing, and perfuming herself. She often said that sexual intercourse was dirty and brutal. She urged him to get it over with quickly, and complained that he was hurting her. If it was true that marriages are made in heaven, Mark often mused, then someone had either erred grievously or played a foul joke on them.

[2]

Mark Meitels always managed to leave the house on time so that he could walk to the Gymnasium. He didn't like the crowded streetcars and wanted to stretch his legs a bit before commencing the lessons.

How odd! He had been born and raised in Warsaw but the city often appeared alien to him. He had little contact with Poles. Although Jews had lived in Poland for eight hundred years, a chasm existed between the two peoples that time couldn't eradicate. However, the Jews were as remote to Mark as the Poles—not only the pious ones with their long gaberdines and small hats, but the modern ones as well. Mark Meitels's father, an assimilated Jew, an architect, a liberal and an atheist, hadn't given his only son any religious training whatsoever. From childhood on, Mark had heard all kinds of mocking remarks about the Hasidim and their rabbis, their filth and fanaticism, but he had never really found out what it was they espoused. After the First World War Jewish nationalism had flourished. The Balfour declaration had been issued and many Chalutzim had sailed off to Palestine. At the Gymnasium where he taught, the curriculum had been enlarged to include more Hebrew studies, but he had never been drawn either to religion or to Palestine, a half-desolate wasteland in Asia Minor. He felt an even stronger aversion against the Jewish Communists and their demonstrations.

His father wouldn't have had any objections had his son converted, but Mark had no interest in Jesus. The assimilated Jews of Warsaw called themselves Poles of Mosaic Faith, but Mark had no faith in anything except scientifically established facts.

Many of his former comrades in the Legion had been issued high military ranks and given important posts in the ministry following Pilsudski's uprising in 1926. Mark Meitels had grown estranged from them and didn't attend their reunions. There was too much brandishing of swords there, and many of them had become anti-Semites. The newspaper, even the semiofficial *Gazeta Polska,* needled the Jewish minority. In Germany the Nazi Party kept gaining new adherents. In Soviet Russia they arrested Trotskyites and sent millions of peasants, so-called kulaks, to Siberia.

Striding along Marshalkowska Street, Mark Meitels felt as if he were a stranger. But where would he feel at home?

Passing Grzybow Place was a source of fresh irritation each day. In the midst of a European capital the Jews had established a ghetto. Women in wigs and bonnets sold rotten fruit, chick-peas with

beans, and potato cakes covered with rags. They hawked their
wares in a gibberish and a whining chant. Men with black or red
beards, stooped shoulders, and heavy boots engaged in surrepti-
tious business. Not infrequently funerals passed by—a black, shiny
hearse, a horse draped in black with holes cut out for the eyes, the
mourners lamenting in shrill voices. Even in Baghdad you couldn't
see such sights, Mark Meitels thought.

In the midst of the whole turmoil, a running and a chasing ensued. Ragged youths with caps pulled down over their eyes had
scrounged up a red flag somewhere and were shouting, "Long live
the Soviet Union! Down with Fascism! All power to the workers
and peasants! . . ." They were pursued by policemen waving guns
and rubber truncheons.

Even the Gymnasium wasn't the same as before. The old teachers
had retired or been dismissed. Others had died. The new teachers
were mostly Jewish nationalists. Teaching most of the girls loga-
rithms and trigonometry served no purpose: their minds weren't on
mathematics, nor would they ever find much use for it. They all
yearned for one thing—to get the diploma so that they could marry
well and have children. Most of them had voluptuously ripened and
their limbs showed an unabashed urge to mate and multiply.

One girl in particular made Mark Meitels feel that all his effort
was for naught. She called herself Bella, but her birth certificate
read Beile Tzypa Zylberstein. Mark taught from the fifth grade up,
and he had the chance to become thoroughly acquainted with his
pupils. Bella came from a poor home. Her father was a clerk in
some store on Gnoyna Street that sold oil and green soap. He had a
half dozen other children at home. The Gymnasium had reduced
her tuition to a minimum, but the father couldn't even pay those
few zlotys. If she had at least been capable! But Bella received the
worst marks. She had gone on to the eight grade, but Mark Meitels
knew that she still didn't grasp the most rudimentary rules of arith-
metic. Actually, she failed in every subject. She had spent two years
each in the sixth and seventh grades and it was obvious to everyone
that she would never graduate.

The principal had called in Bella's parents and had advised that
they enroll her in a vocational school, but they were determined
that their oldest daughter should get a diploma, enter the university, and become a doctor or, at the very least, a dentist.

On top of all this, Bella was ugly—the homeliest girl in the school. Her head was too big for her body, her low brow seemed sunken, her eyes were black and bulging—calf's eyes—her nose curved; her bosom was large, her hips wide, and her legs bowed. Her mother took care that the girl should be decently dressed but whatever Bella wore looked ridiculous. The other girls called her the Freak.

Mark Meitels realized that it was his duty to explain the principles of mathematics to Bella again and again. He began with axioms: Ten groschen added to ten groschen made twenty groschen. If equal numbers were added to each unit of ten groschen, the results would remain equal. If equal numbers were subtracted, they would still remain equal . . . But even though by definition axioms are self-evident truths, Bella still couldn't grasp them. She opened her thick lips, exposing a mouthful of uneven teeth, and smiled in guilty fear, with the submissiveness of an animal trying to grasp human concepts.

But in one area at least Bella was overendowed—that of emotions. She sat on her bench and didn't turn her big black eyes away from Mark. They exuded a love and a reverence like that seen occasionally in a dog's eyes. She followed Meitels with her gaze and her lips repeated every word he uttered. When Mark called her name, she paled and trembled. On the rare occasions he called her to the blackboard, she approached with quaking step and Mark was afraid that she would faint. The piece of chalk fell from her fingers, and the class jeered.

One time Mark Meitels asked her to stay after the others had gone. He tried to give her individual instruction. He sat her down on the bench and began from the beginning. How had primitive man discovered numbers? By ticking off the fingers of his hands . . . Mark took Bella's wrist. Her hand was damp and it shook. Her bosom heaved. She stared at him in fear and in a rapture that astounded him. What can it be she sees in me? he wondered.

He put the tip of his index finger to her pulse. It beat as quickly and strong as in a high fever. Mark asked, "What is it, Bella, are you ill?"

She tore her hand from his and broke out in childish weeping. Within a second her face grew contorted and wet like that of a small girl who has just suffered an unbearable blow.

[3]

Lena frequently doctored herself. She was forever taking medicines. When she said that she wasn't feeling well, Mark didn't take it too seriously, but soon he noticed that her face was assuming a yellow tinge. It soon turned out that she suffered from a grave illness, cancer of the spleen. The doctors didn't tell Lena this, but apparently she gathered that her chances were slim. A team of consulting specialists decided that she should enter the hospital— she couldn't get the help she needed at home—but Lena refused to consider even a private clinic. Her mother came and tried to persuade her to take the doctors' advice, but Lena stuck to her decision and the mother hired a private nurse to care for her at home.

Three women—her mother, Stasia, and the nurse—watched over Lena. A doctor came each day, but she didn't improve. The doctor told Mark the truth—the cancer had spread to the other organs and there was no chance whatsoever.

Mark looked on with amazement as the once-spoiled Lena, who made a fuss when a fingernail broke or a filling fell out of her tooth, now accepted her fate with silence and resignation. She lay in bed in a silk robe, all powdered, rouged, perfumed, coiffed, and manicured, and read the same fashion magazines as before. Her mother brought her the latest Polish and French novels and illustrated magazines both Polish and foreign.

Lena had few girl friends, two or three former schoolmates from the Gymnasium, one of them a cousin, and she wrote a will designating who would get what after her death—the fur coat, the dresses, the jewelry, and the rest of the trinkets.

Only now did Mark Meitels realize that Lena's egotism was actually the instinct of one with insufficient powers who didn't want to dissipate them too soon. One night when they were alone he knelt at her bedside and apologized for his sharp words and reproaches, for the misunderstandings that had evolved in their relationship. Lena stroked his hair (which was already thinning in the middle, the beginning of a bald spot) and said, "You were good to me. It's not your fault. Next time find yourself someone healthier."

"No, Lena, I don't want anyone else."

"Why not? You always yearned for a child, but I didn't want to leave any orphans."

"Does that mean she knew she wouldn't live long?" Mark asked himself later. "Did she live with the knowledge that she would die young?" But how was this possible? Had the doctors told her? Was there something in a person that foresaw the future?

It was all a puzzle—his falling in love with Lena, the alienation that had evolved later between them, the years that had passed without any real intimacy, and the present finale. He might have fallen in love with Lena anew, but she was apparently no longer receptive to sentiment. She grew more rigid, more taciturn, completely absorbed in herself. She demanded he sleep on the sofa in the living room. She grew more preoccupied with the illustrated magazines, the shallow stories about royal courts, American millionaires, and Hollywood film stars. Did this really interest her or was it all merely to forget? Mark Meitels realized that the estrangement between him and Lena would never be eased. It became ever more obvious to him that she wished to avoid him. She never addressed him first, and when he spoke to her, she replied curtly and in such a way that it left nothing more to be said. She didn't even look up from the magazine. She probably felt some resentment against him, but was determined to take it with her to the grave.

The doctor told Mark frankly that all that could be done for her was to keep her drugged to ease her pain until she died.

After a while Lena gave up reading almost entirely. When Mark opened the door to the bedroom he often found her asleep. Other times she lay there with her eyes open, deep in thoughts to which no healthy person could be privy. Gradually she grew indifferent to her appearance, stopped using cosmetics, and no longer spoke on the telephone to her mother.

Lena now seemed to have but one wish—to be left alone. But the visitors kept coming. The girl friends she had named in her will brought flowers, all kinds of delicacies that Lena wouldn't taste, and magazines that no longer interested her. The doctor mouthed the same banalities calculated to encourage the patient: "She drank the soup? Good, fine. She took her pill? Wonderful!" He ordered the window to be opened to let in fresh air. When the nurse announced that she had bathed the patient with cologne, he exclaimed, "Excellent!" If Mark Meitels was home when the doctor came, he would advise him as he was leaving, "Don't neglect your own health. You don't look too well yourself." He told Mark to take vitamins, which were then still something of a novelty in Poland.

During the whole crisis Mark had to continue teaching at the Gymnasium and to finish a textbook on geometry that was scheduled to go to press at a specific date.

The winter passed and spring had come. The girls in the eighth grade now behaved as if the school were some kind of joke. They stopped treating Mark like the teacher, didn't rise when he entered the classroom, and addressed him smilingly, insinuatingly, ironically. They dressed in a provocative way that was forbidden to students. Although they were preparing for their final examinations and spent nights poring over textbooks, they looked on the subjects as if they were merely husks to be cracked and discarded. The core of it all was to find the proper husband, to marry, and to bear children. Their mothers waited impatiently for the satisfaction grandchildren would bring. The fathers yearned to be free of the burden of raising daughters. It seemed to Mark that he had been deceiving these girls all the while and that they had finally uncovered his deception—shapely legs and a chiseled nose were more important than all the Euclidian theorems. The only worth of a diploma was that it might help secure a more favorable match.

The girls looked at Bella just as Lena's friends looked at Lena—as a hopeless case. Bella hadn't the slightest chance of getting her diploma. It was actually a bad mark against the Gymnasium that it had allowed this girl to get as far as the eighth grade. The principal was determined to keep her from taking the final examinations. There were a few other girls in the eighth grade who had received poor marks, but these came from affluent families and were pretty besides. One of them was even engaged, and her fiancé waited outside for her every afternoon.

Mark Meitels avoided looking at Bella. There was no way he could help her. She sat there on the bench and gaped at him, half laughing, half pleadingly, with veneration in her eyes. She had apparently persuaded herself that he could swing things in her favor. But she was wrong. When examination time came around, he would have no choice but to vote against her.

[4]

Lena's final weeks continued to be a gradual decline. The doctors kept her drugged all the while, but she suffered pain nevertheless. Her face had changed almost beyond recognition. It became brown-yellow, congealed, similar to the faces one sees in a wax museum. They prepared pullets for her but she didn't touch them. She was fed medicines, which frequently dribbled out of her mouth. Even when she did say something, her voice was too weak to hear.

Lena waited for death, but death was apparently in no hurry to take her. Her heart went on beating, even if weakly and with hesitation. The other organs still went on functioning too, one way or another.

Lena's mother had never maintained friendly relations with Mark. She felt that her daughter could have done better than to marry a teacher. Since Lena's sickness, the mother had stopped speaking to him altogether. She glared at him and hinted that he was responsible for her daughter's death. He didn't even have enough money for the doctors, medicines, and nurses, and she had to cover all these expenses.

Shortly before the final examinations Lena died. She asked the nurse to turn her toward the wall. The nurse went into the kitchen to boil some water, and when she came back, Lena was gone. Mark didn't take part in the examinations. After the funeral someone from the Gymnasium called to say that Bella hadn't been allowed to take the tests, and of those who had, two had failed to graduate.

The mother-in-law proposed to Mark that he observe the seven days of mourning at her house, but Mark told her that he didn't believe in such rituals. He even declined to say Kaddish over Lena's grave. Why participate in rites in which he didn't believe? What sense did it make to pray to a God who was eternally silent, whose goals could never be established, nor even his existence? If Mark had ever acknowledged that a person possessed a soul, Lena's illness convinced him that this was sheer absurdity. Lena's body disintegrated along with her so-called spirit. During her entire illness, she didn't utter a word to indicate that she was passing over into some other sphere. Well, and what would Lena's soul do even

if it did survive? Again read fashion magazines? Dawdle along Marshalkowska Street window-shopping? On the other hand, if Lena's
soul became different from what it had been here on earth, it would
no longer be Lena's soul! . . . Mark Meitels had heard a lot about
the Polish medium Kluski, at whose séances the dead allegedly left
their palm imprints in a basin of paraffin. He read the essays of the
Polish occultist Professor Ochorowicz, as well as those of Conan
Doyle, Barrett, Sir Oliver Lodge, and Flammarion. He had had
moments when he thought, Maybe yes? After all, what do we know
about nature and her secrets? But Lena's sickness had erased all his
illusions. Nothing remained after her death but a deep emptiness
and the feeling that all was vanity. There wasn't, nor could there
be, any basic difference between Lena and the pullets which had
been prepared for her and which, the following day, were thrown
into the garbage.

Mark Meitels had received a number of condolence letters, tele-
grams, and even a few bouquets of flowers, but hardly anyone came
to pay a consolation call. The teachers had all dispersed for the
summer and Stasia the maid had gone back to her parents' village.
He hadn't a close friend in Warsaw. Out of habit he took long
walks during the day and spent the evenings at home alone. He was
in no hurry to turn on the lights, and sat in the dark. In his childhood he had been afraid of the dead. A funeral would cast a pall
over him. But what did he have to fear from Lena now? Mentally
he called to her: "Lena, if you exist, give me some sign . . ."

At the same time he knew that no sign would be forthcoming.

Strange, but for all his sorrow over Lena's senseless life and premature death, Mark's mind kept turning to Bella. This puzzled him.
What reason did he have to think about some homely girl who was
a dimwit besides? But the moment he stopped sulking about Lena
and her fate, his thoughts inevitably turned to Bella. What was she
doing? How had she taken her failure? Did she know that he had
lost his wife? The other pupils—the pretty, able, and popular ones
—were almost forgotten by him, but Bella's face hovered before
his eyes. In the dark he saw her as if she were present—the narrow
forehead, the humped nose, the thick lips, the great bulging eyes.
In his fantasy he stripped her naked. How loathsome she must be
with her huge breasts, jutting hips, and bowed legs!

This girl bore a streak of madness within her. Within her there laughed and cried out generations of primitive women who lived in caves and struggled against wild animals, lice, hunger, and men—throwbacks to the apes.

For all his preoccupation, Mark had to smile as he recalled how he had tried to teach her mathematics. Intellectually she was thousands of years behind Euclid, but her parents wanted her to become a scholar, no less. What would the parents of such a girl look like? She had to carry someone's genes within her. A strange urge began to take form within Mark Meitels—to seek out Bella. He didn't have her address and such paupers would have no telephone. Her address was surely kept somewhere at the Gymnasium, but it was closed during the vacation. Mark was well aware how pointless all this was. A mourner didn't go to comfort others. And what could he say to her? Her kind was best left to their own devices. Nature, which watched over everything from a bacterium and a bedbug to a whale, would somehow provide for Bella or bring about her perdition, which from a higher standpoint was a kind of provision, too.

Mark told himself that he must put an end to such idle thoughts. Normally he had means of disciplining his mind, but Bella's image wouldn't let itself be shunted aside. Am I going crazy or what? Mark wondered.

One evening he suddenly reminded himself that her father worked in an oil and soap store on Gnoyna Street. Gnoyna was a short street. How many such shops could it contain? However, it was too late by now—all the stores would be closed. Tomorrow . . .

Mark began to pace through the dark rooms filled with a restlessness that baffled him. He was consumed by curiosity about that repulsive girl, along with something akin to passion. "Is this possible? Am I in love with her? It can't be otherwise but that I've lost my senses . . ." He listened in astonishment to the chaos raging within his own brain. For reasons that defied explanation, this Bella obsessed him more and more. He suffered from what might be called an *idée fixe*. At times he had the strange feeling that Bella was calling to him, shouting his name. He saw her with striking clarity, all the curves of her face, the whole deformity of her body. The urge to find her and speak to her grew stronger from minute to minute . . . "I'll walk over to Gnoyna," he decided. "Sometimes they stay open late there . . . Someone might give me the information I need."

Mark rushed to go out. He had the feeling that if he ran he would get there before it was too late. At the same time the sober spirit within him asked, "What's happened to you? Where are you running to? What kind of madness are you heading for?" He slammed the front door, ready to skip down the stairs, when he heard the sharp, insistent ringing of the telephone inside the apartment. "It's she! I've summoned her up with my mind!" he cried to himself.

He grabbed the key to unlock the door again and fumbled momentarily in the keyhole. In the hallway he bumped against a chair and hurt his knee. The phone didn't stop ringing the whole time. When he finally reached the instrument, it became silent. Mark seized the receiver and exclaimed, "Hello? Who is it? Answer! . . ."

He felt a wave of heat and in a flash his body became wet with perspiration. He put down the receiver with a crash and said aloud, "It's she, the beast! . . ."

He was seized by rage and shame. He was no longer Mark Meitels but some superstitious dupe driven by a compulsion or, as it might be described in Jewish terms, possessed by a dybbuk.

[5]

Mark again prepared to leave, this time no longer with the intention of going to Gnoyna Street but to some restaurant for dinner. True, he had lost his appetite, but it made no sense to neglect himself completely. "First thing tomorrow I'll go away some place," he decided. "To Zakopane, or maybe to the seashore . . ." He was half-way to the door when the telephone rang again. He ran up to the instrument in the dark and in a muffled breath exclaimed, "Hello?"

There was a stammering at the other end. Yes, it was Bella. He caught scattered words that lacked cohesion. She was making an effort not to choke on her words. Mark listened in amazement. Would anyone believe this? he wondered. There is such a thing as telepathy. Aloud he asked, "Is this Bella Zylberstein?"

"Teacher recognizes my voice?"

"Yes, Bella, I recognize your voice."

She paused a moment.

"I'm calling because I heard of your tragedy," she went on haltingly. "I'm very sorry . . . The whole class sympathized . . . I myself suffered a misfortune, but compared to yours—" She grew silent.

Mark asked, "Where are you?"

"Eh? On Prosta Street . . . That's where we live."

"You have a phone at home?"

"No, I'm speaking from a delicatessen store."

"Maybe you'd like to come over to my place?"

An oppressive silence ensued; then she said with a flutter in her voice, "If that is Teacher's wish . . . It would be a great honor for me . . . Teacher could never know how much—"

And she did not finish the sentence.

"Come over and don't call me Teacher any more."

"What shall I call you?"

"Whatever you want. It can be simply Mark."

"Oh, Teacher is joking. I felt so sorry . . . I suffered terribly for you . . . The idea that—"

Mark gave her precise instructions on how to get to his house. She thanked him again and again. She kept repeating how she had suffered in his behalf. "Terribly, terribly. Simply day and night . . ."

After a while Mark hung up the receiver.

"Well, what kind of madness is this?" he asked himself. "Is it telepathy, hypnotism? It certainly was no coincidence. I must be careful with this girl," he warned himself. "Her kind go off their head immediately." He switched on the light. "She'll probably be hungry and I'll have to offer her something." He went into the kitchen and began to rummage about in the pantry. He seldom ate at home since Lena's death, and all he could find now was a stale loaf of bread and several cans of sardines. "I'll take her down some place," he decided. But where? One of his acquaintances was liable to drop in and spot him. He was ashamed to be seen with a girl so soon after Lena's death—especially one so ugly. There was an unwritten law at the Gymnasium that teachers must never fraternize with a student. "I'll bring up some rolls and sausage," he finally decided.

He went downstairs, bought sausage, rolls, and fruit. He hurried lest Bella come too early (assuming she took a taxi) and found no one at home. What if Lena's soul is here and sees what I'm doing? it occurred to him. If there can be such a thing as telepathy, why can't souls linger on after death? . . . No, it has to be that from all my troubles I've simply lost my reason.

He waited a long time, but no one came. Earlier he had lit all the lights in the living room, then put them out again, leaving only a small lamp burning. He sat down on the sofa and cocked his ears for any sound at the front door. She might have gotten lost. She was hopelessly ineffectual in every respect . . .

The doorbell resounded in a long, piercing ring. Mark ran to open it and found Bella in a black dress and a straw hat. She carried a bouquet of flowers. She seemed older. She was perspiring and out of breath.

He said, "Oh, flowers! For me?"

"Yes, for you . . . you shouldn't know of any more grief," she said, translating the Yiddish expression into Polish.

Mark took her wrist and led her into the living room. He put the flowers in a pot and ran water into it. Where did she get money for flowers? he wondered. Probably spent her last groschen . . . I'll be nice to her, but I dare not give her even the slightest hope! he warned himself.

Bella took off her hat and it struck Mark for the first time that she had pretty hair. It was chestnut-colored, thick, and exuded a natural gleam. She sat on a chair and looked down at her feet in the black shoes and stockings. She seemed ashamed of her clumsy appearance —the overblown bosom, the wide hips, the hawk nose, the popping eyes. No, those aren't calf eyes, Mark decided. They're reflecting fear and a love as old as the female species itself.

She kept both her hands on her purse—hands too big for a schoolgirl. Mark noticed that they were stained with ink, as if she had just come from the Gymnasium. She said, "We heard about everything that happened and the whole class was beside itself . . . The others couldn't go to the funeral because it was during examination time, but I wasn't allowed to take them . . . But surely Teacher didn't notice me?"

"Eh? No. Unfortunately I didn't."

"Yes, I was there."

"What are you doing now?"

"Oh, what can I do? Everyone in the house is disappointed in me. Bitterly so. Wasted all that money on me for nothing, and all the rest. After all, the diploma isn't everything. I did learn something—literature, history, a little drawing. I'll never be any good at mathematics. It's a lost cause."

"You can be a good person without mathematics."

"Maybe. I'm looking for some kind of work, but everyone in the house says that without a diploma you can't get a job. There was an ad for a girl to work in the chocolate store and I went there. They said it was already filled. They didn't ask about any diploma."

"Our grandmothers had no diplomas either, but they were pretty good women."

"Of course. My mother can't read the Yiddish paper, yet they wanted to make a doctor out of me. I don't have the knack for it."

"What would you like to do—marry and have children?"

Bella's eyes filled momentarily with laughter. "Yes, that, but who would have me? I love children. I love them terribly. It wouldn't have to be my own children. I would take a widower with children and I would raise them as if they were my own. Even better—"

"Why not have your own children?"

"Oh, I'm only saying that. Naturally that would be better, but—"

It became quiet. A clock tolled in the other room.

"Maybe I could do something for Teacher?" Bella asked. "I can sweep, dust, wash—everything. But nothing for pay, God forbid!"

"Why would you work for me for nothing?" Mark asked.

Bella thought it over a moment and a smile showed on her lips. Her eyes looked at him—black and burning. "Oh, I would do anything for Teacher. As they say in Yiddish, Wash the feet and drink the water . . ."

[6]

Mark came up and put his hands on her shoulders. His knees pressed against hers. He asked, "Is what you just said the truth?"

"Yes, the truth."

"Do you love me that much?"

"More than anything in the world."

"More than your parents?"

"Much more."

"Why?"

"Oh, I don't know. Because Teacher is wise and I'm a dumb cow. When Teacher smiles, it's so interesting, and when he is stern, he draws up his brows and everything is somehow so—" She didn't finish. Heat emanated from her, the warmth one feels occasionally standing next to a horse.

Mark asked, "Can I do with you what I want?"

"Anything."

"Slit your throat?" he asked, astounded at his own words.

Bella trembled. "Yes! The blood would gush and I'd kiss the blade . . ."

He was overcome by a lust such as he hadn't felt in years, perhaps never. "Don't do anything stupid!" an inner voice warned. "Send her straight home!" Aloud he said, "Good, I'm going for the knife."

"Yes."

He went into the kitchen, opened a pantry drawer in the dark, and took a knife out from among the utensils. He realized full well that it was all a game, yet he was possessed by a sense of grave earnestness. He came back with the knife. Bella sat in the chair, her face pale, her eyes full of expectation. A pagan ecstasy exuded from her, an eagerness that frightened him.

He said, "Bella, you'll soon be dead. Say what you have to say."

"I love you."

"Are you ready to die?"

"Yes, ready."

He put the blade to her throat. "Shall I slash?"

"Yes."

Mark put the knife down deliberately on the dresser. He recalled the story from the Bible in which God ordered Abraham to slay his son Isaac and the Angel cried out: "Lay not thy hand upon the lad . . ." It was all like a repetition of something that had happened before.

"How long has this love of yours lasted?" he asked in the grave tone of a doctor treating a dangerously ill patient. He sensed the rattling of his own teeth.

"From the day I first saw you."

"The whole time?"

"Day and night."

He stood still and listened to his own breathing. His nose snorted of its own volition. He said, "You knew, after all, that I had a wife."

Bella didn't answer for a long time. "Yes, I knew, but I put a curse on her. That's why she died."

"What are you, a witch?"

"Yes, a witch."

At that moment it struck Mark that Bella looked just like the pictures and carvings of witches in ancient volumes. All she lacked were the elflocks and the wrinkles. Well, those witches hadn't been born old, either. They had probably started practicing sorcery in their youth. Mark told himself that this was all superstition, but Lena's death *had* been a mystery. Even the doctors had said that her illness had been puzzling, flaring up as suddenly as it did. Lena had observed all the rules of hygiene. She ate no fat foods, she didn't smoke, or drink alcohol. The cancer had spread incredibly fast. Mark reminded himself now of what Lena had said: "Someone has cursed me. They envied my good fortune . . ."

The ecstasy dimmed in Bella's eyes and she looked at him gravely, with preoccupation and anxiety.

He said, "I don't believe in such junk. It's all nonsense. But since you do believe it, from your standpoint you murdered a person."

"True. God will punish me for it."

"Did you think that I would marry you?"

"I didn't know myself."

"How did you put a curse on her?"

"Oh, I wished for her death. I woke up in the middle of the night and prayed for her to die."

"You didn't even know her."

"I did know her. I've already been here many times before. Not in the house, but outside. I waited till she looked out the window. One time I rang the door and asked her if she needed a maid. She said, 'I wouldn't take in anyone from the street,' and she slammed the door in my face."

"Wasn't what you did crazy?"

"Yes, crazy."

Mark glanced toward the dresser, where he had put down the

knife. "You deserve to die, but I'm no murderer. In that respect I'm still a Jew. But I'll never have anything to do with you. Go and never come back. You can put a curse on me, too."

"No, I'll bless you to my dying breath."

Bella made a gesture as if to rise, but she remained seated.

Mark said, "That means all you babbled about sympathy was nothing but lies. You were glad she died."

"No. I didn't know I possessed such powers. When I heard the news I became flabbergasted and—"

"You're a stupid ass, that's what you are," Mark said, not certain where his tongue would lead him. "Had you put your mind to your studies instead, you might have gotten your diploma. What will become of you now? You see me today for the last time. I loved Lena dearly, and from now on I'll hate you as I would a spider."

Bella's face drained of color. "And I will go on loving you till I'm in my grave."

"It's all idiocy, hysteria."

"No."

"Did you try calling me earlier this evening?" Mark asked. "I had started out and the phone rang. By the time I got to it, it was too late. Was that you?"

"Yes."

"Why this evening of all times?"

"Oh, I had to."

"It's all self-delusion. You're still stuck back somewhere in the Middle Ages. I'm beginning to understand why they burned witches. Those like you deserve to die. You actually look like a witch," he said, regretting his own words.

"Yes, I know."

"Well, I don't mean that for real. Are you ready to become my lover?" he asked, bewildered at his own words. "I mean a mistress, not a wife. I'd be ashamed to be seen with you in the street. I'm completely frank with you."

Something like anger and mockery flashed in Bella's eyes. "You can do what you want with me."

"When?"

"Now . . ."

[7]

At three o'clock in the morning Bella began to get dressed. A
red lamp gleamed in the bedroom. Mark was too tired to help her.
He lay in bed with one eye closed and watched her struggling to fit
her bosom into the dress. At twenty, her pendulous breasts dangled. Her stomach was wide and bloated. Black hair sprouted on
her belly. The hips bulged at either side like two basins. Her hair
fell over her short brow and crooked nose. The protruding eyes
looked out, frightened, like hunted animals from between bushes.

A witch, a witch! Mark said to himself. He wouldn't have believed that this young girl, and a virgin besides, could fall into such
a frenzy. She had clawed at his flesh, bitten his shoulders, spoken
strange words, and cried in such a wild voice that he was afraid it
might rouse his neighbors. He had sworn to marry her. "How
could this happen? Have I lost my mind? Can there really be such a
thing as black magic?" Mark heard Bella say, "Mother will kick up
such a fuss! They might have called the police by now. No doubt of
it. If only the janitor will open the gate for me!"

"Do you have any change?"

"Eh? No, I spent it on the taxi."

"There is change in my pants pocket."

"Where are your pants? There they are, on the floor. . . ."

She picked up his pants and went through the pockets. Mark
looked on agape. She was acting like a wife already. "Well, I'm
finished," he decided.

Bella took out a few coins and laid the trousers carefully out on
the dresser. She ambled around on her hairy legs. How can such
large feet fit into women's shoes? Mark wondered. He heard Bella
ask, "What shall I tell Mama and Papa? They'll make a frightful
scandal!"

"Tell them whatever you want."

"If you have any regrets, I can go straight to the Vistula and put
an end to it," Bella said.

"I have no regrets."

"Life to me isn't worth two groschen. I can go where your wife
is. She'll take revenge upon me in any case."

"The dead can't take revenge," Mark said in a dull voice.

"They can, they can. She came to me in a dream. She held a dagger and a kerchief full of blood. She screamed at me and spat—"

Mark didn't answer. He had had other women in his life but none who had exhausted him like this girl. She was undoubtedly impregnated, too. He had forgotten to take precautions. Well, this is suicide, he thought. Everything within him filled with a sense of wonder. How had it all come about? What had happened to his reason? All Warsaw would ridicule him. He wouldn't be able to stay on at the Gymnasium. The pupils would laugh in his face.

Bella said, "Well, I'll be going. At least take me to the door."

He got out of bed and shuffled after her. How odd she looked in the black dress and straw hat with the tousled hair dangling from underneath! He took her hand, which was damp and hot. She stood so close to him that she pressed him with her bosom. She said, "If only I didn't have to go home. They will make me miserable. Do you really love me? I beg you, don't deceive me. If it was nothing more than a lark to you, say so."

"What for? So that you can run to the Vistula?"

"That means that it was all a big lie!"

"Bella, I can't marry you."

It grew quiet. In the dimness of the early morning he could see only her eyes. They reflected something mad and savage. He was afraid she would spring at him like some animal and he was too weak now to defend himself.

She said, "Well, all right. It's all over. Good night."

"Where are you going?"

"What's that to you? But don't think badly of me. The way I love you, no one will ever love you again."

"Bella, I beg you, don't do anything foolish!"

"Death isn't foolishness."

"Bella, stay here!" he cried. It was no longer he, Mark Meitels speaking, but some force that had the final say. He went on: "We can't stay here in Warsaw, but there's a big world out there. We'll go to Kraków, or maybe even abroad. I heard one can still get a visa to Cuba or Honduras. What does it matter so long as we are together."

"I'm ready to follow you to the end of the world."

They stood in the dark, brooding. Bella's breath came heavy and hot. He was overcome with a fresh passion.

"Come back!"

"Wait. Mama has a weak heart. She's liable to die from worry."

"She won't die. And if she does, too bad!"

"You sweet murderer of mine!"

"You really are a witch, aren't you?"

"Yes, but don't tell anybody."

"How do you do it?"

"Oh, I pray to God, or maybe it's to the devil. I don't know myself who I pray to. I lie in bed and it just comes out of me. You can't untangle yourself from me and that's the truth. We're like two dogs locked together . . ."

"Come back!"

"If you want us to run away from Warsaw, let's do it right now," she said.

"This minute?"

"Today."

"I have furniture. Books."

"Leave everything behind. Mama and Papa will die of worry, but since I've already murdered one person, what difference does it make?"

"They don't have to die. We'll telegraph them from the road."

"Well, all right. From that first day in the fifth grade, when you came in to give the math lesson, I started wanting you, and a minute hasn't gone by that I haven't thought of you. Where is Honduras, in Africa?"

"You've studied geography, you should know."

"I don't remember a thing. For the whole four years I studied only you, nothing else."

"Come!"

He took her around and they stumbled back to the bedroom, past the living room. The sun had risen and it cast a red glow through the windows. Bella's face seemed to be bathed in blood. Clusters of fire ignited within her eyes. He stood by her, half naked, and they stared into a mirror.

He said, "If there is such a thing as black magic, maybe there is a God, too."

He couldn't wait to get to the bedroom and pushed her down onto the rug—a witch drenched in blood and semen, a monster that the rising sun transformed into a beauty.

Translated by Joseph Singer

Moment of Truth

GERRY LEVINSON

GERRY LEVINSON, *a former Wisconsinite and till recently an arts development executive for a New York philanthropic organization, now serves in a similar capacity with the ASCAP Foundation. In the following short-short story, she grants the reader a hellish glimpse of witchcraft at the end of the world.*

Cassandra was raising the bowl high above her head when it happened. Flames seared her flesh, reaching around from her back, climbing up her arms, her neck, leaping high from her head only to be constantly replaced by new flames at her feet. She knew then that the final conflict was over. The world as she knew it was vanishing, burning in a final conflagration of nuclear fire. The curse she spoke in the church that day long ago was coming true.

Laughter burst out of her mouth to join the flames, climbing up toward the heavens, carrying her message of joy and triumph. No women priests. Hah. She was powerful, invincible. She commanded the flames to begin, and they did.

She watched as the walls of the room caught fire and turned to ashes. The coven, standing below her in two semicircles, followed. She watched, the moment lengthening for her alone, as one after the other of her followers was seared, burned, and eliminated. They didn't have her spells of protection.

She had enjoyed developing her power and control over them, and was sorry to see the faithful die. Especially Allen. So amusing. Such a pretty boy. She planned to introduce him to some of the deeper mysteries later that night. Now, it was too late. Really a shame, she thought, watching him vanish. They might have been together in eternity.

Rebecca, her acolyte, was the last. She had more power than the others, of course, and held off the flames long enough to look once at Cassandra. But her plea for help came too late. Haunted by the despair in her eyes, Cassandra continued to see it long after Rebecca's ashes were consumed by the flames.

As she stood waiting, her hands still holding the bowl high, Cassandra wondered at the stillness of the moment. It should be done, she thought. By now her pain should be over, the firestorm should have passed her by, consuming the trappings of that paternalistic world which so needed to be ended. Her victory over it should be complete.

She looked around, peering through the flames which still seared her body. There was nothing left of the room, the building, her coven. All was consumed, even the earth. She stood on charred rock. Yet the flames still burned her flesh. The world's pain was ended, but hers continued. This wasn't how it was supposed to be.

From a short distance away, her familiar stared at her, his green eyes the narrowest of slits against the brilliance of the flames still licking at her. Always a handsome cat, his black fur was still sleek, and he rested his paws on the charred rock without any apparent pain at the heat. No flames touched his body.

She knew her familiar was a powerful demon, but until this moment didn't realize how powerful. When he first appeared in her apartment, materializing in front of her as a result of her spell, she named him Beelzebub for Satan's most powerful assistant, and bound him to her will with another ancient spell, held to his earthly shape by a silken collar he wore. Now she saw that the collar was gone, burned away with all the rest of the material world. Humbled, she realized that he must have used his power to enhance hers, making her more powerful. Making her able to cast the spell that destroyed the world.

The flames burned. She knew without looking that her robe was gone. All that was left of the world in this place was the bowl, Beelzebub, and herself.

Beelzebub watched her, watched the flames licking at her flesh. She was aware of searing pain, the flames burning her body never-endingly.

Beelzebub changed before her eyes. The familiar cat shape blurred, expanded, and re-formed. She saw the demon as he really was. Beelzebub. Himself. In truth. She saw his malicious smile as he slowly vanished, returning to his own realm, to his true Master, his horrible eyes watching the flames searing her body, his smile lingering in her mind long after she could no longer see him.

The old folktales were wrong. She knew that now. The witch's existence did not end with her familiar. Beelzebub was gone from this world, but she remained.

The flames burned, but they didn't consume. Her spells of invulnerability and everlasting life were holding.

And then she knew. The priest was right when he cast her out of the church that day long ago.

She would burn in hellfire forever.

The Magic Shop

H. G. WELLS

H. G. WELLS (1866–1946), the prolific British fantasist, wrote a body of oft-dramatized novels and short stories, among them The Invisible Man, The Time Machine, The Island of Dr. Moreau, The War of the Worlds, and The Food of the Gods. Wells may well have been acquainted with retail establishments devoted to the sale of professional conjuring equipment, but the shop described in the following tale presumably caters to a somewhat different clientele.

I had seen the Magic Shop from afar several times; I had passed it once or twice, a shop window of alluring little objects, magic balls, magic hens, wonderful cones, ventriloquist dolls, the material of the basket trick, packs of cards that *looked* all right, and all that sort of thing, but never had I thought of going in until one day, almost without warning, Gip hauled me by my finger right up to the window, and so conducted himself that there was nothing for it but to take him in. I had not thought the place was there, to tell the truth —a modest-sized frontage in Regent Street, between the picture shop and the place where the chicks run about just out of patent incubators—but there it was sure enough. I had fancied it was down nearer the Circus, or round the corner in Oxford Street, or even in Holborn; always over the way and a little inaccessible it had been,

with something of the mirage in its position; but here it was now
quite indisputably, and the fat end of Gip's pointing finger made a
noise upon the glass.

"If I was rich," said Gip, dabbing a finger at the Disappearing
Egg, "I'd buy myself that. And that"—which was The Crying Baby,
Very Human—"and that," which was a mystery, and called, so a
neat card asserted, "Buy One and Astonish Your Friends."

"Anything," said Gip, "will disappear under one of those cones.
I have read about it in a book.

"And there, dadda, is the Vanishing Halfpenny—only they've
put it this way up so's we can't see how it's done."

Gip, dear boy, inherits his mother's breeding, and he did not
propose to enter the shop or worry in any way; only, you know,
quite unconsciously he lugged my finger doorward, and he made
his interest clear.

"That," he said, and pointed to the Magic Bottle.

"If you had that?" I said; at which promising inquiry he looked
up with a sudden radiance.

"I could show it to Jessie," he said, thoughtful as ever of others.

"It's less than a hundred days to your birthday, Gibbles," I said,
and laid my hand on the door-handle.

Gip made no answer, but his grip tightened on my finger, and so
we came into the shop.

It was no common shop this; it was a magic shop, and all the
prancing precedence Gip would have taken in the matter of mere
toys was wanting. He left the burthen of the conversation to me.

It was a little, narrow shop, not very well lit, and the door-bell
pinged again with a plaintive note as we closed it behind us. For a
moment or so we were alone and could glance about us. There was
a tiger in *papier-mâché* on the glass case that covered the low counter
—a grave, kind-eyed tiger that waggled his head in a methodical
manner; there were several crystal spheres, a china hand holding
magic cards, a stock of magic fish-bowls in various sizes, and an
immodest magic hat that shamelessly displayed its springs. On the
floor were magic mirrors; one to draw you out long and thin, one
to swell your head and vanish your legs, and one to make you short
and fat like a draught; and while we were laughing at these the
shopman, as I suppose, came in.

At any rate, there he was behind the counter—a curious, sallow, dark man, with one ear larger than the other and a chin like the toe-cap of a boot.

"What can we have the pleasure?" he said, spreading his long, magic fingers on the glass case; and so with a start we were aware of him.

"I want," I said, "to buy my little boy a few simple tricks."

"Legerdemain?" he asked. "Mechanical? Domestic?"

"Anything amusing?" said I.

"Um!" said the shopman, and scratched his head for a moment as if thinking. Then, quite distinctly, he drew from his head a glass ball. "Something in this way?" he said, and held it out.

The action was unexpected. I had seen the trick done at enter-tainments endless times before—it's part of the common stock of conjurers—but I had not expected it here. "That's good," I said, with a laugh.

"Isn't it?" said the shopman.

Gip stretched out his disengaged hand to take this object and found merely a blank palm.

"It's in your pocket," said the shopman, and there it was!

"How much will that be?" I asked.

"We make no charge for glass balls," said the shopman, politely. "We get them"—he picked one out of his elbow as he spoke—"free." He produced another from the back of his neck, and laid it beside its predecessor on the counter. Gip regarded his glass ball sagely, then directed a look of inquiry at the two on the counter, and finally brought his round-eyed scrutiny to the shopman, who smiled. "You may have those too," said the shopman, "and if you *don't* mind, one from my mouth— *So!*"

Gip counselled me mutely for a moment, and then in a profound silence put away the four balls, resumed my reassuring finger, and nerved himself for the next event.

"We get all our smaller tricks in that way," the shopman re-marked.

I laughed in the manner of one who subscribes to a jest. "Instead of going to the wholesale shop," I said. "Of course, it's cheaper."

"In a way," the shopman said. "Though we pay in the end. But not so heavily—as people suppose. . . . Our larger tricks, and our daily provisions and all the other things we want, we get out of that hat. . . . And you know, sir, if you'll excuse my saying it, there *isn't* a wholesale shop, not for Genuine Magic goods, sir. I don't know if you noticed our inscription—the Genuine Magic shop." He drew a business-card from his cheek and handed it to me. "Genuine," he said, with his finger on the word, and added, "There is absolutely no deception, sir."

He seemed to be carrying out the joke pretty thoroughly, I thought.

He turned to Gip with a smile of remarkable affability. "You, you know, are the Right Sort of Boy."

I was surprised at his knowing that, because, in the interests of discipline, we keep it rather a secret even at home; but Gip received it in unflinching silence, keeping a steadfast eye on him.

"It's only the Right Sort of Boy gets through that doorway."

And as if by way of illustration, there came a rattling at the door, and a squeaking little voice could be faintly heard. "N yar! I *warn* a' go in there dadda, I WARN 'a go in there. Nya-a-a-ah!" and then the accents of a down-trodden parent, urging consolations and propitiations. "It's locked, Edward," he said.

"But it isn't," said I.

"It is, sir," said the shopman, "always—for that sort of child," and as he spoke we had a glimpse of the other youngster, a small, white face, pallid from sweet-eating and over-sapid food, and distorted by evil passions, a ruthless little egotist, pawing at the enchanted pane. "It's no good, sir," said the shopman, as I moved, with my natural helpfulness, doorward, and presently the spoilt child was carried off howling.

"How do you manage that?" I said, breathing more freely.

"Magic!" said the shopman, with a careless wave of the hand, and behold! sparks of coloured fire flew out of his fingers and vanished into the shadows of the shop.

"You were saying," he said, addressing himself to Gip, "before you came in, that you would like one of our 'Buy One and Astonish your Friends' boxes?"

Gip, after a gallant effort, said "Yes."

"It's in your pocket."

And leaning over the counter—he really had an extraordinarily long body—this amazing person produced the article in the customary conjurer's manner. "Paper," he said, and took a sheet out of the empty hat with the springs; "string," and behold his mouth was a string-box, from which he drew an unending thread, which when he had tied his parcel he bit off—and, it seemed to me, swallowed the ball of string. And then he lit a candle at the nose of one of the ventriloquist's dummies, stuck one of his fingers (which had become sealing-wax red) into the flame, and so sealed the parcel. "Then there was the Disappearing Egg," he remarked, and produced one from within my coat-breast and packed it, and also The Crying Baby, Very Human. I handed each parcel to Gip as it was ready, and he clasped them to his chest.

He said very little, but his eyes were eloquent; the clutch of his arms was eloquent. He was the playground of unspeakable emotions. These, you know, were *real* Magics.

Then, with a start, I discovered something moving about in my hat—something soft and jumpy. I whipped it off, and a ruffled pigeon—no doubt a confederate—dropped out and ran on the counter, and went, I fancy, into a cardboard box behind the *papier-mâché* tiger.

"Tut, tut!" said the shopman, dexterously relieving me of my headdress; "careless bird, and—as I live—nesting!"

He shook my hat, and shook out into his extended hand two or three eggs, a large marble, a watch, about half-a-dozen of the inevitable glass balls, and the crumpled, crinkled paper, more and more and more, talking all the time of the way in which people neglect to brush their hats *inside* as well as out, politely, of course, but with a certain personal application. "All sorts of things accumulate, sir. . . . Not *you*, of course, in particular. . . . Nearly every customer. . . . Astonishing what they carry about with them. . . ." The crumpled paper rose and billowed on the counter more and more and more, until he was nearly hidden from us, until he was altogether hidden, and still his voice went on and on. "We none of us know what the fair semblance of a human being may conceal, sir. Are we all then no better than brushed exteriors, whited sepulchres—"

His voice stopped—exactly like when you hit a neighbour's gramophone with a well-aimed brick, the same instant silence, and the rustle of the paper stopped, and everything was still. . . .

"Have you done with my hat?" I said, after an interval.

There was no answer.

I stared at Gip, and Gip stared at me; and there were our distortions in the magic mirrors, looking very rum, and grave, and quiet. . . .

"I think we'll go now," I said. "Will you tell me how much all this comes to? . . .

"I say," I said, on a rather louder note, "I want the bill; and my hat, please."

It might have been a sniff from behind the paper pile. . . .

"Let's look behind the counter, Gip," I said. "He's making fun of us."

I led Gip round the head-wagging tiger, and what do you think there was behind the counter? No one at all! Only my hat on the floor, and a common conjurer's lop-eared white rabbit lost in meditation, and looking as stupid and crumpled as only a conjurer's rabbit can do. I resumed my hat, and the rabbit lolloped a lollop or so out of my way.

"Dadda!" said Gip, in a guilty whisper.

"What is it, Gip?" said I.

"I *do* like this shop, dadda."

"So should I," I said to myself, "if the counter wouldn't suddenly extend itself to shut one off from the door." But I didn't call Gip's attention to that. "Pussy!" he said, with a hand out to the rabbit as it came lolloping past us; "Pussy, do Gip a magic!" and his eyes followed it as it squeezed through a door I had certainly not remarked a moment before. Then this door opened wider, and the man with one ear larger than the other appeared again. He was smiling still, but his eye met mine with something between amusement and defiance. "You'd like to see our showroom, sir," he said, with an innocent suavity. Gip tugged my finger forward. I glanced at the counter and met the shopman's eye again. I was beginning to think the magic just a little too genuine. "We haven't *very* much time," I said. But somehow we were inside the showroom before I could finish that.

"All goods of the same quality," said the shopman, rubbing his flexible hands together, "and that is the Best. Nothing in the place that isn't genuine Magic, and warranted thoroughly rum. Excuse me, sir!"

I felt him pull at something that clung to my coat-sleeve, and then I saw he held a little, wriggling red demon by the tail—the little creature bit and fought and tried to get at his hand—and in a moment he tossed it carelessly behind a counter. No doubt the thing was only an image of twisted indiarubber, but for the moment—! And his gesture was exactly that of a man who handles some petty biting bit of vermin. I glanced at Gip, but Gip was looking at a magic rocking-horse. I was glad he hadn't seen the thing. "I say," I said, in an undertone, and indicating Gip and the red demon with my eyes, "you haven't many things like *that* about, have you?"

"None of ours! Probably brought it with you," said the shopman —also in an undertone, and with a more dazzling smile than ever. "Astonishing what people *will* carry about with them unawares!" And then to Gip, "Do you see anything you fancy here?"

There were many things that Gip fancied there.

He turned to this astonishing tradesman with mingled confidence and respect. "Is that a Magic Sword?" he said.

"A Magic Toy Sword. It neither, bends, breaks, nor cuts the fingers. It renders the bearer invincible in battle against anyone under eighteen. Half-a-crown to seven and sixpence, according to size. These panoplies on cards are for juvenile knights-errant and very useful—shield of safety, sandals of swiftness, helmet of invisibility."

"Oh, dadda!" gasped Gip.

I tried to find out what they cost, but the shopman did not heed me. He had got Gip now; he had got him away from my finger; he had embarked upon the exposition of all his confounded stock, and nothing was going to stop him. Presently I saw with a qualm of distrust and something very like jealousy that Gip had hold of this person's finger as usually he has hold of mine. No doubt the fellow was interesting, I thought, and had an interestingly faked lot of stuff, really *good* faked stuff, still—

I wandered after them, saying very little, but keeping an eye on this prestidigital fellow. After all, Gip was enjoying it. And no doubt when the time came to go we should be able to go quite easily.

It was a long, rambling place, that showroom, a gallery broken up by stands and stalls and pillars, with archways leading off to other departments, in which the queerest-looking assistants loafed and stared at one, and with perplexing mirrors and curtains. So perplexing, indeed, were these that I was presently unable to make out the door by which we had come.

The shopman showed Gip magic trains that ran without steam or clockwork, just as you set the signals, and then some very, very valuable boxes of soldiers that all came alive directly you took off the lid and said— I myself haven't a very quick ear and it was a tongue-twisting sound, but Gip—he has his mother's ear—got it in no time. "Bravo!" said the shopman, putting the men back into the box unceremoniously and handing it to Gip. "Now," said the shopman, and in a moment Gip had made them all alive again.

"You'll take that box?" asked the shopman.

"We'll take that box," said I, "unless you charge its full value. In which case it would need a Trust Magnate—"

"Dear heart! *No!*" and the shopman swept the little men back again, shut the lid, waved the box in the air, and there it was, in brown paper, tied up and—*with Gip's full name and address on the paper!*

The shopman laughed at my amazement.

"This is the genuine magic," he said. "The real thing."

"It's almost too genuine for my taste," I said again.

After that he fell to showing Gip tricks, odd tricks, and still odder the way they were done. He explained them, he turned them inside out, and there was the dear little chap nodding his busy bit of a head in the sagest manner.

I did not attend as well as I might. "Hey, presto!" said the Magic Shopman, and then would come the clear, small "Hey, presto!" of the boy. But I was distracted by other things. It was being borne in upon me just how tremendously rum this place was; it was, so to speak, inundated by a sense of rumness. There was something vaguely rum about the fixtures even, about the ceiling, about the floor, about the casually distributed chairs. I had a queer feeling that whenever I wasn't looking at them straight they went askew, and moved about, and played a noiseless puss-in-the-corner behind my back. And the cornice had a serpentine design with masks— masks altogether too expressive for proper plaster.

Then abruptly my attention was caught by one of the odd-looking assistants. He was some way off and evidently unaware of my presence—I saw a sort of three-quarter length of him over a pile of toys and through an arch—and, you know, he was leaning against a pillar in an idle sort of way doing the most horrid things with his features! The particular horrid thing he did was with his nose. He

did it just as though he was idle and wanted to amuse himself. First
of all it was a short, blobby nose, and then suddenly he shot it out
like a telescope, and then out it flew and became thinner and thinner until it was like a long, red, flexible whip. Like a thing in a
nightmare it was! He flourished it about and flung it forth as a fly-
fisher flings his line.

My instant thought was that Gip mustn't see him. I turned about,
and there was Gip quite preoccupied with the shopman, and thinking no evil. They were whispering together and looking at me. Gip
was standing on a stool, and the shopman was holding a sort of big
drum in his hand.

"Hide and seek, dadda!" cried Gip. "You're He!"

And before I could do anything to prevent it, the shopman had
clapped the big drum over him.

I saw what was up directly. "Take that off," I cried, "this instant!
You'll frighten the boy. Take it off!"

The shopman with the unequal ears did so without a word, and
held the big cylinder towards me to show its emptiness. And the
stool was vacant! In that instant my boy had utterly disappeared! . . .

You know, perhaps, that sinister something that comes like a
hand out of the unseen and grips your heart about. You know it
takes your common self away and leaves you tense and deliberate,
neither slow nor hasty, neither angry nor afraid. So it was with me.

I came up to this grinning shopman and kicked his stool aside.

"Stop this folly!" I said. "Where is my boy?"

"You see," he said, still displaying the drum's interior, "there is
no deception—"

I put out my hand to grip him, and he eluded me by a dexterous
movement. I snatched again, and he turned from me and pushed
open a door to escape. "Stop!" I said, and he laughed, receding. I
leapt after him—into utter darkness.

Thud!

"Lor' bless my 'eart! I didn't see you coming, sir!"

I was in Regent Street, and I had collided with a decent-looking
working man; and a yard away, perhaps, and looking extremely
perplexed with himself, was Gip. There was some sort of apology,
and then Gip had turned and come to me with a bright little smile,
as though for a moment he had missed me.

And he was carrying four parcels in his arm!

He secured immediate possession of my finger.

For the second I was rather at a loss. I stared round to see the door of the magic shop, and, behold, it was not there! There was no door, no shop, nothing, only the common pilaster between the shop where they sell pictures and the window with the chicks! . . .

I did the only thing possible in that mental tumult; I walked straight to the kerbstone and held up my umbrella for a cab.

" 'Ansoms," said Gip, in a note of culminating exultation.

I helped him in, recalled my address with an effort, and got in also. Something unusual proclaimed itself in my tail-coat pocket, and I felt and discovered a glass ball. With a petulant expression I flung it into the street.

Gip said nothing.

For a space neither of us spoke.

"Dadda!" said Gip, at last, "that *was* a proper shop!"

I came round with that to the problem of just how the whole thing had seemed to him. He looked completely undamaged—so far, good; he was neither scared nor unhinged, he was simply tremendously satisfied with the afternoon's entertainment, and there in his arms were the four parcels.

Confound it! what could be in them?

"Um!" I said. "Little boys can't go to shops like that every day."

He received this with his usual stoicism, and for a moment I was sorry I was his father and not his mother, and so couldn't suddenly there, *coram publico*, in our hansom, kiss him. After all, I thought, the thing wasn't so very bad.

But it was only when we opened the parcels that I really began to be reassured. Three of them contained boxes of soldiers, quite ordinary lead soldiers, but of so good a quality as to make Gip altogether forget that originally these parcels had been Magic Tricks of the only genuine sort, and the fourth contained a kitten, a little living white kitten, in excellent health and appetite and temper.

I saw this unpacking with a sort of provisional relief. I hung about in the nursery for quite an unconscionable time. . . .

That happened six months ago. And now I am beginning to believe it is all right. The kitten had only the magic natural to all kittens, and the soldiers seem as steady a company as any colonel could desire. And Gip—?

The intelligent parent will understand that I have to go cautiously with Gip.

But I went so far as this one day. I said, "How would you like your soldiers to come alive, Gip, and march about by themselves?"

"Mine do," said Gip. "I just have to say a word I know before I open the lid."

"Then they march about alone?"

"Oh, *quite,* dadda. I shouldn't like them if they didn't do that."

I displayed no unbecoming surprise, and since then I have taken occasion to drop in upon him once or twice, unannounced, when the soldiers were about, but so far I have never discovered them performing in anything like a magical manner. . . .

It's so difficult to tell.

There's also a question of finance. I have an incurable habit of paying bills. I have been up and down Regent Street several times, looking for that shop. I am inclined to think, indeed, that in that matter honour is satisfied, and that, since Gip's name and address are known to them, I may very well leave it to these people, whoever they may be, to send in their bill in their own time.

Fat Chance

THOMAS D. SADLER

THOMAS D. SADLER *is a municipal employee who resides with his wife, children ("two of each kind"), and pets ("cats and goldfish") in a small town some sixty-five miles southwest of Detroit. In his spare time, he writes fantasy and science fiction that has appeared in several periodicals, includ-ing* Beyond, Dark Starr, *the* Minnesota Review, *and* Starsong. *"Fat Chance" is an amusing tale whose moral might have been expressed by Cardinal Wolsey in Shakespeare's* Henry VIII: *"O, how wretched is that poor man that hangs on princes' favours . . . unless he be a canny wiz-ard!"*

The last thing the Duke of Armburster expected to see from his balcony that sunny morning was a fair-sized army encamped outside his castle. As he looked at the men massed below, the Duke franti-cally searched his memory for instances where he might have of-fended someone in the past. But he couldn't come up with anything which could have provoked something as serious as an army. Had he been a man of less substance he might have run back inside and hidden under his bed and tried to wish the army away. But the Duke of Armburster liked to think he was made of much sterner stuff. After making sure he hadn't imagined the army, the Duke returned to his chambers and summoned the captain of his castle guard.

"What's the meaning of that mob of people out there, Skrenk?" the Duke bellowed at the stick-thin, quavering man who slunk into the room. "Why wasn't I told of it?"

"How should I know, sir?" Skrenk nervously stroked his slicked-down black hair. "I thought perhaps they were friends of yours."

"An entire army? Never mind. Go down there and find out what they want."

"M-me, sir?" Skrenk turned white.

"Yes. You. You are captain of my household guard. If you want to remain the captain you'll do as you were told."

"Yes, sir. Right away, Duke." Skrenk backed out the door and softly closed it.

The Duke dressed quickly, muttering to himself as he did. When he was done he went out onto the balcony to see what was going on. The army was still there, as he feared, and from the look of it intended to stay for a long time. Armburster leaned over the railing and glared down at the strange soldiers. After a moment, he saw Skrenk creeping out to where the largest tent stood with a small group of men outside it. The man looked thoroughly terrified, as usual.

"I think I'll have to look for a more courageous captain," the Duke muttered. "That one looks as if he'll die of fear."

Armburster watched as Skrenk finally reached the tent and got the attention of the tallest knight in the group. The man, clad in gleaming armor, looked down at the cowering Skrenk and said something.

Although he knew he was too far away, the Duke leaned out as far as he could to hear what was going on. He saw Skrenk waving his arms and pointing at the castle. The knight listened intently for a few seconds, then looked up in the Duke's direction. To the Duke's dismay and alarm, the man drew his sword and pointed it at the balcony. Armburster backed into his chamber and locked the balcony door.

"I don't like the looks of this at all," the Duke said as he wiped his face with a corner of his bedsheet. But then the memory of all his illustrious Armburster ancestors dropped into his mind. They would never stand for a coward in their midst, no matter what the situation. He couldn't let them down, no matter what.

"Very well," the Duke said aloud to his mirror and the portly figure therein. "I'll defend my castle as well as I can." He almost leaped over the mirror at a loud knock on the door. "Come in," he said when his breathing was normal.

Skrenk, still pale and shaking, entered. His head was bowed and he was breathing hard. The Duke gave the man a few seconds to near a normal state.

"Well, did you find out what that army's doing out there?"

"Yes, Duke. Their commander told me they're on their way to Carlonga to join with another army. It seems Carlonga is going to war with Aspeldia and our King has consented to help the Carlongans out."

"Is that all? I wish them luck. Let's go to breakfast. I'm starved."

"Uh—your pardon, Duke. There's one more thing."

"Out with it so I can get to breakfast."

"The Commander brought a letter from King Luthvig. It's for you. He said the King requests that you and some of your best fighting men go along with the army."

"He what?" The Duke turned white and fell backward onto his bed, then quickly sat up. "Let me see that letter!" He snatched the missive out of Skrenk's trembling hands and hastily read it. "This is disastrous! I've got to get out of it somehow. Do you have any ideas?"

"Me, sir?"

"There's no one else in the room! Help me come up with a way to get out of this or I will personally see to it that you're put in the very front when the fighting starts."

"I'll do my very best. Would you like to take your breakfast first?"

"No. I've lost my appetite. Wait! Is that magician still here? The one who supposedly fell off the parapet and broke both his legs?"

"Yes, Duke. You gave him a room in the west wing."

"Fetch him here, then. Maybe he'll know of some way to help me."

"I'll get him right away, sir. It won't take long." Bowing and scraping, Skrenk backed out of the room and fled back to the main portion of the castle.

While he waited, the Duke crept to one of the windows and peeped out. The army was still there. He had never fought a battle in his life and didn't want to start this late in life. The Duke went to the window one last time and looked out.

"Go away," he shouted down at the army. But he knew he was too high up for anyone to hear him.

Fifteen minutes later there was a hesitant knock on the door and a moment later it slowly swung open. Skrenk tiptoed in, followed by a very fat man with long blond hair who was dressed in a shabby navy-blue robe. There was a slight smile on this man's face. The Duke turned to look at them.

"There you are—uh . . ."

"Blouch, Duke Armburster," the magician said. "Your captain here told me you have a problem and need my help."

"I do indeed. Did he tell you what it is?"

"He was babbling and crying a lot, but, yes, I managed to get the substance of it.

"Well, can you do anything?"

"I might be able to. Of course, I would expect some sort of payment for my services."

"Naturally. What would you like? Gold, silver, jewels?"

"Nothing like that. I understand you have a fine collection of rare decorated dragon's eggs. That's what I want in payment."

"My dragon's egg collection!" The Duke clutched at his stomach. "Not that! Do you know how much it's worth?"

"Will you be able to enjoy it while you're away fighting?" Blouch countered. "Of course, you could take it with you into battle if you've a mind to."

"Very well! If you can get me out of this mess, the collection is yours, curse you."

"A very wise decision, Duke. Shall we go to my rooms? My magical books and such are there."

"Yes. Yes! The sooner the better." The Duke took one last look out the window and shuddered at the army below. "This had better work or you'll also be joining that army down there."

"A most distressing thought," Blouch said as he led the Duke and Skrenk down the narrow, winding passages in the castle.

"I haven't been in this part of the castle in some time," the Duke

observed as he followed the others into Blouch's two-room suite.
"Well, Grouch, what do we do first?"

"The name is Blouch, Duke. All you have to do is wait while I
search my books for a suitable spell. Amuse yourself however you
wish. It shouldn't take me long."

The Duke nodded as Blouch waddled into the next room. While
he waited, the Duke looked around. Lush tapestries covered the
walls, and a huge canopied bed stood on one side of the room with
an ornate armoire nearby.

"I had no idea I gave this fellow such a nice place to stay, Skrenk.
It's almost as nice as my own chambers."

"He brought all these things himself when he moved in here,
Duke."

"Indeed? It looks as if the fellow planned on staying here quite
some time."

"You did promise he could live here the rest of his life."

"I did what? No. I don't want to know."

Just then Blouch re-entered with a triumphant smile on his face.

"I think I have it. Come into the next room with me, please.
Skrenk can come too if he wants."

Feeling lighthearted, the Duke strode into the next room. Skrenk
was close behind him with a terrified look on his face and trembling
worse than ever. Blouch brought up the rear.

The next room was lit by eight tall, fat candles in wall sconces as
well as by a four-candle lamp suspended from the ceiling. A large
workbench with a thick, scarred top sat directly under the ceiling
light. Another, narrower bench stood along the rear wall. A large
locked cabinet stood against another wall, with a small forge close
by. There was a reddish glow in the forge, and thin tendrils of
smoke curled in the air above it.

"All right, magician, what do I do now?"

"Lie down on the table here while I work my spell. Do you think
you can manage that?"

"With great ease. Uh—has it been cleaned off? Is there any—uh
—anything unpleasant on it?"

"It's clean. I made sure of it. If you want me to help, you'll have
to do as I say."

"Very well. There's no need to become so upset."

"I'm not upset. I just want to get this over with."

"No more than I do." The Duke hopped onto the table backward and lay down. "This table smells funny, like dead fish on a hot day. Do you eat your dinner on it, or what?"

"No. I take my meals in the kitchen. Now be quiet or I'll forget the whole thing."

"I wonder what the weather is like where that army is going," the Duke mused aloud. "I know someone who'll find out firsthand. I'll bet it's hot there this time of year."

Blouch sighed but said nothing. He gathered up several bottles, emptied their contents into a large stone bowl, and mixed them all together with an obsidian stirrer. Using what resembled a gigantic eyedropper, he outlined the Duke with the liquid. Next he unlocked the cabinet, removed a long-necked bottle, and poured purple powder all over the Duke.

"What is that stuff?" the Duke demanded. "It smells worse than the table."

"What it is is none of your business. Be silent. I need quiet for the last part of this for it to work properly."

The Duke clamped his mouth shut and watched Blouch. The magician took four large, fat candles the color of slime and put one on each side of the Duke's head and the remaining two at his feet. Finally, he lit the candles with a taper taken from the forge. They burned with a vile green color, and the smoke they emitted was the same color.

"I'm not sure I want to go through with this now," the Duke said nervously as the smoke curled around him like long, thin fingers reaching for his face and throat.

"Silence," Blouch hissed. "Another word and I'll take away your power of speech." He nodded with satisfaction when the Duke bit his upper lip to keep quiet. Slowly circling the table, Blouch chanted an eerie rhyme which made the Duke sleepy.
Several moments later he gave in and dozed off.

Duke Armburster awoke some time later and looked around. The candles had gone out and the smoke was gone. Blouch stood nearby reading a small, dusty book. There was no sight of Skrenk. The Duke sat up.

"I fell asleep," he said unnecessarily. "How long was I out?"

"Not very long. Less than an hour. You may get down now."

"It's about time." The Duke swung his legs over the side of the table and stood. "I don't feel any different. Are you sure the spell worked?"

"Oh yes. Trust me. It may take a little while for it to take full effect, but it did work."

"I'll take your word for it. By the way, where's Skrenk?"

"He was beginning to look ill, so I sent him from the room. My spells sometimes have that effect."

"Oh no! Does that mean I'm disfigured? Let me have a mirror. I want to see how I look."

"I assure you that you look the same as always."

Duke Armburster thought that statement over for a moment, then decided to let it pass. He ran from the magician's chambers in search of Skrenk. He found the other man standing just outside the main entrance looking as if he had eaten or smelled something that had turned his stomach. Skrenk straightened at the sight of the Duke.

"It's finally over? And you're all right!"

"Of course I am. I feel great. Why shouldn't I?"

"Because of the—uh—smoke, the fire, the smell, all those strange noises the magician was making. I thought that maybe you'd—uh—never mind."

The Duke looked at Skrenk curiously, then went back into the castle. The first thing he did was return to his chambers to change his clothes. He gave the ones he'd worn during the spell to one of the servants with instructions to burn them. Then he and Skrenk went to one of the watchtowers to see what the army was doing. All the while, Skrenk kept a close, furtive eye on the Duke as if he expected the man to turn into a demon or something foul.

Nothing noteworthy happened. The Duke watched the soldiers drilling until he grew tired of the sight and his stomach told him it was lunchtime. By the time they reached the dining hall, the Duke decided he was feeling different in some way.

He looked down at his plate and suddenly realized how hungry he was. He picked up a knife and began eating. The Duke cleaned his plate and called for more food. While he waited for a second portion he nibbled away on a loaf of bread.

Skrenk stood by, his stomach gnawing at him in hunger, and tried to get up the courage to ask the Duke's leave to go eat his own lunch. He watched in amazement as the Duke wolfed down a second helping and summoned a third. It looked as if the Duke hadn't eaten in over a month. The sight of the Duke's gluttony only increased Skrenk's hunger. When the third plate of food arrived, Skrenk quietly slipped off to the kitchen to get something to eat before it was all gone. Duke Armburster never noticed Skrenk's absence.

The next two days were unbelievable to Skrenk. He watched the Duke eat enough for three men but gain enough weight for six men. Duke Armburster was too busy eating to connect his increased appetite with Blouch's spell. By the time the day came for the army to leave, the Duke was so fat his sides scraped when he went through doorways. His appetite had eased up somewhat by then, but it was too late to help his weight.

On the morning of the day the army was to leave, Duke Armburster rolled out of his broken bed and waddled over to his armoire. By that time, none of his clothes fit. The best he could do was wrap a bedsheet around himself. He summoned Skrenk to have his horse ready, then slowly, laboriously, he waddled down to the castle's front gate.

"I know I'll never make it onto that horse," the Duke muttered as he crept down the stairs, hugging the wall for support. "But I'll put on a good show for them. Curse that Blouch character—this is not what I had in mind to protect me."

Duke Armburster finally waddled out the main entrance and into the bright sunlight. Skrenk stood nearby holding onto the Duke's horse. The animal whinnied and backed away when it saw the huge shape coming at it. Skrenk clutched the reins tightly and tried to keep the animal calm.

"Keep him good and still, Skrenk," the Duke puffed. "I want to make this look good."

While Skrenk desperately fought to control the horse, Duke Armburster tried to climb onto it. Naturally the attempt drew a lot of attention from the soldiers. They watched the Duke's repeated efforts and failures until at last the commander couldn't take it any longer. He strode up to the Duke, put his fists on his hips, and glanced at the porcine man.

"Stop it, fool. You've put the horse through enough torment. I don't know how you managed it but it's obvious you're unfit for military service in that condition. There's no way you can go into battle like that. I don't think we can use you."

The Duke hesitated not at all.

"Skrenk, put my horse back in its stall. And put my armor away; I won't be needing it." The Duke turned to leave, then stopped and looked over a shoulder with a wide grin on his face. Finally, he waddled back toward his castle.

After passing through the main entrance, he headed straight for the dining hall. "Skrenk, find that magician fellow. I need to cut a new deal with him."

The relieved but still nervous guard captain scurried off on his usual errand while Armburster sat down to his usual breakfast of two dozen eggs, five pounds of smoked ham, a peck of boiled potatoes, and three loaves of bread.

A few minutes later Blouch appeared and stood at the far end of the table. "You wanted to see me, Duke?"

"Yes, Blouch. As you doubtless know from Skrenk, I'm not going with that army, thanks to you. You held up your end of the bargain admirably."

"I try to do the best I can, Duke."

"I'm sure you do—especially when the reward is high enough. But that's neither here nor there. You can do one more thing for me: remove this spell so I can get back to normal."

"I'd like to, Duke Armburster, I really would. But, you see, well, I can't."

"You what?" The Duke roared, standing up and shoving the table ahead with his huge stomach.

"Just what I said. I can't remove the spell because there isn't any counterspell. That was a curse I put on you, and people generally don't remove curses."

"Does that mean I'm going to be like this for the rest of my life? No. It can't be!"

Blouch shrugged. "That's the way things happen sometimes. At least you'll never have to worry about going into the army."

"Or doing much of anything else either." Armburster dropped into his chair, which promptly collapsed. He ignored his current position and buried his face in his hands. "There must be a way to get me back to normal. There must be."

"I can always look for a way," Blouch said with an evil leer, "for a price."

The Traveler

RAY BRADBURY

In this age of instant renown and fast-to-follow obscurity, the fame of RAY
BRADBURY *has deservedly grown with each passing year. His poignant
and poetic imaginative fiction includes such popular science-fantasy as* The
Martian Chronicles, Fahrenheit 451, The Illustrated Man, I Sing the
Body Electric, Something Wicked This Way Comes, *and* The Octo-
ber Country, *a revised version of his first collection of supernatural stories,*
Dark Carnival. *But quite a few entries in that scarce volume published by
Arkham House were not reprinted in* The October Country; *one such
tale is "The Traveler," in which Bradbury introduces Cecy, the April
Witch. (For further information, see Appendix II, page 520.)*

Father looked into Cecy's room just before dawn. She lay upon her
bed. He shook his head uncomprehendingly and waved at her.

"Now, if you can tell me what good she does, lying there," he
said, "I'll eat the crepe on my mahogany box. Sleeping all night,
eating breakfast, and then lying on top her bed all day."

"Oh, but she's so helpful," explained Mother, leading him down
the hall away from Cecy's slumbering pale figure. "Why, she's one
of the most adjustable members of the Family. What good are your
brothers? Most of them sleep all day and do nothing. At least Cecy
is *active.*"

They went downstairs through the scent of black candles; the black crepe on the banister, left over from the Homecoming some months ago and untouched, whispering as they passed. Father unloosened his tie, exhaustedly. "Well, we work nights," he said. "Can we help it if we're—as you put it—old-fashioned?"

"Of course not. Everyone in the Family can't be modern." She opened the cellar door; they moved down into darkness arm in arm. She looked over at his round white face, smiling. "It's really very lucky I don't have to sleep *at all.* If you were married to a night-sleeper, think what a marriage it would be! Each of us to our own. None of us the same. All wild. That's how the Family goes. Some times we get one like Cecy, all mind; and then there are those like Uncle Einar, all wing; and then again we have one like Timothy, all even and calm and normal. Then there's you, sleeping days. And me, awake all and all of my life. So Cecy shouldn't be too much for you to understand. She helps me a million ways each day. She sends her mind down to the greengrocers for me, to see what he sells. She puts her mind inside the butcher. That saves me a long trip if he's fresh out of good cuts. She warns me when gossips are coming to visit and talk away the afternoon. And, well, there are six hundred other things—!"

They paused in the cellar near a large empty mahogany box. He settled himself into it, still not convinced. "But if she'd only contribute more," he said. "I'm afraid I'll have to ask her to find some sort of work."

"Sleep on it," she said to him. "Think it over. You may change your mind by sunset."

She was closing the lid down on him. "Well," he said, thoughtfully. The lid closed.

"Good morning, dear," she said.

"Good morning," he said muffled, enclosed, within the box.

The sun rose. She hurried upstairs to make breakfast.

Cecy Elliott was the one who Traveled. She seemed an ordinary eighteen year old. But then none of the Family looked like what they were. There was naught of the fang, the foul, the worm or wind-witch to them. They lived in small towns and on farms across the world, simply, closely re-aligning and adapting their talents to the demands and laws of a changing world.

Cecy Elliott awoke. She glided down through the house, humming. "Good morning, Mother!" She walked down to the cellar to recheck each of the large mahogany boxes, to dust them, to be certain each was tightly sealed. "Father," she said, polishing one box. "Cousin Esther," she said, examining another, "here on a visit. And—" she rapped at a third, "Grandfather Elliott." There was a rustle inside like a piece of papyrus. "It's a strange, cross-bred family," she mused, climbing to the kitchen again. "Night siphoners and flume-fearers, some awake, like Mother, twenty-five hours out of twenty-four; some asleep, like me, 59 minutes out of 60. Different species of sleep."

She ate breakfast. In the middle of her apricot dish she saw her mother's stare. She laid the spoon down. Cecy said, "Father'll change his mind. I'll show him how fine I can be to have around. I'm family insurance; he doesn't understand. You wait."

Mother said, "You were inside me awhile ago when I argued with Father?"

"Yes."

"I thought I felt you looking out my eyes," the mother nodded.

Cecy finished and went up to bed. She folded down the blankets and clean cool sheets, then laid herself out atop the covers, shut her eyes, rested her thin white fingers on her small bosom, nodded her slight, exquisitely sculptured head back against her thick gathering of chestnut hair.

She started to Travel.

Her mind slipped from the room, over the flowered yard, the fields, the green hills, over the ancient drowsy streets of Mellin Town, into the wind and past the moist depression of the ravine. All day she would fly and meander. Her mind would pop into dogs, sit there, and she would feel the bristly feels of dogs, taste ripe bones, sniff tangy-urined trees. She'd hear as a dog heard. She forgot human construction completely. She'd have a dog frame. It was more than telepathy, up one flue and down another. This was complete separation from one body environment into another. It was entrance into tree-nozzling dogs, men, old maids, birds, children at hopscotch, lovers on their morning beds, into workers asweat with shoveling, into unborn babies pink, dream-small brains.

Where would she go today? She made her decision, and went!

When her mother tiptoed a moment later to peek into the room, she saw Cecy's body on the bed, the chest not moving, the face quiet. Cecy was gone already. Mother nodded and smiled.

The morning passed. Leonard, Bion and Sam went off to their work, as did Laura and the manicuring sister; and Timothy was dispatched to school. The house quieted. At noon time the only sound was made by Cecy Elliott's three young girl-cousins playing Tisket Tasket Coffin Casket in the back yard. There were always extra cousins or Uncles or grand-nephews and night-nieces about the place; they came and went; water out a faucet, down a drain.

The Cousins stopped their play when the tall loud man banged on the front door and marched straight in when Mother answered.

"That was Uncle Jonn!" said the littlest girl, breathless.

"The one we hate?" asked the second.

"What's he want?" cried the third. "He looked mad!"

"*We're* mad at *him,* that's what," explained the second, proudly. "For what he did to the Family sixty years ago, and seventy years ago and twenty years ago."

"Listen!" They listened. "He's run upstairs!"

"Sounds like he's cryin'."

"Do grown-ups cry?"

"Sure, silly!"

"He's in Cecy's room! Shoutin'. Laughin'. Prayin'. Cryin'. He sounds mad, and sad, and fraidy-cat, all together!"

The littlest one made tears, herself. She ran to the cellar door. "Wake up! Oh, down there, wake up! You in the boxes! Uncle Jonn's here and he might have a cedar stake with him! I don't want a cedar stake in my chest! Wake up!"

"Shh," hissed the biggest girl. "He hasn't a stake! You can't wake the Boxed People, anyhow. Listen!"

Their heads tilted, their eyes glistened upward, waiting.

"Get off the bed!" commanded Mother, in the doorway.

Uncle Jonn bent over Cecy's slumbering body. His lips were misshaped. There was a wild, fey and maddened focus to his green eyes.

"Am I too late?" he demanded, hoarsely, sobbing. "Is she gone?"

"Hours ago!" snapped Mother. "Are you blind? She might not

be back for days. Sometimes she lies there a week. I don't have to feed the body, she finds sustenance from whatever or whoever she's in. Get away from her!"

Uncle Jonn stiffened, one knee pressed on the springs.

"Why couldn't she wait?" he wanted to know, frantically, looking at her, his hands feeling her silent pulse again and again.

"You heard me!" Mother moved forward curtly. "She's not to be touched. She's got to be left as she is. So if she comes home she can can get back in her body exactly right."

Uncle Jonn turned his head. His long hard red face was pocked and senseless, deep black grooves crowded the tired eyes.

"Where'd she go? I've *got* to find her."

Mother talked like a slap in the face. "I don't know. She has favorite places. You might find her in a child running along a trail in the ravine. Or swinging on a grape vine. Or you might find her in a crayfish under a rock in the creek, looking up at you. Or she might be playing chess inside an old man in the court-house square. You know as well as I she can be anywhere." A wry look came to Mother's mouth. "She might be vertical inside me now, looking out at you, laughing, and not telling you. This might be her talking and having fun. And you wouldn't know it."

"Why—" He swung heavily around, like a huge pivoted boulder. His big hands came up, wanting to grab something. "If I *thought*—"

Mother talked on, casual quiet. "Of course she's *not* in me, here. And if she was there'd be no way to tell." Her eyes gleamed with a delicate malice. She stood tall and graceful, looking upon him with no fear. "Now, suppose you explain what you want with her?"

He seemed to be listening to a distant bell, tolling. He shook his head, angrily, to clear it. Then he growled. "Something . . . inside me . . ." He broke off. He leaned over the cold, sleeping body. "Cecy! come back, you hear! You can come back if you want!"

The wind blew softly through the high willows outside the sun-drifted windows. The bed creaked under his shifted weight. The distant bell tolled again and he was listening to it, but Mother could not hear it. Only he heard the drowsy summer-day sounds of it, far far away. His mouth opened obscurely:

"I've a thing for her to do to me. For the past month I've been kind of going—insane. I get funny thoughts. I was going to take a train to the big city and talk to a psychiatrist but he wouldn't help. I know that Cecy can enter my head and exorcise those fears I have. She can suck them out like a vacuum cleaner, if she wants to help me. She's the only one can scrape away the filth and cobwebs and make me new again. That's why I need her, you understand?'' he said, in a tight, expectant voice. He licked his lips. "She's *got* to help me!''

"After all you've done to the Family?" said Mother.

"I did nothing to the Family!"

"The story goes," said Mother, "that in bad times, when you needed money, you were paid a hundred dollars for each of the Family you pointed out to the law to be staked through the heart."

"That's unfair!" he said, wavering like a man hit in the stomach. "You can't prove that. You lie!"

"Nevertheless, I don't think Cecy'd want to help you. The Family wouldn't want it."

"Family, Family!" He stomped the floor like a huge, brutal child. "Damn the Family! I won't go insane on their account! I need help, God damn it, and I'll get it!"

Mother faced him, her face reserved, her hands crossed over her bosom.

He lowered his voice, looking at her with a kind of evil shyness, not meeting her eyes. "Listen to me, Mrs. Elliott," he said. "And you, too, Cecy," he said to the sleeper. "If you're there," he added. "Listen to this." He looked at the wall clock ticking on the far, sun-drenched wall. "If Cecy isn't back here by six o'clock tonight, ready to help clean out my mind and make me sane, I'll—I'll go to the police." He drew himself up. "I've got a list of Elliotts who live on farms all around and inside Mellin Town. The police can cut enough new cedar stakes in an hour to drive through a dozen Elliott hearts." He stopped, wiped the sweat off his face. He stood, listening.

The distant bell began to toll again.

He had heard it for days. There was no bell, but he could hear it ringing. It rang now, near, far, close, away. Nobody else could hear it save himself.

He shook his head. He shouted to cover the sound of those bells, shouted at Mrs. Elliott. "You heard me?"

He hitched up his trousers, tightened the buckle clasp with a jerk, walked past Mother to the door.

"Yes," she said. "I heard. But even I can't call Cecy back if she doesn't want to come. She'll arrive eventually. Be patient. Don't go running off to the police—"

He cut her. "I can't wait. This thing of mine, this noise in my head's gone on eight weeks now! I can't stand it much longer!" He scowled at the clock. "I'm going. I'll try to find Cecy in town. If I don't get her by six—well, you know what a cedar stake's like. . . ."

His heavy shoes pounded away down the hall, fading down the stairs, out of the house. When the noises were all gone, the mother turned and looked, earnestly, painfully, down upon the sleeper.

"Cecy," she called, softly, insistently. "Cecy, come home!"

There was no word from the body. Cecy lay there, not moving, for as long as her mother waited.

Uncle Jonn walked through the fresh open country and into the streets of Mellin Town, looking for Cecy in every child that licked an ice-pop and in every little white dog that padded by on its way to some eagerly anticipated nowhere.

The town spread out like a fancy graveyard. Nothing more than a few monuments, really—edifices to lost arts and pastimes. It was a great meadow of elms and deodars and hackmatack trees, laid out with wooden walks you could haul into your barn at night if the hollow sound of walking people irked you. There were tall old maiden houses, lean and narrow and wisely wan, in which were spectacles of colored glass, upon which the thinned golden hair of age-old bird nests sprouted. There was a drug shop full of quaint wire-rung soda fountain stools with plywood bottoms, and the memorious clear sharp odor that used to be in drug stores but never is any more. And there was a barber emporium with a red-ribboned pillar twisting around inside a chrysalis of glass in front of it. And there was a grocery that was all fruity shadow and dusty boxes and the smell of an old Armenian woman, which was like the odor of a rusty penny. The town lay under the deodar and mellow-leaf trees, in no hurry, and somewhere in the town was Cecy, the one who Traveled.

Uncle Jonn stopped, bought himself a bottle of Orange Crush, drank it, wiped his face with his handkerchief, his eyes jumping up and down, like little kids skipping rope. I'm afraid, he thought. I'm afraid.

He saw a code of birds strung dot-dash on the high telephone wires. Was Cecy up there laughing at him out of sharp bird eyes, shuffling her feathers, singing at him? He suspicioned the cigar store Indian. But there was no animation in that cold, carved, tobacco-brown image.

Distantly, like on a sleepy Sunday morning, he heard the bells ringing in a valley of his head. He was stone blind. He stood in blackness. White, tortured faces drifted through his inturned vision.

"Cecy!" he cried, to everything, everywhere. "I know you can help me! Shake me like a tree! Cecy!"

The blindness passed. He was bathed in a cold sweating that didn't stop, but ran like a syrup.

"I know you can help," he said. "I saw you help Cousin Marianne years ago. Ten years ago, wasn't it?" He stood, concentrating.

Marianne had been a girl shy as a mole, her hair twisted like roots on her round ball of head. Marianne had hung in her skirt like a clapper in a bell, never ringing when she walked; just swithering along, one heel after another. She gazed at weeds and the sidewalk under her toes, she looked at your chin if she saw you at all—and never got as far as your eyes. Her mother despaired of Marianne's ever marrying or succeeding.

It was up to Cecy, then. Cecy went into Marianne like fist into glove.

Marianne jumped, ran, yelled, glinted her yellow eyes. Marianne flickered her skirts, unbraided her hair and let it hang in a shimmery veil on her half-nude shoulders. Marianne giggled and rang like a gay clapper in the tolling bell of her dress. Marianne squeezed her face into many attitudes of coyness, merriment, intelligence, maternal bliss, and love.

The boys raced after Marianne. Marianne got married.

Cecy withdrew.

Marianne had hysterics; her *spine* was gone!

She lay like a limp corset all one day. But the habit was in her now. Some of Cecy had stayed on like a fossil imprint on soft shale rock; and Marianne began tracing the habits and thinking them over and remembering what it was like to have Cecy inside her, and pretty soon she was running and shouting and giggling all by herself; a corset animated, as it were, by a memory!

Marianne had lived joyously thereafter.

Standing with the cigar store Indian for conversation, Uncle Jonn now shook his head violently. Dozens of bright bubbles floated in his eyeballs, each with tiny, slanted, microscopic eyes staring in, in at his brain.

What if he never found Cecy? What if the plain winds had borne her all the way to Elgin? Wasn't that where she dearly loved to bide her time, in the asylum for the insane, touching their minds, holding and turning their confetti thoughts?

Far-flung in the afternoon distance a great metal whistle sighed and echoed, steam shuffled as a train cut across valley trestles, over cool rivers through ripe cornfields, into tunnels like finger into thimble, under arches of shimmering walnut trees. Jonn stood, afraid. What if Cecy was in the cabin of the engineer's head, now? She loved riding the monster engines across country far as she could stretch the contact. Yank the whistle rope until it screamed across sleeping night land or drowsy day country.

He walked along a shady street. Out of the corners of his eyes he thought he saw an old woman, wrinkled as a dried fig, naked as a thistle-seed, floating among the branches of a hawthorne tree, a cedar stake driven into her breast.

Somebody screamed!

Something thumped his head. A blackbird, soaring skyward, took a lock of his hair with it!

He shook his fist at the bird, heaved a rock. "Scare me, will you!" he yelled. Breathing rawly, he saw the bird circle behind him to sit on a limb waiting another chance to dive for hair.

He turned slyly from the bird.

He heard the whirring sound.

He jumped about, grabbed up. "Cecy!"

He had the bird! It fluttered, squalled in his hands.

"Cecy!" he called, looking into his caged fingers at the wild black creature. The bird drew blood with its bill.

"Cecy, I'll crush you if you don't help me!"

The bird shrieked and cut him.

He closed his fingers tight, tight, tight.

He walked way from where he finally dropped the dead bird and did not look back at it, even once.

He walked down into the ravine that ran through the very center of Mellin Town. What's happening now, he wondered. Has Cecy's mother phoned people? Are the Elliotts afraid? He swayed drunkenly, great lakes of sweat bursting out under his armpits. Well, let *them* be afraid awhile. He was tired of being afraid. He'd look just a little longer for Cecy and then go to the police!

On the creek bank, he laughed to think of the Elliotts scurrying madly, trying to find some way around him. There was no way. They'd have to make Cecy help him. They couldn't afford to let good old Uncle Jonn die insane, no, sir.

B-b-shot eyes lay deep in the water, staring roundly up at him.

On blazing hot summer noons, Cecy had often entered into the soft-shelled greyness of the mandibled heads of crayfish. She had often peeked out from the black egg eyes upon their sensitive filamentary stalks and felt the creek sluice by her, steadily, and in fluid veils of coolness and captured light. Breathing out and in the particles of stuff that floated in water, holding her horny, lichened claws before her like some elegant salad utensils, swollen and scissor-sharp. She watched the giant strides of boy feet progressing toward her through the creek bottom, heard the faint, water-thickened shout of boys searching for crayfish, jabbing their pale fingers down, tumbling rocks aside, clutching and tossing frantic flippery animals into open metal cans where scores of other crayfish scuttled like a basket of waste-paper come to life.

She watched pale stalks of boy legs poise over her rock, saw the nude loin-shadows of boy thrown on the sandy muck of the creek floor, saw the suspenseful hand hovered, heard the suggestive whisper of a boy who'd spied a prize beneath a stone. Then, as the hand plunged, the stone rolled, Cecy flirted the borrowed fan of her inhabited body, kicked back in a little sand explosion and vanished downstream.

On to another rock she went to sit fanning the sand, holding her claws before her, proud of them, her tiny glass-bulb eyes glowing black as creek-water filled her bubbling mouth, cool, cool, cool. . . .

The realization that Cecy might be this close at hand, in any live thing, drove Uncle Jonn to a mad fury. In any squirrel or chipmunk, in a disease germ, even, on his aching body, Cecy might be existing. She could even enter amoebas. . . .

On some sweltering summer noons, Cecy would live in an amoeba, darting, vacillating, deep in the old tired, philosophical dark waters of a kitchen well. On days when the world high over her, above the unstirred water, was a dreaming nightmare of heat printed on each object of the land, she'd lie somnolent, quivering and cool and distant, settling in the well-throat. Up above, trees were like images burned in green fire. Birds were like bronze stamps you inked and punched on your brain. Houses steamed like manure sheds. When a door slammed it was like a rifle shot. The only good sound on a simmering day was the asthmatic suction of well water drawn up into a porcelain cup, there to be inhaled through an old skelatinous woman's porcelain teeth. Overhead, Cecy could hear the brittle clap of the old woman's shoes, the sighing voice of the old woman baked in the August sun. And, lying lowermost and cool, sighting up up through the dim echoing tunnel of well, Cecy heard the iron suction of the pump handle pressed energetically by the sweating old lady; and water, amoeba, Cecy and all rose up the throat of the well in sudden cool disgorgement out into the cup, over which waited sun-withered lips. Then, and only then, did Cecy withdraw, just as the lips came down to sip, the cup tilted, and porcelain met porcelain. . . .

Jonn stumbled, fell flat into the creek water!

He didn't rise, but sat dripping stupidly.

Then he began crashing rocks over, shouting, seizing upon and losing crayfish, cursing. The bells rang louder in his ears. And now, one by one, a procession of bodies that couldn't exist, but seemed to be real, floated by on the water. Worm-white bodies, turned on their backs, drifting like loose marionettes. As they passed, the tide bobbed their heads so their faces rolled over, revealing the features of the typical Elliott family member.

He began to weep, sitting there in the water. He had wanted Cecy's help, but now how could he expect to deserve it, acting a fool, cursing her, hating her, threatening her and the Family?

He stood up, shaking himself. He walked out of the creek and up the hill. There was only one thing to do now. Plead with individual

members of the Family. Ask them to intercede for him. Have them
ask Cecy to come home, quickly.

In the undertaking parlor on Court Street, the door opened. The
undertaker, a short, well-tonsored man with a moustache and sensi-
tively thin hands, looked up. His face fell.

"Oh, it's *you*, Uncle Jonn," he said.

"Nephew Bion," said Jonn, still wet from the creek, "I need
your help. Have you seen Cecy?"

"Seen her?" Said Bion Elliott. He leaned against the marble table where he was working on a body. He laughed. "God, don't ask
me *that!*" he snorted. "Look at me, close. Do you know me?"

Jonn bristled. "You're Bion Elliott, Cecy's brother, of course!"

"Wrong." The undertaker shook his head. "I'm Cousin Ralph,
the butcher! Yes, the *butcher.*" He tapped his head. "Here, inside,
where it counts, I'm Ralph. I was working in my refrigerator a
moment ago over at the butcher shop when suddenly Cecy was
inside me. She borrowed my mind, like a cup of sugar. And
brought me over here just now and sifted me down into Bion's
body. Poor Bion! What a joke!"

"You're—you're *not* Bion!"

"No, ah, no, dear Uncle Jonn. Cecy probably put Bion in *my*
body! You see the joke? A meat-cutter exchanged for a meat-cutter!
A dealer in cold-cuts traded for another of the same!" He quaked
with laughter. "Ah, that Cecy, what a child!" He wiped happy tears
from his face. "I've stood here for five minutes wondering what to
do. You know something? Undertaking isn't hard. Not much
harder than fixing pot-roasts. Oh, Bion'll be mad. His professional
integrity. Cecy'll probably trade us back, later. Bion never was one
to take a joke on himself!"

Jonn looked confused. "Even *you* can't control Cecy?"

"God, no. She does what she does. We're helpless."

Jonn wandered toward the door. "Got to find her somehow," he
mumbled. "If she can do this to you, think how she'd help me if she
wanted. . . ." The bells rang louder in his ears. From the side of
his eyes he saw a movement. He whirled and gasped.

The body on the table had a cedar-stake driven through it.

"So long," said the undertaker to the slammed door. He listened
to the sound of Jonn's running feet, fading.

. . .

The man who staggered into the police station at five that afternoon was barely able to stand up. His voice was a whisper and he retched as if he'd taken poison. He didn't look like Uncle Jonn any more. The bells rang all the time, all the time, and he saw people walking behind him, with staked chests, who vanished whenever he turned to look.

The sheriff looked up from reading a magazine, wiped his brown moustache with the back of one claw-like hand, took his feet down off a battered desk and waited for Uncle Jonn to speak.

"I want to report a family that lives here," whispered Uncle Jonn, his eyes half-shut. "A wicked family, living under false pretenses."

The sheriff cleared his throat. "What's the family's name?"

Uncle Jonn stopped. "What?"

The sheriff repeated it, "What's the family's name?"

"Your voice," said Jonn.

"What about my voice?" said the sheriff.

"Sounds familiar," said Jonn. "Like—"

"Who?" asked the sheriff.

"Like Cecy's mother! That's who you sound like!"

"Do I?" asked the sheriff.

"That's who you are inside! Cecy changed you, too, like she changed Ralph and Bion! I can't report the Family to you, now, then! It wouldn't do any good!"

"Guess it wouldn't," remarked the sheriff, implacably.

"The Family's gotten around me!" wailed Uncle Jonn.

"Seems that way," said the sheriff, wetting a pencil on his tongue, starting on a fresh crossword puzzle. "Well, good day to you, Jonn Elliott."

"Unh?"

"I said 'Good day'."

"Good day." Jonn stood by the desk, listening. "Do you—do you *hear* anything?"

The sheriff listened. "Crickets?"

"No."

"Frogs?"

"No," said Uncle Jonn. "Bells. Just bells. Holy church bells. The kind of bells a man like me can't stand to hear. Holy church bells."

The sheriff listened. "No. Can't say as I hear 'em. Say, be careful of that door there; it slams."

The door to Cecy's room was knocked open. A moment later, Uncle Jonn was inside, moving across the floor. The silent body of Cecy lay on the bed, not moving. Behind him, as Jonn seized Cecy's hand, her mother appeared.

She ran to him, struck him on head and shoulders till he fell back from Cecy. The world swelled with bell sounds. His vision blacked out. He groped at the mother, biting his lips, releasing them in gasps, eyes streaming.

"Please, please tell her to come back," he said. "I'm sorry. I don't want to hurt any one any more."

The mother shouted through the clamor of bells. "Go downstairs and wait for her there!"

"I can't hear you," he cried, louder. "My head." He held his hands to his ears. "So loud. So loud I can't stand it." He rocked on his heels. "If only I knew where Cecy was—"

Quite simply, he drew out a folded pocket knife, unfolded it. "I can't go on—" he said. And before the mother moved he fell to the floor, the knife in his heart, blood running from his lips, his shoes looking senseless one atop the other, one eye shut, the other wide and white.

The mother bent down to him. "Dead," she whispered, finally. "So," she murmured, unbelievingly, rising up, stepping away from the blood. "So he's dead at last." She glanced around, fearfully, cried aloud.

"Cecy, Cecy, come home, child, I need you!"

A silence, while sunlight faded from the room.

"Cecy, come home, child!"

The dead man's lips moved. A high clear voice sprang from them.

"Here! I've been here for days! I'm the fear he had in him; and he never guessed. Tell Father what I've done. Maybe he'll think me worthy now. . . ."

The dead man's lips stopped. A moment later, Cecy's body on the bed stiffened like a stocking with a leg thrust suddenly into it, inhabited again.

"Supper, mother," said Cecy, rising from bed.

Between the Minute and the Hour

A. M. BURRAGE

ALFRED M. BURRAGE, *a British journalist born in Middlesex in 1889, wrote poetry and tales of terror and the supernatural, including the chilling "Smee," which may be found in* Ghosts *(Doubleday, 1981), and "Between the Minute and the Hour," which tells of one of the strangest curses that witch ever hurled on unfortunate mortal.*

There is no more commonplace stretch of thoroughfare in the United Kingdom than the London Road at Nesthall between Station Road and Beryl Avenue. A row of small, dingy villas and a row of new and diminutive shops face each other across the tram-lines which stretch between Hammersmith and a distant suburb, once a country town. Nearly all of these shops are for the sale of sweets, tobacco, and newspapers, so that it seems strange that there should be a livelihood in any one of them.

Charles Trimmer kept the fifth shop down, as you would count them with your back to London. His commonplace name appeared above his one commonplace window, with "Newsagent" on one side of it and "Tobacconist" on the other. The window displayed an assortment of cheap sweets in bottles and open boxes, picture-postcards in doubtful taste, flies when in season, and dummy packets of tobacco and cigarettes.

Trimmer himself was commonplace in mind and appearance to match his surroundings and his avocation. If I lay particular stress on this, it is because it serves to make this strange narrative the stranger. He was short, turned forty, slightly bald, with a slim, dark, waxed moustache. His hobbies may be said to have consisted of watching professional football—he was a firm "supporter" of Brentford whenever he could get away—and putting odd shillings on horses which seldom won. As he had only his own mouth to feed, the shop kept him without hardship. He lived alone, but an elderly woman came in daily to cook his dinner and do the rougher housework. For the rest, you must imagine him to be a colourless individual, almost without personality, and with, of course, an atrocious accent, part Cockney and part peculiar to the Middlesex suburbs. Yet to this colourless little man in his squalid surroundings befel an adventure the like of which had never before been dreamed.

It was eight o'clock on a Wednesday evening in March, the end of a gusty, drizzling day without a hint of spring in the air. Trimmer's day's work was nearly over. His cold supper lay awaiting him, and in half an hour he would be free to stroll down to the Station Hotel and drink his usual two half-pints of bitter beer. With a cigarette hanging from his under-lip, he was approaching the shop door, to close it, when two ragged figures entered.

The first was a woman, short, swarthy, grey-haired, and indescribably dirty, with an enormous cast in her left eye which seemed in perpetual contemplation of the bridge of her nose. She was followed by a tall, rickety boy in rags who might have been either her son or her grandson. Trimmer, knowing from experience that these were not likely to be customers, immediately assumed an air of hostility.

"Spare us a copper or a mouthful o' food, kind gentleman!" the woman whined. "I've got two dear little bybies starvin'—"

Trimmer made a gesture towards the door.

" 'Op it!" he said. "I've got precious little for myself, let alone for you."

"I'll give you a wish in exchange, pretty gentleman—a good wish, a wish o' wonderment for you. You wouldn't grudge a bit o' bread for my precious children, pretty gentleman? You—"

Trimmer advanced upon her almost threateningly.

"Pop orf!" he cried. "Did you 'ear what I said? Pop orf!"

The ragged woman drew herself up so that she seemed to grow much taller. She stared at him with an intensity that made him fall back a step as if her very gaze were a concrete thing which had pushed him. She raised her open hands above the level of her shoulders.

"Then may the bitterest curse—"

In a moment the boy had caught one of her hands and was trying to clap his own hand over her mouth.

"Mother, mother," he cried, "for God's sake . . ."

Trimmer stared at the pair in something like horror. He did not believe in curses. He had all the materialism of the true Cockney. But the intensity of the woman's manner, the sudden queerness in her eyes for which the cast did not wholly account, and the boy's evident fear worked on his undeveloped imagination.

"All right, missus," he said, a little surprised at his own soothing tone. "You don't want to tyke on like that."

The intensity of the woman's manner subsided a little.

"A bite o' food for me and my starvin' family. 'Twas all I asked."

Trimmer persuaded himself that he was sorry for her. He was not essentially ill-natured. Casting about in his mind for something that he could give her without leaving himself the poorer, he bethought him of some biscuits which had gone soft and pappy through having been kept too long in stock. He went to the tin, emptied its contents into a large bag, and handed the bag to the woman.

She took it without thanks, picked out a biscuit, and nibbled at it. He saw the queerness come back into her eyes.

"A strange gift you have given me, master," she said, "and a strange gift I give you in return. When night turns to morning, between the minute and the hour is your time."

Once more the boy seemed disturbed.

"Mother!" he cried, in expostulation.

"I have said what I have said," she answered. "The end shall be of his own seeking. Between the minute and the hour!"

With that, slowly, they passed out of the shop. Trimmer, as he locked the door behind them, reflected that it was a "rum start." He noticed that his hand trembled as it turned the key.

• • •

For no reason that he could translate into the language of his own thoughts the woman's words haunted Trimmer. He denied to himself that he was in any way afraid; he was merely curious as to what meaning might be attached to what she had said. Had she a real thought in her head, or had she been trying to frighten him with meaningless rubbish?

Several days passed and Trimmer, in his leisure, still vexed his mind with the conundrum. He answered it in a half satisfactory manner. When night turned to morning was technically twelve o'clock midnight. After that it was called A.M., which to him meant nothing. Between the minute and the hour! That must mean the minute before midnight. But why was that *his* time? What had she meant by her vague threat, if, indeed, she had meant anything at all?

Trimmer was generally in bed before eleven and asleep very shortly afterwards, but about ten days later he sat up late in the closed shop, working at his accounts. He was almost done when he glanced up at the little striking clock which he kept on the shelf behind the counter. It wanted just two minutes to the hour of midnight.

Trimmer was not nervous by temperament, but a man sitting up late alone and at work may be excused if he finds himself the victim of strange fancies. In another minute it would be what the old woman had called *his* time, and once again he asked himself what she had meant by that. Had she meant that he would die at that hour?

He rose and went to the door of the shop, his gaze still on the clock. The upper panels of the door were glass and screened by a green linen blind. Outside he could hear a late tram, moaning on its way to the depôt. He was grateful for this friendly sound from the familiar workaday world.

He lifted the curtain and peered through the glass, and then, before his eyes were accustomed to the darkness outside and he could see anything save his own wan reflection, something happened which sent a sudden rush of blood to his heart. The noise of the tram had ceased, and ceased in such a way that the crack of a pistol would have been less startling than this sudden silence. It was not that the tram had suddenly stopped. Afterwards, fumbling for phrases, he recorded that the sound "disappeared." This is a contradiction in terms, but it is sufficiently graphic to serve for what he intended to express.

A moment later, and he was looking out upon an altered world. There was no tram-lines, no pavement, no houses opposite. He saw coarse, greyish grasses stirring in a wind which cried out in an unfamiliar voice. Trembling violently, he unlocked the door and looked out.

A slim crescent of moon and a few stars dimly illumined a landscape without houses, a place grown suddenly strange and dreadful. Where the opposite villas should have been was the edge of a forest, thick and black and menacing. He stepped out, and his foot slid through spongy grass, ankle-deep in mud and slime. He looked back fearfully, and there was his shop with its open door, standing alone. The other jerry-built shops which linked up with it had vanished. It seemed forlorn and ridiculous and out of place, a toy shop standing alone in a wilderness.

Something cold fell on to his hand and made him start. Instantly he knew that it was a drop of sweat. His hair was saturated, his face running. Then he told himself that this was nightmare, that if he could but cry out aloud he would wake up. He cried out and heard his voice ring out hoarsely over the surrounding desolation. From the forest, the cry of some wild animal answered him.

No, this was no dream, or, if it were, it was one of a kind altogether beyond his experience. Where was he? And how had he come to step out of his door into some strange place thousands of miles away from Nesthall?

But was he thousands of *miles* or—thousands of years? An unwontedly quick perception made him ask the question of himself. The land around him was flat, after the dreary nature of Middlesex. Fronting him, a few miles away, was the one hill which he had seen every day of his life, so that he knew by heart the outline of it against the sky. But it was Harrow Hill no more. A dense forest climbed its slope. And over all there brooded an aching silence charged with terror.

Curiosity had in him, to some extent, the better of fear. Cautiously he moved a little away from his shop, but cast continual backward glances at it to make sure that it was still there, while he stepped lightly and carefully over the swampy ground. Away to the left were open marshlands, and he could see a wide arc of the horizon. He could see no river, but vaguely he made out the contours of what he knew to be the Thames Valley. And not a house nor any living thing in sight!

He turned once more to look at his shop. It was still there, its open door spilling light on the bog grasses which grew to the edge of the threshold. And as he turned he saw a low hill away to his half-left—a hill which he could not recognize. He had taken a dozen steps towards it when his heart missed a beat, and he heard himself scream out aloud in an agony of terror.

The hill moved!

It was not a slow movement. There was something impetuous and savage in this sudden heaving-up of the huge mound. With movement the mass took shape from shapelessness. He saw outlined against the dim sky a pair of blunt ears set on a flat, brainless, reptilian head. Shapeless webbed feet tore at the ground in the ungainly lifting of the huge and beastly carcase. Two dull red lights suddenly burned at Trimmer, and he realized that the monster was staring at him.

As it stared he saw the long slit of a mouth open, and a great tongue, a dirty white in colour, passed in slobberly expectation over the greenish lips. There was that about the movement which caused the soul of Trimmer to grow sick within him.

New terror broke the spell cast by the old. The nerves of motion were given back to him. He turned and ran, screaming wildly, arms outflung, towards the open door of his shop.

Behind him he heard the Thing lumbering in clumsy pursuit. The ground reverberated suddenly under its huge webbed feet. He heard the long reptilian body flopping heavily in his wake, heard its open mouth emitting strange wheezing cries full of a hateful yearning.

It was moving quickly, too. The sounds behind him gained upon him with a maddening rapidity. He could smell the creature's hot fetid breath. With one last despairing effort he gained the door of his shop and flung himself across the threshold into what seemed but a paltry chance of safety. Frenziedly he kicked out behind him at the door, closing it with a crash, and fell gasping across his counter.

Almost on the instant the little clock on the shelf began to strike.

And sharp upon the stroke he heard a sudden moaning outside. His strained heart leaped again, but in the fraction of a moment he had recognized the sound. It was the tram resuming what had seemed to him its interrupted journey.

The clock went on striking. He looked at it in blank bewilderment. It was striking the hour of twelve, midnight.

Now he had paid little attention to time, but estimated that he had spent something like half an hour in the strange and awful world outside his shop. Yet it had turned a minute to twelve when the change happened. And now here was his clock only just striking the hour.

He staggered to the door, and as he did so the tram passed, throwing a procession of twinkling lights along the top of his window. The curtain on the door was still raised a little, showing where he had peeped out. He looked through and saw gleaming tramrails, the familiar pillar-box on the corner, the garden gate of Holmecroft opposite. Wherever he had been he was—and he thanked God for it—back in To-day.

The clock finished striking the hour, the sounds of the tram grew fainter in the distance, and silence recaptured her hold upon the night.

Trimmer edged away from the door. He was still sweating profusely, and his heart was still racing. He looked down at his feet. His cheap, worn boots were quite dry.

"God!" he ejaculated aloud. "What a dream!"

A fit of shuddering seized him.

"That thing! Ugh! It was like one of them things on the postcards what chase the pre'istoric blokes—only worse! I didn't dream that! I couldn't have done! I couldn't have run like that and yelled like I did, in a dream. I couldn't have been so surprised, and reasoned things out so clear! Besides, 'ow could I have fallen asleep like that in one second? No, it wasn't no dream! Then what—what in God's name *was* it?"

Next day Trimmer's few regular customers noticed that he looked ill and preoccupied. He handed the wrong article and the wrong change. His lips moved as if he were talking to himself.

As a matter of fact, he was trying to convince himself that his experience of the night before was a dream—trying and failing.

What he half believed was something at which his Cockney common-sense rose in rebellion. By some law contrary to that of Nature he had been free to wander in another age while Time, as we count it, had stood still and waited for him. Either that or he was mad.

He determined to keep his clock exactly right according to Greenwich time, and be on the watch that night just before the stroke of twelve to see if the same thing happened again. But this time he would not venture out of To-day, would not leave his shop and risk the nameless dangers that awaited him in another age.

Eagerly and yet fearfully he awaited the coming of night. At nine o'clock he went down to the Station Hotel and stayed there until closing time, drinking brandy. Having returned to his shop, he paced the parlour at the back until ten minutes to twelve, when he took a candle into the shop and waited.

Fearfully he stared through the lifted blind on the door and out over the steam-tarred road. It was raining gently, and he saw the drops dancing on the surface of a puddle. He watched them until he had almost hypnotised himself; until—

He felt himself start violently. It was as if the road and the house opposite had given themselves a sudden, convulsive twitch. Suddenly and amazingly it was not dark, but twilight. Opposite him, instead of a row of houses, was a hedge, with a rude rustic gate set in it. He found himself looking across fields. He saw a cluster of cows, a haystack, beyond a further hedge the upturned shafts of a derelict plough.

The road was still there, but it had changed out of knowledge. It was narrower, rutted, and edged with grass. As he looked he heard a jingling of bells, and a phaeton, with big yellow wheels, drawn by a high-stepping white horse, came gliding past.

Wonder rather than fear was his predominating emotion. The musical tooting of a horn startled him, and he heard the crisp sound of trotting horses and the lumbering of heavy wheels.

Into view came a coach and four, with passengers inside and out, a driver, with many capes, and a guard perched up behind pointing his long, slim horn at Harrow Hill. Immediately he recognized their clothes as something like those he had seen in pictures, on the covers of the boys' highwaymen stories he read and sold.

"It's safe enough," he reflected, with a strange elation. "Why, it ain't more than a hundred and fifty years ago!"

He wrenched open the door of his shop and passed out into the twilight of a June evening in the eighteenth century. Looking back, he saw that his shop stood alone as before, but this time it broke the line of a hawthorn hedge, on which red and white blossom was decaying and dying. The scent of it blended in his nostrils with the odour of new-mown hay.

He felt now eager and confident, entirely fearless. He was safe from the prehistoric horror that had attacked him the night before. Why, he was in an age of beer and constables and cricket matches.

With light steps he began to walk up the road towards London. It was his privilege now to wander without danger in another age, and see things which no other living man had ever seen. An old yokel, leaning against a gate, stared at him, went on staring, and, as he drew nearer, climbed the gate and made his way hurriedly across a hayfield. This reminded him that he looked as strange to the people of this age as they looked to him. He wished he had known, so that he could have hired an old costume and thus walked inconspicuously among them.

He must have walked half a mile without coming upon one single familiar landmark. A finger-post told him what he already knew —that he was four miles from Ealing Village. He paused outside an inn to read a notice which announced that the stagecoach High-flyer, plying between London and Oxford would arrive at the George at Ealing (D.V.) at 10.45 a.m. on Mondays, Wednesdays and Fridays. He was turning away, having read the bill, when he first saw Miss Marjory.

She was, if you please, a full seventeen years of age, and husband-high according to the custom of her times. She wore a prim little bonnet, a costume of royal blue, and carried a silk parasol which, when open, must have looked ludicrously small. He had one full glance at her piquantly pretty face and saw, for the fraction of an instant, great blue eyes staring at him in frank wonderment. She lowered her gaze abruptly, with an air of conscious modesty, when she saw that he had observed her.

Hitherto, as far as the strange circumstances permitted, Trimmer had felt entirely normal. That is to say that his emotions and outlook were in keeping with a man of his age, station, education and habit of mind. Now came a change, sudden, bewildering, well-nigh overwhelming.

Once he had been in a state which, for want of a better phrase, he called being "in love." He had "walked out" with a young lady who was a draper's assistant. After a while she had deserted him because of the superior attractions of a young clerk in a warehouse. He had been wounded, but not deeply wounded. Marriage was not necessary to his temperament, or, as he put it, he could get along without women. Not for the last sixteen years had he thought of love until that moment, when he, the waif of another century, beheld Miss Marjory.

It was as if some strange secret were revealed to him on the instant. The ecstasy of love which engulfed him like a wave told him that here was his true mate, his complement according to Nature, born into this world, alas! one hundred and fifty years too early for him. Yet, for all that, by a miracle, by witchcraft, by some oversetting of the normal laws, the gulf had been bridged, and they stood now face to face. He walked towards her, fumbling in his mind for something to say, some gallantry preliminary to street flirtations such as happened around him every day.

"Good evening, miss," he said.

He saw the blush in her cheek deepen, and she answered without regarding him:

"Oh, sir, I pray you not to molest me. I am an honest maiden alone and unprotected."

"I'm not molestin' you, miss. And you needn't be alone and unprotected unless you like."

The maiden's eyelids flickered up and then down again.

"Oh, fie on you, sir!" she said. "Fie on you for a bold man! I would have you know that my father is a highly respected mercer and drives into London daily in his own chaise. I have been brought up to learn all the polite accomplishments. 'Twould not be seemly for me to walk and talk with strangers."

"There's exceptions to every rule, miss."

Once more she gave him a quick modest glance.

"Nay, sir, but you have a pretty wit. 'Tis said that curiosity is a permitted weakness to us women. I vow that you are a foreigner. Your accents and strange attire betray you. Yet I have not the wit to guess whence you come, nor the boldness to ask."

"I'm as English as you are, miss," Trimmer protested, a little hurt.

The ready blush came once more to her cheek.

"Your pardon, sir, if I did mistake you for one of those mincing Frenchies. Nay, be not offended. I have heard tell that there is something vastly attractive about a Frenchy, so, if I made the error, I— Oh, why does my tongue betray my modesty!"

"I don't know, miss. But what about a little walk?"

She broke into a delightful little laugh.

"Sir, you speak a strange tongue and wear strange clothes. Yet I confess I find both to my mind. Doubtless you wonder how it is that you find a young lady like myself promenading alone at fall of evening. Ah, me, I fear that Satan is enthroned in my heart! I am acting thus to punish my papa."

Trimmer made an incoherent noise.

"He promised to take me to Bath, and broke his promise," she continued. "Oh, sir, what crimes are done to the young in the name of Business! He has not the time, if I would credit such a tale! So, to serve him, he shall hear that his daughter walked abroad at evening unattended, like any common Poll or Moll. You may walk with me a few yards if it be your pleasure, sir—but only a few yards. I would not have my papa *too* angry with his Marjory."

From then he had no count of time. He walked with her in a sort of dream-ecstasy, while veil after veil of darkness fell over the fields of pasture and half-grown corn. When at last she insisted that the time had come for parting he stole a kiss from her, a theft at which she more than half connived. In a low voice she confessed to him that she was not so sure of her heart as she had been at sunset.

Trimmer walked back on air to where his shop stood, alone and incongruous. He had learned the true meaning of love, and was drunk with an emotion which hitherto he had scarcely sipped. They had made an assignation for the following evening; for he believed that he had been fated to meet her, and that his shop door would let him out once more into the eighteenth century.

When he returned to his shop he was aware of one strange thing —that while it was visible to him it was invisible to others in the world to which it gave him access. He expected to find a crowd around it on his return, so queer and incongruous must it have looked to eighteenth-century eyes. But only a rustic couple was strolling in the moonlight, on the other side of the road, and as he crossed the threshold it must have seemed to them that he had vanished into thin air, for he heard a shrill scream, which ceased on the instant as the clock struck the first beat of twelve.

He was back once more in the twentieth century, his heart full of a girl who was a hundred and fifty years away. He was like a boy after his first kiss under a moonlit hedge. To-morrow night, he promised himself, if he could get back to the eighteenth century, he would remain in it, marry Marjory and live out his life, secure in the knowledge that Time was standing still and awaiting his return.

Next morning the change in Charles Trimmer was still more marked. There was a far-off look in his eyes and a strange smile on his lips.

"If I didn't know ole Charlie," said Mr. Bunce, the butcher, to a friend, over the midday glass, "I should think he was in love."

Trimmer cared little about what his neighbours thought of him, nor had he any longer a regard for his business. His whole mind was centred upon the coming of midnight when, perhaps, he could step out across the years and take Marjory into his arms. He had no thought for anything else. Not having heard of *La Belle Dame Sans Merci* he saw no danger in his obsession. If he had it would have been the same.

Strangely enough he did not trouble himself greatly as to how he had come by this strange gift. He gave little thought to the old cross-eyed woman who had bestowed it upon him, nor did he speculate much as to what strange powers she possessed. Enough that the gift was his.

It was a world of dazzling white which Trimmer saw when he peeped through the blind that night. It startled him a little, for he had not thought of seeing snow. There was no saying now what period he would step into outside his shop. Snow was like a mask on the face of Nature.

For a thinking space he was doubtful if he should venture out, but the fear of missing Marjory compelled him. His teeth chattered as he plunged knee-deep into a drift, but he scrambled up over a small mound, on which the snow was only ankle-deep, and beneath him the surface was hard, possibly that of a road. He turned his face towards London, wondering whether the snow concealed the friendly pastures of the eighteenth century or the wilderness of some unguessed-at period of time.

Away to his left, looking in a straight line midway between Harrow Hill and London, he could see a forest holding aloft a canopy of snow. He had forgotten if he had seen a wood in that direction on the occasion when he had met Marjory. He tried to rack his brains as he trudged on, shivering, hands deep in pockets.

He had walked perhaps half a mile on what certainly seemed some sort of a track, without passing a house or any living person, when a sound, which he associated with civilization, smote upon his ears. It was the low, mournful howling of a dog.

The howling was taken up by other dogs, he could not guess how many, but the effect of it was weird and infinitely mournful. As nearly as he was able to locate them, the sounds came from the direction of the forest.

Vaguely he wondered whose dogs they were and why they were howling. Perhaps they were cold, poor devils. People in less advanced times were very likely cruel to their dogs. They left them out, even on such nights as this.

He trudged on, listening to this intermittent howling and baying, which became more frequent and sounded nearer. Vague fears began to assail him. He was not afraid of dogs which had been made domestic pets—the Fidos and Rovers and Peters of the happy twentieth century. But suppose these were savage—wild?

He halted doubtfully, and as he halted he saw some of them for the first time. There were six of them, and they were streaming across the snow-field from the direction of the forest, one slightly in advance of the others. They were barking and squealing, like hounds hot upon a scent. Their leader, a lean grey brute, raised his head, and uttered a loud yelp, and as he did so Trimmer saw that his eyes were luminous and burning, like two red coals.

In response to the creature's yelp the whole fringe of the wood became alive with his kind. The darkness was specked with vicious luminous eyes. Over the snowfield came the pack, as a black cloud crosses the sky. Trimmer uttered a little sharp cry of fear.

"Wolves!" he gasped aloud. "Wolves!"

As he turned and ran an echo of an old history lesson came back to his mind. He remembered having been told that hundreds and hundreds of years ago the English forests were haunted by wolves, which, maddened by hunger in the winter-time, would attack and kill whomsoever ventured abroad. He ran like a blind man, stumbling and slipping, with horror and despair storming at his heart.

In the distance he could see his shop, with the safe warm light gleaming like a beacon, but he knew that he could never reach it. The yelping of his pursuers grew nearer every moment. Already he could hear their scampering in the snow behind him. A minute later, and a lean body shot past his thigh, just missing him. He heard the snap of the brute's jaws as it rolled over in the snow. Then sharp teeth gripped and tore the calf of one of his legs, and he heard amid his terror a worrying snarl as he tried to kick himself free.

More teeth gripped his shoulder. There was a weight on his back —more weight—and terror which drugged physical pain. One arm was seized above the elbow. They were all over him now, snapping, snarling, tearing and worrying. Down they dragged him— down into the snow—down. . . .

The policeman, passing the shop of Charles Trimmer at nine in the morning, was surprised to find it not yet open. The daily papers had been left in a pile on the doorstep by the van-boy who had evidently despaired of making anyone hear. Being suspicious, the constable examined the door and found that the green blind was lifted a little. Through the chink he could see an eye peering out; but it was an eye which seemed not to see.

Having called out several times and rapped on the glass without evoking any reply, the policeman broke in at the back. He found Charles Trimmer kneeling by the shop door, peering out under the green blind. He was quite dead.

There was not a mark on him, but a doctor giving evidence before the coroner explained that his heart was in a bad way—it weighed a great deal more than a man's heart ought to weigh—and he had been liable for some time to die suddenly. A nightmare or any sudden shock might have brought this about at any time.

The verdict was in accordance with the evidence.

Wizard Crystal

DANIEL PINKWATER

DANIEL PINKWATER *is the author of such brilliantly hilarious books as* Young Adults, The Snarkout Boys and the Avocado of Death, Fat Men from Space, Lizard Music, The Hoboken Chicken Emergency *and many others. Though most of Pinkwater's fiction is distinguished by an addictive brand of lunacy that like all great comedy is rooted in the wisdom of pain (and vice versa), a gentler whimsy infuses a few of his works, notably his Thurberesque* Blue Moose *and the following amphibious saga of a discontented wizard who longs to discover the secret of happiness.*

There were some frogs in a pond. All the frogs were happy. There was enough to eat. There were logs and lily pads to sit on. No danger ever came to that pond.

At night the frogs would sing. Their voices carried over the smooth water:

> *Gunk* this pond, *gunk* this pond,
> *Gagunk* warm sun, *gagunk* warm sun,
> *Gunk* bright stars, *gunk* bright stars,
> *Gagunk* safe home, *gagunk* safe home,
> *Gunk* happy place, *gunk* happy place.

In the pond, at the very bottom, was a magic crystal. The frogs did not know it was magic, but they liked it very much. It made them happy to swim down and see the crystal shining and sparkling. It made them happy to take care of the crystal and keep it free of weeds and moss. It made them happy just to think about their wonderful crystal.

There was a wizard living near. He had been sitting in one place for 100 years reading a book of magic. It was a hard book full of secrets. The wizard was looking for the secret of being happy. He had been unhappy every day for 307 years and he was tired of it.

One day he read in the book about a magic crystal. He read that whoever has the crystal will always be happy, so the wizard made up his mind that he would find it.

To find the crystal was not easy. The book did not say where it was. The wizard built a sort of magic compass to find the crystal. A compass points North, but this one pointed to the crystal.

With the magic compass, the wizard started through the forest searching for the crystal. The needle of the compass pointed to the crystal and the wizard walked in that direction. Because he was looking at the compass while he walked, the wizard bumped into a lot of trees and fell in some holes in the forest. When he came to the frog pond, he fell in that, too.

The wizard walked around the pond, and as he walked the needle moved, always pointing to the middle of the pond. Then the wizard knew that the crystal was there. With a long-handled net, the wizard scooped out the crystal on the first try. "How easy it is to get the thing which will make you happy!" he thought.

When the frogs saw this, they started after the wizard to get their crystal back, but frogs are slow and wizards are fast. When the frogs reached the wizard's house, it was night and he was inside with the door locked. Through the locked window the frogs could see the crystal shining on the table and the wizard asleep. He was dreaming of being happy always.

The frogs did not know what to do. They sat in a circle around the wizard's house and sang a song to help themselves think.

> *Gunk* think hard! *Gunk* think hard!
> *Gagunk* what to do, *gagunk* what to do.
> *Gunk* think hard! *Gunk* think hard!

They sang of their home in the pond. They sang of the sun and the stars. They sang all through the night. The wizard never woke up, but he heard the songs in his sleep and dreamed of frogs and stars and lily pads. And while the frogs sang and the wizard dreamed, magic happened. The place in the forest changed. The house of the wizard changed. The wizard changed. The crystal shone brighter than ever before.

Morning came. When the wizard woke up he was not unhappy any more. He was not a wizard any more, either. He was a frog. The house was gone. In its place in the forest was a pond. In that pond all the frogs were happy. There was enough to eat. There were logs and lily pads to sit on. No danger ever came to that pond. At night the frogs would sing:

> *Gunk* this pond, *gunk* this pond,
> *Gagunk* warm sun, *gagunk* warm sun,
> *Gunk* bright stars, *gunk* bright stars,
> *Gagunk* safe home, *gagunk* safe home,
> *Gunk* happy place, *gunk* happy place.

Perifidious Amber

TANITH LEE

The wise sorcerer knows that evil comes in both mundane and supernatural guises. TANITH LEE, *winner of both the British and World Fantasy Awards, here tells an unusual tale of a wizard who might well pass for a distant ancestor of Sherlock Holmes.*

"It is true they say the ring is cursed," the young man said quietly. "But for myself, I discount such things. I do not believe in demons."

"The more unsanguine for you, should you ever meet one," said Cyrion, with a melancholy smile.

"Well, then, what should I do? My family fortune was lost to me in stupid excesses of my adolescence. Scurrilous acquaintances led me astray. Bitterly regretting these faults, I strove to rebuild my vanished wealth. In the midst of this struggle, walking one morning through the city, I beheld an angel carried in a litter, the most lovely maiden in Andriok: Berdice, Sarmur the silk merchant's daughter. Sarmur is rich; I, at that time, penniless. But, for the sake of my lineage, he permitted me to wed his child, and settled on her an excellent dowry. What can I offer in return? Nothing? Naturally, I thought of this ring, the one possession I never squandered.

My family has owned it, seven generations. Should it lie in a box, or jewel the hand of my exquisite wife?"

Blond, handsome and apparently just a touch politely bored, Cyrion observed the ring in question.

It lay in a nest of azure velvet that made it, by contrast, all the bloodier and more rich; an amber intaglio, set in heavy gold, its surface engraved with the design of a lily, a swallow in flight, and a rayed sunburst. Certainly, it was splendid. Certainly, Cyrion had heard of it. It had a nickname: *Farewell.*

"What do you say, Cyrion? How do you advise me? I admit the *legend* of the curse, but no one has died because of it for a hundred years."

"Neither has anyone worn it during that time."

The young man sighed. He had a strong, attractive face, augmented by bright blue eyes, betrayed by a dissipated mouth. Volf, he was called. He came from the west, though his bride and his ring were eastern in their origins. He had met Cyrion at an expensive tavern on the Street of Heaven. The meeting had been casual, but Volf had seemed to recognize Cyrion's person and cognomen. It was possible he had sought Cyrion out purposely for counsel for, here and there, Cyrion had a reputation for ruthless wisdom.

"I am interested by the engraving," said Cyrion.

"Oh, yes. The lily, symbol of the soul; the flying swallow, symbol of freedom; the sun, symbol of the sky."

"I see you have pondered the matter," said Cyrion blandly. "But now, tell me what you know about the curse itself."

Volf grinned. "What I know proves the legend to be merely that, a tale to scare off thieves, no more. Allegedly, an eastern queen had the ring made as a token of her passion for her husband. But, in order to attain the best, she required a demon to fashion it. Hence the symbols, each connected with the power of Good—lily, swallow, sun—which she had the demon incise in the amber to negate any evil it might be planning. The demon paid no heed to these symbols, however. The queen gave the ring to her husband as he rode out to battle, hoping it would guard him. But no sooner had he raised his sword and spurred his horse to meet the enemy than the king fell dead from the saddle. There was no wound upon him, but his countenance was fixed in a grimace of extreme horror.

"The battle was lost, and the ring passed to the conqueror, who dismissed the event. He wore the ring successfully for three years, though he was an irreligious scoundrel. Then one day he went hunting lions in the desert. No one was near him, but suddenly his horse stumbled. Next moment he was dead. Again no visible assailant, no wound, and a grimace of horror. But this is patently absurd. It offends our reason. Must I go on?"

"If it tires you, there is no need." Cyrion rose.

"No, no. Wait. I rely upon your advice, dear sir. I will continue. The ring was inherited by the son of the conqueror, but the son was afraid to wear it. A century later, the ring was stolen from his treasury by a mage, intrigued by its magic properties. He wore it without harm for some months. Then an earthquake destroyed his house and he perished. The ring was extracted from the ruin by bandits. The leader of these wore the ring only a day. He was captured by warriors of the prince of those parts, but dropped lifeless on the way to his execution. The ring was appropriated by one of the warriors, who gifted it to his pregnant wife. During childbirth she died—her face fixed in horror, of course, and the child was stillborn. Thereafter, the ring was buried with her, and came into my family as loot from the rifled tomb. Three of my ancestors reputedly died through it, but I would credit their deaths to mischance. One met his end by falling from a wall when the parapet gave way. One died during a storm at sea. One died of a fit during an eclipse of the sun. Since then, the ring has gone unworn."

"And have you never worn it?" Cyrion inquired innocently.

"I never thought to, in my penury. But I am not afraid to do so. Mark." Volf drew the amber ring from its velvet and slid it onto the small finger of his left hand. He laughed, decidedly without nervousness. "If a malign fate resides in the ring, let it mow me down. But I do not believe in it. Men have always been prone to death. The termini of my forebears are explicable without recourse to a curse. Even the deaths recounted in the legend are explicable."

"Nevertheless," said Cyrion, "death and the ring go hand in hand."

"But without a pattern—men who died after three years, three months, a day, or less! And such variable deaths. Some without apparent cause, some by earthquake, water—and one a woman in labor. No. Coincidence, Cyrion. If not, I, too, will die. I mean to wear this ring one day and no longer. If we are to credit that all who wear the intaglio are slain by it, the demon has no choice but to kill me during this period. Do you agree?"

"It seems," said Cyrion, "feasible."

"At midnight tonight," said Volf, his eyes shining, "I will remove the ring. At that hour I will give it to my wife. Will you visit us tonight? Eat with us, and remain till midnight. I do not reckon on any danger, but even so, they say you have mastered demons, or what passed for such. In your company, Berdice will be doubly protected."

Cyrion moved toward the door.

"Until tonight, then. Providing you are happy to linger alone with the demon of the ring."

"More than happy," said Volf, and laughed again. Cyrion took his leave.

The house of Volf, a portion of the dowry Sarmur's daughter had brought him, was an opulent one. Gates of wrought iron led from the street into a courtyard of flowers and fountains. Two stories of white and pink washed stone followed, palm-wood pillars and suitable silken hangings.

Nowhere was there more silk than in the apartment of Berdice herself. Hangings fine as smoke and heavy as syrup gleamed on their rings, draped by silken ropes, blue, green and purple. Mirrors of real glass stood in silver frames. Rainbow birds twittered in ornate wicker cages. In the middle of the bower, Berdice herself, twittering too.

Undoubtedly, she was beautiful. Jet black hair poured unbound to her tiny waist. A flawless complexion of most delicate olive flushed into faint rose at her cheeks and lips. Gazelle eyes, dainty hands, full breasts, gave further evidence of perfection. Beauty and to spare she had. She had also, from the age of thirteen, been paralyzed from the tiny waist down.

Regardless of the disposition of Berdice, her physical attributes and her wealth, the affliction had proved a bar in the matter of husbands. Then handsome Volf, poor, but of honorable name and useful western blood, had been smitten by Berdice, and, finding out the truth, had simply wept on Sarmur's shoulder, saying it made her but the dearer to him, that eventually his adoration might cure her of her trouble, that even if it did not, she was the only woman he could ever love.

Luckily, Berdice was empty-headed. It had helped her to brush aside her grievances. She twittered, and twittered. She hardly ever stopped. It could have been irritating, despite her grace and her bravery. It *was* irritating.

Now there was a brief pause. A maid had entered and said: "There is a woman at the gate. She asks to read your hand. I never saw anyone like her before, nor so grand. Shall I tell her to be off?"

"Tell her to come in wight away," twittered Berdice.

She liked to be occupied during the long hours when her husband was absent, at a tavern or similar resort. All manner of charlatans came and went through the house. Now one came who was not like the others.

She was a very tall woman, with imperious chiseled features. These she had plastered skillfully but heavily with paint and powder, which did not hide that her face was far too masculine for beauty, though somehow she was still as beautiful as Berdice, and probably more so. Her head was bound by a black scarf stitched with pearls, her figure swathed in a sack-like robe. Enameled bracelets clanked on her wrists. Her large but well-shaped hands blazed with rings. She bowed herself almost to the ground before Sarmur's daughter, with the flamboyant courtesy of one who secretly rules the kingdom.

"Ethereal mistress," she whispered in a hoarse yet strangely musical voice, "will you allow me to unlock for you the occult lore of the universe?"

"Pwobably," said Berdice. "But what is your pwice?"

"I will inform you presently, maiden mistress." The tall charlatan seated herself at Berdice's feet, and took up the girl's hand in a thrilling, ringed clasp. "You suffer," pronounced the charlatan.

"No." Berdice looked surprised.

"Yes," said the charlatan. "You are unable to walk."

"How clever," said Berdice. For a moment her gazelle eyes were naked and wretched. Then they glazed, and she twittered again: "How ever did you know?"

Most of Andriok knew about Sarmur's daughter.

"My talent for divination," murmured the charlatan modestly.

"But," she hissed, "what can have instigated this tragedy? An accident—"

"It was a—*cat,*" Berdice blurted, blanching.

"I see in your hand a cat," swiftly interrupted the charlatan. "You are afraid of cats. The cat frightened you."

"I was asleep," Berdice confided. "I woke to discover the—*cat*—sleeping across my lap. I scweamed and scweamed, but it only stared with its evil fiery stare. Then it bit me and wan away. Since then I have not walked. I never could bear—*cats.*" Berdice shivered and closed her eyes. "God deliver me," she moaned.

"Does your husband know your fear?" asked the charlatan.

"Oh, yes," said Berdice. She cheered up. She twittered: "What will happen tomowwow?"

"Night will come before day," said the charlatan. "Understand, maiden, I have read your stars. You are in danger's jaws, at the brink of your grave."

The maids, but not Berdice, uttered outraged shrieks. The charlatan silenced them with one glare of her brilliant, kohl-caked eyes. "Send out these bats," commanded the charlatan.

The bats were sent out.

"I speak to save your life," said the charlatan to Berdice.

"God deliver me," said Berdice again.

"Here are amulets to protect you," said the charlatan. "Wear them, and do not reveal their source or their nature. By their efficacy you will live."

Berdice looked at the amulets and tried to twitter. The twitter faded.

"But—" said Berdice.

"Do as you are told," said the charlatan, "or I cannot be responsible."

Kissing Berdice on the forehead, and adorning it thus with the likeness of two carmined lips, the charlatan rose.

"Am I to pay you?" gasped Berdice.

"I will take this," and plucking carelessly undid the purple silken cord from one of the drapes; the charlatan stalked from the chamber, ignoring the resultant gallon of loosed silk which plummeted upon Berdice's head.

• • •

Night clothed Andriok soberly. Andriok retaliated by gaudily
bejeweling itself with lights. Volf's house was no exception.
Scented resins flared and perfumed the air, golden filigree lamps
smoldered.

Volf welcomed Cyrion like a long-lost brother he had not seen in
ten years but for whose company he had continuously pined. In the
satin of Askandris and the silver of Daskiriom, not to mention his
own impeccable glamour, Cyrion was fair set to outshine the house.

Entering the dining chamber, Volf displayed his left hand. On
the small finger, the amber intaglio lay like a great bead of rufus
honey.

"Again, mark, my Cyrion. It and I are yet together, and I thrive.
Only two hours remain to midnight."

"My congratulations," said Cyrion. "This far."

"Pardon me," said Volf. "I assume, from your appearance, you
never lacked for money. I have now only what my wife has brought
me. And I am sick with wanting to give her something of my own."

Just then, two servants came in, carrying Volf's wife in an ornate
chair, which they put beside the open window. She was prettily (if
over) dressed. A gown embroidered with good omens, gold chains
—oddly impressed—at her throat, bracelets hung with small medal-
lions of jade and malachite, sapphire earrings in the shape of
charms, a girdle of striped silk pinned with a lucky golden snake, a
rose in her hair pinned with another, and a pair of thin silk gloves,
rather stiff.

"Here is my light of love, Berdice, my beloved wife," enthused
Volf.

"Madam," said Cyrion bowing. "You seem to be in fear of something. I trust it is not of me?"

Berdice, who had been rather pale, regained her color violently.
Her eyes widened in alarm on Cyrion.

"My dove must fear nothing," said Volf. "At midnight I shall
give her this amber ring, which will thereafter safeguard her from
all ills. You see, Cyrion, I believe in Fortune's smiling face, if not
her frown."

Berdice viewed the ring and paled once more.

"This is the wing they call 'Farewell.' Oh, Volf—it will harm
you!"

Volf laughed loudly, and explained his scheme.

Berdice recoiled.

"God deliver me!" she wailed.

At that, Volf laughed even more loudly.

"Have faith in me, beloved," he sang. "Let us prove to the world that superstition is idiocy and all the demons are dust. Besides, we have Cyrion here to insure our health. Cyrion is a hero of unsurpassable wit and gallantry."

"You will cause me to blush," opined Cyrion.

Berdice gazed at him in confused suspicion.

Dinner was served.

They ate the several courses, Berdice mute, Volf voluble. Through the open window, framing Berdice in spangles, stars shone. The scents of night-blooming flowers also wandered in from that direction, and the trilling of a sulky nightingale. In a corner of the room, meanwhile, a gilded clepsydra dripped away the minutes, quarters, a half hour, an hour. And then began to waste a fresh hour, by minutes, quarters, halves. . . .

It was almost midnight.

Suddenly Berdice started frantically to twitter.

"This afternoon, Volf—such a peculiar thing. A huge tall woman, a palm-weader and astwologer, she said. She burst into my apartment and told me I should die—"

Volf jumped, and dropped his winecup. The wine spilled across the napkins, the mosaic table, sinking in its crevices.

"But the silliest item of all," piercingly twittered Berdice, with a maniacal glance at Cyrion, "is that I wealize the woman to have been—"

"Forgive me, madam," smoothly interposed Cyrion. "But I fancy your water-clock is slow. Is that not the midnight bell from the citadel?"

Volf and his wife froze. Sure enough, the bell was being rung.

As the bell finished, Volf leaped up and clasped Berdice's gloved right hand.

"My darling, I wear the ring and live. And now—" he drew the amber from his finger—"I no longer wear the ring. The demons are defeated. These demons who never existed. Here, my angel. The ring is innocuous. Take it, with my heart." And with these words, Volf slid the amber intaglio onto her index finger. Then, raising his arms aloft in an ecstasy, Volf roared: "Heaven be praised!"

Somewhere in the dark courtyard outside, there was a muffled oath, and a scuffling.

Something hurtled through the window.

It flailed and revolved and kicked and spat and yowled.

In the midst of flailing, revolving, kicking, spitting, yowling, it landed in the lap of Berdice, and to the symphony of noises was added a sound of ripping claws and a single awful scream.

"A—*cat!*" cried Berdice in maddened terror. "A—*cat—a—cat!* Oh—God deliver me!"

"Berdice" Volf shouted, ecstasy replaced by agony. He flung himself on her and gathered her limp form into his arms. He wept uncontrollably. "Cyrion, even you could not save her. I was a fool. The curse is true. The demon of the ring has struck her down, and it is my fault. I am to blame, in my stupidity. You warned me. Demons exist. Now I am left with nothing."

"Not quite," said Cyrion mildly. "Her fortune will be yours upon her death."

Volf shot him a livid, tear-spattered glare.

"What use are riches to me, when my love is slain? I am a broken man."

Cyrion in turn was nursing the cat. Initially furious at its propelled entry through the window, it had now relapsed into a purring drapery for his shoulder. Thoughtfully, Cyrion spoke. "Your grief is premature, Volf. Your wife is not dead."

"Foul mockery. She is."

"No. She has fainted, and will presently revive. Much to your chagrin, dear Volf."

Volf tremblingly peered into Berdice's face, and gasped.

"You are correct—she lives. But—"

The cat kissed Cyrion on the lips.

"Your scurrilous acquaintance, by the way," said Cyrion, "the man you paid to throw a cat in upon your wife, has probably already been apprehended. I gave a warning to the night-watch, earlier this evening."

Volf set Berdice back in her chair, and straightened. His look was currently one of wary incredulity.

"What are you saying?"

"What am I saying?" Cyrion asked the cat.

"You impugn I paid a man to shock my wife to her death?"

"Frankly, my dear," Cyrion reproved him, "if you were clever enough to solve the secret of the intaglio, you should have been capable of a better plot than this."

"Explain yourself."

"Shall I? Why not. It will fill the time until the watch proceed to your gate.

"To begin with, despite your protestations, Berdice was a burden you never intended to shoulder very long. Having married her, you would next get rid of her, so inheriting all her wealth, not to mention her father's, after his demise. Your only problem was method, some tool which would leave you, ostensibly, blameless. It was easy. Sarmur and his daughter are both highly superstitious, while you have been at pains to show yourself an unbeliever in all things intangible. Hence, the amber intaglio, which you knew could kill anyone, given the relevant circumstance.

"The legend of the ring is precise, for it was written up in the woman's tomb, was it not, from which your family pilfered it? The deaths among your forebears are also well documented. Though there appeared to be no pattern, nevertheless, unfailingly, deaths occurred. How long did it take you to answer the riddle? Let me reiterate the fatalities. A king spurring toward a battle. A conqueror on a stumbling horse. A mage in an earthquake. A bandit en route to the gallows. A woman in childbirth. And in your own family, a man falling from a wall, a man in a storm at sea, a man throwing a fit during an eclipse of the sun. And what is the common denominator? How long did you say it took you to unravel the mystery?"

Volf snarled: *"Two years."*

Cyrion diluted a smile. It had taken him two minutes, a little less.

"Danger is the key," said Cyrion. "Danger and its complement, fear. And one further thing, dependent upon danger and fear."

Cyrion was silent.

"Say the rest."

"Must I?"

"I want to hear . . . if you have it right. You owe me that."

"I owe you nothing. It shall be a gift. That further thing, then. I remember how swiftly you named the symbols engraved in the amber—a lily was the soul, a swallow was freedom, the sun was the sky. But, like most symbols of picture-writing, the meaning can be accepted as slightly more exact. The soul-lily may also represent the ego, thus 'I' or 'me.' The swallow does not only signify freedom, but freedom from bondage—deliverance. As for the sun, it is the ancient cipher, not only for the sky, but for God. So the lily, the swallow, the sun offer us, you agree, a sentence of picture-writing to be translated as *God deliver me.* An established religious phrase in most languages, then or now. The king riding to battle whispering a last prayer. The man on the stumbling horse calling out in alarm. The mage, feeling the house shake with the earth-tremor—who could guess him slain before the walls buried him? The bandit uttering the traditional orison on the road to the gallows. The woman in the pain of childbirth, shrieking. And your ancestor tumbling from the broken parapet, dead before he hit the ground. The second dead before the water closed over his head. The third, appalled by the darkness of the eclipse—*God deliver me* they each cried. And the ring killed them instantly, as its engraving warns it will. Those words, spoken by the wearer, activate a device under the stone. A hair-fine sliver darts into the skin of the finger. Poison runs. A demon poison, so virulent it can dispatch in seconds. The victim sinks prostrate, with a look of horror and no visible wound.

"Knowing all this, you could wear the ring and avoid death. But when a cat descended on your cat-fearing wife, you knew she would exclaim the fatal phrase and die immediately. And I, with what you foolishly deduce to be an heroic reputation, was to attend the scene as your witness to inescapable Fate."

"But Berdice has not died," Volf said. He looked drained, no longer angry or malevolent. His weak mouth wobbled, and his feigned tears for his wife had altered to genuine tears spilled for himself.

"Luckily for the lady," said Cyrion, "a witch-woman happened to visit her this afternoon, and persuaded her to wear two amulets. These." He pointed to the silken gloves on Berdice's hands, the fingers of which gloves were all internally lined with thin but impregnable jointed steel of Daskiriom—unpierceable by any venomous sliver, no matter how fine.

Berdice was stirring. Cyrion gently divested himself of the cat, leaned over the girl and took her by the elbows. He pulled her suddenly to her feet.

"The shock of the second cat has cured you," said Cyrion sternly. "Now you can walk. Do so."

Berdice gaped at him, then took a faltering step.

She screamed, and took another.

Still screaming and still walking, she permitted Cyrion to aid her from the room. On the threshold he placed in her grasp a purple silken cord, but she barely noticed. She seemed to have forgotten Volf, too, which forgetfulness would presently stand her in good stead.

When Cyrion returned to the dining chamber, the watch were already hammering at the gate.

Volf huddled in a chair.

Cyrion set beside him, on the mosaic, the ring.

"To hang is a prolonged and unpleasing business," Cyrion murmured, fastidiously.

When they reached the dining chamber, the watch found one man alone in it, and he was quite dead. Volf lay across the table, with the amber intaligo on his hand, a look of horror on his face, and no visible wound.

St. John's Eve

NIKOLAI GOGOL

NIKOLAI VASILEVICH GOGOL *(1809–1852), a native of Ukrainian Russia, probably made history's greatest sacrifice to religious orthodoxy. Ten days before his death, in a fit of prayer and fasting, he burnt most of the second half of the manuscript of* Dead Souls, *which, even in its remaining incomplete state, is considered one of the great comic masterpieces of world literature. Gogol also wrote the hilarious farce* The Inspector General, *a play that in a watered-down version served as the basis for a popular Danny Kaye film. Though Gogol is best remembered as a satirist, he occasionally produced a first-rate horror story, such as the following bloody tale of witchcraft and satanism.*

Thoma Grigorovich had a very strange sort of eccentricity: to the day of his death he never liked to tell the same thing twice. There were times when, if you asked him to relate a thing afresh, behold, he would interpolate new matter, or alter it so that it was impossible to recognize it. Once on a time one of those gentlemen (it is hard for us simple people to put a name to them, to say whether they are scribblers, or not scribblers: but it is just the same thing as the usurers at our yearly fairs; they clutch and beg and steal every sort of frippery and issue mean little volumes, no thicker than an A B C book, every month, or even every week)—one of these gentlemen wormed this same story out of Thoma Grigorovich, and he completely forgot about it. But that same young gentleman in the pea-green caftan, whom I have mentioned, and one of whose tales you have already read, I think, came from Poltava, bringing with him a little book and, opening it in the middle, showed it to us. Thoma Grigorovich was on the point of setting his spectacles astride of his nose but recollected that he had forgotten to wind thread about them, and stick them together with wax, so he passed it over to me. As I understand something about reading and writing and do not wear spectacles, I undertook to read it. I had not turned two leaves, when all at once he caught me by the hand and stopped me.

"Stop! Tell me first what you are reading."

I confess that I was a trifle stunned by such a question.

"What! What am I reading, Thoma Grigorovich? These were your very words."

"Who told you that they were my words?"

"Why, what more would you have? Here it is printed: 'Related by such and such a sacristan.' "

"Spit on the head of the man who printed that! He lies, the dog of a Moscow peddler! Did I say that? ''Twas just the same as though one hadn't his wits about him!' Listen, I'll tell it to you on the spot."

We moved up to the table, and he began.

My grandfather (the kingdom of heaven be his! may he eat only wheaten rolls and *makovniki** with honey in the other world!) could tell a story wonderfully well. When he used to begin on a tale you wouldn't stir from the spot all day but keep on listening. He was no match for the storyteller of the present day, when he begins to lie, with a tongue as though he had had nothing to eat for three days, so that you snatch your cap and flee from the house. As I now recall it, my old mother was alive then; in the long winter evenings when the frost was crackling out of doors and had so sealed up hermetically the narrow panes of our cottage, she used to sit before the hackling comb, drawing out a long thread in her hand, rocking the

---

* Poppy-seeds cooked in honey and dried in square cakes.

cradle with her foot, and humming a song which I seem to hear
even now.

The fat lamp, quivering and flaring up as though in fear of something, lighted us within our cottage; the spindle hummed, and all of
us children, collected in a cluster, listened to Grandfather, who had
not crawled off the stove for more than five years, owing to his
great age. But the wondrous tales of the incursions of the
Zaporogian Cossacks, the Poles, the bold deeds of Podkova, of
Poltor-Kozhukh, and Sagaidatchnii did not interest us so much as
the stories about some deed of old which always sent a shiver
through our frames and made our hair rise upright on our heads.
Sometimes such terror took possession of us in consequence of
them that, from that evening on, Heaven knows what a marvel
everything seemed to us. If you chanced to go out of the cottage
after nightfall for anything, you imagine that a visitor from the
other world has lain down to sleep in your bed; and I should not be
able to tell this a second time were it not that I had often taken my
own smock, at a distance, as it lay at the head of the bed, for the
Evil One rolled up in a ball! But the chief thing about Grandfather's stories was that he never had lied in his life, and whatever he
said was so, was so.

I will now relate to you one of his marvelous tales. I know that
there are a great many wise people who copy in the courts and can
even read civil documents, who, if you were to put into their hand
a simple prayer book, could not make out the first letter in it and
would show all their teeth in derision—which is wisdom. These
people laugh at everything you tell them. Such incredulity has
spread abroad in the world! What then? (Why, may God and the
Holy Virgin cease to love me if it is not possible that even you will
not believe me!) Once he said something about witches. . . .
What then? Along comes one of these head-breakers—and doesn't
believe in witches! Yes, glory to God that I have lived so long in
the world! I have seen heretics to whom it would be easier to lie in
confession than it would for our brothers and equals to take snuff,
and those people would deny the existence of witches! But let them
just dream about something, and they won't even tell what it was!
There's no use in talking about them!

• • •

No one could have recognized this village of ours a little over a hundred years ago: a hamlet it was, the poorest kind of hamlet. Half a score of miserable *izbás*, unplastered, badly thatched, were scattered here and there about the fields. There was not an enclosure or a decent shed to shelter animals or wagons. That was the way the wealthy lived; and if you had looked for our brothers, the poor—why, a hole in the ground—that was a cabin for you! Only by the smoke could you tell that a God-created man lived there. You ask why they lived so? It was not entirely through poverty: almost everyone led a wandering, Cossack life, and gathered not a little plunder in foreign lands; it was rather because there was no reason for setting up a well-ordered *khata.** How many people were wandering all over the country—Crimeans, Poles, Lithuanians! It was quite possible that their own countrymen might make a descent and plunder everything. Anything was possible.

In this hamlet a man, or rather a devil in human form, often made his appearance. Why he came, and whence, no one knew. He prowled about, got drunk, and suddenly disappeared as if into the air, and there was not a hint of his existence. Then again, behold, and he seemed to have dropped from the sky and went flying about the street of the village, of which no trace now remains, and which was not more than a hundred paces from Dikanka. He would collect together all the Cossacks he met; then there were songs, laughter, money in abundance, and vodka flowed like water. . . . He would address the pretty girls and give them ribbons, earrings, strings of beads—more than they knew what to do with. It is true that the pretty girls rather hesitated about accepting his presents: God knows, perhaps they had passed through unclean hands. My grandfather's aunt, who kept a tavern at the time, in which Basavriuk (as they called that devil-man) often had his carouses, said that no consideration on the face of the earth would have induced her to accept a gift from him. And then, again, how avoid accepting? Fear seized on everyone when he knit his bristly brows and gave a sidelong glance which might send your feet God knows whither; but if you accept, then the next night some fiend from the swamp, with horns on his head, comes to call and begins to squeeze

* Wooden house.

your neck when there is a string of beads upon it; or drag you by the hair, if ribbons are braided in it. God have mercy, then, on those who owned such gifts! But here was the difficulty: it was impossible to get rid of them; if you threw them into the water, the diabolical ring or necklace would skim along the surface and into your hand.

There was a church in the village—St. Pantelei, if I remember rightly. There lived there a priest, Father Athanasii of blessed memory. Observing that Basavriuk did not come to church, even on Easter, he determined to reprove him and impose penance upon him. Well, he hardly escaped with his life. "Hark ye, *pannotche!*" he thundered in reply. "Learn to mind your own business instead of meddling in other people's, if you don't want that goat's throat of yours stuck together with boiling *kutya.*"* What was to be done with this unrepentant man? Father Athanasii contented himself with announcing that anyone who should make the acquaintance of Basavriuk would be counted a Catholic, an enemy of Christ's church, not a member of the human race.

In this village there was a Cossack named Korzh, who had a laborer whom people called Peter the Orphan—perhaps because no one remembered either his father or mother. The church *starost,* it is true, said that they had died of the pest in his second year, but my grandfather's aunt would not hear to that and tried with all her might to furnish him with parents, although poor Peter needed them about as much as we need last year's snow. She said that his father had been in Zaporozhe, taken prisoner by the Turks, underwent God only knows what tortures, and, having by some miracle disguised himself as a eunuch, had made his escape. Little cared the black-browed youths and maidens about his parents. They merely remarked that, if only he had a new coat, a red sash, a black lambskin cap with dandified blue crown on his head, a Turkish saber hanging by his side, a whip in one hand, and a pipe with handsome mountings in the other, he would surpass all the young men. But the pity was that the only thing poor Peter had was a gray *svitka* with more holes in it than there are gold pieces in a Jew's pocket. And that was not the worst of it, but this: that Korzh had a daugh-

---

* Rice or wheat flour with honey and raisins, a dish brought to church on celebration of memorial masses.

ter, such a beauty as I think you can hardly have chanced to see. My deceased grandfather's aunt used to say—and you know that it is easier for a woman to kiss the Evil One than to call anybody a beauty, without malice be it said—that this Cossack maiden's cheeks were as plump and fresh as the pinkest poppy when just bathed in God's dew and, glowing, it unfolds its petals and coquets with the rising sun; that her brows were like black cords, such as our maidens buy nowadays, for their crosses and ducats, of the Moscow peddlers who visit the villages with their baskets, and evenly arched as though peeping into her clear eyes; that her little mouth, at sight of which the youth smacked their lips, seemed made to emit the songs of nightingales; that her hair, black as the raven's wing and soft as young flax (our maidens did not then plait their hair in clubs interwoven with pretty, bright-hued ribbons), fell in curls over her *kuntush.** Eh! may I never intone another alleluia in the choir, if I would not have kissed her, in spite of the gray which is making its way all through the old wool which covers my pate, and my old woman beside me, like a thorn in my side! Well, you know what happens when young men and maids live side by side. In the twilight the heels of red boots were always visible in the place where Pidórka chatted with her Petrus. But Korzh would never have suspected anything out of the way, only one day—it is evident that none but the Evil One could have inspired him—Petrus took it into his head to kiss the Cossack maiden's rosy lips with all his heart in the passage, without first looking well about him; and that same Evil One—may the son of a dog dream of the holy cross!—caused the old graybeard, like a fool, to open the cottage door at the same moment. Korzh was petrified, dropped his jaw, and clutched at the door for support. Those unlucky kisses had completely stunned him. It surprised him more than the blow of a pestle on the wall, with which, in our days, the muzhik generally drives out his intoxication for lack of fusees and powder.

Recovering himself, he took his grandfather's hunting whip from the wall and was about to belabor Peter's back with it, when Pidórka's little six-year-old brother Ivas rushed up from somewhere or other and, grasping his father's legs with his little hands, screamed out, "Daddy, Daddy! Don't beat Petrus!" What was to

* Uppergarment.

be done? A father's heart is not made of stone. Hanging the whip
again upon the wall, he led him quietly from the house. "If you
ever show yourself in my cottage again, or even under the windows, look out, Petró! By Heaven, your black mustache will disappear; and your black locks, though wound twice about your ears,
will take leave of your pate, or my name is not Terentii Korzh." So
saying, he gave him a little taste of his fist in the nape of his neck, so
that all grew dark before Petrus, and he flew headlong. So there
was an end of their kissing. Sorrow seized upon our doves; and a
rumor was rife in the village that a certain Pole, all embroidered
with gold, with mustaches, saber, spurs, and pockets jingling like
the bells of the bag with which our sacristan Taras goes through the
church every day, had begun to frequent Korzh's house. Now, it is
well known why the father is visited when there is a black-browed
daughter about. So one day Pidórka burst into tears and clutched
the hand of her Ivas. "Ivas, my dear! Ivas, my love! Fly to Petrus,
my child of gold, like an arrow from a bow. Tell him all: I would
have loved his brown eyes; I would have kissed his white face, but
my fate decrees not so. More than one towel have I wet with burning tears. I am sad; I am heavy at heart. And my own father is my
enemy. I will not marry that Pole, whom I do not love. Tell him
they are preparing a wedding, but there will be no music at our
wedding: ecclesiastics will sing instead of pipes and kobzas. * I shall
not dance with my bridegroom; they will carry me out. Dark, dark
will be my dwelling—of maple wood; and, instead of chimneys, a
cross will stand upon the roof."

Petró stood petrified, without moving from the spot, when the
innocent child lisped out Pidórka's words to him. "And I, unhappy
man, thought to go to the Crimea and Turkey, win gold and return
to thee, my beauty! But it may not be. The evil eye has seen us. I
will have a wedding, too, dear little fish, I, too; but no ecclesiastics
will be at that wedding. The black crow will caw, instead of the
pope, over me; the smooth field will be my dwelling; the dark blue
clouds my rooftree. The eagle will claw out my brown eyes; the
rain will wash the Cossack's bones, and the whirlwinds will dry
them. But what am I? Of whom, to whom, am I complaining? 'Tis

* An eight-stringed musical instrument.

plain, God willed it so. If I am to be lost, then so be it!" And he went straight to the tavern.

My late grandfather's aunt was somewhat surprised on seeing Petrus in the tavern, and at an hour when good men go to morning Mass; and she stared at him as though in a dream, when he demanded a jug of brandy, about half a pailful. But the poor fellow tried in vain to drown his woe. The vodka stung his tongue like nettles and tasted more bitter than wormwood. He flung the jug from him upon the ground. "You have sorrowed enough, Cossack," growled a bass voice behind him. He looked round— Basavriuk! Ugh, what a face! His hair was like a brush, his eyes like those of a bull. "I know what you lack; here it is." Then he jingled a leather purse which hung from his girdle, and smiled diabolically. Petró shuddered. "He, he, he! Yes, how it shines!" he roared, shaking out ducats into his hand. "He, he, he! And how it jingles! And I only ask one thing for a whole pile of such shiners."

"It is the Evil One!" exclaimed Petró: "Give them here! I am ready for anything!"

They struck hands upon it. "See here, Petró, you are ripe just in time: tomorrow is St. John the Baptist's day. Only on this one night in the year does the fern blossom. Delay not. I will await thee at midnight in the bear's ravine."

I do not believe that chickens await the hour when the woman brings their corn with as much anxiety as Petrus awaited the evening. And, in fact, he looked to see whether the shadows of the trees were not lengthening, if the sun were not turning red toward setting; and, the longer he watched, the more impatient he grew. How long it was! Evidently, God's day had lost its end somewhere. And now the sun is gone. The sky is red only on one side, and it is already growing dark. It grows colder in the fields. It gets dusky, and more dusky, and at last quite dark. At last! With heart almost bursting from his bosom, he set out on his way and cautiously descended through the dense woods into the deep hollow called the bear's ravine. Basavriuk was already waiting there. It was so dark that you could not see a yard before you. Hand in hand they penetrated the thin marsh, clinging to the luxuriant thornbushes and stumbling at almost every step. At last they reached an open spot. Petró looked about him; he had never chanced to come there before. Here Basavriuk halted.

"Do you see, before you stand three hillocks? There are a great many sorts of flowers upon them. But may some power keep you from plucking even one of them. But as soon as the fern blossoms, seize it, and look not round, no matter what may seem to be going on behind thee."

Petró wanted to ask—and behold, he was no longer there. He approached the three hillocks—where were the flowers? He saw nothing. The wild steppe grass darkled around and stifled everything in its luxuriance. But the lightning flashed, and before him stood a whole bed of flowers, all wonderful, all strange; and there were also the simple fronds of fern. Petró doubted his senses and stood thoughtfully before them, with both hands upon his sides.

"What prodigy is this? One can see these weeds ten times in a day; what marvel is there about them? Was not devil's-face laughing at me?"

Behold! The tiny flower bud crimsons and moves as though alive. It is a marvel, in truth. It moves and grows larger and larger, and flashes like a burning coal. The tiny star flashes up; something bursts softly, and the flower opens before his eyes like a flame, lighting the others about it. "Now is the time," thought Petró, and extended his hand. He sees hundreds of shaggy hands reach from behind him, also for the flower; and there is a running about from place to place in the rear. He half shut his eyes, plucked sharply at the stalk, and the flower remained in his hand. All became still. Upon a stump sat Basavriuk, all blue like a corpse. He moved not so much as a finger. His eyes were immovably fixed on something visible to him alone; his mouth was half open and speechless. All about, nothing stirred. Ugh! It was horrible! But then a whistle was heard, which made Petró's heart grow cold within him; and it seemed to him that the grass whispered, and the flowers began to talk among themselves in delicate voices, like little silver bells; the trees rustled in waving contention. Basavriuk's face suddenly became full of life and his eyes sparkled. "The witch has just returned," he muttered between his teeth. "See here, Petró: a beauty will stand before you in a moment; do whatever she commands; if not—you are lost forever." Then he parted the thornbush with a knotty stick, and before him stood a tiny izbá, on chicken's legs, as they say. Basavriuk smote it with his fist, and the wall trembled. A large black dog ran out to meet them, and with a whine, transforming itself into a cat, flew straight at his eyes. "Don't be angry, don't be angry, you old Satan!" said Basavriuk, employing such words as would have made a good man stop his ears. Behold, instead of a cat, an old woman with a face wrinkled like a baked apple, and all bent into a bow; her nose and chin were like a pair of nutcrackers. "A stunning beauty!" thought Petró, and cold chills ran down his back. The witch tore the flower from his hand, bent over, and muttered over it for a long time, sprinkling it with some kind of water. Sparks flew from her mouth; froth appeared on her lips.

"Throw it away," she said, giving it back to Petró.

Petró threw it, and what wonder was this? The flower did not fall straight to the earth, but for a long while twinkled like a fiery ball through the darkness and swam through the air like a boat; at last it began to sink lower and fell so far away that the little star, hardly larger than a poppy seed, was barely visible. "Here!" croaked the old woman in a dull voice; and Basavriuk, giving him a spade, said, "Dig here, Petró: here you will find more gold than you or Korzh ever dreamed of."

Petró spat on his hands, seized the spade, applied his foot, and turned up the earth, a second, a third, a fourth time. . . . There was something hard; the spade clinked and would go no farther. Then his eyes began to distinguish a small ironbound coffer. He tried to seize it, but the chest began to sink into the earth, deeper, farther, and deeper still; and behind him he heard a laugh, more like a serpent's hiss. "No, you shall not see the gold until you procure human blood," said the witch, and led up to him a child of six, covered with a white sheet, indicating by a sign that he was to cut off his head. Petró was stunned. A trifle, indeed, to cut off a man's or even an innocent child's head for no reason whatever! In wrath he tore off the sheet enveloping his head, and behold! before him stood Ivas. And the poor child crossed his little hands and hung his head. . . . Petró flew upon the witch with the knife like a madman and was on the point of laying hands on her. . . .

"What did you promise for the girl?" thundered Basavriuk, and like a shot he was on his back. The witch stamped her foot: a blue flame flashed from the earth; it illumined it all inside, and it was as if molded of crystal; and all that was within the earth became visible, as if in the palm of the hand. Ducats, precious stones in chests and kettles were piled in heaps beneath the very spot they stood on.

His eyes burned; his mind grew troubled. . . . He grasped the
knife like a madman, and the innocent blood spurted into his eyes.
Diabolical laughter resounded on all sides. Misshaped monsters
flew past him in herds. The witch, fastening her hands in the headless trunk, like a wolf, drank its blood. . . . All went round in his
head. Collecting all his strength, he set out to run. Everything
turned red before him. The trees seemed steeped in blood and
burned and groaned. The sky glowed and glowered. . . . Burning
points, like lightning, flicked before his eyes. Utterly exhausted, he
rushed into his miserable hovel and fell to the ground like a log. A
deathlike sleep overpowered him.

Two days and two nights did Petró sleep, without once awakening. When he came to himself, on the third day, he looked long at
all the corners of his hut; but in vain did he endeavor to recollect;
his memory was like a miser's pocket, from which you cannot entice
a quarter of a kopek. Stretching himself, he heard something clash
at his feet. He looked—two bags of gold. Then only, as if in a
dream, he recollected that he had been seeking some treasure, that
something had frightened him in the woods. . . . But at what
price he had obtained it, and how, he could by no means understand.

Korzh saw the sacks—and was mollified. "Such a Petrus, quite
unheard of! Yes, and did I not love him? Was he not to me as my
own son?" And the old fellow carried on his fiction until it reduced
him to tears. Pidórka began to tell him some passing Gypsies had
stolen Ivas; but Petró could not even recall him—to such a degree
had the Devil's influence darkened his mind! There was no reason
for delay. The Pole was dismissed, and the wedding feast prepared;
rolls were baked, towels and handkerchiefs embroidered; the
young people were seated at table; the wedding loaf was cut;
banduras, cymbals, pipes, kobzi sounded, and pleasure was
rife. . . .

A wedding in the olden times was not like one of the present
day. My grandfather's aunt used to tell—what doings!—how the
maidens—in festive headdresses of yellow, blue, and pink ribbons,
above which they bound gold braid; in thin chemisettes embroidered on all the seams with red silk, and strewn with tiny silver
flowers; in morocco shoes, with high iron heels—danced the *gorlitza*
as swimmingly as peacocks, and as wildly as the whirlwind; how the

youths—with their ship-shaped caps upon their heads, the crowns of gold brocade, with a little slit at the nape where the hair net peeped through, and two horns projecting, one in front and another behind, of the very finest black lambskin; in kuntushas of the finest blue silk with red borders—stepped forward one by one, their arms akimbo in stately form, and executed the *gopak;* how the lads—in tall Cossack caps, and light cloth svitkas, girt with silver embroidered belts, their short pipes in their teeth—skipped before them and talked nonsense. Even Korzh could not contain himself, as he gazed at the young people, from getting gay in his old age. Bandura in hand, alternately puffing at his pipe and singing, a brandy glass upon his head, the graybeard began the national dance amid loud shouts from the merrymakers. What will not people devise in merry mood! They even began to disguise their faces. They did not look like human beings. They are not to be compared with the disguises which we have at our weddings nowadays. What do they do now? Why, imitate Gypsies and Moscow peddlers. No! Then one used to dress himself as a Jew, another as the Devil; they would begin by kissing each other, and end by seizing each other by the hair. . . . God be with them! You laughed till you held your sides. They dressed themselves in Turkish and Tartar garments. All upon them glowed like a conflagration, and then they began to joke and play pranks. . . . Well, then away with the saints!

An amusing thing happened to my grandfather's aunt, who was at this wedding. She was dressed in a voluminous Tartar robe, and, wineglass in hand, was entertaining the company. The Evil One instigated one man to pour vodka over her from behind. Another, at the same moment, evidently not by accident, struck a light and touched it to her; the flame flashed up; poor aunt, in terror, flung her robe from her, before them all. . . . Screams, laughter, jests arose as if at a fair. In a word, the old folks could not recall so merry a wedding.

Pidórka and Petrus began to live like a gentleman and lady. There was plenty of everything, and everything was handsome. . . . But honest people shook their heads when they looked at their way of living. "From the Devil no good can come," they unanimously agreed. "Whence, except from the tempter of orthodox people, came this wealth? Where else could he get such a lot of gold? Why, on the very day that he got rich, did Basavriuk vanish as if into thin air?" Say, if you can, that people imagine things! In fact, a month had not passed, and no one would have recognized Petrus. Why, what had happened to him? God knows. He sits in one spot and says no word to anyone; he thinks continually and seems to be trying to recall something. When Pidórka succeeds in getting him to speak, he seems to forget himself, carries on a conversation, and even grows cheerful; but if he inadvertently glances at the sacks, "Stop, stop! I have forgotten," he cries, and again plunges into reverie, and again strives to recall something. Sometimes when he has sat long in a place, it seems to him as though it was coming, just coming back to mind . . . and again all fades away. It seems as if he is sitting in the tavern: they bring him vodka; vodka stings him; vodka is repulsive to him. Someone comes along and strikes him on the shoulder; but beyond that everything is veiled in darkness before him. The perspiration streams down his face, and he sits exhausted in the same place.

What did not Pidórka do? She consulted the sorceress; and they poured out fear and brewed stomach-ache ("To pour out fear" is done with us in case of fear; when it is desired to know what caused it, melted lead or wax is poured into water and the object whose form it assumes is the one which frightened the sick person; after this the fear departs. *Sónyashnitza* is brewed for giddiness and pain in the bowels. To this end, a bit of stump is burned, thrown into a jug, and turned upside down into a bowl filled with water, which is placed on the patient's stomach; after an incantation he is given a spoonful of this water to drink)—but all to no avail. And so the summer passed. Many a Cossack had mowed and reaped; many a Cossack, more enterprising than the rest, had set off upon an expedition. Flocks of ducks were already crowding our marshes, but there was not even a hint of improvement.

It was red upon the steppes. Ricks of grain, like Cossacks' caps, dotted the fields here and there. On the highway were to be encountered wagons loaded with brushwood and logs. The ground had become more solid, and in places was touched with frost. Already had the snow begun to besprinkle the sky, and the branches of the trees were covered with rime like rabbitskin. Already on frosty days the red-breasted finch hopped about on the snow heaps like a foppish Polish nobleman and picked out grains of corn; and children, with huge sticks, chased wooden tops upon the ice, while their fathers lay quietly on the stove, issuing forth at intervals with lighted pipes in their lips, to growl, in regular fashion, at the orthodox frost, or to take the air and thresh the grain spread out in the barn. At last the snow began to melt, and the ice rind slipped away, but Petró remained the same; and, the longer it went on, the more morose he grew. He sat in the middle of the cottage as though nailed to the spot, with the sacks of gold at his feet. He grew shy; his hair grew long; he became terrible, and still he thought of but one thing; still he tried to recall something and got angry and ill-tempered because he could not recall it. Often, rising wildly from his seat, he gesticulates violently, fixes his eyes on something as though desirous of catching it; his lips move as though desirous of uttering some long-forgotten word—and remain speechless. Fury takes possession of him: he gnaws and bites his hands like a man half crazy, and in his vexation tears out his hair by the handful, until, calming down, he falls into forgetfulness, as it were, and again begins to recall, and is again seized with fury and fresh tortures. . . . What visitation of God is this?

Pidórka was neither dead nor alive. At first it was horrible to her to remain alone in the cottage; but, in course of time, the poor woman grew accustomed to her sorrow. But it was impossible to recognize the Pidórka of former days. No blush, no smile; she was thin and worn with grief and had wept her bright eyes away. Once, someone who evidently took pity on her advised her to go to the witch who dwelt in the bear's ravine and enjoyed the reputation of being able to cure every disease in the world. She determined to try this last remedy; word by word she persuaded the old woman to come to her. This was St. John's Eve, as it chanced. Petró lay insensible on the bench and did not observe the newcomer. Little by little he rose and looked about him. Suddenly he trembled in every limb, as though he were on the scaffold; his hair rose upon his head, and he laughed such a laugh as pierced Pidórka's heart with fear. "I have remembered, remembered!" he cried in terrible joy; and, swinging a hatchet round his head, he flung it at the old woman with all his might. The hatchet penetrated the oaken door two *vershok*.* The old woman disappeared, and a child of seven in a

---

* Three-and-one-half inches.

white blouse, with covered head, stood in the middle of the cottage. . . . The sheet flew off. "Ivas!" cried Pidórka, and ran to him; but the apparition became covered from head to foot with blood and illumined the whole room with red light. . . . She ran into the passage in her terror, but, on recovering herself a little, wished to help him; in vain! The door had slammed to behind her so securely that she could not open it. People ran up and began to knock; they broke in the door, as though there were but one mind among them. The whole cottage was full of smoke; and just in the middle, where Petrus had stood, was a heap of ashes, from which smoke was still rising. They flung themselves upon the sacks: only broken potsherds lay there instead of ducats. The Cossacks stood with staring eyes and open mouths, not daring to move a hair, as if rooted to the earth, such terror did this wonder inspire in them.

I do not remember what happened next. Pidórka took a vow to go upon a pilgrimage, collected the property left her by her father, and in a few days it was as if she had never been in the village. Whither she had gone, no one could tell. Officious old women would have dispatched her to the same place whither Petró had gone, but a Cossack from Kiev reported that he had seen, in a cloister, a nun withered to a mere skeleton, who prayed unceasingly; and her fellow villagers recognized her as Pidórka, by all the signs—that no one had ever heard her utter a word; that she had come on foot and had brought a frame for the icon of God's mother, set with such brilliant stones that all were dazzled at the sight.

But this was not the end, if you please. On the same day that the Evil One made away with Petrus, Basavriuk appeared again; but all fled from him. They knew what sort of bird he was—none else than Satan, who had assumed human form in order to unearth treasures; and, since treasures do not yield to unclean hands, he seduced the young. That same year, all deserted their earth huts and collected in a village; but, even there, there was no peace, on account of that accursed Basavriuk. My late grandfather's aunt said that he was particularly angry with her, because she had abandoned her former tavern, and tried with all his might to revenge himself upon her. Once the village elders were assembled in the tavern, and, as the saying goes, were arranging the precedence at the table, in the middle of which was placed a small roasted lamb, shame to say.

They chattered about this, that, and the other—among the rest about various marvels and strange things. Well, they saw something; it would have been nothing if only one had seen it, but all saw it; and it was this: the sheep raised his head; his goggling eyes became alive and sparkled, and the black, bristling mustache, which appeared for one instant, made a significant gesture at those present. All, at once, recognized Basavriuk's countenance in the sheep's head; my grandfather's aunt thought it was on the point of asking for vodka. . . . The worthy elders seized their hats and hastened home.

Another time, the church starost himself, who was fond of an occasional private interview with my grandfather's brandy glass, had not succeeded in getting to the bottom twice, when he beheld the glass bowing very low to him. "Satan take you, let us make the sign of the cross over you!" . . . And the same marvel happened to his better half. She had just begun to mix the dough in a huge kneading trough, when suddenly the trough sprang up. "Stop, stop! Where are you going?" Putting its arms akimbo, with dignity, it went skipping all about the cottage. . . . You may laugh, but it was no laughing matter to your grandfathers. And in vain did Father Athanasii go through all the village with holy water and chase the Devil through the streets with his brush; and my late grandfather's aunt long complained that, as soon as it was dark, someone came knocking at her door and scratching at the wall.

Well! All appears to be quiet now, in the place where our village stands; but it was not so very long ago—my father was still alive—that I remember how a good man could not pass the ruined tavern, which a dishonest race had long managed for their own interest. From the smoke-blackened chimneys smoke poured out in a pillar, and rising high in the air, as if to take an observation, rolled off like a cap, scattering burning coals over the steppe; and Satan (the son of a dog should not be mentioned) sobbed so pitifully in his lair that the startled ravens rose in flocks from the neighboring oak-wood and flew through the air with wild cries.

Dark Music

JACK SNOW

*Many a sorcerer seeks simple domination over his fellow man, but the mage
of "Dark Music" wields a much weirder power.* JACK SNOW *(1907–
1956), a native of Piqua, Ohio, had a career in radio which eventually
brought him to New York as an NBC executive. His writings include
fantasy short stories and two of the best post–L. Frank Baum novels,* Magical Mimics in Oz *and* The Shaggy Man of Oz. *He also wrote a delightful guidebook for Oz aficionados,* Who's Who in Oz.

I was the first person in the United States to see the sun rise that
morning late in June, 1929. I stood in the doorway of my cabin on
Moccasin Mountain and watched the fiery steeds draw mighty
Apollo's chariot into the heavens for another journey across the
blue summer sky. Located in central Maine, this was the highest
eastward elevation in the United States—a little more than half a
mile above the sea—and it pleased my vanity to picture myself
there. A lonely human mite, the only one of a continent of several
hundred millions who was touched at this moment by the sun's
rays. For I was alone. There was no one else on the mountain top;
of that I was sure.

My family had owned most of the mountain, and my father, who had loved wild places and wilderness life, had kept it scrupulously free from the taint of the human kind. This rude little log cabin was the only man-made structure on the entire mountain. Years before my father had gone to the Heaven that for him must not be much different from this mountain, and my mother had not waited long to follow him. A young man then, I had come into the family fortune and Moccasin Mountain. In those days I had little taste for solitude or the outdoor life. I was too absorbed—fascinated is a better word—with the life that teems in that human jungle known as Manhattan. I had taken a full part in the riotous life that was New York in the Prohibition era of the roaring twenties. I had worked hard and played harder. I had made money—for that was part of the New York game—but the summer of 1929 found me on the verge of a nervous breakdown. I was thin. I had no appetite. I slept fitfully and awoke exhausted. I was taut to the breaking point. My doctor warned me. A complete rest was imperative: quiet; the great outdoors; plain, wholesome food; no more boot-leg liquor, and no more work.

It was then that my memory harked back across the mad New York years to the cleanly sanity of Moccasin Mountain. And that was how I happened to be the first greeter of the sun on the Northern Hemisphere that morning early in June, 1929. Now that I am approaching old age, I feel compelled to put down on paper the experiences that befell me on Moccasin Mountain those long years ago—experiences so terrifying that I shut them out of my mind for years, closed memory's doors so that they could not obtrude in my waking hours. God knows I have suffered for years with recurring visions in my sleep of that summer's experiences. So frightful was the final horrific crescendo of the series of happenings, that I was unimpressed by the stock crash in the autumn of '29, and the wiping out of the greater part of my personal fortune. That, somehow, did not seem important. I had changed. Money no longer was my obsession. Nor was I ever to return to the round of New York life that had occupied me in the preceding years. I was perfectly content to salvage from the wreck of my fortune a modest sum which permitted me to set myself up in business in a small town in the Middle West.

Within a few years I had married and my whole life was devoted to my family. Outwardly I was a normal man. Few people knew that I suffered agonies when I was forced to listen to music. Years before I had loved music. The opera and the concert hall were an established part of my New York life. But after the summer on Moccasin Mountain the sound of music was a cacophony of horror in my ears. Nor have the passing years lessened my apparent aversion to music. I had thought that perhaps the sharp terror that melody inspired in me would wear off as the years went by. But it has not. The revulsion, the repugnance I experience upon hearing a once beloved symphony melody is as keen today as it was those long years ago when it was first inspired. But I should not use the word "inspired" in connection with so horrible an experience. Rather, my soul and spirit were branded with a dark scar that will endure into my grave.

[2]

At first my way of life on Moccasin Mountain was simple enough. I was utterly alone. In my large touring car I had brought enough supplies of salted meats and tinned goods to last through the summer. Firewood was plentiful for the open fireplaces—and it was often needed, for Maine nights at a mile-high elevation are cool even in August.

I had brought with me a plentiful supply of the books I had been meaning to read for years; and between the simple duties of preparing my meals and cleaning the cabin, and reading, sleeping and taking long walks, the days and nights passed peacefully and uneventfully. Before I had been on Moccasin Mountain two weeks my health had improved noticeably. My appetite was more nearly normal, the bow-string tautness of my nerves had relaxed, and I was able to sleep soundly for hours at a time.

The first intimation I received of the series of events that began innocently enough, but mounted to a climax of vocal horror, came when I discovered that I was not alone.

It was a hot, sleepy afternoon, early in July. I was on one of my exploration tours of the mountain, and I had discovered a spot that enchanted and delighted my spirit. It was a valley, not more than a half mile long, and perhaps four hundred feet wide. It dropped steeply in the stone of the mountain, and looking down into it was for all the world like surveying a sea of greenly waving tree tops.

Carefully I picked my way into the depths of the glen, pushing through tangled vines and undergrowth, and threading my way through those copses where the tall pines grew so closely that they seemed like minions, guarding the depths of this tiny valley against intruders. But once through the trees, I found myself in the heart of the valley, and there paused in wonder and delight. For I was confronted with a cleared space of several hundred feet where no trees grew—only a grass as soft and fine as moss, dappled with wild flowers. Above me the trees met overhead, entirely shutting out the direct rays of the sun. The light that bathed this bit of paradise was screened through millions of living leaves, and was subdued and faintly glowing with green. At one end of the cleared space bubbled a tiny spring of frosty, clear water. I sighed and sank to the ground, stretching my legs before me, and supporting myself on my arms, my palms flat on the soft grass.

Never had man built so lovely a structure as this. The tall pines that encircled me, the green vines that ran lacily up the trees, the fronds that hung from the limbs, the lichen that mellowed on the ancient boles—all combined to give a natural reproduction of the Gothic cathedrals of the Old World. Nature, the master craftsman, had duplicated in vegetation the noblest architectural achievements of man. Or wait, would it not be more truthful to say that some unnamed architect of the remote past had on some late summer afternoon such as this wandered into just such a Gothic cathedral of trunks and leaves and vines as I found myself in? Then, the Gothic in architecture was not a creation of man, but of nature—magnificence on a scale that man could only borrow from and copy.

I sank back on a soft bank of moss and listened to the little sounds that echoed in the hush of that green chamber. The luminous green of the light that filled the enchanted hollow was as clear as that one perceives when gazing into the depths of a flawless gem. Closing my eyes, I lay in perfect peace. For the first time in many a year, I was at rest with myself and my surroundings.

The last thing I remembered was the sleepy chirruping of the crickets, and the remote buzz of a solitary bee as it settled on one of the blossoms that lay scattered over the grass, like the floral pattern of an exquisite carpet.

[3]

I had spent much of the day walking, and my weariness, combined with the sense of peace and rest that pervaded the glen, must have caused me to drowse. I awoke suddenly, startled, with the feeling that I was not alone. Looking up from my couch of moss, I saw an old man standing a few paces away, staring at me curiously through the green gloom. How long I had slept, I did not know, but when I awoke the lambent green light had deepened several shades. Around the edges of the clearing, where the trees grew, the shadows were deep, indicating that the afternoon was wearing into evening.

I leaped to my feet and regarded the stranger. He was a perfect gargoyle of a man. I was amazed at his appearance of extreme age. There was no estimating it. Human beings just don't live the number of years that this dotard had seemed to accumulate. His long, white hair hung down his back in braids. His snowy beard fell to his knees. His face was lined and in turn the lines were broken and interwoven into networks and lacements of incredibly minute detail. His skin was faded to the pallor of age-worn parchment. He stared at me from pale, blue eyes that looked out from under twin canopies of enormous, shaggy, white eyebrows. As curious as the ancient one himself, was his garb. It was simply a tunic woven of reeds and dried grasses, and hung about his shoulders. When, at last he spoke, his voice sounded like wind rustling through dead leaves.

"Go," the old man said. "Go away."

It was a command, nothing less.

"I intend to go," I replied, noting the deepening gloom. "But I will come back, and then I want to talk with you."

"No," murmured the aged one. "You must never come back. You must go now and forget you were ever here."

"But see here," I flared up, annoyed with the old fellow, "I happen to be the owner of this land. You are the one to be told to get off it—not I."

The old man regarded me steadily for a moment, then replied in that strange, tone-faded voice that I was to learn to know so well in the weeks that followed: "The valley is mine. I care for it. I tend it. It wants no one but me. You must go."

It struck me oddly that conversing with the old fellow was like talking with an echo. I shivered. I was lightly clad and already the chill of evening was setting in. It was foolish to waste more time talking, and chance losing my way in the dark, back to the warmth of my cabin.

Apparently the old man was satisfied that he had spoken the final word and settled the matter, for he now turned his back on me and walked toward the opposite end of the valley. He moved with surprising speed and agility for one weighted down with so many years. I noted that he was thin to the point of emaciation, and I wondered how he endured the cold in his frock of woven grasses. Then in the dusk he literally melted away from my sight. The brownish green of his tunic blended into the darkening green of the fading light, and like a phantom or a wavering dream the old fellow was gone.

I turned and started my climb up the steep side of the glen. It was not easy in the thickness of those trees where almost no light penetrated. It took me nearly an hour to find my way back to my cabin. I was tired, cold and hungry, so I set about immediately to prepare my meal. It seemed a long time ago when the sight and smells of steaming hot food inspired in me only boredom and a faint nausea.

After dinner I threw a log on the fire, and settled into an easy chair with my thoughts and my pipe. So now I was no longer alone on the mountain. Who was the old man? How did he live? How long had he been there in the glen? Over and over I pondered these questions, but of course there were no answers—only theories and speculations. That the old man was alone—a solitary—I was convinced. Perhaps he was merely a harmless crackpot who had given up human society many years ago. The longer I pondered, the less important the pitiful old man seemed. The valley—that was the important thing! I closed my eyes and again saw its unearthly beauty. Stay away from it, as the old man had commanded? I smiled to myself.

Later that night, as I lay on my cot looking out of the window at the stars that glowed so bright and clear above, I knew that the very next day would find me making my way to the secluded glen.

But the next day I did not go to the glen. Early in the morning, the sky darkened, a swift wind swept through the trees scudding black clouds before it, and a slow drizzle began. It kept up intermittently all day long; a slow, drawn out, summer rain storm.

I was confined to my cabin, and spent the day trying to read. But my attention remained fixed on the print only fitfully. Somehow the dull day finally passed, and with the coming of evening the rain stopped. A great silver disc of a moon rolled from behind the dispersing clouds. The night grew clear, with air that was freshened and sweetened by the cleansing rain.

I was tempted to go then and there to the glen. I wanted to view the marvel of the place lighted by the faintest of silvery radiance. I imagined the raindrops clinging to the leaves—the glen showered with a myriad of shimmering jewels. The sight would be a magical one, I knew, but reason prevailed, and I retired early, only to toss the night in fitful slumber, haunted by a dream of nightmare quality.

In this vision I was again in the green illuminated hollow, and I was not alone. I was seated in the center of the clearing, when suddenly before me appeared the old man I had seen the day before. As I blinked there appeared another old man, and then another and another and another, until I was surrounded by a hundred old men. They were identically alike to the last flowing white whisker and delicate wrinkle.

While I stared the old men solemnly joined hands and began a macabre dance. There was music now in my dream—such music as Mahler, Berlioz or Schoenberg might have written. It was tortured, twisted, music that cried out in protest even as it sang of vanished and lamented joys. It wove maniacal chords with notes of exquisite purity and beauty.

And all the time the old men danced, solemnly with stately tread, as though they were performing a religious rite. At last it seemed the dance was over. The music stopped, and for a moment the circle of old men was motionless, each standing with his back to me. Then, like a flash, and with an evil jack-in-the-box-like agility the circle of oldsters leaped, turning completely about in the air so that they faced me. I saw that a metamorphosis had come over their faces. They were now bare skulls, and from eyeless sockets flowed luminous green rays that focused on me. As the circle of skulls peered at me, the music crashed into being again. It was a perfect fury of screaming discord. The skull headed men were advancing slowly toward me, closer and closer. The green eyes, beamed upon me, were becoming stronger and stronger. As in all such dreams I was powerless to move. When the skull headed men were almost upon me the music stopped, and the green rays flashed out so that I was in utter darkness and silence. Then in the darkness and silence I heard the jaws of the skulls snap rapidly open and shut, while a hundred dried-leaf, wispish voices shouted at me in whispers these words:

"The Dance of Life Begins and Ends in the Skull."

With the echoes of those words still in my ears, I awoke to find my forehead beaded with perspiration, while my face and body were bathed in the silver luminescence of the full moon that shone through my window.

At the time I dismissed the dream for what it seemed—mere nightmare. But later in the light of what happened, I found myself recalling the eerie dream and the wild, demented music as strangely and weirdly prophetic.

[4]

The following day dawned bright and clear. I awoke feeling weary and listless. Even thoughts of the green hollow could not inspire me. Apathetically I set about preparing my breakfast and doing the morning chores. Somewhat half-heartedly I promised myself that I would visit the glen that day. It was not until afternoon that my spirits rose a bit, and I resolved to go at once to the hollow. It was a beautiful day, the air crisp and clear, and the sun brilliant. My dream of the night before seemed very far away and wholly unreal.

Slowly I picked my way between the trees down the steep grade into the hollow. As before the sunlight trailed reluctantly behind me. There was a steady and progressive darkening, a deepening of the shadows as the trees grew more and more dense. The fancy came to me that a gigantic rheostat controlled the sunlight, and the knob of the rheostat was now being slowly turned by some monstrous hand to the "off" position. But the hand stopped turning just short of the "off" marking, and I found the hollow suffused with the same soft green glow that had enchanted me on my initial visit.

There was no sign of the old man. So, yielding to the perfect peace and quiet of the place, I couched myself on a bank of moss and fell to reading the book I had brought with me. The long afternoon passed all too swiftly, and towards its end, as the light deepened into the emerald hue that marked the coming of evening to the valley, my book slipped from my hands and I dropped into a light sleep. Almost instantly I was awakened by a presence. I opened my eyes to find the old man standing quietly before me. From whence had he come? Apparently he had materialized out of the green vapor that filled the hollow. I raised myself on one elbow and stared at the stranger speculatively.

"You should not have come back," the old man stated in his wind and dead leaves voice.

"I told you I was coming back," I replied. "I am not trespassing —this land legally belongs to me, and I have every right to be here, which you haven't."

The ancient stranger flared up. "Laws! What have your laws to do with me? What can you know of my valley—you, a stranger! This is my home, and it is not right for you to invade it!"

I stared at the old man curiously. "Look," I began in a patient, gentle tone, "I am sorry if you do not want me here. But I find the place restful and soothing to my nerves. There is plenty of room for both of us. You ought to be glad that I didn't drive to the village and return with the Sheriff and have you thrown off my land. I could do that very easily, you know."

At these words the old man started and began trembling with such violence that I feared he was about to collapse. Contrite over the unexpected effect my words had wrought on the ancient, I leaped to my feet and supported him in my arms. The old fellow was shaking alarmingly and seemed to be unconscious of my presence. His eyes were glassed over, uncomprehending as though stricken with unutterable tragedy. Gently I lowered him to the mossy couch on which I had reclined. Then I saw that he was trying to talk. His lips moved but no sound came from them. Slowly he turned his eyes and gave me so piteous and appealing a look that it went straight to my heart. Finally he managed to gasp, "You—you —you won't make me go? I—I can't leave—I have no other world."

I grasped the old fellow's withered hand in mine and held it firmly. "Of course you may stay," I found myself telling him. "Stay as long as you like. Why, as you say, this is your home."

"Thank you," the old man muttered, and something appeared on his face that was wanly like a smile.

That marked the beginning of my friendship with Old Aaron—such was the only name he ever gave me.

By that time the shadows of evening were fast encroaching, and after a few more words of reassurance, I left Old Aaron in his beloved hollow, and made my way to my cabin. But the following day and the day after that and on many succeeding summer days I visited the lonely glen and drowsed away the sleepy hours, lulled by the odd voice of the old man, so much like the soft rustling of dead leaves that I often fancied I was listening to the forest speak through him.

For Old Aaron had come to accept me. Indeed, he looked forward to my visits to the hollow. When rain caused me to be absent, he made no attempt to conceal his pleasure upon my reappearance in the hollow. But never was I able to persuade him to leave the glen, even to visit me in my cabin. He told me much about himself, but he was most elusive regarding his life before he had come to the hollow. When I asked him how long he had lived there, he replied, "always." That was manifestly untrue, but I am convinced that the old man's memory stopped with his existence in the glen. Perhaps something so horrible had befallen him in the outside world, that when he retired to this tiny paradise his mind had blotted out his previous existence.

Early in our acquaintanceship, I brought him food from my ample supply in the cabin. But he would have nothing to do with it. Somewhere in his mind there operated a powerful censor that stubbornly rejected anything from outside the hollow. The "foreign" foods I offered him were not part of the glen, therefore they were to be shunned. In the same manner the old fellow had attempted to reject me, but when I turned the tables and threatened to reject *him* his mental censor was forced to make me the exception to its rule. I offered to bring Old Aaron some of my cast-off clothing. But again he would not hear of it. He asserted that his woven garments were sufficiently warm for the summer, and he had heavier ones for winter wear. When I queried him about how he lived through the long, cold winters when Moccasin Mountain was covered with deep snow, he explained that not much snow penetrated to the hollow.

It was at this point that Old Aaron revealed to me his living place in the glen. He led me to a spot in the hollow where the trees that bordered the clearing were broken by a huge, mossy out-cropping of rock. Stooping over, the old man seized a tendril of vine, and pulled upon it. A little door not more than two feet in diameter opened into a cave in the rock. Here Old Aaron found shelter. He had discovered the cave when he first arrived in the hollow, and had concealed the entrance with a door woven of vines and reeds. Old Aaron would not permit me to enter the cave, and he made me promise solemnly that I would never attempt to do so against his wishes. I was entirely convinced by this time of the ancient hermit's harmlessness, so I readily agreed to stay out of his cave. Let the old fellow have his secrets, if he liked.

Old Aaron was perfectly willing to describe the cave to me. He said that it was quite large and very high. Somewhere there was another opening—probably high up in the roof, or in the side of rock that cropped out above the hollow—for the air inside was fresh and pure, although there were no drafts or currents. Inside, the old man had made himself a bed of soft, dried grasses, and had stored a supply of nuts, roots and berries that lasted him through the winter. Outside the cavern the little spring supplied him with water. The cavern was a snug retreat for the old fellow, and as he seemed to require astonishingly little food, there was nothing to prevent his survival of so hardy an existence.

I recall that Old Aaron brought to a close his story of the cave and his physical life in the hollow with these words:

"Yes, I am quite well provided for—I and my pets." The latter he added absent-mindedly, as though he were speaking to himself, in that strange voice that was half a whisper.

"Your what?" I asked quickly.

The old man looked as though he had let slip something he hadn't meant to speak of. "Just my pets—nothing of any interest," he replied hesitantly in an attempt to dismiss the subject.

But I was interested, and after much arguing I finally succeeded in wheedling out of the old man a promise that sometime he would show me his pets. Whether they were dogs, cats or some woodland creatures, I could not get him to state. I believe that subconsciously he was eager to talk about his pets, but his long years of solitude had rendered him so reticent and shy that his mind rebelled against each new encroachment I made on his hermit existence.

It wasn't until days later, during which I brought up the subject of his pets at every opportunity, that I was rewarded. I was about to leave the hollow and go back to my cabin late one afternoon, when the old man stopped me and haltingly asked:

"You, you really are interested in my pets—you would like to see them?"

"Yes, of course," I replied.

"Then," said the old man, "come back to the hollow tonight after dark, and I will show them to you."

"But why after dark?" I asked. "Can't you show them to me now, or tomorrow perhaps?"

"No, no," the old man insisted earnestly. "They may be seen only at night. You must come then, if you want to see them."

I reflected that I had a powerful electric lantern and with its aid the descent into the hollow wouldn't be too difficult. Also, there was going to be a full moon tonight—and I had never seen the hollow after dark. Of course I yielded, promising Old Aaron that I would return after I had my evening meal.

[5]

Shortly after nine I was on my way to the hollow. The moonlight was so strong that I had no use for my lantern until I entered the shadows of the trees surrounding the glen. With the strong beacon of light shed by my lantern, the descent was not at all difficult. Reaching the glen, I switched off the light and looked about me. It was a truly lovely sight. The moonlight penetrated the canopy of leaves much as the sunlight did, only now the faint green glow was more vaporous and was tinged most delicately with the faintest of silver hues. Gone was the golden-edged light of daytime, and in its place a ghost-luminance of eerie beauty.

A moment later I espied Old Aaron approaching me from the far side of the glen. He was alone. There was no sign of his pets.

"Where are they?" I asked.

And then I noted that he carried something at his side. As I approached, I saw that it was a small cage of woven reeds. What it contained, I could not tell at the moment.

Old Aaron smiled a greeting, and pointing to the cage, said with pride, "My pets."

Impulsively I switched on my lantern and flashed the light on the cage. Immediately there sounded a squeaking like a disturbed nest of mice. The effect of my action on Old Aaron was astounding.

"Don't!" shrieked the old man, leaping frenziedly at me. "The light—put it out—and never turn it on down here!"

There again was that passionate revulsion against anything from outside the hollow. To pacify the old man who was trembling and staring wildly at me, I switched off the lantern. Then, to divert his attention, I said with perfect calmness, as if nothing unusual had happened, "Your pets, Aaron—you were going to show them to me."

"Yes, yes, my pets," mumbled the ancient one, slowly regaining his composure. The old man stooped over and lifted the woven lid of the cage. Inside were a dozen bats.

"Ugh!" I exclaimed with distaste. "So these are your pets."

Old Aaron didn't trouble to answer me. He walked slowly with his cage to the center of the clearing. There he placed the opened cage on the ground, and stepped back from it a few paces. Curiously I watched as the old fellow placed a thin reed to his lips and blew through it. There sounded a weird, piping whistle. Immediately a dozen bats arose from the cage, and circled through the night air. To my amazement they did not squeak or squeal as they flew. Instead there sounded through the glen the oddest, most eerie music I have ever heard. That it was coming from the bats, I could not doubt, because the intensity of the pitch rose and fell as the bats approached and then passed me in their circling. I can not possibly describe the music. It might have been the pipes of fairyland that were sounding. It was the last touch needed to give the glen the ultimate in unearthly, night beauty. The instinctive revulsion one feels for bats vanished for the time being from my mind. I recalled Ariel's song from "The Tempest":

> In a cowslip's bell I lie;
> There I couch when owls do cry;
> On the bat's back I do fly

After summer merrily.
Merrily, merrily shall I live now,
Under the blossom that hangs on the bow.

Had a band of tiny, shimmering fairy folk or a troop of woodland elves suddenly appeared in the glen, I do not think I would have been surprised at that moment. The magic of the silver-green moonlight, the night-loveliness of the glen, the unreal beauty of the music—all conspired to weave about me as potent a spell as any fairy creature ever cast.

Nor did Old Aaron present a discordant appearance in this picture. He might have been an ancient Druidic Priest or the Father Spirit of the forest itself. It was I, I reflected, who was the alien—the lucky alien, I thought then. For surely all too few humans had witnessed such magic as I was seeing and hearing. Delight filled my ears, as I watched Old Aaron with wonder. As the bats wove their airy circles above him, the old man raised and lowered his arms, and for all the world like an orchestra conductor directed the motions and flight of the creatures.

It was wonderful the control Old Aaron exercised over the bats. In some miraculous manner that was as enchanting as the music and the glen, he had trained these creatures to do his will. As his hands rose and fell, so did the flight of the bats in the circles they wove in the green vapor of the valley. I had emerged sufficiently from the thralldom of the music to begin to wonder. Question after question rose to the surface of my mind, and exploded like shooting stars on a summer's eve.

How had Old Aaron trained these wild creatures of the night to do his will? How had he taught them to sing thus beautifully? What had he done to their vocal chords to make it possible for them to utter such opiate notes? Could there possibly be natural answers to these questions, or were the answers to partake of the unreal and mystic qualities of the marvels I was witnessing?

Now I noted that Old Aaron's motions were more confined. The bats were flying in smaller and smaller circles. In a few seconds they circled directly over the open cage. The music had fallen to an echo, an echo of Pan pipes from the far land of faery. I strained my ears to catch the last paean—the last memory of melody. And then the bats had dropped one by one into their basket cage, and silence once more filled the glen. Old Aaron closed the lid of the cage and picked it up.

Immediately I let loose a torrent of questions. The old man was obviously pleased that I had enjoyed his concert, but it took a great deal of questioning to extract any kind of answers to my many questions. About the training of the bats, Old Aaron would say little except that the most important element involved was infinite patience. He spoke of the nights of early training when he tied light cords of dried grass to the bats and thus confined and directed their flight. Later, he dispensed with the woven cords, and the motions of his hands alone sufficed to guide the creatures.

As for the music, the old man stooped, opened the cage and removed one of the bats. Spreading the creature's wings, he showed me tiny pipes or flutes fashioned from reeds and fastened ingeniously with delicate sinews of grass to the under surface of the bat's wings. As the creature flew, the passage of air through the pipes caused the music I had heard. By fashioning the pipes of various sizes, Old Aaron managed to vary the notes produced by each pipe. The old man told me of an ancient Chinese custom of fashioning such pipes and attaching them to the wings of pigeons to produce music in their flight. The art was as old as Chinese history, having been handed down from father to son through generation after generation, and was still practiced today. Old Aaron had no pigeons in the hollow, so he used bats, which were plentiful in his cave.

Long ago I had learned the futility of questioning the old man about his past before he had come to the glen, so now I said nothing, but deduced from what he told me, and from what I had observed, that he had at one time lived or traveled in China, where he had learned the art of fashioning the pipes. Also, it seemed obvious to me that Old Aaron must most certainly have been a gifted musician or composer during his years in the outside world. I had to content myself with these speculations, for I was convinced that as long as Old Aaron lived, he would never speak to any living person of his life outside the glen.

It was nearly midnight when I stumbled into my cabin—moonstruck if ever a mortal was. And small wonder, for I had just lived a waking midsummer night's dream. For a long time I lay on my cot, while the moonlight poured through the window. I don't know when sleep came to me. Perhaps it was when I heard once more the ghost music of the glen, and smiled through the dream.

[6]

A spell of chill, rainy weather kept me away from the hollow for nearly a week. I thought of little else than the elfin music. I fretted the long hours away trying to read, while my eyes wandered continually to the rain-streamered windows.

On the first clear day I hurried to the glen, determined to ask Old Aaron to stage another concert for me that very night. But the old man refused positively to bring forth his "pets." He would not even discuss them, far less the music. He seemed now to regret that he had violated his solitude so far as to share his music with me.

Knowing the workings of Old Aaron's mind as I did, I adopted a new strategy. I acted as if I had never seen nor heard of the piping bats. This did the trick. Before two weeks had passed, the old man was making veiled references to the bats. Then came the day when he openly and of his own accord introduced the creatures into our conversation. Although my heart leapt, I successfully concealed the eagerness I felt. I could see that Old Aaron was affected by this—hurt that what I saw and heard in the glen that night had made so little impression upon me, and that I should so quickly forget. This was just what I wanted as I knew that wheedling and coaxing would only frighten the old man into silence. The idea must be his own.

My scheme was more successful than I had planned. If only it had failed and I had learned nothing more about the piping bats, today I would have only the memory of an enchanted summer evening. But that memory was doomed to be blasted by another as foul and evilly horrible as the first was mystic and lovely.

There came that fateful day when Old Aaron had taken as much of my disinterest and unconcern as he could. Hermit, recluse and eccentric he might be, but Old Aaron was also a human being, and I had sorely wounded his vanity. He determined now to "give me the works," to impress me so that I would never forget. God knows he succeeded.

I was on the point of leaving the glen for my cabin late one afternoon toward the end of August. Earlier in the day I had told Old Aaron that within the next few days—around the first of September—I was going to pack my belongings, lock up the cabin, and go back to the city. The news had visibly affected him and he had been more silent than usual. It was apparent that he was silently debating what was to him a most important question. Just as I was about to leave the hollow, the old man laid his hand on my shoulder and said:

"Once you asked to hear my bats again."

"Yes?" I replied, evincing only idle curiosity.

"Before you go away," the old man went on in his rustling voice, "I want to confess that I have kept much back. I have not told you all about my work. What you saw and heard was but a hint of what I have accomplished."

"Yes?" I repeated with the same laconic interest, although inwardly I was consumed with curiosity and excitement.

Then he came out with it, and it was with difficulty indeed that I maintained my air of unconcern.

"I want you to come to the hollow tonight—a little before midnight"—Old Aaron said, "and you will see and hear something you will never forget."

In an off-hand manner I replied that if I could manage to stay awake that late, I would keep the rendezvous. Then, secretly exulting, I turned and left Old Aaron.

[7]

Stay awake! I could no more have slept in the intervening hours than I could have stayed away from the glen. The evening tip-toed by on leaden feet. I could not read. I could not rest. Most of the time I paced the floor of the cabin, impatiently consulting my watch, which to my excited fancy seemed to tick with deadly slowness.

At about 11:30 I left the cabin. Unlike the first night I had visited the hollow, there was no moon tonight, nor any stars. I required my lantern for the entire journey. The night was so dark that it was lit with shadows.

Finally, I was inching my way down the hollow's steep incline. I had made my way there so many times during the summer, that I had beaten out a faint trail. But even so, it was rough going in the utter gloom of that night.

I stepped from the last of the trees that formed the sides of the glen. Then I stopped, staring in amazement. I needed my flashlight no longer. The hollow was truly enchanted. From each delicate tip of grass that carpeted the glen, there arose a wisp of bluish flame. The sight was indescribably unreal. Millions of tiny grass blades, each tipped with the cold, greenish blue of pale fox-fire. A phosphorescent deposit in the soil of this secluded spot seeped into the roots of the grass and tinged the blades with cold flame.

Here was a fairy glade as entrancing as any ever conjured by mortal fancy! No longer was I in the world of men, I had stepped into that airy realm where Queen Titania and King Oberon held nightly court. Had impish Puck, riding a wild hare across the silver greensward, suddenly confronted me, I would not have been surprised. How perfect a setting this was for the elfin music!

Slowly I advanced over the glowing grass. The ghostly light wavered and gleamed, illuminating the entire glen, faintly but wonderfully, and dissolving into the blackness of the night above. Of course the phosphorescence had been present on my previous visit, I reflected, but then it had blended into the diffused silver-green moonlight.

I made out the figure of Old Aaron, standing quietly beside the entrance to his cave. He greeted me silently. In some strange manner the old man divined the time.

"It is midnight," he stated quietly.

A glance at my wrist watch told me he was correct to the second. Then Old Aaron guided me to a spot on the far edge of the glen, and said solemnly, "Remain here."

The old man left me and returned to the entrance of his cave. Slowly and carefully he opened the door of woven reeds. But he did not produce the cage, as I had thought he would. Instead, he stood before the opening and uttered a long, low, weird whistle.

Immediately bats began issuing from the cave—not twelve—not twenty—not thirty—but literally hundreds and hundreds of the creatures. They flapped and flopped from the cave entrance in what seemed to me an unending, black river of beating wings. In spite of their dread appearance, I could not help thinking that once they were in rapid flight and the air was whistling through the pipes on their wings, they would produce music of truly symphonic proportions.

Old Aaron moved to the center of the glade. What a curious figure the ancient one presented, standing in a sea of wavering, green-blue light, while flopping about him were those hundreds of bats! The old man lifted his arms, and like marionette creatures the bats soared aloft. The black horde filled the air above Old Aaron. Then, in answer to the motions of the old man's arms, they began their dizzy, spiraling flight. They rose so high that I could just make out their shadow shapes. The vapour they showered over the glen was fetid and noxious.

I listened in stunned amazement. What were these sounds I was hearing? Certainly they had no kinship to the fairy music that had so enchanted me. Horror mounted as the sounds shaped themselves into a macabre symphony. I heard a melody—but it was all wrong, musically. There were notes that dropped below the musical scale, to depths of sound never meant to be heard. I was horribly disappointed and shocked. I wanted to bolt from the glen as swiftly as possible. But something forced me to stay and listen to the evil fascination.

The music abruptly shifted to a dance tempo. Dance? The only dancers to such a tempo were those who writhed through the hottest pits of Hades. How long could I endure it? How much punishment could my sensory system withstand? For the music affected not only my hearing—it set my teeth on edge—it crept into my eyes like thick smoke—it rippled my flesh with horror—it filled my mouth with a taste that brought me to the verge of retching—it assaulted my nostrils with a succession of charnel house odors.

And through it all, there stood Old Aaron, passionately and furiously waving and weaving his emaciated arms in a mad pattern of gestures that was in itself revolting and inhuman. I was forced to the realization that *he* was the evil genius—he was the author and the inspiration of these black sounds. Old Aaron was no harmless recluse. He was mad, unutterably mad. No sane man could conceive such horrors and then delight in forcing them upon an innocent spectator.

In the next instant I knew that the symphony was approaching its finale. The bats had increased their pace so that they flew dizzily in wild arcs, crazy spirals, and insane circles. The beating of their leather wings sounded a subtle background, like the applause of an audience of corpses in mold-green dress suits, and tattered lace that tangled with shreds of grave-stale flesh.

The end came with the most horrific blast of sound I have ever heard. Old Aaron was leaping about in a perfect frenzy of motion. As he gestured, first one group of bats would dive earthward, another plunge upward, and another whirl like dark lightning to a far edge of the glen. The result was that the hollow was filled with a demoniac throng of banshee sounds that shrieked with exultance and sobbed with impotent fury, torturing me until I was faint with revulsion.

In its last stages the symphony went utterly mad. There was no restraint whatever. This was the crashing finale, music turned blackly evil, music that sneered and sniveled and reviled any sense of beauty. Howling discords ranged over the glen and sawed through my nerves. The air was transformed into an insane maze of ululating reverberations.

I could endure no more. I clapped my hands to my ears, and staggered up the side of the glen. I dared not use the lantern which swung from my belt, for that would mean removing a hand from my ear, and then I should hear again. Through the intense gloom of the trees, I stumbled on, endlessly it seemed, until at last I stepped forth in a clearing above the hollow. When I removed my hands from my ears, there was utter silence. But never was a human so thankful to *hear* silence. The air was clean again. The night was fresh about me. I sobbed with relief and hurried to my cabin.

Later that night, or rather early that morning, lying on my cot in silence and solitude, I realized with a shudder that I could still hear the dark music. It echoed and reverberated in my tortured mind. I rolled and tossed until dawn, striving to rid myself of the memory of the symphony of the beast-birds.

I arose weary and desolate. During the hours I had tossed on my cot, the realization had come to me that never again would I be able to listen to music, however beautiful, without intense suffering. For there had been something in the torrent of sounds I heard that night that mocked and jibed and snickered obscenely at all that is noble and transcendently beautiful in man's inspired musical creations. There had been planted in my mind innuendoes, hinting,

slurred notes that sullied and contaminated every strain of music I
heard thereafter.

More than that, I soon discovered that not even my *memory* of
music was free from the blight of that night's experience. When a
familiar song or melody ran through my mind, immediately there
would intrude a haunting, jeering echo of the music of the bats.
The original melody became so twisted and blackened, that I strove
quickly to banish it from my mind. The world of music that I had
loved so well was lost to me.

[8]

Weary though I was that morning, I knew what must be done,
and that I should lose no time in doing it. I took the remainder of
my kerosene supply, about two gallons, and went to the hollow. It
was mid-morning when I arrived, and the glen was suffused with
the luminous green glow of the sunlight. Upon emerging from the
trees, I looked instantly toward Old Aaron's cave. The entrance was
open, and beside it lay the old man. Breaking into a run that carried
me across the valley in a matter of seconds, I stopped short with a
gasp of horror.

Old Aaron was dead. There was no doubt of that, nor was there
any doubt as to the cause of his death. His body was literally de-
nuded of the little flesh that had clothed it. There was not a morsel
of flesh that had not been rent and torn from the bones of the old
man. His eyeballs were gone, and the sockets were mere ruddy
holes. The old one might have been attacked by a thousand, razor-
keen knives.

The bats had done this. For some reason, which was soon to be
made obvious to me, they had turned against their master, and in a
wild blood orgy had ripped and torn the flesh from his bones.
Despite my conviction that the old man had been mad, I could not
but feel compassion for him and the frightful manner in which he
had died.

But this must not stop me from my purpose. Upon completing
their massacre, and surfeited with the blood of their Saturnalia, the
creatures had sought their cave. My task was to make sure that they
would never again leave it.

I collected a large amount of dead wood from among the trees, and laboriously conveyed it to the center of the cave. I had no curiosity regarding the extent of the place, I was too intent on my purpose. Next I carried the remains of Old Aaron into the cave and placed them on top of the bier of wood. Finally, I saturated the body, the wood and the floor of the cave with kerosene. The cave's floor was strewn with dried reeds and grasses, which would burn readily. Then I lighted a match, touched it to the bier, and fled to the cave's entrance. In an instant, I was outside, while behind me the cave was livid with crackling flame. My one, hurried, backward glance revealed towering streamers of fire, casting tortured shadows on the jutting stone walls of the cavern. The crackling of the flames was accompanied by a melee of unearthly noises and the mad beating of leathery wings. I did not pause for more than that one glance. That was enough to give me understanding of the visions that must have haunted Dante when he wrote his "Inferno."

Once outside the cave, I determined that not one of the bats should escape. I was about to block the entrance with a large boulder I had procured for that purpose, when one of the bats flopped and fluttered out, almost overcome by the heat and smoke. Viciously I ground its head under my heel, and quickly placed the stone before the entrance.

That was the end—the end of Old Aaron—and the end of the piping bats. For a moment I stood in silence.

Then, curiously I picked up the dead bat at my foot. I wanted another look at those pipes. I spread the bat's wings and stared, puzzled. There were no pipes, and there was no evidence that any had ever been attached to the creature's wings.

I was standing with the bat in my hand, so that the golden-green luminance of the glen shone full upon it. I looked more closely at the creature's face. Clots of half-dried blood were darkly smeared about its mouth and nostrils—human blood—Old Aaron's blood. I felt faintly ill. Suddenly the bat's mouth gaped open. It was not dead, as I had supposed.

And then occurred the final horror, the ultimate loathsomeness. As the bat's mouth gaped wide, I couldn't escape seeing that deep in its mouth, protruding from its throat—inserted there with what must have been astounding skill so that it formed an integral part of the bat's breathing apparatus—was one of Old Aaron's tiny pipes.

While my skin crawled, the bat breathed its death gasp. From the little pipe there burst an obscene bleat of sound that was an echo of the demoniac symphony that had shrieked through the glen the night before.

The Magic Egg

FRANK R. STOCKTON

Some miracles owe more to charlatanism than unholy compact, as is discovered in this strange story by FRANK R. STOCKTON, *who was born in Philadelphia in 1834, best remembered today for his maddening puzzle tale, "The Lady or the Tiger?" and its equally irritating sequel, "The Discourager of Hesitancy."*

The pretty little theater attached to the building of the Unicorn Club had been hired for a certain January afternoon by Mr. Herbert Loring, who wished to give therein a somewhat novel performance to which he had invited a small audience consisting entirely of friends and acquaintances.

Loring was a handsome fellow about thirty years old, who had traveled far and studied much. He had recently made a long sojourn in the far East, and his friends had been invited to the theater to see some of the wonderful things he had brought from that country of wonders. As Loring was a clubman, and belonged to a family of good social standing, his circle of acquaintances was large, and in this circle a good many unpleasant remarks had been made regarding the proposed entertainment—made, of course, by the people who had not been invited to be present. Some of the gossip on the subject had reached Loring, who did not hesitate to say that he could not talk to a crowd, and that he did not care to show the curious things he had collected to people who would not thoroughly appreciate them. He had been very particular in regard to his invitations.

At three o'clock on the appointed afternoon nearly all the people who had been invited to the Unicorn theater were in their seats. No one had stayed away except for some very good reason, for it was well known that if Herbert Loring offered to show anything it was worth seeing.

About forty people were present, who sat talking to one another, or admiring the decoration of the theater. As Loring stood upon the stage—where he was entirely alone, his exhibition requiring no assistants—he gazed through a loophole in the curtain upon a very interesting array of faces. There were the faces of many men and women of society, of students, of workers in various fields of thought, and even of idlers in all fields of thought, but there was not one which indicated a frivolous or listless disposition. The owners of those faces had come to see something, and they wished to see it.

For a quarter of an hour after the time announced for the opening of the exhibition Loring peered through the hole in the curtain, and then, although all the people he had expected had not arrived, he felt it would not do for him to wait any longer. The audience was composed of well-bred and courteous men and women, but despite their polite self-restraint Loring could see that some of them were getting tired of waiting. So, very reluctantly, and feeling that further delay was impossible, he raised the curtain and came forward on the stage.

Briefly he announced that the exhibition would open with some fireworks he had brought from Korea. It was plain to see that the statement that fireworks were about to be set off on a theater stage, by an amateur, had rather startled some of the audience, and Loring hastened to explain that these were not real fireworks, but that they were contrivances made of colored glass, which were illuminated by the powerful lens of a lantern which was placed out of sight, and while the apparent pyrotechnic display would resemble fireworks of strange and grotesque designs, it would be absolutely without danger. He brought out some little bunches of bits of colored glass, hung them at some distance apart on a wire which was stretched across the stage just high enough for him to reach it, and then lighted his lantern, which he placed in one of the wings, lowered all the lights in the theater, and began his exhibition.

As Loring turned his lantern on one of the clusters of glass lenses, strips, and points, and, unseen himself, caused them to move by means of long cords attached, the effects were beautiful and marvelous. Little wheels of colored fire rapidly revolved, miniature rockets appeared to rise a few feet and to explode in the air, and while all the ordinary forms of fireworks were produced on a diminutive scale, there were some effects that were entirely novel to the audience. As the light was turned successively upon one and another of the clusters of glass, sometimes it would flash along the whole line so rapidly that all the various combinations of color and motion seemed to be combined in one, and then for a time each particular set of fireworks would blaze, sparkle, and coruscate by itself, scattering particles of colored light, as if they had been real sparks of fire.

This curious and beautiful exhibition of miniature pyrotechnics was extremely interesting to the audience, who gazed upward with rapt and eager attention at the line of wheels, stars, and revolving spheres. So far as interest gave evidence of satisfaction, there was never a better satisfied audience. At first there had been some hushed murmurs of pleasure, but very soon the attention of everyone seemed so completely engrossed by the dazzling display that they simply gazed in silence.

For twenty minutes or longer the glittering show went on, and not a sign of weariness or inattention was made by any one of the assembled company. Then gradually the colors of the little fireworks faded, the stars and wheels revolved more slowly, the lights in the body of the theater were gradually raised, and the stage curtain went softly down.

Anxiously, and a little pale, Herbert Loring peered through the loop-hole in the curtain. It was not easy to judge of the effects of his exhibition, and he did not know whether or not it had been a success. There was no applause, but, on the other hand, there was no sign that anyone resented the exhibition as a childish display of colored lights. It was impossible to look upon that audience without believing that they had been thoroughly interested in what they had seen, and that they expected to see more.

For two or three minutes Loring gazed through his loophole and then, still with some doubt in his heart, but with a little more color in his cheeks, he prepared for the second part of his performance.

At this moment there entered the theater, at the very back of the house, a young lady. She was handsome and well-dressed, and as she opened the door—Loring had employed no ushers or other assistants in this little social performance—she paused for a moment and looked into the theater, and then noiselessly stepped to a chair in the back row, and sat down.

This was Edith Starr, who, a month before, had been betrothed to Herbert Loring. Edith and her mother had been invited to this performance, and front seats had been reserved for them, for each guest had received a numbered card; but Mrs. Starr had a headache, and could not go out that afternoon, and for a time her daughter had thought that she too must give up the pleasure Loring had promised her, and stay with her mother. But when the elder lady dropped into a quiet sleep, Edith thought that, late as it was, she would go by herself, and see what she could of the performance.

She was quite certain that if her presence were known to Loring he would stop whatever he was doing until she had been provided with a seat which he thought suitable for her, for he had made a point of her being properly seated when he gave the invitations. Therefore, being equally desirous of not disturbing the performance and of not being herself conspicuous, she sat behind two rather large men, where she could see the stage perfectly well, but where she herself would not be likely to be seen.

In a few moments the curtain rose, and Loring came forward, carrying a small, light table, which he placed near the front of the stage, and for a moment stood quietly by it. Edith noticed upon his face the expression of uncertainty and anxiety which had not yet left it. Standing by the side of the table, and speaking very slowly, but so clearly that his words could be heard distinctly in all parts of the room, he began some introductory remarks regarding the second part of his performance.

"The extraordinary, and I may say marvelous, thing which I am about to show you," he said, "is known among East Indian magicians as the magic egg. The exhibition is a very uncommon one, and has seldom been seen by Americans or Europeans, and it was by a piece of rare good fortune that I became possessed of the appliances necessary for this exhibition. They are indeed very few and simple, but never before, to the best of my knowledge and belief, have they been seen outside of India.

"I will now get the little box which contains the articles necessary for this magical performance, and I will say that if I had time to tell you of the strange and amazing adventure which resulted in my possession of this box, I am sure you would be as much interested in that as I expect you to be in the contents of the box. But, in order that none of you may think this is an ordinary trick, executed by means of concealed traps or doors, I wish you to take particular notice of this table, which is, as you see, a plain, unpainted pine table with nothing but a flat top, and four straight legs at the corners. You can see under and around it, and it gives no opportunity to conceal anything." Then, standing for a few moments as if he had something else to say, he turned and stepped toward one of the wings.

Edith was troubled as she looked at her lover during these remarks. Her interest was great—greater, indeed, than that of the people about her—but it was not a pleasant interest. As Loring stopped speaking, and looked about him, there was a momentary flush on his face. She knew this was caused by excitement, and she was pale from the same cause.

Very soon Loring came forward, and stood by the table.

"Here is the box," he said, "of which I spoke, and as I hold it up I think you can all see it. It is not large, being certainly not more than twelve inches in length and two deep, but it contains some very wonderful things. The outside of this box is covered with delicate engraving and carving which you can not see, and these marks and lines have, I think, some magical meaning, but I do not know what it is. I will now open the box, and show you what is inside. The first thing I take out is this little stick, not thicker than a lead-pencil, but somewhat longer, as you see. This is a magical wand, and is covered with inscriptions of the same character as those on the outside of the box. The next thing is this little red bag, well filled, as you see, which I shall put on the table, for I shall not yet need it.

"Now I take out a piece of cloth which is folded into a very small compass, but as I unfold it you will perceive that it is more than a foot square, and is covered with embroidery. All those strange lines and figures in gold and red, which you can plainly see on the cloth as I hold it up, are also characters in the same magic language as those on the box and wand. I will now spread the cloth on the table, and then take out the only remaining thing in the box, and this is nothing in the world but an egg—a simple, ordinary hen's egg, as you all see as I hold it up. It may be a trifle larger than an ordinary egg, but then, after all, it is nothing but a common egg—that is, in appearance; in reality it is a good deal more.

"Now I will begin the performance," and as he stood by the back of the table over which he had been slightly bending, and threw his eyes over the audience, his voice was stronger, and his face had lost all its pallor. He was evidently warming up with his subject.

"I now take up this wand," he said, "which, while I hold it, gives me power to produce the phenomena which you are about to behold. You may not all believe that there is any magic whatever about this little performance, and that it is all a bit of machinery; but whatever you may think about it, you shall see what you shall see.

"Now with this wand I gently touch this egg which is lying on the square of cloth. I do not believe you can see what has happened to this egg, but I will tell you. There is a little line, like a hair, entirely around it. Now that line has become a crack. Now you can see it, I know. It grows wider and wider! Look! The shell of the egg is separating in the middle. The whole egg slightly moves. Do you notice that? Now you can see something yellow showing itself between the two parts of the shell. See! It is moving a good deal, and the two halves of the shell are separating more and more! And now out tumbles this queer little object. Do you see what it is? It is a poor, weak, little chick, not able to stand, but alive—alive! You can all perceive that it is alive. Now you can see that it is standing on its feet, feebly enough, but still standing.

"Behold, it takes a few steps! You can not doubt that it is alive, and came out of that egg. It is beginning to walk about over the cloth. Do you notice that it is picking the embroidery? Now, little chick, I will give you something to eat. This little red bag contains grain, a magical grain, with which I shall feed the chicken. You must excuse my awkwardness in opening the bag, as I still hold the wand; but this little stick I must not drop. See, little chick, there are some grains. They look like rice, but, in fact, I have no idea what they are. But he knows, he knows! Look at him! See how he picks it up! There! He has swallowed one, two, three. That will do, little chick, for a first meal.

"The grain seems to have strengthened him already, for see how lively he is, and how his yellow down stands out on him, so puffy and warm! You are looking for some more grain, are you? Well, you can not have it just yet, and keep away from those pieces of egg-shell, which, by the way, I will put back into the box. Now, sir, try to avoid the edge of the table, and to quiet you, I will give you a little tap on the back with my wand. Now, then, please observe closely. The down which just now covered him has almost gone. He is really a good deal bigger, and ever so much uglier. See the little pin-feathers sticking out over him! Some spots, here and there, are almost bare, but he is ever so much more active. Ha! Listen to that! He is so strong that you can hear his beak as he pecks at the table. He is actually growing bigger and bigger before our very eyes! See that funny little tail, how it begins to stick up, and quills are showing at the end of his wings.

"Another tap, and a few more grains. Careful, sir! Don't tear the cloth! See how rapidly he grows! He is fairly covered with feathers, red and black, with a tip of yellow in front. You could hardly get that fellow into an ostrich egg! Now, then, what do you think of him? He is big enough for a broiler, though I don't think anyone would want to take him for that purpose. Some more grain, and another tap from my wand. See! He does not mind the little stick, for he has been used to it from his very birth. Now, then, he is what you would call a good half-grown chick. Rather more than half grown, I should say. Do you notice his tail? There is no mistaking him for a pullet. The long feathers are beginning to curl over, already. He must have a little more grain. Look out, sir, or you will be off the table! Come back here! This table is too small for him, but if he were on the floor you could not see him so well.

"Another tap. Now see that comb on the top of his head; you scarcely noticed it before, and now it is bright red. And see his spurs beginning to show—on good thick legs, too. There is a fine young fellow for you! Look how he jerks his head from side to side, like the young prince of a poultry-yard, as he well deserves to be!"

The attentive interest which had at first characterized the audience now changed to excited admiration and amazement. Some leaned forward with mouths wide open. Others stood up so that they could see better. Ejaculations of astonishment and wonder were heard on every side, and a more thoroughly fascinated and absorbed audience was never seen.

"Now, my friends," Loring continued, "I will give this handsome fowl another tap. Behold the result—a noble, full-grown cock! Behold his spurs; they are nearly an inch long! See, there is a comb for you; and what a magnificent tail of green and black, contrasting so finely with the deep red of the rest of his body! Well, sir, you are truly too big for this table. As I can not give you more room, I will set you up higher. Move over a little, and I will set this chair on the table. There! Up on the seat! That's right, but don't stop; there is the back, which is higher yet! Up with you! Ha! There, he nearly upset the chair, but I will hold it. See! He has turned around. Now, then, look at him. See his wings as he flaps them! He could fly with such wings. Look at him! See that swelling breast! Ha, ha! Listen! Did you ever hear a crow like that? It fairly rings through the house. Yes; I knew it! There is another!"

At this point, the people in the house were in a state of wild excitement. Nearly all of them were on their feet, and they were in such a condition of frantic enthusiasm that Loring was afraid some of them might make a run for the stage.

"Come, sir," cried Loring, now almost shouting, "that will do; you have shown us the strength of your lungs. Jump down on the seat of the chair, now on the table. There, I will take away the chair, and you can stand for a moment on the table, and let our friends look at you, but only for a moment. Take that tap on your back. Now do you see any difference? Perhaps you may not, but I do. Yes; I believe you all do. He is not the big fellow he was a minute ago. He is really smaller; only a fine cockerel. A nice tail that, but with none of the noble sweep that it had a minute ago. No; don't try to get off the table. You can't escape my wand. Another tap. Behold a half-grown chicken, good to eat, but with not a crow in him. Hungry, are you? But you need not pick at the table that way. You get no more grain, but only this little tap. Ha! Ha! What are you coming to? There is a chicken barely feathered enough for us to tell what color he is going to be.

"Another tap will take still more of the conceit out of him. Look at him! There are his pin-feathers, and his bare spots. Don't try to get away; I can easily tap you again. Now, then. Here is a lovely little chick, fluffy with yellow down. He is active enough, but I shall quiet him. One tap, and now what do you see? A poor feeble chicken, scarcely able to stand, with his down all packed close to him as if he had been out in the rain. Ah, little chick, I will take the two halves of the egg-shell from which you came, and put them on each side of you. Come now, get in! I close them up; you are lost to view. There is nothing to be seen but a crack around the shell! Now it has gone! There, my friends, as I hold it on high, behold the magic egg, exactly as it was when I first took it out of the box, into which I will place it again, with the cloth and the wand and the little red bag, and shut it up with a snap. I will let you take one more look at this box before I put it away behind the scenes. Are you satisfied with what I have shown you? Do you think it is really as wonderful as you supposed it would be?"

At these words the whole audience burst into riotous applause, during which Loring disappeared; but he was back in a moment.

"Thank you!" he cried, bowing low, and waving his arms before him in the manner of an Eastern magician making a salaam. From side to side he turned, bowing and thanking, and then with a hearty, "Good-bye to you, good-bye to you all!" he stepped back, and let down the curtain.

For some moments the audience remained in their seats as if they were expecting something more, and then they rose quietly and began to disperse. Most of them were acquainted with one another, and there was a good deal of greeting and talking as they went out of the theater.

When Loring was sure the last person had departed, he turned down the lights, locked the door, and gave the key to the steward of the club.

He walked to his home a happy man. His exhibition had been a perfect success, with not a break or a flaw in it from beginning to end.

"I feel," thought the young man, as he strode along, "as if I could fly to the top of that steeple, and flap and crow until all the world heard me."

• • •

That evening, as was his daily custom, Herbert Loring called upon Miss Starr. He found the young lady in the library.

"I came in here," she said, "because I have a good deal to talk to you about, and I do not want interruptions."

With this arrangement the young man expressed his entire satisfaction, and immediately began to inquire the cause of her absence from his exhibition in the afternoon.

"But I was there," said Edith. "You did not see me, but I was there. Mother had a headache, and I went by myself."

"You were there!" exclaimed Loring, almost starting from his chair. "I don't understand. You were not in your seat."

"No," answered Edith; "I was on the very back row of seats. You could not see me, and I did not wish you to see me."

"Edith!" exclaimed Loring, rising to his feet, and leaning over the library table, which was between them. "When did you come? How much of the performance did you see?"

"I was late," she said; "I did not arrive until after the fireworks, or whatever they were."

For a moment Loring was silent, as if he did not understand the situation.

"Fireworks!" he said. "How did you know there had been fireworks?"

"I heard the people talking of them as they left the theater," she answered.

"And what did they say?" he inquired, quickly.

"They seemed to like them very well," she replied, "but I do not think they were quite satisfied. From what I heard some persons say, I inferred that they thought it was not very much of a show to which you had invited them."

Again Loring stood in thought, looking down at the table; but before he could speak again, Edith sprang to her feet.

"Herbert Loring," she cried, "what does all this mean? I was there during the whole of the exhibition of what you called the magic egg. I saw all those people wild with excitement at the wonderful sight of the chicken that came out of the egg, and grew to full size, and then dwindled down again, and went back into the egg, and, Herbert, there was no egg, and there was no little box, and there was no wand, and no embroidered cloth, and there was no red bag, nor any little chick, and there was no full-grown fowl, and there was no chair that you put on the table! There was nothing, absolutely nothing, but you and that table! And even the table was not what you said it was. It was not an unpainted pine table with four straight legs. It was a table of dark polished wood, and it stood on a single post with feet. There was nothing there that you said was there; everything was a sham and a delusion; every word you spoke was untrue. And yet everybody in that theater, excepting you and me, saw all the things that you said were on the stage. I know they saw them all, for I was with the people, and heard them, and saw them, and at times I fairly felt the thrill of enthusiasm which possessed them as they glared at the miracles and wonders you said were happening."

Loring smiled. "Sit down, my dear Edith," he said. "You are excited, and there is not the slightest cause for it. I will explain the whole affair to you. It is simple enough. You know that study is the great object of my life. I study all sorts of things, and just now I am greatly interested in hypnotism. The subject has become fascinating to me; I have made a great many successful trials of my power, and the affair of this afternoon was nothing but a trial of my powers on a more extensive scale than anything I have yet attempted. I wanted to see if it were possible for me to hypnotize a considerable number of people without anyone suspecting what I intended to do. The result was a success. I hypnotized all those people by means of the first part of my performance, which consisted of some combinations of colored glass with lights thrown upon them. They revolved, and looked like fireworks, and were strung on a wire high up on the stage.

"I kept up the glittering and dazzling show—which was well worth seeing, I can assure you—until the people had been straining their eyes upward for almost half an hour; and this sort of thing—I will tell you if you do not know it—is one of the methods of producing hypnotic sleep.

"There was no one present who was not an impressionable subject, for I was very careful in sending out my invitations, and when I became almost certain that my audience was thoroughly hypnotized, I stopped the show, and began the real exhibition, which was not really for their benefit, but for mine.

"Of course, I was dreadfully anxious for fear I had not succeeded

entirely, and that there might be at least some one person who had
not succumbed to the hypnotic influences, and so I tested the matter by bringing out that table, and telling them it was something it
was not. If I had had any reason for supposing that some of the
audience saw the table as it really was, I had an explanation ready,
and I could have retired from my position without anyone supposing that I had intended making hypnotic experiments. The rest of
the exhibition would have been some things that any one could see,
and as soon as possible I would have released from their spell those
who were hypnotized. But when I became positively assured that
everyone saw a light pine table with four straight legs, I confidently
went on with the performances of the magic egg."

Edith Starr was still standing by the library table. She had not
heeded Loring's advice to sit down, and she was trembling with
emotion.

"Herbert Loring," she said, "you invited my mother and me to
that exhibition. You gave us tickets for front seats, where we would
be certain to be hypnotized if your experiment succeeded, and you
would have made us see that false show, which faded from those
people's minds as soon as they recovered from the spell; for as they
went away they were talking only of the fireworks, and not one of
them mentioned a magic egg, or a chicken, or anything of the kind.
Answer me this: Did you not intend that I should come and be put
under that spell?"

Loring smiled. "Yes," he said, "of course I did; but then your
case would have been different from that of the other spectators,
for I should have explained the whole thing to you, and I am sure
we would have had a great deal of pleasure, and profit too, in
discussing your experiences. The subject is extremely—"

"Explain to me!" she cried. "You would not have dared to do it!
I do not know how brave you may be, but I know you would not
have had the courage to come here and tell me that you had taken
away my reason and my judgment, as you took them away from all
those people, and that you had made me a mere tool of your will—
glaring and panting with excitement at the wonderful things you
told me to see where nothing existed. I have nothing to say about
the others; they can speak for themselves if they ever come to know
what you did to them. I speak for myself. I stood up with the rest of
the people. I gazed with all my power, and over and over again I

asked myself if it could be possible that anything was the matter with my eyes or my brain, and if I could be the only person there who could not see the marvelous spectacle that you were describing. But now I know that nothing was real, not even the little pine table, not even the man!"

"Not even me!" exclaimed Loring. "Surely I was real enough!"

"On that stage, yes," she said; "but you there proved you were not the Herbert Loring to whom I promised myself. He was an unreal being. If he had existed he would not have been a man who would have brought me to that public place, all ignorant of his intentions, to cloud my perceptions, to subject my intellect to his own, and make me believe a lie. If a man should treat me in that way once he would treat me so at other times, and in other ways, if he had the chance. You have treated me in the past as today you treated those people who glared at the magic egg. In the days gone by you made me see an unreal man, but you will never do it again! Good-bye."

"Edith," cried Loring, "you don't—"

But she had disappeared through a side door, and he never spoke to her again.

Walking home through the dimly lighted streets, Loring involuntarily spoke aloud:

"And this," he said, "is what came out of the magic egg!"

The Curse of the Wandering Gypsy

PATRICIA MULLEN

Tea parlors where "Gypsies" tell your fortune may sound like a bygone pleasure, but last time I looked there was still such a fortune-telling establishment in Manhattan's East Fifties, and it may well have been the model for the following charming story. PATRICIA MULLEN, *a former resident of Vermont, now lives in her native New York City, where she trains actors at the Circle-in-the-Square theatrical company. She says she is "the mother of two cats and a parakeet."*

Get it straight right now, I'm a businessman. I don't believe in fortunetelling, palm reading, or any of that, but a lot of people do, and that's all right. There's guys who come in week after week and swear they're making a fortune in stocks or at the track because of my place. And there's the little old ladies—who are most of the trade—who cry and say thank you so often I sometimes end up a good day feeling like a rat. And each one has to see Madame Zenobia or Madame Tasha or Swami Ben Ali. Sometimes they sit together over tea and watercress sandwiches, which is the house specialty, and argue about who of my Gypsies is the most gifted. Which is kind of funny and kind of sad, too, because every one of my Gypsies is a fake. Madame Tasha's really Janice Weinroth and

Swami Ben's a retired carnival barker named Benjamin Francis
Pagnarro.

Out on the shopwindow it says, "Teapot of the Wandering
Gypsy, Fortunes While You Wait." Inside I got everything fixed up
so it looks like it's a hundred years old. You want to make people
believe you can read the future? Remind them of the past. If I had
everything done up with chrome and plastic, would you believe this
is a fortunetelling shop? Not for a minute. The only thing I got in
the place that's plastic is the big crystal ball. If a real Gypsy ever
wandered in here he'd run right back out in sheer terror. A business is what I got.

I get a lot of kooks coming in looking for jobs. They're best
friends with the spirit of Harry Houdini or Napoleon or they've
got their purse full of gooey ectoplasm to prove their powers. I'm
usually polite and show them the door. The last thing I need is my
help taking this stuff seriously and going all spiritual on me. My
customers are bad enough.

Usually I hire out-of-work actors or carney people like Ben.
Once I had this guy who'd run a confidence racket in Cincinnati.
He was beautiful for about six weeks. Old ladies loved him. But
then he picked up this diamond ring—a real rock, I had it checked
out by the best. But one thing led to another and before I know it I
own a hunk of paste and he's split for Cincinnati again.

But not to digress, you get my point about the kind of soothsay-
ers I keep around here. They have to be sharp and size people up
quick and give them what they want to hear. And that doesn't take
any mystic stuff or crystal balls, just good old savvy and common
sense.

So a while back when this old lady walks into the place and starts
mumbling how she gets messages from The Great Beyond I'm already figuring how I'm going to get her out the door. It was right
after the Cincinnati Kid split and my self-esteem was still pretty
bent, so I wasn't as nice as I could have been. I told her what to do
with her Great Beyond and goodbye and went back to folding tea
napkins for the afternoon crowd I was hoping to get when the
matinees got out.

She just stands there for a minute and her lower lip sort of
quivers and she goes, "Oh, rats," picks up her bag and leaves. I'm
watching her go, and I'm a little impressed because spirit people

usually don't talk that way. And I notice that though she's all done up, she looks a little down at the heels, like she doesn't want anybody to know how bad she needs a job.

It gets to me to see old ladies who look like they're on the thin edge. I'd have called her back right then except Tony, never what you call a quiet guy, throws a tantrum 'cause a new waitress calls five minutes after she's due on the floor and says she's moving that afternoon to Wyoming.

I can't get him to quiet down till I've fired him for the third time that week, and by that time the lady is halfway up the block and I'm feeling like a slime bucket for yelling at everybody all morning. So I tell Tony to go and find her while I change into my gypsy suit and try to get the place straightened out before customers start to show up.

After a while he's back with the lady, who sits down and we talk over tea. I apologize for being nasty and then I ask her, "Why'd you fake all that Great Beyond stuff?"

"I need a job and I figured you were some kind of nut," she says.

I can't help but like somebody who's straight like that so we get to talking. Turns out she's an old trouper. Her name is Mrs. Bringley, she used to be married to The Great Anselmo years back. I warm up to people in that trade because my dad was a magic man. In fact, it turns out she and Anselmo knew my father, who was one of the best, though he came to it too late, when the craze for it was nearly over. I don't remember her but I don't let on, 'cause I hate to hurt an old lady's feelings.

But she's got lots of stories to tell and before long the matinee crowd is in and I tell Tony to bring us some sandwiches. Over lunch she tells me how the Great Anselmo passed away. Nice getting the inside story on a mystery. I mean, you remember the furor in the papers when it happened. And who could blame them? A great magician dies mysteriously like that, everybody wants to know what happened. But she tells it just like it was in the papers at the time. She can't figure it any more than anybody else.

So the upshot of it all is, I hire her. I didn't really need her right then 'cause it was summer, when business is slack, but I figure that maybe, if she works out, she can fill in and my regulars can take vacations.

The first week she's there, commotion starts. Tony comes to me on a Wednesday afternoon right in the middle of the matinee crowd. "Better check booth two, boss," he says.

"I'm running a cash register, Tony, I got better things to do than check booth two," I tell him. He just nods and goes on serving watercress sandwiches and weak tea.

Five minutes later I've been stewing long enough and I ask him, "What's with booth two?"

"Maybe nothing," he says, "and maybe you're losing Mrs. Boomanger." And then goes back to his tea and sandwich routine.

Mrs. Boomanger is a big lady who got rich a long time ago. Since her first husband, who started the business with her, popped off, she's been searching for the second one, or so she claims. She wears a heavy perfume which is always hanging around the place long after she's left, sports several carloads of jewelry and has a voice like an ambulance siren in a closed garage. But she comes in once a week regular and leaves tips like Mohammed Ali. She has a lot of friends she brings to the place, too, who tip the same way. So I got to investigate.

Fortunes are told in these little booths with curtains around them so you can't see what's going on, but I don't have to stand very close to hear Mrs. Boomanger.

"Nothing?" she says.

"Oh, no, the cards say you have a very active life," I hear Mrs. Bringley say. "You have an important business trip coming up in about three weeks. A letter soon will bring you money. . . ."

"No tall, dark strangers?" Mrs. Boomanger sounds like she's going to cry.

"Not that I can see," says Mrs. Bringley. "Your cards are all clubs and diamonds, good fortune and money. No hearts to speak of, and not one spade . . ."

"But what about that three of hearts?"

I hear Mrs. Bringley sigh. "Well that, yes. A bit of unpleasantness, but nothing serious, I'm sure. Overall, I would say that this is the fortune of a very capable businesswoman. . . ."

I grab Ben and send him in to get Mrs. Bringley out of there.

"You said to just generally follow the cards," Mrs. Bringley protests when I haul her into my office.

"And tell them what they want to hear!" I say, trying to keep my voice down so the customers can't hear me. "Why do you think we take the ace of spades out of the decks? There's a lot of things people just don't want to hear."

"But I didn't tell her anything bad," Mrs. Bringley argues. "She's going to take a trip, make a lot of money. . . ."

I had to sit down. "Look, Mrs. B.," I tell her. "First lesson in reading fortunes, whether it's crystal balls, tea leaves, cards, palms, or ear lobes. You get a sharp lady like Mrs. Boomanger, she's already got all the money she needs and can go anywhere she wants. She doesn't want to hear about that. She wants to hear about how she's wonderful. How this tall, romantic guy is going to go ga-ga over her, 'cause she's never had that. Comprendo?"

"No," says Mrs. Bringley. "It sounds unethical."

"Look," I say. "A bimbo with a wedding ring and a slick mink coat walks in here, right? I don't care what the cards say, are you going to tell her she's going to meet the man of her dreams and be rich? That's yesterday's news!"

She hesitates.

"If you want her to come back, you tell her she's really got brains that nobody appreciates and you see her writing the Great American Novel. It's what people want. They already know what they have. They come to us so we'll tell 'em they can get the other things."

"It sounds unethical," she repeats, stubborn as the traffic on the street.

"What's unethical?" I ask. "You can't lie about this stuff 'cause you don't know what's going to happen anyway. What's so different about making some mark of an old lady happy or rupturing rabbit ears pulling them out of hats? Huh? Where were your ethics then?"

"That was just entertainment, Harvey!" She's still indignant, but I'm making sense to her.

"Fine," I tell her. "So go entertain some old ladies. Go back to work and take booth six."

Well, she can listen, this lady, cause that afternoon she works over a beat-up old horseplayer I never saw before but who's back the next day and tells me that if he'd understood her right he'd of had a forty-five hundred dollar exacta. So the customers are all right again, I'm happy, and Mrs. Bringley is not scaring people anymore.

Now, you should know, I like all my help, but Ben is an old

devil. He's a good-looking man with a lot of white teeth that are all his, and big dark eyes that the little old ladies love. When he's out of his gypsy costume, he wears a suit with a carnation in the lapel. He'll kiss the hand of a total stranger if she's a good-looking woman, and for some reason otherwise sensible women get breathless and turn all sorts of colors when he smiles. But he's good at his work, so I ask Ben to give Mrs. Bringley some tips. And it works out all right, too, at first.

Now, Mrs. Bringley is old enough to be my mother, but so's Ben. And she's a pretty lady. Her hair is grey, but it curls all around her face, and there's a fullness in her lips and something in her eye that says it's not all over yet. So I'm not surprised when Ben begins to hang around.

He starts with flowers like he usually does, so everybody at the shop will know what he's up to. Janice tries to warn Mrs. Bringley, but she won't listen.

"She's so happy, Harvey," Janice tells me. "Maybe Ben's serious this time."

"And maybe politicians are honest," I tell her. "Don't hold your breath."

Mrs. Bringley has me and the gypsies over to her apartment on a Monday night when the shop is closed. She cooks a nice dinner and sits Ben right beside her where he can cut the meat and she can keep feeding him.

But Mrs. Bringley is looking good. She loses a few pounds and gets a glow on her face. After a while she and Ben don't make it a secret that they're seeing each other, and they show up together in the morning and leave together at night. But I know Ben. He's like a big old tomcat who's found an easy mark. He's not figuring to stick around, but he'll purr and act nice till he finds a better berth.

Sometimes I have lunch with Mrs. Bringley because I like to hear her talk about the old days, touring with The Great Anselmo and all the people she knew. Then one afternoon she says to me, "Oh, Harvey, all my life it's been hard, but now I'm so happy."

"Well, that's nice," I tell her.

"I was engaged twice before I married Anselmo, you know," she goes on. "They both just disappeared without a word of warning. And now that I'm older, well, you don't know how hard it is to find a job at my age. Especially one where the money's good and the people are nice. I used to think sometimes that I had bad luck."

"Oh, come on," I tell her. "Don't go thinking like that."

"But that's all over. I'm so happy now. Ben is wonderful and I like you so much, Harvey. I feel at home here." She pats the back of my hand, and I am no pushover or anything like that but I got tears in my eyes when she says that.

"You got friends, Mrs. Bringley, don't you worry," I tell her. And I mean it.

And it works out all right at first. Mrs. Bringley fills in for Janice for a couple of days so Janice can go visit her mother. Sophie gets a vacation, and I offer one to Ben, but he just licks his chops and says, "Not now." Business is good and Mrs. Bringley even begins to get her own clientele from the Wednesday matinee set.

But nothing stays easy. There is this lady from Oklahoma City who comes to town. She's just lost her husband and inherited the biggest tractor dealership in the Midwest, Sophie tells me. She gets to be a regular customer, and I see how she's always asking for Ben. I get the idea there's more going on in Ben's booth than fortune-telling.

And after this lady from Oklahoma City's been in town a couple of weeks, Mrs. Bringley loses the glow in her cheeks and doesn't look so good. After a while, she and Ben don't show up together anymore, and once I see her on her break, sitting in the kitchen and crying.

"You gotta buckle down," I tell her one day. "You gotta get interested in things again. Go to the movies. Don't hang around here and get depressed. He's not the first rat in your life, right?" And after a while she cheers up a little. She doesn't go to the movies, instead she works real hard and I can see she's learning the business.

Now, Ben's been with me seven years. He's one of the best tea-leaf hustlers in the business and I'm lucky to have him. It's like he's the star of *The Wandering Gypsy* and I guess he's got to liking that. Thing is, Madame Tasha and Madame Zenobia are nice ladies, but they're not world beaters as fortunetellers. But Mrs. Bringley, when she gets into the swing of it, is good. Maybe better than Ben.

Anyway, a little at a time, Ben starts getting cancellations and Mrs. Bringley picks up his trade. I figure a little competition never hurt anybody and there's enough business to go around. Besides, she's new and everybody wants to know what she's about, and it's a phase and it'll pass. And it serves him right.

But Ben can't let it pass. The lady from Oklahoma City's gone home and he's all upset about Mrs. Bringley. He's getting all out of joint and accusing her of stealing his clients. He doesn't say anything to her, but I think she knows what he's up to. Instead he comes to me and tells me how she's messing clients up. Now, I remember Mrs. Boomanger and at first I'm worried, but I stop by her booth every so often and I can hear that she's all straightened out and giving the marks what they want to hear.

But Ben is like a star who thinks a bit player is trying to take the stage from him. Madame Tasha and Madame Zenobia don't care that much, but Ben gets them all upset and the next thing I know I got all my gypsies in the office talking about policy. "Tell the boss what we were talking about, Janice," Ben says after a while.

Janice looks like she'd rather have stayed home. "Well," she hems and haws, "I thought that, since we've all got to make a living, Harvey, it would be nice if we could all fill our schedules first," she tells me.

"And Mrs. Bringley should get our overload," Ben chimes in. "You hired her for overflow, Boss, and that's the marks she should get. Right, girls?"

I spread my hands out flat on the desk. "Whose clients is she taking?" I ask. "Janice? Have you lost any of your reliables?" She looks away from me. "Sophie?" I ask Madame Zenobia. "Who've you lost to Mrs. Bringley lately?"

Sophie, who's a big lady who flutters, glances at Ben and then back to me. "There's Peter Famish," she says after a minute. "And Mrs. Botnovik." Ben is smiling like he's proud of himself and I just can't let him get away with it.

"Peter Famish is a creep who's gone through every one of you," I say. "And Mrs. Botnovik never tipped more than a dime in her life, so what's to lose?" The smile is coming off Ben's face now. I raise my voice. "What's this all about, anyway? You guys aren't happy with your jobs? You want to go work somewhere you gotta pay tax and Social Security? What's going on here?"

Ben stands up. "Harvey," he says, "that woman took two of my clients last week and another one asked for her just this morning. It's my clients she's taking, that's no secret, and it's not fair."

"Don't give me 'fair,' mister," I tell him. "Changing the ground rules on somebody 'cause they're good doesn't sound fair to me."

I walk to the door and throw it open. "Mrs. Bringley!" I yell. "Come here a minute!" She comes in all smiles till she sees Ben's face. "These meatballs have got something to say that concerns you," I say and motion her to sit down on the folding stool by the door. "Janice, Sophie, tell her what you told me."

Janice just turns her head away like she might see something interesting on the wall. Sophie flutters her fingers and sighs half a dozen times before she reaches out and pats Mrs. Bringley's hand. "I assure you, dear, I don't mean a word of it," she says. I figure I have Ben against the wall, but it's not the first time I underestimate him. I didn't realize how angry he was. He stands up with a glare at me and bows before Mrs. Bringley.

"Madame," he says. "What the girls are trying to say is that we have been talking and we have all agreed. Since you are the junior member in this organization, you should not be allowed to work on an equal basis with the rest of us. Henceforth you will only see clients after the girls and I have filled our schedules."

Mrs. Bringley turns to me. "Harvey, that's not what we agreed on," she says and she's right. "I can't pay my rent if I have to work that way."

"I know that," I say. "Tell these fools."

She turns to Janice who's still looking longingly at the wall. "You so rarely work a filled schedule," she says. "If we work that way it will mean that I get hardly anything. I've never tried to take clients from anyone, you know that."

"It's all right, Mrs. B.," Janice says. "I don't mind it at all."

"Well, I mind!" Ben interrupts. "If Harvey chooses to ignore my request, then I will leave this establishment. The Gypsy Caravan on Forty-seventh Street has already made me an offer." He glares at me. "I needn't say that if I go, my clients will come with me."

He's right, they will. The Gypsy Caravan is new and Rocco Bonducci who owns it is always looking for a way to twist my tail. I sigh and sit down. "Ben," I say, "this is a lousy thing to do." It kills me, but I got to say to her, "Mrs. Bringley, I'm sorry."

She has tears in her eyes and bright splotches of color in her cheeks. She stands up and turns to Ben. "This is the first job I've had in years where I've been happy," she says. "And you've ruined that for no reason except that you're a selfish old man." She pulls off her turban and throws it on the desk in front of him. "God damn you," she says and turns and walks out.

Sophie and Janice are embarrassed. I don't think they like what they've just done or intended it to go this far. They probably just sit around agreeing with Ben while he complains and now they're in this mess. Anyway, they look miserable and leave not saying a word. Even Ben looks uneasy, but he's got what he wanted.

"That was the meanest thing I ever saw," I tell him. But he's the star again, and gets more clients than anybody else. And I hate him so bad I almost feel good when something happens.

The first time, it's not so bad. Ben's car gets run over by a truck. He's not in it and I laugh a lot that day because it seems like justice. He's stuck out in Staten Island, so I call Mrs. Bringley but she can't come in on short notice and the day is hectic.

But a little while later, Ben comes down with boils. I mean, these are *boils*. He goes to the doctor, he gets shots, everything. For a while he comes in to work cause you can't see them under his robes. But then it gets so bad he can't go anywhere. I visit him to bring him groceries sometimes. He can hardly sit down and he's rough to look at close up. I feel real bad for him.

But I have to call Mrs. Bringley, who comes back full time and the shop's doing all right. I actually miss Ben a little, but without his star act everybody gets along better, so I'm thinking that maybe it's all right.

It's just after Christmas when me and Janice Weinroth decide we're going to get married. We keep it a secret from everybody else for about fifteen minutes when Janice tells Sophie, and then there's nothing to do but go ahead and do it.

I close the place early and everybody comes down to City Hall with us and stands in the corridor and cheers and throws tea leaves cause nobody's had time to pick up rice. Then we go back up to The Gypsy and I crack the cash register for some bucks to buy champagne and bagels and lox. We're there till all hours, not a sober head or a dry eye in the house.

At the peak of the festivities, Mrs. Bringley, who's been dancing with Tony while one of the waiters plays the accordion, comes over

and flings her arms around my neck. She's happy for us and has a
lot of champagne under her belt.

"You're a good man, Harvey," she says, her eyes brimming.
"You're the best. You've been good to me."

"Aw, come on, Mrs. B.," I tell her, trying to pry her off.

"No, you're the best," she repeats and then spies Janice. "And
Janice, you're like a daughter to me." And with that she begins to
blubber and Janice begins to cry and Tony gets his handkerchief out
and the whole place looks like it's going to sink any minute.

Mrs. Bringley's face powder is all over my lapel but I don't really
care all that much at that point. Then she raises high her teacup full
of champagne, sloshing my other lapel with it, and proposes a toast.
"I wish Janice and Harvey health, wealth, and happiness. God bless
you both." Everybody cheers, we drink a lot more champagne and
all go home in an illegal condition.

I can't take wine, never could, but the next morning neither
Janice or I have any hangover so we decide to go for an early walk
in the park. It's a Wednesday so we have to get down to the shop,
but just as we're leaving the telephone rings. First I think it's Tony
playing a joke, but finally I realize the guy's on the level. A while
before, I bought Janice a lottery ticket as a dumb thing to do to
impress her. And this guy tells me it won. This lottery ticket has
won nine million dollars and Janice and I are seriously rich. Or at
least Janice is, but she's more than happy to split it.

So we go into the shop and after I close we have another party.
And this time I drink way too much, but again the next morning
neither Janice or I have hangovers. I think it over for a couple of
days and then I call Natty Teitelbaum. He's a detective with what
we used to call the bunco squad and his real name's Nathan only he
dresses like he bought his clothes from an out-of-luck horseplayer.
He comes in sometimes to ask about the Cincinnati Kid and get
Madame Tasha to read the bumps on his head. So I ask him to find
out what he can about The Great Anselmo.

"Ask me to catch you a murderer, Harvey," he complains, "and
for you I'll do it. But that's a long time ago. Those files are down in
the basement and it's dark and dirty down there." But he does it. In
a couple of days he tells me what I know already. That's how I can
tell you this for a fact. The Great Anselmo died of third-degree
burns suffered while he sat with an unknown female in the lobby of

the Algonquin Hotel. "Fire of unknown origin," the report called it. The fire consumed him and the chair he sat in, but nothing else. I tell Natty thanks.

"I wonder," I ask her the next day at lunch, "did you often fight with The Great Anselmo?"

She nods and pats my hand. "Yes, I did, Harvey, but don't let it bother you, married couples often fight. It doesn't mean they don't love each other. Are you and Janice . . . ?"

"No, we're fine, Mrs. B.," I tell her. "Were you and the Great Anselmo getting along just before he died?"

Her eyes fill with tears. "Oh, Harvey, I've regretted that for so long. I almost always keep my temper, but he did try it so . . . and I just couldn't stand it anymore. He was a handsome devil. Handsomer than even Ben. And he flirted with every chorus girl he ever saw. He just plain out and told me his last night that that's the way he was and he wouldn't change."

"And what did you say to him, Mrs. Bringley?" I ask. "Can you remember exactly?"

"Of course I can, Harvey. It's haunted me for all these years. I told him . . . Well, I was trying to keep my temper, not to swear, you know. But I told him to go to hell. I was so mad."

"As mad as you were at Ben," I want to say. But I don't. I tell her it's all right and not to feel guilty or anything, although I can see why she does. And then I spend a long time thinking over whether I should keep her on at the job or not.

Mostly it's harmless. And what she wished on Janice and me is hard to believe but wonderful just the same. But it's dangerous. What happened to The Great Anselmo and to Ben is awful, and I have to think about that. I don't believe in fortunetelling or purses full of ectoplasm, but this I have to treat with respect. If Mrs. Bringley is happy she isn't given to swearing much and everything's all right. So I'm going to keep her on and make sure she's happy. I like the old girl, so do the customers. Besides, I can't figure any way of firing her without making her mad.

The Sorcerers

W. B. YEATS

WILLIAM BUTLER YEATS *(1865–1939) was born in Dublin and became one of Ireland's most important poets, playwrights and statesmen. Director of the famous Abbey Theatre, he served as a senator of the Irish Free State in 1922 and a year later received the Nobel Prize for Literature. Best remembered for such poems as "The Lake Isle of Innisfree" and "The Song of Wandering Aengus" and plays like* The Countess Cathleen, Yeats, *early in his career, wrote three studies of Irish myth:* Fairy and Folk Tales of the Irish Peasantry, The Secret Rose, *and* The Celtic Twilight, *from which latter work is taken this glimpse at some self-styled sorcerers that Yeats knew personally.*

In Ireland we hear but little of the darker powers,* and come across any who have seen them even more rarely, for the imagination of the people dwells rather upon the fantastic and capricious, and fantasy and caprice would lose the freedom which is their breath of life, were they to unite them either with evil or with good. And yet the wise are of opinion that wherever man is, the dark powers who

---

* I know better now. We have the dark powers much more than I thought, but not as much as the Scottish, and yet I think the imagination of the people does dwell chiefly upon the fantastic and capricious.

would feed his rapacities are there too, no less than the bright beings who store their honey in the cells of his heart, and the twilight beings who flit hither and thither, and that they encompass him with a passionate and melancholy multitude. They hold, too, that he who by long desire or through accident of birth possesses the power of piercing into their hidden abode can see them there, those who were once men or women full of a terrible vehemence, and those who have never lived upon the earth, moving slowly and with a subtler malice. The dark powers cling about us, it is said, day and night, like bats upon an old tree; and that we do not hear more of them is merely because the darker kinds of magic have been but little practised. I have indeed come across very few persons in Ireland who try to communicate with evil powers, and the few I have met keep their purpose and practice wholly hidden from those among whom they live. They are mainly small clerks and the like, and meet for the purpose of their art in a room hung with black hangings. They would not admit me into this room, but finding me not altogether ignorant of the arcane science, showed gladly elsewhere what they would do. "Come to us," said their leader, a clerk in a large flour-mill, "and we will show you spirits who will talk to you face to face, and in shapes as solid and heavy as our own."

I had been talking of the power of communicating in states of trance with the angelical and faery beings,—the children of the day and of the twilight—and he had been contending that we should only believe in what we can see and feel when in our ordinary everyday state of mind. "Yes," I said, "I will come to you," or some such words; "but I will not permit myself to become entranced, and will therefore know whether these shapes you talk of are any the more to be touched and felt by the ordinary senses than are those I talk of." I was not denying the power of other beings to take upon themselves a clothing of mortal substance, but only that simple invocations, such as he spoke of, seemed unlikely to do more than cast the mind into trance, and thereby bring it into the presence of the powers of day, twilight, and darkness.

"But," he said, "we have seen them move the furniture hither and thither, and they go at our bidding, and help or harm people who know nothing of them." I am not giving the exact words, but as accurately as I can the substance of our talk.

On the night arranged I turned up about eight, and found the leader sitting alone in almost total darkness in a small back room. He was dressed in a black gown, like an inquisitor's dress in an old drawing, that left nothing of him visible except his eyes, which peered out through two small round holes. Upon the table in front of him was a brass dish of burning herbs, a large bowl, a skull covered with painted symbols, two crossed daggers, and certain implements shaped like quern stones, which were used to control the elemental powers in some fashion I did not discover. I also put on a black gown, and remember that it did not fit perfectly, and that it interfered with my movements considerably. The sorcerer then took a black cock out of a basket, and cut its throat with one of the daggers, letting the blood fall into the large bowl. He opened a book and began an invocation, which was certainly not English, and had a deep guttural sound. Before he had finished, another of the sorcerers, a man of about twenty-five, came in, and having put on a black gown also, seated himself at my left hand. I had the invoker directly in front of me, and soon began to find his eyes, which glittered through the small holes in his hood, affecting me in a curious way. I struggled hard against their influence, and my head began to ache. The invocation continued, and nothing happened for the first few minutes. Then the invoker got up and extinguished the light in the hall, so that no glimmer might come through the slit under the door. There was now no light except from the herbs on the brass dish, and no sound except from the deep guttural murmur of the invocation.

Presently the man at my left swayed himself about, and cried out, "O god! O god!" I asked him what ailed him, but he did not know he had spoken. A moment after he said he could see a great serpent moving about the room, and became considerably excited. I saw nothing with any definite shape, but thought that black clouds were forming about me. I felt I must fall into a trance if I did not struggle against it, and that the influence which was causing this trance was out of harmony with itself, in other words, evil. After a struggle I got rid of the black clouds, and was able to observe with my ordinary senses again. The two sorcerers now began to see black and white columns moving about the room, and finally a man in a monk's habit, and they became greatly puzzled because I did not see these things also, for to them they were as solid as the table before them. The invoker appeared to be gradually increasing in power, and I began to feel as if a tide of darkness was pouring from him and concentrating itself about me; and now too I noticed that the man on my left hand had passed into a death-like trance. With a last great effort I drove off the black clouds; but feeling them to be the only shapes I should see without passing into a trance, and having no great love for them, I asked for lights, and after the needful exorcism returned to the ordinary world.

I said to the more powerful of the two sorcerers—"What would happen if one of your spirits had overpowered me?" "You would go out of this room," he answered, "with his character added to your own." I asked about the origin of his sorcery, but got little of importance, except that he had learned it from his father. He would not tell me more, for he had, it appeared, taken a vow of secrecy.

For some days I could not get over the feeling of having a number of deformed and grotesque figures lingering about me. The Bright Powers are always beautiful and desirable, and the Dim Powers are now beautiful, now quaintly grotesque, but the Dark Powers express their unbalanced natures in shapes of ugliness and horror.

Sanguinarius

RAY RUSSELL

RAY RUSSELL, *the first executive editor of* Playboy *magazine, is the prolific author of award-winning poetry and prose, including novels and many fine science-fantasy short stories. In the 1960s, Russell wrote three popular neo-Gothic horror novellas: "Sardonicus" (in* Masterpieces of Terror and the Supernatural, *Doubleday, 1985), "Sagittarius," and the following grisly tale of black magic and vampirism. (For a startling footnote to "Sanguinarius," see Appendix II, page 520.)*

I. A KEY TO SECRET PLACES

O Lord,

High on its jutting promontory, gaunt and austere, Castle Csejthe still stands, dark and muted now, its tenants none but rats and spiders, nesting birds, and one lone wretch, Elisabeth, Thy servant. In my sleepless desolation, I think upon those great rooms I am constrain'd to see no more, and roam in fancy through them, gliding like an insubstantial phantom through those high, broad, livid veils of dust that, when they catch the moonlight and a vagrant breeze, shimmer and ponderously sway, thus doubtless spawning village talk of ghosts—vast, shapeless, silent, silver minions now that once were solid men and women. Sometimes a bird, flapping and cawing, will start a shrill reverberation drifting through those bleak, abandon'd halls, filling their enormous emptiness with memories of screaming, and of pitiless laughter, and of the sharp cries of fleshly lust.

I do not starve for food, but pine for faces, and for the cherish'd sound of speech. The serfs whose task it is to hand my fare in through the narrow chink risk death by the whispers they afford me in their pity, yet they are good of heart, and when I plead with them and beg them but to speak, to utter any words, be they ever so plain and paltry, these lowly folk cannot gainsay me.

From them, I glean that in the village, in every inn and cottage, the church itself not excepted, all but one colour may be seen in draperies and raiment and every manner of trapping: no soul will dare display a thing of crimson. The sun itself is shunn'd when, at the close of day, it sinks into its scarlet bath; and should a wayfarer, ignorant of this strange conceit, enter the village, and he attir'd in red, be it no more than a kerchief of the offending hue, that garment is stripp'd from him, and burnt, and he is told, "We of Nyitra are sore surfeited with that colour; by firm decree we do not name it, we think not of it, we have forbade our eyes to look upon it evermore."

Soon I will die, O Lord, and the fetters of mortality will be stricken from my limbs, and I will straightway fly into Thy Presence, into the waiting embrace of Thine Arms. The thought of that liberation is the sole thing that sustains me in my harsh imprisonment, and allows me to endure these final solitary days, seal'd off by stone and mortar from this world, from the blue of the very sky, denied all human congress, speaking naught, seeing no one, inaccessible to all save Thee.

The others are already dead—some dispatch'd mercifully, some torn and broken by protracted torture, then burnt while yet they liv'd. I alone (and how alone!) remain, passing the cheerless days with this my screed, a captive in a single room of this which was my castle.

Fifteen I was, and lovely, when first I came to Castle Csejthe as the bride of Ferencz Nadasdy. My flesh was as pearl, lit from within, the faint blue tracery of the veins lightly visible; my hair, a tumble of raven's plumage that fell to below my waist; mine eyes, large and lustrous; my mouth, full-lipp'd and carmine. (Do women of the village now, I wonder, blanch the proscrib'd colour of their lips?)

We had met not many months before, in my father's house, where Nadasdy had been an honour'd guest. He was handsome and masterful, a scant six years older than mine own few years. His sweet demeanour, the lightning flashes of his eyes, his melodious laugh, his arms, hard with latent puissance: these things commended him to me, and quicken'd my blood. No man had yet enjoy'd me, but I knew full well that Ferencz yearn'd to do so. He paid me compliments, bestow'd flowers and other gifts upon me, seldom left my side.

I took refuge in coyness, and reciprocated by presenting him with a dainty wooden box made of interlocking panels, a product of Cathayan cunning, impossible to open lest one knew the secret sequence of its intricate design. It had belong'd to my mother.

"There is a sweetmeat within," I told him. "It is thine to savour, if thou canst extract it."

At first, he tried without success to gain entry, his fingers vainly prodding and prying. "Canst find no way into that little toy, Count Ferencz?" I said, amus'd at his efforts. "How wilt thou find thy way into my heart?"

He laugh'd, and solv'd the problem simply—by crushing the box between his two strong hands and victoriously chewing the sweetmeat, his eyes aglint with mischief.

I feign'd vexation. "Brute strength," I coldly said. "It is a thing to please foolish girls . . ."

"But it does not please Elisabeth Bathory," he rejoin'd, "kin to bishops, cardinals, princes, kings. So be it. Pose me other problems, little Bathory, and Ferencz of Nyitra will solve them all!"

"Sayest thou? Then look upon these . . ." I shew'd him three eggs, which artisans had stain'd with divers patterns, each delightful, yet each different.

"Painted eggs," said Ferencz, with a shrug. "Dost think I cannot open them, as thou thought I could not open that little box?"

He reach'd for the eggs, but I stay'd his hand. "This is a problem for thy *mind*, Count Ferencz, not thy sinews," I explain'd. "Each of these eggs is pleasing to the eye, and yet each is different from its sisters. It is hard to choose among them, they are so beautiful. Is it not so?"

"It is so—if that be thy wish."

"But once the pretty shells are peel'd away, one egg will taste much like another."

"Doubtless. Does thy discourse have a theme?"

"Only this," I said: "It is even so with women. Outwardly, one of us may seem more fair than others; but when our shells are crack'd . . ."

He smil'd; his white teeth gleam'd. "The riddling wisdom of the Bathorys is well-renown'd," he admitted, "but Nadasdy wit can match it. Look thou here . . ." He gestur'd toward three carafes which stood on my father's table. "Outwardly, all these are quite the same," he said, "but do not be deceiv'd. One contains strong Bathory wine . . ." He drank deeply from the wine carafe. "One contains water . . ." He drank of the water. "And one is full of emptiness." He flung the empty carafe to the floor's stone flagging, where it was sunder'd into shards. He walk'd closer to me and look'd long into mine eyes before he spoke. "It is even so with women," he said, echoing my words. "Elisabeth, God willing, I would quench my thirst with strong Bathory wine—not tasteless water."

"And if . . ." I found it difficult to speak. "And if I fain prove full of emptiness, Count Ferencz?"

"My love should fill thee," he swore.

That same night, when my old nurse, Ilona Joo, was undressing me, I ask'd of her, "What think thee of the young Nadasdy?"

"A noble gentleman," she replied, "and all report him gracious, brave, and godly."

"But of his person, what of that, Ilona? Is he not comely and well-favour'd?"

Ilona laugh'd at this, and said, "The time is past, my lady, when such things caught my fancy; and yet I deem Count Ferencz most agreeable to the eye."

"Ilona," I said as I climb'd into my bed, "would marriage to him suit me, dost think?"

"Thou art young," she answer'd, "but it may be that thou art ready for reaping. The Bathorys are people of high blood. Thy brother, since the time his cheek first sprouted pallid down, has never yet been sated, and neither green-bud maids nor matrons far past ripe have been enough to glut him. Thine aunts and uncles, all, crave without end; thy noble cousin Zsigmond . . . tut, tut, thou mak'st me talk of things not meet."

"Is marriage, then, not meet? For it is *that* I bade thee speak of, dear old goose."

"Marriage, my child," she said, after smoothing my coverlet, "is a key to a lock'd casket, full of many things."

"What kind of things?" I ask'd her.

"Things unknown," she said. "Bright things, most oft, but . . ."

"But *what*, Ilona?"

"But naught. It is time thou wert asleep." She blew out the candles. "Good night, my little bud, and dream of pleasing things."

I did. I dream'd of Ferencz. That same week, he ask'd for and receiv'd my hand, for he was look'd upon with favour by my father.

The wedding feast was prodigal, and spoken of throughout the land. Hundreds of guests attended, pounds of viands and gallons of drink were consum'd. The king himself was present, and his Prime Minister, my cousin. Another kinsman of mine, a great prince of Transylvania, sent gifts and lordly greetings across the miles. There was dancing, and there were songs of minstrels; and some of the men, my brother among them, giddy with the fumes of wine, quarrel'd and brawl'd and laugh'd and, I doubt not, had their way of serving maids in the priviest recesses of my father's house.

Through all of this, my glance would catch the eye of Ilona; but she said naught, proffer'd me scant regard, and I was sore distress'd at this and could, at length, endure her silence no whit more; hence went to her, and took her two old hands in mine.

"Dear friend," I chided, "whence come these glances? Have I done ought to vex thee?"

"No, my lady," she said.

"Why, then, rejoice with me," I begg'd her. "This is a merry time. Put off thy glumness and thy frowns, or I will think thou dost not wish to see me happy." I then perceiv'd that both her cheeks were wet. "Dear nanny, weepest thou? Pray do not, lest mine own tears flow."

"I weep to think of time's too hurried passage," she replied. "For fifteen years thou hast been my tender charge, and now . . ."

"Ilona," I said, "dost think I am a heartless ingrate who would leave thee behind? Thou'lt come with us, and be with me alway."

"Oh, lady," she said in a rush of warmth, "those words are a benison to mine ears!"

And so, on that same day, I, my husband, and my nurse departed for Nyitra; and soon I was to behold Castle Csejthe for the first time.

Vasty, it stood upon high ground, o'erlooking all the country-side, and was, in truth, a bastion'd citadel, for the rich and noble of that region, in times past, being much given to feuds and blood-shed, had need of suchlike strongholds to subdue their equals and oppress their lessers. Such castles, too, gave protection 'gainst the invading Turk, rampant in our land. In the months to come, Ferencz was to shew me every inch of this his home, but this detailing was to wait upon his ardour: we had not been within the walls of Csejthe ten minutes ere he lifted me aloft in his strong arms, and with a lusty laugh, carried me up a winding, wide, stone staircase to our chambers.

"Now, Elisabeth; pale, trembling little Bathory," he whisper'd when we were quite alone, "I will do that I swore to do: fill thy maiden emptiness with my love."

In later days, I was to recollect the words of old Ilona Joo, and her likening of marriage to a key that opened seal'd and secret places, denizen'd by things unknown. For such it prov'd.

II. A Courier in the Night

It was, at first, a key to joy.

As in the old tale of the slumbering princess, Nadasdy's kiss awaken'd me, open'd mine eyes to piercing colours I had not hith-erto beheld. I flourish'd, ripen'd, thriv'd, like some lush tropic bloom. Each sense was made more keen, the air itself more sharp and clear, lung-lancing, as is air upon a mountain top, for indeed to peaks of pleasure Ferencz led me, slowly to start with, step by timo-rous step, then setting out with more audacity, striving together, each succouring the other, climbing, first to one ledge, then to a higher, and then to yet a higher and more dizzying ridge, finally to soar as if on wings and to attain, both in the same heart-bursting moment, that cloud-capp'd ultimate point.

This arduous and ardent mountain scaling was not the work of any single night; rather, it was a task spread over many weeks and months. Not ever had I known such blinding gladness; its very existence this side of Heaven's gates I had not once suspected. And thus I fell to worshipping my Ferencz as I would a god. His lithe young body was a shrine at which I knelt, bowing happily before his might, paying him tender homage, grateful, humble, awed by the majesty and marvel of his transfiguring power.

He, too, was close to Heaven in such moments, for he would cry aloud: "God! O, God! My God!" as if the Deity had appear'd, in a supernal flash, before his eyes.

Once, in the dark, I, in my foolish innocence, ask'd him: "Why dost thou call upon God when thou art with me thus?" He seemed bemus'd by my question, and I was oblig'd to mimic him as best I could, calling out as was his wont: " 'O God! My God!' " until he laugh'd. "Why sayest that?" I ask'd again.

"In faith, I do not know," he said, and I could feel him smiling in the darkness, for with my fingertips I trac'd his lips. "It is a thing men say; no more." We lay not speaking for a time, and I knew that he was thinking on my question. At length, he spoke again: "Perchance 'tis this . . ." He held me closer, and his voice was quiet. "This joy that we twain make together is but a gift; a gift from Him; the brightest thing of all that He has given us. It gilds the drabness of our world, makes music out of silence. When I say that, when any man or woman says it, we are thanking Him for the gift."

This I could well understand, for in this wise I thank'd my private god, my Ferencz, for his bounty.

Our life together was an idyll. Having no need for other folk, we saw but few, content within our universe of love. Troubadours, from time to time, would pass our way and sing some lay or other and pass on; the reverend father from the village church would come to say a simple mass and hear confession; messengers would bring dispatches to Ferencz, which he would read, and frown upon, and give grumbling reply; purported wizards of the woods and flame-hair'd Gypsies would wander near the castle, gathering weeds and herbs, and would smile up at us and we would nod from out our window; villagers would bring provender to the castle kitchens; but these were all.

When love did not demand our urgent services, Ferencz and I would roam the whole of Csejthe, within and without. Mighty it was, and arrogant, its arrogance proclaim'd by its high, unbroken, battlemented walls; its overhanging bartizans and galleries from which attackers could be shower'd with missiles and archers' shafts; its projecting turrets, palisades, and towers. Ferencz would extol the main wall's strength and the loftiness of its parapet, pointing with family pride to every bulwark and rampart, praising the crenels and merlons, explaining patiently the purposes of glacis, escarp, counterscarp, and machicolation, until my brain would spin and I would yawn, and he would make a show of anger, causing us both to laugh.

The castle's depths we plumb'd, descending into dungeons where, in former times, dread punishments were suffer'd by unhappy captives. There stood the infernal rack, and branding irons and thumbscrews, and that grim table called in French *peine forte et dure,* whereon helpless wretches were constrain'd to lie under intolerable iron weights until the breath of life was press'd from them. "Tokens of bygone tyranny," my husband call'd these fell objects. "God grant no human soul again scream out his final hours here."

"Amen to that," I said.

It was my husband's custom, when we address'd ourselves to the sweet rites of Venus, to allow no mortal thing to interrupt us. Minstrels were silenc'd at such times, no messengers admitted to the castle, no thing or person given leave to sully the unmingled rapture of our love.

It yet befell, one rain-thick night, when the lightning and the thunder fill'd the eyes and ears, and we oblivious to it all, so deep immur'd within our love were we, that a wayfarer approach'd the castle. He came on foot, his pummel'd body bent forward into the driving slant of the rain, his clinging raiment heavy and dark with wet. More than once, he slipp'd in the slick brown mud and fell, sliming himself from head to foot, but each time he rose and clamber'd on, desperate to reach the castle, his eyes intent upon the great portcullis that barr'd his entry. At length, his vigour spent, his bosom heaving, he fell against the outer wall and tried to regain his breath. This done, he commenc'd to pound and shout, raising his voice high above the shriek of the wind, demanding word with Count Nadasdy. A wracking cough shook him more than once, and nearby twists of lightning balefully blanch'd his face, but when the spasms were subsided, he resum'd. All this, I learn'd of later.

From one of the castle bartizans, a helmeted guard at last looked down. "Away with thee!" he cried to the forlorn figure below.

The wayfarer persisted: "Grant me entrance! Raise the portcullis, I beseech thee!"

"Have done with that!" the guard call'd down. "Count Ferencz will see no one! Be off!" And he fix'd an arrow to his crossbow.

"Scullion!" the wayfarer cried. "Is this the welcome thou affordest a courier of the king?"

"A courier?" the guard rejoin'd. "Unmounted, like a churl?"

"My steed lies dead a league from here. Open, I say!"

"King's courier?" the guard call'd down again. "What sign proclaims thee this?"

"Sign enough!" the fellow roared: "Thy caitiff head upon a pike, when the king hears how thou useth me!"

By this time, the tumult had reach'd my husband's ears, and disengaging himself from mine arms, he gave orders to admit the man. With a sour creaking of chains and winches, the portcullis was rais'd, and at length the courier enter'd the great hall. A stoup of hot wine was put into his hands, and this he drank off at a draught. "My lord," he then said to Ferencz, "these from His Majesty." And handed certain papers to my husband.

When he had read them, frowning more deeply even than his wont, he pass'd them to me, but I could make small substance of them, darken'd as they were by bristling words such as "defense" and "border," "the marauding Turk" and "loyal Magyar lords." Looking up, I ask'd, "What mean these papers, Ferencz?"

"They may be digested and distill'd to one hard word." He turn'd to me, and I could see his gentle nature reinforc'd with manly steel as he, with sorrow, spoke that one word: "War."

The happenings of that night were swift and melancholy. I found myself helping Ferencz into his battle garb and gear, asking him tearful questions touching upon his return, but answers had he none, and I could see his thinking was already far from Nyitra and from me. Then, at the open portal, clad though I was but in my nightdress, my bare feet wet and cold upon the drench'd flagging, the raging elements all wild and out of tune around us, he bade me kiss him.

This I did, in a frenzy, throwing my arms about him, crying, "Live, Ferencz! Live for me!"

He smiled down upon my upturn'd face. "Little Bathory," he said, "player with painted eggs and Cathay boxes. God's my guardian, thou my guerdon: how else, then, can it be but I will triumph over Death and foe alike?"

And, on these words, he rode into the whirling storm.

I stood, I know not how long, in the portal, nearly naked, the icy rain pasting my nightdress to my body as 'twere a shining skin; until Ilona, rous'd from her sleep, clucking words of comfort, led me back to my bed, peel'd the dripping garment from me, warm'd me with blankets, and sat with me until I wept myself at last to troubled sleep.

III. AN ANGRY BURNING EMBER

Now stretch'd a span of time bereft of bliss, like to an arid desert waste which one traverses without hope, on bleeding feet, one's skin aflame, the flesh and humours parch'd beyond endurance, the very soul a festering cicatrix. Such was my lot, with Ferencz gone.

By dint of tender arts, Nadasdy had, as 'twere, spread out for my delight a table heap'd with dishes exquisite and rare, delicious Afric fruits, pungent sauces, succulent meats, all hitherto untasted by my palate—cruelly to sweep away that feast with harsh abruptness, consigning me again to the flat gruel that had been my erstwhile fare.

Cozen'd by heartless war, I pin'd, I mourn'd; the hours of my husband's absence were like the heavy weights of the *peine forte et dure*, each more insupportable than the last, pil'd upon my bosom without pity by a tormenting fiend, until my heart was crush'd within my breast and I cried out in bitter anguish. Daytime was passing desolate; but in the night, my bed transmogrified into an hideous rack on which my aching flesh was torn, I writh'd and thrash'd upon the sheets, despairing and distrait, my teeth worrying the coverlet as might a bitch, my briny tears making the pillow sodden.

From such nights would I wake dull, unrestor'd, and pale, with swollen eyes, my spirit bleak. In such sorry case was I that I would rage at the servants who brought my morning morsel, even at my faithful old Ilona; and at one such time she said, "What pains my lady?"

"Love," I sigh'd, "no other thing than love for my departed consort."

She took my hand. "It is as I have fear'd would come to pass," she said, nodding her gray head. "Thou wast dry tinder till Count Ferencz struck his flint and spark'd thee; now, lacking his cool quenching, thou art an angry ember, my poor child; thou burnest."

"Oh, my old friend, indeed I burn!" I moan'd, tears brimming in mine eyes. "Red glowing irons sear me to the bone, impale me deep, plunge hot into my vitals. I am in dire distraction!"

As if alone and speaking to herself, Ilona murmur'd, "Abandon'd thus to such a scorching fever, what fearsome, all-consuming blaze might not this child become?" Then, looking down at me, she said, "No other thing within this mortal sphere do I desire but thy happiness. There, there, my child, there, there . . ." And she strok'd my dry, hot hand.

"Thou art so wise, Ilona," I said, my head in her ample lap, "are there not medicines to avail against such sore distress?"

"None, none, my lady," she replied. "Fasting and prayer excepted, I know none."

"These have I tried, at the priest's urging, but they are unavailing. Dost know of some diversions, then? Puzzles and games to tease the mind away from the throbbing wound?"

"None, child; none that are wholesome."

"Are there unwholesome pastimes, then?" I marvell'd. "My fancy cannot picture pleasures that are vile. To be vile, yet pleasing? This surely is a paradox, Ilona."

"I chatter'd idly; think not of this," she said. Patting my hand more heartily, she further spake: "Thou passeth thy days too much alone here, now that thy good Count is gone. None but serfs and servants, and cold priests, hold discourse with thee. This must not be, for thou art young, and have sore need of merriment. In attendance should be those whose arts would fain relume thy heart, as pipers, poets, minstrels."

"Sweet nanny, they are with their warlike masters, striking tabours, and bawling songs of brave exploits. All men of mettle or of mirth are far away."

"Then what of ladies?" ask'd Ilona.

I pouted and pac'd. "The ladies hereabout are lackwits," I rejoin'd, "who prate of naught but gowns and silly gossip."

Thus did it go, and thus I languish'd for full many a day, and word of my distemper spread slowly through all Nyitra. From time to time, but all too seldom, letters would be brought from Ferencz, swearing his love anew, importuning me to free my mind of worry. These messages would I press to my bosom, and to my thirsting lips, and place beneath my pillow when I slept.

One morn, when I was lolling in my bath, Ilona, as she fetch'd my towel, disclos'd that there awaited in the adjacent chamber a lady, who, hearing of my drear existence, had forthwith come to cheer me.

"Name her," I said, with some alacrity.

"Alas, I cannot," said Ilona, drying my glistening limbs as I stepp'd from the tub, "and, indeed, I know naught of her station, or if it is meet that you have concourse with her. She is not, I think, a gentlewoman, and yet, in sooth, her aspect is most gracious and commends her . . ."

"Ilona, leave off prattling! Go to the lady, use her with courtesy, ask what her name be, and—"

"My name," now spake a purring voice, "is Dorottya."

I looked up, undrap'd as I was, to see my visitant standing in the archway, tall, full-bodied, beautiful, attir'd all in black, her skin paler than mine, her tresses red as fire. It was one of the persons I had glimps'd, now and again, from out my window, quietly gathering barks and grasses. "Have I leave to enter, Countess?" she ask'd, most deferentially.

I nodded, and she mov'd soundlessly into the chamber, her eyes not once leaving mine. Then, her glance flickering quickly down the length of my dewy frame, she enquir'd, "Is it my lady's pleasure, after bathing, to be rubb'd with scented oil?"

Once more I nodded, and Ilona held out for her to see the phial of oil with which she customarily anointed me. "With my lady's permission," said Dorottya, "may I proffer a balm of mine own concoction, distill'd of aromatic woodland herbs?" She pull'd the stopper from a tiny urn, and instantly the air was all infus'd with heady fragrance. "To soft skins such as thine, Countess, it is as sweet as lover's lips," she said.

I smiled my approval, and Ilona reach'd for the urn, but Dorottya did not surrender it. "Let not rough hands perform this subtle office," she urg'd. "Rather, if it please my lady, let myself be thine anointer."

Again I smil'd, words frozen on my lips by the unswerving eyes of my new friend, and discarding my towel, I reclin'd upon my bench to await the soothing unction.

Dorottya knelt beside the bench, and pour'd the olent oil into her palm. "Leave us," she bade Ilona.

IV. THE VILLAGE GIRL

How shall I say what comfort Dorottya afforded me; what panacea flow'd from her, in the days that follow'd, to ease my loneliness? Her voice, as rich and dark as sable, was in itself a healing balsam; her gentle, stroking hands unparallel'd in smoothing cares away. To her, I felt that I could speak of all things: trifles, fears, delights, puzzles that piqued my curiosity, small vexing shames too delicate to confess even to Ilona. Dorottya was a vessel that receiv'd and understood them all. She assuag'd my fears, confirm'd my joys, bestow'd upon me peace and absolution beyond the gifts of any priest.

Of herself, she spoke little. "Dorottya," I asked her straight one day, "whence comest thou; what are thy people?"

"I am a woman of the wood, Countess," she said. "Some call us Gypsies, others deem us fairies. Those who fear our wisdom and our crafts say we are witches."

"That is no answer at all," I told her, laughing, "but let it pass."

She said, "I would not leave my lady unsatisfied."

"It is no matter," I assur'd her, "but tell me this: are there others of thine ilk or kin hereabout?"

"More than my lady might suppose," she said.

"Why do thy people keep their own counsel, and eschew the company of others?"

"Our ways are oft misrender'd, and false readings put on what we do: out of such ill perceivings rise discord and strife."

"Do I misrender or misread thee, Dorottya? Doth discord come of these fair hours together?"

"No, my lady. But thine affections complement mine own."

At first, Dorottya paid visits to the castle of an hour or more; these visits I persuaded her to lengthen; finally I gave instructions to Ilona that the woman of the wood was to be granted domicile in chambers next to mine.

It must not be suppos'd that Dorottya's ministrations dislodg'd all thought of Ferencz from my mind, or that my love for him had lessen'd with the lessening of my loneliness. Indeed, some of my new friend's arts seem'd meant by fate to cleave Ferencz more close to me, and fan our love, and sanctify it with issue. For Dorottya's discourse of herbs and vegetals and suchlike held me blandish'd: how ragwort and colewort do enliven virile humours, whereas chaste-tree and water lily quench the generative powers of the man; how mugwort, pennyroyal, fetherfew, and savine are most benefi-cent to the womb; how saffron is so priz'd for its medicinable effects that, in Nuremberg, if pharmacists adulterate or otherwise dilute it, they are some burnt and some interr'd alive. By this and other learned talk did Dorottya amuse me, likewise by suave anointings and by little games most easing to my nature.

From all of this, Ilona drew away, her aspect clouded by disap-probation. Anger'd by this, I call'd her to task. "Fie, Ilona," I said. "It speaks most ill of thee to mope thus."

"I beg my lady's pardon," she said coldly.

"Was it not thee, Ilona," I pursu'd, "who said that she desir'd, above all else, my happiness? Why, then, these frowns?"

"My lady," she said haltingly, "this Gypsy woman is not of thy station . . ."

"No more are thee."

". . . And yet, ye twain are lock'd for hours together; I hear the plashing of thy bath, and laughter, and low talking, and strange long silences, and sudden cries . . ."

"Dost decree, then, that I weep and groan, which heretofore has been my portion?"

Ilona gabbl'd on, as if I had not spoken: "Such silences, such laughter, and such cries, as I was wont to hear more happily, when thou wert closeted with thy lord the Count . . ."

"Enough of this!" I shouted in displeasure. "Thy brain is addl'd with thine age, and poison'd with ignoble jealousy! What, shall a married lady, the mistress of a mighty castle, be censur'd and dimin-ish'd by her ancient nurse? Hath the fair structure and proportion of mankind been now inverted, dangled by its heels? Do lackeys reign, and servants sit in judgment? Oh, then is Chaos surely come!"

So generous and open was Dorottya that, learning of old Ilona's foolish opposition, she ventur'd to suggest a remedy. "Among my people, there are cordials, broths, and simples to charm away these cholers, and to lull and pacify such peevish minds . . ."

"I would not drug the good old woman," I said.

"She will no more be drugg'd than is the fever'd, raving patient, when physick'd into calm by healthful draughts. I prithee, Countess, place thy trust in me and in my arts."

And so, with sprinkling of some powdery dust into Ilona's nightly cup of mead, that source of sad annoy was purg'd. My nurse, quite cur'd of retrograde and waspish thoughts, was coax'd into a smiling mollitude, her eye no longer darken'd by unseemly doubts, but well-content and fix'd as on some distant blissful scene.

"She is the happier now," I was assur'd by Dorottya.

"Yes, it is good," I quite agreed. "I would not have the dear dame vex'd and sorrow'd."

With fresh zeal, then, did I address myself to all those revels which Dorottya had devis'd to fill my heart, made empty by my warrior husband's fealty to the king.

"What would my lady say," croon'd Dorottya one eve, "if I were to bid welcome to such others as would cheer thee?"

"Bid welcome *here,* dear Dorottya? What sort of others?"

"Some, as myself, of Gypsy breed," she said. "Others, maybe, of different stamp—young village maids of jolly temper, whose rustic songs and dances would regale thee."

I thought upon this before answering, "I know not if such company would find favour with the Count."

"The Count?" laughed Dorottya. "I see no Count. Say, rather, if such company would find favour with the Countess."

I knew not what to answer: fill my husband's home with wild Gypsies and ungentle village girls, suffer rude songs and peasant gambols to taint these ancestral halls? I waver'd, said not yes or no; and Dorottya did not persist. "If thou art hesitant, I will not press," she said, "for it is only thine own merriment, and my sworn duty to preserve it, that brought the notion to my thoughts. Let us say no more of this. At any rate, it is past time for my lady's bath . . ."

Never had I enjoy'd such frequency of bathing and oiling, save since the day Dorottya had come to me. Surrendering to her services, I let my imagination dwell upon the sport she had suggested, the singing and the dancing of the simple village folk, the carefree ways of Gypsies. As Dorottya rubb'd me from head to foot with scented ointment (I sipping all the while from a chalice of wine she had mull'd for me), my presentments fell away, and in a drowsy voice I let her know that it would not be untoward if, at some time soon, she invited certain gay companions to the castle.

"I would not do a thing the Countess thinks unseemly," she replied.

"Nay," I said, with clos'd eyes, "do it, sweet Dorottya, I pray. I give you leave . . ." And, with this, I was asleep, warm'd by the wine, naked and bath'd and oil'd upon my bench.

Whether an hour I doz'd, or more, I never knew, but when I awaken'd, I was irk'd to see a stranger in my chambers, a young girl, scarcely out of childhood, rudely garbed but comely. I reach'd out, startl'd, for my towel, and with it covered most of my nakedness, crying out, "Who art thou? What dost thou here?"

"Please m'lady," the girl stammer'd, afrighted and distrait. " 'Twas Mistress Dorottya commanded me to appear before thee . . ." And she look'd, with some trepidation I bethought me, over my shoulder, where, I now discover'd, Dorottya stood.

" '*Commanded*'?" I said to Dorottya sharply. "Dost now command here, Gypsy woman?"

"The girl is mewling," smiled Dorottya. "She is but a village simpleton I had brought hither for thy diversion, Countess. For, sure, thou gavest leave to do so."

"I may have done," I said, my brain still wrapp'd in foggy sleep, "I do not now recall. But whilst I am all ungirt, can it be meet?"

"Faith, lady," chided Dorottya, "are we not all women here, whatever our condition? No harm can come of such an audience, surely."

Dorottya's words calm'd my first misgivings. "Thou art welcome," I said, extending my hand for the girl to kiss. But she instead fell forward on her knees and kiss'd mine unshod foot.

This much surpris'd me, and I giggl'd, drawing my foot away and saying, "Nay, foolish girl, I am no pope that thou must pay me homage thus."

"But Mistress Dorottya—" the girl began to say.

"Silly wench," said Dorottya, "dost thou so soon offend the Countess?"

I interven'd: "But there is no offense. Arise, girl, do not kneel thus, as if at thy prayers."

"Truly," said Dorottya, with a merry laugh, "we hope to be more jocund than folk are wont to be at vespers!"

With this I did concur with all my heart, and ask'd of Dorottya, "What frolic, then, shall we try with our new friend?"

"None at all," said Dorottya, "whilst she is thus begrim'd with village dirt." (And true it was, the girl was most uncleanly.)

"What then?" I ask'd, still clutching at my towel.

"Why," said Dorottya, "would it not prove saucy sport for us to play at being handmaidens to the girl? To let this lowly person once enjoy the ministrations highborn ladies do?"

"It is thy thought, then . . . ?"

"But a passing thought, a vagrant fancy," Dorottya answer'd with a shrug. "If thou likest it not . . ."

"It suits me well," I rejoin'd. "To bathe the girl, and then anoint her?"

"For a beginning," Dorottya made reply, adding: "Surely it is innocent, and Christian?"

"So it is!" I laugh'd.

And thus, with many a smile and slap and sportive cry, Dorottya and I stripp'd bare the girl of her mean attire, and lifted her into my tub. She squeal'd to feel the water, and howl'd as we scrubb'd her with the brush. Such squirming did she do that I was drench'd from head to foot, but this was no great matter for I was still unclad, and Dorottya, in concord with the occasion, had divested herself of her garments, as well.

It was at this time that Ilona enter'd the chamber, was gaily told to be about her business and leave us young ladies to our play, but persisted, and through the girl's pretty shrieks, at length made her message understood; it was none other than the news that, from the highest parapet of Csejthe, a vigil guard had seen and made known the approach of mounted men.

"What men?" I laugh'd, still in the spirit of our romp. "We have no need of men!"

"Count Ferencz and his retinue," my nurse replied.

V. Sins Without Faces

Ferencz! The mention of that cherish'd name at once restor'd me to my former self. "Dorottya," I quickly said, "this girl must not be found here; secrete her where my lord will not come upon her . . ."

"It will be done," Dorottya replied, urging the girl out of the tub.

"Ilona, dear," I said, "fetch here my nightdress, remove the tub and blot away this water."

These things were swiftly done, and it was not long ere Dorottya, now dress'd, appear'd again within my chamber and assur'd me that the girl was safely hid away. "Is it my lady's wish," she ask'd, "that I, as well, hide from the Count?"

"No, good Dorottya!" I said. "Thou art my trusted friend. Stand here at my side, for the Count will wish to meet thee, I am certain. Later, thou wilt be given leave to retire to thine own chamber, for the Count will wish to be alone with me."

"Oh, that is sure," said Dorottya, with a tinct of slyness that made my cheeks all roseate with blushing.

And, while my face was yet thus flush'd, my dear Ferencz, he gone from me these many weeks, enter'd my chamber. His face was made gaunt by weariness, and he walk'd with a halting step that spoke, with mute eloquence, of grievous wounds. I rush'd into his arms, and felt him crush me hungrily to his bosom; I wept with joy; and neither of us spoke for many moments.

Then what a torrent of sweet words cascaded from us twain! What sighs, what vows, what bright renewals of our love! Until, at length, his eye first catching sight of Dorottya, Ferencz ask'd, "And this lady: who is she?"

"A dear and valu'd friend, by name Dorottya," I replied. "She hath done much to make my days less bleak."

"Why, then," he said to her, "I am beholden to thee, mistress."

"Such duty is but pleasure, good m'lord," said Dorottya. "But now I see thou'rt tired, and I beg leave to retire."

Ferencz nodded graciously, and Dorottya repair'd to her own rooms. This caus'd my husband to lift his eyebrows: "She dwelleth here?" he ask'd.

"Sweet Ferencz, do not scold," I said. "She is a kind and most devoted lady; without her, I fear I would have gone quite mad with sorrow. Pray let her stay."

"It matters not," he answer'd, with a wan smile. "For a while, at least, she may stay."

Then did I help remove my husband's battle gear, and rubb'd his wounds, and coo'd soft words into his ear as we lay upon our bed; and soon had brought him to a pitch of glowing love, and we did cleave as we were wont to do before his leaving.

How happy was I then! how luminous! how tingling and alive!

After a time, Ferencz turn'd to me and said, "Elisabeth, a secret hides behind thine eyes, a darkness. Tell me of it."

"I have no secrets from thee, Ferencz," I replied, "and if a darkness thou divinest in me, it is the shadow of the loneliness I felt when thou wert far away."

"Is not that shadow now dispell'd by my return?"

"It is, beloved husband, oh it is!"

But still did Ferencz stubbornly persist.

"This Dorottya," he said. "What traffic does she have with thee?"

"Friendship, gentle Ferencz, nothing more. Solace for my lonely hours. Am I to pine without companions? May no one cheer my heart when thou art gone from me?"

He then did stroke my hair, and spoke more low, and call'd me his little raven. "Elisabeth, there are abroad in this world things thou know'st not of, such things that were better thou shouldst be struck blind than look upon, struck deaf than bend thine ear to."

"What breed of things, Ferencz?" I ask'd, masking my fearfulness, for his voice had taken on a thickness much disquieting to me.

"Things of black night," he said, in hollow tones.

"Thy words afright me, though I glean them not," I said.

"My little one, my pearl: in elder time, before Christ shed his blood for us, unholy joys were known . . ."

"Why dost thou tell me of them, Ferencz, and in a voice so full of haunt that I am chill'd unto my marrow?"

"I do *not* tell thee of them," he said, "I do *not*. For these sweet ears, such stuff would not be meet. And yet, I do most earnestly abjure thee: pray to God, read deeply of thy Scripture."

"I do, I have; both prayer and Book have always fill'd my days."

"Let them fill thy nights as well, Elisabeth," he said, "for there are sins without faces; sins that, in their shame, shun the glare of honest day and creep unseen into the soul. Such guileless souls as thine are lodestones to them. Therefore, pray; steep thyself in Holy Writ. Be mindful of that blessed Paul of Tarsus, and those of whom he wrote."

"Wrote what, Ferencz?"

"Of those who 'changed the glory of the uncorruptible God into an image made like to corruptible man,' " he answered, " 'and worshipp'd and serv'd the creature more than the Creator . . .' "

"Ferencz, these words are naught but fumes to make me giddy! Desist, I do beseech thee, and let us talk of blither things!"

Fatigue of battle took its toll, however, and soon Ferencz was in a deep sleep. I, rested by my earlier nap, and made still more awake by my returning warrior's kisses, lay for a time, with open eyes, beside him. Then, sleep evading me, I arose and crept quietly into Dorottya's rooms, thinking to talk with her if she be still awake.

Her bed was empty. This was most curious, and I went in search of her. I walk'd through halls and antechambers, peeped within alcoves and nooks, and still I found her not. Then, from far off, I thought I heard a cry.

So faint it was, that I at first deem'd it a figment or, at most, a passing bird. Then, as I turn'd into another corridor, I heard the sound again, more clearly and much closer, and knew with certainty it was a human cry; or more precisely, scream.

Again it rang out: high and sharp and piercing, the scream of one so sore excruciated that all mark of sex or age was lost—man, woman, child, crone, any of these could have utter'd it in dire extremity.

Downward I delv'd into the castle's bowels, into dominions dark and rank with damp effluvium of must, on stone steps slick with parlous grume—and, of a sudden, very near to me, that scream reach'd shrilly out once more, and I was much afraid, for, turning, I perceiv'd that it had issued from no other place than that horrendous dungeon wherein, long since, despairing victims had been tortur'd unto death!

Chill'd by fear, my flesh acrawl and prickl'd, I yet did muster courage and approach'd, on timorous feet, that evil room.

VI. THE SMELL OF PAIN

The torture chamber's heavy iron door was but an inch ajar, and yellow torchlight flicker'd out through this discrepancy. The screams had stopp'd, but now I heard another sound: the voice of Dorottya.

"I will return to thee at dawn," she said, "at which hour wilt thou be more acquiescent to my wishes. Indeed, by that time thou wilt beg, if need be, on thy knees for the privilege of serving me."

The door, with shriek of hinges, open'd wider, and I back'd into the shadows. Dorottya appear'd, her dark eyes smouldering, her face agleam with sweat. She turn'd to close and lock the iron door, but ere she did so, I stepp'd forth and challeng'd her by name. She spun around, astonish'd, then, making out my face in the half-dark, spake: "My lady here, and at such an hour?"

"That question should be mine," I said.

"A matter of mere discipline," she smil'd. "Nothing of such high import that it should trouble thee." And, so saying, she began to lock the dungeon door.

"No happening in this castle is too low of import for mine ears," I said. "What dost thou here, Dorottya?"

She sigh'd. "Why, then, I see thou art distrustful. It is no more than this: when, earlier, thou bad'st me hide the village girl in some recess where Count Nadasdy would not find her, I, in my haste, could think of no place better than these dungeons, where no one treads. I lock'd the girl herein, and charg'd her to be silent. Later, as I lay alone abed, I heard the silence of this night disturb'd by the foolish wench's cries. Fearing the Count would hear them, I arose, descended hither, and abjur'd her to be quiet. She would not; she demanded I release her; I told her to be patient and she would gain thereby, with fair rewards and bounty; but the stubborn creature still persisted until, at last, I was oblig'd to chastise her. That, my lady, is the simple sum."

"How chastise her?" I ask'd.

"Such trifling things must not concern my lady."

"*How* chastise her, Dorottya?" I repeated sternly.

She stood unspeaking for a moment, her eyes as hard as flint. Then, smiling thinly, she replied: "By means most honour'd with long use and old tradition the world over, even in far-off heathen lands, and most particularly in the noble canons of thy Christian law." She push'd open the dungeon door. "Will it please my lady pass approval on my handiwork?"

I fear'd to step inside that place of ancient horror, but the steady eyes of Dorottya, narrow with mockery, goaded me, and with a shuddering breath, I took heart and pass'd through the iron door. In the erratic, twitching torchlight, I saw again the rack, the brazier of old irons and ashes, the cages, chains, the instruments of crushing and of tearing, the ghastly slab of the *peine forte et dure*. And then my breath caught suddenly in my lungs, as I saw the village girl.

Naked from head to toe, she hung motionless and silent in this place that smell'd of pain. Her feet dangled inches off the dungeon floor. Her arms stretch'd straight above her head, and the weight of her small body, slight though it was, dragg'd upon her thumbs, purpled and swollen in the leathern thongs that bound them. Her back and nates were cover'd by a tangle of glistering welts. Briny blood ooz'd thickly from the freshest of these, making its sluggish way down the serpentine length of her body in thin rivulets, thence to gather into heavy droplets at her toetips and drip evenly into a pool of ruby slime under her feet. The metrical slow dripping of her lifeblood was the only sound in the dungeon, and the foetid air hung still as Death.

I whisper'd in revulsion, "Oh, God in Heaven, Dorottya—hast slain this unoffending child?"

"Nay," Dorottya said, grinning, "she is but senseless from the blows. A little salt rubb'd briskly on her rawest weals, and she will shew thee life enough! Wouldst have me demonstrate?"

"Pile one abomination on another?" I cried.

"Tut, lady, 'twould be healthful to the wretch," Dorottya rejoin'd.

"This is a monstrous thing," I said. "How dar'd thou trespass thus, and so abuse my confidence?"

"My lady likes it not?"

"Thou knowest well I like it not!"

"My lady finds some flaw?" she said with a sneering lilt. "Some thing not done or poorly wrought? My lady would *improve* my efforts?" She thrust into my hand a coil'd black whip, still thick with blood: my fingers jump'd from it as they would jump from a venomous reptile, and the ugly length of hide fell to the floor.

Dorottya pick'd up the whip. "Wilt add thy signature to this
piece of work?" she taunted.

I dash'd it from her hand. "Art mad?"

She cluck'd her tongue in mocking admonition. "So squeamish
art thou, Countess?" And ere I could reply, she added: "So squeamish—*and a Bathory?*"

"Thy words lack all concord and sense," I told her. "In what
wise does my name have aught to do with this?"

"Oh, lady, 'tis a large and lustrous name, known far and wide,
familiar to the ears of great and humble . . ."

"Thou speakest wildly, Dorottya!" I said, and stepp'd forward to
cut down the hapless girl.

"Sayest thou so?" snapp'd Dorottya, seizing my shoulder and
staying me. "Here is a marvel, then, indeed! What? Thou, a
Bathory, unknowing of the fame that shineth from thy family's escutcheon? This is surpassing modesty, my lady; innocence so pure,
unspoilt, and rare that Reason's own sweet self is ravag'd!"

"Let loose mine arm," I said, "and help me dress this poor girl's
sorry gashes, or *thou* wilt hang thus in her stead, I swear!"

"Ah!" crow'd Dorottya in triumph. "Now speaks the true
Bathory voice!"

"What meanest thou, by this vain harping on my name?"

Dorottya shook her head in wonderment. "Dost thou, in truth,
not know?"

My blank looks gave reply; and Dorottya, with a bestial snarl,
look'd past me, toward the dungeon door, and said, *"Enlighten
her."*

I swiftly turn'd, and gave a cry of sharp surprise. There in the
open door of that vile chamber—not livid in disgust and loathing,
not mouth agape and wide of eye with unbelieving awe, but,
rather, with lips curving in a calm and curious smile—stood my
husband.

VII. THE ENLIGHTENMENT

Ferencz stood in the doorway for an unending moment, not
speaking, his eye darting from me, to Dorottya, to the tormented

victim hanging from the ceiling; then he advanc'd into the chamber, easefully, unhurried, his smile broadening the while. "Enlighten my little spouse?" he said at last. "Cast her out naked from that Eden of sweet ignorance she hath so happily inhabited? Crease that unlin'd brow? Darken those starry eyes? Bow those alabaster shoulders with the heavy, horrid burthen of knowledge? What saith Elisabeth: shall I indeed enlighten thee?"

Terror and fearful portent rose like a freezing mist, enveloping my body, choking the words in my throat. My Ferencz, who was my world, my god, to look and speak thus cold, ironical, and strange? To be so alter'd and unlike his own fair self in every aspect? If this could be, then nothing in this sphere or in the vast eternal firmament was constant, staunch, or true. Heaven and Hell were, then, but painted pictures, and love itself a lie.

Yet, though fear transfix'd me, my first words were of the unlucky village girl, for I said: "Enlighten me if't please thee, Ferencz, but not until that blameless maid is loos'd from out her crippling bonds."

He look'd up at the hanging girl, and at her blackening thumbs, and said to Dorottya: "The purpose hath been serv'd, methinks, the lesson learn'd. Cut down the little drab."

With one of sundry cruel blades that lay about the cell, Dorottya sever'd the thongs from the wall-hook whereat they were affix'd; the ceiling pulley squeak'd; and the girl slump'd to the damp stone floor, a silent, naked, bleeding heap of flesh.

"Enlightenment hath been ask'd for," Ferencz said when this was done, "and indeed it seems most timely. Enlightenment by dint of words; but first by dint of action . . ."

What follow'd then was so abhorrent, that to think upon it even now, after the lapse of years, makes my gorge to seethe and rise within me.

"Sit thee down," said Ferencz, and push'd me into a chair affix'd with manacles, and these he lock'd upon my hands and feet. "Thou'lt not be much discomfited," he said, "for I do not mean to light the pan of coals that lieth under the iron seat. This is but to assure thy fixity." A kind of vise he tighten'd, not ungently, at my temples, saying: "And this to keep thy head from motion." He then display'd two small iron rings, about the same circumference as florins. "And these?" he chuckl'd. "Why, these will make it certain thou'lt not miss the smallest trifle of thy enlightenment." He, quickly and with deftness, forc'd the iron rings around my very eyeballs, in such wise as to keep my lids from lowering, obliging me to stare, unblinking, at whatever lay before me.

Ferencz then, to my mounting anguish, gather'd the gloating Dorottya into his arms, and kiss'd her with excess of zeal; and did not stop with kissing, that perfidious pair, but, unmindful of all decency, like ruttish beasts that lack the benefit of soul to guide them, did foully slake their lusts in that rank cell, amongst the cunning tools of agony, within an arm's length of the insensate village girl, whilst I, unable to turn my head from the infernal scene, beheld, with stinging, bulging eyes, each moment of that union, unto its final hideous gasp.

Arising then from his depravity, Ferencz walk'd over to the chair in which I was constrain'd to sit, saying, "My little wife is shaken by this entertainment, Dorottya: see, her face is all o'ercast with sickly pallor." And he laugh'd. "What, Elisabeth? Hast lost thy pretty tongue? No epithets, no pious cries? Quite mum? Thine eyes do stream with tears—but whether they be drops of sorrow, or no more than that liquor Nature doth provide to lave thy parching orbs withal, I know not. Let me affirm my fondness for thee, sweetest chuck, and relieve thy lovely eyes of their hindrances."

So saying, he remov'd the iron rings, and I blink'd, my lids comforting my burning eyeballs like healing poultices.

"Know, then," Ferencz continu'd, "that I intend thee nothing hurtful, unless thou dost prove tiresome by stubborn protestations —yet this thou wilt not, I believe. Art silent still? 'Tis well, for thou hast much to learn, and it is meet that thou shouldst meekly listen:

"This wanton, wise, and artful Gypsy wight, this Dorottya, hath been my ardent mistress since before thine own fair beauty snar'd my heart. With her, I have known deep delights surpassing those pale, milky pleasures other folk enjoy. For most men and their dames are plodding, stale, proscrib'd, bound in by limitation, fear, denial, an host of guilty doubts and shames. To but a few is granted spirits broad and questing, undismay'd, which freely vault o'er petty confines, to range in unexplor'd demesnes; and such an one am I, for those of my blood have ever been impatient with the shackles other men clap round themselves. Thus, from an early age,

I sought out bypaths little trod, and cleav'd to those whose passions match'd mine own.

"Dorottya was one such, yet it is too small a thing to call her 'one such'—rather, has she been the paramount and chiefest sharer of my joys: pupil and tutor both, purveying and receiving; yet not permitting jealousies to hinder her from being the avenue whereby I met with other congenial spirits.

"Our pleasures were not look'd upon with favour when, from time to time, a whisper would escape from some disgruntled creature we had used; but I would quell such rumours with a show of piety, and all would then again be well.

"But for how long would soothing words and seeming virtue still these grumblings? Not forever, surely. Much need had we to join our forces with those who, sympathetic to our tastes, would yet be sturdy shields, protectors, with blood alliances to noble ministers of mighty sway. 'Twas then we learn'd there liv'd, in a purlieu not far distant from our own, a fair young maid, in whose comely person nubility with nobility were conjoin'd; who counted cardinals and kings among her line; who was a most beloved cousin of that high-placed Gyorgy Thurzo, Prime Minister to His Majesty . . ."

I found my voice at last. "Oh God! Myself!"

"Thyself," Ferencz confirm'd.

"But . . ." I stammer'd haltingly: "didst thou not say, just now, that such highborn allies must needs be 'sympathetic to thy tastes'?"

"Ay, little wife. And art thou not of Bathory breed?"

"I am, but what of this?"

"Come, art so innocent? Dost thou not know full well the maim'd repute thy family bears—yet suffers not a jot of open censure, by reason of its powerful affiliates?"

" 'Tis slander!"

"Truly? Is it slander, then, to say thy brother is an unsated ram who spends himself on young and old alike by main force, yet goes unpunish'd? Is't calumny to recall to thee thine aunt, whose lusts consume the choicest youthful blooms her influence and riches can procure, distinguishing not betwixt their genders? Is't falsehood to evoke that uncle who is call'd a warlock, concocter of dread alchemies, whose prayers are offered not to God, but Satan? And, dear Elisabeth, what of thy princely cousin Mad Zsigmond, he of Transylvania? Art thou indeed unknowing of his ways, of how, to entertain him whilst he sups (as others might be cheer'd by songs or stories) he hath serfs dragg'd before his table, that he may watch their coupling, and if he be not pleas'd with their performance, bids his varlets torture them to death, their screams concordant carols to his ears?"

"Nay, these are lies!" I cried.

He did not heed me, but went on. "And so, on Dorottya's urging, I paid thee court, was welcom'd by thy father, found thee most beauteous, and set about persuading thee to wed me. Young thou wert, and as young mares must needs be broken to the saddle, so must young maids. During this time of tutelage, Dorottya did absent herself from Csejthe. Thine untried ardour soar'd, but still did I refrain from leading thee to arcane joys, for fear of shocking thee and marring all. The mask of sanctimony I put on, and prated like a monk, and anxiously awaited such a time when it would be propitious to bring Dorottya to thee, for different teachings. The king's command well serv'd my purpose; I rode off to rout the Turk; thine unquench'd passions rag'd; and Dorottya, as was my plan, came unto thee to sate them."

"To . . . sate them?" I said. "Nay, Dorottya but calm'd me with anointings and sport . . ."

Dorottya, long silent, threw back her head and laugh'd. "Is't innocence or idiocy?" she said. "Wert thou indeed purblind, that thou wast unaware how interdicted and unlawful was our congress? Did not these 'calmings' and 'anointings' and our romps, from which thou didst derive such glee, not once seem contraband or guilty?"

"Nay . . . nay, never!" I rejoin'd.

Ferencz then spake. "I do believe it, Dorottya. For when, to-night, she lay clasp'd within mine arms, I did attempt to sound her, by talk of 'secrets' hidden from me, hints of things unholy in the world, righteous warnings of the faceless sins that 'creep unseen into the soul.' And not once was she disquieted by guilt or shame, she is so pure. I press'd the point e'en further, bade her read Scripture, spoke of Paul, recited verses that I hop'd would lead her on to fuller guessings." He look'd down upon me, still manacled, by hand and foot, unto that chair. "Dost recollect, Elisabeth? Those pagans who, 'tis writ, 'worshipp'd and serv'd the creature more than the Creator'? The Holy Book has ever fill'd thy days, thou saith. Then canst thou not recite the words that follow? 'For this cause . . .' "

In memory, the page of Scripture rose before mine eyes: *For this cause God gave them up into vile affections: for even their women did change the natural use into that which is against nature* . . .

"Then I . . ." My voice falter'd and broke.

"Ay, little one," said Ferencz. "Thou, either by the fault of too excessive innocence, or the strain of Bathory perverseness in thy veins, hath done things call'd uncleanly and corrupt."

Dorottya said, "Thou art now one of us, Elisabeth."

"Bound to us by bands stouter than the ties of blood," said Ferencz.

"Ay," said I in hollow answer, "and likewise damn'd with ye."

"If that be so," said Ferencz, "then let thine arms embrace damnation like a lover . . ."

"And let us lead thee onward," added Dorottya, "to keen delights far stranger and more bold than those thou hast already savour'd . . ."

"Ay, wife," said Ferencz, "and be thou Bathory not but in name, but in hot deed, as well!"

"And let us seal this compact with a solemn pledge," Dorottya said, "a ceremonial bath to signalize our fealty to sin."

"We three to bathe?" said Ferencz. " 'Tis well. And what, of all thy unctions, Dorottya, shall we bathe ourselves withal?"

"One richer far than all the others," she replied, pointing to the girl who lieth, scourg'd and raw, upon the floor. "That which floweth in her veins."

VIII. GREX SANGUINARIUS

Thou knowest, Lord, that blood bath was the first, but not the last, in which I would immerse myself in all the years that follow'd. As if a gate of Hell had been thrown open, Ferencz and Dorottya, made confident by the bastion of my family name, now steep'd us all in reeking devilish rites, and vilest pleasures; whilst I, like unto one in whom the soul has died, became a stunn'd, obedient creature, sharing both dark lust and blame.

Whether 'twas truly some streak of grainèd foulness in my stirps that made me such an unobjecting partner in those crimes; or whether disenchantment with my Ferencz and with all humanity had stifled gentler humours; or whether Dorottya's cunning simples had a part in blunting my fair nature (as they had blunted poor Ilona's), I know not. I only know that I became as despicable and perjur'd as Ferencz and Dorottya, for all of us would make a show of most devout obeisance when the village priest would call to say mass; and our confessions were but cynical recitals of small vices and transgressions, nothing more.

As hideous vermin crawl from under lifted stones, now bloated, grinning cohorts stream'd to Csejthe, call'd hither by Dorottya. Thou wert long familiar with them, Lord: the sorcerers Ujvary and Thorko, the first a skillful crafter of new tormentry which far surpass'd in cruel genius those of rack or wheel or any hitherto invented; another witch, call'd Darvula, whose energies and hungers rivall'd those of Dorottya; two serving maids, Otvos and Barsovny, to tend my person, chosen by Ferencz for youth and beauty and total absence of all scruple; and troops of others, nameless to me now.

Pitiful were those who came to Csejthe unwillingly: the blossoming young girls, who, in the mounting hundreds, were requir'd to fan and then appease our raging appetites. Entic'd from the village by pretty Otvos and Barsovny, who told of fair employment and reward at Csejthe; or drugg'd by Dorottya or Darvula; or overwhelm'd and beaten by the hulking Thorko or the slavering Ujvary; these pathetic creatures (all young and fair, for none else did we crave), were herded like swine into our cellars and our dungeons, to await the most deprav'd extremity of our pleasure.

Dorottya told me once she was far older than she seem'd, and that she held the years in check and retain'd the youthful freshness of her skin by bathing in the blood of virgins. She bade me join her, and I did. If such a thing be horrible—the draining of young veins for such a purpose—how much more horrible, and to no purpose whatsoever, was the manner by which these hapless prisoners were put to death: not with the swift, blunt mercy that is dealt even to dumb cattle, but by prolong'd and calculated tortures, which I have not stomach to set down here, so degraded and inhuman were they.

Inhuman, saith I? Nay: the beasts of field and forest, lacking all humanity, e'en the most terrible among these, slay not by long deliberate delaying and for lust. Human, then, indeed, were those fell crimes.

From time to time, my brain—like to a wanderer lost in fog which sometimes lifteth, showing clary sun, only to weave greyly 'round the stumbling wretch again—would comprehend the fullest, deepest horror of our acts; and I would then resolve to end them, by freeing our poor victims, allowing them to spread the tale of our decay throughout the village, till it was arous'd. But never did I this, and now, upon reflection, I do think it was somehow for love of Ferencz that I refrain'd; some shred of former feeling clung to me, and I could not bear to think of him haul'd up before tribunals and punish'd.

Then, on one day, fate took that fear from me.

Ferencz was summon'd to the battlefield again to fight the Saracen. As on that night years before, I bade farewell to him whilst cannonades of thunder boom'd through Csejthe and pelting rain curtain'd the countryside.

"Dost recollect," I ask'd him, "what words thou spake that other time thou left me for the wars?"

"Nay," he answer'd, "what said I then?"

"Thou didst declare: 'God's my guardian, thou my guerdon: how else, then, can it be but I will triumph over Death and foe alike?' "

"A pretty speech," he said, and mounted his palfry.

"Say it now!" I bade him.

"Art silly still?" he scoff'd.

"Say it, Ferencz!"

"Nay, have done. Fare thee well, and—" (irony congeal'd his face) "—prithee, do not pine away in solitude!" He goaded his mount, and rode into the night.

Less than a score of days from then, a courier deliver'd unto me the news: Ferencz was dead, "honourably slain in battle, by the heathen Turk who long hath ravag'd and lain waste our land." The King himself had signed it.

O fortunate husband! Dead with honour; whilst I still languish'd in a filthy sty of sin. 'Twas then I cast from me all caution, and conspir'd to let the world know of the foul blight Castle Csejthe had now become.

One morning, my gore-streak'd companions still abed, so worn were they by ghastly revels in the night, I stole into the dungeons and unlock'd the shackles from the limbs of a single youthful captive, destin'd soon for torture and for death. I bade her flee to the village, and tell all—"Spare nothing," I beseech'd her, "relate all horrors thou hast seen, all gushings of fair maidens' blood, all gloating torments, all!"

The frighten'd maid, at first, thought 'twas some trick, some game design'd to raise her hope, then dash it to the ground and thus torment her further. I begg'd her to believe me, trust in me (why *should* she trust in one who had partaken of such infernal rites?), and perchance for some sincerity that shineth from mine eyes, she believ'd me and did as she was bidden.

She was not miss'd by Dorottya or the others ('twas for this reason I but set free a single prisoner), and word soon spread. Grumblings commenc'd to reach us at the castle; village girls no longer were so easefully accessible to our procurers.

But there it stopp'd: rumblings and rumours; frighten'd glances cast toward Csejthe; a need by us of greater stealth; from the village church, veil'd sermons which, by indirections, weakly touch'd on a certain "bloody band" abhorr'd by God, yet even these pale warnings couch'd in Latin—*"grex sanguinarius"*—which the villagers could scarce divine. And still our base carousals went uncheck'd!

Slowly, my dull mind fathom'd why: and, in its own way, the cause was far more crushing to my spirit than the grossest horrors we had wrought in Castle Csejthe.

IX. THE CURSE OF CATS

For Ferencz had spoke true.

My name was too refulgent, my family too high-plac'd: who dar'd chastise us? My cousin, Gyorgy, Prime Minister to the King, ignor'd all tales he heard of our debauches, so that his own escutcheon might not be stain'd thereby.

When this execrable truth became clear to me, my heart sank. Was this humanity? Was this nobility? Was this the Christian glory that presum'd to hold itself above the heathen Turk? To suffer innocents be sacrific'd on an altar of corruption, merely that a lofty family be spar'd discomfiture? Oh, this was tenfold more abominable than the crime itself, that high authority should wink at it! Dismay'd, revolted, heartsick, I in that moment of black revelation forswore mankind, abjur'd all ties of family, renounc'd and disavow'd sweet Christ Himself.

Why did I not, disgusted by the perfidious world, plunge with refreshen'd appetite into those hellish orgies? I know not. Some almost dead, not quite extinguish'd lamp of good, perchance, prevented me; and I instead sought out Ilona.

I spoke to her as in far bygone days: "Sweet nanny . . . dear old lady, dost thou hear? Put by thy dreaming ways, and list. Nay, nanny, do not drowse—thou must needs hear me! I'll give to thee a letter, which I'll straightway indite, and this I charge thee carry to good King Matthias—ay, to His Majesty, Ilona! Dost grasp my words?"

The good old lady nodded; the clouds lifted from her eyes. "What kind of letter, child?" she ask'd.

"A document describing all heinous, dire iniquities that hath sprouted here like poisonous weeds. An humble, penitent confession of mine own part in them. A strong entreaty that His Majesty send troops to storm this castle and ensnare this whole foul company of demons! Such a letter shalt thou bear, Ilona."

The old nurse strok'd my hand, as she was wont to do of yore. "Dear child," she said, "my little babe, thou wilt be tried before stern judges, put to torture . . ."

"It is no matter. I yearn to be dismember'd on the rack, or disembowell'd, or burnt alive, to expiate my sins! No penance less will serve, Ilona; the time for pious mutterings of *mea culpa* is long past, it is too late! Thou *must,* dear nanny, do this thing for me!"

"Send *thee,* Elisabeth, to such judgement? . . ."

" 'Twere best, Ilona. In thine own unblemish'd conscience, thou know'st it must be done."

My old nurse said no more, but obediently awaited my writing of the letter. This I did; and seal'd it with the signets of both Bathory and Nadasdy; and put it in her hand; and watch'd her until she was safe away from Csejthe.

The rest Thou knowest, too, O Lord:

How clement Matthias grew outrag'd, and made Gyorgy Thurzo storm my castle on the very eve of the New Year; how those captives left alive were freed; how all my despicable minions were put

in chains and carried off to trial; how all, save me, were put to
death.

Ay, all save me: that mercy was as bitter gall to me, who crav'd
atonement. I, who wish'd for rack and fire, wast but condemn'd to
stay in solitude, wall'd here within my chamber for the remainder
of my days—for even when the grisly truth was told, my cousin
interceded for me, and my life and comfort spar'd.

In all this tainted record, in all this sorry blot on privilege and
authority, is there not one redeeming ray? One good and golden
thing to shine in Heaven's book and expiate, in some small part,
this race of man?

Verily, there is one. One who, from loyalty and love, could not
endure to see me dragg'd before the seat of mortal judgement; one
who, lest such a fate befall me, took all blame, all censure, all
chastisement, said, " 'Twas not the Countess brought these witches
to the castle; nay, 'twas I, and only I."

Too late I learn'd of dear Ilona's act: of how she made her way to
His Majesty's court, was recogniz'd as my old nurse and so admitted, and how she then (having destroy'd my letter) told the King an
host of horrid truths, and one unselfish lie: her false confession.

And, for that glorious sacrifice, which I neither desir'd nor
deserv'd, the noble dame was grimly martyr'd: for though Ujvary,
Thorko, Darvula, Otvos, and Barsovny were swift despatch'd by
the headsman's axe, a most particular doom was meted out to those
two thought the most despicable of that band: Dorottya and Ilona.
Both luckless women (one a fiend, and one a blessed saint) were
condemn'd to have their fingers, one by one, ripp'd off their hands,
before they were conducted to the stake and burnt alive.

And soon I, too, will die, for I have left untouch'd for many days
the food that has been brought me. Before I die, O Lord, I ask that
I be granted but one boon:

I ask that Thou send cats—lean, vicious cats with teeth and claws
as sharp as daggers—and set them on all pious souls who, when
they knew full well what things were being done at Csejthe, sat idly
by and mumbl'd orisons, and cross'd themselves, and did no other
thing. On my too generous cousin, Thurzo, set these clawing
beasts; on that o'ercautious priest down in the village, who water'd
down his Christian zeal into an insipid broth; and on all others of

their ilk, rain yellow-eyed, mad, scratching, squawling cats! Do this,
O Lord, I beg!

And, if Thou dost, why, when I see Thee soon, I'll thank Thee.
For what should such an inky soul as mine do in the jasper halls of
Heaven? I am so dipp'd in blood of innocents that my intolerable
stench would cause the angels to stop up their nostrils at me! And
so, instead, I have consign'd myself to Thee, for in Thy realm I am
assur'd of welcome. I come, then, like a mistress, to Thy terrible
Arms, and offer up mine own immortal soul to Thee—my Sover-
eign Lord, great Lucifer!

Thine own
ELISABETH

Vasilisa and the Witch

A RUSSIAN FOLK TALE

VASILISA THE BEAUTIFUL *is a Russian folk tale that may well be the Slavic equivalent of* Cinderella. *The two tales contain similar elements: a wicked stepmother, a witch and a happily-ever-after royal marriage. The witch, however, is on the side of good—though it is clear that this is not her usual policy. (For further details, see Appendix II, page 520.)*

Once upon a time in old Russia there dwelt a merchant who had a beautiful daughter named Vasilisa. When she was only eight years old, her mother called the child to her bedside and said, "My darling, I am dying, but I am leaving you something wonderful that will always protect you from harm. Reach beneath the bed and see what it is."

Vasilisa did as she was told and found a magic doll. Her mother said she must always keep it near her and if ever trouble came, Vasilisa must feed the doll and then ask for its advice. The little girl promised she would. Then Vasilisa's mother blessed her, gave her one last kiss, and died.

For a long time the merchant mourned his wife, but eventually decided to marry a widow who had two daughters the same age as Vasilisa, thinking that she would be a fine mother for his child. However, he was mistaken. Because Vasilisa was the loveliest little girl in the whole village, her stepsisters were jealous of her, and so her stepmother gave Vasilisa the most wearisome household chores to perform, in hopes that hard labor would turn her thin and wan. But though Vasilisa toiled uncomplainingly in wind and rain and hot weather, she grew more and more beautiful, while her stepmother and stepsisters, though they did nothing in the way of hard work, became thinner and plainer as spitefulness worked in their spirits like poison.

In truth, Vasilisa never could have accomplished all her chores alone. Her stepmother and stepsisters did not know about the magic doll. Each night, when they were fast asleep, Vasilisa fed scraps of food saved from her own dinner to the doll, and afterward would say, "Though I live in my dear father's house, my wicked stepmother robs me of all joy. What shall I do?" Then the magic doll would comfort Vasilisa and advise her how to deal with the following day. The next morning, while Vasilisa played in shady places and picked flowers, the doll would weed and water the flower beds and light the stove. Once she even pointed out to Vasilisa a plant that would protect her skin from sunburn. In this fashion, the years passed and Vasilisa grew up to be the most attractive young woman in the village. She was sought after in marriage by all the eligible bachelors, but her stepmother told all of them she never would permit Vasilisa to marry until her elder sisters were wed. Whenever she sent a disappointed suitor away, the malicious woman would beat her stepdaughter.

There came a time when Vasilisa's father had to travel to distant countries on business. As soon as he was gone, Vasilisa's wicked stepmother moved her family into a house near a great forest where Baba Yaga dwelt.

Now Baba Yaga was a witch who lived in a hut on fowl's legs and ate bad little girls and boys as if they were poultry. As soon as Vasilisa's family settled in their new home, the stepmother began finding excuses to send her stepchild into the woods, hoping that Baba Yaga would catch her and gobble her up. But the magic doll always told Vasilisa which paths to take to avoid the witch.

One evening that autumn, the stepmother assigned her eldest daughter to make lace and her second child to knit stockings, while Vasilisa was told to spin. While the three young women were thus occupied, the spiteful woman extinguished all the lights in the house except for one candle in the chamber where her daughters worked.

When the last candle burned low, the stepmother said, "There is hardly any light left in the house and you must all finish your tasks. Someone hurry to our neighbor Baba Yaga and borrow light from her." Instantly, her daughters shoved Vasilisa out of the room, saying she must do what their mother demanded.

Terrified, Vasilisa ran to her bedroom, fed her doll, and said, "Dear friend, I need your help more than ever. They are sending me to Baba Yaga. She will eat me up!"

"Do not be afraid, sweet Vasilisa," the doll comforted her. "Go to the witch, but take me with you and Baba Yaga will not harm you." So Vasilisa put the doll in her pocket, left the house, and entered the deep woods.

Time passed. Vasilisa fearfully walked in the direction the doll told her to take. Suddenly a whey-faced horseman all in white galloped by her on a pale horse. Dawn rose and a little later, when the sun grew bright, a second horseman with ruddy complexion and scarlet garments rode past on a red steed. Vasilisa journeyed all day long and at last, as evening drew nigh, she spied the clearing where Baba Yaga's house stood.

The hut rested on living legs like the feet of an enormous chicken. A fence of human bones surmounted by skulls enclosed the house. Instead of a lock, the front door contained a mouth agape with pointed teeth. As Vasilisa stood rooted to the spot, numb with horror, an ebony horseman clad in black charged by on a coal-black stallion, disappeared into the darkness—and it was night. A sickly yellow gleam began to glitter from the eye sockets of the skulls atop the fenceposts, making the glade as bright as if it were lit by moonlight. Soon the terrified young lass heard a strange pounding noise coming from the heart of the woods, headed in her direction. Branches cracked and leaves rustled; Baba Yaga flew into the clearing, riding in the bowl of a huge mortar which she pounded with an enormous pestle. When she saw the motionless girl waiting for her outside her hut, she demanded to know who she was and what she wanted.

From its haven in Vasilisa's pocket, the doll whispered, "Answer her truthfully and with great respect."

"Grandmother Yaga," the young woman said, "my name is

Vasilisa. Your neighbor my stepmother sent me here to borrow some light."

Now Baba Yaga knew all about Vasilisa's wicked stepmother and understood that she had sent the girl to her so she might eat her up. This annoyed the witch, who only devoured bad children, but in hopes that she might discover some appetizing nasty trait in Vasilisa, she cackled, "Come into my house, child, and I will give you the light you ask for, but first you must perform my chores, and if you do not work hard enough, I will swallow you whole!" With that, she said some magic words and the gate and door of the house both opened and the mortar flew inside with her, leaving Vasilisa to follow. The girl entered the hut, and portal and gate snapped shut behind her.

Inside, Baba Yaga sat down upon an old chair. She told the girl the first thing she must do was serve dinner, so Vasilisa opened up the stove and found enough food inside to feed a dozen laborers famished from a day's toil. The witch devoured it all, accompanying her meal with great draughts of whisky, wine, beer, and honey liqueur that Vasilisa had to fetch up from the basement. After she finished eating, Baba Yaga permitted her new servant to sup off a scrap of leftover meat, the heel end of a loaf of black bread, and a scant bowl of cabbage broth.

The witch yawned. "It's bedtime. Tomorrow, you must wash my clothes, clean the house, tidy the glade outside, make me dinner, and haul up a bushel of wheat from the cellar. If you don't get everything done by the time I return home, I'll make you the main course at tomorrow's evening meal!" With that, she went to bed.

Vasilisa fed her doll leftovers gleaned from the witch's feast, then told her how much work she must do the next day. The doll comforted her and told her to go to sleep, saying that things would not seem nearly so bleak in the morning.

The next day when Vasilisa woke up, Baba Yaga was already away doing mischief. The beautiful young woman rubbed her eyes, then looked round in wonder—the hut was spotlessly clean! She jumped out of bed and ran to the window and looked out; the clearing, too, was neat as a pin. Just then she heard a noise coming from the basement. Vasilisa turned and saw her doll hauling up a bushel of wheat from below.

"There, that's the lot!" the doll said. "Now all you have to do is prepare the witch's dinner."

That night, Baba Yaga could not help but be impressed by Vasilisa's industry, but she kept her feelings to herself. After she ate, the crone murmured a few magic words under her breath and three pairs of hands appeared in midair; these she commanded to grind her wheat into flour. Then she said to Vasilisa, "Tomorrow you must perform the same tasks that you did today, but you must also remove the poppy seeds from the old cellar bin and dust each grain. If I find even one speck of dust on a single seed, I'll eat your tender flesh tomorrow night."

When the witch went to bed, Vasilisa fed her doll and told her the impossible chore she must perform the next day, but the doll just said, "Go to sleep, my sweet, and let tomorrow take care of itself."

In the morning, Vasilisa awoke early. Baba Yaga was already gone. Once again, the hut was clean, the witch's laundry was done, another bushel of wheat had already been brought up from the basement, and the doll was seated by the stove swiftly dusting the poppy seeds, grain by grain. When the doll saw her, it said, "Ah, good morning, Vasilushka. All you have to do now is cook for the witch."

When Baba Yaga came back that night, she was even more impressed than the day before, but still she said nothing. After she called up the three pairs of magic hands to press the oil from her poppy seeds, she sat at her table, gobbled down her dinner, then, eying Vasilisa curiously, said, "Child, why do you never talk to me?"

"I have been afraid to."

"I give you leave to speak. I suppose," the witch slyly suggested, "that you have a thousand questions in your head you would like to ask me."

Now Vasilisa knew Baba Yaga was deliberately testing her, for it was common knowledge that whenever Baba Yaga answered a question, she immediately aged an entire year. "Grandmother Yaga," she prudently replied, "I have but one question I would like to ask. As I journeyed through the woods on my way to your house, three horsemen passed me. The first was whey-faced, wore white garments, and rode a pale charger, the second had a ruddy complexion, was clad in scarlet, and sat upon a red horse, while the third's skin and clothing and steed were all coal black. I wonder who they are—but as it is truly said that not all curiosity deserves to be satisfied, therefore I hesitate to burden you with mine."

Baba Yaga was so pleased with Vasilisa's tactfulness that she actually decided to answer her question. "The man in white is the dawn. His red and black brothers, respectively, are daylight and dark night. All of them are my servants." No sooner had the words left her mouth than Baba Yaga began to tremble like a leaf shaken by storm. Vasilisa watched in fascination and dread as in a twinkling the old woman aged a full year.

"Have you any other questions, child?"

Vasilisa would have liked to learn about the mysterious hands that ground the wheat and pressed the oil from the poppy seeds, but her doll whispered, "Do not yield to temptation," so she declined Baba Yaga's offer.

"A wise decision, Vasilisa. I eat anyone who displays too much curiosity. And now I shall ask you a question. How have you managed to perform the tasks I set for you these past two days?"

"With the help of my late mother's blessing," Vasilisa truthfully replied.

"No wonder!" the witch shuddered. "The house of a witch is no place for the blessed. You must leave at once." Baba Yaga led the girl outside, plucked a skull with gleaming eye sockets from the gate of bones, muttered magic words over it, and made a mystical pass before handing the skull to Vasilisa, saying, "Here is the light your stepmother sent you to borrow. Take it and go away."

Vasilisa did not have to be told twice. Grateful to be free of the witch, she hurried into the forest with the frightful yellow glow guiding her. When day broke, the magic light went out. "By now," Vasilisa thought, "my stepmother must have found another light-source." She was just about to discard the skull when it spoke to her in the witch's voice, saying, "You must not throw me away. Take me to your stepmother and stepsisters."

Vasilisa's return journey lasted all day. As night fell, the eye sockets again glimmered eerily. When the girl reached home, she saw no light in the windows, so she entered and found her stepmother and stepsisters sitting in the dark. As soon as they saw the glowering skull, they all cried out and tried to hide their eyes.

"What evil thing is this that you have dared to bring to us?" Vasilisa's stepmother shrieked.

"This is the light you sent this innocent to fetch," the skull replied in the voice of Baba Yaga. "Now look upon your own wickedness and see your doom!" With that, the skull's baleful glare burned into the eyes and minds and spirits of the three evil women, who first lost their sight and then their reason and lastly their lives. When morning dawned, nothing remained of them but three heaps of ashes.

Vasilisa moved back to town and the house of her father, where one fine day the czar himself saw her and proposed marriage. When Vasilisa's father at last returned from overseas, he found the grief of losing a second wife much assuaged by the news that in his absence his daughter had become a princess. With the help of her mother's doll, Vasilisa the Beautiful (for so her people called her) long and lovingly ruled her country.

As for Baba Yaga, scholars wonder whether she aged yet another year when her voice emerged from the skull and answered the wicked stepmother's final question. Some maintain that the witch merely wove a magic spell so the skull might imitate her voice, while others believe she willingly sacrificed a second year to the good and beautiful Princess Vasilisa, but a third school of thought sullenly contends that the stepmother's last question was directed to Vasilisa, so Baba Yaga risked nothing by replying. The issue has been argued long and heatedly, yet no one ever seeks out the witch to ask her the truth.

English adaptation by Marvin Kaye

The Mirror

MARGARET MAYO McGLYNN

MARGARET MAYO McGLYNN, *a resident of New York City, has been a book editor at two major publishing firms. Her gently feminist witch tale "The Mirror" invites favorable comparison with certain stories by Tanith Lee (represented elsewhere in this volume).*

The Queen is tired of waiting.

She sits on a rich eiderdown bed, looking at the diamond panes of her window. Her black hair is bound by tight golden cords. Rubied drops of silver waggle at her earlobes. Mica dust pinks her eyelids, getting in her eyes—she must rub them to see clearly—and white powder tints her face dead white. Silver links yoke her throat. Voices and the pounding of hooves rise from the yard, rattling the panes.

The lords are going.

They have left her the castle, which should be safe for her and Princess Blanche, since it is deep within a dark wood. Safe until the Council of Lords decides upon suitable matches for them.

Somewhere in the castle, the Princess plays, or cleans, or performs some other task to keep her busy, Queen Rosamond supposes. One of the nobles' wives informed Rosamond of the girl's uncertain future, now that her father, the great King Harcourt, is dead. *Uncertain future,* thinks the queen. *Blanche and I are alike in that.* "You need a protector," the ladies told Rosamond today.

The Queen sighs. Rising, she unbinds her hair, removes the silver at her ears and throat, pours water into the basin, and scrubs her face clean. She unlaces her bodice, removes her gown, and puts it away with careful habit—it is her finest—and draws on her simple nightdress. She paces a length of wall.

On another wall of the chamber between dark tapestries hangs a mirror, framed in carved, gilded, curvaceous wood. Catching her reflection in it, Rosamond pauses.

Too old to marry again, she thinks, her mind's eye casting a fresh, unlined image over the one she sees.

Long ago, her nursemaids told her a man would come.

And so he came. His battle-scarred body quaking in his armor, he rode from the north with his entourage, over the warm green hills of her dead father's land. The man's dull features were casqued in shadow; from his lips, sparse words, culled in sorrow. Great King Harcourt, tired of war, widowed.

Yes, he came. Grey-headed, bereaved, carrying a pretty, white-skinned girl child in his arms.

To Princess Rosamond, sole descendent of her line, the noble ladies said, "You are merely a daughter, this is your lot. He is strong, he is powerful, his kingdom borders yours. It is not right for a woman to rule alone."

He is old, he is homely, Rosamond thought. *And I am young. Is this to be my freedom?* But she said nothing, knowing her place too well.

They were married in a grand ceremony, and the Council of Lords and their ladies celebrated the auspicious match with a day-long feast of venison, fruit and wine. In their church, a priest set a circlet of gold on Rosamond's dark head, naming her queen. Escorted by the King's liveried guard, she journeyed to her husband's fortress.

Passing through King Harcourt's cold land, Rosamond found it a benighted forest, a country of old battlegrounds—like its ruler. His humpbacked home loomed ahead, a thick-walled stone enclosure with small windows and heavy locked doors. Within the dark castle the king's leaden silence shrouded Rosamond by day, his icy indifference by night—even as he pierced her and spent himself inside her. His silver yoke lay ever on her body.

In the afternoons she passed Princess Blanche's nursery. Harcourt sat there, murmuring to his daughter, his gray head bent gently over her while he told her heroic tales of his many battles. "Sire," said Rosamond, "may I read to the child?"

He flashed blue, vexed eyes at her. "No need. I read to her. Only men read here."

"But I can. I would like to—"

"Don't talk back, girl. Your duty lies elsewhere. Get me a son, my dear. Then you will please me." He waved her away with thick, clumsy hands. The King's heart was full up with Blanche.

Blanche. With her bright, dark eyes and pale, lustrous skin, the princess is the ideal of beauty in this chilly land. Women here are kept inside, in darkness, to preserve their fairness. In the mirror, Rosamond's face is brown from riding and hunting. *Dark skin, prized in the South. I too was lovely, but not fair.*

Rosamond did not blame the King for his coldness at first—Blanche's mother was so recently gone—nor did she blame the princess. But years later, Blanche remained Harcourt's only issue, and her face fulfilled its promise of beauty. Quietly the Queen resolved herself to barrenness, to wifely failure. And late at night, tatting strips of tightly knotted lace, she thought blackly of precious little Blanche.

Grooming his daughter to be a queen, Harcourt paid Rosamond's conduct little mind. One day, boldly, she began riding in the morning, then hunting in the gnarled royal wood in the afternoon, dressed in a man's habit. *Out from behind doors, but even the sun is pale and distant here.* This was her second girlhood, but she did not revel in it. *What am I for?* she thought, and could find no answer. Letting her lamp burn deep into the night, she read and reread the books in Harcourt's library. Rosamond did not yet open those left to her by her mother—those tomes containing secrets of the magical arts.

Then the King's sighing death passed by her one night, as much a struggle as falling asleep. His coffin, his shroud, his crypt, his fallow lands he left Rosamond. And his daughter.

For one moment, the Queen allowed herself to believe freedom had come to her. Later she cursed her foolishness. Reason told her the truth as the lords whispered fervently to their ladies over great King Harcourt's splendid burial.

Now Rosamond's yoke is heavier. Today the lords visited her, hungry for the land. And their ladies chattered at her, saying, "A man will come again for you—a match that can mean peace for decades. Aren't you lucky?"

A new husband, Rosamond thinks as night falls and she lights her lamp. Yet another kingdom for her to rule. *Was ever woman so powerful?* She laughs bitterly.

The man will arrive within the month.

But Rosamond awaits no He, covets no His. She sits in her chamber, watching the lamp dapple her thick tapestries with shadow, hand rubbing the black head of her cat. The lords will never leave her alone. This scorching ache is anger, she realizes. *Anger—they tried to breed it out of me before the wedding.* She scratches the cat's ear too hard, and it snarls, ready to bite. Tossing it off her lap, Rosamond wishes she could fight, command armies, rout the lords from her kingdom. But it is not to be. She does have some recourse—the arts her mother taught her. Yet conscience forbids it. After her mother died, the nursemaids scolded Rosamond, "Witchcraft is a low, vile thing. No wonder God took your dam so young."

The next evening, bringing her forgotten dinner plates down to the kitchen, Rosamond overhears the cook talking to the scullery maid. "The villagers say she is a witch. Foreign bitch," the cook drawls distortedly, probably picking at her teeth, "paints her face to hide its darkness, charmed the King's seed dead in her womb, stopped his breath with evil wiles as he slept." The plates crash on the flagstones, and the two servants run from the castle, making signs against evil conjuring.

My subjects—Rosamond grimaces, sweeping up a staircase to her chamber—*damn them! Damn God and conscience and delicate ladies and their simpering snow-white faces!* She flies into the library, slams and locks the door. Opening a dusty chest with a key she has hidden for years, she takes out her mother's books and begins to read.

Soon the ancient arts are fresh to her once more, as if she has rediscovered the dog-eared map of her childhood country. Full up with spells and mysteries, Rosamond mixes and boils a philtre in her chamber hearth, chants through the night, calling a spirit to her.

It comes, a pale spectre whirling in upon itself like a dust devil, and slips behind the glass of her gilded mirror. Rosamond speaks to it, and it advises her. Sometimes she imagines it looks like her mother. It has a ghostly, calm visage. It speaks with a woman's voice. While the servants attend to the castle and stable and gardens, while Blanche, forgotten somewhere below, seeks to amuse herself, the queen stays behind the locked door of her chamber. Sometimes she grinds herbs, berries, and seeds with her mortar and pestle, sometimes she chants softly—all to keep the spirit with her. Rosamond no longer feels quite so alone.

She listens now, four weeks since the spirit came.

It whispers smoothly, *"He is coming. Hear the hoof's thud upon the mud? He nears."*

"Send him away, Mirror." Rosamond tosses black dust from her mortar onto the hearthfire. The fire sputters.

"Yes, Mistress, it is good."

The man does not come. The queen knows the spirit has made him lose his way in a deep wood. Perhaps a large beast will eat him. She sits uncaring, glad that he is gone.

One week later, as the setting sun bleeds colors into the sky beyond her narrow window, the spirit informs Rosamond that an army approaches. With the innards of certain nocturnal animals, with urine and blood—magic a shade darker, but stronger—she weaves another spell. The spirit looks on approvingly. Soon, around the forest cloaking the dark castle, grows a wall of thorns, adamantine, impenetrable by man.

Now she is safe, but something irks Rosamond. Still she waits in her chamber, although no one is coming now, and as the spirit whispers dull words of encouragement, her senses blur and she feels all this has happened before. Sometimes at night there is a knock on her door, but she does not answer, and time unwinds like a roll of coarse cotton.

Awakening Rosamond from a formless reverie one evening, the spirit prompts, *"The Princess, mistress."*

"What of her?" sighs the Queen, her head propped on her palm as she gazes at a ripe, red-skinned apple sitting on her trunk. Where has it come from?

"She is as you were."

"As I was?" The Queen turns to look at the mirror. It frowns admonishingly.

"Yes."

"Lonely?" Rosamond wonders at the spirit's meaning.

"Yes. But more beautiful than before."

Now she understands. "It is not good," she says, her eyes drawn back to the apple.

"She is a woman now, and she waits for someone to come. The lords will come for her. For her this time, and when she weds a king, you will be nothing."

The Queen ponders the problem. "Mirror, bring her to me."

"Listen first, to her song."

And the spirit's lips grow round, spewing out the sparkling tones of Blanche's voice. Bright notes dancing up from a courtyard where every day a girl plays alone, muses Rosamond, not sure why she has never quite heard the sound before. It is as flesh to the dry bones of her desires. Implacably, it wounds her. The girl's song—its lyrics are "him," "his," "thou," "thine."

Surprised that tears prick her eyes, Rosamond furtively wipes her face with her sleeve—the spirit must not see her weakness.

Without thinking, she says, "Mirror, can I teach her?"

"Mistress," the spirit reproves in a sharp voice, *"that is not what you must say now. The huntsman, the heart. . . ."* The smooth planes of the spirit's face harden to oddly familiar lines. Rosamond feels a loop of destiny tighten around her. *"Do you not wish revenge, Mistress? She has denied you everything. Kill her and Harcourt's lands are yours alone."* The spirit's lips curve cruelly. Then its face becomes Blanche's, mockingly exquisite.

Rosamond's brow furrows. "Oh, I am old, wasted, Mirror. The Princess—"

". . . is lovely." The spirit reassumes its own cold, pale mask. *"Beside her, you fade. But if she were to die . . ."*

Rosamond recalls the afternoons passing the happy King in his daughter's nursery—*always left outside that door, never welcomed in*—the nights brooding over her own empty womb, and the laughter of a child through the halls of the castle, shrill noise, cutting into her.

"You know the way of it," whispers the Mirror.

If the Princess were to die . . . "Yes—" the Queen's witch-green eyes burn with old fury "—I know the way." Her hands trembling, she reaches for her spell book.

A feeble knock at the door. The Queen's head snaps toward it. "Who is it?" The spirit in the mirror transpares itself.

"Blanche, Mother," says the girl from beyond the door. "Please let me in."

"Nothing, it is nothing," sighs the spirit.

"Please, Mother, open the door tonight. I won't bother you ever again."

Rosamond glowers at her tapestries, but something in the girl's voice lances her. She goes to the door and, uncertain, unlocks and opens it. "What do you want, child?"

The Princess's eyes widen in her face, too big for it.

She fears me. Rosamond remembers how severely her hair is pulled from her face, how deathly white she has painted it of late. "What happened? Tell me quickly," she snaps.

The girl squares her shoulders, says bravely, "Well, I . . . I have nightmares. Tonight I saw a thousand men riding here to hack down the thicket around our castle, and when they slashed at it, it screamed and bled from its wounds. It died, and we had no defense." Blanche's face is red and puffy, her black hair in tangles over her shoulders, her blood-red lips swollen as if she'd been biting them.

"Blanche, dreams are not real," says the Queen, still half-wishing the girl would go back to bed, but unsettled by the dream.

"Your dreams can be real, can't they, Mother? You make them real, like the thicket around us." The girl is shaking.

"Yes. But the hedge will not die unless I will it, and I do not will it. Do you understand, girl?"

"Yes . . ." For a moment, biting her lips again, the princess mulls over her stepmother's words.

Then before Rosamond can pull out of reach, Blanche grasps her hand.

"We are safe because of what you have done. Thank you, Mother." She squeezes the hand gently and smiles, eyes gleaming dark. "You are right, and I was foolish to bother you. I am sorry." The girl turns, says, "Good night," and disappears down the torch-lit corridor.

The Queen stares at her hand, amazed that Blanche's warmth can remain on her skin, palpable, vivid still. And the girl's cheeks were rosy with health, even though she had been crying. And her frame had the gawkiness . . . the clumsiness of all girls entering womanhood. Too soon, always too soon. *How unhappy she must be, and yet she asks so little of me.*

"Mistress, *her land could be yours,*" hisses the mirror from over the Queen's shoulder.

She spins toward it, certain now where her fury belongs.

"These lands will never be mine, even if they were by birthright. I have no army. And the blasted lords want the land. Oh, how I tire of this game!"

"*Game? I do not understand. Mistress, the dagger, the apple—*"

"—The spell, the harridan! No, I have seen these things before somehow. Enough! You are like the rest—the ladies who told me to wait! Only the castle is left to us, and that, not for long. So do I take revenge on Blanche because she is pretty and young? Because I am childless? Because her dead father loved her more than me?" Rosamond picks up the apple.

"*You cannot deny me! You made me, woman, and I am no spirit,*" says the thing in the mirror.

It cackles at her, the sound playing along Rosamond's spine. She gasps. "No . . ." Rosamond backs away from it, almost tripping over her long gown.

She knows the thing's face.

I am there—all that I am—my stoppered bitterness, hatred of those of greater power, my idiotic complacency, my own icy, impregnable mask!

"*Yes. You know what I am . . .*" it says.

"Leave me," moans Rosamond.

The mirror chuckles softly. "*I cannot. Mistress, this is the only—*"

"The only way?" cries the Queen. "I will not have it so! I do not believe it." She gathers herself up, staring boldly into the glass. "You are hideous—I see that now—but not so frightening," she tells it, her voice growing soft and low, "now that I know you."

The spirit scowls in silence, waiting.

"Here is the apple you would have me poison." Rosamond gazes at the fruit. In its polished, russet skin, she sees her tear-streaked face. Not the fairest face she has seen.

But she smiles. And draws back her arm. And throws.

The mirror shatters.

• • •

Two tall figures stand in the castle courtyard, saddling their horses—a man of middling years, broad and burly, and a lanky boy, apparently the man's son.

For the last week, only the footsteps and voices of these two have echoed through the dark castle. The servants are gone. Grass pushes up between the cobblestones of the court. Already the castle walls seem to shift and crumble, but the dissolution of the structure will occur only when it is entirely abandoned. The elder of this pair has seen to that.

"Mother," says Blanche, buckling a saddlebag to her mare, "when will you tell me where we are going?"

Rosamond turns to her with a serious face—only Blanche will see it as a woman's. "I will tell you when I know, which will be when we arrive."

"Don't you know where?"

"No, I don't."

Blanche's response is a smile of admiration, which still has the power to touch her stepmother. Perhaps, thinks Rosamond, it always will.

"Then we will discover it at the same time. But something bothers me. When will *he* come for me?"

"Your cloaking spell is strong, Blanche. No one will know you for a girl. You have learned so quickly. Faster than I did." Rosamond pulls herself up onto her mare.

"Mother," says the girl firmly, "answer my question."

The Queen considers for a moment. "When will who come?"

"You know. A man. A husband. I do want children someday." Instantly Blanche winces at her callous remark and regretfully mounts her horse. But Rosamond only smiles slightly, not looking at her.

"He will come—when we find a place where we can show ourselves as we are. What of it? Tomorrow comes, too, and sooner. Are you ready?"

"Mother, that is no answer!"

"It is my answer, girl. Are you afraid to find your own?" Blanche's brow furrows and she looks down at her small gloved hands, weighing the leather reins resting in them. But as she lifts her gaze to the open gate of the castle—beyond its cumbersome arch, no wall of thorns, only curded hills of deep emerald cut by a trail winding toward the horizon—her burgeoning smile is reply enough.

"Not too afraid," she whispers, a breeze lifting her dark hair away from her cheeks. They share a grin. "Let's go," says Blanche, spurring her mare first. And Queen Rosamond and her stepdaughter thunder through the gate, out onto the long road.

The Tiger's Eye:
A Jungle Fairy Tale

L. FRANK BAUM

L. FRANK BAUM (1856–1919), *author of that American classic* The
Wonderful Wizard of Oz *as well as* The Magical Monarch of Mo,
Queen Zixi of Ix, John Dough and the Cherub, *numerous Oz sequels
and many other delightful children's books, in 1905 wrote a group of
amusing "Animal Fairy Tales" to which the following story belongs,
though it never was published during Baum's lifetime. (For details, see
Appendix II, page 521.) "The Tiger's Eye," according to* The Baum
Bugle, *the official magazine of the International Wizard of Oz Club,
"comes closer to being a pure horror story than anything else he ever wrote."*

This is a fairy tale of Pocofo, which is an island of the South Seas,
where the people are black and have never heard of telephones or
chocolate caramels.

One half the Island of Pocofo is a dense jungle, filled with wild
beasts which devour one another when they cannot get black people to eat. The other half of the island is inhabited by warring tribes
of natives who fight and rob each other when they are not hunting
the wild beasts. So it is not very peaceful in Pocofo, and I have
often wondered how the wee brown children and baby animals
manage to grow up where they are surrounded by so many dangers.

But they do grow up, and become strong men and women and fierce beasts. They take their part in the wars and worries of their day.

Once on a time a baby tiger was born in the jungle, and it was found to be blind in one eye. The father and mother tiger loved their baby and were sorry it had but one eye to see with.

"The black people may easily kill our darling," said the mother, "for when they approach it on the blind side it cannot see them."

"The leopards and lions will do the same," added the father tiger, sadly. "We really need three or four eyes, to be able to watch all our enemies, and one eye is no protection for a baby tiger at all."

So they decided something must be done, and resolved to visit a Magic-Maker who lived near the edge of the jungle.

This Magic-Maker had the heart of a beast and the form of a man. He understood the language spoken by the animals and that spoken by the black men, and he served anyone who brought him payment for his magic. So the father and mother tigers took their baby to the straw hut in which Nog the Magic-Maker lived, and told him they must have another eye for their darling one.

"A glass eye?" asked Nog.

"No; one that can see," was the reply.

"That is impossible," declared the Magic-Maker. I have much wisdom, and considerable skill in magic, but I cannot give your baby an eye that will see."

"Is there absolutely no way it can be done?" enquired the mother, in a grieved and disappointed voice.

"Oh, there is one way," said Nog, carelessly. "I could transform myself into an eye that could see; but in that case I would destroy my own form forever and become helpless except as an eye. Therefore, as I said, the thing is impossible."

"It may be from your point of view," growled the father tiger; "but to us it is more important that our baby has the eye than that you continue to live in your present form—an unlovely shape at the best. So we insist upon your transforming yourself into an eye."

"Nonsense!" exclaimed Nog, beginning to be frightened. "You don't suppose I'll consent to destroy myself for your foolish whim, do you?"

"Not willingly," admitted the tiger. "But here is the alternative;

either you transform yourself into an eye for our child, or I and my dear wife will tear you into shreds."

The Magic-Maker, hearing this dreadful threat, looked around for a way to escape. But the mother tiger was crouched on one side of him and the father tiger upon the other, while the baby tiger was glaring hungrily at Nog with its one eye, as if longing to eat him.

Nog was a wise man. He knew that tigers were merciless and had little respect for Magic-Makers—or anything else, for that matter. So he thought over this uncomfortable alternative and decided it would cause him extreme pain to be torn to shreds by sharp tiger claws and teeth, whereas it would not hurt at all to transform himself into an eye. Moreover, as an eye he would still be alive, with a faint—a very faint—hope that some day he might be saved, whereas to be torn into shreds would kill him in the operation.

"I will have revenge if you make me do this dreadful thing," he threatened.

"We are determined to make you do it," declared the father tiger. "What do we care for your revenge?"

Finding escape impossible Nog heaved a deep sigh and transformed himself into an eye. It was just like a tiger's eye and it hopped into the empty eyesocket in the baby tiger's face and rolled around with a fierce and wicked expression, for the Magic-Maker was angry because he had been trapped and transformed against his will.

All the way home the baby tiger leaped here and there about the jungle, growling ferociously and never at rest. It even snarled at its mother when she tried to quiet it. And the very next day the child deserted the safety of the lair where it was born and wandered through the jungle in search of prey.

So sharp and far-seeing was the new eye that nothing escaped it, and so fierce was the temper of the wearer that the baby tiger boldly attacked animals twice its own size and defeated them all. It could not devour all the slain, so the bodies of the young tiger's victims littered all the jungle, and the animals complained bitterly of this awful destruction. One of the laws of the jungle is that no animal may kill except for food, yet here was the baby tiger killing for the wicked sport of murder. The animals straightway condemned the murderer and banded together to destroy the tiger which wore Nog the Magic-Maker for an eye.

But the baby tiger avoided the stronger beasts and conquered the weaker ones. Meantime it grew wonderfully until it became a full sized tiger and a greater terror to the jungle folk than ever. One day it savagely fought its own father, who barely escaped with his life.

By this time the animals had become so angry and annoyed that they declared war upon the lawless tiger. They formed their army in line of battle and hunted the outlaw through the jungle till he was forced to fly to that part of the island where the black people lived.

Here the tiger's plan was to lie hidden by day and prowl over the country at night, killing all with whom he met. The people began to fear this enemy more than all the other animals of the jungle, yet few were brave enough to face the ferocious beast. These few he usually succeeded in killing before the fight was over.

Terror filled all the land and mothers kept their children in the huts so the cruel tiger could not find them.

Titticontoo was the little son of a native chieftain, and some time, if he lived to grow up, would rule a thousand black men himself. He was a pretty child, with sparkling brown eyes and soft hair, and he laughed all day at his play, being joyous of heart and quite happy.

Titticontoo did not know the meaning of clothes. He wore a cloth around his middle, woven of cocoanut fibre, but aside from that his little brown body was bare both night and day. He had no toys, so his only playthings were a small spear and a bow and arrows. With these he learned to skillfully shoot small birds, and so lithe were his muscles that he won every leaping and running contest from the other boys. He swam in the streams as nimbly as a fish. He said little and thought much. All the black people loved him because he was so smiling and cheerful, and Titticontoo loved his people in return and was generous and kind to all.

About the time the fierce tiger made its appearance in the land the boy's mother began to keep him shut up in the hut, fearing he might be killed. And at about the same time a horde of strange warriors from some unknown distant island landed on the coast of Pocofo and began to burn and slay and pillage wherever they went. So all the black men, headed by the chieftain who was Titticontoo's father, marched away to fight these strangers, while the women stayed at home to protect the children from the dreadful tiger.

One afternoon, as Titticontoo sat upon the floor of the hut playing with his little spear, a fierce growl was heard and suddenly there bounded into the room a great tiger. Its teeth were terrible to look at and its bared claws might well make the bravest shudder. One of its eyes—the left one—rolled with a glare so wicked and cruel that Titticontoo's mother screamed and fainted with fear.

The boy, with the spear clutched in his little hand, sat still and looked at his enemy. The tiger snarled and crouched for a spring. Then its lean yellow body shot forward, the dreadful claws extended to clutch and rend its victim.

Titticontoo had never been afraid in his life, and he was not afraid now. He knew the tiger was dangerous and realized his mother had fainted and could not help him. So he must do his best to help himself. He set one end of his spear against the ground and pointed the other—the sharp end—at the leaping tiger.

Next moment the beast was upon him. A blow from its sharp claw sent the boy flying against the wall of the hut and tore out his left eye, leaving two livid gashes on his cheek. But the spear pierced the heart of the tiger and it fell dead.

In spite of the burning pain in his eye the brave boy crept forward to examine his fallen enemy. And then a strange thing happened. The eye that had once been the Magic-Maker popped out of the tiger's head and popped into the head of Titticontoo, where it took the place of the eye which had been torn out by the tiger's claw. For Nog was still alive, although he was now only an eye, and he realized there was no use in remaining in the head of a dead tiger. He could do many more wicked and vengeful deeds, he thought, if he was in the head of the boy.

Strangely enough, Titticontoo's pain began to pass away as soon as the new eye popped into his head. He was glad at first to have the eye to see with, for he did not know it would try to influence him to evil deeds. When his mother recovered from her swoon she found the tiger dead and Titticontoo trying to bandage the gashes in his cheek. The eye did not pain him at all now.

All the women in the village, hearing the glad news that the tiger was slain, came running to the hut to congratulate Titticontoo upon his bravery; but the boy returned surly and ungracious answers and seemed to have lost his old merry ways and his kindly disposition.

Just then a band of the black men came running into the village to say their chieftain had been defeated and slain by the invaders and telling the women and children to fly to the jungle or they would all be captured and made slaves.

Hearing this Titticontoo sprang up angrily and cried out:

"You are cowards—every man of you! How dare you be alive when your chieftain is dead? Follow me, and do not fear, for I will defeat these strangers and drive them from our island."

"You! What can you do—you who are a mere boy?" asked the men, wonderingly.

"I have slain the tiger," replied Titticontoo, pointing proudly to the body of the beast.

They were amazed at this masterful feat, and when they looked upon the boy they noticed that his left eye flashed in a cruel and ferocious manner that was terrible to see. So they consented to return to the fight with the boy as their leader, and in spite of his mother's wails and protests Titticontoo seized his spear, pulled it from the tiger's heart, and with the blood still dripping from the weapon rushed away to lead his men.

They met the enemy not far from the village, and so bravely and desperately did the boy fight that his black men were encouraged and fought better by his side than they had ever fought before. Presently the strangers who had invaded the island became afraid and started to flee, for they could not bear the awful gleam of the tiger's eye when it was turned upon them.

Titticontoo pursued his foe, killing many with his spear and more with his bow and arrows. And when the strangers reached their boats they hastily tumbled into them and rowed away home; nor did they ever dare to invade Pocofo again.

Titticontoo returned with his victorious warriors to the village, where there was great rejoicing. Everyone declared he was the greatest chieftain and the fiercest fighter they had ever known; although he was but a boy.

Yet Titticontoo was strangely silent and ill at ease. He retired from the feasting and merrymaking to his mother's hut, where a great struggle took place in his heart.

Being by nature kind and gentle the boy was alarmed to find

himself so cruel and bloodthirsty as he had been in the recent fight. He had begun to hate even his own people, and when his mother entered the hut to speak with him he drove her out in a fit of unreasonable anger.

"I know I am growing wicked and doing unmanly and unjust things," said he to himself; "and I believe it is all because of the tiger's eye which is in my head. I am becoming as fierce as the tiger was, and unless I pluck out this dreadful eye I shall soon be unable to resist its wicked influence. Then my life will be ruined and my people and my friends come to hate me."

Titticontoo realized it would hurt dreadfully to pluck out the eye. He remembered the burning pain he had felt when his own eye was torn out. But after a brief struggle his gentle heart and true manly courage finally triumphed. He suddenly clutched the eye with his fingers, pulled it out and cast it upon the floor. Then he bore the pain courageously and bathed his wound in clear water and bound it up.

I am inclined to think this noble act proved what a great chieftain Titticontoo really was. His good heart saved him from a dreadful fate, for as soon as the tiger's eye was cast away he regained his finer nature and all his old gentleness.

The boy was ill and in pain for several days. Then he slowly recovered and his wound healed. "Titticontoo, the One-Eyed" he was always called after that; but every person on that island grew to love and respect him. He is now known as the greatest chieftain of his race.

Oh; I must tell you what became of the tiger's eye.

For many days, while Titticontoo was ill, the eye lay upon the floor of the hut, and no one dared to touch it. For it glared as fiercely now as ever, since the spirit of old Nog the Magic-Maker was still alive within it. And what do you suppose Nog thought all this time? He knew he had his revenge for being obliged to transform himself into an eye, yet perhaps he wondered anxiously what was to be his future fate.

After a time the boy came and looked at the eye, and its cruel expression made him shudder. He was glad the evil thing was lying there upon the floor instead of being in his own head; but it seemed alive, and he did not know what to do with it.

That night he cast it into the fire; but when the embers had burned away there lay the eye among the ashes, as bright and watchful as ever. Then Titticontoo tried to stamp upon it, but it slipped from underneath his heel and remained uninjured.

The boy knew it would never do to leave the dreadful eye in his hut, where it would glare upon him constantly and watch with its intent gaze every movement he made. So he tied the thing to an arrow and shot the arrow from his bow far into the air, in the direction of the jungle. For it was a tiger's eye, and the jungle was the home of tigers.

The arrow sailed far over the tangled trees and then descended. It struck a dappled deer, glancing past its cheek and putting out the poor creature's left eye. The thing which Titticontoo had tied to the arrow became loosened and rolled upon the ground; but as the deer stood trembling with terror and pain the tiger's eye suddenly popped into the place of the one which had been dislodged, and so the spirit of Nog the Magic-Maker found a new resting place.

It is said the deer is the most timid and harmless of animals, but this creature now seemed inspired by a new and evil nature. It dashed away through the jungle, fighting every beast it met and transfixing its victims upon its sharp horns with wicked glee. And all the while the tiger's eye glared viciously and thrilled the hearts of all who looked upon it with fear and dismay.

Finally the demon deer, panting and exhausted by the desperate war it had waged upon its fellow creatures, reached a pool of water and bent its head to drink.

Aha! That was just what old Nog the Magic-Maker had been looking for. Only one charm would restore him to his natural form: the tiger's eye must first be bathed in fire and then in water. Already Titticontoo had given it the test of fire, and now, as the deer bent over the pool, the eye which contained the spirit of Nog dropped out of the deer's head and fell into the water.

How wonderful these magic charms are! Here in the shallow pool stood the old Magic-Maker himself, while the startled deer screamed at sight of him and dashed into the forest.

The cry was heard by the father tiger, who stalked out of the thicket to find Nog scrambling from the water and grinning an evil grin of joy at regaining his natural form.

"Oh," said the father tiger, clicking his teeth together. "I believe

I owe you a debt for destroying my child. Prepare to die, Magic-Maker!"

The yellow body made a spring, but Nog dodged it and sped away through the jungle, trying to reach the safety of his home. The father tiger followed in pursuit, and an interesting race took place. Fear made the old wizard's feet to fly, and the tiger's leaps were long and swift, for his heart was bursting with rage and sorrow.

Near the edge of the jungle a vine tripped Nog and he fell flat upon his face. An instant later the great body of the tiger fell upon the Magic-Maker—and so the story ends.

It is a fairy tale told me by a black man who once lived on that same island of Pocofo.

A Smell of Sulphur

MARVIN KAYE

"A Smell of Sulphur," which was first published in Amazing Stories, *belongs to an as-yet-unclassified subcategory of fiction akin to pastiche but sufficiently differing in tone as to warrant a new label. I suggest that they might be called "tangentia." (For further comment, see Appendix II, page 521.)*

Wrinkling her nose at the acrid stink of sulphur she'd never learned to tolerate, the crone plucked a fatal sprig of Saluria from the crock. An ominous tremor shook her crooked spine. She deposited the poisonous herb on a cracked plate and hobbled to the window.

All morning she'd sensed the burgeoning danger. Her sister might scoff at her disquiet, but the omen was nevertheless real . . . an almost *welcome* warning. Her sibling delighted in more flamboyant magicks, but the crone knew the play and tension of opposing powers—for that and herbal grammarye comprised her most profound province of lore. She could hardly mistake the tang of foreboding stirring outward from an inimical source of strength.

Peering through the window of her hut, she scanned the bright blue skies and fields and thought spitefully of her elder sister. The lowering portent surely stemmed from her morning's labors, but if she only dared scotch her sibling's needlessly cruel scheme, the growing threat would probably dissipate.

A sudden breeze gusted a saffron patch of sulphur up her crooked nose. She sneezed. Wiping her long beak with a tattered sleeve, the crone plopped onto a low wooden stool, dismayed that even so slight an effort winded her.

The cheat of the bargain, she told herself, not for the first time. Centuries earlier, when the dark things, her masters, first whispered, she was hardly more than a child, full of vitality and hope. What did she know then of wickedness? *And now the years stretch ever on, and all action is wearisome . . .*

The surface of the seeing-glass clouded. Dark smoke billowed within its depths; as it cleared, the loathsome visage of her sister sprang up, staring dourly out at her.

"Is it ready?" she shrilled. Her voice had a naked edge like a steel razor slicing silver. It chilled the crone, set her teeth on edge, resonated in her bones. *"Or are you dawdling, as usual?"*

Rising from the stool with difficulty, she complained, "I'm tired, and my fingers ache. The stuff still must be stirred and set out to cool."

"Be brisk, you decrepit fool! I want that potion today!"

The tremor happened again, stronger. "So you have taken the first steps?"

"Aye!" The older woman laughed, a series of terse, ear-piercing stabs. *"The King's deposed, they'll never find him! As for his brat—"* She held up a lovely sleeping infant so her sister could see her in the crystal.

"Then you've kidnapped her," the crone said, a vague, undefinable emotion stirring in her breast, "isn't that enough? Why murder her? Our cousin agrees to work a metamorphosis to—"

"To her own purposes!" The crystal momentarily darkened; her sister was angry. *"That doddering dunderhead simply wishes to flatter her ego by having royalty serve her! I'll take no chances the princess will be found and restored to the throne. She dies!"*

"But not within these borders!"

"Of course not, fool! When you've prepared the potion, I'll transport her far beyond the sands and bury her at sea."

"But why? We have all we need. Till now, our sorceries have been tolerated, even overlooked. Why tempt the Fates?"

"After today, I shall be Fate in this land!"

"Yes," the crone grumbled, sourly stirring the Saluria into the mixture in the kettle, "power always was your chief weakness. Mine, knowledge."

Her sister sneered. *"Regret after all these years, sister? Perhaps, then, you wish to retire? Cede me your territory, dear—I'll see you well provided for in your dotage."*

Contempt welled up in the crone, her old pride. She nearly dematerialized with rage, but managed to pull herself together, sulphur exuding from her pores. (She *hated* the stench!)

"Cede to you? I'd sooner take service with the Red Witch!"

"Shh! Name her not!" The mere mention made her sister quail. *"She suspects nothing!"*

A bubbling plop. The Saluria was working up the broth. "Well, well," the crone reluctantly said, "the mixture's nearly done."

"Splendid. I'll be by in two hours to fetch it. Have it cooled and bottled."

"Don't presume to give *me* orders!" The crone waved a wooden spoon angrily at the face in the sphere. "It's all *your* fault!"

Her sister appeared genuinely puzzled. *"My fault? What is?"*

"That I signed the pact!"

"Dredging up ancient history, aren't we?"

"What did *I* know then? The dark things spoke first to *you*. And you tempted *me*."

"I don't recall needing a great deal of persuasion to get you to make up your mind."

"Everyone knows you're wickeder than I!"

"And you're inconstant! And craven!" The hag grimaced horribly. *"Bah! I'll not bandy words. Cool and bottle that potion or I'll see you suffer, sister. Two hours!"*

With a contemptuous sneer, she vanished. The crystal clouded, cleared and was blank once more.

All, all now was wearisome, and all because of her sister's unslakable lust for power. It was she who, long ago, seduced her innocence to the ways of the night.

"All *her* fault," the crone muttered.

. . .

When she removed the kettle from the fire, she felt the ominous tremble along her spine yet again. Its potency had doubled since the last time she sensed it looming ever nearer. It was so strong she knew its wrathful shadow eventually would extend to her sister as well, despite her greater skills at magick.

The scheme was foolish at best, and her withered heart dared whisper it was more than that: a foulness even she could not contemplate. Enchanting the child, enslaving her . . . those were choices that could be countenanced, at least for a time, in the tacit cosmic battle. But to kill the King's sole daughter was not only difficult to accomplish, but fraught with risk.

The sensible thing to do—though it would arouse the terrible wrath of her sister—would be to pitch the poison out the back door.

Instead, the crone, smiling bleakly, set the kettle on the windowsill to cool.

Once, long ago, she *might* have refused her sister. She *could* have entered the service of the Red Witch. *Couldn't she?*

A long sigh. *No way of knowing now.* She could not alter the course of her destiny. She was proscribed to evil. And yet, she toyed with the notion of upsetting the kettle, actually reached out her hand to do so. *But I dare not! I must not! She's my sister, after all. We serve the same masters!* Her gnarled hand dropped to her side.

The skies darkened.

The pettiness of evil! How it corrodes! How it renders the years endless, all alike. Clasping her knees, she rocked miserably on the stool. *Turns and dodges, all winding down toward Eternal Entropy.*

And the smell of sulphur always offending her nose.

The wind rose. The kettle teetered on the ledge.

The old woman rose painfully to her feet and stumped to the sill, steadying the mixture lest the gale dash it on the floor. *Spill it out!*

The kettle felt cool. She lifted the pot with an enormous effort. *Spill it out!*

"I can't," she protested. "She'd merely chain and torture me till I succumbed and mixed a new quantity of potion."

Spill it, spill it, do!

"I haven't the strength to resist."
"That's it!"

The answer had been with her all morning, niggling at her thoughts. Now it finally stood out square and plain.

"Yes," she exclaimed feebly, *"yes!* The only way to oppose her is —*to acquiesce!"*

Putting down the kettle, she scuttled feverishly to her cabinet of implements and flung wide the doors. She grasped a large empty bottle and a cork big enough to stop it.

The wind roared.

As she dipped a spoon into the kettle, she taunted the Fates. "See what I'm doing! *See!* All babes need their bottles. Here's one for the princess!" She ladled the poison, cackling fiendishly while the hut pitched and rocked in the hurricane's fury.

Momentary fear. But she shunted the irrelevant emotion aside and stuck the cork tight into the neck of the filled flask.

The crone donned her favorite slippers and hobbled out into the storm, clutching the bottle in one claw-like hand. The wind whipped her white hair, plucked at her spindly legs. But the sorcery of her enchanted footwear rooted her to the spot.

Now a giant cloud blotted out the straggling rays of the pallid sun. She looked up and saw the shape of her Destiny.

Resigned, yet wearily triumphant, the crone muttered, "Ah, well, I know not what may be coming but . . . let it come down . . ."

The last vestige of breeze died away. The land was calm once more. The sun sparkled on the dead hag's resplendent shoes.

A door opened in the battered remnant of what was once a rustic house and a small girl emerged holding a dog under her arm.

Dorothy, savior of the infant ruler Ozma, wondered why such a lovely country stank so of sulphur.

Young Goodman Brown

NATHANIEL HAWTHORNE

NATHANIEL HAWTHORNE *(1804–1864), born in Salem, Massachu-*
setts, was a descendant of Major William Hawthorne, one of America's
somber Puritan settlers. Hawthorne's masterpieces, the novels The Scarlet
Letter *and* The House of the Seven Gables, *seem to me essentially*
composed of a series of "still-life" studies of sin and the regenerative force of
penitence, yet despite their slow pace—and sometimes because of it—each
possesses enormous cumulative power. "Young Goodman Brown," compara-
tively swifter in pace, is one of the darkest depictions of moral corruption ever
penned.

Young Goodman Brown came forth at sunset into the street at
Salem village; but put his head back, after crossing the threshold, to
exchange a parting kiss with his young wife. And Faith, as the wife
was aptly named, thrust her own pretty head into the street, letting
the wind play with the pink ribbons of her cap while she called to
Goodman Brown.

"Dearest heart," whispered she, softly and rather sadly, when
her lips were close to his ear, "prithee put off your journey until
sunrise and sleep in your own bed to-night. A lone woman is troubled with such dreams and such thoughts that she's afeared of her-

self sometimes. Pray tarry with me this night, dear husband, of all nights in the year."

"My love and my Faith," replied young Goodman Brown, "of all nights in the year, this one night must I tarry away from thee. My journey, as thou callest it, forth and back again, must needs be done 'twixt now and sunrise. What, my sweet, pretty wife, dost thou doubt me already, and we but three months married?"

"Then God bless you!" said Faith, with the pink ribbons; "and may you find all well when you come back."

"Amen!" cried Goodman Brown. "Say thy prayers, dear Faith, and go to bed at dusk, and no harm will come to thee."

So they parted; and the young man pursued his way until being about to turn the corner by the meeting-house, he looked back and saw the head of Faith still peeping after him with a melancholy air, in spite of her pink ribbons.

"Poor little Faith!" thought he, for his heart smote him. "What a wretch am I to leave her on such an errand! She talks of dreams, too. Methought as she spoke there was trouble in her face, as if a dream had warned her what work is to be done to-night. But no, no; 'twould kill her to think it. Well, she's a blessed angel on earth; and after this one night I'll cling to her skirts and follow her to heaven."

With this excellent resolve for the future, Goodman Brown felt himself justified in making more haste on his present evil purpose. He had taken a dreary road, darkened by all the gloomiest trees of the forest, which barely stood aside to let the narrow path creep through, and closed immediately behind. It was all as lonely as could be; and there is this peculiarity in such a solitude, that the traveller knows not who may be concealed by the innumerable trunks and the thick boughs overhead; so that with lonely footsteps he may yet be passing through an unseen multitude.

"There may be a devilish Indian behind every tree," said Goodman Brown to himself; and he glanced fearfully behind him as he added, "What if the devil himself should be at my very elbow!"

His head being turned back, he passed a crook of the road, and, looking forward again, beheld the figure of a man, in grave and decent attire, seated at the foot of an old tree. He arose at Goodman Brown's approach and walked onward side by side with him.

"You are late, Goodman Brown," said he. "The clock of the Old

South was striking as I came through Boston, and that is full fifteen minutes agone."

"Faith kept me back a while," replied the young man, with a tremor in his voice, caused by the sudden appearance of his companion, though not wholly unexpected.

It was now deep dusk in the forest, and deepest in that part of it where these two were journeying. As nearly as could be discerned, the second traveller was about fifty years old, apparently in the same rank of life as Goodman Brown, and bearing a considerable resemblance to him, though perhaps more in expression than features. Still they might have been taken for father and son. And yet, though the elder person was as simply clad as the younger, and as simple in manner too, he had an indescribable air of one who knew the world, and who would not have felt abashed at the governor's dinner table or in King William's court, were it possible that his affairs should call him thither. But the only thing about him that could be fixed upon as remarkable was his staff, which bore the likeness of a great black snake, so curiously wrought that it might almost be seen to twist and wriggle itself like a living serpent. This, of course, must have been an ocular deception, assisted by the uncertain light.

"Come, Goodman Brown," cried his fellow-traveller, "this is a dull pace for the beginning of a journey. Take my staff, if you are so soon weary."

"Friend," said the other, exchanging his slow pace for a full stop, "having kept covenant by meeting thee here, it is my purpose now to return whence I came. I have scruples touching the matter thou wot'st of."

"Sayest thou so?" replied he of the serpent, smiling apart. "Let us walk on, nevertheless, reasoning as we go; and if I convince thee not thou shalt turn back. We are but a little way in the forest yet."

"Too far! too far!" exclaimed the goodman, unconsciously resuming his walk. "My father never went into the woods on such an errand, nor his father before him. We have been a race of honest men and good Christians since the days of the martyrs; and shall I be the first of the name of Brown that ever took this path and kept—"

"Such company, thou wouldst say," observed the elder person, interpreting his pause. "Well said, Goodman Brown! I have been as

well acquainted with your family as with ever a one among the
Puritans; and that's no trifle to say. I helped your grandfather, the
constable, when he lashed the Quaker woman so smartly through
the streets of Salem; and it was I that brought your father a pitch-
pine knot, kindled at my own hearth, to set fire to an Indian village,
in King Philip's war. They were my good friends, both; and many a
pleasant walk have we had along this path, and returned merrily
after midnight. I would fain be friends with you for their sake."

"If it be as thou sayest," replied Goodman Brown, "I marvel
they never spoke of these matters; or, verily, I marvel not, seeing
that the least rumor of the sort would have driven them from New
England. We are a people of prayer, and good works to boot, and
abide no such wickedness."

"Wickedness or not," said the traveller with the twisted staff, "I
have a very general acquaintance here in New England. The deacons of many a church have drunk the communion wine with me;
the selectmen of divers towns make me their chairman; and a majority of the Great and General Court are firm supporters of my
interest. The governor and I, too— But these are state secrets."

"Can this be so?" cried Goodman Brown, with a stare of amazement at his undisturbed companion. "Howbeit, I have nothing to
do with the governor and council; they have their own ways, and
are no rule for a simple husbandman like me. But, were I to go on
with thee, how should I meet the eye of that good old man, our
minister, at Salem village? Oh, his voice would make me tremble
both Sabbath day and lecture day."

Thus far the elder traveller had listened with due gravity; but
now burst into a fit of irrepressible mirth, shaking himself so violently that his snake-like staff actually seemed to wriggle in sympathy.

"Ha! ha! ha!" shouted he again and again; then composing himself, "Well, go on, Goodman Brown, go on; but, prithee, don't kill
me with laughing."

"Well, then, to end the matter at once," said Goodman Brown,
considerably nettled, "there is my wife, Faith. It would break her
dear little heart; and I'd rather break my own."

"Nay, if that be the case," answered the other, "e'en go thy
ways, Goodman Brown. I would not for twenty old women like the
one hobbling before us that Faith should come to any harm."

As he spoke he pointed his staff at a female figure on the path, in whom Goodman Brown recognized a very pious and exemplary dame, who had taught him his catechism in youth, and was still his moral and spiritual adviser, jointly with the minister and Deacon Gookin.

"A marvel, truly, that Goody Cloyse should be so far in the wilderness at nightfall," said he. "But with your leave, friend, I shall take a cut through the woods until we have left this Christian woman behind. Being a stranger to you, she might ask whom I was consorting with and whither I was going."

"Be it so," said his fellow-traveller. "Betake you to the woods, and let me keep the path."

Accordingly the young man turned aside, but took care to watch his companion, who advanced softly along the road until he had come within a staff's length of the old dame. She, meanwhile, was making the best of her way, with singular speed for so aged a woman, and mumbling some indistinct words—a prayer, doubtless —as she went. The traveller put forth his staff and touched her withered neck with what seemed the serpent's tail.

"The devil!" screamed the pious old lady.

"Then Goody Cloyse knows her old friend?" observed the traveller, confronting her and leaning on his writhing stick.

"Ah, forsooth, and is it your worship indeed?" cried the good dame. "Yea, truly is it, and in the very image of my old gossip, Goodman Brown, the grandfather of the silly fellow that now is. But—would your worship believe it?—my broomstick hath strangely disappeared, stolen, as I suspect, by that unhanged witch, Goody Cory, and that, too, when I was all anointed with the juice of smallage, and cinquefoil, and wolf's bane—"

"Mingled with fine wheat and the fat of a new-born babe," said the shape of old Goodman Brown.

"Ah, your worship knows the recipe," cried the old lady, cackling aloud. "So, as I was saying, being all ready for the meeting, and no horse to ride on, I made up my mind to foot it; for they tell me there is a nice young man to be taken into communion to-night. But now your good worship will lend me your arm, and we shall be there in a twinkling."

"That can hardly be," answered her friend. "I may not spare you my arm, Goody Cloyse; but here is my staff, if you will."

So saying, he threw it down at her feet, where, perhaps, it assumed life, being one of the rods which its owner had formerly lent to the Egyptian magi. Of this fact, however, Goodman Brown could not take cognizance. He had cast up his eyes in astonishment, and, looking down again, beheld neither Goody Cloyse nor the serpentine staff, but his fellow-traveller alone, who waited for him as calmly as if nothing had happened.

"That old woman taught me my catechism," said the young man; and there was a world of meaning in this simple comment.

They continued to walk onward, while the elder traveller exhorted his companion to make good speed and persevere in the path, discoursing so aptly that his arguments seemed rather to spring up in the bosom of his auditor than to be suggested by himself. As they went, he plucked a branch of maple to serve for a walking stick, and began to strip it of the twigs and little boughs, which were wet with evening dew. The moment his fingers touched them they became strangely withered and dried up as with a week's sunshine. Thus the pair proceeded, at a good free pace, until suddenly, in a gloomy hollow of the road, Goodman Brown sat himself down on the stump of a tree and refused to go any farther.

"Friend," said he, stubbornly, "my mind is made up. Not another step will I budge on this errand. What if a wretched old woman do choose to go to the devil when I thought she was going to heaven: is that any reason why I should quit my dear Faith and go after her?"

"You will think better of this by and by," said his acquaintance, composedly. "Sit here and rest yourself a while; and when you feel like moving again, there is my staff to help you along."

Without more words, he threw his companion the maple stick, and was as speedily out of sight as if he had vanished into the deepening gloom. The young man sat a few moments by the roadside, applauding himself greatly, and thinking with how clear a conscience he should meet the minister in his morning walk, nor shrink from the eye of good old Deacon Gookin. And what calm sleep would be his that very night, which was to have been spent so wickedly, but so purely and sweetly now, in the arms of Faith! Amidst these pleasant and praiseworthy meditations, Goodman Brown heard the tramp of horses along the road, and deemed it advisable to conceal himself within the verge of the forest, conscious of the guilty purpose that had brought him thither, though now so happily turned from it.

On came the hoof tramps and the voices of the riders, two grave old voices, conversing soberly as they drew near. These mingled sounds appeared to pass along the road, within a few yards of the young man's hiding-place; but, owing doubtless to the depth of the gloom at that particular spot, neither the travellers nor their steeds were visible. Though their figures brushed the small boughs by the wayside, it could not be seen that they intercepted, even for a moment, the faint gleam from the strip of bright sky athwart which they must have passed. Goodman Brown alternately crouched and stood on tiptoe, pulling aside the branches and thrusting forth his head as far as he durst without discerning so much as a shadow. It vexed him the more, because he could have sworn, were such a thing possible, that he recognized the voices of the minister and Deacon Gookin, jogging along quietly, as they were wont to do, when bound to some ordination or ecclesiastical council. While yet within hearing, one of the riders stopped to pluck a switch.

"Of the two, reverend sir," said the voice like the deacons, "I had rather miss an ordination dinner than to-night's meeting. They tell me that some of our community are to be here from Falmouth and beyond, and others from Connecticut and Rhode Island, besides several of Indian powwows, who, after their fashion, know almost as much deviltry as the best of us. Moreover, there is a goodly young woman to be taken into communion."

"Mighty well, Deacon Gookin!" replied the solemn old tones of the minister. "Spur up, or we shall be late. Nothing can be done you know until I get on the ground."

The hoofs clattered again; and the voices, talking so strangely in the empty air, passed on through the forest, where no church had ever been gathered or solitary Christian prayed. Whither, then, could these holy men be journeying so deep into the heathen wilderness? Young Goodman Brown caught hold of a tree for support, being ready to sink down on the ground, faint and overburdened with the heavy sickness of his heart. He looked up to the sky, doubting whether there really was a heaven above him. Yet there was the blue arch, and the stars brightening in it.

"With heaven above and Faith below, I will yet stand firm against the devil!" cried Goodman Brown.

While he still gazed upward into the deep arch of the firmament and had lifted his hands to pray, a cloud, though no wind was stirring, hurried across the zenith and hid the brightening stars. The blue sky was still visible, except directly overhead, where this black mass of cloud was sweeping swiftly northward. Aloft in the air, as if from the depths of the cloud, came a confused and doubtful sound of voices. Once the listener fancied that he could distinguish the accents of towns-people of his own, men, and women, both pious and ungodly, many of whom he had met at the communion table, and had seen others rioting at the tavern. The next moment, so indistinct were the sounds, he doubted whether he had heard aught but the murmur of the old forest, whispering without a wind. Then came a stronger swell of those familiar tones, heard daily in the sunshine at Salem village, but never until now from a cloud of night. There was one voice of a young woman, uttering lamentations, yet with an uncertain sorrow, and entreating for some favor, which, perhaps, it would grieve her to obtain; and all the unseen multitude, both saints and sinners, seemed to encourage her onward.

"Faith!" shouted Goodman Brown, in a voice of agony and desperation; and the echoes of the forest mocked him, crying, "Faith! Faith!" as if bewildered wretches were seeking her all through the wilderness.

The cry of grief, rage, and terror was yet piercing the night, when the unhappy husband held his breath for a response. There was a scream, drowned immediately in a louder murmur of voices, fading into far-off laughter, as the dark cloud swept away, leaving the clear and silent sky above Goodman Brown. But something fluttered lightly down through the air and caught on the branch of a tree. The young man seized it, and beheld a pink ribbon.

"My Faith is gone!" cried he, after one stupefied moment. "There is no good on earth; and sin is but a name. Come, devil; for to thee is this world given."

And, maddened with despair, so that he laughed loud and long, did Goodman Brown grasp his staff and set forth again, at such a rate that he seemed to fly along the forest path rather than to walk or run. The road grew wilder and drearier and more faintly traced, and vanished at length, leaving him in the heart of the dark wilderness, still rushing onward with the instinct that guides mortal man to evil. The whole forest was peopled with frightful sounds—the creaking of the trees, the howling of wild beasts, and the yell of Indians; while sometimes the wind tolled like a distant church bell, and sometimes gave a broad roar around the traveller, as if all Nature were laughing him to scorn. But he was himself the chief horror of the scene, and shrank not from its other horrors.

"Ha! ha! ha!" roared Goodman Brown when the wind laughed at him. "Let us hear which will laugh loudest. Think not to frighten me with your deviltry. Come witch, come wizard, come Indian powwow, come devil himself, and here comes Goodman Brown. You may as well fear him as he fear you."

In truth, all through the haunted forest there could be nothing more frightful than the figure of Goodman Brown. On he flew among the black pines, brandishing his staff with frenzied gestures, now giving vent to an inspiration of horrid blasphemy, and now shouting forth such laughter as set all the echoes of the forest laughing like demons around him. The fiend in his own shape is less hideous than when he rages in the breast of man. Thus sped the demoniac on his course, until, quivering among the trees, he saw a red light before him, as when the felled trunks and branches of a clearing have been set on fire, and throw up their lurid blaze against the sky, at the hour of midnight. He paused, in a lull of the tempest that had driven him onward, and heard the swell of what seemed a hymn, rolling solemnly from a distance with the weight of many voices. He knew the tune; it was a familiar one in the choir of the village meeting-house. The verse died heavily away, and was lengthened by a chorus, not of human voices, but of all the sounds of the benighted wilderness pealing in awful harmony together. Goodman Brown cried out, and his cry was lost to his own ear by its unison with the cry of the desert.

In the interval of silence he stole forward until the light glared full upon his eyes. At one extremity of an open space, hemmed in by the dark wall of the forest, arose a rock, bearing some rude, natural resemblance either to an altar or a pulpit, and surrounded by four blazing pines, their tops aflame, their stems untouched, like candles at an evening meeting. The mass of foliage that had overgrown the summit of the rock was all on fire, blazing high into the night and fitfully illuminating the whole field. Each pendent twig and leafy festoon was in a blaze. As the red light arose and fell, a numerous congregation alternately shone forth, then disappeared in shadow, and again grew, as it were, out of the darkness, peopling the heart of the solitary woods at once.

"A grave and dark-clad company," quoth Goodman Brown.

In truth they were such. Among them, quivering to and fro between gloom and splendor, appeared faces that would be seen next day at the council board of the province, and others which, Sabbath after Sabbath, looked devoutly heavenward and benignantly over the crowded pews, from the holiest pupils in the land. Some affirm that the lady of the governor was there. At least there were high dames well known to her, and wives of honored husbands, and widows, a great multitude, and ancient maidens, all of excellent repute, and fair young girls, who trembled lest their mothers should espy them. Either the sudden gleams of light flashing over the obscure field bedazzled Goodman Brown, or he recognized a score of the church members of Salem village famous for their especial sanctity. Good old Deacon Gookin had arrived, and waited at the skirts of that venerable saint, his revered pastor. But, irreverently consorting with these grave, reputable, and pious people, these elders of the church, these chaste dames and dewy virgins, there were men of dissolute lives and women of spotted fame, wretches given over to all mean and filthy vice, and suspected even of horrid crimes. It was strange to see that the good shrank not from the wicked, nor were the sinners abashed by the saints. Scattered also among their pale-faced enemies were the Indian priests, or powwows, who had often scared their native forest with more hideous incantations than any known to English witchcraft.

"But where is Faith?" thought Goodman Brown; and, as hope came into his heart, he trembled.

Another verse of the hymn arose, a slow and mournful strain, such as the pious love, but joined to words which expressed all that our nature can conceive of sin, and darkly hinted at far more. Unfathomable to mere mortals is the lore of fiends. Verse after verse was sung; and still the chorus of the desert swelled between like the deepest tone of a mighty organ; and with the final peal of that dreadful anthem there came a sound, as if the roaring wind, the rushing streams, the howling beasts, and every other voice of the unconcerted wilderness were mingling and according with the voice of guilty man in homage to the prince of all. The four blazing pines threw up a loftier flame, and obscurely discovered shapes and visages of horror on the smoke wreaths above the impious assembly. At the same moment the fire on the rock shot redly forth and formed a glowing arch above its base, where now appeared a figure. With reverence be it spoken, the figure bore no slight similitude, both in garb and manner, to some grave divine of the New England churches.

"Bring forth the converts!" cried a voice that echoed through the field and rolled into the forest.

At the word, Goodman Brown stepped forth from the shadow of the trees and approached the congregation, with whom he felt a loathful brotherhood by the sympathy of all that was wicked in his heart. He could have well-nigh sworn that the shape of his own dead father beckoned him to advance, looking downward from a smoke wreath, while a woman, with dim features of despair, threw out her hand to warn him back. Was it his mother? But he had no power to retreat one step, nor to resist, even in thought, when the minister and good old Deacon Gookin seized his arms and led him to the blazing rock. Thither came also the slender form of a veiled female, led between Goody Cloyse, that pious teacher of the catechism, and Martha Carrier, who had received the devil's promise to be queen of hell. A rampant hag was she. And there stood the proselytes beneath the canopy of fire.

"Welcome, my children," said the dark figure, "to the communion of your race. Ye have found thus young your nature and your destiny. My children, look behind you!"

They turned; and flashing forth, as it were, in a sheet of flame, the fiend worshippers were seen; the smile of welcome gleamed darkly on every visage.

"There," resumed the sable form, "are all whom ye have reverenced from youth. Ye deemed them holier than yourselves, and shrank from your own sin, contrasting it with their lives of righteousness and prayerful aspirations heavenward. Yet here are they all in my worshipping assembly. This night it shall be granted you to know their secret deeds: how hoary-bearded elders of the church have whispered wanton words to the young maids of their households; how many a woman, eager for widows' weeds, has given her husband a drink at bedtime and let him sleep his last sleep in her bosom; how beardless youths have made haste to inherit their fathers' wealth; and how fair damsels—blush not, sweet ones—have dug little graves in the garden, and bidden me, the sole guest to an infant's funeral. By the sympathy of your human hearts for sin ye shall scent out all the places—whether in church, bedchamber, street, field, or forest—where crime has been committed, and shall exult to behold the whole earth one stain of guilt, one mighty blood spot. Far more than this. It shall be yours to penetrate, in every bosom, the deep mystery of sin, the fountain of all wicked arts, and which inexhaustibly supplies more evil impulses than human power—than my power at its utmost—can make manifest in deeds. And now, my children, look upon each other."

They did so; and, by the blaze of the hell-kindled torches, the wretched man beheld his Faith, and the wife her husband, trembling before that unhallowed altar.

"Lo, there ye stand, my children," said the figure, in a deep and solemn tone, almost sad with its despairing awfulness, as if his once angelic nature could yet mourn for our miserable race. "Depending upon one another's hearts, ye had still hoped that virtue were not all a dream. Now are ye undeceived. Evil is the nature of mankind. Evil must be your only happiness. Welcome again, my children, to the communion of your race."

"Welcome," repeated the fiend worshippers, in one cry of despair and triumph.

And there they stood, the only pair, as it seemed, who were yet hesitating on the verge of wickedness in this dark world. A basin was hollowed, naturally, in the rock. Did it contain water, reddened by the lurid light? or was it blood? or, perchance, a liquid flame? Herein did the shape of evil dip his hand and prepare to lay the mark of baptism upon their foreheads, that they might be partakers of the mystery of sin, more conscious of the secret guilt of others, both in deed and thought, than they could now be of their own. The husband cast one look at his pale wife, and Faith at him. What polluted wretches would the next glance show them to each other, shuddering alike at what they disclosed and what they saw!

"Faith! Faith!" cried the husband, "look up to heaven, and resist the wicked one."

Whether Faith obeyed he knew not. Hardly had he spoken when

he found himself amid calm night and solitude, listening to a roar of the wind which died heavily away through the forest. He staggered against the rock, and felt it chill and damp; while a hanging twig, that had been all on fire, besprinkled his cheek with the coldest dew.

The next morning young Goodman Brown came slowly into the street of Salem village, staring around him like a bewildered man. The good old minister was taking a walk along the graveyard to get an appetite for breakfast and meditate his sermon, and bestowed a blessing, as he passed, on Goodman Brown. He shrank from the venerable saint as if to avoid an anathema. Old Deacon Gookin was at domestic worship, and the holy words of his prayer were heard through the open window. "What God doth the wizard pray to?" quoth Goodman Brown. Goody Cloyse, that excellent old Christian, stood in the early sunshine at her own lattice, catechizing a little girl who had brought her a pint of morning's milk. Goodman Brown snatched away the child as from the grasp of the fiend himself. Turning the corner by the meetinghouse, he spied the head of Faith, with the pink ribbons, gazing anxiously forth, and bursting into such joy at sight of him that she skipped along the street and almost kissed her husband before the whole village. But Goodman Brown looked sternly and sadly into her face, and passed on without a greeting.

Had Goodman Brown fallen asleep in the forest and only dreamed a wild dream of a witch-meeting?

Be it so if you will; but, alas! it was a dream of evil omen for young Goodman Brown. A stern, a sad, a darkly meditative, a distrustful, if not a desperate man did he become from the night of that fearful dream. On the Sabbath day, when the congregation were singing a holy psalm, he could not listen because an anthem of sin rushed loudly upon his ear and drowned all the blessed strain. When the minister spoke from the pulpit with power and fervid eloquence, and, with his hand on the open Bible, of the sacred truths of our religion, and of saint-like lives and triumphant deaths, and of future bliss or misery unutterable, then did Goodman Brown turn pale, dreading lest the roof should thunder down upon the gray blasphemer and his hearers. Often, waking suddenly at midnight, he shrank from the bosom of Faith; and at morning or eventide, when the family knelt down at prayer, he scowled and muttered to himself, and gazed sternly at his wife, and turned away. And when he had lived long, and was borne to his grave a hoary corpse, followed by Faith, an aged woman, and children and grandchildren, a goodly procession, besides neighbors not a few, they carved no hopeful verse upon his tombstone, for his dying hour was gloom.

The Chaney Legacy

ROBERT BLOCH

Though no warlock appears in the next tale, it is evident that "The Chaney Legacy" was set in motion by someone intimately acquainted with dark forces. ROBERT BLOCH, *one of America's most popular horror writers, is best known for such stories as "Yours Truly, Jack the Ripper," "Enoch," "The Sorcerer's Apprentice," "The Skull of the Marquis de Sade" and, of course,* Psycho. *"The Chaney Legacy" was the cover story of the Fall 1986 issue of the late lamented* Night Cry *magazine.*

Nobody thought Dale was crazy until the trouble started.

True, he'd been a film buff ever since he was a kid, the way other youngsters sometimes get hung-up on baseball, football, or even chess. If they follow their hobby into adult life such interests can become an obsession, yet no one thinks it's a sign of insanity.

In Dale's case his studies led him into teaching a course on film history at the university, which seemed sensible enough. Certainly he appeared to be normal; he wasn't one of those wimpy professors seen in comedy films aimed at the junk-food generation.

Actually Dale was rather attractive. Debbie Curzon thought so. She was a newscaster on local radio where she met and interviewed many of the stud celebrities in sports or films; Dale must have had some *charisma* for her to choose him as a lover.

The two of them might have ended up together on a permanent basis if Dale hadn't leased the Chaney house.

That's what the realtor called it—"the Chaney house"—although Dale couldn't verify the claim and the ancient escrow was clouded. The place was really just a small cottage halfway up Nichols Canyon in the Hollywood hills. Huddled amidst a tangle of trees and underbrush on a dirt side-road which turned to quicksand during the rainy season, the weatherbeaten frame dwelling offered no exterior charm or interior comfort. Debbie's reluctance to share it was understandable, but once he found it Dale couldn't wait to move in.

"All right, do as you please," Debbie told him. "If that dump is more important to you than sharing a brand-new condo with me—"

"It's not just a dump," Dale protested. "This is the *Chaney* house. Can't you understand?"

"Frankly, no. What makes you want to hole up in a place like this just because some dumb actor may or may not have hung out here sixty years ago?"

"Lon Chaney wasn't dumb," Dale said. "He happens to be one of the finest performers in silent films, perhaps the greatest of them all."

"Who cares?" Debbie's voice honed to a cutting-edge. "I just hope your wonderful Mr. Chaney knows how to cook and is good in bed, because from now on you'll be living with him, not me."

It was open warfare, but Dale found no weapon to pierce the armor of feminine logic. In the end Debbie told him to bug off, and he had no choice but to obey the entomological injunction.

A week later Dale moved into the Chaney house and by then everybody thought he'd flipped out. Turning down a renewal of his teaching contract now at the end of the fall semester meant losing his chance at tenure, and that certainly was a crazy decision, because he gave no reason for leaving.

But Dale knew exactly what he was going to do. He would vindicate himself in the eyes of Debbie and the academic world by writing a Hollywood history of his own—a definitive work which would answer the questions which lurked behind the legends. Who killed William Desmond Taylor, and why? Did Thomas Ince meet his death because of illness or was it murder? What really kept Garbo from returning to the screen? Had there been cover-ups in the cases of Thelma Todd or Marilyn Monroe? So much had been surmised, so little verified. And for a starter, he meant to solve the Chaney mystery.

Of all the stars of silent films, Lon Chaney was by far the most mysterious. There were books on his films but no full-length biographies except for a reporter's inaccurate magazine series following Chaney's untimely death from cancer in 1930. Chaney's first wife died without breaking silence and his second left no memoir. His son Creighton, who later changed his name to Lon Chaney Jr., was estranged from his father for many years and avoided painful memories. To this day Chaney's private life remains an enigma. "Between pictures," he told reporters, "there is no Lon Chaney."

The coincidence of moving into one of the actor's former residences challenged Dale. Come what may, he meant to learn Lon Chaney's secret.

But first there were more practical questions to deal with. Once furniture arrived and utilities installed, he had to renovate his surroundings. The cottage had been unoccupied for many years—no wonder the realtor offered him such a bargain rental—and it was time for a thorough housecleaning.

So Dale called an agency and secured the services of an Hispanic lady named Juanita. She was short, plump, but surprisingly strong; perched on a rickety ladder she scrubbed away at the ceiling and side-walls, then descended to attack the floors with mop and brush. And on the second day she made her discovery.

Finishing up her work, she cleared out old boxes and empty cartons from the bedroom closet. The last carton, wedged in back under a jumble of debris, was not entirely empty.

"Look what I find," Juanita said, holding up her trophy for Dale's inspection.

He took the tin box from her, hefting it with both hands. Then he lifted the lid and his eyes widened.

"What is it?" Juanita asked.

The box was empty but its interior was divided into a number of small compartments lined with smudged cloth. And the underside of the lid was covered by a mirror.

"Some kind of a kit," Dale said.

It was hard to keep his voice from quavering, hard to conceal rising excitement as he paid and dismissed Juanita. When she left

Dale picked up the box again and now his hands were trembling. His hands, holding Lon Chaney's makeup kit.

Dale had seen publicity stills of Chaney displaying a different and much larger kit with side trays, so this obviously wasn't the only one. What made it unique was that this box was here, in Chaney's secret hideaway.

Or was it?

Dale forced himself to face facts. In spite of the realtor's claim, he couldn't be certain that Lon Chaney ever lived here. For all he knew, the kit might have belonged to any one of a thousand actors residing in these hills when Hollywood was young.

What Dale needed was proof. And staring at the bottom of the box, he found it.

Wedged against the base was a coil of paper, a small square scrap which must have peeled off after being pasted below the mirror. Dale picked it up, smoothed it out, then read aloud the lettering typed across its surface.

"Property of Leonidas Chaney."

Leonidas!

This was proof and no mistake. While the general public knew the actor as Lon and most filmographies listed his first name as Alonzo, Dale was one of the few aware that the star's birth certificate identified him as Leonidas.

Chaney, born on April Fool's Day, had fooled his public. And considering his passion for privacy it seemed odd he'd put his real name here. But perhaps he'd fixed on this deception later in his career. Dale's inspection told him this battered box was old, perhaps dating back to pre-Hollywood days when Chaney was a struggling actor in traveling shows. Could this actually be his very first makeup kit?

One thing seemed certain—Chaney *had* lived here. But when?

Dale pondered the question as he sat in gathering darkness alone, with the makeup kit on the table before him.

From what little he knew, Chaney's homes were modest by Hollywood standards, even after he attained stardom, but he would never have settled his family here. Which left only one other plausible answer.

Suppose this place was really a hideaway, a place his family didn't know about, a place he came to secretly and alone? According to publicity he did have a cabin up in the mountains where he went fishing between films. Could it be that he actually spent some of that time here, perhaps even without his wife's knowledge?

And if so, why? Dale quickly dismissed the notion of a secret love-life; Chaney was never a womanizer, and even had he been, this was hardly the setting for a romantic rendezvous. Nor was he a closet alcoholic or drug-addict. In any case there'd be no reason for him to keep a makeup kit hidden here.

Dale leaned forward, peering at the box through the twilight shadows which fell across its murky mirror.

But the mirror wasn't murky now. As he stared, something in the mirror stared back.

For a moment Dale thought it was his own face, distorted by a flash of fading sunlight amidst the coming of the dark. Even so, he realized that what he saw was not a reflection. There was another face, a face *in* the mirror, a ghastly white face with painted features that glowed and grinned.

With a shock he realized what it was—the face of a clown. And before Dale's widened eyes the face was melting, changing, so that now a second clown loomed leering out at him—cheeks spotted with paint and tufts of hair suddenly sprouting above a bony brow.

Dale turned, seeking a glimpse of someone else, some intruder who must have stolen silently into the bedroom to stare over his shoulder.

But save for himself the room was empty. And when his eyes sought the mirror again the face—or faces—had vanished. All he saw now was his own face reflected in the glass, its features fading in the dark.

Dale rose, stumbling across the room to switch on the overhead light. In its welcome glare he saw the makeup box and the perfectly ordinary mirror mounted within.

The clown-images were gone. They had existed only in his imagination—or was it his memory? For there had been two clowns in Chaney's life.

Hastily Dale sought his bookshelves, fumbling and finding the volume containing Lon Chaney's filmography. He riffled through it until a page fell open upon a photograph of the actor in the title role of *He Who Gets Slapped.* And now it was Dale who felt the slap

of recognition. The picture showed the face of the first clown he'd
seen in the mirror.

Turning pages, he located the still photo of another clown with
daubed cheeks and patches of hair clumped on the bone-white
skull. Chaney again, in *Laugh, Clown, Laugh.*

But there was no mirth in the painted face, and none in Dale's as
he banged the book shut and left the room. Left the room, left the
cottage, left the canyon to drive down to the shelter and sanity of
lighted streets below.

He parked on Fairfax and entered a restaurant, taking comfort in
its crowded quarters and the presence of a friendly waitress who
urged him to try tonight's special. But when his order came he had
no appetite for it.

Tonight had already been too special for him, and he couldn't
forget his confrontation at the cottage. Had he really glimpsed
those faces in the mirror, or had the images been evoked from
memories of the films seen in retrospective showings long ago? A
mirror is just a sheet of silvered glass, and what it reflected must
have come from his mind's eye.

Dale forced himself to eat and gradually the tension ebbed. By
the time he finished and drove back up the canyon his composure
had returned.

Inside the cottage the lights still blazed upon commonplace surroundings, safeguarding against shadows and dispelling doubts. If
Chaney had lived here at all, that time was long-gone and the actor
himself was long-dead. There were no ghosts, and the box on the
bedroom table was merely an old makeup kit, not a miniature
haunted house.

For a moment Dale had an impulse to lift the lid and examine the
mirror for added reassurance, but he dismissed it. There was no
point in dignifying his apprehensions; what he needed was a good
night's sleep and a clear head for tomorrow.

Truth to tell, he felt drained after the emotional stress of the day,
and once he undressed and sought his bed Dale quickly fell into
dreamless slumber.

Just when the change occurred he did not know, but there *was* a
change, and the dream came.

In the dream he found himself awakened, sitting up in bed and
staring through darkness at the black blur of the box on the table.

And now the impulse he'd rejected upon entering the bedroom returned with an urgency he could not deny.

Sometimes dreams seem oddly like films—movies of the mind in which one's own movements are silently commanded by an unseen director—a series of jump-cuts and sudden shifts in which one is both actor and audience.

Thus it was that Dale both felt and saw himself rise from the bed, captured in a full shot as he moved across the room. Now a cut to another angle, showing him poised above the makeup kit. Then came a close shot of his hand moving down to raise the lid.

Moonlight from the window sent a silvery shaft to strike the surface of the makeup mirror, flooding it with a blinding brightness that seethed and stirred.

Faces formed in the glass—contorted countenances which seemed frighteningly familiar, even in the depths of dream. Faces changed, and yet there was a lurking linkage between them, for all were oriental.

Some Dale had seen before only in photographs—the evil China- man from the lost film, *Bits of Life,* the benevolent laundryman in *Shadows.* Then, in rapid shifts, the vengeful mandarin of *Mr. Wu,* the bespectacled elderly image of Wu's father, and a final, frighten- ing glimpse of the chinless, sunken-cheeked, shrivelled face of the aged grandfather. They formed and faded, smiling their secret smiles.

Now others appeared—the two pirates, Pew and Merry, from *Treasure Island,* a bearded Fagin out of *Oliver Twist,* followed by figures looming full-length in the mirror's depths. Here were the fake cripples of *The Miracle Man, The Blackbird, Flesh and Blood.* Then the real cripple of *The Shock* and the legless Blizzard in *The Penalty.* Now came a derby-hatted gangster, a French-Canadian trapper, a tough sergeant of Marines, a scarred animal-trapper, an elderly railroad engineer, and Echo, the ventriloquist of *The Unholy Three.*

In his dream Dale stood frozen before the glass as faces flashed forth in faster flickerings—the faces of madmen. Here was a crazed wax-museum attendant, a bearded victim of senile delusions, a de- ranged Russian peasant, the insane scientists of *A Blind Bargain* and *The Monster.* They were laughing at him, grinning in glee as Dale closed his eyes, hands clawing out to close the lid of the makeup kit.

Then he staggered back to the bed. There were no images here, only the darkness, and Dale fell into it, fleeing the faces and seeking surcease in sleep.

It was morning when Dale's eyes blinked open, welcoming the sanity of sunlight. He stirred, conscious now that last night had been a dream, knowing he'd seen nothing in the mirror; indeed, he had never even left his bed.

As he rose he glanced over at the box resting on the table, remembering how he'd closed it in reality before retiring, then closed it again in his nightmare.

But now the lid was up.

For a moment Dale recoiled, fighting the irrational explanation until sunlight and common sense prevailed.

The makeup kit was old, its hinges worn or even sprung. Sometime during the night the catch must have loosened and the lid popped up.

It was a logical answer, but even so he had to force himself toward the table, steel himself to gaze down into the mirror set inside the lid and gaze on what was reflected there.

Sunshine formed a halo around the image in its glassy surface— the image of his own face.

And as his features formed a smile of rueful relief, Dale turned away. The mirror in the makeup kit held no terrors for him now, any more than the one he faced as he shaved. He dressed and sought the makeshift kitchen, taking comfort in the familiar ritual of preparing his breakfast, then eating eggs and toast with a copy of the morning *Times* propped up before his coffee cup. Even the news offered an odd comfort of its own—the familiar headlines and stories of wars, terrorist bombings, political corruption, street crime, drug-busts, accidents, epidemics, natural and unnatural disasters that filled the newspaper pages. However grim, these were realities; realities which he and everyone else in the world faced with fortitude born of long familiarity. They had nothing to do with the unhealthy fantasies which took form when Lon Chaney stalked the screen—fantasies which existed now only in Dale's imagination.

Glancing at his watch, he folded the paper and rose quickly. There was a busy day ahead, and time was already running short.

Leaving the cottage, he drove down to Hollywood Boulevard, turned right, then made a left on Fairfax. He reached Wilshire and headed west, weaving through noonday traffic until he found a parking space before the imposing structure of the Motion Picture Academy of Arts and Sciences.

Here, upstairs in the Margaret Herrick Library, he turned his attention to the files he requested. Lon Chaney wasn't the only movie monster he meant to deal with in his projected history; there was research to be done on other stars of the horror film. And unlike the case with Chaney, there was ample material on men like Karloff, Lorre, and Lugosi.

But even as he scribbled notes Dale found something lacking in the interviews and biographical data of these celebrated actors who seemingly made no mystery of their careers.

The one missing element common to all was that of explanation. Why had a gentle gentleman like Boris ended up playing monsters? What led Peter Lorre, the rabbi's grandson, to the portrayal of psychopaths? How did Bela Lugosi, who played parts ranging from Romeo to Jesus Christ in early European appearances, transform himself into Dracula?

William Henry Pratt, Laszlo Loewenstein, Bela Blasko—all three men had changed their names, but what had changed their natures?

Dale found no answer in the files, but the last item he read before leaving the Academy offered a hint. It was an interview with an actress who toured with Lugosi in *Dracula.*

She told of how the genial cigar-smoking Hungarian prepared for his famous role, sitting before his dressing-room mirror and donning the costume and makeup of the vampire. But that was only a preliminary to performing. The next and most crucial step came as he rose, wrapped in the black cape, face contorted and eyes blazing. As he confronted himself in the mirror his deep voice invoked an incantation. "I am Dracula," he intoned. *"I* am Dracula. I *am* Dracula."* Over and over again he repeated the words, and by the time he strode out upon the stage the words became reality. Lugosi *was* Dracula.

"He psyched himself up," the actress explained. And as the years passed, a part of him became the part he played; when he died he was buried in Dracula's cape, with Dracula's ring on his finger.

Dale jotted down his notes, then hurried out into the afternoon sunshine. Now it was time to drive into Beverly Hills for a medical appointment.

It had been made a month ago, just an annual checkup, as a matter of routine. But now, as he arrived and took a seat in the crowded waiting room, Dale felt uptight. He felt no worry about possible physical illness, but what about psychological stress? Last night's dreams might be a symptom of mental disturbance. What if Dr. Pendleton told him he was cracking up?

By the time the receptionist called his name and a nurse led him to the examining room he knew his pulse was pounding and his blood-pressure had risen. So it came as a pleasant surprise when the doctor made no comment on his readings other than remarking he thought Dale was underweight and seemed overtired. Reports on blood-tests and urine-specimen would be available in a few days, but nothing indicated cause for concern.

"Slow down a little," Dr. Pendleton said. "Pace yourself. And it won't hurt if you put on a few pounds."

Armed with that advice Dale left. Relieved, he headed for a seafood restaurant on Brighton Way and there he ordered and actually enjoyed his meal. The doctor was probably right, Dale decided; he *had* been working too hard, and the tension flaring up after his break with Debbie took an added toll. He resolved to follow orders, rest, and relax. Then, perhaps, it might be possible to come to terms with himself, and with Debbie too. He really missed her, missed the hours they spent together, and the breach must be mended. All in good time.

As Dale left the restaurant he sensed a change in the air; the chill breeze hinted at rain and muted murmur of distant thunder confirmed its coming.

The first drops spattered the windshield as he turned onto the canyon side-road, and by the time he parked in the driveway a flicker of lightning heralded the downpour that followed. Dale hurried into the cottage beneath the wind-tossed trees. Once inside he flipped the light switches as he moved from room to room. It was only upon reaching the bedroom that he halted when its overhead light came on.

Standing in the doorway he stared at the open makeup box on the table, forehead furrowed in doubt.

Hadn't he closed the lid before he left? Dale shrugged in uncertainty. Perhaps the loose catch was the culprit once again; he'd better examine it and put his mind to rest.

Rain drummed the rooftop in a faster tempo and lightning flashed outside the window as he crossed to the table. Then, as he reached it, a clap of thunder shook the walls and the lights went off, overhead and throughout the cottage.

Power-outages were not uncommon hereabouts during a storm and Dale wasn't alarmed; perhaps the lights would come back on in a moment. He waited, but the darkness persisted and prevailed. Perhaps he'd better look for his flashlight.

Then its illumination was unnecessary as the lightning bolt struck somewhere close outside the window, filling the bedroom with a greenish glare. As it did so Dale peered down at the mirror inside the lid of the makeup kit and froze.

The reflection peering up at him was not his own.

It was the face of Singapore Joe—the role Chaney played in *The Road to Mandalay*—the half-blind man whose left eye was covered with a ghastly white cast.

But the image seemed strangely blurred; Dale blinked to clear his vision as lightning faded and the room plunged into darkness again.

Dale's shudder wasn't prompted by the roar of thunder. It was what he'd seen that traumatized him. *The Road to Mandalay* was one of the lost films; he knew of no print in existence. But Singapore Joe existed, in the mirror, existed in an indelible image leering up at him through the dark.

And the dark must be dispelled. Dale turned and blundered his way into the hall. Reaching the kitchen he stooped and opened the cabinet beneath the sink. Lightning outside the kitchen window came to his aid and in its moment of livid life he found and grasped the flashlight. It was not just an ordinary cylinder-type but one which terminated in a square base, projecting a strong beam of almost lanternlike intensity.

Dale switched it on, and the ray guided him back to the bedroom. As he walked his relief faded with the realization that his vision had faded too.

He was seeing only with his right eye now. The left was blind. Blind—like the eye of Singapore Joe.

You're having a nightmare, he told himself. But he wasn't asleep, and if there was a nightmare it had to be in the mirror of the makeup kit. Unless, of course, he was hallucinating.

There was only one way to find out, and Dale knew what he must do. Rain swept across the rooftop above, doors creaked and groaned against the onslaught of the wind, lightning glimmered, thunder growled. Only the light he gripped in his hand was reassurance; a magic lantern to protect him on his way. *Magic Lantern*— that's what they called the movies in the old days. Was there such a thing as magic?

Forcing himself toward the bedroom table, he gazed down at the glass reflected in the lantern light.

Half blind, he stared, but what he saw with his right eye was just a mirror after all. A shining surface reflecting his own familiar face.

And now his left eye cleared and he could see again. Dale took a deep breath, then expelled it hastily—for now the mirror blurred and a piercing pain shot through his lower limbs, causing him to crouch. Something pressed heavily against his spine, bowing his back.

He was changing, and the image in the mirror was changing too. He saw the tousled hair, the gargoyle grimace, the twisted limbs, the body bent beneath the hideous hump. No need to ask the identity of this image—he was gazing at Quasimodo—the Hunchback of Notre Dame.

It was Chaney he saw in the glass but he himself felt the weight of the hump, the constriction of the harness binding it to his body, the pain inflicted by the mass of makeup covering his face, the jagged teeth wired into his mouth, the mortician's wax masking his right eye.

Realization brought relief. It was makeup, and only makeup after all. Gradually the image diffused and Dale's feeling of physical restraint faded until once again he stood erect.

Thunder rolled as the image dispelled. Dale sighed with relief; now was the time to slam down the lid of the kit once and for all.

He started to reach for it, but his hands were gone.

His hands—and his arms.

Illusion, of course, like the illusion of Chaney's face and form coming into focus beneath the mirror's shiny surface. Dale's eyes met those of the visage peering out at him from under the broad brim of a Spanish sombrero. Chaney was armless, and now Dale felt the agony of numbed circulation, the constriction of his own arms bound against his body by a tight, concealing corset. That, he remembered, had been Chaney's device when portraying the armless knife-thrower in *The Unknown.*

With the recollection his panic ebbed, and once more features and form receded into the mirror's depths. The numbness was gone from his arms now; he could lift his hands and close the lid.

Then he fell.

His legs gave way and he slumped to the floor, sprawling helplessly, the box on the table beyond his reach. All he could do was elevate his gaze, see the shaven-headed creature crawling across the glass, dead legs dragging behind him.

It was Phroso, the paralyzed cripple in *West of Zanzibar.*

No makeup had been involved in the simulation of the man who had lost the use of his lower limbs; it had been Chaney's artistry which made the role seem reality.

Knowing that, Dale strove to rise, but there was no feeling in his legs—he couldn't command them. The face in the mirror glowered at him in the lamplight, bursting into brightness as lightning flashed outside the window. The eyes were mocking him, mocking his plight, and now Dale realized that the mirror's monsters sensed his purpose and were summoned to prevent it. Their appearance in the mirror gave them life, his awareness gave them strength to survive, and that strength was growing. Closing the kit would condemn them to darkness and it was this they fought against. They knew he couldn't close the lid, not if he were blind, armless, or paralyzed.

Frantically Dale balanced himself on the palm of his left hand, extending his right arm upward, inching to the table-top. Then his fingers gripped the lid of the makeup kit, wrenching it down. With a rasp of rusty hinges the box slammed shut.

The mirror disappeared from view, but Dale's paralysis persisted. Try as he would, he couldn't raise himself. All he could do was wriggle, wriggle across the floor like a snake with a broken back, and lever his arms against the side of the bed. Pulling his body upward, he lifted himself, gasping with effort, then collapsed upon the cool sheets which dampened with the sweat of fear pouring from his fevered forehead.

Fever. That was the answer; it had to be. The doctor was wrong in his diagnosis. Dale was coming down with something, something that twisted mind and body. Labeling it psychosomatic brought no relief.

Dale rolled over to face the telephone resting on the nightstand beside the bed. If he could reach it he could call the paramedics. But as his hand moved forward he felt a sudden tingling in his legs, then kicked out with both feet. The paralysis, real or imaginary, was gone.

No reason to summon paramedics now, but he still needed help. In the dim light cast by the flash-lantern standing on the table across the room he dialled Dr. Pendleton's number. The ringing on the line gave way to the mechanical message of an answering-service.

"Dr. Pendleton is not in. Please leave your name and number and he will get back to you—"

Dale cradled the receiver, frowning in frustration. Sure, the doctor would get back to him, perhaps in an hour, maybe two or three. And then what?

How could he explain all this? If he minimized his condition he'd get that take-two-aspirins-and-call-me-in-the-morning routine. And if he came on too strong the doctor would probably order up an ambulance on his own. Pendleton was a practitioner of modern medicine; he wouldn't come out in the storm to make a house-call merely to humor a hysterical patient with his presence.

But Dale had to have someone's presence here, someone to talk to, someone like—

"Debbie?"

He'd dialled her number automatically and now the very sound of her voice brought relief.

"Dale! I was hoping you'd call."

Then she *did* care. Thank God for that! He listened intently as the warmth of her response gave way to concern.

"What's wrong? Are you sick or something?"

"Something," Dale said. "That is, I'm not sure. No, I can't explain it on the phone. If you could just come over—"

"Tonight? In all this rain?"

"Debbie, please. I know it's asking a lot, but I need you. I need you now—"

"And I need you." Debbie sighed. "All right. Give me half an hour."

The phone went dead, but as he replaced the receiver Dale came alive again. She was coming and he'd told the truth; he did need her, needed her desperately.

Listening, he realized the rain was slowing. It was a good sign. Perhaps by the time she arrived the storm would be over and they could talk without the punctuation of thunder. He'd tell her what had happened, make her understand.

But just what *had* happened—and why?

Dale rolled over on his back, staring at the shadows on the ceiling, facing up to the shadows surrounding the question in his own mind.

And the answer came.

He'd found it today at the Academy, found it when he read the actress's description of Bela Lugosi preparing for his portrayal.

"He psyched himself up." That was her explanation of how Lugosi became Dracula, and that was what Lon Chaney must have done.

No wonder he'd established a secret hideaway! Here, in this very room, he did more than experiment with physical disguise. Dale pictured him sitting alone on a night like this, creating contrivances to deform his body, refashioning his face, staring into the mirror at the creature reflected there. And then, the final transformation.

"Make up your mind." A figure of speech, but Chaney had given it a literal application, one beyond the mere application of makeup from his kit. Seated here in the shadowed silence, this man of mystery—this son of deaf-mute parents whom he communicated with through the power of pantomime—confronted the reflections of monsters in the mirror and whispered the words. "I am the Frog. I am Blizzard. I am Dr. Ziska, Sergei, Alonzo the Armless, the Blackbird, Mr. Wu." Each time a different incarnation, each time a new *persona*, each time a litany repeated hour after hour from midnight to dawn, willing himself into the role until the role became reality.

And psyching himself up, he'd psyched-up the mirror too. The intensity of total concentration had been captured in the glass forever, just as it was later captured on the blank surface of nitrate film used for silent pictures. The filmed images decayed in time but the makeup kit mirror preserved Chaney's psychic power forever—a long-latent power revived by Dale's own glimpses into the glass, a power that grew greater with each succeeding gaze.

Dale remembered the first apparitions—how fleetingly they appeared and how little effect they had beyond the initial shock of recognition. It was his repeated viewing which gave strength to the shifting shapes until they transformed his body into a semblance of what he saw.

But he wouldn't repeat the mistake. From now on the makeup kit would remain closed and he'd never look into that mirror again.

The rain had ended now and so had his fear. Thunder and lightning gave way to a calm matching his own. Knowing the truth was enough; he wouldn't repeat all this to Debbie or try to convince her. Instead he'd just tell how much he needed her, and that was true too.

But first he must dispose of the kit.

Dale shifted himself over to the side of the bed, sitting up and swinging his feet to the floor. The power-outage hadn't ended; he'd shut the kit away in the closet, then take the flash-lantern with him and guide Debbie up the path when she arrived.

All was quiet as he crossed the room to the table where the lantern-light shone on the closed box beside it. That's what the kit was, really; just a battered old box. Lon Chaney's box—Pandora's box, which opened for evils to emerge. But not to worry; the lid was down and it would stay down forever.

His hand went to the flash-lantern.

At least that was his intention, until he felt the chill of cold metal at his fingertips and found them fixed upon the lid of the makeup kit.

He tried to pull away but his hand remained fixed, fixed by a force commanding his movement and his mind, a power he could not control.

It was the power that raised the lid of the box, a power that seethed and surged, and in the uptilted mirror he saw its source.

Two eyes blazed from a face surmounted by a beaver hat and framed by matted hair; a face that grinned to display the cruel, serrated teeth. But it was from the cruel eyes that the power poured —the burning eyes of the vampire in *London After Midnight*. Dale knew the film, though he'd never seen a print; knew its original title was *The Hypnotist*. And it was a hypnotist who glared up at him, a hypnotist's power which had compelled him to open the box and stand transfixed now by the vision in the glass.

Then suddenly the face was fading and for a moment Dale felt a glimmer of hope. But as the face disappeared into the mirror's distorted depths, another face took form.

It was a face Dale knew only too well, one which had lain buried in his brain since childhood when he'd first seen it fill the screen from behind a ripped-away mask. The face of madness, the face of Death incarnate, the face of Chaney's supreme horror; the face of Erik in *The Phantom of the Opera*.

No wonder he'd blotted out all memory of the terror which tormented his nightmares as a child, the terror he'd hidden away in adulthood but which still survived in his unconscious. It was suppressed fear that lay behind his inexplicable interest in Lon Chaney, a fright disguised as fascination which guided him to this ultimate, inevitable confrontation with the gaping fangs, the flaring nostrils, the bulging eyes of a living skull.

The Phantom stared and Dale felt the flooding force of the death's-head's overwhelming power, to which he responded with a power of his own, born of utter dread.

For an instant, for an eternity, his gaze locked with that of the monster and he realized a final fear. The face was looming larger, moving forward—attempting to emerge from the mirror!

And then, with savage strength, Dale gripped the box in both hands, raising it high; panting, he dashed it down upon the floor. The makeup kit landed with a crash as the Phantom's image shattered into shards of splintered glass glinting up in the lantern-light.

Chaney's power was broken at last, and with it the power of the Phantom. Dale gasped, shuddering in relief as he felt full control return.

As the knocking sounded its summons he picked up the flash-lantern and carried it with him down the hall to the front door. Debbie was here now, his hope, his angel of salvation. And he went to her proudly and unafraid because he was free of Chaney, free of the mirror's magic, free of the Phantom forever. This was the beginning of a new life, a life of love and beauty.

Dale opened the door and saw her standing there, smiling up at him. It was only when he lifted the lantern and Debbie saw his face that she began to scream.

Lorelei

WILHELM RULAND

*I found the following tale in an obscure book of legends about the River
Rhine that I purchased in a secondhand store. The Lorelei is a water witch
akin to sirens and undines.*

Above Coblentz where the Rhine flows through hills covered with
vineyards, there is a steep rock, round which many a legend has
been woven—the Lurlei Rock. The boatman gazes up at its gigantic
summit with awful reverence when his boat glides over the waters
at twilight. Like chattering children the restless waves whisper
round the rock, telling wonderful tales of its doings. Above on its
gray head, the legend relates that a beautiful but false nymph,
clothed in white with a wreath of stars in her flowing hair, used to
sit and sing sweet songs, until a sad tragedy drove her forever away.

Long long ago, when night in her dark garment descended from
the hills, and her silent comrade, the pale moon, cast a silver bridge
over the deep green steam, the soft voice of a woman was heard
from the rock, and a creature of divine beauty was seen on its
summit. Her golden locks flowed like a queenly mantle from her
graceful shoulders, covering her snow-white raiment so that her
tenderly-formed body appeared like a cloud of light. Woe to the
boatsman who passed the rock at the close of day! As of old, men

were fascinated by the heavenly song of the Grecian hero, so was the unhappy voyager allured by this being to sweet forgetfulness, his eyes, even as his soul, would be dazzled, and he could no longer steer clear of reefs and cliffs, and this beautiful siren only drew him to an early grave. Forgetting all else, he would steer towards her, already dreaming of having reached her; but the jealous waves would wash round his boat and at last dash him treacherously against the rocks. The roaring waters of the Rhine would drown the cries of agony of the victim who would never be seen again.

But the virgin to whom no one had ever approached, continued every night to sing soft and low, till darkness vanished in the first rays of light, and the great star of day drove the gray mists from the valley.

Ronald was a proud youth and the boldest warrior at the court of his father, the Palatinate Count. He heard of this divine, enchanting creature, and his heart burned with the desire to behold her. Before having seen the water-nymph, he felt drawn to her by an irresistible power.

Under pretence of hunting, he left the court, and succeeded in getting an old sailor to row him to the rock. Twilight was brooding over the valley of the Rhine when the boat approached the gigantic cliff; the departing sun had long sunk below the mountains, and now night was creeping on in silence; the evening star was twinkling in the deep blue firmament. Was it his protecting-angel who had placed it there as a warning to the deluded young man?

He gazed at it in rapture for some time, until a low cry from the old man at his side interrupted him. "The Lorelei!" whispered he, startled, "do you see her—the enchantress?" The only answer was a soft murmur which escaped from the youth. With wide-open eyes he looked up and lo! there she was. Yes, this was she, this wonderful creature! A glorious picture in a dark frame. Yes, that was her golden hair, and those were her flowing white garments.

She was hovering up above on the rocks combing her beautiful hair; rays of light surrounded her graceful head, revealing her charms in spite of the night and the distance, and as he gazed, her lips opened, and a song thrilled through the silence, soft and plaintive like the sweet notes of a nightingale on a still summer evening.

From her height she looked down into the hazy distance and cast at the youth a rapturous look which sank down into his soul, thrilling his whole frame.

His eyes were fixed on the features of this celestial being where he read the sweet story of love . . . Rocks, stream, glorious night, all melted into a mist before his eyes, he saw nothing but the figure above, nothing but her radiant eyes. The boat crept along, too slowly for him, he could no longer remain in it, and if his ear did not deceive him, this creature seemed to whisper his name with unutterable sweetness, and calling to her, he dashed into the water.

A death-like cry echoed from the rocks . . . and the waves sighed and washed over the unhappy youth's corpse.

The old boatman moaned and crossed himself, and as he did so, lightning tore the clouds asunder, and a loud peal of thunder was heard over the mountains. Then the waves whispered gently below, and again from the heights above, sad and dying away, sounded the Lurlei's song.

The sad news was soon brought to the Palatinate Count, who was overpowered with grief and anger. He ordered the false enchantress to be delivered up to him, dead or alive.

The next day a boat sailed down the Rhine, manned by four hardy bold warriors. The leader looked up sternly at the great rocks which seemed to be smiling silently down at him. He had asked permission to dash the diabolical seducer from the top of the rocks into the foaming whirlpool below, where she would find a certain death, and the count had readily agreed to this plan of revenge.

The first shades of twilight were gliding softly over mountain and hill.

The rock was surrounded by armed men, and the leader, followed by some daring comrades, was climbing up the side of the mountain the top of which was veiled in a golden mist, which the men thought were the last rays of sunset. It was a bright gleam of light enshrouding the nymph who appeared on the rocks, dreamingly combing her golden hair. She then took a string of pearls from her bosom, and with her slender white hand bound them round her forehead. She cast a mocking glance at the threatening men approaching her.

"What are the weak sons of the earth seeking up here on the

heights?" said she, moving her rosy lips scornfully. "You sorceress!" cried the leader enraged, adding with a contemptuous smile,
"You! We shall dash you down into the river below!"

An echoing laugh was heard over the mountain.

"Oh! the Rhine will come himself to fetch me!" cried the
maiden.

Then bending her slender body over the precipice yawning below, she tore the jewels from her forehead, hurling them trium-
phantly into the waters, while in a low sweet voice she sang:—

> "Haste thee, haste thee oh father dear!
> Send forth thy steeds from the waters clear.
> I will ride with the waves and the wind!"

Then a storm burst forth, the Rhine rose, covering its banks with
foam. Two gigantic billows like snow-white steeds rose out of the
depths, and carried the nymph down into the rushing current.

Seeing Them

DARRELL SCHWEITZER

Flying saucers are usually associated with science fiction, but in the follow-
ing story DARRELL SCHWEITZER *ingeniously links up UFOs with witch-*
craft. A Pennsylvanian who has written many imaginative novels and short
stories, Schweitzer is also a critic and the coeditor of the recently revived
Weird Tales *magazine.*

I never knew Barry Atwood well. We moved in the same circles in
college, but only because mutual friends led us to a casual acquaintance. We went to the same parties. We belonged to the same literary society.

And we both knew Laura Howard.

That was all. That was enough. Kismet, fate, inscrutable destiny.
"There are no coincidences," Laura used to say. In the end, I believed her.

But the beginning was what we used to call a *flash from the past.* I
had settled down to a quiet Sunday afternoon of marking test papers when the phone rang. Quasimodo, my terrier, yelped and ran
in circles around the telephone stand.

A *flash*—

"Phil? It's Barry."

For a moment, I didn't recognize the voice.

"Barry *who?*"

"Barry Goldwater, who do you think, old buddy? I'm running for president . . . and your . . . contribution could make all the damn difference—" He faked a laugh, but even over the phone I could tell it was a fake. His voice was hoarse, strained. He sounded as if he'd been crying.

"Barry Atwood," I said. "I haven't heard from you in—what is it? Fifteen years, I think."

"Yeah. Look, Phil, I know I may be intruding, but if you have some time, I'd like to see you. It's *important.*"

I glanced at the pile of ungraded test papers, but some instinct told me this was indeed important.

"Sure. Where are you?"

"Here. In Philadelphia. I can be over to your place in half an hour."

"Fine."

The year we graduated, Barry Atwood had moved to the West Coast. Los Angeles, undoubtedly. He'd wanted to get into films. I think he actually had worked on a few commercials. Now he was back. It had indeed been fifteen years.

There are no coincidences.

Quasimodo barked with customary fierceness when the doorbell rang, then scooted under his favorite stuffed chair.

I opened the door.

Barry looked tired. That was the overwhelming impression I got. Stooped slightly, his hair thinning in front instead of going gray, but mostly *tired,* almost haggard. And he was thin. For most people, the difference between twenty-two and thirty-seven is at least twenty pounds, but he looked thinner than he had the last time I'd seen him. Not at all well, really.

"Phil?"

I noticed that he squinted.

"Come in, Barry."

He sat in the chair beneath which the dog had tactically withdrawn. Quasimodo kept still.

I fetched us a couple of beers. Barry sipped his occasionally. Then he started talking, nervously at first, and finally in a great torrent of words.

"It was really funny when it started," he said. "I mean, I laughed—"

He hesitated, as if he'd lost the train of thought.

I settled back, nursing my beer.

"What was funny?"

"Meeting Laura again after so long. This is getting to be a goddamn class reunion, Phil—"

"Laura *Howard?* Miss Occult U.S.A. 1970, teen witch, number-one groupie of the ghost of Aleister Crowley, *that* Laura?"

He put down his beer, folded his hands in his lap, and said very quietly, "Don't joke about it, Phil. You went to her little sessions too."

"I mostly went to see her naked. Who could forget the sight of her crawling around by candlelight in her birthday suit, chalking circles on the basement floor at her mom's place. She had . . . a great ass."

"She still does."

I leaned forward and slapped my fist into the palm of my hand. "Hey, hey— Know what I mean? Nudge-nudge? Wink-wink?"

He didn't laugh at my borrowed witticism.

"There's so much to fill in." He sighed. "It's been *such* a long time. There are things you're no doubt wondering, Phil. I'm wondering too. What have *you* been doing all this time?"

"Living. I think I'm the only member of the Villanova Literary Society to actually go off and commit literature. I even get published occasionally. But mostly I teach ninth grade in the public schools."

"Are you married, Phil?"

"Almost a couple of times, but no."

"Well, I was. Her name was Anne Harris. You don't know her. After our divorce, she moved to New York. I'm in Philly so I can commute up every other weekend and see Jason, our son. He's five and the only good thing that came out of our marriage, which otherwise went very sour. Anne hates me."

"I'm . . . sorry."

Suddenly I was very embarrassed, listening to this near stranger tell me such intimate things, and at the same time a little resentful that he had invited himself over to spill his guts on my living room rug, so to speak.

"Barry, aren't we off the subject?"

"No, we're not. It all has to do with Laura Howard. I met her just a block from here, a week ago yesterday, in Clark Park. I saw a poster about a rock concert, and I had this whim. I hadn't been to a real, live rock concert in a long, long time, and . . . well, I actually put on a pair of genuine 1960s bell bottoms and a tastefully shrieking blue and red dashiki I hadn't worn in *decades*. But the concert was quite a disappointment."

"They always are. I've never been to a Clark Park event that wasn't—"

"*Tawdry,* Phil. That's what it was. A festival of some sort, but really an overblown flea market with some local group on a stage at the far end putting up a wall of noise. The whole thing was depressing. I realized how silly I'd been, dressing like an aging hippie when all the kids around me wore black leather, safety pins, and mohawks and carried boom-boxes the size of suitcases—as if the alleged music wasn't shattering eardrums quite efficiently enough.

"But I stayed long enough to flip through a record dealer's wares, boxes of albums on a table and on the ground underneath. It was underneath the table that I found myself face-to-face with a woman in her upper thirties. I didn't know who she was at first, but then she grinned hugely and said, 'Hey, man! Far out! We could be the Boobsey Twins!'

"I tried to stand up, but hit my head on the underside of the table. All I could say was, 'Huh?'

"When we got out from under the table, I could see what she meant. We were wearing identical dashikis.

"It was Laura Howard, unquestionably. The first thing she did was grab my wrist and say, 'Wait. Wait. Anachronism check. You're wearing a Timex. There were no digital watches in the Summer of Love—'

" 'My God,' I said.

" 'My God,' she said. 'You haven't seen me since the Upper Paleolithic. Hey—look what I found!'

"She waved a record in front of me. It was by the Fugs. *Golden Filth.* She read from the back of the sleeve in her finest mock-oratorical manner: '*If you hesitate to hear about the cold fork of naked reality . . . then you'd better flip this record back into the rack and go dig up some old Monkees' albums—*'

" 'Right on,' I said. 'Let's hear it for naked forks.'

" 'Barry, give me a hug—'

"I did, and a kiss too, and pretty soon we both sort of *fell* down onto the curb, laughing hysterically. One or two of the teenagers glanced our way. The band let fly with another peal of electronic thunder.

" 'Hey,' I said. 'People are *staring. . . .*'

" 'They probably wonder what us crazily garbed old farts are *on*. Or else they assume we're having heart attacks in stereo. I mean, look at us. You're, what? Thirty-seven? Your hair's thinning. Mine's got a goddamn racing stripe down the middle—'

" 'Laura, it's been a long time—'

" 'Let's get out of here,' she said. 'This is getting maudlin.'

"She paid for the record and dragged me along toward a streetcar.

" 'Were there any more treasures back there?'

" 'Not unless you want old Monkees' albums. Come on.'

I interrupted. "Barry, you loved her once, didn't you?"

He trembled slightly, then caught onto the armrests, hard. Underneath, Quasimodo started to whine. Barry didn't seem to notice.

"Yeah. Once."

"But not now." I said that as a statement, not a question.

"No, not in years. But for a moment there, I almost fooled myself."

"Barry, level with me. It's great to see old school chums, but you don't suddenly come over here and—"

He stood up, as if to attention.

"I quite understand. I see. You're right, of course. Sorry to be of any bother. I'll just go now—"

I got up, caught him by the shoulder, and pushed him gently back into the chair.

"No, you don't have to go. But I do think you have to tell me the real story, the *whole* story. For friendship's sake, at least, I'll listen."

"Will you, for friendship's sake, *believe me?*"

That gave me a start. For the first time I was a little bit afraid.

"Has something happened? Involving Laura?"

He took a long draw on his beer, then said in a voice of the utmost sadness: "You could say that. Yes. No. Maybe. I'm not sure anymore, Phil."

"Just tell me everything," I said.

"When we were on the subway, I asked her where we were going, and she told me she had a business here in town. Would I like to see? Well, it did seem *wonderful* to meet up with her again. It brought back so many memories.

"She took me to a part of the city I'd never even known existed before. Somewhere along the way, the subway burst out of the ground and became the elevated. It was sunset. I remember that distinctly. The sky was bright orange.

"She told me a little of her own adventures in the intervening years, but I did most of the talking, about Anne, about Jason. Maybe I told her too much.

" 'Well, look at it this way,' she said. 'If you're not married, you're free. Like in the old days.'

" 'It's fun to pretend,' I said, 'but you know perfectly well that we can't go back and be young again, make everything different—'

"Then she looked at me sharply and said something I didn't understand, not then.

" 'What if we're not pretending?'

"When our stop came, she led me down rusty stairs to a place where the El runs over Frankford Avenue like a roof and the stores are all blaring lights and iron bars. Every third one was boarded up. The street smelled like a subway tunnel, dirty and damp.

" 'You live here?'

" 'Like I said, my business. Opportunity is where you find it.'

" 'A bit capitalistic for an over-the-hill flower child—'

"She smiled ever so sweetly and said, 'Well, fuck you too. Here we are.'

"She got out a set of keys and unlocked a door I hadn't even noticed as we had come upon it, squeezed in between two vacant storefronts. A wooden sign swung overhead, a faded picture of a bare-breasted mermaid in a top hat waving a magician's wand, and slightly newer lettering which said merely *This is THE PLACE*. A plastic "Closed" sign dangled behind glass and bars.

"Inside, she fumbled for a light. The switch clicked, but no light came on.

" 'Shit—'

"We groped our way along in the musty dark, past crates and piles of boards. Paint chips rattled from the walls at my touch. Once something scurried before us.

"At the end of the corridor was another switch. This time the light worked, or at least one of its two uncovered bulbs came on, its harsh glare revealing a room filled with shelves of books and bottles and what looked like very peculiar pottery half hidden in the deep shadows. That was my first impression: a typical back-street junk shop. But then I followed her gaze upward and saw huge, brightly painted masks hanging from the walls.

" 'Isn't this *wild?*'

" 'Wild.'

" 'Those are Mardi Gras masks. Some of them are very old. Once in a great while I sell one, but mostly they're my lares and penates.'

" 'Larry *who?*'

" 'Guardian spirits. Never mind. Classical.'

"I started browsing and I saw at once that Laura Howard was still very much on her occult kick, as we used to call it. The books were all on witchcraft and 'ancient mysteries,' that sort of thing, including the inevitable *Necronomicon.* Packs of tarot cards hung from hooks on a pegboard. There was even a baggie of something labeled 'Devil Dust.'

"I held it up to her. *'Devil Dust?'* I said.

" 'For them that needs it, Devil Dust.'

"Amid the potions and herbs and black candles were a wide assortment of more conventional stage-magic paraphernalia: wands, hats, disguises, glasses with funny eyes, blindfolds, trick knives, and even a rubber chicken. Crystal balls gleamed in a locked case, each of them held in a pair of carved wooden hands.

" 'You sell this stuff?'

" 'The old guy I bought the place from used to supply Ernie Kovacs with gimmicks. I deal to an exclusive clientele.'

"On the wall at the end of an aisle was a huge poster that glowed in the semi-darkness: three flying disks and the legend *SEEING THEM by L. Allen Weinstein.* There were more books, mostly about UFOs, but also Atlantis, Bigfoot, the Bermuda Triangle, and a whole stack of the Weinstein volume. I held up a copy quizzically.

" 'I haven't changed,' she said softly.

" 'You don't still get yourself all yucky driving nails through rat hearts, do you?'

"She didn't smile at that.

" 'You might as well ask me if I still suck my thumb. One *does* make progress over the years.'

"She took me by the arm and led me through a bead curtain. Behind us, something rattled. Glass fell and broke.

"She jerked me around suddenly, back toward the shop room. *'Esmeralda!'* she hissed.

"The only reply was a creaking, like the sound of an old house settling, followed by silence.

" 'Your cat?'

"She didn't answer, but directed me back into the other room. I saw a lava lamp glowing in a corner, more posters of flying saucers on the walls, and a mattress on the floor. Beside the lamp was what looked like an altar, with a six-fingered wooden hand rising from it. Colored glass sparkled on the fingertips.

" 'Barry, I am sure it meant something that we met today.'

" 'Destiny, my dear. It's written in the stars. Your sign is Scorpio. Mine is Right Turn Keep Moving—'

"She put her finger to my lips. 'Now, don't be cynical about things you don't understand. It *meant* something. I *knew* to go to that place. I knew that I'd meet you—or someone else who mattered—there today.'

" 'It's a wonderful coincidence, that's all.'

" 'There are no coincidences, Barry Atwood. Not even this is a coincidence.' She tugged at her dashiki, then mine.

"She knelt down on the mattress and pulled me down after her, then proceeded to demonstrate that not all her magic was of the ethereal, abstract kind . . . and as we lay there afterwards, sweaty with love, it was easy to pretend—to *forget* otherwise—that no time at all had passed since those nights we used to spend secretly together in the *Lynx* magazine office at Villanova University.

"I remarked on this, and she said, 'It's only in your mind that any time has passed, any distance. That's what I've learned over the past decade and more. That's why I don't need rat hearts and chalk circles anymore. It's hard to explain, but once your spirit has become attuned to . . . I suppose you'd call it cosmic energy, although there are different words the adepts use . . . you can see

the Masters on other worlds, where there is no war or disease or
death. You don't have to grow old. That's what you want, isn't it?'
   " 'Like Peter Pan,' I muttered, mostly to myself. I folded my
hands behind my head and stared up at the ceiling. 'I won't grow
up, I *won't*—'
   " 'You're so damned narrow-minded. You think you know everything with your goddamn *science*. I'm trying to give you the greatest
gift you can ever receive. I can move you back and forth through
time, like a needle through cloth, out of the reach of age and death.
Once your eyes are opened, once you understand, you will be able
to do it too. Once you *see them*—'

Barry stopped talking, as if he'd run out of words. He closed his
eyes. For a moment I almost thought he was asleep. Then he sud-
denly sat bolt upright and all but shouted at me.
   "I did something really stupid, Phil. Really stupid."
   "Hey, calm down. What did you do? Just tell me."
   "I *laughed* at her."

   "I knew I was being cruel, but I couldn't help myself. You know
how it was back in college. We used to smirk about her being a
witch and all. It was a big joke. You and me, Phil, we never took it
seriously for an instant. And then, to hear her talk like that, so
deadpan earnestly, it brought all the laughter back.
   "She glared at me, furious. As if on cue, the whole place shook.
For a moment, I thought it was an earthquake. A *lot* of merchandise
fell in the next room. The lava lamp slipped in its base, sending
jerky shadows over the walls and ceiling.
   " 'That Esmeralda,' I said somewhat nervously, 'is going to put
you out of business yet.'
   "She crawled away from me, toward the lamp. Despite everything, the one thought that percolated into my brain was, *After all
these years, she still has a great ass.*
   "I laughed again, but broke off in mid-chuckle when she flung
my clothes into my face.
   " 'I think you had better fucking *go*—'
   "I sat up. 'I'm sorry,' I said. 'Really I am. I like you a lot, and I
hope you'll always be my friend, but—it's just too much to listen to

you offering to take me on a flying-saucer ride to see the perfect spiritual masters of Mars—'

"The bead curtain rattled at the bottom, as if something small had just entered the room. But when I turned and looked, I saw nothing.

"I dressed quickly and rose to go. 'Look, I really am sorry. I apologize. Can I make it up to you? Take you out to dinner, maybe?'

"She just sat there, staring into space, oblivious of my presence. When she began to speak, it was as if to the whole universe.

" 'This is a very special day.'

" 'I'm sorry I wrecked it for you. I've apologized. What more can I do?'

"She got to her feet and walked toward me, still naked. She reached out to touch my face. I raised my hand to push hers away, but hesitated. She closed my eyes with two outstretched fingers.

" 'When it is the proper time,' she said, 'you will see everything. You will open your eyes. Yours will not be a fleeting glimpse, a mere streak across the heavens. For you, there shall be no mysteries. Open your eyes. Come to understand that we are bound together now, you and I, by the magic of the flesh. Understand the special meaning of this day, of this encounter. It is a kind of graduation for me. I have worked so many years to reach this point. Open your eyes. For you it is but a beginning, a first step. Open your eyes. *See them.* Open your eyes.'

"I drew back from her and stood in the doorway, gazing at her—her nakedness, her undeniable beauty. Still my mind entertained undergraduate wolf thoughts, even though it hurt to see her angry.

"And I told myself that on some level I still loved her. I couldn't explain the hurt any other way.

"There was one thing more: She looked distinctly younger in the half-light. It was something about the way her skin gleamed. And something else, too, which didn't come to me until I was away from there.

"Her hair was completely black. The white streak, the racing stripe as she'd called it, was definitely gone."

Barry paused again, as if he couldn't go on.

"Now, wait a minute," I said after a while. "Parts of this are getting distinctly impossible. People don't *really* get younger now, do they?"

"I saw what I saw."

"It was the bad light. You said so yourself."

"Phil, I *saw* it."

"Okay," I said, sensing that it would be futile to pursue this point. "Tell me what happened next."

"What happened next was I went home. The Indian-summer daytime weather had given out, and it was quite cold. I shivered all the way in that damned dashiki.

"Of course I couldn't sleep. I was rattled, to put it mildly. So I sat up listening to music. I tried to read. I tried to work on a script I'm doing. But I couldn't concentrate.

"Eventually I lay on my bed in the dark, watching the hands move on the glowing face of my alarm clock. Regardless of what I tried to think about, I always came back to Laura, to what it had been like before with her, the sights and sounds and *scents*—the faint perfume she used to wear—and it was all so vivid I seemed to be reliving my youth. I was halfway moved to turn on the radio and see if I could pick up a 1970 newscast, but at the same time I was afraid that I might succeed.

"Eventually I dozed off and had a dream. I *knew* I was dreaming, and it seemed that inside my dream I awoke. Someone was rapping gently at the front door, almost like an animal clawing to get in.

"I padded downstairs, barefoot, and opened the door.

"A huge, orange, laughing face floated before me in the darkness. It was one of the Mardi Gras masks. It spoke to me in the voice of my five-year-old boy.

" '*Daddy, I'm lost. Daddy, it's dark here.*'

"Then I realized that a child was wearing the mask. It covered his whole body. Untied sneakers stuck out beneath the orange chin.

" '*Jason?*'

"I snatched the mask away, but it wasn't Jason. It was Laura, her adult head on a little boy's body, distorted, gnarled, like a hideous dwarf. And her voice was cracked, grating.

" '*I am the way. I am the truth. I am the light of the other world. Come, follow me.*'

"Then she laughed at me, a harsh, ugly laugh, and ran off my porch, down the steps, into the street. I ran after her in my bare feet, for blocks. The city was empty, silent, dark. The padding of my footsteps was the only sound, impossibly magnified, like the thunderous beating of an enormous heart. Still the huge-headed dwarf ran, vanished between two parked cars, then appeared again in the middle of the street only to disappear once more around a turn in an alley.

"At last we reached an open place, bare ground, a vacant lot or maybe a park. The dwarf-child just stood there waiting for me to catch up.

"Suddenly the sky was filled with blinding light. I looked up, shielding my eyes, into a glowing, whirling, humming disk, and I heard Laura's voice.

" *'Like a needle through the cloth of time. Forever and ever.'*

"The light dimmed and the saucer had clock hands on it, turning slowly at first, then faster, backward, then forward, then backward again—

"The alarm went off and I awoke in my bedroom, damp with sweat."

"That was quite some dream, Barry."

He sipped his beer, then gagged.

"You okay?"

"Yeah, yeah. I'm okay. Now you're thinking I woke up and found my pajamas torn and my feet dirty from running in the street, but it wasn't like that."

"It wasn't." A statement, not a question.

"But the dream was more than just mind-static. It was what occultists, sorcerers, or whatever call a *sending,* a message, clear as a phone call, from Laura—"

"You can't really believe—"

Now I was beginning to think I should stop Barry's story right there. This was not healthy for him to bring it up with such conviction.

He clearly believed every word he said. I thought he was truly going insane, just then.

But there was no stopping him.

• • •

"That Sunday—just a week ago—was visiting day, when I could go up to New York and see my boy. That was why the alarm had been set. I was exhausted. I'd had almost no sleep. But I got up anyway. I never wanted to let Jason down.

"I fell asleep once I was on the train and dreamed of Laura, scenes from our past, pleasant moments, but somehow they seemed forced to me, a kind of threat.

" 'No,' I said in my dream. 'Get away from me—'

"Then the conductor was nudging me awake, a worried look on his face.

" 'Hey buddy, dis your stop?'

"I thanked him, embarrassed, and hurried from the train. I was looking forward to seeing Jason. I was *dreading* seeing Anne. Whenever we met, we always ended up screaming at one another. I hoped she had left Jason in custody of the maid and gone shopping or something.

"Her apartment was in the East Nineties, right off Central Park. I— I—"

Once more Barry broke off. He put his hands over his face and sobbed.

I felt I had to say something, anything.

"Hey, East Nineties. You must have done very well for yourself—"

He pulled his hands away from his face and glared at me. Instantly I felt like a total jerk for having said that.

"She did very well by me, that bitch-and-a-half!"

"But there was . . . there *is* your son."

"Yes, Jason. But, you know, Phil? I realize now that even Jason was bait. Anne used him as bait. And beyond that, *Laura* was pulling all the strings like a fucking *puppet-master . . .* and I had to choose between *realities,* between *lives,* one with Jason in it, and Anne too, or else just Laura. Not that I had much choice."

"Barry, listen to what you're saying. This is seriously crazy. Paranoid. It'll destroy you."

He pounded hard on the arms of the chair. *"Not that I had any fucking choice!"*

Just then Quasimodo the terrier squealed as if he'd been stepped on and darted out from under the chair and into my lap, whining. Barry let out a yelp too, almost a scream, and jumped up, nearly tipping the chair over. It was like the stereotypical woman's reaction to a mouse. At any other time, it might have seemed funny. But I didn't doubt that he had just mistaken my dog for Esmeralda the . . . what? Familiar? Semi-housebroken poltergeist?

Then Barry was laughing, humorlessly, desperately.

"*Jesus*, Phil, this *is* crazy. I'm acting like such an asshole. You have every right to toss me out on my ear—"

"No, Barry. I'm not going to do that. Meet Quasimodo."

"Hi, Quasimodo," Barry said, waving his hand feebly. "Nice to get to know ya."

"I went up to Anne's apartment and rang the bell. I knew where I was going, of course. I couldn't have gotten *lost*. No, I had stood in this very hallway and rung this bell many times before.

"But there was no answer. I rang again, waited, rang. At last the door opened with a jolt, hooked on a chain. A sixtyish woman I had never seen before in my life stared out at me suspiciously.

" 'Yes? What do you want?'

"I was momentarily too startled to say anything.

" 'What do you *want?*'

"At last I managed to say, 'I've come to pick up Jason. I'm—'

" '*Who?*' She almost spat the word.

"Somewhat more in control, I asked, 'Does Anne Harris live here anymore?'

" 'I don't know anyone by that name.'

" 'But . . . this is *her* apartment. Do you know where she's gone? Did you just move in here? The previous tenant—'

"The woman slammed the door in my face. I heard a bolt click. I raised my fist to knock, but staggered away and hit the opposite wall so hard I cracked the plaster. Then I realized I'd best be gone before someone called the police, so I hurried from the building.

"Outside, I sat on the garden wall and said over and over, '*The bitch. The goddamn bitch.*'

"I thought I was talking about Anne, who had moved away without telling me, taking Jason with her. I thought my anger and my hurt came from the realization that I'd never see my son again.

"If it had really been Anne, if I'd truly believed she had moved, I would have called information. I would have called my lawyer, or maybe even her lawyer.

"But I was actually talking about Laura.

"And I looked up in the sky and I *saw one,* a glowing disk, as clear a sign as any burning bush.

"I knew there was only one thing left for me. So I came back to Philadelphia on the next train. I didn't fall asleep this time. My mind turned endlessly in fantasies of revenge. By the time I reached Thirtieth Street Station my eyes were truly opened, and, just as Laura had predicted, I was *seeing them—*"

"Barry, what did you see? Think carefully."

"The saucers, Phil. Flying saucers, thousands of them at once, passing over the city like an incredible migration of suns. You didn't see anything unusual that day, Phil, nor did most people, but *I* did, because Laura had opened my eyes. She'd brought me that far, and my hatred and my fear provided the extra power I needed.

"I saw them, and I understood why the stupid Air Force with its Project Blue Book never turned up anything. They're not space-ships with little green men from Mars. They're spiritual *powers,* like angels, miraculous messengers, apparitions, but neither good nor evil. Most people never see them. A few catch a glimpse, just a glimpse, and they don't know what they've seen. But I *knew* that they're like the living cells in the bloodstream of the universe, all around us constantly, if only we can *see them.* That was what was happening. It was as if the painted backdrop of our reality were torn away, and I was seeing the bare stage behind."

"By the time I reached the Market–Frankford El," Barry continued, "I was alone, no longer quite in *your* world, Phil, or at least perceiving it very differently. The city was deserted, the streets as empty and silent as in my dream, the flying saucers gliding overhead like a burning cloud.

"The train came just for me. There was no one in the attendant's booth, so I climbed over the turnstile and boarded. And that train didn't stop until it came to the place with the rusty stairs, where the street smelled like a damp tunnel.

"I got off, went down the stairs, and the saucers flickered

through the tracks above me like a rain of fire. My footsteps echoed.

"Something ran ahead of me, something small and dark, rattling behind trashcans. Once a window flew open and a blast of air from within sent curtains flapping. I heard things falling in there, breaking.

"The door to Laura's shop was unlocked. I had expected that. I groped my way along the cluttered corridor, paint chips raining down on me. The main room seemed to be swaying like the cabin of a ship in a storm, glass tinkling, books tumbling from shelves.

"The masks on the walls swayed and rattled. Then they began to speak. One of them had my ex-wife's voice, Anne's.

" 'Barry? Where are you? Goddamnit—*Barry!'*

"And another screamed. It was Jason.

" 'Daddy! Help me! I'm scared! *Daddy!'*

"I tore aside the bead curtain. Laura was sitting there, naked, on the edge of the mattress. She held a glowing disk in her hands. Then she released it and it floated in the air, expanding and whirling until it filled the room and its light was blinding. I staggered back into the shop room. The masks rattled.

" 'Daddy! Daddy!' Jason screamed from behind one mask, then another, and another, as if he were running along a corridor behind them, shouting out of each mouth in turn.

"The room went dark. I rubbed my eyes. When I could see again, I went back into the bedroom, through the bead curtain. Laura was still sitting there.

" 'It will be wonderful,' she said. 'The two of us together. We won't have to age. We won't have to die.'

" '*Why?'* I said. 'Why are you doing this?'

" 'I *take* what I *want* and I want *you.* '

"Furiously, I yanked on the bead curtain, tearing the curtain rod loose. Beads rattled to the floor. 'What about my son?'

"She smiled, and her smile was utterly malevolent. 'Think of the good old days, Barry, my love. You didn't have a son then. The needle passes in and out, back and forth, forward and back. That is all.'

"I was without words. 'You—you—*witch*—'

"Now it was her turn to laugh at me, and her voice was horrible, like the dwarf in my dream.

" *'Do what thou wilt,'* she said. *'That is the whole of the law.* And I have done so.' "

The phone rang. Barry looked at it in absolute, abject terror.

"Excuse me," I said.

"No, Phil— Please! Don't answer it!"

The story had gone on for hours. I stood in the semi-darkness, flicked on a lamp, and went for the phone.

"Phil!"

Just then an avalanche of pots and pans fell in the kitchen. The phone kept ringing.

"Quasimodo? Is that you?"

But my dog peeked fearfully out of a nearby closet, whined, and retreated back in again.

The phone still rang.

"Phil! For God's sake!"

Something rattled across the floor upstairs, like the hooves of a goat.

"Phil!"

He lunged for me, but I picked up the receiver and he froze where he was.

There was no voice on the other end of the line at first, just utter silence. Then, very faintly, something stirred. I thought of the sound of a crab scratching against the side of a bucket.

Finally there was a voice I had not heard in fifteen years. But I knew it certainly enough. It was Laura Howard.

"I am the way. I am the door to the other world. I have seen the frozen suns of Orion, and sailed on fiery ships into the darkness beyond, where there is no more suffering, only joy—"

I replaced the receiver carefully. I felt sick then, terrified. I grasped desperately at any possible rational explanation, and, not finding one, felt my own sanity fraying, about to snap.

"Phil," Barry said. "It was her." No question. Plain statement.

I nodded.

"I knew it would be."

"You knew?"

"Yes, because I killed her."

The lamp flickered, then went out. I could see out the window that the whole neighborhood had gone dark.

I regarded Barry Atwood with horror, and with awe.

And, sitting in the darkness, he told me the rest of the story.

"I hurled the glass part of the lava lamp at her. It shattered against her temple and she fell back onto the mattress. Then I grabbed the wooden hand-thing from the altar and beat her with it again and again, while the building shook and the floor heaved, and darkness flashed into brilliant light and back into darkness. Even then, she wouldn't die. I had to strangle her.

"I felt like I was killing myself, but I had my hands around her throat for a long time.

"And, much later, I stumbled out into the silent, dark center room. I think some light came in through a skylight. I could see that all the masks had fallen. Many were broken. None of them spoke.

"I found the key to the shop in a drawer. I locked the door behind me as I left.

"Outside, the train rattled on its track overhead. There were people on the sidewalks, cars moving in the streets, and no flying saucers."

"I killed her, Phil."

"But, *murder*—" I didn't know what to say. Just then I felt that Barry Atwood was far saner than I.

"It's been a week," he said. "The police haven't come looking for me. There was nothing in the papers. I don't think it was quite . . . murder."

"Is she really dead, then?"

"In this world, in the body, she's dead, all right. But I think it was all part of her plan. I think she *needed* me to somehow help her make the transition into . . . another state. Now she wants me to join her there. I know this, Phil, just like I knew it was her on the phone.

"When I got home that night, there was a single saucer hovering outside my window. It was for me, again, invisible to everyone else, I'm certain. And it has been there every night since. It isn't angry. It tells me, in her voice, how happy we were once and how we can be happy like that again. Together."

With great effort, I asked, "Barry, do you want to go with her?"

"Part of me does, Phil, the same part that wants to be twenty-two forever. I'm not sure I can . . . stay away much longer. You understand?"

"I think so, Barry."

"That's why I came to you, Phil. I thought you would understand. I looked in the phone book, and you were the only one of my old friends I could find, the only one who knew Laura Howard. So I knew you would help me, even though we actually never knew each other very well. There are no coincidences, Phil. Somehow it has to be you. I want you to do something for me after I'm gone."

And for an instant everything snapped into a different focus, and I thought: *He's going to kill himself.*

But, no, by the crazy logic of his story, everything fit.

"What do you want me to do?" I asked quietly.

"Find my boy. Laura canceled Jason out somehow. She did something with time. Pulled a few stitches maybe. But he's out there somewhere. I know it. Help him find his way back, if you can."

"But *how?*"

Barry rose from his seat and closed my eyes with two extended fingers.

"When it is time, open your eyes."

"I'll try," I said.

"Thank you, Phil. Now, I think, Laura is waiting. Goodbye, Phil."

"Goodbye, Barry."

"You may need this."

He pressed a key into my hand, and he whispered an address.

I sat in the darkness and listened to him leave. He opened the door. The iron gate of the porch railing creaked. Then he was gone.

I opened my eyes, and after a minute there was light flickering in through the open doorway and through the Venetian blinds, as if the whole city were on fire.

I went to the doorway and looked out.

Barry was standing in the middle of the street.

And there in the darkness, as silent as falling snow, the flying saucers began to land.

Doll-Baby

C. H. SHERMAN

C. H. SHERMAN *frequently appears on national television commercials and, under another name, in a recurring role on a popular daytime drama. If Erskine Caldwell had a mind to write about rural witchcraft, he might have produced a horror story rather like Sherman's "Doll-Baby."*

The mistletoe branch snapped against Lonnie Mae's leg as she stepped into the clearing. The welt rose up fast and it stung like twenty bees. Lonnie Mae grabbed the branch and broke it from the bush. It made her mad when she got marks on her legs. She had pretty legs, her daddy said, and she meant to keep them white and smooth. Not like her ma's legs. They were lumpy with ugly purple and blue veins showing through the hairs. And her ma's hairs were dark. Not like Lonnie Mae's golden fuzz. That's what her daddy called it. Her golden fuzz.

She knelt down and looked at the red mark on her calf.

"Miz Big Belly's fault."

A little mud would have taken the color down but the ground was dry as graveyard dust. She mashed the stem of a polecat weed covered with white foam her ma called frog spit and rubbed it on the tender place. At least it would heal before she got home. Unless the birthing was early. She would wish for that. Then her daddy

could tend to the mark, make it better. Good thing it didn't break
the skin.

Lonnie Mae sat down on the ground and stared at the shack in
the clearing. Smoke rose from the chimney. At least Miz Pritchard
wasn't too far gone to let the fire die. Having babies happened all
the time and a woman shouldn't need the help of a twelve-year-old
girl. Especially during County Fair week. But Miz Pritchard was
having her first and she was old for that. Lonnie Mae heard her ma
telling her daddy that Mr. Pritchard was going to throw Miz Pritchard out if she couldn't bear him any children. They'd been married
since before Lonnie Mae lost her first baby teeth and it was high
time they were in the family way. Lonnie Mae heard her daddy say
he'd be glad to service the missus since he knew for a fact that Mr.
Pritchard's tiny pecker was the cause of all the trouble. Lonnie
Mae's ma made the mistake of hitting her daddy and she wore a
pair of swelled eyes for a week. Lonnie Mae put salve on her daddy's knuckles each morning till the bruises healed.

The shack was kind of pretty, though, set back against a brace of
laurel trees. Lots of sunshine in the front, lots of shade in back.
Even a skinny little creek not too far away. At least she wouldn't
break her back hauling water during the birthing. Lord, she wished
her ma had come instead of sending her to babysit this woman.

Lonnie Mae brushed the drying stem away and broke the mistletoe branch, then tossed the pieces into the brush. She wondered if
Miz Pritchard was watching her take care of herself. Could she tell
Lonnie Mae wasn't rushing like a goose to its gizzard to help some
baby get born? The six times she helped her ma she'd stayed at
home and taken care of her daddy too. Only good thing about
helping Miz Pritchard was her sugar beet dumplings. Lonnie Mae
meant to stock up on those.

She smoothed her dress as she stood up and walked a walk that
would let a spying Miz Pritchard know she was tired of this business
before she got started. When no one came out onto the porch she
pounded on the oak front door just in case the pregnant lady was
sleeping.

"Hey, Miz Pritchard, it's Lonnie Mae."

She was just fixing to go on in when the door swung open. There
stood Miz Pritchard, big-bellied and freckled. Twenty-six or -seven

with swollen cheeks, swollen fingers, swollen ankles. A leather-handled knife gleamed in her hand. She was smiling.

"Lonnie Mae, it sure good to see you! Come in and help me cut my hair!"

Lonnie Mae had expected Miz Pritchard to be dragging herself about but here she was waddling around like a hog heading for the trough. A woman about to deliver a child wasn't supposed to have that much energy. And she probably didn't have much tolerance for those who didn't feel the need to rush. She wouldn't give Lonnie Mae a minute's rest. It'd be "Do this, do that!" the whole time. Lonnie Mae figured she could stand it for a week at most. She'd pray to the Lord that the water would break tonight so she'd get home faster. She didn't like this joyful woman.

"I really appreciate you helping me, Lonnie Mae, 'specially since you be missin' the fair and all."

"Where's Mr. Pritchard?"

Miz Pritchard took Lonnie Mae's blanketful of belongings and laid them on the floor in the corner. "Fixin' the dam up river. My time's comin' fast and I don't know when he'll be back. That's why your mama sent you. Help me with my hair, Lonnie Mae. I don't want my baby screamin' its head off at the sight of me."

No wonder her husband was away from home. Who could stand all that yakking? Lonnie Mae shuffled over to the stool where Miz Pritchard was trying to squat down without losing her balance.

"Gimme your arm, girl, this baby rocks so much it like to make me tip over." And she giggled a little-girl giggle that made Lonnie Mae wonder if mothering hadn't made all her brains leave her head and fall into her belly to get squashed by the baby.

"I got one side sorta cut but I know it ain't straight and I ain't even got a lookin' glass to show me. Make me pretty, Lonnie Mae, make me pretty for my brand-new child."

Lonnie Mae took the knife. Miz Pritchard's hair fell in grey-brown strings down to her shoulders, straight as the stitching on her daddy's suspenders. No two strands were the same length. She had bangs in front with one great chunk missing near her left ear. Even if she got everything else the same length she was still going to be lopsided. But Lonnie Mae didn't much care. She smelled something good cooking. The faster she cut, the sooner she'd eat. The knife was a poor one, though. Cutting hair even using a sharp knife took time but this knife was so dull Lonnie Mae could have sawed across the back of Miz Pritchard's neck without so much as piercing the skin.

"Dull knife don't cut good."

"Get the sharpnin' stone on the table. Hurry up, Lonnie Mae. This baby's kickin' to get out. He won't let me set here too long. And then we'll be needin' more firewood. The wind's blowin' from the east and the fire's cracklin' too loud. Big storm comin' for sure. We'll be needin' a sizable heap."

Lonnie Mae dragged herself to the table. She scraped the knife blade across the stone while Miz Pritchard talked and talked and talked. About nothing and everything. Lord, the woman was duller than the knife. Rattling on about babies and such didn't interest Lonnie Mae at all. She'd been caring for them all her life. Nothing exciting about babies.

"When you're done with my hair I want you should see my baby's clothes. They's so sweet. Just like my baby. You hear that, baby child? You are sweet like them clothes I'm set to wrap you up in. Soft and sweet-smellin'. And Miss Lonnie Mae is makin' things easy for your poor mama, makin' her pretty for you, little baby, little baby, my little baby come to stay, thank the Lord, come and pray, thank the Lord."

Sakes, singing was worse than talking. Hungry or not, Lonnie Mae had to get away.

"Storm's comin' fast. I best get firewood."

She stuck the knife in the table before Miz Pritchard could argue and ran out of the shack faster than she'd moved all day. She hadn't lied too much. A storm was blowing up but she figured it wouldn't hit for a while. She could take her time getting logs and kindling.

The air was cool and blessedly quiet. How was she going to put up with that horrible cheerful woman? Maybe if she acted put upon, which she was, the old lady would leave her alone and just hurry up and have her damn baby.

Lonnie Mae decided to get the kindling first since the logs were already stacked at the side of the little shed next to the shack. That way she wouldn't have to go back in right away. The woods round back were dark, thick with moss and saplings trying to make a life of their own in a world of giants. She picked up a twig here, a branch there, holding them in the hollow of her skirt. She wanted to run and play hide-and-seek with the sun. She wanted to run away from sappy Miz Pritchard and get on home, back to her daddy.

"Hurry up and get born, damn baby!"

Her voice rang through the trees. A brush rabbit sprang from a fallen log and did a zigzag scamper in front of her. It crossed left to right, a sure bad-luck sign. Lonnie Mae tore the hem of her dress just a little to take off the curse. Most of the kindling fell to the ground.

"Damn rabbit! Damn baby!"

She gave the log a mighty kick but then stopped short. Sometimes rabbits left their babies hidden and tried to lure you away from them. A little dead bunny rabbit would be fun to hide somewhere in the shack for Miz Pritchard to find. Maybe a good scare would get the labor started.

She dropped the rest of the kindling and snuck forward. Squatting by the log she peered into its open end. She couldn't see any rabbit babies but there was something sticking out from under a mound of rocks and dead leaves. It looked like a piece of flowery material. She poked at it with her finger, then gingerly pulled it out from its hiding place. The material was wrapped around something. A knotted piece of string held it together.

Lonnie Mae set it on her lap and carefully untied the string. The material fell away and there staring up at her was a cornshuck doll only as big as her hand. It had little cut-out arms and legs and dried peas for its eyes, ears, nose, and mouth. Straight pins kept them from falling off. On its head was a clump of brownish hair stuck on with sorghum by the smell of it. It was wearing a little cloth diaper. Lonnie Mae looked under it. The doll had a tiny carrot pecker and two dried pea balls. She laughed out loud.

A little boy doll-baby hidden in a log. Somebody's secret doll-baby. And Lonnie Mae had found it. She kissed it and rocked it while she sang a lullaby her ma used to sing.

"Bye-o my baby, bye-o my baby, bye-o my baby, go to sleep."

She'd only had one doll in her whole life. Her daddy whittled her a beautiful lady doll when she was five but it had got passed on to her three sisters and one day it turned up lost. Lonnie Mae beat all three of them but it couldn't be found. Her daddy never made her another one even though she asked him real nice and always rubbed his back that special way when he asked her to.

Lonnie Mae knew she should put the doll back where she found it. But it was so tiny and cute she wanted to play with it. She kissed the little doll-baby's face and rocked it some more.

"You hungry, child?"

She unbuttoned the two buttons still holding the top of her dress together and gently pushed the cornshuck baby's face to her small pink nipple. She imagined her doll-baby sucking milk from her even though her breasts weren't full grown yet. Big enough to stretch her dress too tight and make her lose buttons. But not big enough to suckle a child of her own. Soon though. She made sucking sounds like she'd heard her baby sisters and brothers make. Once when her ma had fallen asleep while nursing Conner, Lonnie Mae had gently pushed his head aside and sucked at her ma's breast like she was a baby again. Conner's bawling woke up her ma and she swatted eight-year-old Lonnie Mae away from her so hard that the girl fell against the wood bin and chipped a new front tooth. Lonnie Mae yelled that her ma's milk didn't even taste as good as an old cow's. She was glad to see blood on her ma's brown nipple where her big-girl teeth had ripped the skin. Lonnie Mae's shouts brought her daddy running. Ma was the one who got the whipping though.

Somebody took real good care to make the little doll-baby look so sweet and to cover it so it wouldn't get cold. This doll-baby was real important to somebody. But why did they hide it in a dirty old log? Maybe they knew only somebody special would find it. Like Lonnie Mae. A special doll-baby for a special girl. A special girl who could feel the tingling in that little cornshuck body shoot right through her body too.

She let her doll-baby nurse at her breast while she sang some more, then laid him on her lap and buttoned her dress. She'd take the little doll-baby with her. To play with. She wrapped it carefully in its calico swaddling and put it in her pocket. It bulged some when her hips swung inside her shapeless dress but she figured nobody would notice. Besides, her pockets were her business.

The sun was sliding down the sky so she headed back to Miz Pritchard with the wood. She gathered as much kindling as she could hold in her skirt without crushing her doll-baby and sauntered back to the shack. She talked to her doll-baby the whole time, telling him the games they were going to play together.

As she clumped up the porch steps she heard her name being called. She had an excuse all ready about a mean wart hog protecting its babies when she opened the door and saw Miz Pritchard on her hands and knees in a pool of water. Her breathing was noisy and fast, whether from pain or fear Lonnie Mae didn't know.

"My time. Get Miz Murley."

Lonnie Mae dropped the kindling in the wood bin and rushed to get Miz Pritchard to the bed. A pregnant woman is heavy but a laboring pregnant woman is a handful even for a full-grown man. The girl had to half-drag, half-carry the panicky woman from the floor across the room to her bed. It would have been easier just to leave her there on the floor but she didn't want the granny-woman scolding her. Besides, Lonnie Mae was thrilled the birthing was happening so soon. Her little doll-baby had brought her luck.

She got Miz Pritchard into the bed and piled the limp pillows on either side of her. She dipped a cloth in the water bucket and wrung it almost dry before laying it on the woman's forehead. Then she covered her up with the comfort at the foot of the bed.

"I'm for Miz Murley. You got lots of time afore the baby gets here. Whyn't you sing it a song?"

Lonnie Mae dumped the water from the bucket onto the floor to rinse away the mother's water, then ran to the creek and filled the bucket with fresh water which she poured into the bigger of the two kettles hanging over the fire. She didn't want Miz Murley yelling at her for not having any water heated up. She was almost out the door when she remembered.

"Miz Pritchard, where's the hornet's nest?"

If the stupid woman didn't have an empty nest hanging in the rafters, the granny-woman might not deliver the child at all and it would be up to Lonnie Mae. And the birth would surely be a bad one. And it would be Lonnie Mae's fault for not making sure everything was right. She pressed her doll-baby against her thigh.

"Hanging over the cupboard!" screamed Miz Pritchard.

Relieved, Lonnie Mae grabbed the knife sticking in the table and speared a chunk of meat boiling in the small kettle. Then she ran for the midwife.

Miz Murley would be expecting someone to fetch her any day now so there was no danger she wouldn't be home. All the same, Lonnie Mae ran as fast as she could just in case she had to find her out picking herbs in the woods. First births could be hard, especially when the mother was past her prime. Lonnie Mae wanted the granny-woman to be there from the start to coax that baby into the world.

Thunder rumbled in the sky. She could feel her doll-baby rubbing against her leg as she ran. He brought her the good luck to get the mother's water to break so soon and he brought her the good luck to find Miz Murley just coming home with a basketful of wild licorice, the best thing for easy childbirth. The granny-woman told Lonnie Mae to run back ahead of her so Miz Pritchard wouldn't be alone for too long. Since Lonnie Mae left the shack, three hours had passed.

The wind was thrashing the trees when Lonnie Mae burst into the Pritchard home and found the mother in the middle of a bad pain. Her howls put the fear of God into Lonnie Mae. She'd never heard a woman in confinement scream so horribly. At the same time, she couldn't help but think how childish this woman was for not being able to stand a little pain.

"Miz Murley's comin'."

"Hurtin' bad. Make it stop, dear Jesus!"

A lot of the kettle water had boiled away while she was gone so Lonnie Mae grabbed the bucket and ran for more water. She filled and emptied four bucketsful until the kettle couldn't hold any more. Then she dragged in two logs and laid them across the kindling from the wood bin. Luckily, the leftover embers were still hot enough so the fire was blazing by the time Miz Murley, drenched with rain, rushed in. Lonnie Mae's face was flushed from standing by the fire so long to keep it good and hot. Her doll-baby's cornshuck body felt warm against her leg. The pregnant woman's howls had turned to screams but the granny-woman slapped the hysterical woman's face.

"Eliza, you are not dyin', you're just givin' birth! Stop raisin' the dead!"

The old woman's gumption made Lonnie Mae smile as Miz Pritchard started to cry like a baby. Some women just can't take pain, she thought as she closed the door Miz Murley had left open. Maybe Miz Pritchard's hips were too small, maybe that's why those bones were having to stretch so much. Lonnie Mae's hips were just right for childbearing. Her daddy had told her so.

"She's burning up. Girl, bring me all the clean cloths you can find."

The granny-woman sounded worried. She knew it was going to be a hard birthing too. Lonnie Mae yanked open the cabinet drawers and pulled out two patched and yellowed sheets. She fairly flung them onto the foot of the bed in her haste. Miz Pritchard's foot jerked as a spasm wrenched her and the clean sheets fell to the floor.

"You stupid girl! Rip off the parts that touched the floor and boil them! Hand them to me next time."

"Yes'm."

Lonnie Mae cursed the stupid old pregnant lady, then cursed the stupid old midwife. It wasn't her fault the sheets got dirty. She tore the thin material with her teeth and tossed the dirtied pieces into the kettle of boiling water. Then she walked extra slow around the bed and leaned against the bedpost to hand the clean leftover pieces to Miz Murley.

"Get more."

"Sweet Jesus, sweet Jeeeee—!"

The prayer ended in an ear-splitting squeal. It sounded to Lonnie Mae just like the time her ma lost her grip while slitting a hog's throat. In bolting away from her with the knife still stuck in its gullet, the hog hit the ground and shoved the knife straight through the back of its neck. None of the family could catch it to put it out of its misery and it broke out of the pen and ran off into the woods, squealing and squealing. Just like a stuck pig, her daddy said. He had made her ma, seven months pregnant with Doria, go after it alone and haul it back. That hog must have weighed forty or fifty pounds. And the knife was ruined. Her daddy was so mad he threatened to use it to cut the baby out of her ma's belly right there over the hog's stinking carcass. When Doria was born the cord was wrapped around her neck and she was marked with a piggish pushed-up nose.

"More cloths!"

Lonnie Mae threw open the cabinet's bottom drawer and lifted out a white tablecloth embroidered all over with tiny yellow and blue daisies. She yearned to have a beautiful cloth of her own one day. The thought of this piece of work covered in blood and birthing muck almost made her cry. She carried it to Miz Murley and held it out to her. Thunder cracked outside.

"Fine. Lay it at the foot of the bed. Then wipe her face with this cloth."

The granny-woman had ripped pieces of the torn sheets into strips and tied Miz Pritchard's feet to the bottom bed posts. Too much thrashing around could cause a lot of damage. The other pieces were soaking in a bowl of water. As she wrung out a wet cloth Lonnie Mae stole a look at the woman waiting for her baby.

The mother lay stiffly as if she was fighting the pain even when it wasn't there. Her eyes were closed and tears from the corners melted into the sweat from her stringy hair. Her thin dress was stretched tight across her huge belly and Lonnie Mae could see lumps moving underneath the material as the baby squirmed to get into the right place to be born. It didn't smell so good around the bed. Everything was wet and fearful. The birthing was going to get harder. Lonnie Mae squeezed her doll-baby hiding in her pocket.

Suddenly Miz Pritchard reared up and screamed. Her eyes bugged wide and even the blue parts looked white. One arm shot out and grabbed Lonnie Mae's wrist hard enough to almost break it. Lonnie Mae yelped and snapped the wet cloth across the woman's face. The pain in her wrist was fierce so she hit her again and again to make her let go. Then she bent forward and bit Miz Pritchard's hand as hard as she could and the laboring woman finally let go. The girl fell to the floor on her side. Her doll-baby dug deep into her skin. Miz Murley yanked her up by her hair. The room was filled with the screams of all three women.

"Lonnie Mae, shut your mouth! You're here to help this poor woman, not make her more fearful!"

The midwife shoved her away and Lonnie Mae fell hip-first against the bedpost. Her poor doll-baby took most of the blow but Lonnie Mae's leg hurt real bad. Miz Pritchard's screams got louder than before. Lonnie Mae limped away from the bed and cursed under her breath.

"Hush now, hush, it's comin' soon now. Your pretty little baby will be here real soon."

The granny-woman fairly crooned to the pain-crazed woman strapped to the bed. She stroked her hair and wiped the sweat and spittle from her face with strong, soothing strokes. The screams turned to whimpers.

"Lonnie Mae, can I trust you to gentle her into drinking this licorice tea while I boil the mouth-bit? It's almost time."

Sullenly, Lonnie Mae crossed to the bed but stood out of reach of any grasping hands. The woman on the bed was so pale she looked almost dead. This was the worst birthing Lonnie Mae had ever seen. How much pain could this woman bear? Lonnie Mae checked to see that Miz Murley was busy at the kettle, then leaned close and whispered into Miz Pritchard's ear.

"You wanna see my doll-baby?"

Lonnie Mae pulled out her little doll for the pregnant woman to see. She unwrapped it and held it in front of the woman's face but was ready to yank it back if she grabbed for it. Miz Pritchard opened her eyes just a slit, thinking in her delirium that it was her own baby being shown to her.

"A boy?"

"Yes'm. It's my little boy doll-baby. You can look at it but don't touch it none."

Miz Pritchard struggled to focus her eyes on the wonder of her creation. Instead she saw dried peas skewered on a cornshuck face with a scraggly piece of human hair on its head. Her eyes opened wide as she croaked in a hoarse voice.

"She tooken my baby. Put it . . . ."

Lonnie Mae tightened her grip on the doll. Another howl ripped the laboring mother's throat. The sound was terrifying. Miz Murley rushed to the bed.

"Damnation, Lonnie Mae, where did you get that doll?"

"I found it."

"Put it back! Now! It the spell for her child. You messin' with a witch's spell, you wicked girl, put it back!"

"I ain't done nothin' wrong! I didn't know it were hers!"

"Put it back where you found it or I'll have the Devil curse you barren!"

"I was just playin' with it!"

Lonnie Mae ran from the shack into the storm. She crushed her doll-baby against her breast as she stumbled through the brambles and dodged the branches that threatened to slap her face. Rain blinded her. She cried as she ran, cried with all the fury in her soul.

Even through her sobs she could still hear Miz Pritchard's screams. Tears clogged her eyes so she tripped on scruffy undergrowth and twisted her ankles on rocks. By the time she reached the log where she'd found her doll-baby she was soaking wet and her breath was choked and gasping. Lightning lit up the sky.

She threw herself down on the slippery grass and writhed, paying no heed to the mud dirtying her dress. Thunder exploded and she howled. Her bare feet kicked and kicked as if the storm were her enemy. Raindrops pelted her twisting body. The wind ripped at her clothes and pulled her hair. She clung to her doll-baby with both hands and rocked back and forth, moaning. She rolled herself sideways into a ball and pressed the little cornshuck figure between her legs. After a time she lay still on the ground, matted grass under her cheek, mud oozing near her mouth.

Lonnie Mae knew she couldn't keep her doll-baby. She had to put it back where she found it or be cursed by the Devil. Miz Murley would know if she kept it. Witch magic was powerful. And Lonnie Mae was holding Miz Pritchard's birthing doll. She had to put it back in its hiding place so the baby could get born.

She brought the doll-baby close to her face. A bolt of lightning lit it up. One of the dried pea eyes was missing and the hair had slid down its back. Her sweet little doll-baby was nothing but a spell doll. An ugly cornshuck spell doll that would never be hers.

She'd put Miz Pritchard's doll-baby back. She'd tell Miz Murley so the old witch wouldn't make her barren. But she'd better hurry. Miz Murley might be mad enough to witch her soon as the baby was born. If her daddy found out he'd whip her good. Of all kinds of punishment that's what he favored most. And she didn't cotton to having a spell put on her *and* getting whipped. Especially since it wasn't her fault.

The rain pelted her hard as Lonnie Mae cradled her doll-baby in her arms one last time. She kissed the tiny face. She lifted the tiny diaper and kissed its tiny pecker.

Then she bit it off.

She did a good job of shoving the doll-baby back inside the log and covering the little figure with a mound of slippery leaves and twigs. Then she ran as fast as she could back to the shack. The sky was almost dark as night with ugly grey-black clouds. Lightning and thunder battled the wind and rain for power. Lonnie Mae shivered and swiped at the hair in her eyes. Lights ahead made her ache for the warmth of the shack.

As she stepped into the clearing she saw a bloodied Miz Murley lurch through the doorway and collapse to her knees, retching. A mother's anguished wails were pierced by the tinny screech of a child in pain.

The Unholy Compact Abjured

CHARLES PIGAULT-LEBRUN

CHARLES ANTOINE GUILLAUME PIGAULT DE L'EPINEY LEBRUN *(1753–1835), to give the (very) full name of the French author of the following tale, began his writing career as a playwright with the renowned Comédie Française in Paris, but later turned to fiction. Many of his works have been translated into English, including* History of a Dog, The Monk of the Grotto *and* The Barons of Felsheim. *"The Unholy Compact Abjured" is a literary retelling of a Gallic legend of demonic witchcraft and vampirism.*

In the churchyard of the town of Salins, department of Jura, may still be seen the remains of a tomb, on which is sculptured in figures as rude as the age in which they were carved, a representation of a soldier, firmly clasped in the arms of a maiden; near them stands the devil in a menacing attitude. Though the inhabitants of the town are all ready to swear to the truth of the story, they are not agreed as to the time when it happened; so that we can only say, that some centuries have rolled away, since a young soldier named St Amand, a native of Salins, was returning after a long absence to the bosom of his family. He walked with quick and cheerful steps, carrying with ease, in a small knapsack, the whole of his worldly goods. Never since he quitted the paternal roof, had he felt so happy; for he hoped ere night, to see his pretty cousin, Ninette, whom he loved with all his heart, and whom he intended to make his wife.

He walked on, gaily carolling, till he saw a cross-road before him, and uncertain of his way, he called to an old woman, with her back towards him, to direct him. She was silent: and, as he approached, he repeated the call, and she raised her head to answer it. The stout heart of the young soldier quailed, as he cast his eyes upon a countenance, such as never before had met his gaze. He had indeed, reason to tremble; for he had just disturbed in the middle of an incantation, one of the most powerful witches in the country. She regarded him with a demoniac smile, and said in a tone which froze his blood, "Turn where thou wilt, thy road is sure,—it leads to death!"

For some moments, he stood as if rooted to the spot; but, soon, fear of the sorceress, who remained gazing upon him, gave him strength to flee. He ran forward, nor stopped till he had completely lost sight of the fearful being, whose dreadful prediction had struck him with such horror. Suddenly a frightful storm arose; the thunder growled, and the lightning flashed round the weary traveller, who, drenched with rain, and overcome with fatigue, had hardly strength to proceed. How great was his joy, when he saw at a distance, a magnificent chateau, the gate of which stood open. He exerted all his remaining strength to reach it, and precipitately entered a large hall. There he stopped, expecting every moment to see some domestics, but no one appeared. He remained some time, watching the progress of the storm: at length it began to abate, and he determined to pursue his way; but as he approached the door, it closed with a loud noise, and all his efforts to open it were vain.

Struck with astonishment and dismay, the young soldier now believed that the prediction of the witch was about to be accomplished, and that he was doomed to fall a sacrifice to magic art. Exhausted by his vain efforts to open the ponderous door, he sank for a moment in helpless despondency, on the marble pavement; put his trust in providence, and soon revived. He said his prayers, and rising, waited with firmness the issue of this extraordinary adventure. When he became composed enough to look round him, he examined the hall in which he was: a pair of folding doors at the further end, flattered him with the hope of escape that way; but they too, were fastened. The hall was of immense size, entirely unfurnished; the walls, pavement and ceiling, were of black marble; there were no windows, but a small sky-light faintly admitted the light of day, into this abode of gloom, where reigned a silence like that of the tomb. Hour after hour passed; this mournful silence remained still undisturbed; and St Amand, overcome with fatigue and watching, at length sunk into a deep, though perturbed slumber.

His sleep was soon disturbed by a frightful dream: he heard all at once, the sound of a knell, mingled with the cries of bats, and owls, and a hollow voice, murmured in his ear, *"Woe to those who trouble the repose of the dead!"* He started on his feet, but what a sight met his eyes! The hall was partially illuminated by flashes of sulphurious fire; on the pavement was laid the body of a man newly slain, and covered with innumerable wounds, from which, a band of unearthly forms, whose fearful occupation, proclaimed the hellish origin, were draining the yet warm blood.

St Amand uttered a shriek of terror, and was in an instant surrounded by the fiends: already were their fangs, from which the remains of their horrid feast still dripped, extended to grasp him, when he hastily made the sign of the cross, and sank senseless upon the ground. When he regained his senses, the infernal band had vanished, and he saw bending over him, an old man, magnificently but strangely dressed: his silken garments flowed loosely around him, and were embroidered with figures of different animals, and mystic devices. His countenance was majestic, and his venerable white beard descended below his girdle: but his features had a wild and gloomy expression: his eyes, above all, had in their glance, that which might appal the stoutest heart. St Amand shrunk from this mysterious being, with awe, mingled with abhorrence, and a cold shudder ran through his veins, as the old man bent upon him his piercing eyes.

"Rash youth," cried he in a severe tone, "how is it that thou hast dared to enter this place, where never mortal foot save mine has trod?"

"I came not willingly," replied St Amand, trembling; "an evil destiny, and not vain curiosity brought me hither."

"Thou wouldst not the less have expiated thy presumption with thy life, but for my aid," returned the old man, austerely. "I have saved thee from the vampires who guard it, and it depends upon me, whether thou shalt not still become their prey."

"Oh! save me, then, I pray thee!"

"And why should I save thee?" demanded the venerable magician. "What price art thou willing to give me for thy life?"

"Alas! I have nothing worthy of thy acceptance," sighed St Amand.

"But thou may'st have; and it is only through thee that I can obtain what I most desire."

"How?"

"The blood of a dove, for me, would be a treasure, but I may not kill one; she must be slain for me, by one whose life I have saved. Should I liberate thee, a dove will fly to thy bosom; swear that thou wilt instantly sacrifice her for me, and thou shalt be free."

"I swear it!"

Hardly had St Amand uttered the words, when he found himself in the chamber of Ninette, who, with a cry of joy, rushed into his arms. He pressed her with transport to his breast; but scarcely had he embraced her, when he saw the magician standing by his side.

"Wretch!" cried he, "is it thus thou keepest thine oath? Pierce her heart—she is the dove that thou must instantly sacrifice, if thou wilt not become a feast for the vampires!"

"Sacrifice her? Never! Never!"

"Then, thou art my prey!" and the fiend assuming his own form, sprang towards his victim; but he stopped suddenly—he dared not seize him: for the maiden held him firmly clasped in her arms, and the little cross of gold, which night and day she wore upon her bosom, had been blest by the venerable priest, whose gift it was. Thus, nought unholy dared approach the maiden, and the baffled fiend fled with a tremendous yell, as the crowing of the cock, announced the approach of dawn.

The cries of the maiden soon brought the neighbours to her chamber, and among them was the pastor, to whom St Amand related his adventure. "Oh, my son!" said the good priest, "what have you done? See you not, that you have entered into a contract with the powers of darkness? Unable to wreak their vengeance on you, when you had guarded yourself with the blessed sign of our redemption, the fiend has had recourse to craft to draw you into his power. You have promised a sacrifice, to the enemy of God and man, but you have done it in ignorance. Abjure then, solemnly, the cursed contract, and dread no longer the vengeance of the fiend."

The young soldier made the required abjuration, during which, the most dreadful noises were heard: it was the last effort of the demon's vengeance; for, from that time, he was never seen, nor heard of. St Amand married Ninette, who had given him such a courageous proof of her love; and the cross transmitted from her, to her descendants, was always considered by them as the most precious part of their inheritance. In process of time, the family became wealthy, and a great grandson of St Amand erected the monument we have described, to commemorate the miraculous escape of his ancestor.

General Andrew Jackson and the Bell Witch

M. V. INGRAM

This eyewitness account of a famous American who visited an allegedly authentic witch comes from a book published in 1894 in Clarksville, Tennessee, and written by one M. V. INGRAM, *who saddled his work with the unwieldy title* An Authenticated History of the Famous Bell Witch. The Wonder of the 19th Century, and Unexplained Phenomena of the Christian Era. The Mysterious Talking Goblin that Terrorized the West End of Robertson County, Tennessee, Tormenting John Bell to His Death. The Story of Betsy Bell and the Haunting Sphinx. *No wonder Stonewall Jackson wanted to see her for himself!*

Grandfather Fort told me the story of Gen. Jackson's visit to the witch, which was quite amusing to me. The crowds that gathered at Bell's, many coming a long distance, were so large that the house would not accommodate the company. Mr. Bell would not accept any pay for entertaining, and the imposition on the family, being a constant thing, was so apparent, that parties were made up and went prepared for camping out. So Gen. Jackson's party came from Nashville with a wagon loaded with a tent, provisions, etc., bent on a good time and much fun investigating the witch. The men were riding on horseback and were following along in the rear of the wagon as they approached near the place, discussing the matter and planning how they were going to do up the witch, if it made an exhibition of such pranks as they had heard of. Just then, within a short distance of the house, traveling over a smooth level piece of road, the wagon halted and stuck fast. The driver popped his whip, whooped and shouted to the team, and the horses pulled with all of their might, but could not move the wagon an inch. It was dead stuck as if welded to the earth. Gen. Jackson commanded all men to dismount and put their shoulders to the wheels and give the wagon a push. The order was promptly obeyed. The driver laid on the lash and the horses and men did their best, making repeated efforts, but all in vain; it was no go. The wheels were then taken off, one at a time, and examined and found to be all right, revolving easily on the axles. Another trial was made to get away, the driver whipping up the team while the men pushed at the wheels, and still it was no go. All stood off looking at the wagon in serious meditation, for they were "stuck." Gen. Jackson after a few moments thought, realizing that they were in a fix, threw up his hands exclaiming, "By the eternal, boys, it is the witch." Then came the sound of a sharp metallic voice from the bushes, saying, "All right General, let the wagon move on, I will see you again tonight." The men in bewildered astonishment looked in every direction to see if they could discover from whence came the strange voice, but could find no explanation to the mystery. Gen. Jackson exclaimed again, "By the eternal, boys, this is worse than fighting the British." The horses then started unexpectedly of their own accord, and the wagon rolled along as light and smoothly as ever. Jackson's party was in no good frame of mind for camping out that night, notwithstanding one of the party was a professional "witch layer," and boasted much of his power over evil spirits, and was taken along purposedly to deal with Kate, as they called the witch. The whole party went to the house for quarters and comfort, and Mr. Bell, recognizing the distinguished character of the leader of the party, was lavishing in courtesies and entertainment. But Gen. Jackson was out with the boys for fun—"witch hunting"—and was one of them for the time. They were expecting Kate to put in an appearance according to promise, and they chose to sit in a room by the light of a tallow candle waiting for the witch. The witch layer had a big flint lock army or horse pistol, loaded with a silver bullet, which he held steady in hand, keeping a close lookout for Kate. He was a brawny man, with long hair, high cheek bones, hawk-bill nose and fiery eyes. He talked much, entertaining the company with details of his adventures, and exhibitions of undaunted courage and success in overcoming witches. He exhibited the tip of a black cat's tail, about two inches, telling how he shot the cat with a silver bullet while sitting on a bewitched woman's coffin, and by stroking that cat's tail on his nose it would flash a light on a witch the darkest night that ever come; the light, however, was not visible to any one but a magician. The party was highly entertained by the vain stories of this dolt. They flattered his vanity and encouraged his conceit, laughed at his stories, and called him sage, Apollo, oracle, wiseacre, etc. Yet there was an expectancy in the minds of all left from the wagon experience, which made the mage's stories go well, and all kept wide awake till a late hour, when they became weary and drowsy, and rather tired of hearing the warlock detail his exploits. Old Hickory was the first one to let off tension. He commenced yawning and twisting in his chair. Leaning over he whispered to the man nearest him, "Sam, I'll bet that fellow is an arrant coward. By the eternals, I do wish the thing would come, I want to see him run." The General did not have long to wait. Presently perfect quiet reigned, and then was heard a noise like dainty footsteps prancing over the floor, and quickly following, the same metallic voice heard in the bushes rang out from one corner of the room, exclaiming, "All right, General, I am on hand ready for business." And then addressing the witch layer, "Now, Mr. Smarty, here I am, shoot." The seer stroked his nose with the cat's tail, leveled his pistol, and pulled the trigger, but it failed to fire. "Try again," exclaimed the witch, which he did with the same result. "Now it's my turn; look out, you old coward, hypocrite, fraud. I'll teach you a lesson." The next thing a sound was heard like that of boxing with the open hand, whack, whack, and the oracle tumbled over like lightning had struck him, but he quickly recovered his feet and went capering around the room like a frightened steer, running over every one in his way, yelling, "Oh my nose, my nose, the devil has got me. Oh lordy, he's got me by the nose." Suddenly, as if by its own accord, the door flew open and the witch layer dashed out, and made a bee line for the lane at full speed, yelling every jump. Everybody rushed out under the excitement, expecting the man would be killed, but as far as they could hear up the lane, he was still running and yelling, "Oh Lordy." Jackson, they say, dropped down on the ground and rolled over and over, laughing. "By the eternal, boys, I never saw so much fun in all my life. This beats fighting the British." Presently the witch was on hand and joined in the laugh. "Lord Jesus," it exclaimed, "How the old devil did run and beg; I'll bet he won't come here again with his old horse pistol to shoot me. I guess that's fun enough for to-night, General, and you can go to bed now. I will come to-morrow night and show you another rascal in this crowd." Old Hickory was anxious to stay a week, but his party had enough of that thing. No one knew whose turn would come next, and no inducements could keep them. They spent the next night in Springfield, and returned to Nashville the following day. . . .

The Party Animal

ALVIN VOGEL

"The Party Animal" is the first in a new series of galumphingly comedic fantasy-mysteries by ALVIN VOGEL, *a resident of Great Neck, New York. The second, "Poppa Bear," appeared in the April 1989 issue of* Beyond Science Fiction and Fantasy. *Mr. Vogel, a consultant for the North American Company for Life and Health, is presently at work on a Nick Merlin novel.*

PROLOGUE

Belarivo moved through the night, his consciousness a thin balloon stretched over emptiness. He was empty—empty of feeling, his sense of self limited to his name, Joachim Belarivo.

He had just left a wedding. He enjoyed the food and wanted company, but everyone ran away when he arrived. That always seemed to happen.

Belarivo continued to move, looking for another party. He shuffled down the darkened streets in a slow shamble, feeling dull, empty. Then there was something there, in his head—a faint gossamer touch, a tiny whine of a mosquito burning louder, louder than a buzz saw, until Belarivo's self ignited in a white heat of blood lust. He raised his arms in ecstasy; his nails, which had continued to grow after he died, glinted orange in the dull beam of the street lamp. Belarivo quickened his pace. Party Time!

[1]

My office is in one of those few remaining old-fashioned buildings. You know, the ones in which you can open and close the windows manually. I was in earlier than was my habit because of an unusually difficult case I was on. The deadline was almost upon me and I was in a vicious mood.

My secretary was surprised to see me. "Hi, Nick. What're you doing in so early?"

I was about to snap at her to mind her own business, but that's what she was doing, wasn't it? So I said, in as reasonable a tone as I could assay prior to my morning coffee, "My case load is running away from me, and I have to finish the Scarsdale matter by the weekend or I'll forfeit my performance bond. Did you hear from Angakuk yet?"

"Not a word, Boss."

"Just like that Eskimo charlatan," I muttered.

"What?"

"Nothing. Reach out for him and tell him if he wants to work with me again he's got to get here before the close of business hours."

"What time is that, Boss?"

"How the hell should I know? Just get him here."

"Ten four, Nick." She reached for the phone and I went into my private sanctorum. I sat behind my desk and unstrapped my .22. Most P.I.s wore .45s, but so long as I stayed within city limits, I saw no need for such firepower. Even when my cases require me to leave the metropolis, the heaviest I carry is a .38. I mean, who needs a silver bullet or wolfbane anymore? The P.D. has controlled the vampires and the weres to such an extent that none have appeared in the last three years. So, why, I ask you, do all the Private Interveners carry .45 potions? A .38 I can understand. I mean you never know when you're going to need essence of bat wings or mandrake root extract. There are still a lot of Doppelgängers causing trouble, and lately the Bendith Y Mamau have escalated their kidnappings. But here in New York, carrying all that stuff is overkill, the way I see it. My phone intercom buzzed.

"I've got Angakuk on the line, Nick."

I punched the button and snarled, "Where the hell are you?"

"Now, now, Nicodemus. That's no way to talk to the Inuits' most distinguished magician."

"Distinguished magician my ass!"

"You sound upset, Nick."

"Sure I'm upset. Why shouldn't I be upset? You were supposed to be here yesterday. What do you care if I get killed or worse playing tag with that Belarivo thing?"

"Joachim Belarivo? Is he still around? I thought he'd been de-planed."

"No, he wasn't. He's still in this plane, and he's been very active in Scarsdale. It's gotten so bad that they just stopped having social events there, so now the bastard has started to show up at family dinners. The capper is that at the last one he turned bad. He didn't like the vegetarian dinner they served so he ate the cook."

"That is terrible! What went wrong?"

"I don't know. All I know is that someone was hired to raise the corpse of Joachim Belarivo for Zombie labor. Some component of the spell must have gone wrong because Belarivo refused to work. Instead, he attended all the neighborhood celebrations. Let's face it, Angy, who wants a mouldering corpse at a celebration?"

"I see your point. What would you want me to do?" he asked, in a suddenly cautious voice.

"I want you to hold him in Arctic Stasis until I can cast a spell to send him out of our plane for good."

"Shouldn't Scarsdale's P.D. handle the matter?"

"Angakuk, your brains must have frozen. Scarsdale is a very social place and does not find Joachim Belarivo to be a very upscale haunt. He's bad for property values. That's why the civic association hired a Private I. That's why I need you. *Here.* Where are you anyway?"

"I'm calling from my sled. It looks like I'm over Philadelphia. If the dogs hold out, I should be with you in about twenty minutes."

"Oh, Jeez! Don't tell me. You're traveling by dog sled again?"

"Nick, how else should an Angakuk travel? You want me to use a broomstick like your girlfriend? Over and out!"

I inadvertently glanced over my shoulder at the window, half
expecting Cassie to be there, center stage: sitting there on her
broom handle, insouciant, legs crossed, showing plenty of inner
thigh, emery board busily smoothing some microscopic chip on her
exquisite nails, waiting for me to open my window for her. It would
have been a sight for my sore eyes if she *were* framed in the window. A damn sight better view than the one that came with the
window in the first place.

I thought I'd better get my mind on my work and opened the
Belarivo file, which I had tried to read all week. If you want to
know, that's really why I'm in such a foul mood. I hate the file. I
hate the *case*. Belarivo's an accident. I can't call him a Mutant, because he's not Human anymore. He's Other. I know, dealing with
Others is my business, but you'd better remember that all of my
considerable experience has been with *standard* Others. Who
knows what spell will or won't work on Belarivo? After reading the
file I was damn sure that if what was supposed to work didn't work,
I could be one dead dick.

A distant sound caught my ear. I went to the window and opened
it. Yep. Dogs. I could hear their yapping and yowling before I
could make out the speck which speedily evolved into a silhouette
of a chubby little man in a fur parka and mukluks standing on the
back runners of a sled pulled through the air by a team of seven
malamutes. He cracked his whip and mushed the dogs in my direction. As he got close, the howling, and yowling became almost
deafening. The dogs' legs were frantically scrabbling for the feel of
the ground, fruitlessly. No wonder they were yowling. They were
terrified! I mean, what do Huskies know about flying ointment?

Angakuk's face smiled at me below his fur hood and long black
bangs. He tapped the window lightly with his whip and motioned
for me to let him in. No way, you crazy bastard! No way are you
coming in here with those ugly-tempered, ugly-smelling animals. I
screamed at him through the closed window, "Park 'em downstairs
and use the elevator like a *Human,* for God's sake!"

Angakuk shook his head at me pityingly, then descended to
street level. Not too long afterward he arrived in my office beaming
with pleasure over the sensation he'd caused. He's such an exhibi-
tionist!

"Well, Nicodemus, you look as unraveled as you've been sounding. You can relax now that I, Shaman and Angkuk of the Inuit, am here to help."

I gritted my teeth and did not rise to the bait. "Aren't you hot in all those furs? It must be sixty degrees outside."

"Oh, no, Nick. I've got plenty of cold cream on." I let that one go too. I'd get even. I just passed the Belarivo file to him. Angakuk removed his mittens and parka and sat down to read the material. He read and grunted here and there and finally finished reading the dossier. He reached into his inside pocket and drew out a black cigar which he clenched between his strong white teeth. He made a flashy gesture and conjured a flame in which he fired up his stogy. He's such a show-off!

He contemplated his cigar with studious pleasure and then spoke. "I hate this case."

"Good! That's the first thing we agree on."

Angakuk nodded. "I see that Belarivo was a caterer up in Westchester—did all the better weddings and bar mitzvahs."

"Yeah, till he died, then Glorious Dishes moved in. The owner . . . what's his name?"

Angakuk glanced down at the open folder, "Bruce Merriman."

"Right. Well, Merriman couldn't find enough experienced night help so he must have hired some cut-rate houngan or other to raise Belarivo. He must have screwed up the spell and created Superzombie instead of a potato peeler."

Angakuk puffed on his cigar and said, "Let's review what we know before trying to formulate our next steps. I'll ask. You answer."

"Shoot."

"You don't know who raised Belarivo," he stated.

"No, I don't."

"Belarivo can move around only at night in a slow shambling walk," Angakuk continued stating his questions.

"Wrong. He hates the daylight, but he's been spotted after dawn." I paused for effect. "And he was moving like greased lightning!"

"So! Eating is not his only aberration then."

"Not by a long shot, Angy."

"Have they tried salt? Even a few grains touching him'll make him realize he's dead and he'll go directly back to his grave."

I snapped at him. "You kidding? Belarivo's been known to taste what's in the pot at parties and add a pinch of salt and pepper here and there if he thought the food was too bland."

"Check. Is it possible that someone or something laid on a re-programme spell after he was raised?"

"It's never been done, but it's possible," I mused. "Well, we're not going to solve the problem sitting here. Let's continue to review the relevant facts on our way to Scarsdale. *By ground car.*"

"If you insist. I'll throw a stasis on the dogs so they'll be asleep and protected while I'm away. Your gal won't even know they're here. While I go get them why don't you bring your car around?"

"It's only four blocks to the garage," I complained. "Why don't you come with me? All the streets are one way the wrong way. It'll take me a half hour to drive back here."

Angakuk waved his cigar vaguely. "We can always take my sled. It's right here."

"Never mind," I said wearily, "I'll get the car."

[2]

It took us about forty minutes, up the Hutchinson River Park-way, to get to Scarsdale, just in time for our appointment with Bruce Merriman, who had contracted for the raising of Belarivo. We arrived at his establishment, a one-story taxpayer-type building. A woman behind a desk looked up from her ledger inquiringly. "We're here to see Mr. Merriman. I'm Nick Merlin and this is my associate, Mr. Angakuk."

She pressed a button and called into a mike, "Bruce! Someone to see you up front!" and went back to her ledger. We stood around uncomfortably and looked the place over.

A door in the rear partition opened and a slim, elegant figure in a dark suit and a boutonniere walked through and approached us. He held out his hand in a position that called for you to kiss it rather than shake it, and said, "Hi . . . I'm Bruce."

"We're Merlin and Angakuk. We are investigating the Belarivo matter."

"You are P.D.?"

"No. Private."

"I see. Who is your client? The Civic Association?"

"Normally, Mr. Merriman, I . . ."

"You can call me Bruce. *Everyone* does."

"Uh, yes. Well, Bruce, as I was saying, normally I would have to safeguard the confidentiality of my client, but in this case it seems all right for me to tell you that it is the Association that hired us. In a way we're working for you too. You're the last remaining caterer in town, and I hear that you haven't had any new business since Belarivo's appearance at the Goldstein bar mitzvah."

Bruce shuddered delicately. "What do you want with me?"

"We'd just like to talk to you. Is there a place where we can sit down?"

"Oh. How rude of me! Please. Walk this way." He pivoted gracefully and we followed him through the door. Merriman turned left and ushered us into his private office, where he gestured toward the two needlepoint upholstered chairs in front of his antique writing table. He sat down, steepled his fingers, pursed his lips, and gave us his full, sincere attention. I felt like giving him the go-ahead for a cocktail party for a hundred or so. Only I didn't know that many people. Come to think of it, I don't know anyone. Not really. I mean you *can't* in my line of work.

Angakuk, noting my lapse of attention, said, "Mr. Bruce, may I ask why you had Belarivo raised?"

Bruce looked at him. "You have such beautiful skin. Whatever do you use?"

Angakuk looked pleased. "Why, thank you. I really don't do anything. Just an occasional face pack at night of whale vomit and polar bear fat."

Bruce looked ill. I took over. "Did the fact that Belarivo was your main competitor have anything to do with you raising him?"

Merriman looked distraught. "My goodness, no."

"Go on."

Merriman complained, "Belarivo never acted like a proper Zombie. He ran amok and there seems to be no way of stopping him." Bruce looked on the verge of tears.

"Don't you worry, Brucie, we'll stop him," Angakuk said.

I jabbed him in the ribs with my elbow viciously, and asked Merriman, "Who'd you use? A houngan or what?"

"I used Carrefou."

"He's very good," I said, surprised. I'd heard of Carrefou. He's rumored to be one of the few zobops still practicing. He'd be too pricey for a Zombie job. Something didn't fit.

Bruce must have seen some doubt in my expression because he rummaged around in the table drawer and thrust forward a performance bond sealed with Carrefou's zange.

Good, I thought. At least Scarsdale could bring a malpractice suit against Carrefou. If they'd dare, that is.

"Well, Bruce, I guess we'll be on our way. I'll want to see you again after talking to Carrefou."

"I'm your obedient servant," Bruce smarmed.

"I'd like to use the facilities, if I may, before we leave," said Angakuk.

"Back there." Merriman waved vaguely.

Angakuk meandered toward the rear, apparently answered the goading urgency of nature and returned quickly. We said goodbye to Merriman and went on our way.

We stopped at a fast food place for coffee and sat in the car sipping and talking over the case. I told Angakuk about my suspicions, and my intention to see Carrefou.

"But Nick, he's in Haiti!"

"Yeah, so what?"

"So I don't have anything to wear. You engaged me to do an Arctic Stasis, not a tropical tour."

"Take along some of your damned cold cream." I smiled, spitefully, and went to phone my secretary about airline reservations.

[3]

The taxi ground its way up the winding, dusty mountain road. The driver turned off into a side road, little more than a path through the rain forest, and wheezed to a stop in front of Carrefou's place. It was a curious mixture of modern architecture and native ambiance. I told the driver to wait.

Chickens flapped out of our way as we approached the house. The door opened and an exceptionally beautiful mulatto woman said, "I am Erzelie, loa to Maître Carrefou." Her French was richly flavored with the Creole patois. "How may the loa give service?" she asked in a formal manner.

Keeping it at that level, I intoned, "I am the Intervenor, Merlin. My partner, the Shaman Angakuk, and I wish to visit the Zobop, Carrefou."

She became less formal. She smiled and said, "Yes, he is expecting you, but he is resting now. He is very old, you see, and does not have much energy these days. I will see if he is awake."

Her EYE flickered. "Maître Carrefou will see you now. Please come this way." She led us to the living room, incongruously furnished in a dark, heavy, Victorian manner, where Carrefou awaited us.

The features of his face, set in a tiny head, were sharp and ferret-like. His skin, once shiny blue-black, was dry and ashy gray. When I got close I realized how very old he was. I gave a grunt of appreciation when I saw the outline of his enormous EYE. He said, "You are wasting your time. I cannot help you."

Angakuk said tentatively, "Could we at least ask you about the Zombie, Joachim Belarivo?"

Perhaps it was my imagination, but I thought I saw Carrefou stiffen for the briefest moment before he answered. "You may speak of It."

I decided to take the direct approach. "What happened to make your Zombie a monster?" Angakuk winced at the word, but it didn't bother the old man.

"Belarivo is not my Other," he said.

"But your client, Bruce Merriman, has your performance bond."

"That is true, but even as a young houngan I called out a loa to do such work. Do you think that now, I, the last of the Zobops, would do a raising?"

"That depends on what you'd get out of it, I imagine," I said. The Zobop closed his eyes, ending the interview.

Erzelie appeared, "Maître Carrefou is tired. You had best leave."

We stood up and I said to Carrefou's shut face, "You know I'll find the loa sooner or later. I appeal to you as a fellow professional to save me the time and tell me who raised Belarivo." He seemed to ignore me for the longest while, then nodded slightly.

Erzelie said, "Her name is Amelia Ogoun, and she resides in Mount Vernon, New York."

[4]

I dialed Amelia Ogoun from Kennedy Airport. She answered on the third ring. I explained our mission and asked if she could see us within the hour. She asked in a West Indian accent if I had any whitethorn. We made a deal. She would see us in exchange for ten grams of whitethorn. Fortunately, I was packing my .38. Whitethorn isn't in my .22.

It was an old neighborhood in a section called Little Haiti. An old crone opened the door before we could knock. She had a rudimentary EYE which she left uncovered. It didn't cause me even a ripple of response because it looked more like a wart than an EYE.

Angakuk covers his with his long black bangs. Cassie Coulis affects a jeweled headband. I just slap a plasti-flesh square over mine. Everybody knows that private intervenors are adepts anyway.

"Vous êtes le Maître Merline?" she asked.

"Oui. C'est moi."

"Bien! Suivez moi."

We followed her into her parlor. Her EYE pulsed faint rose and blue as she strove, with no effect, to LOOK at us. She seated us in a circle of three chairs set on an elaborate pentagram.

"Please, Madame Ogoun," I began. "Here is the whitethorn you requested."

She hefted the plastic bag. "It is more than ten grams."

"A pourboir por vous, alors. To thank you for seeing us."

"And for giving you information. *N'est-ce pas?"*

"Yes. The Belarivo matter, madame. You raised him?"

"Yes, but I prefer doing erotic love spells, which are my specialty." She smirked hideously at Angakuk. "You have such wonderful skin, Shaman. What is your spell?"

"Madame!" I recaptured her attention. "Belarivo?"

"Ah, oui. The revered Maître Carrefou called me out to zombie Belarivo. *C'est tout."*

"That's all?" Angakuk repeated.

"Would you let me SEE your ritual?" I asked.

She bowed her head in acquiescense. "We must move off my pentagram. You cannot SEE within its confines." This time it was my turn to nod.

We moved the chairs off the design and I removed my EYEpatch. As always, I opened it slowly. My EYE is as fully developed as my eyes. The color, however, is quite as different as its function. As I raised my lid I first saw the infrareds, then the spectrum and into the ultraviolets. It took me a while to adjust to the light, because I hadn't opened my EYE in over a week. Eventually, I achieved clarity and could clearly SEE the intersecting lines between planes. I LOOKED at Angakuk and Amelia.

It's been what, about two years since I SAW Angakuk? He'd changed somewhat. His aura was clearly receding and was beginning to streak blue here and there. He flung a sharply pointed icicle right at my EYE. I involuntarily winced and blinked shut. Of course it was an illusion, but it still scared the hell out of me!

"I didn't say you could *LOOK*," Angakuk said.

He's so vain! I turned my attention to Amelia Ogoun. She was beautiful. Her aura had gracefully blued and attenuated, like a beautifully sunny sky after a brief spring snow. I bowed to her in appreciation. She smiled and asked me if I was ready. I nodded and matched frequencies with her EYE. I felt a stab of pity for her. It was like LOOKING through a heavy veil. Nevertheless, I got enough out of her ritual to know that she wasn't responsible for Belarivo's aberrations. But someone, or something, sure was. I closed my EYE and slapped on the plasti-flesh. I kissed Amelia on the cheek and we left the fine old loa to her erotic love potions.

When we were in the car and headed back to my Manhattan apartment, Angakuk said, "I could have told you that there was nothing wrong with the raising."

"Oh yeah? I suppose you could also tell me what did go wrong." I said with as much sarcasm as I could muster.

"Yes, Merlin. As a matter of fact, I can."

"You can?"

"Yes."

"What then? *What?*" I took my eye off the road and almost went over the divider. "You want to kill us? Speak, you Arctic turd!" He was driving me crazy.

"There's another adept at work. An inept adept, I might add. Is that an oxymoron?"

"Angie, I swear. I'll lay a curse on you that will last a hundred lifetimes if you don't tell me."

"Now, now, Nick. It's a capital offense to magic a Human without his consent."

"I don't care. It'll be worth it. You're not strictly human anyway."

"We adepts were given full Human status in the Magica Carta of 1215." He chuckled. "The Humans almost didn't make it past 1214. The Others were rampant then. We would have had such fun, Nick! There was such exotic game around! Now all we get to hunt is dreck. Why, I remember—"

"Okay, Angakuk. You win. I'm very sorry that I was rude. Won't you please give me the benefit of your thinking on this?"

"Do you also apologize for LOOKING at me?"

"Yes. I'm very sorry about that too."

"I'm starting to show my age, aren't I?"

"No. Not at all, Angie. You LOOKED great."

"Well, even though I know you don't mean it, it's still nice to hear. Our boy Brucie Merriman's been messing around with stuff he doesn't understand."

"Merriman's an adept?" I asked, incredulously.

"No. Not even a latent EYE there. I LOOKED."

"Without his permission? What if he *was* an adept? He could've had you thrown out of the Guild!"

"Well, he wasn't. Anyway, when I asked to go to the bathroom I did a quick reconnoiter. Yes, Nick—without a search warrant. In a side room there was a pentagram on the floor. I didn't have time to LOOK at it but it was a very complicated sign. Too bad we'll never SEE it. If we went for a warrant Merriman would no doubt get rid of it."

"We'll see about that," I said as I slammed the gear into drive. We were at Glorious Dishes in twenty minutes and went through the same routine that we did the first time. When we were once again seated across the writing table from Merriman, I said, "Bruce, you are in very bad trouble."

Perturbed, he said, "What do you mean?"

"I'm not going to fool around with you, Bruce. You know the penalty for a human to practice magic without a license."

"I'm an apprentice. There is—that is—I mean, I have a latent EYE."

"Oh!" I responded in a cheerful manner. "In that case, when I cast a spell to take away your sense of taste and smell, your latent EYE will counter it." I removed my plasti-flesh patch.

Merriman blanched. "No! Stop! I don't know what happened. Everything just went wrong. I'm sorry. Truly sorry." He put his head in his hands and wept. I felt awkward.

Angakuk was just patting his bangs in place when I turned to him for help. The rascal had been LOOKING again. "Brucie, my boy," Angie said, "you disappoint me. Not only are you a mercenary putz who took advantage of a lovely old loa and screwed up her Zombie, you're not even gay! Now you let my partner LOOK at your pentagram or *I'll* throw you in Arctic Stasis and put you on an ice floe forever, or until you die, whichever comes first."

Old Brucie turned vicious. "Go ahead, you fat faggot. I dare you! I know my rights. You can't use magic on Humans. It's a capital offense."

For the second time in as many hours I repeated myself. "It'll be worth it." I peeled off my patch and opened my EYE. Merriman threw his hands up in a blocking motion.

"Close it! I can't stand those things. Close it!"

"Sure sign of a guilty conscience," I said to Angakuk in a stage whisper. But I lowered my lid when I turned back to Merriman. "Are you going to show me your sign or not?"

"It's in the storage room two doors down."

I took that as implied consent and tugged his sleeve. We went to the designated place. Yep. There it was. I took my time. For a Human, it wasn't a bad job. The symbols within the pentagram were fairly specific. Overlaying the pattern on Amelia's ritual was the hard part. If her EYE was better developed, he'd never have gotten away with it.

I kept my EYE closed while I inspected the design. Bruce watched me fearfully. I turned to him and said, "I see what you did. You modified Belarivo's behavior to make him a partying Zombie. What was your scheme? Unleash Belarivo on your competitor's catered parties and when it became apparent that only *your* parties were safe from that gruesome gate crasher, you'd get all the orders?"

Merriman looked like he wanted to run, but I was blocking the door. Then all at once it burst forth. "Yes, that's right, I did it. But you've got to believe me. I didn't know this would happen. All I wanted was to scare people. It didn't seem so bad. I could have taken over all of Westchester County's business. I swear I didn't know what would happen."

Neither did I, but I found the probable cause after bending down and LOOKING. I could SEE that Bruce Merriman had not completed the pentagram he had laid over Amelia's in one continuous movement. My blood ran cold. He'd left a gap at the third point! He'd left a gap wide enough to let in any kind of Demon— excuse me, any kind of Other—which happened to be in the neighborhood. Who, or rather, *What* was inhabiting poor Joachim Belarivo's Zombie?

I reached for my .38 and drew my brush and paint and closed the gap, inscribing my personal seal at the edited portion. I was sure, however, that I had closed the proverbial barn door too late.

I said to Merriman, "Here's the deal. You cooperate with me and I'll forget what I SAW. You don't, I turn you over to the P.D. If I do, you *know* they'll coma you forever. What'll it be?"

"What do you want me to do?"

"A party."

"You want me to do a party?"

"A biggie. Lots of guests, great food, champagne. The works."

"You think Belarivo will show?" Merriman asked.

"He'd better, or your ass is grass," I told him. "And I want this party to take place tomorrow night—my deadline."

"I'll never get it done in time."

"Why not? I'm the only customer in town. Tomorrow, at the Country Club. Right?"

"Yes, all right," he sighed.

"Good boy, Brucie. Come on, Angie, we've got to make plans."

We got up and motored back to Manhattan. As soon as we were settled in my apartment, Angakuk called up for Chinese takeout. "Champagne is excellent with Chinese," he said. "Do you have some?" Deep in thought, I gestured toward the fridge.

After Shun Lee delivered, we popped the wine and ate from the containers with the ivory scrimshaw chopsticks Angakuk always carries. "So," he said around a honey-fried prawn, "we're going to throw a party! Too bad the guest of honor is a runaway Zombie who may not show. Is there a Plan B?"

"Yeah, there's a Plan B all right," I said. "We get some blood-

hounds, arm the villagers with smoking torches and garden implements, and rush muttering and shouting into the woods where we
corner the monster."

"Yes." Angakuk picked up the tale. "Then the monster turns and
snarls and everyone falls over himself running away."

We screamed with laughter. I guess the bubbly got to us. "We'd
better come up with something better than that," he said.

"Let's try," I said, peeling off my patch.

"Well . . ."

"Oh, come *on*, Angie. You really LOOK great. Don't be self-
conscious just because your aura is getting a few blue streaks. You
look quite distinguished, Shaman."

"Well . . . all right." He parted his bangs and we slowly
opened our EYES and synchronized. After RE-VIEWING the interview with the loa, Amelia Ogoun, and how she did the Belarivo
design, we VIEWED Merriman's overlaid pentagram as Angakuk
originally saw it, then as I SAW it and repaired it. Angakuk became
pensive.

"Angie, are you all right?" I asked.

"Yes, Nick. Fine. Wasn't her aura charming?"

"Yes. To the point of distraction, I'd say."

"You're something, Nick! All you need is for a gal to flash a
pretty aura and you go BLIND."

"What are you talking about?" I said.

"There was something there. I don't know what but there was
something there," Angakuk said, his EYE looking inward. "The
thing is, *you* were so distracted by her aura you didn't notice."

"Okay, okay! But what did you SEE?"

"I can't be sure, but I think that Amelia Ogoun LOOKED different, somehow, after she completed the Belarivo spell. Here,
LOOK here."

Yep. There was a difference, all right. When she was doing the
Belarivo spell, I could see—there, just below her aura, on her
shoulder—another aura, the size of a flea. A mosquito, I should say,
because I'd seen that aura in the mug books. It was a loup-garou
and I was willing to bet it was Carrefou's. What Angie noticed was
that it was gone after the loa had cast her spell. What happened was
pretty clear and it bothered me. I hated this case.

Angakuk wanted a break. "You go ahead," I said. "I'd like to think for a while."

"Okay, then. I'll check on the dogs and maybe visit some friends in the Village." Left alone, I began my analysis of what might be needed for an effective programme. Hours later, dozens of sketches later, five LOOKS and twenty potions later, I had my answers. I wearily pressed on my plasti-flesh patch and dropped off to sleep with my head in my arms.

Angakuk showed up at seven-thirty with lox and bagels and a mound of triple cream cheese and began to set the table. I made coffee and tidied up the place and took a shower. We were on our second cup of coffee when we reluctantly faced the problem. Angakuk said, "Well, Nick. What's the story?"

"I hated this case from the beginning. How did I ever get—"

"Nicodemus, you're starting to whine. You know I hate that," Angakuk said.

"Yeah, well that's too bad." I thought, What a way to start the day that very well could be my last! Shaking off my foreboding, I said, "Listen, I think I've figured this out. You were right. Amelia Ogoun is not the author of the design under investigation. She had a ghost writer, so to speak." Angakuk shook his head at me in despair. "Sorry. The adept we're dealing with has to be Amelia's boss, Carrefou. My view is that his loup-garou sat on Amelia's shoulder and caused Merriman to leave a gate in the pentagram. Then it slipped through that gate and turned a decent Zombie into a monster. Sorry!" I hadn't meant to use profanity but I hated this case!

Angakuk said, "Excellent, Holmes. Why'd the blighter do it, d'ya suppose?" The crazy Eskimo was playing Dr. Watson. He's such a clown!

"Will you let me finish? Carrefou is one of the few remaining male Zobops and he was on his last legs when we saw him. When a Zobop ages and feels his powers declining, he can project a loup-garou, a kind of ghost mosquito, to find a host which will provide it with human blood. The loup-garou grows as it consumes the blood and when it reaches man size, it returns to its master and is absorbed. The Zobop is then renewed, so to speak."

"I say, Holmes, quite the blood transfusion!" Angakuk was still in his Dr. Watson manifestation. "So Carrefou's loup-garou slipped through the gap in Merriman's pentagram and seized control of Belarivo to hunt human blood for it."

"Yep. Count on it. And that's what turned him vicious. And that's what I've got to deplane tonight if he shows up at the party," I said.

"If I can hold him in Stasis," Angakuk said.

"If I can figure the right spell," I said.

I hated this case.

[5]

The party was warming up, thanks to the bartender's lavish pouring. Most of the Country Club members and their families were present along with invited guests and staff. The band eased into the groove and the dancing began. As a matter of fact, everybody was having a fine time. Bruce Merriman had come through. No one was looking apprehensively at the entrance to the ballroom anymore. Well . . . Angakuk and I were looking. Apprehensively.

At the end of the number the band leader announced a break. As everyone left the dance floor, and the Vienna Tables, laden with cakes and desserts, were being wheeled in, Belarivo arrived. I shouldn't say Belarivo "arrived" any more than I should say a tornado "arrived." It had the same effect. There was an explosion of people outward and away from the source of the power. The party-goers flattened out along the perimeter of the room as if they were all spun there by a centrifuge. Angie and I stood our ground in front of the Vienna Table. Belarivo stood quietly inside the double doorway.

He was not a pretty sight. His hair, like his nails, had continued to grow after he died and drooped from his head like rotted grass. His lips were mostly gone, leaving him with a skeletal grin that was totally devoid of mirth. His clothes and his skin hung in tatters around him, so encrusted in dirt and filth that it was impossible to determine where one left off and the other began.

I had seen the Polaroids and listened to eyewitness descriptions of Belarivo, but nothing prepared me for the malevolence he emanated. And nothing could have prepared me for the smell. Funny, it had not been reported before. It was the smell of a scavenger, a whiff of corruption, the smell of a vulture. And vulturelike, his skinny tattered arms ended with bony, taloned claw hands.

Our stunned paralysis was broken when a tipsy young woman returning from her visit to the lady's room stumbled full tilt into Belarivo's back. He whirled with incredible speed and seized his prey. We pulled at our EYEcovers and started toward him. Too late! He held her close. His claws slashed, tearing at the poor girl's throat. Her helpless screams were cut off and bright blood spurted. He buried his face in her torn throat, chewing, drinking, withered lips sucking inefficiently, making obscene, slobbering sounds. His eyes glowed red as if his head was filling with blood. The droning of a mosquito filled the room.

"For God's sake, Angie! Do your thing!" I screamed, grabbing for my .38. I yanked out the talisman in the shape of St. Christopher I'd fashioned painstakingly from a block of rocksalt. It was strung on a noose of braided hair from a virgin. I had arranged the knots and braids in a programme powerful enough to deplane a rogue elephant. Assuming I'd gotten everything right, the St. Christopher zange should take care of Carrefou's loup-garou. Then the salt should take care of Belarivo. All I had to do was hang the talisman around Belarivo's neck, locate a contiguous plane, and activate the program with a LOOK.

I turned to Angakuk, ready to boot him into action but it wasn't necessary. His hair had turned into an ice cap. His face was bristled with a mustache and beard of icicles. His breath formed a fog of frost which slowly fell to the floor. He LOOKED magnificent. He was the Angakuk, Shaman of the Inuit, and he was casting cold from his pointing finger upon Belarivo. Cold so intense that all molecular activity would cease. Belarivo froze in his tracks. I advanced, the amulet on its noose, stretched wide in my hands, ready to loop over Belarivo's head. At minus 273 degrees Kelvin, he should be motionless. But he wasn't. His mouth was working from his efforts to throw off the Arctic Stasis. The loup-garou's drone had changed to an almost unbearable shriek as it strove to generate counteracting heat. The forces of Carrefou's equatorial tropics blazed against the heavy coldness from Angakuk's arctic spirit.

Belarivo began to turn away. He was very slow and sluggish, but he was moving. I threw a glance at Angakuk. His icicle whiskers were starting to drip water from the tips. He was losing it! I couldn't wait anymore. I had to try. I rushed Belarivo, arms out-stretched, the magic loop spread wide between my hands, ready to place it around Belarivo's neck—like so! Damn!

Belarivo managed to duck his head, so the loop fell harmlessly along his back. The only thing that kept him from tearing out my throat was that he needed both his hands to keep my amulet away. My wrists were freezing from the grasp of his hands. My crawling gooseflesh had nothing to do with the cold.

Belarivo bent his head toward me, his skeletal mouth all teeth. He bent to me, slowly, inexorably. I struggled hysterically. I was going to die horribly. I opened my EYE and desperately searched for a contiguous plane. There *was* one coming into confluence! If I could just get my hands free for a few seconds. I tried to pull away with all my strength, but there was no give to the frozen, granite grip. My effort was so great I started to black out.

The mosquito dirged his triumph. A long pointed icicle whizzed past my scalp and squished Belarivo directly in the eye. It pene-trated and thunked to a stop inside the thing's head. Newly con-sumed blood spurted around the protruding icicle like an obscene ejaculation.

The mosquito keened and Belarivo let go, convulsively throwing me away from him. As I fell back and away I tossed the loop. A ringer! I had kept my EYE on the rapidly intersecting planes and at the instant of confluence LOOKED, projecting the pattern of the programme knitted into the virgin's hair. I was praying that she wasn't lying when I hit the floor and my lights went out.

I came to with my head cushioned on a folded tablecloth. Hot compresses were on my wrists and cold cream was on my face. Angakuk was looking down on me anxiously. "What happened?" I blurted out.

"He's outta here," Angakuk said smugly.

I sat up and groaned. "You sure screwed that up," I said, feeling awful.

Angakuk was simmering. "Screwed up?" He pointed to himself elaborately and said, "I screwed up? You ungrateful lout, the only way I screwed up was to save your life!"

"Oh, yeah? I ordered a stasis. A *stasis,* understand? Not a slow motion. If you would have frozen him properly, you wouldn't have had to save my life." I was feeling better. I grinned at Angakuk and said, "Did you see me—my fall-away shot? Pure poetry in motion."

Angakuk was now boiling. He drew himself up to his full five feet three inches and said, "I screwed up, huh? You were poetry in motion, huh? Well, to hell with you!"

I was glad his EYE was closed when he said that. I was too bushed to ward off a real curse. He's really a good guy.

The Horned Women

LADY WILDE

This folk tale of a gaggle of Irish peasant witches has been recounted by more than one Celtic author. This version is drawn from Ancient Legends, Mystic Charms and Superstitions of Ireland *by Lady* JANE FRANCESCA WILDE *(1826–1896) a well-known literary hostess who wrote under the pen-name "Speranza" and was the mother of Oscar Wilde, whose own witch story immediately follows.*

A rich woman sat up late one night carding and preparing wool, while all the family and servants were asleep. Suddenly a knock was given at the door, and a voice called—"Open! open!"

"Who is there?" said the woman of the house.

"I am the Witch of the One Horn," was answered.

The mistress, supposing that one of her neighbours had called and required assistance, opened the door, and a woman entered, having in her hand a pair of wool carders, and bearing a horn on her forehead, as if growing there. She sat down by the fire in silence, and began to card the wool with violent haste. Suddenly she paused and said aloud: "Where are the women? They delay too long."

Then a second knock came to the door, and a voice called as before—"Open! open!"

The mistress felt herself constrained to rise and open to the call, and immediately a second witch entered, having two horns on her forehead, and in her hand a wheel for spinning the wool.

"Give me place," she said; "I am the Witch of the Two Horns," and she began to spin as quick as lightning.

And so the knocks went on, and the call was heard, and the witches entered, until at last twelve women sat round the fire—the first with one horn, the last with twelve horns. And they carded the thread, and turned their spinning wheels, and wound and wove, all singing together an ancient rhyme, but no word did they speak to the mistress of the house. Strange to hear, and frightful to look upon were these twelve women, with their horns and their wheels; and the mistress felt near to death, and she tried to rise that she might call for help, but she could not move, nor could she utter a word or a cry, for the spell of the witches was upon her.

Then one of them called to her in Irish and said—

"Rise, woman, and make us a cake."

Then the mistress searched for a vessel to bring water from the well that she might mix the meal and make the cake, but she could find none. And they said to her—

"Take a sieve and bring water in it."

And she took the sieve and went to the well; but the water poured from it, and she could fetch none for the cake, and she sat down by the well and wept. Then a voice came by her and said—

"Take yellow clay and moss and bind them together and plaster the sieve so that it will hold."

This she did, and the sieve held the water for the cake. And the voice said again—

"Return, and when thou comest to the north angle of the house, cry aloud three times and say, 'The mountain of the Fenian women and the sky over it is all on fire.' "

And she did so.

When the witches inside heard the call, a great and terrible cry broke from their lips and they rushed forth with wild lamentations and shrieks, and fled away to Slieve-namon, where was their chief abode. But the Spirit of the Well bade the mistress of the house to enter and prepare her home against the enchantments of the witches if they returned again.

And first, to break their spells, she sprinkled the water in which she had washed her child's feet (the feet-water) outside the door on the threshold; secondly, she took the cake which the witches had made in her absence, of meal mixed with the blood drawn from the sleeping family. And she broke the cake in bits, and placed a bit in the mouth of each sleeper, and they were restored; and she took the cloth they had woven and placed it half in and half out of the chest with the padlock; and lastly, she secured the door with a great crossbeam fastened in the jambs, so that they could not enter. And having done these things she waited.

Not long were the witches in coming back, and they raged and called for vengeance.

"Open! open!" they screamed. "Open, feet-water!"

"I cannot," said the feet-water, "I am scattered on the ground and my path is down to the Lough."

"Open, open, wood and tree and beam!" they cried to the door.

"I cannot," said the door, "for the beam is fixed in the jambs and I have no power to move."

"Open, open, cake that we have made and mingled with blood," they cried again.

"I cannot," said the cake, "for I am broken and bruised, and my blood is on the lips of the sleeping children."

Then the witches rushed through the air with great cries, and fled back to Slieve-namon, uttering strange curses on the Spirit of the Well, who had wished their ruin; but the woman and the house were left in peace, and a mantle dropped by one of the witches in her flight was kept hung up by the mistress as a sign of the night's awful contest; and this mantle was in possession of the same family from generation to generation for five hundred years after.

The Fisherman and His Soul

OSCAR WILDE

OSCAR FINGAL O'FLAHERTIE WILLS WILDE *(1854–1900) was born
in Dublin, the son of Sir William Wilde, a surgeon, and Lady Jane
Francesca Wilde, a popular writer (see the preceding selection). Though
Wilde's literary fame probably rests most firmly upon his excellence as a
playwright* (Lady Windermere's Fan, The Importance of Being Earnest, Salomé, *etc.), he also wrote several fine works of fantasy fiction,
including "The Canterville Ghost" (included in* Ghosts, Doubleday,
1981*) and that unforgettable study of corruption and hypocrisy,* The Picture of Dorian Gray. *"The Fisherman and His Soul," a haunting morality tale whose mischief begins with witchcraft, is one of several fairy tales
that Wilde wrote for his sons.*

Every evening the young Fisherman went out upon the sea, and
threw his nets into the water.

When the wind blew from the land he caught nothing, or but
little at best, for it was a bitter and black-winged wind, and rough
waves rose up to meet it. But when the wind blew to the shore, the
fish came in from the deep, and swam into the meshes of his nets,
he took them to the marketplace and sold them.

Every evening he went out upon the sea, and one evening the
net was so heavy that hardly could he draw it into the boat. And he

laughed, and said to himself, "Surely I have caught all the fish that swim, or snared some dull monster that will be a marvel to men, or some thing of horror that the great Queen will desire," and putting forth all his strength, he tugged at the coarse ropes till, like lines of blue enamel round a vase of bronze, the long veins rose up on his arms. He tugged at the thin ropes, and nearer and nearer came the circle of flat corks, and the net rose at last to the top of the water.

But no fish at all was in it, nor any monster or thing of horror, but only a little Mermaid lying fast asleep.

Her hair was as a wet fleece of gold, and each separate hair as a thread of fine gold in a cup of glass. Her body was as white ivory, and her tail was of silver and pearl. Silver and pearl was her tail, and the green weeds of the sea coiled round it; and like sea-shells were her ears, and her lips were like sea-coral. The cold waves dashed over her cold breasts and the salt glistened upon her eyelids.

So beautiful was she that when the young Fisherman saw her he was filled with wonder, and he put out his hand and drew the net close to him, and leaning over the side he clasped her in his arms. And when he touched her, she gave a cry like a startled seagull and woke, and looked at him in terror with her mauve-amethyst eyes, and struggled that she might escape. But he held her tightly to him, and would not suffer her to depart.

And when she saw that she could in no way escape from him, she began to weep, and said, "I pray thee let me go, for I am the only daughter of a King, and my father is aged and alone."

But the young Fisherman answered, "I will not let thee go save thou makest me a promise that whenever I call thee, thou wilt come and sing to me, for the fish delight to listen to the song of the Sea-folk, and so shall my nets be full."

"Wilt thou in very truth let me go, if I promise thee this?" cried the Mermaid.

"In very truth I will let thee go," said the young Fisherman.

So she made him the promise he desired, and sware it by the oath of the Sea-folk. And he loosened his arms from about her, and she sank down into the water, trembling with a strange fear.

Every evening the young Fisherman went out upon the sea, and called to the Mermaid, and she rose out of the water and sang to him. Round and round her swam the dolphins, and the wild gulls wheeled above her head.

And she sang a marvellous song. For she sang of the Sea-folk who drive their flocks from cave to cave, and carry the little calves on their shoulders; of the Tritons who have long green beards and hairy breasts, and blow through twisted conches when the King passes by; of the palace of the King which is all of amber, with a roof of clear emerald, and a pavement of bright pearl; and of the gardens of the sea where the great filigrane fans of coral wave all day long, and the fish dart about like silver birds, and the anemones cling to the rocks, and the pinks bourgeon in the ribbed yellow sand. She sang of the big whales that come down from the north seas and have sharp icicles hanging to their fins; of the Sirens who tell of such wonderful things that the merchants have to stop their ears with wax lest they should hear them, and leap into the water and be drowned; of the sunken galleys with their tall masts, and the frozen sailors clinging to the rigging, and the mackerel swimming in and out of the open portholes; of the little barnacles who are great travellers, and cling to the keels of the ships and go round and round the world; and of the cuttlefish who live in the sides of the cliffs and stretch out their long black arms, and can make night come when they will it. She sang of the nautilus who has a boat of her own that is carved out of an opal and steered with a silken sail; of the happy Mermen who play upon harps and can charm the great Kraken to sleep; of the little children who catch hold of the slippery porpoises and ride laughing upon their backs; of the Mermaids who lie in the white foam and hold out their arms to the mariners; and of the sea-lions with their curved tusks, and the sea-horses with their floating manes.

And as she sang, all the tunny-fish came in from the deep to listen to her, and the young Fisherman threw his nets round them and caught them, and others he took with a spear. And when his boat was well-laden, the Mermaid would sink down into the sea, smiling at him.

Yet would she never come near him that he might touch her. Oftentimes he called to her and prayed of her, but she would not; and when he sought to seize her she dived into the water as a seal might dive, nor did he see her again that day. And each day the sound of her voice became sweeter to his ears. So sweet was her voice that he forgot his nets and his cunning, and had no care of his craft. Vermilion-finned and with eyes of bossy gold, the tunnies went by in shoals, but he heeded them not. His spear lay by his side unused, and his baskets of plaited osier were empty. With lips parted, and eyes dim with wonder, he sat idle in his boat and listened, listening till the sea-mists crept round him, and the wandering moon stained his brown limbs with silver.

And one evening he called to her, and said: "Little Mermaid, little Mermaid, I love thee. Take me for thy bridegroom, for I love thee."

But the Mermaid shook her head. "Thou hast a human soul," she answered. "If only thou wouldst send away thy soul, then could I love thee."

And the young Fisherman said to himself: "Of what use is my soul to me? I cannot see it. I may not touch it. I do not know it. Surely I will send it away from me, and much gladness shall be mine." And a cry of joy broke from his lips, and standing up in the painted boat, he held out his arms to the Mermaid. "I will send my soul away," he cried, "and you shall be my bride, and I will be thy bridegroom, and in the depth of the sea we will dwell together, and all that thou hast sung of thou shalt show me, and all that thou desirest I will do, nor shall our lives be divided."

And the little Mermaid laughed for pleasure, and hid her face in her hands.

"But how shall I send my soul from me?" cried the young Fisherman. "Tell me how I may do it, and lo! it shall be done."

"Alas! I know not," said the little Mermaid; "the Sea-folk have no souls." And she sank down into the deep, looking wistfully at him.

Now early on the next morning, before the sun was the span of a man's hand above the hill, the young Fisherman went to the house of the Priest and knocked three times at the door.

The novice looked out through the wicket, and when he saw who it was, he drew back the latch and said to him, "Enter."

And the young Fisherman passed in, and knelt down on the sweet-smelling rushes of the floor, and cried to the Priest who was reading out of the Holy Book and said to him: "Father, I am in love with one of the Sea-folk, and my soul hindereth me from having my desire. Tell me how I can send my soul away from me, for in truth I have no need of it. Of what value is my soul to me? I cannot see it. I may not touch it. I do not know it."

And the Priest beat his breast, and answered: "Alack, alack, thou art mad, or hast eaten of some poisonous herb, for the soul is the noblest part of man, and was given to us by God that we should nobly use it. There is no thing more precious than a human soul, nor any earthly thing that can be weighed with it. It is worth all the gold that is in the world, and is more precious than the rubies of the kings. Therefore, my son, think not any more of this matter, for it is a sin that may not be forgiven. And as for the Sea-folk, they are lost, and they who would traffic with them are lost also. They are as the beasts of the field that know not good from evil, and for them the Lord has not died."

The young Fisherman's eyes filled with tears when he heard the bitter words of the Priest, and he rose up from his knees and said to him: "Father, the Fauns live in the forest and are glad, and on the rocks sit the Mermen with their harps of red gold. Let me be as they are, I beseech thee, for their days are as the days of flowers. And as for my soul, what doth my soul profit me, if it stand between me and the thing that I love?"

"The love of the body is vile," cried the Priest, knitting his brows, "and vile and evil are the pagan things God suffers to wander through His world. Accursed be the Fauns of the wood-land, and accursed be the singers of the sea! I have heard them at night-time and they have sought to lure me from my beads. They tap at the window, and laugh. They whisper into my ears the tale of their perilous joys. They tempt me with temptations, and when I would pray they make mouths at me. They are lost, I tell thee, they are lost. For them there is no heaven nor hell, and in neither shall they praise God's name."

"Father," cried the young Fisherman, "thou knowest not what thou sayest. Once in my net I snared the daughter of a King. She is fairer than the morning star, and whiter than the moon. For her body I would give my soul, and for her love I would surrender heaven. Tell me what I ask of thee, and let me go in peace."

"Away! Away!" cried the Priest; "thy leman is lost, and thou shalt be lost with her." And he gave him no blessing, but drove him from his door.

And the young Fisherman went down into the market-place, and he walked slowly, and with bowed head, as one who is in sorrow.

And when the merchants saw him coming, they began to whisper to each other, and one of them came forth to meet him, and called him by name, and said to him, "What hast thou to sell?"

"I will sell thee my soul," he answered: "I pray thee buy it of me, for I am weary of it. Of what use is my soul to me? I cannot see it. I may not touch it. I do not know it."

But the merchants mocked at him, and said: "Of what use is a man's soul to us? It is not worth a clipped piece of silver. Sell us thy body for a slave, and we will clothe thee in sea-purple, and put a ring upon thy finger, and make thee the minion of the great Queen. But talk not of the soul, for to us it is nought, nor has it any value for our service."

And the young Fisherman said to himself: "How strange a thing this is! The Priest telleth me that the soul is worth all the gold in the world, and the merchants say that it is not worth a clipped piece of silver." And he passed out of the market-place, and went down to the shore of the sea, and began to ponder on what he should do.

And at noon he remembered how one of his companions, who was a gatherer of samphire, had told him of a certain young Witch who dwelt in a cave at the head of the bay and was very cunning in her witcheries. And he set to and ran, so eager was he to get rid of his soul, and a cloud of dust followed him as he sped round the sand of the shore. By the itching of her palm the young Witch knew his coming, and she laughed and let down her red hair. With her red hair falling around her, she stood at the opening of the cave, and in her hand she had a spray of wild hemlock that was blossoming.

"What d' ye lack? What d' ye lack?" she cried, as he came panting up the steep, and bent down before her. "Fish for thy net, when the wind is foul? I have a little reed-pipe, and when I blow on it the mullet come sailing into the bay. But it has a price, pretty boy, it has a price. What d' ye lack? What d' ye lack? A storm to wreck the ships, and wash the chests of rich treasure ashore? I have more storms than the wind has, for I serve one who is stronger than the wind, and with a sieve and a pail of water I can send the great galleys to the bottom of the sea. But I have a price, pretty boy, I have a price. What d' ye lack? What d' ye lack? I know a flower that grows in the valley, none knows it but I. It has purple leaves, and a star in its heart, and its juice is as white as milk. Shouldst thou touch with this flower the hard lips of the Queen, she would follow thee all over the world. Out of the bed of the King she would rise, and over the whole world she would follow thee. And it has a price, pretty boy, it has a price. What d' ye lack? What d' ye lack? I can pound a toad in a mortar, and make broth of it, and stir the broth with a dead man's hand. Sprinkle it on thine enemy while he sleeps, and he will turn into a black viper, and his own mother will slay him. With a wheel I can draw the Moon from heaven, and in a crystal I can show thee Death. What d' ye lack? What d' ye lack? Tell me thy desire, and I will give it thee, and thou shalt pay me a price, pretty boy, thou shalt pay me a price."

"My desire is but for a little thing," said the young Fisherman, "yet hath the Priest been wroth with me, and driven me forth. It is but for a little thing, and the merchants have mocked at me, and denied me. Therefore am I come to thee, though men call thee evil, and whatever be thy price I shall pay it."

"What wouldst thou?" asked the Witch, coming near to him.

"I would send my soul away from me," answered the young Fisherman.

The Witch grew pale, and shuddered, and hid her face in her blue mantle. "Pretty boy, pretty boy," she muttered, "that is a terrible thing to do."

He tossed his brown curls and laughed. "My soul is nought to me," he answered. "I cannot see it. I may not touch it. I do not know it."

"What wilt thou give me if I tell thee?" asked the Witch, looking down at him with her beautiful eyes.

"Five pieces of gold," he said, "and my nets, and the wattled house where I live, and the painted boat in which I sail. Only tell me how to get rid of my soul, and I will give thee all that I possess."

She laughed mockingly at him, and struck him with the spray of hemlock. "I can turn the autumn leaves into gold," she answered, "and I can weave the pale moonbeams into silver if I will it. He whom I serve is richer than all the kings of this world, and has their dominions."

"What then shall I give thee," he cried, "if thy price be neither gold nor silver?"

The Witch stroked his hair with her thin white hand. "Thou must dance with me, pretty boy," she murmured, and she smiled at him as she spoke.

"Nought but that?" cried the young Fisherman in wonder, and he rose to his feet.

"Nought but that," she answered, and she smiled at him again.

"Then at sunset in some secret place we shall dance together," he said, "and after that we have danced thou shalt tell me the thing which I desire to know."

She shook her head. "When the moon is full, when the moon is full," she muttered. Then she peered all round, and listened. A blue bird rose screaming from its nest and circled over the dunes, and three spotted birds rustled through the coarse grey grass and whistled to each other. There was no other sound save the sound of a wave fretting the smooth pebbles below. So she reached out her hand, and drew him near to her and put her dry lips close to his ear.

"To-night thou must come to the top of the mountain," she whispered. "It is a Sabbath, and He will be there."

The young Fisherman started and looked at her, and she showed her white teeth and laughed. "Who is He of whom thou speakest?" he asked.

"It matters not," she answered. "Go thou to-night, and stand under the branches of the hornbeam, and wait for my coming. If a black dog run towards thee, strike it with a rod of willow, and it will go away. If an owl speak to thee, make it no answer. When the moon is full I shall be with thee, and we will dance together on the grass."

"But wilt thou swear to me to tell me how I may send my soul from me?" he made question.

She moved out into the sunlight, and through her red hair rippled the wind. "By the hoofs of the goat I swear it," she made answer.

"Thou art the best of the witches," cried the young Fisherman, "and I will surely dance with thee to-night on the top of the mountain. I would indeed that thou hadst asked of me either gold or silver. But such as thy price is thou shalt have it, for it is but a little thing." And he doffed his cap to her, and bent his head low, and ran back to the town filled with a great joy.

And the Witch watched him as he went, and when he had passed from her sight she entered her cave, and having taken a mirror from a box of carved cedar-wood, she set it up on a frame, and burned vervain on lighted charcoal before it, and peered through the coils of the smoke. And after a time she clenched her hands in anger. "He should have been mine," she muttered; "I am as fair as she is."

And that evening, when the moon had risen, the young Fisherman climbed up to the top of the mountain, and stood under the branches of the hornbeam. Like a targe of polished metal the round sea lay at his feet, and the shadows of the fishing boats moved in the little bay. A great owl, with yellow sulphurous eyes, called to him by his name, but he made it no answer. A black dog ran towards him and snarled. He struck it with a rod of willow, and it went away whining.

At midnight the witches came flying through the air like bats. "Phew!" they cried, as they lit upon the ground, "there is someone here we know not!" and they sniffed about, and chattered to each other, and made signs. Last of all came the young Witch, with her red hair streaming in the wind. She wore a dress of gold-tissue embroidered with peacocks' eyes, and a little cap of green velvet was on her head.

"Where is he, where is he?" shrieked the witches when they saw her, but she only laughed, and ran to the hornbeam, and taking the Fisherman by the hand she led him out into the moonlight and began to dance.

Round and round they whirled, and the young Witch jumped so high that he could see the scarlet heels of her shoes. Then right across the dancers came the sound of the galloping of a horse, but no horse was to be seen, and he felt afraid.

"Faster," cried the Witch, and she threw her arms about his neck, and her breath was hot upon his face. "Faster, faster!" she cried, and the earth seemed to spin beneath his feet, and his brain grew troubled, and a great terror fell on him, as of some evil thing that was watching him, and at last he became aware that under the shadow of a rock there was a figure that had not been there before.

It was a man dressed in a suit of black velvet, cut in the Spanish fashion. His face was strangely pale, but his lips were like a proud red flower. He seemed weary, and was leaning back toying in a listless manner with the pommel of his dagger. On the grass beside him lay a plumed hat, and a pair of riding-gloves gauntleted with gilt lace, and sewn with seed-pearls wrought into a curious device. A short cloak lined with sables hung from his shoulder, and his delicate white hands were gemmed with rings. Heavy eyelids drooped over his eyes.

The young Fisherman watched him, as one snared in a spell. At last their eyes met, and wherever he danced it seemed to him that the eyes of the man were upon him. He heard the Witch laugh, and caught her by the waist, and whirled her madly round and round.

Suddenly a dog bayed in the wood, and the dancers stopped, and going up two by two, knelt down, and kissed the man's hands. As they did so, a little smile touched his proud lips, as a bird's wing touches the water and makes it laugh. But there was disdain in it. He kept looking at the young Fisherman.

"Come! let us worship," whispered the Witch, and she led him up, and a great desire to do as she besought him seized on him, and he followed her. But when he came close, and without knowing why he did it, he made on his breast the sign of the cross, and called upon the holy name.

No sooner had he done so than the witches screamed like hawks and flew away, and the pallid face that had been watching him twitched with a spasm of pain. The man went over to a little wood, and whistled. A jennet with silver trappings came running to meet him. As he leapt upon the saddle he turned round, and looked at the young Fisherman sadly.

And the Witch with the red hair tried to fly away also, but the Fisherman caught her by her wrists, and held her fast.

"Loose me," she cried, "and let me go. For thou hast named what should not be named, and shown the sign that may not be looked at."

"Nay," he answered, "but I will not let thee go till thou hast told me the secret."

"What secret?" said the Witch, wrestling with him like a wild cat, and biting her foam-flecked lips.

"Thou knowest," he made answer.

Her grass-green eyes grew dim with tears, and she said to the Fisherman, "Ask me anything but that!"

He laughed, and held her all the more tightly.

And when she saw that she could not free herself, she whispered to him, "Surely I am as fair as the daughters of the sea, and as comely as those that dwell in the blue waters," and she fawned on him and put her face close to his.

But he thrust her back frowning, and said to her, "If thou keepest not the promise that thou madest to me I will slay thee for a false witch."

She grew grey as a blossom of the Judas-tree, and shuddered. "Be it so," she muttered. "It is thy soul and not mine. Do with it as thou wilt." And she took from her girdle a little knife that had a handle of green viper's skin, and gave it to him.

"What shall this serve me?" he asked of her, wondering.

She was silent for a few moments, and a look of terror came over her face. Then she brushed her hair back from her forehead, and smiling strangely she said to him: "What men call the shadow of the body is not the shadow of the body, but is the body of the soul. Stand on the sea-shore with thy back to the moon, and cut away from around thy feet thy shadow, which is thy soul's body, and bid thy soul leave thee, and it will do so."

The young Fisherman trembled. "Is this true?" he murmured.

"It is true, and I would that I had not told thee of it," she cried, and she clung to his knees weeping.

He put her from him and left her in the rank grass, and going to the edge of the mountain he placed the knife in his belt and began to climb down.

And his Soul that was within him called out to him and said: "Lo! I have dwelt with thee for all these years, and have been thy servant. Send me not away from thee now, for what evil have I done thee?"

And the young Fisherman laughed. "Thou hast done me no evil, but I have no need of thee," he answered. "The world is wide, and there is Heaven also, and Hell, and that dim twilight house that lies between. Go wherever thou wilt, but trouble me not, for my love is calling to me."

And his Soul besought him piteously, but he heeded it not, but leapt from crag to crag, being sure-footed as a wild goat, and at last he reached the level ground and the yellow shore of the sea.

Bronze-limbed and well-knit, like a statue wrought by a Grecian, he stood on the sand with his back to the moon, and out of the foam came white arms that beckoned to him, and out of the waves rose dim forms that did him homage. Before him lay his shadow, which was the body of his Soul, and behind him hung the moon in the honey-coloured air.

And his Soul said to him: "If indeed thou must drive me from thee, send me not forth without a heart. The world is cruel; give me thy heart to take with me."

He tossed his head and smiled. "With what should I love my love if I gave thee my heart?" he cried.

"Nay, but be merciful," said his Soul; "give me thy heart, for the world is very cruel, and I am afraid."

"My heart is my love's," he answered, "therefore tarry not, but get thee gone."

"Should I not love also?" asked his Soul.

"Get thee gone, for I have no need of thee," cried the young Fisherman, and he took the little knife with its handle of green viper's skin, and cut away his shadow from around his feet, and it rose up and stood before him, and looked at him, and it was even as himself.

He crept back, and thrust the knife into his belt, and a feeling of awe came over him. "Get thee gone," he murmured, "and let me see thy face no more."

"Nay, but we must meet again," said the Soul. Its voice was low and flute-like, and its lips hardly moved while it spake.

"How shall we meet?" cried the young Fisherman. "Thou wilt not follow me into the depths of the sea?"

"Once every year I will come to this place, and call to thee," said the Soul. "It may be that thou wilt have need of me."

"What need should I have of thee?" cried the young Fisherman; "but be it as thou wilt," and he plunged into the water, and the Tritons blew their horns, and the little Mermaid rose up to meet him, and put her arms around his neck and kissed him on the mouth.

And the Soul stood on the lonely beach and watched them. And when they had sunk down into the sea, it went weeping away over the marshes.

And after a year was over the Soul came down to the shore of the sea and called to the young Fisherman, and he rose out of the deep, and said, "Why dost thou call to me?"

And the Soul answered, "Come nearer, that I may speak with thee, for I have seen marvellous things."

So he came nearer, and couched in the shallow water, and leaned his head upon his hand and listened.

And the Soul said to him: "When I left thee I turned my face to the East and journeyed. From the East cometh everything that is wise. Six days I journeyed, and on the morning of the seventh day I came to a hill that is in the country of the Tartars. I sat down under the shade of a tamarisk-tree to shelter myself from the sun. The land was dry, and burnt up with the heat. The people went to and fro over the plain like flies crawling upon a disk of polished copper.

"When it was noon a cloud of red dust rose up from the flat rim of the land. When the Tartars saw it, they strung their painted bows, and having leapt upon their little horses they galloped to meet it. The women fled screaming to the waggons, and hid themselves behind the felt curtains.

"At twilight the Tartars returned, but five of them were missing, and of those that came back not a few had been wounded. They harnessed their horses to the waggons and drove hastily away. Three jackals came out of a cave and peered after them. Then they sniffed up the air with their nostrils, and trotted off in the opposite direction.

"When the moon rose I saw a camp-fire burning on the plain, and went towards it. A company of merchants were seated round it on carpets. Their camels were picketed behind them, and the negroes who were their servants were pitching tents of tanned skin upon the sand, and making a high wall of the prickly pear.

"As I came near them, the chief of the merchants rose up and drew his sword, and asked me my business.

"I answered that I was a Prince in my own land, and that I had escaped from the Tartars, who had sought to make me their slave.

The chief smiled, and showed me five heads fixed upon long reeds of bamboo.

"Then he asked me who was the prophet of God, and I answered him Mohammed.

"When he heard the name of the false prophet, he bowed and took me by the hand, and placed me by his side. A negro brought me some mare's milk in a wooden dish, and a piece of lamb's flesh roasted.

"At daybreak we started on our journey. I rode on a red-haired camel by the side of the chief, and a runner ran before us carrying a spear. The men of war were on either hand, and the mules followed with the merchandise. There were forty camels in the caravan, and the mules were twice forty in number.

"We went from the country of the Tartars into the country of those who curse the Moon. We saw the Gryphons guarding their gold on the white rocks, and the scaled Dragons sleeping in their caves. As we passed over the mountains we held our breath lest the snows might fall on us, and each man tied a veil of gauze before his eyes. As we passed through the valleys the Pygmies shot arrows at us from the hollows of the trees, and at night-time we heard the wild men beating on their drums. When we came to the Tower of Apes we set fruits before them, and they did not harm us. When we came to the Tower of Serpents we gave them warm milk in bowls of brass, and they let us go by. Three times in our journey we came to the banks of the Oxus. We crossed it on rafts of wood with great bladders of blown hide. The river-horses raged against us and sought to slay us. When the camels saw them they trembled.

"The kings of each city levied tolls on us, but would not suffer us to enter their gates. They threw us bread over the walls, little maize-cakes baked in honey and cakes of fine flour filled with dates. For every hundred baskets we gave them a bead of amber.

"When the dwellers in the villages saw us coming, they poisoned the wells and fled to the hill-summits. We fought with the Magadae who are born old, and grow younger and younger every year, and die when they are little children; and with the Laktroi who say that they are the sons of tigers, and paint themselves yellow and black; and with the Aurantes who bury their dead on the tops of trees, and themselves live in dark caverns lest the Sun, who is their god, should slay them; and with the Krimnians who worship a crocodile, and give it earrings of green glass, and feed it with butter and fresh fowls; and with the Agazonbae, who are dog-faced; and with the Sibans, who have horses' feet, and run more swiftly than horses. A third of our company died in battle, and a third died of want. The rest murmured against me, and said that I had brought them an evil fortune. I took a horned adder from beneath a stone and let it sting me. When they saw that I did not sicken they grew afraid.

"In the fourth month we reached the city of Illel. It was night-time when we came to the grove that is outside the walls, and the air was sultry, for the Moon was travelling in Scorpion. We took the ripe pomegranates from the trees, and brake them, and drank their sweet juices. Then we lay down on our carpets and waited for the dawn.

"And at dawn we rose and knocked at the gate of the city. It was wrought out of red bronze, and carved with sea-dragons and drag-ons that have wings. The guards looked down from the battlements and asked us our business. The interpreter of the caravan answered that we had come from the island of Syria with much merchandise. They took hostages, and told us that they would open the gate to us at noon, and bade us tarry till then.

"When it was noon they opened the gate, and as we entered in the people came crowding out of the houses to look at us, and a crier went round the city crying through a shell. We stood in the market-place, and the negroes uncorded the bales of figured cloths and opened the carved chests of sycamore. And when they had ended their task, the merchants set forth their strange wares: the waxed linen from Egypt and the painted linen from the country of the Ethiops, the purple sponges from Tyre and the blue hangings from Sidon, the cups of cold amber and the fine vessels of glass and the curious vessels of burnt clay. From the roof of a house a com-pany of women watched us. One of them wore a mask of gilded leather.

"And on the first day the priests came and bartered with us, and on the second day came the nobles, and on the third day came the craftsmen and the slaves. And this is their custom with all merchants as long as they tarry in the city.

"And we tarried for a moon, and when the moon was waning, I wearied and wandered away through the streets of the city and came to the garden of its god. The priests in their yellow robes moved silently through the green trees, and on a pavement of black marble stood the rose-red house in which the god had his dwelling. Its doors were of powdered lacquer, and bulls and peacocks were wrought on them in raised and polished gold. The tiled roof was of sea-green porcelain, and the jutting eaves were festooned with little bells. When the white doves flew past, they struck the bells with their wings and made them tinkle.

"In front of the temple was a pool of clear water paved with veined onyx. I lay down beside it, and with my pale fingers I touched the broad leaves. One of the priests came towards me and stood behind me. He had sandals on his feet, one of soft serpent-skin and the other of birds' plumage. On his head was a mitre of black felt decorated with silver crescents. Seven yellows were woven into his robe, and his frizzed hair was stained with antimony.

"After a little while he spake to me, and asked me my desire.

"I told him that my desire was to see the god.

" 'The god is hunting,' said the priest, looking strangely at me with his small slanting eyes.

" 'Tell me in what forest, and I will ride with him,' I answered.

"He combed out the soft fringes of his tunic with his long pointed nails. 'The god is asleep,' he murmured.

" 'Tell me on what couch, and I will watch by him,' I answered.

" 'The god is at the feast,' he cried.

" 'If the wine be sweet I will drink it with him, and if it be bitter I will drink it with him also,' was my answer.

"He bowed his head in wonder, and, taking me by the hand, he raised me up, and led me into the temple.

"And in the first chamber I saw an idol seated on a throne of jasper bordered with great orient pearls. It was carved out of eb-ony, and in stature was of the stature of a man. On its forehead was a ruby, and thick oil dripped from its hair on to its thighs. Its feet were red with the blood of a newly-slain kid, and its loins girt with a copper belt that was studded with seven beryls.

"And I said to the priest, 'Is this the god?' And he answered me, 'This is the god.'

" 'Show me the god,' I cried, 'or I will surely slay thee.' And I touched his hand, and it became withered.

"And the priest besought me, saying, 'Let my lord heal his servant, and I will show him the god.'

"So I breathed with my breath upon his hand, and it became whole again, and he trembled and led me into the second chamber, and I saw an idol standing on a lotus of jade hung with great emeralds. It was carved out of ivory, and in stature was twice the stature of a man. On its forehead was a chrysolite, and its breasts were smeared with myrrh and cinnamon. In one hand it held a crooked sceptre of jade, and in the other a round crystal. It ware buskins of brass, and its thick neck was circled with a circle of selenites.

"And I said to the priest, 'Is this the god?' And he answered me, 'This is the god.'

" 'Show me the god,' I cried, 'or I will surely slay thee.' And I touched his eyes, and they became blind.

"And the priest besought me, saying, 'Let my lord heal his servant, and I will show him the god.'

"So I breathed with my breath upon his eyes, and the sight came back to them, and he trembled again, and led me into the third chamber, and lo! there was no idol in it, nor image of any kind, but only a mirror of round metal set on an altar of stone.

"And I said to the priest, 'Where is the god?' And he answered me: 'There is no god but this mirror that thou seest, for this is the Mirror of Wisdom. And it reflecteth all things that are in heaven and on earth, save only the face of him who looketh into it. This it reflecteth not, so that he who looketh into it may be wise. Many other mirrors are there, but they are mirrors of Opinion. This only is the Mirror of Wisdom. And they who possess this mirror know everything, nor is there anything hidden from them. And they who possess it not have not Wisdom. Therefore is it the god, and we worship it.' And I looked into the mirror, and it was even as he had said to me.

"And I did a strange thing, but what I did matters not, for in a valley that is but a day's journey from this place have I hidden the Mirror of Wisdom. Do but suffer me to enter into thee again and be thy servant, and thou shalt be wiser than all the wise men, and Wisdom shall be thine. Suffer me to enter into thee, and none will be as wise as thou."

But the young Fisherman laughed. "Love is better than Wisdom," he cried, "and the little Mermaid loves me."

"Nay, but there is nothing better than Wisdom," said the Soul.

"Love is better," answered the young Fisherman, and he

plunged into the deep, and the Soul went weeping away over the marshes.

And after the second year was over, the Soul came down to the shore of the sea, and called to the young Fisherman, and he rose out of the deep and said, "Why dost thou call to me?"

And the Soul answered, "Come nearer, that I may speak with thee, for I have seen marvellous things."

So he came nearer, and couched in the shallow water, and leaned his head upon his hand and listened.

And the Soul said to him: "When I left thee, I turned my face to the South and journeyed. From the South cometh everything that is precious. Six days I journeyed along the highways that lead to the city of Ashter, along the dusty red-dyed highways by which the pilgrims are wont to go did I journey, and on the morning of the seventh day I lifted up my eyes, and lo! the city lay at my feet, for it is in a valley.

"There are nine gates to this city, and in front of each gate stands a bronze horse that neighs when the Bedouins come down from the mountains. The walls are cased with copper, and the watch-towers on the walls are roofed with brass. In every tower stands an archer with a bow in his hand. At sunrise he strikes with an arrow on a gong, and at sunset he blows through a horn of horn.

"When I sought to enter, the guards stopped me and asked of me who I was. I made answer that I was a Dervish and on my way to the city of Mecca, where there was a green veil on which the Koran was embroidered in silver letters by the hands of the angels. They were filled with wonder, and entreated me to pass in.

"Inside it is even as a bazaar. Surely thou shouldst have been with me. Across the narrow streets the gay lanterns of paper flutter like large butterflies. When the wind blows over the roofs they rise and fall as painted bubbles do. In front of their booths sit the merchants on silken carpets. They have straight black beards, and their turbans are covered with golden sequins, and long strings of amber and carved peach-stones glide through their cool fingers. Some of them sell gelbanum and nard, and curious perfumes from the islands of the Indian Sea, and the thick oil of red roses, and myrrh and little nail-shaped cloves. When one stops to speak to them, they throw pinches of frankincense upon a charcoal brazier and make the air sweet. I saw a Syrian who held in his hands a thin rod like a reed. Grey threads of smoke came from it, and its odour as it burned was as the odour of the pink almond in spring. Others sell silver bracelets embossed all over with creamy blue turquoise stones, and anklets of brass wire fringed with little pearls, and tigers' claws set in gold, and the claws of that gilt cat, the leopard, set in gold also, and earrings of pierced emerald, and finger-rings of hollowed jade. From the teahouses comes the sound of the guitar, and the opium-smokers with their white smiling faces look out at the passers-by.

"Of a truth thou shouldst have been with me. The wine-sellers elbow their way through the crowd with great black skins on their shoulders. Most of them sell the wine of Shiraz, which is as sweet as honey. They serve it in little metal cups and strew rose-leaves upon it. In the market-place stand the fruit-sellers, who sell all kinds of fruit: ripe figs, with their bruised purple flesh; melons, smelling of musk and yellow as topazes; citrons and rose-apples and clusters of white grapes, round red-gold oranges, and oval lemons of green gold. Once I saw an elephant go by. Its trunk was painted with vermilion and turmeric, and over its ears it had a net of crimson silk cord. It stopped opposite one of the booths and began eating the oranges, and the man only laughed. Thou canst not think how strange a people they are. When they are glad they go to the bird-sellers and buy of them a caged bird, and set it free that their joy may be greater, and when they are sad they scourge themselves with thorns that their sorrow may not grow less.

"One evening I met some negroes carrying a heavy palanquin through the bazaar. It was made of gilded bamboo, and the poles were of vermilion lacquer studded with brass peacocks. Across the windows hung thin curtains of muslin embroidered with beetles' wings and with tiny seed-pearls, and as it passed by a pale-faced Circassian looked out and smiled at me. I followed behind, and the negroes hurried their steps and scowled. But I did not care. I felt a great curiosity come over me.

"At last they stopped at a square white house. There were no windows to it, only a little door like the door of a tomb. They set down the palanquin and knocked three times with a copper hammer. An Armenian in a caftan of green leather peered through the wicket, and when he saw them he opened, and spread a carpet on the ground, and the woman stepped out. As she went in, she turned round and smiled at me again. I had never seen anyone so pale.

"When the moon rose I returned to the same place and sought for the house, but it was no longer there. When I saw that, I knew who the woman was, and wherefore she had smiled at me.

"Certainly thou shouldst have been with me. On the feast of the New Moon the young Emperor came forth from his palace and went into the mosque to pray. His hair and beard were dyed with rose-leaves, and his cheeks were powdered with a fine gold-dust. The palms of his feet and hands were yellow with saffron.

"At sunrise he went forth from his palace in a robe of silver, and at sunset he returned to it again in a robe of gold. The people flung themselves on the ground and hid their faces, but I would not do so. I stood by the stall of a seller of dates and waited. When the Emperor saw me, he raised his painted eyebrows and stopped. I stood quite still, and made him no obeisance. The people marvelled at my boldness, and counselled me to flee from the city. I paid no heed to them, but went and sat with the sellers of strange gods, who by reason of their craft are abominated. When I told them what I had done, each of them gave me a god and prayed me to leave them.

"That night, as I lay on a cushion in the tea-house that is in the Street of Pomegranates, the guards of the Emperor entered and led me to the palace. As I went in they closed each door behind me, and put a chain across it. Inside was a great court with an arcade running all round. The walls were of white alabaster, set here and there with blue and green tiles. The pillars were of green marble, and the pavement of a kind of peach-blossom marble. I had never seen anything like it before.

"As I passed across the court two veiled women looked down from the balcony and cursed me. The guards hastened on, and the butts of the lances rang upon the polished floor. They opened a gate of wrought ivory, and I found myself in a watered garden of seven terraces. It was planted with tulipcups and moonflowers, and silver-studded aloes. Like a slim reed of crystal a fountain hung in the dusky air. The cypress-trees were like burnt-out torches. From one of them a nightingale was singing.

"At the end of the garden stood a little pavilion. As we approached it two eunuchs came out to meet us. Their fat bodies swayed as they walked, and they glanced curiously at me with their yellow-lidded eyes. One of them drew aside the captain of the guard, and in a low voice whispered to him. The other kept munching scented pastilles, which he took with an affected gesture out of an oval box of lilac enamel.

"After a few moments the captain of the guard dismissed the soldiers. They went back to the palace, the eunuchs following slowly behind and plucking the sweet mulberries from the trees as they passed. Once the elder of the two turned round, and smiled at me with an evil smile.

"Then the captain of the guard motioned me towards the entrance of the pavilion. I walked on without trembling, and drawing the heavy curtain aside I entered in.

"The young Emperor was stretched on a couch of dyed lion skins, and a gerfalcon perched upon his wrist. Behind him stood a brass-turbaned Nubian, naked down to the waist, and with heavy earrings in his split ears. On a table by the side of the couch lay a mighty scimitar of steel.

"When the Emperor saw me he frowned, and said to me: 'What is thy name? Knowest thou not that I am Emperor of this city?' But I made him no answer.

"He pointed with his finger at the scimitar, and the Nubian seized it, and rushing forward struck at me with great violence. The blade whizzed through me, and did me no hurt. The man fell sprawling on the floor, and when he rose up his teeth chattered with terror and he hid himself behind the couch.

"The Emperor leapt to his feet, and taking a lance from a stand of arms, he threw it at me. I caught it in its flight, and broke the shaft into two pieces. He shot at me with an arrow, but I held up my hands and it stopped in mid-air. Then he drew a dagger from a belt of white leather, and stabbed the Nubian in the throat lest the slave should tell of his dishonour. The man writhed like a trampled snake, and a red foam bubbled from his lips.

"As soon as he was dead the Emperor turned to me, and when he had wiped away the bright sweat from his brow with a little napkin of purfled and purple silk, he said to me: 'Art thou a prophet, that I may not harm thee, or the son of a prophet, that I can do thee no hurt? I pray thee leave my city to-night, for while thou art in it I am no longer its lord.'

"And I answered him: 'I will go for half of thy treasure. Give me half of thy treasure, and I will go away.'

"He took me by the hand, and led me out into the garden. When the captain of the guard saw me, he wondered. When the eunuchs saw me, their knees shook and they fell upon the ground in fear.

"There is a chamber in the palace that has eight walls of red porphyry, and a brass-scaled ceiling hung with lamps. The Emperor touched one of the walls and it opened, and we passed down a corridor that was lit with many torches. In niches upon each side stood great wine-jars filled to the brim with silver pieces. When we reached the centre of the corridor the Emperor spake the word that may not be spoken, and a granite door swung back on a secret spring, and he put his hands before his face lest his eyes should be dazzled.

"Thou couldst not believe how marvellous a place it was. There were huge tortoise-shells full of pearls, and hollowed moon-stones of great size piled up with red rubies. The gold was stored in coffers of elephant-hide, and the gold-dust in leather bottles. There were opals and sapphires, the former in cups of crystal, and the latter in cups of jade. Round green emeralds were ranged in order upon thin plates of ivory, and in one corner were silk bags filled, some with turquoise-stones, and others with beryls. The ivory horns were heaped with purple amethysts, and the horns of brass with chalcedonies and sards. The pillars, which were of cedar, were hung with strings of yellow lynx-stones. In the flat oval shields there were carbuncles, both wine-coloured and coloured like grass. And yet I have told thee but a tithe of what was there.

"And when the Emperor had taken away his hands from before his face he said to me: 'This is my house of treasure, and half that is in it is thine, even as I promised to thee. And I will give thee camels and camel drivers, and they shall do thy bidding and take thy share of the treasure to whatever part of the world thou desirest to go. And the thing shall be done to-night, for I would not that the Sun, who is my father, should see that there is in my city a man whom I cannot slay.'

"But I answered him: 'The gold that is here is thine, and the silver also is thine, and thine are the precious jewels and the things of price. As for me, I have no need of these. Nor shall I take aught from thee but that little ring that thou wearest on the finger of thy hand.'

"And the Emperor frowned. 'It is but a ring of lead,' he cried, 'nor has it any value. Therefore take thy half of the treasure and go from my city.'

" 'Nay,' I answered, 'but I will take nought but that leaden ring, for I know what is written within it, and for what purpose.'

"And the Emperor trembled, and besought me and said: 'Take all the treasure and go from my city. The half that is mine shall be thine also.'

"And I did a strange thing, but what I did matters not, for in a cave that is but a day's journey from this place have I hidden the Ring of Riches. It is but a day's journey from this place, and it waits for thy coming. He who has this Ring is richer than all the kings of the world. Come therefore and take it, and the world's riches shall be thine."

But the young Fisherman laughed. "Love is better than Riches," he cried, "and the little Mermaid loves me."

"Nay, but there is nothing better than Riches," said the Soul.

"Love is better," answered the young Fisherman, and he plunged into the deep, and the Soul went weeping away over the marshes.

And after the third year was over, the Soul came down to the shore of the sea, and called to the young Fisherman, and he rose out of the deep and said, "Why dost thou call to me?"

And the Soul answered, "Come nearer, that I may speak with thee, for I have seen marvellous things."

So he came nearer, and couched in the shallow water, and leaned his head upon his hand and listened.

And the Soul said to him: "In a city that I know of there is an inn that standeth by a river. I sat there with sailors who drank of two different-coloured wines, and ate bread made of barley, and little salt-fish served in bay-leaves with vinegar. And as we sat and made merry, there entered to us an old man bearing a leathern carpet and a lute that had two horns of amber. And when he had laid out the carpet on the floor, he struck with a quill on the wire strings of his lute, and a girl whose face was veiled ran in and began to dance before us. Her face was veiled with a veil of gauze, but her feet were naked. Naked were her feet, and they moved over the carpet like little white pigeons. Never have I seen anything so marvellous, and the city in which she dances is but a day's journey from this place."

Now when the young Fisherman heard the words of his Soul, he remembered that the little Mermaid had no feet and could not dance. And a great desire came over him, and he said to himself, "It is but a day's journey, and I can return to my love," and he laughed, and stood up in the shallow water, and strode towards the shore.

And when he had reached the dry shore he laughed again, and held out his arms to his Soul. And his Soul gave a great cry of joy and ran to meet him, and entered into him, and the young Fisherman saw stretched before him upon the sand that shadow of the body that is the body of the Soul.

And his Soul said to him, "Let us not tarry, but get hence at once, for the Sea-gods are jealous, and have monsters that do their bidding."

So they made haste, and all that night they journeyed beneath the moon, and all the next day they journeyed beneath the sun, and on the evening of the day they came to a city.

And the young Fisherman said to his Soul, "Is this the city in which she dances of whom thou didst speak to me?"

And his Soul answered him: "It is not this city, but another. Nevertheless let us enter in."

So they entered in and passed through the streets, and as they passed through the Street of the Jewellers the young Fisherman saw a fair silver cup set forth in a booth. And his Soul said to him, "Take that silver cup and hide it."

So he took the cup and hid it in the fold of his tunic, and they went hurriedly out of the city.

And after that they had gone a league from the city, the young Fisherman frowned and flung the cup away, and said to his Soul, "Why didst thou tell me to take this cup and hide it, for it was an evil thing to do?"

But his Soul answered him, "Be at peace, be at peace."

And on the evening of the second day they came to a city, and the young Fisherman said to his Soul, "Is this the city in which she dances of whom thou didst speak to me?"

And his Soul answered him: "It is not this city, but another. Nevertheless let us enter in."

So they entered in and passed through the streets, and as they passed through the Street of the Sellers of Sandals, the young Fisherman saw a child standing by a jar of water. And his Soul said to him, "Smite that child." So he smote the child till it wept, and when he had done this they went hurriedly out of the city.

And after that they had gone a league from the city the young Fisherman grew wroth, and said to his Soul, "Why didst thou tell me to smite the child, for it was an evil thing to do?"

But his Soul answered him, "Be at peace, be at peace."

And on the evening of the third day they came to a city, and the young Fisherman said to his Soul, "Is this the city in which she dances of whom thou didst speak to me?"

And his Soul answered him, "It may be that it is in this city, therefore let us enter in."

So they entered in and passed through the streets, but nowhere could the young Fisherman find the river or the inn that stood by its side. And the people of the city looked curiously at him and he grew afraid and said to his Soul, "Let us go hence, for she who dances with white feet is not here."

But his Soul answered, "Nay, but let us tarry, for the night is dark and there will be robbers on the way."

So he sat him down in the market-place and rested, and after a time there went by a hooded merchant who had a cloak of cloth of Tartary, and bare a lantern of pierced horn at the end of a jointed reed. And the merchant said to him, "Why dost thou sit in the market-place, seeing that the booths are closed and the bales corded?"

And the young Fisherman answered him, "I can find no inn in this city, nor have I any kinsman who might give me shelter."

"Are we not all kinsmen?" said the merchant. "And did not one God make us? Therefore come with me, for I have a guest-chamber."

So the young Fisherman rose up and followed the merchant to his house. And when he had passed through a garden of pomegranates and entered into the house, the merchant brought him rose-water in a copper dish that he might wash his hands, and ripe melons that he might quench his thirst, and set a bowl of rice and a piece of roasted kid before him.

And after that he had finished, the merchant led him to the guest-chamber, and bade him sleep and be at rest. And the young Fisherman gave him thanks, and kissed the ring that was on his hand, and flung himself down on the carpets of dyed goat's-hair. And when he had covered himself with a covering of black lamb's-wool he fell asleep.

And three hours before dawn, and while it was still night, his Soul waked him and said to him, "Rise up and go to the room of the merchant, even to the room in which he sleepeth, and slay him, and take from him his gold, for we have need of it."

And the young Fisherman rose up and crept towards the room of the merchant, and over the feet of the merchant there was lying a curved sword, and the tray by the side of the merchant held nine purses of gold. And he reached out his hand and touched the sword, and when he touched it the merchant started and awoke, and leaping up seized himself the sword and cried to the young Fisherman, "Dost thou return evil for good, and pay with the shedding of blood for the kindness that I have shown thee?"

And his Soul said to the young Fisherman, "Strike him," and he struck him so that he swooned, and he seized then the nine purses of gold, and fled hastily through the garden of pomegranates, and set his face to the star that is the star of morning.

And when they had gone a league from the city, the young Fisherman beat his breast, and said to his Soul: "Why didst thou bid me slay the merchant and take his gold? Surely thou art evil."

But his Soul answered him, "Be at peace, be at peace."

"Nay," cried the young Fisherman, "I may not be at peace, for all that thou hast made me to do I hate. Thee also I hate, and I bid thee tell me wherefore thou hast wrought with me in this wise."

And his Soul answered him, "When thou didst send me forth into the world thou gavest me no heart, so I learned to do all these things and love them."

"What sayest thou?" murmured the young Fisherman.

"Thou knowest," answered his Soul; "thou knowest it well. Hast thou forgotten that thou gavest me no heart? I trow not. And so trouble not thyself nor me, but be at peace, for there is no pain that

thou shalt not give away, nor any pleasure that thou shalt not receive."

And when the young Fisherman heard these words he trembled
and said to his Soul, "Nay, but thou art evil, and hast made me
forget my love, and hast tempted me with temptations, and hast set
my feet in the ways of sin."

And his Soul answered him: "Thou hast not forgotten that when
thou didst send me forth into the world thou gavest me no heart.
Come, let us go to another city, and make merry, for we have nine
purses of gold."

But the young Fisherman took the nine purses of gold, and flung
them down, and trampled on them.

"Nay," he cried, "but I will have nought to do with thee, nor
will I journey with thee anywhere, but even as I sent thee away
before, so will I send thee away now, for thou hast wrought me no
good." And he turned his back to the moon, and with the little
knife that had the handle of green viper's skin he strove to cut from
his feet that shadow of the body which is the body of the Soul.

Yet his Soul stirred not from him, nor paid heed to his command,
but said to him: "The spell that the Witch told thee avails thee no
more, for I may not leave thee, nor mayest thou drive me forth.
Once in his life may a man send his Soul away, but he who
receiveth back his Soul must keep it with him forever, and this is his
punishment and his reward."

And the young Fisherman grew pale and clenched his hands and
cried, "She was a false Witch in that she told me not that."

"Nay," answered his Soul, "but she was true to Him she wor-
ships, and whose servant she will be ever."

And when the young Fisherman knew that he could no longer
get rid of his Soul, and that it was an evil Soul and would abide with
him always, he fell upon the ground weeping bitterly.

And when it was day the young Fisherman rose up and said to his
Soul: "I will bind my hands that I may not do thy bidding, and close
my lips that I may not speak thy words, and I will return to the
place where she whom I love has her dwelling. Even to the sea will
I return, and to the little bay where she is wont to sing, and I will
call to her and tell her the evil I have done and the evil thou hast
wrought on me."

And his Soul tempted him and said: "Who is thy love, that thou shouldst return to her? The world has many fairer than she is. There are the dancing-girls of Samaris who dance in the manner of all kinds of birds and beasts. Their feet are painted with henna, and in their hands they have little copper bells. They laugh while they dance, and their laughter is as clear as the laughter of water. Come with me and I will show them to thee. For what is this trouble of thine about the things of sin? Is that which is pleasant to eat not made for the eater? Is there poison in that which is sweet to drink? Trouble not thyself, but come with me to another city. There is a little city hard by in which there is a garden of tulip-trees. And there dwell in this comely garden white peacocks and peacocks that have blue breasts. Their tails when they spread them to the sun are like disks of ivory and like gilt disks. And she who feeds them dances for their pleasure, and sometimes she dances on her hands and at other times she dances with her feet. Her eyes are coloured with stibium, and her nostrils are shaped like the wings of a swallow. From a hook in one of her nostrils hangs a flower that is carved out of a pearl. She laughs while she dances, and the silver rings that are about her ankles tinkle like bells of silver. And so trouble not thyself any more, but come with me to this city."

But the young Fisherman answered not his Soul, but closed his lips with the seal of silence and with a tight cord bound his hands, and journeyed back to the place from which he had come, even to the little bay where his love had been wont to sing. And ever did his Soul tempt him by the way, but he made it no answer, nor would he do any of the wickedness that it sought to make him to do, so great was the power of the love that was within him.

And when he had reached the shore of the sea, he loosed the cord from his hands, and took the seal of silence from his lips, and called to the little Mermaid. But she came not to his call, though he called to her all day long and besought her.

And his Soul mocked him and said: "Surely thou hast but little joy out of thy love. Thou art as one who in time of dearth pours water into a broken vessel. Thou givest away what thou hast, and nought is given to thee in return. It were better for thee to come with me, for I know where the Valley of Pleasure lies, and what things are wrought there."

But the young Fisherman answered not his Soul, but in a cleft of the rock he built himself a house of wattles, and abode there for the space of a year. And every morning he called to the Mermaid, and every noon he called to her again, and at night-time he spake her name. Yet never did she rise out of the sea to meet him, nor in any place of the sea could he find her, though he sought for her in the caves and in the green water, in the pools of the tide and in the wells that are at the bottom of the deep.

And ever did his Soul tempt him with evil, and whisper of terrible things. Yet did it not prevail against him, so great was the power of his love.

And after the year was over, the Soul thought within itself: "I have tempted my master with evil, and his love is stronger than I am. I will tempt him now with good, and it may be that he will come with me."

So he spake to the young Fisherman and said: "I have told thee of the joy of the world, and thou hast turned a deaf ear to me. Suffer me now to tell thee of the world's pain, and it may be that thou wilt hearken. For of a truth pain is the Lord of this world, nor is there anyone who escapes from its net. There be some who lack raiment, and others who lack bread. There be widows who sit in purple, and widows who sit in rags. To and fro over the fens go the lepers, and they are cruel to each other. The beggars go up and down on the highways, and their wallets are empty. Through the streets of the cities walks Famine, and the Plague sits at their gates. Come, let us go forth and mend these things, and make them not to be. Wherefore shouldst thou tarry here calling to thy love, seeing she comes not to thy call? And what is love, that thou shouldst set this high store upon it?"

But the young Fisherman answered it nought, so great was the power of his love. And every morning he called to the Mermaid, and every noon he called to her again, and at night-time he spake her name. Yet never did she rise out of the sea to meet him, nor in any place of the sea could he find her, though he sought for her in the rivers of the sea, and in the valleys that are under the waves in the sea that the night makes purple, and in the sea that the dawn leaves grey.

And after the second year was over, the Soul said to the young Fisherman at night-time, and as he sat in the wattled house alone: "Lo! now I have tempted thee with evil, and I have tempted thee with good, and thy love is stronger than I am. Wherefore will I tempt thee no longer, but I pray thee to suffer me to enter thy heart, that I may be one with thee even as before."

"Surely thou mayest enter," said the young Fisherman, "for in the days when with no heart thou didst go through the world thou must have much suffered."

"Alas!" cried his Soul, "I can find no place of entrance, so compassed about with love is this heart of thine."

"Yet I would that I could help thee," said the young Fisherman.

And as he spake there came a great cry of mourning from the sea, even the cry that men hear when one of the Sea-folk is dead. And the young Fisherman leapt up, and left his wattled house, and ran down to the shore. And the black waves came hurrying to the shore, bearing with them a burden that was whiter than silver. White as the surf it was, and like a flower it tossed on the waves. And the surf took it from the waves, and the foam took it from the surf, and the shore received it, and lying at his feet the young Fisherman saw the body of the little Mermaid. Dead at his feet it was lying.

Weeping as one smitten with pain he flung himself down beside it, and he kissed the cold red of the mouth, and toyed with the wet amber of the hair. He flung himself down beside it on the sand, weeping as one trembling with joy, and in his brown arms he held it to his breast. Cold were the lips, yet he kissed them. Salt was the honey of the hair, yet he tasted it with a bitter joy. He kissed the closed eyelids, and the wild spray that lay upon their cups was less salt than his tears.

And to the dead thing he made confession. Into the shells of its ears he poured the harsh wine of his tale. He put the little hands round his neck, and with his fingers he touched the thin reed of the throat. Bitter, bitter was his joy, and full of strange gladness was his pain.

The black sea came nearer, and the white foam moaned like a leper. With white claws of foam the sea grabbled at the shore. From the palace of the Sea-King came the cry of mourning again, and far out upon the sea the great Tritons blew hoarsely upon their horns.

"Flee away," said his Soul, "for ever doth the sea come nigher, and if thou tarriest it will slay thee. Flee away, for I am afraid, seeing that thy heart is closed against me by reason of the greatness of thy love. Flee away to a place of safety. Surely thou wilt not send me without a heart into another world?"

But the young Fisherman listened not to his Soul, but called on the little Mermaid and said: "Love is better than wisdom, and more precious than riches, and fairer than the feet of the daughters of men. The fires cannot destroy it, nor can the waters quench it. I called on thee at dawn, and thou didst not come to my call. The moon heard thy name, yet hadst thou no heed of me. For evilly had I left thee, and to my own hurt had I wandered away. Yet ever did thy love abide with me, and ever was it strong, nor did aught prevail against it, though I have looked upon evil and looked upon good. And now that thou art dead, surely I will die with thee also."

And his Soul besought him to depart, but he would not, so great was his love. And the sea came nearer, and sought to cover him with its waves, and when he knew that the end was at hand he kissed with mad lips the cold lips of the Mermaid, and the heart that was within him brake. And as through the fulness of his love his heart did break, the Soul found an entrance and entered in, and was one with him even as before. And the sea covered the young Fisherman with its waves.

And in the morning the Priest went forth to bless the sea, for it had been troubled. And with him went the monks and the musicians, and the candle-bearers and the swingers of censers, and a great company.

And when the Priest reached the shore he saw the young Fisherman lying drowned in the surf, and clasped in his arms was the body of the little Mermaid. And he drew back frowning, and having made the sign of the cross, he cried aloud and said: "I will not bless the sea nor anything that is in it. Accursed be the Sea-folk, and accursed be all they who traffic with them. And as for him who for love's sake forsook God, and so lieth here with his leman slain by God's judgment, take up his body and the body of his leman, and bury them in the corner of the Field of the Fullers, and set no mark above them, nor sign of any kind, that none may know the place of their resting. For accursed were they in their lives, and accursed shall they be in their deaths also."

And the people did as he commanded them, and in the corner of the Field of the Fullers, where no sweet herbs grew, they dug a deep pit, and laid the dead things within it.

And when the third year was over, and on a day that was a holy day, the Priest went up to the chapel, that he might show to the people the wounds of the Lord, and speak to them about the wrath of God.

And when he had robed himself with his robes, and entered in and bowed himself before the altar, he saw that the altar was covered with strange flowers that never had been seen before. Strange were they to look at, and of curious beauty, and their beauty troubled him, and their odour was sweet in his nostrils. And he felt glad, and understood not why he was glad.

And after that he had opened the tabernacle, and incensed the monstrance that was in it, and shown the fair wafer to the people, and hid it again behind the veil of veils, he began to speak to the people, desiring to speak to them of the wrath of God. But the beauty of the white flowers troubled him, and their odour was sweet in his nostrils, and there came another word into his lips, and he spake not of the wrath of God, but of the God whose name is Love. And why he so spake, he knew not.

And when he had finished his word the people wept, and the Priest went back to the sacristy, and his eyes were full of tears. And the deacons came in and began to unrobe him, and took from him the alb and the girdle, the maniple and the stole. And he stood as one in a dream.

And after that they had unrobed him, he looked at them and said, "What are the flowers that stand on the altar, and whence do they come?"

And they answered him, "What flowers they are we cannot tell, but they come from the corner of the Fullers' Field." And the Priest trembled, and returned to his own house and prayed.

And in the morning, while it was still dawn, he went forth with the monks and the musicians, and the candle-bearers and the swingers of censers, and a great company, and came to the shore of the sea, and blessed the sea, and all the wild things that are in it. The Fauns also he blessed, and the little things that dance in the woodland, and the bright-eyed things that peer through the leaves. All the things in God's world he blessed, and the people were filled

with joy and wonder. Yet never again in the corner of the Fullers'
Field grew flowers of any kind, but the field remained barren even
as before. Nor came the Sea-folk into the bay as they had been
wont to do, for they went to another part of the sea.

The Up-to-Date Sorcerer

ISAAC ASIMOV

For an author whose literary fame principally rests on science fiction (notably the Foundation *series and the "robot" short stories and novels, including* The Naked Sun, The Robots of Dawn, The Caves of Steel *and* I, Robot) ISAAC ASIMOV *has assayed pure fantasy quite a few times in his illustrious career. In "The Up-to-Date Sorcerer" he indulges his lifelong love of Gilbert and Sullivan in a tale that offers a plausible solution to a problem that puzzles all Gilbertian scholars: why does G&S's third operetta end so unsatisfactorily? (Though it is not absolutely necessary to be familiar with* The Sorcerer *to enjoy Asimov's story, for the curious reader's convenience a précis of the Gilbert and Sullivan operetta is provided in Appendix II, page 522.)*

It always puzzled me that Nicholas Nitely, although a Justice of the Peace, was a bachelor. The atmosphere of his profession, so to speak, seemed so conducive to matrimony that surely he could scarcely avoid the gentle bond of wedlock.

When I said as much over a gin and tonic at the Club recently, he said, "Ah, but I had a narrow escape some time ago," and he sighed.

"Oh, really?"

"A fair young girl, sweet, intelligent, pure yet desperately ardent, and

*withal most alluring to the physical senses for even such an old fogy as
myself."*

I said, "How did you come to let her go?"

*"I had no choice." He smiled gently at me and his smooth, ruddy com-
plexion, his smooth gray hair, his smooth blue eyes, all combined to give him
an expression of near-saintliness. He said, "You see, it was really the fault
of her fiancé—"*

"Ah, she was engaged to someone else."

*"—and of Professor Wellington Johns, who was, although an endocri-
nologist, by way of being an up-to-date sorcerer. In fact, it was just that—"
He sighed, sipped at his drink, and turned on me the bland and cheerful
face of one who is about to change the subject.*

*I said firmly, "Now, then, Nitely, old man, you cannot leave it so. I
want to know about your beautiful girl—the flesh that got away."*

*He winced at the pun (one, I must admit, of my more abominable efforts)
and settled down by ordering his glass refilled. "You understand," he said,
"I learned some of the details later on."*

Professor Wellington Johns had a large and prominent nose, two
sincere eyes and a distinct talent for making clothes appear too
large for him. He said, "My dear children, love is a matter of
chemistry."

His dear children, who were really students of his, and not his
children at all, were named Alexander Dexter and Alice Sanger.
They looked perfectly full of chemicals as they sat there, holding
hands. Together, their age amounted to perhaps 45, evenly split
between them, and Alexander said, fairly inevitably, *"Vive la
chémie!"*

Professor Johns smiled reprovingly, "Or rather endocrinology.
Hormones, after all, affect our emotions and it is not surprising that
one should, specifically, stimulate that feeling we call love."

"But that's so unromantic," murmured Alice. "I'm sure I don't
need any." She looked up at Alexander with a yearning glance.

"My dear," said the professor, "your blood stream was crawling
with it at that moment you, as the saying is, fell in love. Its secretion
had been stimulated by"—for a moment he considered his words
carefully, being a highly moral man—"by some environmental factor involving your young man, and once the hormonal action had

taken place, inertia carried you on. I could duplicate the effect easily."

"Why, Professor," said Alice, with gentle affection. "It would be delightful to have you try," and she squeezed Alexander's hand shyly.

"I do not mean," said the professor, coughing to hide his embarrassment, "that I would personally attempt to reproduce—or, rather, to duplicate the conditions that created the natural secretion of the hormone. I mean, instead, that I could inject the hormone itself by hypodermic or even by oral ingestion, since it is a steroid hormone. I have, you see," and here he removed his glasses and polished them proudly, "isolated and purified the hormone."

Alexander sat erect. "Professor! And you have said nothing?"

"I must know more about it first."

"Do you mean to say," said Alice, her lovely brown eyes shimmering with delight, "that you can make people feel the wonderful delight and heaven-surpassing tenderness of true love by means of a . . . a pill?"

The professor said, "I can indeed duplicate the emotion to which you refer in those rather cloying terms."

"Then why don't you?"

Alexander raised a protesting hand. "Now, darling, your ardor leads you astray. Our own happiness and forthcoming nuptials make you forget certain facts of life. If a married person were, by mistake, to accept this hormone—"

Professor Johns said, with a trace of hauteur, "Let me explain right now that my hormone, or my amatogenic principle, as I call it—" (for he, in common with many practical scientists, enjoyed a proper scorn for the rarefied niceties of classical philology).

"Call it a love-philtre, Professor," said Alice, with a melting sigh.

"My amatogenic cortical principle," said Professor Johns, sternly, "has no affect on married individuals. The hormone cannot work if inhibited by other factors, and being married is certainly a factor that inhibits love."

"Why, so I have heard," said Alexander, gravely, "but I intend to disprove that callous belief in the case of my own Alice."

"Alexander," said Alice. "My love."

The professor said, "I mean that marriage inhibits extra-marital love."

Alexander said, "Why, it has come to my ears that sometimes it does not."

Alice said, shocked, "Alexander!"

"Only in rare instances, my dear, among those who have not gone to college."

The professor said, "Marriage may not inhibit a certain paltry sexual attraction, or tendencies toward minor trifling, but true love, as Miss Sanger expressed the emotion, is something which cannot blossom when the memory of a stern wife and various unattractive children hobbles the subconscious."

"Do you mean to say," said Alexander, "that if you were to feed your love-philtre—beg pardon, your amatogenic principle—to a number of people indiscriminately, only the *un*married individuals would be affected?"

"That is right. I have experimented on certain animals which, though not going through the conscious marriage rite, do form monogamous attachments. Those with the attachments already formed are not affected."

"Then, Professor, I have a perfectly splendid idea. Tomorrow night is the night of the Senior Dance here at college. There will be at least fifty couples present, mostly unmarried. Put your philtre in the punch."

"What? Are you mad?"

But Alice had caught fire. "Why, it's a heavenly idea, Professor. To think that all my friends will feel as I feel! Professor, you would be an angel from heaven. —But oh, Alexander, do you suppose the feelings might be a trifle uncontrolled? Some of our college chums are a little wild and if, in the heat of the discovery of love, they should, well, kiss—"

Professor Johns said, indignantly, "My dear Miss Sanger. You must not allow your imagination to become overheated. My hormone induces only those feelings which lead to marriage and not to the expression of anything that might be considered indecorous."

"I'm sorry," murmured Alice, in confusion. "I should remember, Professor, that you are the most highly moral man I know—excepting always dear Alexander—and that no scientific discovery of yours could possibly lead to immorality."

She looked so woebegone that the professor forgave her at once.

"Then you'll do it, Professor?" urged Alexander. "After all, assuming there will be a sudden urge for mass marriage afterward, I can take care of that by having Nicholas Nitely, an old and valued friend of the family, present on some pretext. He is a Justice of the Peace and can easily arrange for such things as licenses and so on."

"I could scarcely agree," said the professor, obviously weakening, "to perform an experiment without the consent of those experimented upon. It would be unethical."

"But you would be bringing only joy to them. You would be contributing to the moral atmosphere of the college. For surely, in the absence of overwhelming pressure toward marriage, it sometimes happens even in college that the pressure of continuous propinquity breeds a certain danger of—of—"

"Yes, there is that," said the professor. "Well, I shall try a dilute solution. After all, the results may advance scientific knowledge tremendously and, as you say, it will also advance morality."

Alexander said, "And, of course, Alice and I will drink the punch, too."

Alice said, "Oh, Alexander, surely such love as ours needs no artificial aid."

"But it would not be artificial, my soul's own. According to the professor, your love began as a result of just such a hormonal effect, induced, I admit, by more customary methods."

Alice blushed rosily. "But then, my only love, why the need for the repetition?"

"To place us beyond all vicissitudes of Fate, my cherished one."

"Surely, my adored, you don't doubt my love."

"No, my heart's charmer, but—"

"*But?* Is it that you do not trust me, Alexander?"

"Of course I trust you, Alice, but—"

"*But?* Again but!" Alice rose, furious. "If you cannot trust me, sir, perhaps I had better leave—" And she did leave indeed, while the two men stared after her, stunned.

Professor Johns said, "I am afraid my hormone has, quite indirectly, been the occasion of spoiling a marriage rather than of causing one."

Alexander swallowed miserably, but his pride upheld him. "She will come back," he said, hollowly. "A love such as ours is not so easily broken."

· · ·

The Senior Dance was, of course, the event of the year. The young men shone and the young ladies glittered. The music lilted and the dancing feet touched the ground only at intervals. Joy was unrestrained.

Or, rather, it was unrestrained in most cases. Alexander Dexter stood in one corner, eyes hard, expression icily bleak. Straight and handsome he might be, but no young woman approached him. He was known to belong to Alice Sanger, and under such circumstances, no college girl would dream of poaching. —Yet where was Alice?

She had not come with Alexander and Alexander's pride prevented him from searching for her. From under grim eyelids, he could only watch the circulating couples cautiously.

Professor Johns, in formal clothes that did not fit although made to measure, approached him. He said, "I will add my hormone to the punch shortly before the midnight toast. Is Mr. Nitely still here?"

"I saw him a moment ago. In his capacity as chaperone he was busily engaged in making certain that the proper distance between dancing couples was maintained. Four fingers, I believe, at the point of closest approach. Mr. Nitely was most diligently making the necessary measurements."

"Very good. Oh, I had neglected to ask: Is the punch alcoholic? Alcohol would affect the workings of the amatogenic principle adversely."

Alexander, despite his sore heart, found spirit to deny the unintended slur upon his class. "Alcoholic, Professor? This punch is made along those principles firmly adhered to by all young college students. It contains only the purest of fruit juices, refined sugar, and a certain quantity of lemon peel—enough to stimulate but not inebriate."

"Good," said the professor. "Now I have added to the hormone a sedative designed to put our experimental subjects to sleep for a short time while the hormone works. Once they awaken, the first individual each sees—that is, of course, of the opposite sex—will inspire that individual with a pure and noble ardor that can end only in marriage."

Then, since it was nearly midnight, he made his way through the happy couples, all dancing at four-fingers distance, to the punch bowl.

Alexander, depressed nearly to tears, stepped out to the balcony. In doing so, he just missed Alice, who entered the ballroom from the balcony by another door.

"Midnight," called out a happy voice. "Toast! Toast! Toast to the life ahead of us."

They crowded about the punch bowl; the little glasses were passed round.

"To the life ahead of us," they cried out and, with all the enthusiasm of young college students, downed the fiery mixture of pure fruit juices, sugar and lemon peel, with—of course—the professor's sedated amatogenic principle.

As the fumes rose to their brains, they slowly crumpled to the floor.

Alice stood there alone, still holding her drink, eyes wet with unshed tears. "Oh, Alexander, Alexander, though you doubt, yet are you my only love. You wish me to drink and I shall drink." Then she, too, sank gracefully downward.

Nicholas Nitely had gone in search of Alexander, for whom his warm heart was concerned. He had seen him arrive without Alice and he could only assume that a lovers' quarrel had taken place. Nor did he feel any dismay at leaving the party to its own devices. These were not wild youngsters, but college boys and girls of good family and gentle upbringing. They could be trusted to the full to observe the four-finger limit, as he well knew.

He found Alexander on the balcony, staring moodily out at a star-riddled sky.

"Alexander, my boy." He put his hand on the young man's shoulder. "This is not like you. To give way so to depression. Chut, my young friend, chut."

Alexander's head bowed at the sound of the good old man's voice. "It is unmanly, I know, but I yearn for Alice. I have been cruel to her and I am justly treated now. And yet, Mr. Nitely, if you could but know—" He placed his clenched fist on his chest, next his heart. He could say no more.

Nitely said, sorrowfully, "Do you think because I am unmarried that I am unacquainted with the softer emotions? Be undeceived.

Time was when I, too, knew love and heartbreak. But do not do as I did once and allow pride to prevent your reunion. Seek her out, my boy, seek her out and apologize. Do not allow yourself to become a solitary old bachelor such as I, myself. —But, tush, I am puling."

Alexander's back had straightened. "I will be guided by you, Mr. Nitely. I will seek her out."

"Then go on in. For shortly before I came out, I believe I saw her there."

Alexander's heart leaped. "Perhaps she searches for me even now. I will go— But, no. Go you first, Mr. Nitely, while I stay behind to recover myself. I would not have her see me a prey to womanish tears."

"Of course, my boy."

Nitely stopped at the door into the ballroom in astonishment. Had a universal catastrophe struck all low? Fifty couples were lying on the floor, some heaped together most indecorously.

But before he could make up his mind to see if the nearest were dead, to sound the fire alarm, to call the police, to anything, they were rousing and struggling to their feet.

Only one still remained. A lonely girl in white, one arm outstretched gracefully beneath her fair head. It was Alice Sanger and Nitely hastened to her, oblivious to the rising clamor about him.

He sank to his knees. "Miss Sanger. My dear Miss Sanger. Are you hurt?"

She opened her beautiful eyes slowly, and said, "Mr. Nitely! I never realized you were such a vision of loveliness."

"I?" Nitely started back with horror, but she had now risen to her feet and there was a light in her eyes such as Nitely had not seen in a maiden's eyes for thirty years—and then only weakly.

She said, "Mr. Nitely, surely you will not leave me?"

"No, no," said Nitely, confused. "If you need me, I shall stay."

"I need you. I need you with all my heart and soul. I need you as a thirsty flower needs the morning dew. I need you as Thisbe of old needed Pyramus."

Nitely, still backing away, looked about hastily, to see if anyone could be hearing this unusual declaration, but no one seemed to be paying any attention. As nearly as he could make out, the air was filled with other declarations of similar sort, some being even more forceful and direct.

His back was up against a wall, and Alice approached him so closely as to break the four-finger rule to smithereens. She broke, in fact, the no-finger rule, and at the resulting mutual pressure, a certain indefinable something seemed to thud away within Nitely.

"Miss Sanger. Please."

"Miss Sanger? Am I Miss Sanger to you?" exclaimed Alice, passionately. "Mr. Nitely! Nicholas! Make me your Alice, your own. Marry me. Marry me!"

All around there was the cry of "Marry me. Marry me!" and young men and women crowded around Nitely, for they knew well that he was a Justice of the Peace. They cried out, "Marry us, Mr. Nitely. Marry us!"

He could only cry in return, "I must get you all licenses."

They parted to let him leave on that errand of mercy. Only Alice followed him.

Nitely met Alexander at the door of the balcony and turned him back toward the open and fresh air. Professor Johns came at that moment to join them all.

Nitely said, "Alexander. Professor Johns. The most extraordinary thing has occurred—"

"Yes," said the professor, his mild face beaming with joy. "The experiment has been a success. The principle is far more effective on the human being, in fact, than on any of my experimental animals." Noting Nitely's confusion, he explained what had occurred in brief sentences.

Nitely listened and muttered, "Strange, strange. There is a certain elusive familiarity about this." He pressed his forehead with the knuckles of both hands, but it did not help.

Alexander approached Alice gently, yearning to clasp her to his strong bosom, yet knowing that no gently nurtured girl could consent to such an expression of emotion from one who had not yet been forgiven.

He said, "Alice, my lost love, if in your heart you could find—"

But she shrank from him, avoiding his arms though they were outstretched only in supplication. She said, "Alexander, I drank the punch. It was your wish."

"You needn't have. I was wrong, wrong."

"But I did, and oh, Alexander, I can never be yours."

"Never be mine? But what does this mean?"

And Alice, seizing Nitely's arm, clutched it avidly. "My soul is intertwined indissolubly with that of Mr. Nitely, of Nicholas, I mean. My passion for him—that is, my passion for marriage with him—cannot be withstood. It racks my being."

"You are false?" cried Alexander, unbelieving.

"You are cruel to say 'false,' " said Alice, sobbing. "I cannot help it."

"No, indeed," said Professor Johns, who had been listening to this in the greatest consternation, after having made his explanation to Nitely. "She could scarcely help it. It is simply an endocrinological manifestation."

"Indeed that is so," said Nitely, who was struggling with endocrinological manifestations of his own. "There, there, my—my dear." He patted Alice's head in a most fatherly way and when she held her enticing face up toward his, swooningly, he considered whether with her alluring lips pursed most swooningly, he considered whether it might not be a fatherly thing—nay, even a neighborly thing—to press those lips with his own, in pure fashion.

But Alexander, out of his heart's despair, cried, "You are false, false—false as Cressid," and rushed from the room.

And Nitely would have gone after him, but that Alice had seized him about the neck and bestowed upon his slowly melting lips a kiss that was not daughterly in the least.

It was not even neighborly.

They arrived at Nitely's small bachelor cottage with its chaste sign of JUSTICE OF THE PEACE in Old English letters, its air of melancholy peace, its neat serenity, its small stove on which the small kettle was quickly placed by Nitely's left hand (his right arm being firmly in the clutch of Alice who, with a shrewdness beyond her years, chose that as one sure method of rendering impossible a sudden bolt through the door on his part).

Nitely's study could be seen through the open door of the dining room, its walls lined with gentle books of scholarship and joy.

Again Nitely's hand (his left hand) went to his brow. "My dear," he said to Alice, "it is amazing the way—if you would release your hold the merest trifle, my child, so that circulation might be restored—the way in which I persist in imagining that all this has taken place before."

"Surely never before, my dear Nicholas," said Alice, bending her fair head upon his shoulder, and smiling at him with a shy tenderness that made her beauty as bewitching as moonlight upon still waters, "could there have been so wonderful a modern-day magician as our wise Professor Johns, so up-to-date a sorcerer."

"So up-to-date a—" Nitely had started so violently as to lift the fair Alice a full inch from the floor. "Why, surely that must be it. Dickens take me, if that's not it." (For on rare occasions, and under the stress of overpowering emotions, Nitely used strong language.)

"Nicholas. What is it? You frighten me, my cherubic one."

But Nitely walked rapidly into his study, and she was forced to run with him. His face was white, his lips firm, as he reached for a volume from the shelves and reverently blew the dust from it.

"Ah," he said with contrition, "how I have neglected the innocent joys of my younger days. My child, in view of this continuing incapacity of my right arm, would you be so kind as to turn the pages until I tell you to stop?"

Together they managed, in such a tableau of preconnubial bliss as is rarely seen, he holding the book with his left hand, she turning the pages slowly with her right.

"I am right!" Nitely said with sudden force. "Professor Johns, my dear fellow, do come here. This is the most amazing coincidence—a frightening example of the mysterious unfelt power that must sport with us on occasion for some hidden purpose."

Professor Johns, who had prepared his own tea and was sipping it patiently, as befitted a discreet gentleman of intellectual habit in the presence of two ardent lovers who had suddenly retired to the next room, called out, "Surely you do not wish my presence?"

"But I do, sir. I would fain consult one of your scientific attainments."

"But you are in a position—"

Alice screamed faintly, "Professor!"

"A thousand pardons, my dear," said Professor Johns, entering. "My cobwebby old mind is filled with ridiculous fancies. It is long since I—" and he pulled mightily at his tea (which he had made strong) and was himself again at once.

"Professor," said Nitely. "This dear child referred to you as an up-to-date sorcerer and that turned my mind instantly to Gilbert and Sullivan's *The Sorcerer*."

"What," asked Professor Johns, mildly, "are Gilbert and Sullivan?"

Nitely cast a devout glance upward, as though with the intention of gaging the direction of the inevitable thunderbolt and dodging. He said in a hoarse whisper, "Sir William Schwenk Gilbert and Sir Arthur Sullivan wrote, respectively, the words and music of the greatest musical comedies the world has ever seen. One of these is entitled *The Sorcerer*. In it, too, a philtre was used: a highly moral one which did not affect married people, but which did manage to deflect the young heroine away from her handsome young lover and into the arms of an elderly man."

"And," asked Professor Johns, "were matters allowed to remain so?"

"Well, no. —Really, my dear, the movements of your fingers in the region of the nape of my neck, while giving rise to undeniably pleasurably sensations, *do* rather distract me. —There is a reunion of the young lovers, Professor."

"Ah," said Professor Johns. "Then in view of the close resemblance of the fictional plot to real life, perhaps the solution in the play will help point the way to the reunion of Alice and Alexander. At least, I presume you do not wish to go through life with one arm permanently useless."

Alice said, "I have no wish to be reunited. I want only my own Nicholas."

"There is something," said Nitely, "to be said for that refreshing point of view, but tush—youth must be served. There *is* a solution in the play, Professor Johns, and it is for that reason that I most particularly wanted to talk to you." He smiled with a gentle benevolence. "In the play, the effects of the potion were completely neutralized by the actions of the gentleman who administered the potion in the first place: the gentleman in other words, analogous to yourself."

"And those actions were?"

"Suicide! Simply that! In some manner unexplained by the authors, the effect of this suicide was to break the sp—"

But by now Professor Johns had recovered his equilibrium and said in the most sepulchrally forceful tone that could be imagined, "My dear sir, may I state instantly, that, despite my affection for the young persons involved in this sad dilemma, I cannot under any circumstances consent to self-immolation. Such a procedure might be extremely efficacious in connection with love-potions of ordinary vintage, but my amatogenic principle, I assure you, would be completely unaffected by my death."

Nitely sighed. "I feared that. As a matter of fact, between ourselves, it was a very poor ending for the play, perhaps the poorest in the canon," and he looked up briefly in mute apology to the spirit of William S. Gilbert. "It was pulled out of a hat. It had not been properly foreshadowed earlier in the play. It punished an individual who did not deserve the punishment. In short, it was, alas, completely unworthy of Gilbert's powerful genius."

Professor Johns said, "Perhaps it was not Gilbert. Perhaps some bungler had interfered and botched the job."

"There is no record of that."

But Professor Johns, his scientific mind keenly aroused by an unsolved puzzle, said at once, "We can test this. Let us study the mind of this—this Gilbert. He wrote other plays, did he?"

"Fourteen, in collaboration with Sullivan."

"Were there endings that resolved analogous situations in ways which were more appropriate?"

Nitely nodded. "One, certainly. There was *Ruddigore.*"

"Who was he?"

"Ruddigore is a place. The main character is revealed as the true bad baronet of Ruddigore and is, of course, under a curse."

"To be sure," muttered Professor Johns, who realized that such an eventuality frequently befell bad baronets and was even inclined to think it served them right.

Nitely said, "The curse compelled him to commit one crime or more each day. Were one day to pass without a crime, he would inevitably die in agonizing torture."

"How horrible," murmured the soft-hearted Alice.

"Naturally," said Nitely, "no one can think up a crime each day, so our hero was forced to use his ingenuity to circumvent the curse."

"How?"

"He reasoned thus: If he deliberately refused to commit a crime, he was courting death by his own act. In other words, he was attempting suicide, and attempting suicide is, of course, a crime—and so he fulfills the conditions of the curse."

"I see. I see," said Professor Johns. "Gilbert obviously believes in solving matters by carrying them forward to their logical conclusions." He closed his eyes, and his noble brow clearly bulged with the numerous intense thought waves it contained.

He opened them. "Nitely, old chap, when was *The Sorcerer* first produced?"

"In eighteen hundred and seventy-seven."

"Then that is it, my dear fellow. In eighteen seventy-seven, we were faced with the Victorian age. The institution of marriage was not to be made sport of on the stage. It could not be made a comic matter for the sake of the plot. Marriage was holy, spiritual, a sacrament—"

"Enough," said Nitely, "of this apostrophe. What is in your mind?"

"Marriage. Marry the girl, Nitely. Have all your couples marry, and that at once. I'm sure that was Gilbert's original intention."

"But that," said Nitely, who was strangely attracted by the notion, "is precisely what we are trying to avoid."

"I am not," said Alice, stoutly (though she was not stout, but, on the contrary, enchantingly lithe and slender).

Professor Johns said, "Don't you see? Once each couple is married, the amatogenic principle—which does not affect married people—loses its power over them. Those who would have been in love without the aid of the principle remain in love; those who would not, are no longer in love—and consequently apply for an annulment."

"Good heavens," said Nitely. "How admirably simple. Of course! Gilbert must have intended that until a shocked producer or theater manager—a bungler, as you say—forced the change."

"And did it work?" I asked. "After all, you said quite distinctly that the professor had said its effect on married couples was only to inhibit extra-marital re—"

"It worked," said Nitely, ignoring my comment. A tear trembled on his eyelid, but whether it was induced by memories or by the fact that he was on his fourth gin and tonic, I could not tell.

"It worked," he said. "Alice and I were married, and our marriage was almost instantly annulled by mutual consent on the grounds of the use of undue pressure. And yet, because of the incessant chaperoning to which we were subjected, the incidence of undue pressure between ourselves was, unfortunately, virtually nil." He sighed again. "At any rate, Alice and Alexander were married soon after and she is now, I understand, as a result of various concomitant events, expecting a child."

He withdrew his eyes from the deep recesses of what was left of his drink and gasped with sudden alarm. "Dear me! She again."

I looked up, startled. A vision in pastel blue was in the doorway. Imagine, if you will, a charming face made for kissing; a lovely body, made for loving.

She called, "Nicholas! Wait!"

"Is that Alice?" I asked.

"No, no. This is someone else entirely: a completely different story. —But I must not remain here."

He rose and, with an agility remarkable in one so advanced in years and weight, made his way through a window. The feminine vision of desirability, with an agility only slightly less remarkable, followed.

I shook my head in pity and sympathy. Obviously, the poor man was continually plagued by these wondrous things of beauty who, for one reason or another, were enamored of him. At the thought of this horrible fate, I downed my own drink at a gulp and considered the odd fact that no such difficulties had ever troubled me.

And at that thought, strange to tell, I ordered another drink savagely, and a scatological exclamation rose, unbidden, to my lips.

Emma's Daughter

ALAN RODGERS

ALAN RODGERS, *recent short-story winner of the coveted* World Fantasy Award, *is one of the finest writers and worst poker players I have the privilege of knowing. Formerly on the editorial staff of* Twilight Zone *magazine, Alan was editor of the excellent but short-lived terror periodical* Night Cry. *"Emma's Daughter" appeared in the Fall 1988 issue of the newly revived* Weird Tales *magazine. It is characterized by a form of vivid horror effect that most genre writers abuse, but I feel Alan renders it palatable by carefully combining shock with compassion. Nevertheless, the reader is warned: "Emma's Daughter" is not for queasy stomachs.*

Emma went drinking the night after the cancer finally got done with her daughter Lisa. Lisa was eight, and she'd died long and hard and painful, and when she was finally gone what Emma needed more than anything else was to forget, at least for a night.

The bar Emma went to was a dirty place called the San Juan Tavern; she sometimes spent nights there with her friends. It was only four blocks from home—two blocks in another direction from the hospital where Lisa died. A lot of people who lived around where Emma did drank at the San Juan.

It made her feel dirty to be drinking the night after her daughter died. She thought a couple of times about stopping, paying up her bill, and going home and going to sleep like someone who had a little decency. Instead she lit cigarettes, smoked them hard until they almost burned her lips. She didn't usually smoke, but lately she felt like she needed it, and she'd been smoking a lot.

The cigarettes didn't help much, and neither did the wine. When she was halfway through her third tumbler of something that was cheap and chalky and red, Mama Estrella Perez sat down across from her and clomped her can of Budweiser onto the Formica table top. Emma expected the can to fall over and spill. It didn't, though —it just tottered back and forth a couple of times and then was still.

Mama Estrella ran the *bodega* downstairs from Emma's apartment. She was Emma's landlord, too—she owned the building. Her *bodega* wasn't like most of them; it was big and clean and well lit, and there was a big *botánica* in the back, shelves and shelves of *santería* things, love potions and strange waters and things she couldn't figure out because she couldn't read Spanish very well. Emma always thought it was cute, but then she found out that *santería* was Cuban voodoo, and she didn't like it so much.

"Your daughter died today," Mama Estrella said. "Why're you out drinking? Why aren't you home, mourning?" Her tone made Emma feel as cheap and dirty as a streetwalker.

Emma shrugged. She knocked back the rest of her glass of wine and refilled it from the bottle the bartender had left for her.

Mama Estrella shook her head and finished off her beer; someone brought her another can before she even asked. She stared at Emma. Emma kept her seat, held her ground. But after a few minutes the taste of the wine began to sour in her throat, and she wanted to cry. She knew the feeling wasn't Mama Estrella's doing, even if Mama was some sort of a voodoo woman. It was nothing but Emma's own guilt, coming to get her.

"Mama, my baby *died* today. She died a little bit at a time for six months, with a tumor that finally got to be the size of a grapefruit growing in her belly, almost looking like a child that was going to kill her before it got born." She caught her breath. "I want to drink enough that I don't see her dying like that, at least not tonight."

Mama Estrella was a lot less belligerent looking after that. Ten minutes later she took a long drink from her beer and said, "You okay, Emma." Emma poured herself some more wine, and someone brought Mama Estrella a pitcher of beer, and they sat drinking together, not talking, for a couple of hours.

About 1:00 A.M. Mama Estrella got a light in her eye, and for just an instant, just long enough to take a breath and let it out, Emma got a bad feeling. But she'd drunk too much by that point to feel bad about anything for long, so she leaned forward and whispered in her conspiracy-whisper, "What's that, Mama Estrella? What're you thinking?"

Mama Estrella sprayed her words a little. "I just thought: hey, you want your baby back? You miss her? I could bring her back, make her alive again. Sort of." She was drunk, even drunker than Emma was. "You know what a zombie is? A zombie isn't a live little girl, but it's like one. It moves. It walks. It breathes if you tell it to. I can't make your baby alive, but I can make what's left of her go away more slowly."

Emma thought about that. She knew what a zombie was—she'd seen movies on television, even once something silly and disgusting at the theater. And she thought about her little Lisa, her baby, whimpering in pain in her sleep every night. For a minute she started to think that she couldn't stand to see her baby hurting like that, even if she would be dead as some crud-skinned thing in a theater. Anything had to be better, even Lisa being completely dead. But after a moment Emma knew that just wasn't so; life was being alive and having to get up every morning and push hard against the world. And no matter how bad life was, even half-life was better than not being alive at all.

Emma started to cry, or her eyes did. They kept filling up with tears even though she kept trying for them not to. "I love my baby, Mama Estrella," she said. It was all she *could* say.

Mama Estrella looked grim. She nodded, picked up her beer, and poured most of it down her throat. "We go to the hospital," she said. "Get your Lisa and bring her home." She stood up. Emma took one last swallow of her wine and got up to follow.

It was hot outside. Emma was sure it was going to be a hot summer; here it was only May and the temperature was high in the eighties at midnight.

The moon was out, and it was bright and full overhead. Usually the moon looked pale and washed out because of the light the city reflected into the sky. But tonight somehow the city was blacker than it should be, and the moon looked full and bright as bone china on a black cloth.

They walked two blocks to the hospital, and when they got to the service door Mama Estrella told Emma to wait and she'd go in and get Lisa.

Mama left her there for twenty minutes. Twice men came out of the door carrying red plastic bags of garbage from the hospital. It was infected stuff in the red bags; dangerous stuff. Emma knew because her job was cleaning patients' rooms in another hospital in another part of the city.

After ten minutes Emma heard a siren, and she thought for a moment that somehow she and Mama Estrella had been found out and that the police were coming for them. But that was silly; there were always sirens going off in this part of the city. It could even have been the alarm on someone's car—some of them sounded just like that.

Then both sides of the door swung open at once, and Mama Estrella came out of the hospital carrying poor dead little Lisa in her arms. Emma saw her daughter's too-pale skin with the veins showing through and the death-white haze that colored the eyes, and her heart skipped a beat. She shut her eyes for a moment and set her teeth and forced herself to think about Lisa at the picnic they had for her birthday when she was five. They'd found a spot in the middle of Prospect Park and set up a charcoal grill, and Lisa had run off into the trees, but she didn't go far enough that Emma had to worry about keeping an eye on her. Just before the hamburgers were ready Lisa came back with a handful of pine straw and an inchworm crawling around on the ends of the needles. She was so excited you'd think she'd found the secret of the world, and Emma got behind her and looked at the bug and the needles from over Lisa's shoulder, and for just a moment she'd thought that Lisa was right, and that the bug and the needles *were* the secret of the world.

Emma forced her jaw to relax and opened her eyes. Lisa was special. No matter what happened to Lisa, no matter what Lisa was, Emma loved the girl with all her heart and soul. She loved Lisa enough that she didn't let it hurt, even when her eye caught on Lisa's midriff and she saw the cancer that made it look like she had a baby in her belly. Emma felt a chill in spite of her resolve; there was something strange about the cancer, something stranger than just death and decay. It frightened her.

"You okay, Emma?" Mama Estrella asked. She looked a little worried.

Emma nodded. "I'm fine, Mama. I'm just fine." When she heard her own voice she realized that she really was fine.

"We need to get to my car," Mama Estrella said. "We need to go to the graveyard." Mama kept her car in a parking garage around the corner from the San Juan Tavern.

"I thought we were just going to take her home," Emma said.

Mama Estrella didn't answer; she just shook her head.

Emma took Lisa from Mama Estrella's arms and carried the body to the garage. She let the head rest on her shoulder, just as though Lisa were only asleep instead of dead. When they got to Mama's car she laid Lisa out on the back seat. She found a blanket on the floor of the car and by reflex she covered the girl to keep her from catching cold.

The drive to the cemetery only took a few minutes, even though Mama Estrella drove carefully, almost timidly. When she came to stop signs she didn't just slow down and check for traffic; she actually stopped. But the only things she had to use her brakes for *were* the stop signs. Somehow the traffic lights always favored her, and whichever street she chose to turn on was already clear of traffic for blocks in either direction.

There was no one minding the gate at the cemetery, so when they got there they just drove through like they were supposed to be there. The full-bright moon was even brighter here, where there were no street lights; it made the whole place even more strange and unearthly than it was by nature.

Mama Estrella drove what felt like half a mile through the cemetery's twisting access roads, and then pulled over in front of a stand of trees. "Are there others coming, Mama? Don't you need a lot of people to have a ceremony?"

Mama Estrella shook her head again and lifted a beer from a bag on the floor of the car that Emma hadn't seen before. She opened the can and took a long pull out of it.

"You wait here until I call you, Emma," she said. She got out of the car, lifted Lisa out of the back, and carried her off into the graveyard.

After a while Emma noticed that Mama'd started a fire on top of someone's grave. She made noise, too—chanting and banging on things and other sounds Emma couldn't identify. Then she heard the sound of an infant screaming, and she couldn't help herself anymore. She got out of the car and started running toward the fire.

Not that she really thought it was her Lisa. Lisa had never screamed as a baby, and if she had she wouldn't have sounded like that. But Emma didn't want the death of someone else's child on her conscience, or on Lisa's.

By the time Emma got to the grave where Mama Estrella had started the fire, it looked like she was already finished. Emma didn't see any babies. Mama looked annoyed.

"I thought I heard a baby screaming," Emma said.

"You shouldn't be here," Mama Estrella said. She stepped away from Lisa for a moment, looking for something on the ground by the fire, and Emma got a look at her daughter. Lisa's eyes were open, but she wasn't breathing. After a moment, though, she blinked, and Emma felt her heart lurch. *Lisa. Alive.* Emma wanted to cry. She wanted to pray. She wanted to sing. But something in her heart told her that Lisa was all empty inside—that her body was just pretending to be alive. But her heart wouldn't let her stop pacing through the steps, either; it wouldn't let her back away without showing, one last time, how much she loved her baby. Emma ran to Lisa and grabbed her up in her arms and sang in her cold-dead ear. *"Lisa, Lisa, my darling baby Lisa."* When her lips touched Lisa's ear it felt like butchered meat. But there were tears all over Emma's face, and they fell off her cheeks onto Lisa's.

Then, after a moment, Lisa started to hug Emma back, and she said "Mommy," in a voice that sounded like dry paper brushing against itself.

Emma heard Mama Estrella gasp behind her, and looked up to see her standing over the fire, trembling a little. When she saw Emma looking at her, she said, "Something's inside her."

Emma shook her head. "Nothing's inside Lisa but Lisa." Emma was sure. A mother *knew* these things. "She's just as alive as she always was."

Mama Estrella scowled. "She shouldn't be alive at all. Her body's dead. If something happened to it . . . *God,* Emma. Her soul could die forever."

"What do you mean?"

"Emma . . . you were hurt so bad. I thought . . . if I could make Lisa's body pretend to be alive for a while it would help you. I could make a zombie from her body. A zombie isn't a daughter, but it's like one, only empty. But if her soul is inside the zombie, it could be trapped there forever. It could wither and die inside her."

Emma felt herself flush. "You're not going to touch my baby, Mama Estrella. I don't know what you're thinking, but you're not going to touch my baby."

Mama Estrella just stood there, gaping. Emma thought she was going to say something, but she didn't.

After a moment Emma took Lisa's hand and said, "Come on, child," and she led Lisa off into the graveyard, toward home. There were a few tall buildings in another part of the city that she could see even from here, and she used the sight of them to guide her. It only took a few minutes to get out of the cemetery, and half an hour after that to get home. She carried Lisa most of the way, even though the girl never complained. Emma didn't want her walking that far in nothing but her bare feet.

When they got home, Emma put Lisa to bed, even though she didn't seem tired. It was long past her bedtime, and God knew it was necessary to at least keep up the pretense that life was normal.

Twenty minutes after that, she went to bed herself.

Emma woke early in the morning, feeling fine. She went out to the corner before she was completely awake and bought herself a paper. When she got back she made herself toast and coffee and sipped and ate and settled down with the news. As she'd got older she'd found herself waking earlier and earlier, and now there was time for coffee and the paper most mornings before she went to work. It was one of her favorite things.

She let Lisa sleep in; there was no sense waking her this early. She kept expecting Mama Estrella to call; she'd really expected her to call last night before she went to sleep. All night she dreamed the sound of telephones ringing, but every time she woke to answer them the bells stopped. After a while she realized that the real telephone wasn't ringing at all, and the rest of the night she heard the bells as some strange sort of music. The music hadn't bothered her sleep at all.

At 9:00 she decided it was late enough to wake Lisa up, so she folded her newspaper, set it on the windowsill, and went to her daughter's bedroom. She opened the door quietly, because she didn't want Lisa to wake to a sound like the creaking of a door on her first day back at home. Lisa was lying in bed resting with her eyes closed—probably asleep, Emma thought, but she wasn't sure. The girl lay so still that Emma almost started to worry about her, until her lips mumbled something without making any sound and she rolled over onto her side. In that instant before Emma went into the room, as she stood watching through the half-open door, she thought Lisa was the most beautiful and adorable thing in the world.

Then she finished opening the door, took a step into the room, took a breath, and *smelled* her.

The smell was like meat left to sit in the sun for days—the smell it has after it's turned gray-brown-green, but before it starts to liquefy. Somewhere behind that was the sulphury smell that'd permeated Lisa's waste and her breath—and after a while even her skin—since a little while after the doctors found the cancer in her.

Emma's breakfast, all acidy and burning, tried to lurch up her throat. Before she knew what she was thinking she was looking at Lisa and seeing something that wasn't her daughter at all—it was some *dead* thing. And who gave a good goddamn what sort of spirit was inside? The thing was disgusting, it was putrefied. It wasn't fit for decent folks to keep in their homes.

Then Emma stopped herself, and she felt herself pale, as though all the blood rushed out of her at once. She felt ashamed. Lisa was Lisa, damn it, and no matter what was wrong with her she was still Emma's baby. And whatever else was going on, no matter how weird and incomprehensible things got, Emma *knew* that Lisa was the same Lisa she'd been before she died.

She tiptoed over to her daughter's bed, and she hugged her good morning—and the smell, strong as it was, was just Lisa's smell.

Which was all right.

"Did you sleep well, baby?" Emma asked. She gave Lisa a peck on the cheek and stepped back to take a look at her. There was a gray cast, or maybe it was blue, underneath the darkness of her skin. That worried Emma. Even just before the cancer killed her Lisa hadn't looked that bad. Emma pulled away the sheets to get a better look at her, and it almost seemed that the tumor in Lisa's belly was bigger than it had been. Emma shuddered, and her head spun. There was something about that cancer that wasn't natural. She couldn't stop herself from staring at it.

"I guess I slept okay," Lisa said. Her voice sounded dry and powdery.

Emma shook her head. "What do you mean, you guess? Don't you know how well you slept?"

Lisa was looking down at her belly now, too. "It's getting bigger, Mommy." She reached down and touched it. "I mean about sleeping that I guess I'm not sure if I was asleep. I rested pretty good, though."

Emma sighed. "Let's get some breakfast into you. Come on, out of that bed."

Lisa sat up. "I'm not hungry, though."

"You've got to eat anyway. It's good for you."

Lisa stood up, took a couple of steps, and faltered. "My feet feel funny, Mommy," she said.

Emma was halfway to the kitchen. "We'll take a good look at your feet after breakfast. First you've got to eat." In the kitchen she broke two eggs into a bowl and scrambled them, poured them into a pan she'd left heating on the stove. While they cooked she made toast and buttered it.

Mama Estrella finally called just after Emma set the plate in front of Lisa. Emma rushed to the phone before the bell could ring a second time; she hated the sound of that bell. It was too loud. She wished there was a way to set it quieter.

"Emma," Mama Estrella said, "your baby could die forever."

Emma took the phone into the living room and closed the door as much as she could without damaging the cord. When she finally responded her voice was even angrier than she meant it to be. "You stay away from Lisa, Mama Estrella Perez. My Lisa's just fine, she's going to be okay, and I don't want you going near her. Do you understand me?"

Mama sighed. "When you make a zombie," she said, "when you make a real one from someone dead, I mean, you can make it move. You can even make it understand enough to do what you say. But still the body starts to rot away. It doesn't matter usually. When a zombie is gone it's gone. What's the harm? But your Lisa is inside that zombie. When the flesh rots away she'll be trapped in the bones. And we won't ever get her out."

Emma felt all cold inside. For three long moments she almost believed her. But she was strong enough inside—she had *faith* enough inside—to deny what she didn't want to believe.

"Don't you say things like that about my Lisa, Mama Estrella," she said. "My Lisa's *alive,* and I won't have you speaking evil of her." She *knew* Lisa was alive, she was certain of it. But she didn't think she could stand to hear anything else, so she opened the door and slammed down the phone before Mama Estrella could say it.

Lisa was almost done with her eggs, and she'd finished half the toast. "What's the matter with Mama Estrella, Mommy?" she asked.

Emma poured herself another cup of coffee and sat down at the table across from Lisa. She didn't want to answer that question. She didn't even want to *think* about it. But she had to—she couldn't just ignore it—so she finally said, "She thinks there's something wrong with you, Lisa."

"You mean because I was dead for a while?"

Emma nodded, and Lisa didn't say anything for a minute or two. Then she asked, "Mommy, is it wrong for me to be alive again after I was dead?"

Emma had to think about that. The question *hurt.* When she realized what the answer was it didn't bother her to say it. "Baby, I don't think God would have let you be alive if it wasn't right. Being alive even once is a miracle, and God doesn't make miracles that are evil."

Lisa nodded like she didn't really understand. But she didn't ask about it anymore. She took another bite of her toast. "This food tastes funny, Mommy. Do I have to eat it all?"

She'd eaten most of it, anyway, and Emma didn't like to force her to eat. "No, sugar, you don't have to eat it all. Come on in the den and let me see those feet you said were bothering you."

She had Lisa sit with her feet stretched out across the couch so she could take her time looking at them without throwing the girl off balance. "What do they feel like, baby? What do you think is the matter with them?"

"I don't know, Mommy. They just feel strange."

Emma peeled back one of the socks she'd made Lisa put on last night before she put her to bed. There wasn't anything especially wrong with her ankle, except for the way it felt so cold in her hands. But when she tried to pull the sock off over Lisa's foot, it stuck. Emma felt her stomach turning on her again. She pulled hard, because she knew she had to get it over with. She expected the sock to pull away an enormous scab, but it didn't. Just the opposite. Big blue fluffs of sock fuzz stuck to the . . . *thing* that had been Lisa's foot.

No. That wasn't so. It *was* Lisa's foot, and Emma loved it, just like she loved Lisa. Lisa's foot wasn't any *thing*. Even if it was all scabrous and patchy, with dried raw flesh poking through in places as though it just didn't have the blood inside to bleed anymore.

Nothing was torn or ripped or mangled, though Emma's first impulse when she saw the skin was to think that something violent had happened. But it wasn't that at all; except for the blood, the foot almost looked as though it'd worn thin, like the leather on an old shoe.

What caused this? Emma wondered. Just the walk home last night? She shuddered.

She peeled away the other sock, and that one was a little worse.

Emma felt an awful panic to *do* something about Lisa's feet. But what could she do? She didn't want to use anything like a disinfectant. God only knew what a disinfectant would do to a dead person who was alive. Bandages would probably only encourage the raw places to fester. She could pray, maybe. Pray that Lisa's feet would heal up, even though everything inside the girl that could heal or rebuild her was dead, and likely to stay that way.

Emma touched the scabby part with her right hand. It was hard and rough and solid, like pumice, and it went deep into her foot like a rock into dirt. It'd probably wear away quickly if she walked on it out on the street. But it was strong enough that walking around here in the house probably wouldn't do any harm. That was a relief; for a moment she'd thought the scab was all soft and pus-y and crumbly, too soft to walk on at all. Emma thought of the worn-old tires on her father's Rambler (it was a miracle that the car still ran; it'd been fifteen years at least since the car company even made Ramblers). The tread on the Rambler's tires was thin; you could see the threads showing through if you knew where to look. It made her shudder. She didn't want her Lisa wearing away like an old tire.

Mama Estrella was right about that, and Emma didn't want to admit it to herself. Lisa wasn't going to get any better. But Emma knew something else, too: things can last near forever if you take the right care of them. Let Mama Estrella be scared. Emma didn't care. The girl was alive, and the important part was what Emma had realized when Lisa asked: even being alive once is a miracle. Emma wasn't going to be someone who wasted miracles when they came to her.

Not even if the miracle made her hurt so bad inside that she wanted to die, like it did later on that day when she and Lisa were sitting in the living room watching TV. It was a doctor show—even while they watched it Emma wasn't quite sure which one it was— and it got her thinking about how tomorrow was Wednesday and she'd have to go back to the hospital where she cleaned patients' rooms for a living. She'd taken a leave of absence while Lisa was in the hospital, and now she realized that she didn't want to go back. She was afraid to leave Lisa alone, afraid something might happen. But what could she do? She had to work; she had to pay the rent. Even taking off as much as she had bled away her savings.

"Lisa," she said, "if anybody knocks on that door while I'm gone at work, you don't answer it. You hear?"

Lisa turned away from the TV and nodded absently. "Yes, Mommy," she said. She didn't look well, and that made Emma hurt some. Even after all those months with the cancer, Emma had never got to be easy or comfortable with the idea of Lisa being sick.

"Come over here and give me a hug, Lisa."

Lisa got out of her seat, climbed onto Emma's lap, and put her arms around her. She buried her face in her mother's breast and hugged, hard, too hard, really. She was much stronger than Emma'd realized; stronger than she'd been before she got sick. The hug was like a full-grown man being too rough, or stronger, maybe.

Emma patted her on the back. "Be gentle, honey," she said, "you're hurting me."

Lisa eased away. "Sorry, Mommy," she said. She looked down, as though she was embarrassed, or maybe even a little bit ashamed. Emma looked in the same direction reflexively, too, to see what Lisa was looking at.

Which wasn't anything at all, of course. But when Emma looked down what she saw was the thing in Lisa's belly, the tumor. It had grown, again: it looked noticeably bigger than it had this morning. Emma touched it with her left hand, and she felt a strange, electric thrill.

She wondered what was happening inside Lisa's body. She wanted to believe that it was something like trapped gas, or even that she was only imagining it was larger.

She probed it with her fingers.

"Does this hurt, Lisa?" she asked. "Does it feel kind of strange?"

"No, Mommy, it doesn't feel like anything at all anymore."

The thing was hard, solid, and strangely lumpy. When she touched it on a hollow spot near the top, it started to throb.

Emma snatched her hand away, afraid that she'd somehow waked up something horrible. But it was too late; something *was* wrong. The thing pulsed faster and faster. After a moment the quivering became almost violent. It reminded Emma of an epileptic at the hospital who'd had a seizure while she was cleaning his room.

"Lisa, are you okay?" Emma asked. Lisa's mouth moved, but no sound came out. Her chest and abdomen started heaving, and choking sounds came from her throat.

The first little bit just dribbled out around the corners of Lisa's mouth. Then she heaved again, more explosively, and the mass of it caught Emma square on the throat. Two big wads of decayed egg spattered on her face, and suddenly Lisa was vomiting out everything Emma had fed her for breakfast. Emma recognized the eggs and toast; they hadn't changed much. They were hardly even wet. The only thing that seemed changed at all about them, in fact, was the smell. They smelled horrible, worse than horrible. Like dead people fermenting in the bottom of a septic tank for years.

"Mommy," Lisa said. It almost sounded like she was pleading. Then she heaved again. But there wasn't much for her stomach to expel, just some chewed egg and bread colored with bile and drippy with phlegm. Lisa bent over the rug and coughed it out. "Mommy," she said again, "I think maybe I shouldn't eat anymore."

Emma nodded and lifted her daughter in her arms. She carried her to the bathroom, where she washed them both off.

[2]

And Emma *didn't* make Lisa eat again, except that she gave the girl a glass of water a couple of times when she seemed to feel dry. It didn't seem to do her any harm not to eat. She never got hungry. Not even once.

Emma went back to work, and that went well enough.

For two months—through the end of May, all of June, and most of July—Emma and Lisa lived quietly and happily, in spite of the circumstances. After a day or two Emma really did get used to Lisa looking and smelling like she was a dead thing. It was kind of wonderful, in a way: Lisa wasn't suffering at all, and the cancer was gone. Or at least it wasn't killing her anymore. She wasn't hurting in any way Emma could see, anyway. Maybe she was uncomfortable sometimes, but it wasn't giving her pain.

The summer turned out to be as hot and rainy and humid as Emma could have imagined, and because it was so warm and wet Lisa's body decayed even faster than Emma had feared it would. After a while the smell of it got hard to ignore again. The evil thing in her belly, the cancer, kept growing, too. By the end of July it was almost the size of a football, and Lisa really did look like a miniature pregnant lady come to term.

It was the last Friday in July when Emma noticed that Lisa's skin was beginning to crack away. She'd just finished getting into her uniform, and she went in to give Lisa a kiss goodbye before she left for work. Lisa smiled and Emma bent over and gave her a peck on the cheek. Her skin felt cold and squishy-moist on Emma's lips, and it left a flavor on them almost like cured meat. Emma was used to that. It didn't bother her so much.

She stood up to take one last look at Lisa before she headed off, and that's when she noticed the crow's-feet. That's what they looked like. Crow's-feet: the little wrinkle lines that older people get in the corners of their eyes.

But Lisa's weren't wrinkles at all. Emma looked close at them and saw that the skin and flesh at the corners of her eyes was actually cracked and split away from itself. When she looked hard she thought she could see the bone underneath.

She put her arms around Lisa and lifted her up a little. "Oh,

baby," she said. She wanted to cry. She'd known this was coming—
it had to. Emma knew about decay. She knew why people tanned
leather. The problem was she couldn't just take her little girl to a
tannery and get her preserved, even if she was dead.

If Lisa's flesh was beginning to peel away from her bones, then
the end had to be starting. Emma'd hoped that Lisa would last
longer than this. There was a miracle coming. Emma was sure of
that. Or she thought she was. Why would God let her daughter be
alive again if she was going to rot away to nothing? Emma wasn't
somebody who went to church every Sunday. Even this summer,
when church seemed more important than it usually did, Emma'd
only been to services a couple of times. But she believed in God.
She had faith. And that was what was important, if you asked her.

Someone knocked on the outer door of the apartment.

That shouldn't be, Emma thought. The only way into the building
was through the front door downstairs, and that was always locked.
You had to have a key or have someone buzz you in. Maybe it was
someone who lived in the building, or maybe Mama Estrella.

Whoever it was knocked again, and harder this time. Hard
enough that Emma heard the door shake in its frame. She could just
picture bubbles of caked paint on the door threatening to flake off.
She set Lisa down and hurried to answer it.

When she got to the door, she hesitated. "Who's there?" she
asked.

No one answered for a long moment, and then a man with a
harsh voice said, "Police, ma'am. We need to speak to you."

Emma swallowed nervously. The police had always frightened
her, ever since she was a child. Not that she had anything to be
afraid of. She hadn't done anything wrong.

She opened the door about halfway and looked at them. They
were both tall, and one of them was white. The other one was East
Indian, or maybe Hispanic, and he didn't look friendly at all.

Emma swallowed again. "How can I help you?" she asked, trying
not to sound nervous. It didn't help much; she could hear the
tremor in her voice.

"We've had complaints from your neighbors about a smell coming from your apartment," the dark-skinned one said. He didn't
have an accent, and he didn't sound anywhere near as mean as he
looked.

"Smell?" Emma asked. She said it before she even thought about it, and as soon as she did she knew it was the wrong thing to do. But she really had forgotten about it. Sure, it was pretty bad, but the only time she really noticed it was when she first got home from work in the evening.

"Lady, it smells like something died in there," the white one said. He was the one with the harsh voice. "Do you mind if we step in and take a look around?"

Emma felt as though all her blood drained away at once. For a moment she couldn't speak.

That was a bad thing, too, because it made the policemen even more suspicious. "We don't have a search warrant, ma'am," the dark one said, "but we can get one in twenty minutes if we have to. It's better if you let us see."

"No," Emma said. "No, I'm sorry, I didn't understand. I'll show you my daughter."

She let the door fall open the rest of the way and led the policemen to Lisa's bedroom. Just before she got there she paused and turned to speak to the dark-skinned man. "Be quiet. She may have fallen back asleep."

But Lisa wasn't asleep, she was sitting up in bed in her nightgown, staring out her open window into the sunshine. For the first time in a month Emma looked at her daughter with a fresh eye, *saw* her instead of just noting the little changes that came from day to day. She didn't look good at all. Her dark skin had a blue-yellow cast to it, a lot like the color of a deep bruise. And there was a texture about it that was *wrong;* it was wrinkled and saggy in some places and smooth and pasty in others.

"She has a horrible disease," Emma whispered to the policemen. "I've been nursing her at home myself these last few months." Lisa turned and looked at them. "These two policemen wanted to meet you, Lisa," Emma said. She read their badges quickly. "This is Officer Gutierrez and his partner, Officer Smith."

Lisa nodded and smiled. It didn't look very pretty. She said, "Hello. Is something wrong?" Her voice was scratchy and vague and hard to understand. "On TV the policemen are usually there because something's wrong."

The dark-skinned policeman, Gutierrez, answered her. "No, Lisa, nothing's wrong. We just came by to meet you." He smiled grimly, as though it hurt, and turned to Emma. "Thank you, ma'am. I think we should be on our way now." Emma pursed her lips and nodded, and showed them to the door.

Before she went to work she came back to say goodbye to Lisa again. She walked back into the hot, sunny room, kissed her daughter on the cheek, and gave her hand a little squeeze.

When Emma took her hand away she saw that three of Lisa's fingernails had come off in her palm.

Lisa wasn't in her bedroom that night when Emma got home. Emma thought at first that the girl might be in the living room, watching TV.

She wasn't. She couldn't have been: Emma would have heard the sound from it if she was.

Emma looked everywhere—the dining room (it was more of an alcove, really), the kitchen, even Emma's own bedroom. Lisa wasn't in any of them. After a few minutes Emma began to panic; she went back to Lisa's room and looked out the window. Had the girl gone crazy, maybe, and jumped out of it? There wasn't any sign of her on the sidewalk down below. Lisa wasn't in any shape to make a jump like that and walk away from it. At least not without leaving something behind.

Then Emma heard a noise come from Lisa's closet. She turned to see it, expecting God knew what, and she heard Lisa's voice: "Mommy . . . ? Is that you, Mommy?" The closet door swung open and Lisa's face peeked out between the clothes.

"Lisa? What are you doing in that closet, child? Get yourself out of there! You almost scared me to death—I almost thought someone had stolen you away."

"I had to hide, Mommy. A bunch of people came in to the house while you were gone. I think they were looking for me. They even looked in here, but not careful enough to see me in the corner behind all the coats."

Emma felt her blood pressing hard against her cheeks and around the sockets of her eyes. "Who? Who was here?"

"I didn't know most of them, Mommy. Mama Estrella was with them. She opened up the door with her key and let them in."

Emma fumed; she clenched her teeth and hissed a sigh out between them. She reached into the closet and grabbed Lisa's hand.

"You come with me. We're going to get some new locks for this place and keep *all* those people out. And then I'm going to have words with that witch."

Emma's arm jarred loose a double handful of hangers that didn't have clothes on them, and hangers went flying everywhere. Seven or eight of them hooked into each other almost like a chain, and one end of the chain latched into the breast pocket of Lisa's old canvas army jacket, which hung from a sturdy wooden hanger.

The chain's other end got stuck on the nightgown Lisa was wearing. It caught hold just below her belly. Emma wasn't paying any attention; she was too angry to even think, much less notice details. When Lisa seemed to hesitate Emma pulled on her arm to yank her out of the closet.

The hanger hook ripped through Lisa's nightgown and dug into the soft, crumbly-rotten skin just below her belly. As Emma yanked on Lisa's arm, the hanger ripped open Lisa's gut.

Lisa looked down and saw her insides hanging loose, and she screamed. At first Emma wasn't even sure it was a scream; it was a screechy, cracky sound that went silent three times in the middle when the girl's vocal cords just stopped working.

Emma tried not to look at what the hanger had done, but she couldn't stop herself. She had to look.

"Jesus, Jesus, O sweet Jesus," she whispered.

A four-inch flap of skin was caught in the hanger. Lisa twisted to get away from the thing, and the rip got bigger and bigger.

Emma said, "Be still." She bit her lower lip and knelt down to work the hanger loose.

There was no way to do it without looking into Lisa's insides. Emma gagged in spite of herself; her hands trembled as she lifted them to the hanger. Up close the smell of putrid flesh was unbearable. She thought for a moment that she'd lose her self-control, but she managed not to. She held herself as careful and steady as she could and kept her eyes on what she had to do.

Lisa's intestines looked like sausage casings left to sit in the sun for a week. Her stomach was shriveled and cracked and dry. There were other organs Emma didn't recognize. All of them were rotting away. Some of them even looked crumbly. An insect scrambled through a nest of pulpy veins and squirmed underneath the tumor.

Emma had tried to avoid looking at that. She'd had nightmares about it these last few weeks. In her dreams it pulsed and throbbed, and sometimes it sang to her, though there were never any words when it was singing. One night she'd dreamed she held it in her arms and sang a lullaby to it. She woke from that dream in the middle of the night, dripping with cold sweat.

Even if those were only dreams, Emma was certain that there was something *wrong* with the cancer, something unnatural and dangerous, maybe even evil.

It was enormous now, a great mottled-grey leathery mass the size of Emma's skull. Blue veins the size of fingers protruded from it. Emma wanted to sob, but she held herself still. Gently, carefully as she could, she took the loose skin in one hand and the hanger in the other and began to work Lisa free. Three times while she was working at it her hand brushed against the cancer, and each time it was like an electric prod had found its way into the base of her own stomach.

She kept the tremor in her hands pretty well under control, but when she was almost done her left hand twitched and tore Lisa open enough for Emma to see a couple of her ribs and a hint of her right lung underneath them.

She set the hanger down and let out the sob she'd been holding back. Her arms and legs and neck felt weak; she wanted to lie down right there on the floor and never move again. But she couldn't. There wasn't time. She had to *do* something—she knew, she just *knew* that Lisa was going to crumble away in her arms if she didn't do something soon.

But again: what *could* she do? Get out a needle and thread and sew her back together? That wouldn't work. If a coat hanger could tear Lisa's skin, then it was too weak to hold a stitch. What about glue? Or tape, maybe—Emma could wrap her in adhesive tape, as though she were a mummy. But that wouldn't solve anything forever, either. Sooner or later the decay would get done with Lisa, and what good would bandages do if they were only holding in dust? Sooner or later they'd slip loose around her, and Lisa would be gone in a gust of wind.

No. Emma knew about rot. Rot came from germs, and the best way to get rid of germs was with rubbing alcohol.

She had a bottle of rubbing alcohol under the bathroom cabinet. That wasn't enough. What Lisa needed was to soak in a bathtub full of it. Which meant going to the grocery to buy bottles and bottles of the stuff. Which meant either taking Lisa to the store—and she was in no condition for that—or leaving her alone in the apartment that wasn't safe from people who wanted to kill her. But Emma *had* to do something. It was an emergency. So she said, "You wait here in the closet, baby," and she kissed Lisa on the forehead. For a moment she thought she felt Lisa's skin flaking away on her lips, thought she tasted something like cured ham. The idea was too much to cope with right now. She put it out of her mind.

Even so, the flavor of preserved meat followed her all the way to the store.

The grocery store only had ten bottles of rubbing alcohol on the shelf, which wasn't as much as Emma wanted. Once she'd bought them, though, and loaded them into grocery bags, she wondered how she would have carried any more anyway. She couldn't soak Lisa in ten bottles of alcohol, but she could stop up the tub and rinse her with it, and then wash her in the runoff. That'd do the job well enough, at least. It'd have to.

When Emma got back to the apartment Lisa was asleep in the closet. Or she looked like she was sleeping. Emma hadn't actually seen her asleep since she'd died. She spent a lot of time in bed, and a lot of time resting, but whenever Emma looked in on her she was awake.

"Lisa?" Emma said. She pulled the clothes aside and looked into the closet. Lisa was curled up in the corner of the closet with her head tucked into her chest and her hands folded over her stomach. "Lisa, are you awake, honey?"

Lisa looked up and nodded. The whites of her eyes were dull yellow. They looked too small for their sockets. "Mommy," she said, "I'm scared." She *looked* afraid, too. She looked terrified.

Emma bit into her lower lip. "I'm scared too, baby. Come on." She put up her hand to help Lisa up, but she didn't take it. She stood up on her own, and when Emma moved aside she walked out of the closet.

"What're you going to do, Mommy?"

"I'm going to give you a bath, baby, with something that'll stop what's happening to your body." Emma looked Lisa over, and the sight made her wince. "You get yourself undressed and get in the bathtub, and I'll get everything ready."

Lisa looked like she didn't really believe what Emma was saying, but she went in and started getting undressed anyway. Emma got the shopping bag with the bottles of alcohol from where she left it by the door and took them to the bathroom. It was an enormous bathroom, as big as some people's bedrooms. The building was old enough that there hadn't been such a thing as indoor plumbing when it was built. Not for tenement buildings, anyway. Emma never understood why the people who put the plumbing in decided to turn a room as big as this one into a bathroom. When she got there Lisa had her nightgown up over her head. She finished taking it off and stepped into the tub without even turning around.

Emma took the bottles out of the bag and lined them up one by one on the counter. She took the cap off each as she set it down, and tossed the cap into the waste basket.

"Put the stopper in the tub for me, would you, honey?" Emma said. She got the last bottle out of the bag, got rid of the cap, and carried it over to Lisa.

She was already sitting down inside the tub, waiting. "This may sting a little, baby. Why don't you hold out your hand and let me make sure it doesn't hurt too much."

Lisa put her hand out over the tub stopper, and Emma poured alcohol on it.

"What does that feel like?"

"It doesn't feel like anything at all, Mommy. I don't feel anything anymore."

"Not anywhere?"

"No, Mommy."

Emma shook her head, gently, almost as though she hoped Lisa wouldn't see it. She didn't like the sound of what Lisa'd said. It worried her. Not feeling anything? That was dangerous. It was wrong, and scary.

But she had to get on with what she was doing; things would only keep getting worse if she let them go.

"Close your eyes, baby. This won't be good for them even if it doesn't hurt." She held the bottle over Lisa's head and tilted it. Clear fluid streamed out of the bottle and into her hair. After a moment it began to run down her shoulders in little rivulets. One of them snaked its way into the big open wound of Lisa's belly and pooled in an indentation on the top of the cancer. For a moment Emma thought something horrible would happen, but nothing did.

Emma poured all ten bottles of alcohol onto Lisa. When she was done the girl was sitting in an inch-deep pool of the stuff, soaked with it. Emma figured that she needed to soak in it for a while, so she told Lisa to wait and left her there.

She went into the kitchen, put on a pot of coffee, and lit a cigarette. It'd been two months since she'd smoked. The pack was very stale, but it was better than nothing. When the coffee was ready she poured herself a cup, opened the morning's paper, and sat down to read.

She'd been reading for twenty minutes when she heard Lisa scream.

The sound made her want to curl up and die; if there was something else that could go wrong, she didn't want to know about it. She didn't want to cope with it. But there wasn't any choice—she *had* to cope. Even doing nothing was a way of coping, when you thought about it. No matter what Emma felt, no matter how she felt, she was a mother. Before she even realized what she was doing she was in the bathroom beside Lisa.

"Mommy," Lisa said, her voice so still and quiet that it gave Emma a chill, "I'm *melting.*"

She held out her right hand, and Emma saw that was just exactly what was happening. Lisa's fingers looked like wet clay that someone had left sitting in warm water; they were too thin, and there was some sort of a milky fluid dripping from them.

Oh, my God, a little voice inside Emma's head whispered. *OhmiGodOhmiGod.* She didn't understand. What was happening? Alcohol didn't make people dissolve. Was Lisa's flesh so rotten that just getting it wet would make it slide away like mud?

She thought she was going to start screaming herself. She managed not to. In fact, it was almost as though she didn't feel anything at all, just numb and weak and all cold inside. As if her soul had oozed away, or died. Her legs went all rubbery, and she felt her jaw go slack. She thought she was going to faint, but she wasn't sure; she'd never fainted before.

Lisa looked up at her, and her shrunken little eyes were suddenly hard and mean and angry. She screamed again, and this time it sounded like rage, not fear. She stood up in the tub. Drippy slime drizzled down from her butt and thighs. *"Mommy,"* she screamed, and she launched herself at Emma. "Stupid, stupid, *stupid* Mommy!" She raised her fist up over her head and hit Emma square on the breast, and *hard.* Harder than Lisa's father'd ever hit her, back when he was still around. Lisa brought her other fist down, just as hard, then pulled them back and hit her again, and again, and again. Emma couldn't even move herself out of Lisa's way. She didn't have the spirit for it.

For a moment it didn't even look like Lisa beating on her. It looked like some sort of a monster, a dead zombie-thing that any moment would reach into her chest, right through her flesh, and rip out her heart. And it would eat her bloody-dripping heart while it was still alive and beating, and Emma's eyes would close, and she'd die.

"All your *stupid* fault, Mommy! All your *stupid, stupid* fault!" She grabbed Emma by the belt of her uniform skirt and shook her and shook her. Then she screamed and pushed Emma away, threw her against the wall. Emma's head and back hit too hard against the rock-thick plaster wall, and she fell to the floor. She lay on her side, all slack and beaten, and stared at her daughter, watching her to see what she'd do next.

Lisa stared at her for three long beats like a fury from Hell, and for a moment Emma thought she really was going to die. But then something happened on Lisa's face, like she'd suddenly realized what she was doing, and her legs fell out from under her and she started crying. It sounded like crying, anyway, and Emma thought there were tears, but it was hard to tell because of the drippy slime all over her.

Emma crawled over to her and put her arms around her and held her. One of her hands brushed up against the open cancer in Lisa's belly and again there was an electric throb, and she almost flinched away. She managed to stop herself, though, and moved her hand without making it seem like an overreaction. "It's okay, baby. Mommy loves you." Lisa's little body heaved with her sobs, and when her back pressed against Emma's breasts it made the bruises hurt. "Mommy loves you."

Emma looked at Lisa's hands, and saw that the flesh had all crumbled away from them. They were nothing but bones, like the skeleton one of the doctors at the hospital kept in his office.

"I want to die, Mommy." Her voice was all quiet again.

Emma squeezed her, and held her a little tighter. *I want to die, Mommy.* It made her hurt a little inside but she knew Lisa was right. Mama Estrella was right. It was wrong for a little girl to be alive after she was dead. Whether faith was right or not, it was wrong to stake a little girl's soul on it.

"Baby, baby, baby, baby, I love my baby," Emma cooed. Lisa was crying even harder now, and she'd begun to tremble in a way that wasn't natural at all.

"You wait here, baby. I got to call Mama Estrella." Emma lifted herself up off the floor, which made everything hurt all at once.

Emma went to the kitchen, lifted the telephone receiver, and dialed Mama's number. While the phone rang she wandered back toward the bathroom. The cord was long enough that it didn't have any trouble stretching that far. Even if it hadn't really been long enough, though, Emma probably would have tried to make it reach; she wanted to look at Lisa, to watch her, to save as much memory of her as she could.

The girl lay on the bathroom floor, shaking. The tremor had gotten worse, much worse, in just the time it'd taken Emma to dial the phone. It seemed to *get* worse, too, while Emma watched.

Mama Estrella finally answered the phone.

"Hello?"

"Mama?" Emma said, "I think maybe you better come up here."

Mama Estrella didn't say anything at all; the line was completely silent. The silence felt bitter and mean to Emma.

"I think maybe you were right, Mama. Right about Lisa, I mean." Emma looked down at the floor and squeezed her eyes shut. She leaned back against the wall and tried to clear her head. "I think . . . maybe you better hurry. Something's very wrong, something I don't understand."

Lisa made a little sound halfway between a gasp and a scream, and something went *thunk* on the floor. Emma didn't have the heart to look up to see what had happened, but she started back toward the kitchen to hang up the phone.

"Mama, I got to go. Come here *now,* please?"

"Emma . . ." Mama Estrella started to say, but Emma didn't hear her; she'd already hung up, and she was running back to the bathroom, where Lisa was.

Lisa was shivering and writhing on the bathroom floor. Her left arm, from the elbow down, lay on the floor not far from her. Was her flesh that corrupt? God in heaven, was the girl going to shake herself to shreds because of some kind of a nervous fit? Emma didn't want to believe it, but she couldn't ignore what she was seeing. She took Lisa in her arms and lifted her up off the floor.

"You've got to be still, honey," Emma said. "You're going to tremble yourself to death."

Lisa nodded and gritted her teeth and for a moment she was pretty still. But it wasn't anything she could control, not for long. Emma carried Lisa to her bedroom, and by the time she got there the girl was shaking just as bad as she had been.

There was a knock on the front door, but Emma didn't pay any attention. If it was Mama she had her own key, and she'd use it. Emma sat down on the bed beside Lisa and stroked her hair.

After a moment Mama showed up in the bedroom doorway, carrying some kind of a woody-looking thing that burned with a real low flame and smoked something awful. It made so much smoke that Emma figured that it'd take maybe two or three minutes for it to make the air in the room impossible to breathe.

Mama Estrella went to the window and closed it, then drew down the shade.

"Water," she said. "Bring me a kettle of hot water."

"You want me to boil water?" There was smoke everywhere already; it was harsh and acrid and when a wisp of it caught in Emma's eye it burned her like something caustic. A cloud of it drifted down toward Lisa, and she started wheezing and coughing. That frightened Emma; she hadn't even heard the girl draw a breath, except to speak, in all the weeks since she'd died.

"No, there isn't time. Just bring a kettle of hot water from the tap."

Then Mama Estrella bent down to look at Lisa, and suddenly it was too late for hot water and magic and putting little girls to rest.

The thick smoke from the burning thing settled onto Lisa's face, Lisa began to gag. She took in a long wheezing-hacking breath, and for three long moments she choked on it, or maybe on the corruption of her own lungs. Then she began to cough, deep, throbbing, hacking coughs that shook her hard against the bed.

Mama Estrella pulled away from the bed. She looked shocked and frightened and unsure.

"Lisa, be *still!*" Emma shouted. It didn't do any good.

Lisa sat up, trying to control herself. That only made things worse—the next cough sent her flying face-first onto the floor. She made an awful smacking sound when she hit; when she rolled over Emma saw that she'd broken her nose.

Lisa wheezed, sucking in air.

She's breathing, Emma thought. *Please, God, she's breathing now and she's going to be fine. Please.*

But even as Emma thought it she knew that it wasn't going to be so. The girl managed four wheezing breaths, and then she was coughing again, and much worse. Emma saw bits of the meat of her daughter's lungs spatter on the hardwood floor.

She bent down and hugged Lisa, hugged her tight to make her still. "Be still, baby. Hold your breath for a moment and be still. Mommy loves you, Lisa." But Lisa didn't stop, she couldn't stop, and the force of her racking was so mean that her shoulders dug new bruises in Emma's breast. When Lisa finally managed to still herself for a moment she looked up at Emma, her eyes full of desperation, and she said, *"Mommy . . ."*

And then she coughed again, so hard that her tiny body pounded into Emma's breast, and her small, hard-boned chin slammed down onto Emma's shoulder.

Slammed down so hard that the force of it tore free the flesh of Lisa's neck.

And Lisa's head tumbled down Emma's back, and rolled across the floor.

Emma turned her head and watched it happen, and the sight filled her nightmares for the rest of her life. The tear began at the back of Lisa's neck, where the bone of her skull met her spine. The skin there broke loose all at once, as though it had snapped, and the meat inside pulled away from itself in long loose strings. The cartilage of Lisa's spine popped loose like an empty hose, and the veins and pipes in the front of her neck pulled away from her head like they weren't even attached anymore.

Her head rolled over and over until it came to a stop against the leg of a chair. Lisa's eyes blinked three times and then they closed forever.

Her body shook and clutched against Emma's chest for a few
more seconds, the way Emma always heard a chicken's does when
you take an ax to its neck. When the spasming got to be too much
to bear Emma let go and watched her daughter's corpse shake itself
to shreds on the bedroom floor. After a while the tumor-thing fell
out of it, and everything was still.

Everything but the cancer. It quivered like grey, moldy-rotten
pudding that you touched on a back shelf in the refrigerator because you'd forgotten it was there.

"Oh, my God," Mama Estrella said.

Emma felt scared and confused, and empty, too, like something
important had torn out of her and there was nothing left inside but
dead air.

But even if Emma was hollow inside, she couldn't force her eye
away from the cancer. Maybe it was morbid fascination, and maybe
it was something else completely, but she knelt down and looked at
it, watched it from so close she could almost taste it. There was
something about it, something wrong. Even more wrong than it
had been before.

"She's dead, Emma. She's dead forever."

Emma shuddered, but still she couldn't force herself away. The
tumor began to still, but one of its ropy grey veins still pulsed. She
reached down and touched it, and the whole grey mass began to
throb again.

"What is it, Mama Estrella? Is it alive?"

"I don't know, Emma. I don't know what it is, but it's dead."

Then the spongy grey tissue at the tumor's crest started to swell
and bulge, to bulge so far that it stretched thin and finally split.

"Like an egg, Mama," Emma said. "It almost looks like an egg
when a chick is hatching. I've seen that on the television, and it
looks just like this."

Emma reached over toward the split, carefully, carefully, imagining some horrible monster would reach up out of the thing and tear
her hand from her wrist. But there was no monster, only hard,
leathery hide. She set the fingers of her other hand against the far
lip of the opening and pried the split wide so that she could peek
into it. But her head blocked what little light she could let in.

Small gurgling sounds came out of the darkness.

Emma crossed herself and mumbled a prayer too quiet for anyone else to hear.

And reached down, into her daughter's cancer.

Before her hand was halfway in, she felt the touch of a tiny hand. It startled her so badly that she almost screamed. To hold it back she bit into her lip so hard that she tasted her own blood.

A baby's hand.

Then a baby girl was crawling up out of the leathery gray shell, and Mama Estrella was praying out loud, and Emma felt herself crying with joy.

"I love you, Mommy," the baby said. Its voice was Lisa's voice, just as it'd been before her sickness.

Emma wanted to cry and cry and cry, but instead she lifted her baby Lisa out of the cancer that'd borne her, and she held her to her breast and loved her so hard that the moment felt like forever and ever.

Light-Headed

JOHN TUNNEY

Monk thought he was buying stuff that would give him and his friends a real high . . . but that was just the half of it! JOHN TUNNEY, *a reporter for* American Metal Market, *lives in Maplewood, New Jersey, "with four fish and no children" but may remedy the situation with a marriage-in-the-offing.*

Monk hurried down Fourth Street on his way to meet his friends, nervously patting his pocket as he went, making sure the small brown envelope was still there.

He didn't want to be late. No way, not today. He had plans. Big plans.

Monk was basically a good kid—smart, did well in school—but a little crazy. Not dangerous nuts, just a little weird, into doing strange things. Like shaving his head.

It happened a couple of months ago. Monk was looking through a *Rolling Stone* when he saw a picture of this band with bald heads. He liked the look, so he got out his mother's old home-barber kit and cut off all his hair.

He thought he looked special, distinguished, like MTV. The rest of the world, however, saw a goofy-looking bald-headed twelve-year-old with big ears, sort of a punked-out Dopey the Dwarf.

Today, Monk and his friends—The Group—were going to get high for the first time. Everything was set. They'd been talking about it for a while and agreed to do it together, the four of them: Mickey, Mike, Monk, and Artie. The Group. By chance, Monk bought the stuff yesterday.

In a way, it was a coup for Monk. Usually Mickey, the oldest and unofficial leader, handled The Group's contacts with the outside world, and he was very jealous of his role. But Monk wasn't big on protocol, so when the opportunity popped up, he grabbed it.

He bought the stuff on his way to school. Every day he took the same route, through the twisting streets of the village out onto the avenue and all its wildness. People and cars whizzed by in every direction, horns blared, sirens screamed, and Monk bopped through the mayhem as usual, until he saw a strange man lurking in an alley.

"Pssst. Pssst. Check it out, check it out," said the short dark man, motioning Monk closer.

Monk passed guys like this every day, and usually he ignored them, but this one was different. He looked like a frog the way he squatted in the shadows, his back to the wall. He had large round eyes, gangly arms, and big feet. Huge feet, gray with grime, and big fat toes: a footful of thumbs drumming the pavement.

Monk stared.

"Check it out, check it out," the man said again.

"Check what out?"

"Whatever you want, man. Whatever you want," he said, and pretended to inhale smoke, making a wet sucking sound.

Monk smiled.

"Got any of that?"

"Any what?"

"You know," Monk said pursing his lips and inhaling in a knowing way.

The little man laughed. "I got some good stuff," he said. "The best, man, I'm telling you, nothing like it."

"How much?"

"The good stuff?"

"Yeah, the good stuff," Monk said looking around nervously.

"Five. Five to make you fly, boy," the little man said, and laughed again.

"Okay." Monk pulled a crumpled five-dollar bill from his pocket and handed it to the man in exchange for a small brown envelope.

"Thank you," Monk said, not sure if he was supposed to say that or not, and then ran off.

That was yesterday. Today The Group cut school to go to the park and smoke. The others were waiting at the park entrance when Monk arrived.

"About time," Mickey said, grumpy as usual.

"What's up, guys?" Monk said.

"You got it?"

"Yup."

"So, we're agreed, then, we're gonna do it?" Mickey asked. "Mike?"

"Yeah, sure."

"Artie?"

"I don't care."

"All right. Let's go."

The Group marched into the park and found a good spot behind some bushes in a dip between two hills.

Mickey pulled out the packet and filled the pipe with the dark stringy stuff.

"That don't look right," Mickey said.

"Yeah, really," Mike agreed. "The stuff I've seen has always been green."

"Where'd you ever see this stuff before?" Artie asked.

"My sister," Mike answered.

"What does she know?"

"More than you."

Coming to his own defense, Monk said, "Well, the guy said it was really good stuff and he looked like he knew what he was talking about. You should've seen this guy. Besides, I asked him for the good stuff. What do you think, I'm stupid or something?"

"Sometimes, yeah," Mike said.

"Funny."

"Come on let's try it. If we don't get high we'll know the bonehead here got robbed," Mickey said.

Monk went first. Taking a big hit, he felt his lungs slowly expand —and suddenly burst in a great convulsion of coughing.

"Looks like fun," Mike said, taking the pipe.

The bowl went around several times and everybody coughed at least once.

When it was finally spent, they sat quietly waiting for something to happen.

"I don't feel anything," Mickey said.

"Me neither."

"Should we do some more?"

"Let's wait a bit," Monk said. "I heard it takes a little while to hit you sometimes."

So they waited.

And waited.

"Ah, this is bullshit," Mickey said with disgust and stood up. "Monk got robbed and we've been sitting here smoking rat hairs or something." Mickey walked around the bush into the sunshine.

They all got up. "You know, I feel kind of different, maybe," Mike said.

"Yeah," Monk added. "Me too. Not real stoned or anything, but kind of light."

"Me too, I think," Artie said as they stepped out from behind the bush.

"Where's Mickey?" Monk asked.

"I'm right here. What are you—blind?"

Monk turned toward Mickey's voice, but couldn't see him.

"Where?" he asked again.

"Here. But, hey, where are you?" Mickey asked.

"Huh?" Monk turned in a complete circle. Not only was Mickey out of sight, but Artie and Mike were gone too.

"Where is everybody? Where'd you guys go?"

"Right here."

"Where?"

"Hey! I can't see you."

"I can't see anyone."

"Me neither."

"Oh, my God!"

"Holy shit, we're blind!" Mike cried.

"I knew we shouldn't have done this," Artie whispered.

"Wait a minute, wait a minute," Monk said, trying to sound calm. "I'm not blind. I can see everything, the bush, the trees, the whole park. I just can't see you guys. You're . . . We're invisible!"

"Holy shit," Mike said again, softly.

"Oh, no," Artie said. "Hey, guys, I don't know, I mean, I'm scared."

"I don't believe this," Mickey said. "Monk, you're such a god-damn idiot, you know that? Look what's happened to us!" He sounded close to tears. "I knew I never should've smoked stuff you got. You can't do anything right."

Monk didn't answer back. He never did. There's no arguing with Mickey. Once Mickey gets bent out of shape about something, he raves away and won't listen to anyone or anything until he's done.

Still, Monk didn't like getting yelled at.

Why's it my fault? Okay, so I bought the stuff, but how was I to know we'd turn invisible?

At least we're not dead.

Besides, invisibility might be fun. It was like having magic powers. Super powers.

Yeah. Super powers.

Ever since he was a little kid Monk dreamed about finding some thing, some stuff, that would give him special abilities. He used to pretend that red M&Ms were a secret power source. He'd save all the red ones until last and then pop them into his mouth one right after the other and crunch 'em up into one giant mushy glob of super substance.

Super Monk would stand on his front porch, the noble hero gazing kindly upon the world he protected, and then dash off down the street on his bicycle to do good.

Monk wanted to grab Mickey and shake him. Couldn't he see it? This was great. They were invincible.

Superheroes.

A scene flashed through Monk's mind.

We're riding the subway, the four of us, invisible. It's late at night and we're the only ones on the train except for two creeps and a beautiful girl sitting by herself.

The creeps leer at the girl and whisper to each other, laughing. Monk, watching, takes a deep breath and prepares for trouble.

The creeps move in on the girl. One grabs her arm; the other steals her purse. She cries out.

"Unhand her!" Monk commands, his voice booming through the subway car like a cannon.

Surprised, the creeps look up, but there's no one there.

"Unhand her or risk the wrath of the Ghostriders," Monk says.

The creeps look at each other, thinking they're going crazy.

Suddenly Monk leaps across the car, grabs the center pole, swings his feet into the air and kicks the biggest creep in the chest, knocking him against the wall. The creep slumps to the floor unconscious. Mickey, Mike, and Artie tackle creep number two.

The beautiful girl stares in teary-eyed disbelief.

"Who . . . what are you?" she asks.

"The Ghostriders, miss," Monk says. "Dedicated to fighting crime, punishing the guilty, and protecting the innocent. You have nothing to fear when the Ghostriders are near."

"Oh, thank you," the beautiful girl replies.

"No need to thank us, miss. We're just doing what we have to do."

To his companions, Monk says, "Ghostriders, away!"

The door between cars opens and the Ghostriders move out into the rushing clatter of the subway train.

Ghostriders. Yeah. Monk giggled at the thought, but Mickey quickly brought him back to reality.

"What do you think this is—funny or something?" Mickey demanded.

"Yeah."

"What?"

"Don't you get it? This is great. We're invisible. Nobody can see us. We can go anywhere and do anything. Nobody can stop us. It's like super powers."

Very slowly, the possibilities dawned on each of them one by one.

"Yeah."

"You know, this could be okay," Mickey said, regaining his confidence.

Their adventures, however, were less than heroic.

They laughed at the dumfounded pretzel vendor as he watched one of his pretzels float through the air and disappear bite by bite. Then there was the orange that peeled itself as it drifted down the avenue. And of course, the copy of *Playboy* that hopped off the stand and hung mysteriously in the air as Miss June unfolded to the accompaniment of phantom whistles.

Full invisibility only worked in direct light, however; otherwise
the boys could be seen. They might look a little ghostly, or washed
out, but were visible just the same, as Monk discovered when he
tried the pretzel trick on a soda vendor who happened to be standing in a shadow.

"Hey! Where you going with that?" the vendor shouted.

"Huh?"

"You gonna pay for the soda or what?"

"You can see me?" Monk asked.

"Can I see you? Yeah, but only cause I got X-ray eyes. What are
you—on drugs? Now gimme that back and get out of here, you
weirdo."

Shadows weren't the only giveaway. When light crested around
their bodies, it created small ripples, like heat waves. That's how
they kept track of each other, by watching for wiggles in the air.

But the hardest thing to get used to about invisibility was the
bouncy feeling of lightness. Their density decreased with their
physical presence. Of course, it affected each of them to a different
degree.

"This is definitely strange," Monk said as they cut across the park
on their way back to the bush for another bowl. "Like being under
water, or sort of swimming through air."

"I feel like a feather," Artie said. "Or a bubble. I don't know,
like I might float away."

"Yeah, it's wild," Mike said. "It's like . . . I don't know what."

"You got to concentrate on keeping your feet on the ground,
Artie," Mickey said.

"Yeah," Monk added. "Lean forward like you're walking into
the wind. Just take it slow. Think down."

"I'll try," Artie said quietly.

Monk, speaking softly so others wouldn't hear, told Artie to stay
close and hold onto him if he wanted.

"Thanks," Artie whispered.

They were in the middle of a field when suddenly the wind
picked up and lifted Artie into the air.

"Monk, help!"

"Artie's getting blown away!"

"Monk, help me!"

"Where is he?" Mickey asked as they all looked around.

"Help," Artie cried again, his voice getting fainter as he drifted off.

"Come on, guys, we've got to find him," Monk pleaded.

"Yeah, but where did he go?"

"There he is!" Mike shouted, seeing the ripples. "He's heading across the park toward the lake. Come on!"

They raced after him, careful not to get caught in the wind like Artie.

Out of breath and panting, they stopped at the edge of the lake by the old boathouse.

"Now where'd he go?"

Monk spotted him first, skimming the treetops.

"There he is, we must've gotten ahead of him."

"Now what?" Mickey asked.

"We need a rope or something," Monk said. "Look for a rope."

"Down there by the boats," Mike said, pointing. The small rowboats for rent during the summer were tied up in front of the boathouse, strung together with one long strand.

They untied the rope and let the boats drift out into the lake. Monk tied the rope around his waist.

Artie, sailing closer, called out, "Monk. You guys. Get me down. Help me."

"Don't worry, Artie," Monk shouted. "I'm coming to get you."

"What are you going to do?" Mickey asked.

"You guys hold onto the rope and just before he floats by I'm going to jump up and grab him. Just don't let go."

"Here he comes. Get ready."

"I'm coming, Artie!" Monk cried as he leaped into the air.

Monk shot upward like a guided missile, straight to his friend. "Grab my hand, Artie," he said as he zeroed in on the ripples.

Monk was still moving higher when Artie reached out and took his hand.

"Gotcha!"

But suddenly the rope went taut and snapped Monk back. Artie slipped from his grasp.

"Monk!"

"Artie!"

He was gone.

Mickey and Mike pulled Monk down. Together the three boys stared up at the sky as their friend drifted away like a stray balloon.

They spent the next several hours frantically scanning the skies for a sign of Artie, but it was no use.

It was dark when the boys materialized.

"Where is he?" Monk asked. "Where did he go?"

"Maybe he floated up to outer space," Mickey suggested.

"Or out to Jersey," Mike added.

Monk groaned. It was all his fault; it was his idea. *Some Ghostrider. Some hero.*

They walked back to their meeting spot. Nobody said anything and only Monk glanced up at the night sky.

"I guess I'm going home," Mickey said.

"And give up?" Monk exclaimed.

"What do you want us to do, Monk?" Mickey replied. "Hang out here all night?"

Mike said, "Look, Artie'll be okay. The stuff has to wear off of him like it did us, right? He's probably home already. We just got separated, that's all."

Monk wanted to believe him.

"Yeah," Mickey said, "he's probably all right, but just in case, we got to have a story in case somebody asks something."

"What?" Monk asked, but he knew what Mickey meant.

"We've all got to say that we don't know anything, that he said he was going home and that's the last we saw of him. Agreed?"

Monk was stunned. "I can't believe you guys. You're talking like Artie's dead or something. What's the matter with you guys?"

"Listen," Mickey said, "we're doing this for you."

"For me?"

"Yeah. You're the one who bought the stuff, you know."

Monk knew. He wanted to cry.

Mike and Mickey left Monk alone on the street corner. He slumped against a wall and sank slowly to the ground.

I'm sorry, Artie. Really, really sorry. I wish I could undo everything, go back in time, make it yesterday and do it all over. Everything'd be different.

Monk played the scene over in his mind, the walk down the street, the little frog man in the alley going, "Pssst!"

This time I'd walk by. I wish I had just walked by. I wouldn't do it again, I wouldn't. I wish I could go back.

But he knew there wasn't enough magic in the city to take him back.

Finally, Monk went home, defeated.

His mother was there. The school called; Artie's mother called. Monk was in big trouble, but he didn't care. He was too depressed.

"I don't know" was all he said to his mother's questions. He hated lying.

He lay in bed thinking that this was the worst day of his life. The frog man said the stuff was good, special. "Five to make you fly, boy."

Sick joke. It's over, now. Can't get any worse.

It seemed like such a good idea at the time, but things never turn out the way you imagine. It was so unfair he wanted to scream. Finally, though, he fell asleep.

Clink!

A noise at the window woke him up.

Clink! Clink!

Monk went to the window and saw a shadowy figure outside throwing pebbles. He opened the window and looked out.

"Who's there?"

"Hey, Monk."

"Artie?"

"Hey, Monk."

"Artie!"

Monk ran downstairs and out into the street in his pajamas.

"Artie!"

"I just got back."

"What happened?"

"It was unreal. I just kept getting lighter and lighter and floating up and up."

"Where did you go?"

"Jersey. I floated the whole way. I had to take a train back."

"Wow."

They were quiet for a few seconds, each thankful that Artie was back, and then Artie said, "Monk, it was the weirdest thing in the world, way up there. I liked it, but I was scared, too. Way up there the blue goes on forever and the clouds are huge, as big as mountains, like islands. Really weird."

"Artie, I'm sorry. I didn't know it would happen like that. I tried to grab you."

"I know. It's okay. I'm all right."

Later that night, after Artie went home, Monk lay awake in bed, unable to sleep, his mind racing, a million ideas burning through his brain. But as the night wore on he kept thinking about a few things in particular.

He thought about the strange frog man and he thought about the Ghostriders.

He also wondered what it would be like to sail through a blue that goes on forever and to touch a mountain-sized cloud.

But mostly he wondered what to do with the rest of the stuff in the small brown envelope in his pants pocket.

The Enchanter Faustus and Queen Elizabeth

ANECDOTE EXTRACTED FROM THE DOCTOR'S UNPUBLISHED MEMOIRS

One of history's most famous wizards is the enchanter Faustus, who, in the following colorful narrative, does his best to put on a good show for the British Crown. (For more details about this mighty warlock, see "Doctor Faustus Journeys to Hell," elsewhere in this volume.)

"I do not say it is possible—I only say it is true."

Elizabeth was a wonderful princess for wisdom, learning, magnificence, and grandeur of soul. All this was fine,—but she was as envious as a decayed beauty—jealous and cruel—and that spoiled all. However, be her defects what they may, her fame had pierced even to the depths of Germany, whence the Enchanter Faustus set off for her court, that great magician wishing to ascertain by his own wits, whether Elizabeth was as gifted with good qualities as she was with bad. No one could judge this for him so well as himself— who read the stars like his A, B, C, and whom Satan obeyed like his dog—yet, withal, who was not above a thousand pleasant tricks, that make people laugh, and hurt no one. Such, for instance, as

turning an old lord into an old lady, to elope with his cook-maid—
exchanging a handsome wife for an ugly one, &c. &c.

The Queen, charmed with the pretty things which she heard of
him, wished much to see him—and from the moment that she did,
became quite fascinated. On his side, he found her better than he
had expected, not but that he perceived she thought a great deal
too much of her wit—though she had a tolerable share of it, and
still more of her beauty—of which she had rather less.

One day that she was dressed with extraordinary splendour, to
give audience to some ambassadors, she retired into her cabinet at
the close of the ceremony, and sent for the Doctor. After having
gazed at herself in all the mirrors in the room, and seeming very
well pleased with their reflection,—for her roses and lilies were as
good as gold could buy—her petticoat high enough to shew her
ankle, and her frill low to expose her bosom,—she sat down *en
attitude,* in her great chair. It was thus the Enchanter Faustus found
her. He was the most adroit courtier that you could find, though
you searched the world over. For though there are good reasons
why a courtier may not be a conjuror, there are none why a conjuror may not be a courtier; and Faustus, both in one—knowing the
Queen's foible as to her imaginary beauty—took care not to let slip
so fine an opportunity of paying his court. He was wonderstruck,
thunderstruck, at such a blaze of perfection. Elizabeth knew how to
appreciate the moment of surprise. She drew a magnificent ruby
from her finger, which the Doctor, without making difficulties
about it, drew on his.

"You find me then passable for a Queen," said she, smiling. On
this he wished himself at the devil, (his old resting-place,) if, not
alone that he had ever seen, but if any body else had ever seen,
either queen or subject to equal her.

"Oh, Faustus, my friend," replied she, "could the beauties of
antiquity return, we should soon see what a flatterer you are!"

"I dare the proof," returned the Doctor. "If your Majesty will it
—but speak, and they are here."

Faustus, of course, never expected to be taken at his word; but
whether Elizabeth wished to see if magic could perform the miracle, or to satisfy a curiosity that had often tormented her, she expressed herself amazingly pleased at the idea, and begged it might
be immediately realised.

Faustus then requested her Majesty to pass into a little gallery near the apartment, while he went for his book, his ring, and his large black mantle.

All this was done nearly as soon as said. There was a door at each end of the gallery, and it was decided that the beauties should come in at one, and go out at the other, so that the Queen might have a fair view of them. Only two of the courtiers were admitted to this exhibition; these were the Earl of Essex and Sir Philip Sydney.

Her Majesty was seated in the middle of the gallery, with the Earl and the Knight standing to the right and left of her chair. The enchanter did not forget to trace round them and their mistress certain mysterious circles, with all the grimaces and contortions of the time. He then drew another opposite to it, within which he took his own station, leaving a space between for the actors.

When this was finished, he begged the Queen not to speak a word while they should be on the stage; and, above all, not to appear frightened, let her see what she might.

The latter precaution was needless; for the good Queen feared neither angel nor devil. And now the Doctor inquired what *belle* of antiquity she would first see.

"To follow the order of time," she answered, "they should commence with HELEN."

The magician, with a changing countenance, now exclaimed, "Sit still!"

Sidney's heart beat quick. The brave Essex turned pale. As to the Queen, not the slightest emotion was perceptible.

Faustus soon commenced some muttered incantations and strange evolutions, such as were the fashion of the day for conjurors. Anon the gallery shook, so did the two courtiers, and the Doctor, in a voice of anger, called out,

> "Daughter of fair Leda, hear!
> From thy far Elysian sphere;
> Lovely as when, for his fee,
> To Paris Venus promised thee.
> Appear—appear—appear!"

Accustomed to command, rather than to be commanded, the fair Helen lingered to the last possible moment; but when the last moment came, so did she, and so suddenly, that no one knew how she got there. She was habited *à la Grecque,*—her hair ornamented with pearls and a superb aigrette. The figure passed slowly onwards—stopped for an instant directly opposite the Queen, as if to gratify her curiosity, took leave of her with a malicious smile, and vanished. She had scarcely disappeared when her Majesty exclaimed—"What! that the fair Helen! I don't pique myself on beauty, but may I die if I would change faces with her!"

"I told your Majesty how it would be," remarked the enchanter; "and yet there she is, as she was in her best days."

"She has, however, very fine eyes," observed Essex.

"Yes," said Sidney, "they are large, dark, and brilliant—but after all, what do they say?" added he, correcting himself.

"Nothing," replied the favourite.

The Queen, who was this day extravagantly rouged, asked if they did not think Helen's tint too *China-white.*

"China!" cried the Earl; "Delf rather."

"Perhaps," continued the Queen, "it was the fashion of her time, but you must confess that such turned-in toes would have been endured in no other woman. I don't dislike her style of dress, however, and probably I may bring it round again, in place of these troublesome hoops, which have their inconveniences."

"O, as to the dress," chimed in the favourite—"let it pass, it is well enough, which is more than can be said for the wearer."

A conclusion, in which Sidney heartily joined, rhapsodying—

> "O Paris, fatal was the hour,
> When, victim to the blind God's power,
> Within your native walks you bore
> That firebrand from a foreign shore;
> Who—ah so little worth the strife!—
> Was fit for nothing, but a wife."

"Od's my life now," said her Majesty,—"but I think she looks fitter for any thing else, Sidney!—My Lord of Essex, how think you?"

"As your Majesty does," returned he;—"there is a meaning in that eye."

"And a minute past they said there was none," thought Faustus.

This liberal critique on the fair Helen being concluded, the Queen desired to see the beautiful and hopeless Mariamne.

The enchanter did not wait to be twice asked; but he did not chuse to invoke a Princess who had worshipped at holy altars in the same manner as he had summoned the fair Pagan. It was then, by way of ceremony, that turning four times to the east, three to the south, two to the west, and only once to the north, he uttered, with great suavity, in Hebrew—

> "Lovely Mariamne, come!
> Though thou sleepest far away,
> Regal spirit! leave thy tomb!
> Let the splendours round thee play,
> Silken robe and diamond stone,
> Such as, on thy bridal-day,
> Flash'd from proud Judea's throne."

Scarcely had he concluded, when the spouse of Herod made her appearance, and gravely advanced into the centre of the gallery, where she halted, as her predecessor had done. She was robed nearly like the high-priest of the Jews, except that instead of the Tiara, a veil, descending from the crown of the head, and slightly attached to the cincture, fell far behind her. Those graceful and flowing draperies, threw over the whole figure of the lovely Hebrew an air of indescribable dignity. After having stopped for several minutes before the company, she pursued her way,—but without paying the slightest parting compliment to the haughty Elizabeth.

"Is it possible," said the Queen, before she had well disappeared—"is it possible that Mariamne was such a figure as that?—such a tall, pale, meagre, melancholy-looking affair, to have passed for a beauty through so many centuries!"

"By my honour," quoth Essex, "had I been in Herod's place, I should never have been angry at her keeping her distance."

"Yet I perceived," said Sydney, "a certain touching languor in the countenance—an air of dignified simplicity."

Her Majesty looked grave.

"Fye, fye," returned Essex, "it was haughtiness—her manner is full of presumption,—aye, and even her height."

The Queen having approved of Essex's decision—on her own part, condemned the Princess for her aversion to her spouse, which, though the world alleged to have been caused by his being the cut-throat of her family, she saw nothing to justify, whatever a husband might be. A wife was a wife; and Herod had done quite right in cutting off the heads of the offenders.

Faustus, who affected universal knowledge, assured her Majesty that all the historians were in error on that point; for he had had it himself from a living witness, that the true cause of Herod's vengeance was his spiteful oldmaid of a sister—Salome's overhearing Mariamne—one day at prayers—beg of Heaven to rid her of her worthless husband.

After a moment of thought, the Queen, with the same indifference with which she would have called for her waiting-maid—desired to see Cleopatra; for the Egyptian queen not having been quite as *comme il faut* as the British, the latter treated her accordingly. The beautiful Cleopatra quickly made her appearance at the extremity of the gallery,—and Elizabeth expected that this apparition would fully make up for the disappointment which the others had occasioned. Scarcely had she entered, when the air was loaded with the rich perfumes of Arabia.

Her bosom (that had been melting as charity) was open as day,— a loop of diamonds and rubies gathered the drapery as much above the left knee, as it might as well have been below it,—and a woven wind of transparent gauze, softened the figure which it did not conceal.

In this gay and gallant costume, the mistress of Antony glided through the gallery, making a similar pause as the others. No sooner was her back turned, than the courtiers began to tear her person and frippery to pieces,—the Queen calling out, like one possessed, for paper to burn under her nose, to drive away the vapours occasioned by the gums with which the mummy was filled, —declared her insupportable in every sense, and far beneath even the wife of Herod, or the daughter of Leda,—shocked at her Diana drapery, to exhibit the most villainous leg in the world,—and protested that a thicker robe would have much better become her.

Whatever the two courtiers might have thought, they were forced to join in these sarcasms, which the frail Egyptian excited in peculiar severity.

"Such a cocked nose!" said the Queen.

"Such impertinent eyes!" said Essex.

Sydney, in addition to her other defects, found out that she had too much stomach and too little back.

"Say of her as you please," returned Faustus—"one she is, however, who led the Master of the World in her chains. But, Madam," added he, turning to the Queen, "as these far-famed foreign beauties are not to your taste, why go beyond your own kingdom, England, which has always produced the models of female perfection —as we may even at this moment perceive—will furnish an object perhaps worthy of your attention in the fair Rosamond." Now Faustus had heard that the Queen fancied herself to resemble the fair Rosamond; and no sooner was the name mentioned, than she was all impatience to see her.

"There is a secret instinct in this impatience," observed the Doctor, craftily; "for, according to tradition, the fair Rosamond had much resemblance to your Majesty, though, of course, in an inferior style."

"Let us judge—let us judge," replied the Queen, hastily, "but from the moment she appears, Sir Sydney, I request of you to observe her minutely, that we may have her description, if she is worth it." This order being given, and some little conjuration made, as Rosamond was only a short distance from London, she made her appearance in a second. Even at the door, her beauty charmed every one, but as she advanced, she enchanted them; and when she stopped to be gazed at, the admiration of the company, with difficulty restrained to signs and looks, exhibited their high approbation of the taste of Henry II. Nothing could exceed the simplicity of her dress—and yet in that simplicity she effaced the splendours of day—at least to the spectators. She waited before them a long time, much longer than the others had done; and, as if aware of the command the Queen had given, she turned especially towards Sydney, looking at him with an expressive smile,—but she must go at last; and when she was gone,—"My lord," said the Queen, "what a pretty creature! I never saw any thing so charming in my life. What a figure! what dignity without affectation! what brilliancy without artifice! and it is said that I resemble her. My lord of Essex, what think you?" My lord thought, would to Heaven you did; I would give the best steed in my stable that you had even an ugly likeness to her. But he said, "Your Majesty has but to make the tour of the gallery in her green robe and primrose petticoat, and if our magician himself would not mistake you for her, count me the greatest—of your three kingdoms."

During all this flattery with which the favourite charmed the ears of the good Queen, the poet Sydney, pencil in hand, was sketching the vision of the fair Rosamond.

Her Majesty then commanded it should be read, and when she heard it, pronounced it very clever; but as it was a real impromptu, not one of those born long before, and was written for a particular audience, as a picture is painted for a particular light—we think it but justice to the celebrated author, not to draw his lines from the venerable antiquity in which they rest, even if we had the MS. copy; but we have not—which at once finishes the business.

After the reading, they deliberated on the next that should succeed Rosamond,—the enchanter, still of opinion, that they need not leave England when beauty was the object in question, proposed the famous Countess of Salisbury—who gave rise to the institution of the garter—the idea was approved of by the Queen, and particularly agreeable to the courtiers, as they wished to see if the *cause* were worthy of the effect, *i.e.* the leg of the garter; but her Majesty declared that she should particularly like a second sight of her lovely resemblance, the fair Rosamond. The doctor vowed that the affair was next to impracticable in the order of conjuration,— the recall of a phantom not depending on the powers submitted to the first enchantments. But the more he declared against it, the more the Queen insisted, until he was obliged, at last, to submit, but with the information, that if Rosamond should return, it would not be by the way in which she had entered or retired already, and that they had best take care of themselves, as he could answer for no one.

The Queen, as we have elsewhere observed, knew not what fear was—and the two courtiers were now a little re-assured on the subject of apparitions. The doctor then set about accomplishing the Queen's wishes.—Never had conjuration cost him so much trouble, and after a thousand grimaces and contortions—neither pretty nor polite, he flung his book into the middle of the gallery, went three times round it on his hands and feet, then made the tree against the wall, head down and heels up; but nothing appearing, he had recourse to the last and most powerful of his spells—what that was must remain for ever a mystery, for certain reasons; but he wound it up by three times summoning with a sonorous voice,—"Rosamond! Rosamond! Rosamond!" At the last of these magic cries, the grand window burst open with the sudden crash of a tempest, and through it descended the lovely Rosamond into the middle of the room.

The Doctor was in a cold sweat, and while he dried himself, the Queen, who thought her fair visitant a thousand times the fairer for the additional difficulty in procuring this second sight, for once let her prudence sleep, and, in a transport of enthusiasm, stepping out of her circle with open arms, cried out, "My dear likeness!" No sooner was the word out, than a violent clap of thunder shook the whole palace; a black vapour filled the gallery, and a train of little fantastic lightnings, serpentined to the right and left in the dazzled eyes of the company.

When the obscurity was a little dissipated, they saw the magician, with his four limbs in air, foaming like a wild boar,—his cap here, his wig there, in short, by no means an object of either the sublime or beautiful. But though he came off the worst, yet no one in the adventure escaped *quite clear,* except Rosamond. The lightning burned away my Lord of Essex's right brow; Sir Sydney lost the left moustachio; her Majesty's head-dress smelt villainously of the sulphur, and her hoop-petticoat was so puckered up with the scorching, that it was ordered to be preserved among the royal draperies, as a warning, to all maids of honour to come, against curiosity.

Ever the Faith Endures

MANLY WADE WELLMAN

In contrast to the vivid gruesomeness of Alan Rodgers' "Emma's Daughter," elsewhere in this volume, is the following quiet tale of brooding menace. MANLY WADE WELLMAN *(1903–1986), one of the grand old men of the science-fantasy genre, was a winner of the World Fantasy Award as well as the Mystery Writers of America's "Edgar" (for fact-crime) and was a Pulitzer nominee for one of his historical novels. "Ever the Faith Endures" first appeared in* The Year's Best Horror Stories VI.

He'd somehow expected it to be like this. What else had he come looking for?

Though he'd never been here, had only wanted to be here. Had saved money for this journey overseas, then had puzzled and striven over railway timetables and guidebooks to get here. Here to the home his ancestors had left to go to America.

The place was swaddled in trees, there a couple of miles from the village where he'd left the train that noon, all among a landscape of tawny hills and softly grassed valleys, gatherings of sheep grazed here and there in the open, under the serene authority of black and white dogs. And no trees out there, only here, heavily marshalled beyond the quickset hedge with its June blossoms. There were yews, rowans, Scotch firs, two or three enormous oaks, with shrubs matted here and there underneath. It was like a solid chunk of forest taken from somewhere else and set here among the meadows and slopes and distant heights.

Wofford Belson stood opposite a driveway gap in the hedge. He was fifty-five, big but not soft, wearing the tweed suit he had bought in London. Gray stitched his heavy black hair. His face was square-jawed, vigorously seamed. He reminded himself that Belsons had been American for three hundred years. Before that, British for how many thousands?

Movement among the trees, and a woman stepped into view. She was tall, slim, in dark blue slacks and a white blouse and a gray jacket. Her hair was a fine toss of syrupy brown. She wore broad spectacles. In one long hand she held a trowel. She came toward him.

"Yes?" she said.

Belson wished he had a hat to take off.

"I wondered—" he began, stopped, and started again. "Does this house happen to be called Belstone?"

"Yes," she said again, clipping the syllables. "It happens to be called Belstone."

"Let me explain." He wondered if he could. "My name's Wofford Belson, but it used to be Belstone." Once more he stopped.

"Used to be?" she prompted. Behind the spectacles her watchful eyes were as blue as deep, clean water, and as calm. She was, he thought, perhaps forty-two or forty-three. And quite pretty.

"I'm American," he said unnecessarily. "The name got changed over there. Back in 1643, in Virginia." He smiled, white-toothed. "That's long ago in America, if it's not long ago here."

"And I daresay you're curious about your British origins, Mr. Belson," she said gently. "I am Anne Belstone, and we must be cousins, at a number of removes." She smiled, ever so slightly, and she had a dimple. "Forgive me if I seemed careful. I live here alone, you know, and I don't get many callers." Her blue eyes appraised him. "But come into the yard if you like."

"Thank you, ma'am," he said. "I ought to say, I'm from North Carolina, a town called Chapel Hill. That's where the State university is."

"You are of the university?" she asked as he walked into the driveway and toward her. "You teach?"

"No, ma'am, but I graduated from there, and I have a book store in town. Now that I'm alone in the world—divorced, my children grown up—I wanted to come here. I always wanted to. Hoped to make it during the war, but they sent me to the Pacific theater." He felt that he was jabbering nervously, and wondered why. "I do know something, not much, about my family before the name got changed."

"Do you know why the name is Belstone?" she asked. "Do come and sit on the porch, I was going to have tea there. Would you care for a cup?"

"I thank you, ma'am, that's right good of you."

"Not at all."

They walked along the pebbled driveway. Overhead, the trees crossed stirring green branches. The driveway curved in around a gaunt, jagged rock, mottled gray in color and almost as tall as Belson. He thought that Anne Belstone drew away from it as she walked, and would have looked at it closely, but there was the house.

He stopped in his tracks to look. It was what he had wanted, without knowing it.

The house was squarely and massively built, with lean windows in its two stories and dormers in the high slate roof. The stone of the walls was gray with a hint of rose. Up the two gable sides sprouted wide chimneys of the same rose-gray stone, built into the walls themselves and each crowned with a row of hatlike pots. Across the front sprawled a paved porch with sturdy posts of cut stones in dark mortar. Inside the windows behind the porch clung tawny curtains. Along the porch's edge stood flower pots with tufts of bloom.

"Is something wrong?" asked Anne Belstone at his shoulder.

"I was admiring the house."

"I suppose it's different from houses in the States."

"The chimneys," he tried to explain his feelings. "They're part of the house, of the walls. Not put on after the house was built, not tacked on as an afterthought."

She chuckled. It was a musical chuckle.

"Well, sir, generations of your forebears lived here. This house, or most of it, goes back to Elizabethan times. I think of it as utilitarian, old-fashioned. You make me wonder if it isn't more than that. But come up and sit on the porch."

They mounted the blocky steps. "Here," she said, and laid a hand on the back of a chair of weathered, solid wood. "Sit here and I'll fetch us out a tray."

Then she was gone. Belson sat in the chair. Next to it was a blocky table. He looked out into the trees of the yard.

Someone stood beside the driveway. No, it was the jagged rock. It was like an ill-proportioned human figure in the shadows. It seemed to have sloping shoulders and a knobby head. Eyes? But they were only scraps of shadow. The mouth-like crack was just a crack. Belson told himself that. For a moment he almost got out of the chair to step from the porch and walk down to examine the rough pillar. Then he lectured himself to wait and ask Anne Belstone about it first.

Behind him he fancied he heard a rustle. He turned in his chair, expecting to see his hostess. There was only a window behind him, and a stir in the stealthy curtains.

Then she came through the door, bringing a broad tray set with heaped dishes. He rose, took the tray from her and set it on the table.

"I hope you don't mind tea," she said, sitting in another chair. "I believe that most Americans prefer coffee."

"Tea suits me fine, ma'am," he said. "Don't fret about Americans not appreciating it. Some of them dumped a whole shipload of it into Boston harbor one time."

She laughed her musical laugh and poured him a cup. He declined cream and sugar and thanked her when she put a roll and a pat of butter on a plate for him. They ate and drank.

"That's a right interesting chunk of rock in your yard," he felt it was time to remark. "For a moment, sitting here, I thought it looked like somebody coming in."

She set down her cup, her eyes moody behind the spectacles. "I'd better tell you about that. That stone is named Belstone, too."

"It is?" he said, smiling, for he had begun to like her company. "Who named it that?"

"Nobody knows. It's been here, probably, since prehistoric times. And the name means a god. Baal."

She sipped tea. Belson gazed at the stone, disliking the fancy that it gazed back at him.

"Baal," he repeated. "That's out of the Bible."

"Out of many places," said Anne Belstone. "Baal was worshipped by Old Testament people, by European pagans, worshipped here in the British Isles. His name's on the land. Balquiddir and Balgonie in Scotland, Baltimore in Ireland—they hark back to Baal, worshipped by the Celts before the Romans."

"And we have the name too, Cousin Anne."

She smiled again when he called her that. "Yes, let's be cousinly. I'll call you cousin—Wofford, you said?"

"That's my mother's family name. I've lots of Wofford kinfolk."

"Kinfolk," she said after him. "Not me. I was an only child, so was my father, and his father before him. Any cousins I have are almost as distant as you, Cousin Wofford. I don't keep in touch with them, and I have no friends you could call friends, not here. People don't come here."

"Not the milkman, the postman?"

"I get milk and letters and supplies yonder in the village. I've a little car out behind, to do my errands. I don't even try to keep up this house, so forgive me for not taking you inside. I live in just a bedroom and a kitchen."

He had a sense of movement at the window, but did not look. "We were talking about the name Belstone," he reminded her.

"And I said the stone was always there where you see it. The Romans invaded and wanted to take it away, but some sort of disaster happened to anyone who tried, so they left it. When Saxon missionaries came along, they learned to let it alone, too."

"Was it that bad?" asked Belson, gazing at the rock.

"Bad enough that someone was told off, about a thousand years ago, to live here and guard it; and he took the name Belstone on account of his job."

"Baal's stone," said Belson, buttering a bit of roll. "Why Baal's stone? Was it an altar?"

Anne Belstone's shoulders drew up, in not quite a shudder. "You can say that. The old pagans had human sacrifices—that's why the Romans were so bitter about them. And where sacrifice has been, a spirit stays. It can't be exorcised."

"The missionaries tried, I reckon."

"Yes, and they failed. This must sound silly to you."

"It sounds fascinating, Cousin Anne."

She dimpled at the name. "Well, the stone's stayed where you see it, all those centuries. And the Belstones have lived here beside it, and sometimes got into trouble and then got out."

"One got to America," said Belson. "My ancestor Thomas."

"What do you know of him?"

"Almighty little," admitted Belson. "His name's in a book about persons of quality coming to America. He arrived at Jamestown in 1643, aboard a ship named *Bristol Venture,* and there's a note saying he had to take a special oath of allegiance to Charles the First. I've wondered about that."

"I can tell you," said Anne Belstone. "He was a younger son—the older son, Alan, was my ancestor. The records say that Thomas Belstone claimed magical powers. One day Matthew Hopkins arrived in this area. Do you know who he was?"

"A witch-hunter, wasn't he?"

"England's Witch-finder General. Thomas Belstone was one of twenty-three accused witches here, and the only one not hanged. He seems to have had money and friends to help him get more or less exiled instead."

"I'm glad he got to America," said Belson, smiling into her spectacled eyes. "He married a girl with Indian blood, and I'm glad for that, too. A drop of the Indian—that's really American."

She pondered that for a moment. Then:

"My ancestor Alan joined Cromwell—the winning side." Her soft voice had music in it. "He profited by that and he enlarged this house. We've lived here ever since, and I hope this much family history will content you, because I don't know much more."

"It's pleasant on this porch." He changed the subject.

"Sometimes, when I sit out here at night, I hear a nightingale sing in the trees."

"Nightingale," he said after her. "We don't have those in America. I've often wondered how they sounded."

But she did not invite him to stay and find out. He set down his teacup.

"You said you won't show me the house, but I'd like to walk out and look at that rock I'm named for."

"Well . . ." That was no permission, but no refusal, either.

He rose and walked into the yard. The gravelled way was bordered with shaggy moss, in which grew tiny red toadstools. He reached the rock. It stood as tall as himself. It was like the outline of a human shape, but if it had been hewn like that, the marks of hewing had long weathered away. Belstone studied the shadowed dints that looked like eyes, the crack that ran across like a mouth. That crack seemed to twist wryly.

"You're not pretty," he addressed it. "No wonder the old Romans wanted to put you away. What if I just shoved you over?"

He lifted a hand, but he did not touch the rock. At that moment, it seemed to blur, as in a mist. He had a sensation of cold. And he heard the murmur of a voice.

That made him jump backward and turn around.

Anne Belstone had come silently out with him. Her hands clasped themselves in front of her. She whispered something. A prayer? But he did not know the words:

"Sobrosto, ekkshilhai—pion fhanfhantishm—"

She sidled away.

"What did you say?" he asked her.

"Old words I was taught when I was a girl."

"Some kind of spell?"

She did not answer that. "Come," she said, and turned to lead him back to the porch. He sat down and lifted his teacup, and silently cursed his hand for trembling.

"You had your wish, saw it at close quarters," she said. "Why did you make fun of it?"

He looked out at the silent rock. "You said, human sacrifices."

"Only in those days before the Romans. Later on, blood sacrifices of animals." Her smooth cheek looked tense. "When a god's overthrown, it becomes a devil."

"And a devil must be bought off," he tried to fall in with her unhappy humor.

"Yes, he must be bought off."

"Let's talk about something else, Cousin Anne. Thanks, I'd like more tea."

She asked about his children. He talked proudly of his lawyer son who had two sons himself, and of his daughter who was finishing her studies for a doctorate in psychology. He told about his book store and how happily he kept it. He said he approved of old shoes and the novels of P. G. Wodehouse, and of vacations in the mountains and at the seaside.

She talked more briefly about herself. She had always lived at Belstone, except when she had gone to school as a girl. When her parents died, she had stayed there, quietly alone.

"Haven't men come visiting?" he teased her, smiling. "I'd think that any man who was a man would want to."

"I know very few men."

"You ought to come and visit in North Carolina."

"You make it sound perfect there," she said.

"Nothing's perfect, but most time things are good. Beautiful spring and summer and fall, and mild winters. And I have friends, some of them professors, scholars. You'd like them." He looked at her earnestly. "They'd like you, too."

At last her own smile came back. "Why do you think that?"

"They'd have to, because I like you so much myself."

"I wish I could come." She sounded as if she meant it. She rose and began to gather up the tea things.

"I hate to bring this to an end, Cousin Wofford."

"Why bring it to an end?" he protested.

Her eyes were blue, blue, behind the spectacles. "You have quite a walk to the village. You'll want to be there by sundown."

"It won't be sundown for quite a while. Look, come with me. We can have dinner at the inn."

She stacked dishes on the tray. "I mustn't, really. But it's been good having you here. You're—well, so healthy, so cheerful."

"You don't look unhealthy, and you could be cheerful if you half tried," he said. "I want to help you to try."

"I might be cheerful if—"

She left it unfinished. He studied the sweet curve of her cheek as she bent over the tray.

"Look here, why didn't you ever marry?" He demanded suddenly, strong in the sense it was none of his business. "You ought to have a family, children."

"No," she said gently, "not for me. If you'll excuse me, I'll take these back to the kitchen."

She carried the tray to the door and turned the knob with her free hand. She stepped inside and closed the door behind her. He heard the click of the catch. Had she locked it from inside? Why?

Rising, he walked to the door and turned the big brass knob. It wasn't locked. He pushed it inward and stepped into the house.

Dim in there, a sort of sandy-brown light. That was from the curtains at the window. He took half a dozen steps along a hall and looked through an open arch into a broad, dim room.

It was walled with darkly aged wooden panels and set with upright timbers, like the ribs of a ship's hold. Furniture stood here and there, draped with dusty sheets. At the far end, a fireplace, and, though it was warm June outside, a nest of coals burned redly on the hearth. Belson felt its heat.

On the hob of the fireplace was built up a little cube of stones. Upon it, as upon an altar, lay what looked like shreds of raw meat.

Belson gazed at the hearth, wondering. Something moved on the far side of the room, beside a draped chair, something black and bulky. Belson turned his gaze upon it.

Only a particularly deep shadow, shifting perhaps in the light of the coals. Or a robe or coat of heavy dark fur, thrown there. Or—

But it stirred again. It rose slowly erect, like a black bear, gross and shaggy. But not a bear either, not with that broad flat face, those glowing pale eyes. Where the nose should be was a damp blob, like soggy brown leather, with staring nostrils. The mouth was a broad cleft. Upper and lower teeth jutted, like splinters of china.

Frozen, unbelieving, Belson looked. The glowing eyes looked back at him. Long, knobby arms lifted, spreading hands like hairy rakes. Talons glinted, as sharp and pale as the teeth. The mouth gaped, made a crooning snarl. It stepped toward him, on long flippers of feet.

"No, you don't!" Belson found his voice. "Stay away from me!"

He turned to run, and bumped into Anne Belstone. She pushed him into the hall. She raised her arms high.

"Athe, pemeath." She was saying more strange words. *"Somiatoai, haliha."*

It stood fast, its eyes flashed pale.

"Ah jathos noio sattis," Belson heard her chant. *"Ishoroh."*

He ran into the hall, leaving her alone there. He scrabbled the door open and was out on the porch, gasping for breath.

"Selu, samhaiah," said her voice in the house behind him. *"Trinu, iamensaha."*

He clung dizzily to the back of a chair. His knees wavered. Something made a noise behind him and he looked back in terror. Anne Belstone was on the porch, closing the door. She walked toward him. Her sweet face was as pale as a pan of fresh milk.

"Now," she said gently. "Now you know why I didn't want to invite you into the house."

"That in there," he mouthed. "A man or an animal or what?"

"Not man or animal." She was precise, informative. "I told you that the Belstones were ordered to look after him."

"A god, is that thing a god?"

"He used to be. Now he's what he is. Always hungry."

Belson gestured. "You said words to drive him back."

"I told you, my parents made me learn them." She shrugged. "I keep him here, so that he won't plague others—plague the world."

Something scraped inside the heavy door. She turned that way. *"Heriel aias stoch nahas,"* she pronounced. The scraping ceased.

"He's not wholly satisfied with pieces of butcher's meat or just rabbits or chickens," she said wearily. "Maybe he thought you were the sort of sacrifice he used to expect."

He blinked at her. "You worship him," he half accused.

"Yes," she agreed. "Yes, I do. That way, I can keep him here. And now, you must go."

"Go?" He looked out at the jagged stone pillar.

"Probably he knows you're of the Belstone blood. That makes it bad for you, very bad. You must never come near this house again."

The drapes stirred at a window.

"How can you possibly live here?" cried Belson, wondering at how steady her stance was, her voice was. "How can you?"

"Because I've always lived here," she replied. "I was brought up to live here, stay here, see that he stays here, too. It's what I'm on earth for."

"No!" he fairly shouted into her calm, pale face. He seized both her slim hands in his big ones. "Come with me."

"Come with you?" she said after him and stared.

"Come home to America with me, Anne. Don't even step back inside there for anything. We'll buy you clothes, whatever you need, in London. We'll go back together, back home. It'll be your home, too." He pressed her hands. "Come with me," he begged. "Please!"

"I can't. If you'll only stop to think, you'll know why I can't. It's for me to live here at Belstone and keep him here, too. Keep him here away from everyone else."

"But when you don't live to keep him any more?" he prodded at her. "When you die at last?"

"Who knows what will happen then?" Her voice rose, her hands gripped his. "Who can know that? I'll be dead, I'll be past knowing. But until I'm dead, I'll stay and keep him here."

Strongly she dragged her hands free of his grip.

"Now, this is my house," she said, "though just now it may not seem quite like that to you. This is my house, and I must tell you to leave."

"I won't leave," he tried to argue.

"Go this instant," she commanded. "If you don't, I'll open the door and let him out here."

Again, a stir at the drapes of the window.

"And you know that I mean what I say," she told him. "Go on, go away, and don't ever come back."

She pushed him toward the steps, with a power he had not expected in her slim body. He blundered down them to the gravel below.

"Go away!" she cried at him once more.

He walked along the driveway. As he came opposite the rock he heard a sound from it, like a sigh of wind. Its eye-patches shone suddenly, as bits of ice shine. The crack of a mouth seemed to twitch.

He quickened his steps. Out on the road, he turned toward the village. He dared not look back. He could not have seen her, anyway. Upon him rushed a grinding sense of loss, of defeat.

His breath shook in his throat. He felt a trickle of wet on his cheeks. He was in tears, for the first time since he had been a little, little boy.

The Old Man of Visions

ALGERNON BLACKWOOD

Not all mystical power derives from the Devil. The tone of transcendental wonder of "The Old Man of Visions" is unusual for ALGERNON BLACKWOOD *(1869–1951), the British author of such justly famous supernatural tales as "The Willows," "The Wendigo," and "The Woman's Ghost Story" (in* Ghosts, Doubleday, 1981*).*

The image of Teufelsdröckh, sitting in his watch-tower "alone with the stars," leaped into my mind the moment I saw him: and the curious expression of his eyes proclaimed at once that here was a being who allowed the world of small effects to pass him by, while he himself dwelt among the eternal verities. It was only necessary to catch a glimpse of the bent grey figure, so slight yet so tremendous, to realise that he carried staff and wallet, and was travelling alone in a spiritual region, uncharted, and full of wonder, difficulty, and fearful joy.

The inner eye perceived this quite as clearly as the outer was aware of his Hebraic ancestry; but along what winding rivers, through what haunted woods, by the shores of what singing seas he pressed forward towards the mountains of his goal, no one could guess from a mere inspection of that wonderful old face.

To have stumbled upon such a figure in the casual way I did

seemed incredible to me even at the time, yet I at once caught
something of the uplifting airs that followed this inhabitant of a
finer world, and I spent days—and considered them well spent—
trying to get into conversation with him, so that I might know
something more than the thin disguise of his holding a reader's
ticket for the Museum Library.

To reach the stage of intimacy where actual speech is a hindrance
to close understanding, one need not in some cases have spoken at
all. Thus by merely setting my mind, and above all, my imagination, into tune with his, and by steeping myself so much in his
atmosphere that I absorbed and then gave back to him with my own
stamp the forces he exhaled, it was at length possible to persuade
those vast-seeing eyes to turn in my direction; and our glances having once met, I simply rose when he rose, and followed him out of
the little smoky restaurant so closely up the street that our clothes
brushed, and I thought I could even catch the sound of his breathing.

Whether, having already weighed me, he accepted the office, or
whether he was grateful for the arm to lean upon, with his many
years' burden, I do not know; but the sympathy between us was
such that, without a single word, we walked up that foggy London
street to the door of his lodging in Bloomsbury, while I noticed
that at the touch of his arm the noise of the town seemed to turn
into deep singing, and even the hurrying passers-by seemed bent
upon noble purposes; and though he barely reached to my shoulder, and his grey beard almost touched my glove as I bent my arm
to hold his own, there was something immense about his figure that
sent him with towering stature above me and filled my thoughts
with enchanting dreams of grandeur and high beauty.

But it was only when the door had closed on him with a little
rush of wind, and I was walking home alone, that I fully realised the
shock of my return to earth; and on reaching my own rooms I
shook with laughter to think I had walked a mile and a half with a
complete stranger without uttering a single syllable. Then the
laughter suddenly hushed as I caught my face in the glass with the
expression of the soul still lingering about the eyes and forehead,
and for a brief moment my heart leaped to a sort of noble fever in
the blood, leaving me with the smart of the soul's wings stirring
beneath the body's crushing weight. And when it passed I found

myself dwelling upon the words he had spoken when I left him at the door:

"I am the Old Man of Visions, and I am *at your service.*"

I think he never had a name—at least, it never passed his lips, and perhaps lay buried with so much else of the past that he clearly deemed unimportant. To me, at any rate, he became simply the Old Man of Visions, and to the little waiting-maid and the old landlady he was known simply as "Mister"—Mister, neither more nor less. The impenetrable veil that hung over his past never lifted for any vital revelations of his personal history, though he evidently knew all the countries of the world, and had absorbed into his heart and brain the experience of all possible types of human nature; and there was an air about him not so much of "Ask me no questions," as "Do not ask me, for I cannot answer you *in words.*"

He could satisfy, but not in mere language; he would reveal, but by the wonderful words of silence only; for he was the Old Man of Visions, and visions need no words, being swift and of the spirit.

Moreover, the landlady—poor, dusty, faded woman—the landlady stood in awe, and disliked being probed for information in a passage-way down which he might any moment tread, for she could only tell me, "He just came in one night, years ago, and he's been here ever since!" And more than that I never knew. "Just came in —one night—years ago." This adequately explained him, for where he came *from,* or was journeying *to,* was something quite beyond the scope of ordinary limited language.

I pictured him suddenly turning aside from the stream of unimportant events, quietly stepping out of the world of straining, fighting, and shouting, and moving to take his rightful place among the forces of the still, spiritual region where he belonged by virtue of long pain and difficult attainment. For he was unconnected with any conceivable network of relations, friends, or family, and his terrible aloofness could not be disturbed by anyone unless with his permission and by his express wish. Nor could he be imagined as "belonging" to any definite set of souls. He was apart from the world—and above it.

But it was only when I began to creep a little nearer to him, and our strange, silent intimacy passed from mental to spiritual, that I began really to understand more of this wonderful Old Man of Visions.

Steeped in the tragedy, and convulsed with laughter at the comedy, of life, he yet lived there in his high attic wrapped in silence as in a golden cloud; and so seldom did he actually speak to me that each time the sound of his voice, that had something elemental in it —something of winds and waters—thrilled me with the power of the first time. He lived, like Teufelsdröckh, "alone with the stars," and it seemed impossible, more and more, to link him on anywhere into practical dealings with ordinary men and women. Life somehow seemed to pass *below* him. Yet the small, selfish spirit of the recluse was far from him, and he was tenderly and deeply responsive to pain and suffering, and more particularly to genuine yearning for the far things of beauty. The unsatisfied longings of others could move him at once to tears.

"My relations with men are perfect," he said one night as we neared his dwelling. "I give them all sympathy out of my stores of knowledge and experience, and they give to me what kindness I need. My outer shell lies within impenetrable solitude, for only so can my inner life move freely along the paths and terraces that are thronged with the beings to whom I belong." And when I asked him how he maintained such deep sympathy with humanity, and had yet absolved himself apparently from action as from speech, he stopped against an area railing and turned his great eyes on to my face, as though their fires could communicate his thought without the husk of words:

"I have peered too profoundly into life and beyond it," he murmured, "to wish to express in language what I *know*. Action is not for all, always; and I am in touch with the cisterns of thought that lie behind action. I ponder the mysteries. What I may solve is not lost for lack either of speech or action, for the true mystic is ever the true man of action, and my thought will reach others as soon as they are ready for it in the same way that it reached you. All who strongly yearn must, sooner or later, find me and be comforted."

His eyes shifted from my face towards the stars, softly shining above the dark Museum roof, and a moment later he had disappeared into the hallway of his house.

"An old poet who has strayed afield and lost his way," I mused; but through the door where he had just vanished the words came back to me as from a great distance: "A priest, rather, who has begun to find his way."

For a space I stood, pondering on his face and words: that mercilessly intelligent look of the Hebrew woven in with the expression of the sadness of a whole race, yet touched with the glory of the spirit; and his utterance—that he had passed through all the traditions and no longer needed a formal, limited creed to hold to. I forget how I reached my own door several miles away, but it seemed to me that I flew.

In this way, and by unregistered degrees, we came to know each other better, and he accepted me and took me into his life. Always wrapped in the great calm of his delightful silence, he taught me more, and told me more, than could ever lie within the confines of mere words; and in moments of need, no matter when or where, I always knew exactly how to find him, reaching him in a few seconds by some swift way that disdained the means of ordinary locomotion.

Then at last one day he gave me the key of his house. And the first time I found my way into his aery, and realised that it was a haven I could always fly to when the yearnings of the heart and soul struggled vainly for recompense, the full meaning and importance of the Old Man of Visions became finally clear to me.

[2]

The room, high up creaky, darkened stairs in the ancient house, was bare and fireless, looking through a single patched window across a tumbled sea of roofs and chimneys; yet there was that in it which instantly proclaimed it a little holy place out of the world, a temple in which someone with spiritual vitality had worshipped, prayed, wept, and sung.

It was dusty and unswept, yet it was utterly *unsoiled;* and the Old Man of Visions who lived there, for all his shabby and stained garments, his uncombed beard and broken shoes, stood within its door revealed in his real self, moving in a sort of divine whiteness, iridescent, shining. And here, in this attic (lampless and unswept), high up under the old roofs of Bloomsbury, the window scarred with rain and the corners dropping cobwebs, I heard his silver whisper issue from the shadows:

"Here you may satisfy your soul's desire and may commune with the Invisibles; only, to find the Invisibles, you must first be able to lose yourself."

Ah! through that stained window-pane, the sight leaping at a single bound from black roofs up to the stars, what pictures, dreams, and visions the Old Man has summoned to my eyes! Distances, measureless and impossible hitherto, became easy, and from the oppression of dead bricks and the market-place he transported me in a moment to the slopes of the Mountains of Dream; leading me to little places near the summits where the pines grew thinly and the stars were visible through their branches, fading into the rose of dawn; where the winds tasted of the desert, and the voices of the wilderness fled upward with a sound of wings and falling streams. At his word houses melted away, and the green waves of all the seas flowed into their places; forests waved themselves into the coastline of dull streets; and the power of the old earth, with all her smells and flowers and wild life, thrilled down among the dead roofs and caught me away into freedom among the sunshine of meadows and the music of sweet pipings. And with the divine deliverance came the crying of sea-gulls, the glimmer of reedy tarns, the whispering of wind among grasses, and the healing scorch of a real sun upon the skin.

And poetry such as was never known or heard before clothed all he uttered, yet even then took no form in actual words, for it was of the substance of aspiration and yearning, voicing adequately all the busy, high-born dreams that haunt the soul yet never live in the uttered line. He breathed it about him in the air so that it filled my being. It was part of him—beyond words; and it sang my own longings, and sang them perfectly so that I was satisfied; for my own mood never failed to touch him instantly and to waken the right response. In its essence it was spiritual—the mystic poetry of heaven; still, the love of humanity informed it, for starfire and heart's blood were about equally mingled there, while the mystery of unattainable beauty moved through it like a white flame.

With other dreams and longings, too, it was the same; and all the most beautiful ideas that ever haunted a soul undowered with expression here floated with satisfied eyes and smiling lips before one —floated in silence, unencumbered, unlimited, unrestrained by words.

In this dim room, never made ugly by artificial light, but always shadowy in a kind of gentle dusk, the Old Man of Visions had only to lead me to the window to bring peace. Music, that rendered the soul fluid, as it poured across the old roofs into the room, was summoned by him at need; and when one's wings beat sometimes against the prison walls and the yearning for escape oppressed the heart, I have heard the little room rush and fill with the sound of trees, wind among grasses, whispering branches, and lapping waters. The very odours of space and mountainside came too, and the looming of noble hills seemed visible overhead against the stars, as though the ceiling had suddenly become transparent.

For the Old Man of Visions had the power of instantly satisfying an ideal when once that ideal created a yearning that could tear and burn its way out with sufficient force to set the will a-moving.

[3]

But as the time passed and I came to depend more and more upon the intimacy with my strange old friend, new light fell upon the nature and possibilities of our connection. I discovered, for instance, that though I held the key to his dwelling, and was familiar with the way, he was nevertheless not always available. Two things, in different fashion, rendered him inaccessible, or mute; and, for the first, I gradually learned that when life was prosperous, and the body singing loud, I could not find my way to his house. No amount of wandering, calculation, or persevering effort enabled me even to find the street again. With any burst of worldly success, however fleeting, the Old Man of Visions somehow slipped away into remote shadows and became unreal and misty. A merely passing desire to be with him, to seek his inspiration by a glimpse through that magic window-pane, resulted only in vain and tiresome pacing to and fro along ugly streets that produced weariness and depression; and after these periods it became, I noticed, less and less easy to discover the house, to fit the key in the door, or, having gained access to the temple, to realise the visions I *thought* I craved for.

Often, in this way, have I searched in vain for days, but only succeeded in losing myself in the murky purlieus of a quite strange Bloomsbury; stopping outside numberless counterfeit doors, and struggling vainly with locks that knew nothing of my little shining key.

But, on the other hand, pain, loneliness, sorrow—the merest whisper of spiritual affliction—and, lo, in a single moment the difficult geography became plain, and without hesitation, when I was unhappy or distressed, I found the way to his house as by a bird's instinctive flight, and the key slipped into the lock as though it loved it and was returning home.

The other cause to render him inaccessible, though not so determined—since it never concealed the way to the house—was even more distressing, for it depended wholly on myself; and I came to know how the least ugly action, involving a depreciation of ideals, so confused my mind that, when I got into the house, with difficulty, and found him in the little room after much searching, he was able to do or say scarcely anything at all for me. The mirror facing the door then gave back, I saw, no proper reflection of his person, but only a faded and wavering shadow with dim eyes and stooping, indistinct outline, and I even fancied I could see the pattern of the wall and shape of the furniture *through* his body, as though he had grown semi-transparent.

"You must not expect yearnings to weigh," came his whisper, like wind far overhead, "unless you lend to them *your own* substance; and your own substance you cannot both keep and lend. If you would know the Invisibles, forget yourself."

And later, as the years slipped away one after another into the mists, and the frontier between the real and the unreal began to shift amazingly with his teachings, it became more and more clear to me that he belonged to a permanent region that, with all the changes in the world's history, has itself never altered in any essential particular. This immemorial Old Man of Visions, as I grew to think of him, had existed always; he was old as the sea and coeval with the stars; and he dwelt beyond time and space, reaching out a hand to all those who, weary of the shadows and illusions of practical life, really call to him with their heart of hearts. To me, indeed, the touch of sorrow was always near enough to prevent his becoming often inaccessible, and after a while even his voice became so *living* that I sometimes heard it calling to me in the street and in the fields.

Oh, wonderful Old Man of Visions! Happy the days of disaster, since they taught me how to know you, the Unraveller of Problems, the Destroyer of Doubts, who bore me ever away with soft flight down the long, long vistas of the heart and soul!

And his loneliness in that temple attic under the stars, his loneliness, too, had a meaning I did not fail to understand later, and why he was always available for me and seemed to belong to no other.

"To everyone who finds me," he said, with the strange smile that wrapped his whole being and not his face alone, "to everyone I am the same, and yet different. I am not really ever alone. The whole world, nay"—his voice rose to a singing cry—"the whole universe lies in this room, or just beyond that window-pane; for here past and future meet and all real dreams find completeness. But remember," he added—and there was a sound as of soft wind and rain in the room with his voice—"no true dream can ever be shared, and should you seek to explain me to another you must lose me beyond recall. You have never asked my name, nor must you ever tell it. Each must find me in his own way."

Yet one day, for all my knowledge and his warnings, I felt so sure of my intimacy with this immemorial being, that I spoke of him to a friend who was, I had thought, so much a part of myself that it seemed no betrayal. And my friend, who went to search and found nothing, returned with the fool's laughter on his face, and swore that no street or number existed, for he had looked in vain, and had repeatedly *asked the way.*

And, from that day to this, the Old Man of Visions has neither called to me nor let his place be found; the streets are strange and empty, and I have even lost the little shining key.

Too Far

FREDRIC BROWN

FREDRIC BROWN *(1907–1972), one of America's most delightful genre writers, distinguished his writing career with such acclaimed mystery novels as* The Fabulous Clipjoint *(which won an "Edgar" from the Mystery Writers of America) and* Night of the Jabberwock *as well as unforgettable science-fantasy such as* What Mad Universe *and* Martians Go Home, *which, according to Roberta Pryor, agent to the Brown literary estate, is soon to be filmed. When he wasn't writing deadly serious fiction, Brown often indulged in punishing humor. "Too Far" is a particularly outrageous example.*

R. Austin Wilkinson was a bon vivant, man about Manhattan, and chaser of women. He was also an incorrigible punster on every possible occasion. In speaking of his favorite activity, for example, he would remark that he was a wolf, as it were, but that didn't make him a werewolf.

Excruciating as this statement may have been to some of his friends, it was almost true. Wilkinson was not a werewolf; he was a werebuck.

A night or two nights every week he would stroll into Central Park, turn himself into a buck and take great delight in running and playing.

True, there was always danger of his being seen but (since he punned even in his thoughts) he was willing to gambol on that.

Oddly, it had never occurred to him to combine the pleasures of being a wolf, as it were, with the pleasures of being a buck.

Until one night. Why, he asked himself that night, couldn't a lucky buck make a little doe? Once thought of, the idea was irresistible. He galloped to the wall of the Central Park Zoo and trotted along it until his sensitive buck nose told him he'd found the right place to climb the fence. He changed into a man for the task of climbing and then, alone in a pen with a beautiful doe, he changed himself back into a buck.

She was sleeping. He nudged her gently and whispered a suggestion. Her eyes opened wide and startled. "No, no, a dozen times no!"

"Only a doezen times?" he asked, and then leered. *"My deer,"* he whispered, *"think of the fawn you'll have!"*

Which went too far. He might have got away with it had his deer really been only a doe, but she was a weremaid—a doe who could change into a girl—and she was a witch as well. She quickly changed into a girl and ran for the fence. When he changed into a man and started after her she threw a spell over her shoulder, a spell that turned him back to a buck and froze him that way.

Do you ever visit the Central Park Zoo? Look for the buck with the sad eyes; he's Wilkinson.

He is sad despite the fact that the doe-weremaid, who is now the toast of New York ballet (she is graceful as a deer, the critics say) visits him occasionally by night and, resumes her proper form.

But when he begs for release from the spell she only smiles sweetly and tells him no, that she is of a very saving disposition and wants to keep the first buck she ever made.

Doctor Faustus
Journeys to Hell

We met Doctor Faustus earlier in this volume in "The Enchanter Faustus and Queen Elizabeth," a latter-day addition to his voluminous myth that directly or indirectly influenced many authors, most notably Johann Wolfgang von Goethe, Christopher Marlowe, and (indirectly) George Gordon, Lord Byron. The Faustian legend, based on the exploits of an itinerant conjurer not unknown to Martin Luther, is Medieval in origin and initially appeared in print as the Faustbuch, *published in 1587 at Frankfurt, Germany, and soon translated into English as* The History of the Damnable Life and Deserved Death of Doctor John Faustus. *I have adapted the following bizarre picaresque from that work. (For further comment, see Appendix II, page 524.)*

Eight years of Doctor Faustus's contracted span elapsed in study, inquiry, and disputation, but as the time drew near for the Devil to come for him the scholar dreamed about Hell, so he called his familiar spirit, Mephistopheles, and told him to summon up his master Belial. Mephistopheles did as requested, but instead of Belial came Beelzebub, an airborne sprite whose dominion lay under Heaven. He demanded to know what Faustus wanted.

Said the mortal, "Is it possible for you to take me into Hell for a visit, so that I may note the quintessential qualities of the Pit?"

"This may be done," Beelzebub replied. "At midnight shall I come for thee."

The fiend kept his word; as the night's darkest hour struck, Beelzebub returned carrying upon his back an enclosed sedan chair fashioned entirely of human bone. Doctor Faustus sat in it, whereupon the evil sprite soared into the air with his passenger, who fell fast asleep and did not rouse till Beelzebub plummeted into a roaring volcano that belched up mountains of brimstone and fire. Though the conflagration raged all around him, Doctor Faustus remained cool as if visited by balmy spring breezes; in the air he heard dulcet music performed by some invisible orchestra that he could not inquire about, for Beelzebub had sternly imposed upon him the condition that on this infernal sojourn, Faustus must ask no questions.

In flight, Beelzebub resembled a dragon, and soon three more diabolical fire-drakes joined him and his passenger as they plunged ever downward. Suddenly a monstrous stag flew at Doctor Faustus and would have plucked him up with its huge antlers and thrown him into Hell, but Beelzebub's three brother-dragons routed the beast. A menacing ring of gigantic serpents loomed up next, only to be chased off by a pride of winged lions, but then a monstrous raging bull shot up from a dark hole and charged the sedan chair, which overturned and pitched both devil and mortal into the abyss. The screaming philosopher, losing sight of his protector demon, was sure that death and eternal punishment were imminent, but just then a wizened ape caught Doctor Faustus and held him until there appeared another pair of dragons pulling a great coach into which the ape set Faustus.

A sulphurous storm began to rage; the coach rattled through mist, thunder, and noisome stench for perhaps a quarter of an hour. When at length the darkness lifted, Doctor Faustus perceived below him a vast roiling sea into which dragons and coach plunged, but the waters of Hell were not wet; they laved Faustus with warm, radiant light. Down, down coach and rider plummeted until they reached the ocean floor, when, to his vast surprise, Faustus discovered himself seated upon the topmost pinnacle of a mighty crag. Looking down, he saw the sea and Hell's burning hole beneath him. He was alone, pitiably alone.

Thus spake Doctor Faustus to himself: "O thou whom even evil sprites hath forsaken, what shalt thou do but drown thyself in this turbid ocean or else hurl thyself into the portal of damnation?" And mad with despair, he leaped into Hell's flame-spitting iris, crying aloud, "O Demon-King, clasp unto your breast this, my vile spirit!"

Now as he fell, a cannonade of thunderous curses and groans assaulted his ears, until at length Doctor Faustus found himself standing upright on the floor of Hell's cellar. Everywhere he looked, he saw torrents of flame licking the limbs and loins of a tormented host of kings and lackeys, clerics and cutthroats, finely attired ladies roasting indiscriminately with their sinful sister-strumpets. At the fire's border, Doctor Faustus perceived a cool stream where the damned were permitted to drink and wash themselves before returning to the conflagration. The philosopher stepped forward and tried to set hands on several of the sufferers, but at his approach, each he attempted to grasp disappeared.

Hell's intense heat and stench and woeful wailing were more than Faustus could stand, but just when he thought he could bear no more, Beelzebub arrived with the bone sedan chair resettled on his back. The mortal gratefully seated himself thereon and the fiend swiftly rose up as Doctor Faustus passed into an exhausted slumber from which he did not rouse till the next morning, when he woke in his own bed.

Doctor Faustus lay in bed for a long while trying to decide whether Beelzebub had actually taken him to Hell or merely deceived him with a vivid dream. At length the philosopher concluded that he had indeed been tricked, and in this he was perfectly correct, for Beelzebub knew that if he had really allowed Doctor Faustus to witness Hell's true aspect, he would have devoted the rest of his mortal life to trying to escape the contract he had signed with Mephistopheles.

English adaptation by Marvin Kaye

The Witch Is Dead

EDWARD D. HOCH

Simon Ark is reticent about discussing his past, but at closest reckoning he is about two thousand years old and once was a Coptic priest. His mission throughout the ages is to hunt down the Devil or his minions and vanquish them. Ark does so with the intuitive skills of the detective, as witness the way he solves the ensuing problem of a self-styled witch's death. EDWARD D. HOCH, *past president of the Mystery Writers of America, has written more than seven hundred tales of espionage, crime, and fantasy.*

Her real name was Helen Marie Carrio, but for more years than anyone could remember she'd been known simply as Mother Fortune. She was a large, plump woman, somewhere near seventy years old, though she might easily have passed for a hundred.

As her name might have implied, Mother Fortune made her meagre living by predicting the future, by peering into a mammoth crystal ball and telling you just what you wanted to hear about yourself. It was a dying profession—especially in Westchester County in the second decade of the Atomic Age—but there were still many to whom her word was almost sacred.

There were others, however, who had widely different views on the subject of Mother Fortune. There were some, in fact, who even accused her of being a modern-day witch.

And perhaps she was.

In any event, Mother Fortune died as all good witches must—in a burst of flames that would have brought cries of envy from the judges of centuries agone.

It was perhaps one of the paradoxes of life, though, that Mother Fortune's death was to prove even more fantastic than had her life. . . .

It was the first week in October, and the twelfth day of an early fall heat wave that had amazed both forecasters and suburbanites by sending the temperatures into the high eighties. I had taken the 5:12 train from New York, as I usually did on nights when things weren't too busy at the office.

Actually, I suppose I noticed the man in the seat ahead of me right from the very start; but it wasn't until he left the train with me at Hudsonville that I actually caught a glimpse of his face. It had been a long time since I'd seen him, but that heavyset, wrinkled, yet somehow handsome, face was one you didn't forget easily.

I caught up with him in front of the tiny building that served to link Hudsonville with the New Haven Railroad, and asked him, "You're Simon Ark, aren't you?"

The smile came at once to his tight lips. "Of course. It has been many years. . . ."

It had been many years. I'd first met Simon Ark in a little Western mining town years before, when I was still a newspaper reporter. I hadn't seen him since; but since he was probably the most unusual man I'd ever know, I wasn't likely to forget him.

I led him to a coffee shop across the street, and over two steaming cups of black coffee I told him of my life during recent years. "I'm with Neptune Books now," I said; "one of these paperbound book publishers. Been there about three years now. It's a lot better than chasing politicians and police cars for a living. I married Shelly Constance, you know."

"I'd heard," Simon Ark said. "It's quite good to see you again after all these years."

"You certainly don't look any older, Simon. What have you been doing with yourself?"

Simon Ark smiled again. "The usual things. I've been traveling mostly. To England, and other places."

"I hope things weren't as bad as in Gidaz."

"Sometimes they were worse," he replied, and the smile was no longer on his lips. "There is evil everywhere these days, and it is most difficult to separate the man-made evil from the more ancient type. . . ."

I'd formed many theories about Simon Ark since our brief encounter several years back, but I could see that I was still a long way from knowing the truth about him. He'd told me once that he was searching, searching for the ultimate evil, searching for the devil himself. And there were times when the look of his face seemed to tell me that he'd been searching a long, long time.

I lit a cigarette and sipped my coffee. "Well, what on earth are you doing up in Westchester, anyway? The most evil things up here are the commuters' trains and this current heat wave."

He frowned slightly at that. "You perhaps have not heard then about the remarkable events at the Hudsonville College for Women, or about the old woman who calls herself Mother Fortune."

"I guess I haven't. Maybe I don't want to, if they're the kind of thing to bring *you* to Hudsonville."

"I hope that I am in time to prevent anything really serious," he said, "but it is hard to say just yet."

"What is it that's happening, anyway?"

"Of course there hasn't been any public announcement of it as yet—and there probably won't be—but it seems that this woman named Mother Fortune fancies herself as something of a modern-day witch. In any event, she has cast a spell of some kind over the girl students of Hudsonville College."

I had to laugh at that. The whole idea of a witch invading a modern girls' college was too much for me. "You're not serious, certainly?"

"I fear that I am," he told me. "Three of the girls are apparently near death, and some forty others have become ill."

"Then there must be some other explanation," I was quick to insist. "Things like that just don't happen any more, at least not around Hudsonville."

"Stranger things than that have happened in this world," Simon Ark replied. "I'm going out to the school now. You may accompany me if you wish. . . ."

. . .

Hudsonville College for Women was like no other institute of higher learning anywhere in the east. Sixty years of traditions, plus millions of dollars from a few lucky endowments, had made it possible to re-create in Westchester some of the great wonders of ancient Rome.

At the very entrance to the campus was a line of pillars suggesting the remains of Apollo's temple at Pompeii, and even the students' chapel was an exact duplicate, in miniature, of the Church of San Francesco at Assisi. The main road through the campus was called, appropriately enough, the Appian Way. And the huge assembly hall, which could never be filled by Hudsonville's moderate enrollment, was of course patterned on the Roman Forum. There was even a small bridge over a creek that bore a remarkable resemblance to Venice's Rialto Bridge.

The whole thing was like taking a tour of all of Italy in a little over an hour; but whether it actually contributed to the task of turning out modern, cultured young ladies prepared for business and marriage was something I didn't know. I suppose it did, however, attract a certain number of students whose mothers would otherwise have sent them up to Vassar or over to Bryn Mawr; and it had the distinction of getting regular picture stories in all the leading magazines by the simple method of staging annual pageants based on some forgotten lore of ancient Rome.

It was apparently Simon Ark's first glimpse of the unusual campus, for he spent some minutes strolling around aimlessly before we finally headed for the administration building, which oddly enough was the only one that failed to carry out the old Roman motif. Instead, it was an ancient limestone structure that apparently dated from the college's founding back in the mid-nineties, and had somehow survived the Romanizing of the remainder of the college.

I'd called Shelly to tell her I'd be late for supper, though I didn't really expect the trip to Hudsonville College to last too long. And I was still quite dubious about the whole thing when we were met at the door by a tall, scholarly-looking gentleman with a Roman nose that fitted in well with the rest of the campus.

"May I help you?" he asked quietly, and though his voice was polite I noticed that he was carefully blocking the doorway and barring our way.

"Possibly. I am Simon Ark, and this is a friend of mine. I heard that you have had some trouble here, and I thought I might be able to offer some assistance. . . ."

"We already have a doctor . . ." the tall man began.

"I'm not a doctor."

"If you're a newspaper reporter or anything like that, I can tell you right now we've nothing to say."

Simon Ark grunted. "I'm not a reporter, either; but before I say any more could you tell us who you are?"

"Sorry," the man said, smiling slightly. "Name's Hugh Westwood. I'm professor of ancient history here. Now, if you could tell me your business. . . ."

"We . . . happened to hear about your troubles here, Professor Westwood. I personally specialize in the investigation of such phenomena, and I thought I might be of some little assistance."

Westwood gazed at Simon Ark with searching eyes. "I don't know how you found out about it, but if you mean you've had experience in dealing with witches, you're certainly the man we want to see."

"Well . . ." Simon Ark hesitated a moment. "I have had some small experience with witches. . . ."

That was all Westwood needed to hear. He led them down a long hall to his office and motioned to two chairs. In a few moments he rejoined them with an older, white-haired man and a middle-aged woman.

"This is our president, Doctor Lampton, and the Dean of Women, Miss Bagly. You said your name was . . . Simon Ark?"

He nodded and introduced me as his assistant. I was amazed at how quickly he seemed to be accepted by these three frightened people. Perhaps it was their fear, coupled with Ark's compelling manner, that made them forget their aversion to publicity.

"It's this woman . . . this . . . this Mother Fortune," Miss Bagly began. "She's some kind of a witch, and she's put a spell over our girls. We . . . we don't know which way to turn, Mr. Ark; we really don't. If we reported something like this to the police, it would get into all the papers and our school would be ruined."

Simon Ark frowned, and I knew a question was coming. "But I

understand that at least a few of these girls are extremely ill. You mean to say they aren't even receiving medical attention?"

"Oh, heavens," Miss Bagly exclaimed, "Dr. Lampton here is a real M.D., you know. He's been looking after them."

"That's correct," the doctor said. "I haven't had any private practice in a good many years, ever since I became president of Hudsonville, but I still know enough to give those girls proper attention."

"Then just what's wrong with them, Doctor?" Simon Ark asked.

"Well . . . by medical standards it's very difficult to say. They just seem . . . well, weak, without energy. Several girls have fainted, and one or two are in a mild coma of some sort."

"I imagine you've thought of narcotics."

"Certainly. There's no possibility of anything like that—not at Hudsonville!"

Simon Ark sighed. "I understand there have been letters. . . ."

I knew better than to wonder how he knew about the letters, because Simon Ark had ways of finding out such things. Doctor Lampton nodded and pulled them from his pocket. They looked like he'd been carrying them and studying them for weeks.

There were three of them in all, dated about a week apart and starting three weeks previous, around the first day of the Fall term. The writing was crude, intentionally crude, I thought. All three letters were identical in their wording: *To the president of Hudsonville College: Your cruel act of fifty years ago is at last avenged. I have cursed your school and every student in it. Before another moon has come your school will be a campus of the dead."* The notes were signed *"Mother Fortune."*

Simon Ark studied them carefully. "This Mother Fortune is a local Gypsy fortune teller, I understand. Do you have any idea just why she should be putting a curse on the college?"

Professor Westwood, who'd remained silent for some time, joined in the conversation then. "Unfortunately, yes. That reference to fifty years ago sent us looking back through the school's old records, but we found it. The woman who calls herself Mother Fortune was once a student here."

This news made it a little easier for me to understand their reluctance to call in the police. It was bad enough to have an exclusive girls' college hexed by a witch, but when it turns out the witch was once a student at the school, that's even worse publicity.

"Her name was Helen Marie Carrio at that time," Westwood continued. "We found from the records that she was expelled just two weeks before she was to have graduated."

"For what reason?" Simon Ark asked.

Doctor Lampton interrupted to answer. "You have to remember that this was fifty years ago, Mister Ark. Many things were different then."

"Why was she expelled?" Ark repeated.

"For smoking cigarettes," Lampton replied weakly. "You must realize that at the time such a thing was unknown among young girls, and at a school like Hudsonville it would have been a most serious offense."

We were silent for a moment while we thought about it. Was it possible that such a girl, grown old fifty years later, should still remember this childhood tragedy? Was it possible that the old woman now known as Mother Fortune somehow had the power to strike down these young girls?

"Have you contacted Mother Fortune about these threats?" Simon Ark asked.

"I went to see her personally," Doctor Lampton said. "Two weeks ago. She admitted sending the notes, and said she'd keep on sending them. She's a very odd woman indeed—half-insane, possibly—yet with a manner about her that almost makes you believe she is some sort of . . . witch." The last word was spoken very quietly, as if the president was afraid someone outside the room might be listening.

Simon Ark frowned once again. "There have been witches in this world, and quite possibly Mother Fortune is one; but it is too early to say for certain. Right now I'd like to see some of these girls who have suffered this odd sickness. Oh, and I'd like a list of their names if possible."

Professor Westwood nodded and pulled a pad of yellow lined paper from his desk. The top sheet was covered with the usual unintelligible notes of a history professor, phrases like *"Tunica Molesta,"* and *"Plato—IX—Jowett."* Westwood tore off the top sheet and began copying names from a typed list on his desk.

There were some forty-odd names on the list, ranging from Abbot, Mary to Yeagen, Bernice. Some had grim-looking stars after them, and I figured correctly that these were the more serious cases. Simon Ark carefully folded the yellow list and we followed the three others out of Westwood's office.

They led us across the mildly rolling hills of the campus, past the ancient Roman columns, to a squat, three-storey structure. "This is Venice Hall, the principal girls' dorm," Miss Bagly informed us. "All of our dorms are named after Italian cities."

We followed her in, amidst a few questioning stares from casually dressed girls relaxing after supper. I gathered that the sick girls were simply being kept in their own rooms.

The first room we visited was a cheerful-looking one on the second floor. There were two girls in it, both of them in bed. One was sitting up and reading a thick historical novel, but the other was asleep.

Simon Ark examined them both with care, but except for a somewhat tired-out expression there was nothing unusual about them. "When did you first begin to feel ill?" Ark inquired.

The girl sat up further in bed, revealing a fantastic pair of plaid pajamas. "Gosh, I don't know. About a week ago, I guess."

"Did you receive any burns or unusual injuries around that time?"

"No, nothing."

"Do you smoke?"

"Sometimes. Not too much."

"Have you had a cigarette recently?"

"Not in over a month; not since I was back home."

I could see that Simon Ark was mildly disappointed at this. He apparently had thought that the perfect weapon of Mother Fortune's revenge would be poisoned cigarettes of some kind. But such was not the case.

The other girl had awakened now, and I could see that she was in much worse shape. I think it gave us all an odd feeling, looking at those girls, realizing that they might be the innocent victims of a terror that couldn't happen, but was.

Later, when we left the room and the building, Simon Ark appeared deep in thought. Once he turned to Professor Westwood and asked, "Have any teachers shown signs of this . . . sickness?"

"No, just the students."

"And what symptoms have the more serious cases shown?"

"Oh . . . vomiting, partial paralysis of various muscles. . . ."

Simon Ark frowned. "Has anyone taken a blood test of the sick girls?"

"A blood test? Why, no, I hardly think so. That would involve calling in the authorities."

"Perhaps you could do it in your own lab. At least I suggest that a blood test of some sort be made as soon as possible."

We left them shortly after that, and Simon Ark and I made our way across the now darkened campus to the street. Even with night upon us, the heat was still there, making us forget the fact that it was already early autumn.

"What do you think about it, Simon?" I asked after we had walked some distance.

Simon Ark gazed off into the night, and I thought for a moment he hadn't heard my question. But then gradually he turned to me. "I think that we should pay a visit to Mother Fortune."

We found her, later that night, in a little street in a little city not too far from Hudsonville College. It was just another city in the southern part of the country called Westchester. And the street, usually, was just another street.

But tonight it was different. Tonight it blazed with light, light from a thousand colored bulbs that spelled out a score of gay designs against the evening sky. From every direction lighted streets shot out from the large old church at their center, the church of St. Francis of Assisi.

"It's a celebration for the saint's feast day," I explained to Simon. "These old Italian churches go big for things like that. The thing is sort of one huge block party that lasts for three or four nights. You certainly don't expect to find Mother Fortune here, do you?"

"I never expect to find evil anywhere," Simon Ark replied, "and yet it is all around us. This poor church, I fear, is no exception."

We walked on, beneath the colored lights and past the booths and trucks and wagons, selling everything from religious statues to hot pizza. Presently we saw a short, fat priest moving among the crowd.

Simon Ark moved quickly through the crowd and caught the priest's arm. "Pardon, Father, but I seek information regarding a woman known as Mother Fortune. I believe she is near here."

The little priest's face turned dark with rage. "Sir, if you seek her out I hope it is to force her to move away from my church and my people. She came two days ago, with her trailer and her crystal ball and her fortune telling. My people—many of them—are simple superstitious Italians, not long in this country."

Simon Ark frowned. "But don't you have any control over who takes part in your celebration?"

"Ah, no," the priest shrugged. "They even come here and sell meat to my people on Fridays. But there are regulations about trailers in Westchester County, as you know, and perhaps the police will force Mother Fortune to leave."

As we'd talked, he had led us to the very end of the lighted area, and there, parked against the curb like some giant sleeping beetle, was a long house trailer with the name of Mother Fortune on its side.

The priest left us, fading into the bright lights at our backs, leaving us alone with the woman who was perhaps a witch. The trailer was a large silver one, and in addition to Mother Fortune's name I noticed the single word *"Erebus"* near the front of the vehicle, like the name on the prow of a ship.

"What kind of a bus is that?" I asked Simon.

He smiled slightly. "Erebus was one of the names for hell used by the poet Milton. A fitting name for the home of a witch."

There was no one down at that end of the street at all, and I imagined correctly that the little priest's campaign against Mother Fortune was meeting with much success. Simon Ark pressed a tiny button by the trailer door and we waited for it to open.

When it finally did, the woman who greeted us was a surprise. I didn't know just what I expected, and certainly Mother Fortune was no beauty, but neither was she the typical concept of a medieval witch. She was simply a very old white-haired woman, who acted as if she might be a little drunk and probably was.

"What you want?" she managed to mumble.

"My name is Simon Ark; I'd like to talk to you."

"Want your fortune told?"

"Possibly."

"Come in, then."

We entered the gleaming silver trailer and found ourselves in another world. I'd expected something unusual, but I hadn't been prepared for the ancient beaded drapes, the musty oriental furnishings, and huge glowing crystal ball that filled the center of the trailer's main room.

The crystal ball, apparently lit by a bulb in its base, was a good three feet in diameter, and the way it gave off illumination reminded me of those big revolving glass globes they used to have in dance halls twenty years ago.

Simon Ark settled himself in one of the big overstuffed chairs with curling dragons for arms and said, "I want to talk about the trouble at Hudsonville College."

The words were hardly out of his mouth when the old woman was on her feet, shouting in a harsh voice that was almost a scream. "They've been here themselves. I already told them it would do no good. It's too late to stop me now. Too late, you hear? Too late! They can have me arrested if they want, but it will do no good. Before many moons have passed, the first of the girls will be dead! After that the rest will die quickly. They'll regret the day they expelled Mother Fortune from their school!"

From the cigarette burns on the sleeve of her robe, it was obvious that she still had the habit that had led to her disgrace those many years before. In a way I felt sorry for this old woman whose aging brain had turned back fifty years for revenge.

"Helen," Simon Ark began, but the woman showed no emotion at the use of her real name. "Helen, you've got to stop all this foolishness. You're not a witch and you haven't put a curse on those girls."

"Haven't I?" she laughed shrilly. "Haven't I? Look at this!"

She opened a drawer and pulled out a thin book with heavily padded covers that I recognized as the yearbook of Hudsonville College. Several long black hatpins had been driven through the covers and the pages.

The sight of it was so incredible that I would have laughed had I not remembered those girls I'd seen back at the college. Something had made them sick, and perhaps this was it. I'd learned a long time ago, at my first meeting with Simon Ark, that there are things in this world beyond our powers of explanation.

She placed the book on a table and gazed into the huge crystal ball. "Back in the Middle Ages it was believed that tobacco was invented by the devil, and that only the devil's priests used it," she said. "When they threw me out of Hudsonville, I began to believe it."

I turned my face from her as she talked, unable to look at the lines of tragedy I saw there. What had happened during fifty years of heartbreak to turn this one-time college girl into a vengeful witch? That was something I never found out, and something that is perhaps better left unknown.

At length she fell silent, and I could see that Simon Ark would learn nothing more from her. "Get out of here now," she said with finality. "I have to change my robe and get ready for the evening business." She gestured toward the wall, where a glistening gold and purple garment decorated with blazing suns and half-moons hung from a hook.

Of course there would be no more customers for her fortunes this late at night, but she didn't seem to realize it. In her vague way, night and day had apparently merged into one.

We left her then, and walked back through the lighted streets to the church of Saint Francis of Assisi. And when I looked at Simon Ark's face in the light of the multi-colored bulbs, I knew that neither one of us was certain whether we had just left a modern-day servant of Satan or simply a confused old woman.

The following morning dawned hot and bright, with the sun beating down upon leaves and grass that waited in vain for the cool slumber of autumn. It was Saturday, and I spent the morning working around the house. Shelly was an avid listener to my account of the previous night's adventures, but by noon I had all but forgotten Simon Ark and Mother Fortune.

It was just after the church bells had sounded the mid-day hour in the distance that Shelly called to me. "Someone wants you on the telephone."

I dropped the garden hose I'd been using and went into the

house. The voice on the phone was familiar at once, but it took me a moment to identify Simon Ark on the other end.

"The witch is dead," he said simply. "Would you like to meet me at the trailer?"

"I'll be right over."

With a shouted few words to Shelly, I jumped into my car and headed south toward the parish of Saint Francis of Assisi. In those first few minutes I didn't even try to think of the meaning of Simon Ark's words. I only knew that something had happened, something strange and unknown.

To the west dark clouds were forming on the horizon, and the shiver that went down my spine told me the barometer was falling fast. The October heat wave was on its last legs.

In the distance I thought I heard the rumble of thunder. . . .

The street by the church, which last night had been a brightly lighted invitation to fun and merriment, was now dark with the threat of approaching rain. It was blocked off completely by nearly a dozen police and private cars, and additional policemen were busy keeping back the crowd of curious neighbors. Some seemed almost indignant that they should be kept from seeing this bit of drama that had been played out on their street. Others simply stood silently, aware that they were in the presence of death.

Simon Ark stood in the door of the trailer, and he signaled to the police to let me through. I had long ago stopped wondering about his strange power over people, and now it seemed only natural that he was already in the confidence of the police.

"Prepare yourself," he told me at the door; "it's not a pleasant sight."

And it wasn't.

It reminded me of a time, a lifetime ago, when we'd had to blast a Japanese machine-gun nest on a lonely Pacific isle. We'd used flame throwers, and the bodies of the dead Japs came back to my memory now as I stared at the thing that had been Mother Fortune.

She lay on top of her giant crystal ball, with her arms hanging down limply almost to the floor. Her clothes had been burnt off her completely, and the withered flesh was black and scorched. Her hair, and much of the skin on her face, had been burnt away, but there was no doubt in my mind that it really was the body of the woman we'd talked to last night.

"What happened?" I asked finally.

Simon Ark continued gazing at the body as he answered. "The police came to tell her she'd have to move the trailer. They looked through the window and saw her like this." He paused a moment before continuing. "The trailer was locked. They had to force the door to get in."

"What started the fire?"

"The police don't know. Even the priest doesn't know. They think it might have been something . . . unnatural."

For the first time I realized that the trailer itself was virtually unmarked by the fire; the blaze apparently had been centered on the body of the woman.

"Do you think somebody killed her, burned her because she was a witch, like they did in Salem?"

"Nobody burned her to death because she was alone in a locked trailer at the time," Simon Ark replied. "And at Salem they hanged the witches—they hanged nineteen and pressed one to death. I know."

And when he said it I knew that he really did know. He knew because he'd been there and seen it, just as I could tell that he'd seen something like this horror before, somewhere in the dark forgotten past of history.

The police were busy removing the body, and examining the crystal ball for some sign of the fire's origin. But of course they found nothing.

As he left the trailer I saw the priest from St. Francis of Assisi Church making the sign of the cross over the body, and I wondered how this man could bless the corpse of a woman who'd opposed him so just a few hours earlier, when she still lived. I was even more astonished when I saw Simon Ark take an odd-looking cross from his pocket and raise it for a second over the body.

As he walked away he mumbled something in a tongue I didn't understand. He'd told me once it was Coptic, and I suspected it was a prayer, a very old prayer from the dawn of civilization.

And then the rain began to fall, in great wet drops that brought wisps of steam from the dry hot pavement. Simon Ark followed me to my car, and we sat in the rain watching the morgue wagon pull slowly away with the body of Mother Fortune. . . .

"Did you ever hear of Charles Fort?" Simon Ark asked me some time later, as we sipped a glass of wine in an almost deserted oak-lined cocktail lounge. "He was a writer of some twenty-five years back who collected odd and unexplained news reports. His writings contain several references to deaths by mysterious burns."

I'd heard of Fort, of course, but I wasn't familiar with his writings. Simon Ark counted them off on his fingers as he mentioned the odd deaths. "There was one in Blyth, England, about fifty years ago. An old woman in a locked house, burned to death on a sofa. And in Ayer, Massachusetts, in 1890—a woman burned to death in the woods. In London, Southampton. Liverpool—always women, always old women. Fort reports only one case of an old man burning to death mysteriously. You want more cases, closer to home? St. Louis in 1889, North Carolina, San Diego. . . . A similar case in Rochester, New York, was blamed on lightning. . . ."

As if on cue a streak of lightning cut through the afternoon sky, followed almost at once by a crash of thunder. "Any chance that lightning could have killed Mother Fortune?" I asked.

"Hardly. The storm just started, and in any event a bolt of lightning would certainly not go unnoticed by the neighbors."

I sipped my wine and glanced behind the bar, where the Notre Dame football team had just faded from the TV set, to be replaced by a dark-haired girl singing "That Old Black Magic." The song seemed appropriate to the occasion.

"Then what killed her?" I asked. "Do you know?"

"I've known since before she died," Simon Ark replied unhappily. "It was one of the most difficult decisions I ever had to make, to let her die like that. But it was the only chance to save those college girls."

"You mean the spell will be lifted now that the witch is dead?"

"Not exactly; but it'll force a very clever killer into the open."

"Then Mother Fortune was murdered, and by natural means!"

"She was murdered, but who is to say that any method of murder is natural? They are all weapons of the devil, in one way or another. Always remember that—every murder, every crime, is supernatural, in the sense that it was inspired by Satan."

The bartender switched off the television set, and we were alone with the constantly irregular crashes of thunder from the outside world.

"Did Satan kill her, then?" I asked, and I knew that Simon Ark would not consider the question a foolish one. "The way all those other people were burned to death?"

"Only indirectly. Perhaps the real killer is a man who's been dead for nearly two thousand years. Because in a way, you see, Mother Fortune was killed by the ancient Roman emperor, Lucius —better known as Nero. . . ."

Simon Ark would say no more on the subject of the old fortune teller's mysterious death. He seemed to dismiss the subject from his mind and turned instead to questioning me about the activities of Hudsonville College.

"Do they have summer courses at all?" he wanted to know.

"No, it's closed up completely all summer. Most of these exclusive girls' colleges are. Why do you want to know that?"

"Just filling in bits of the picture. Now I must make an important telephone call to Washington. To the Atomic Energy Commission. Perhaps then we can return to the college."

He talked on the telephone for some time, and when he came out of the booth he seemed pleased. We left the bar and drove through the gentle rain toward the campus of Hudsonville College.

It was almost dark by the time we arrived, and already the remains of the heat wave had given way to an autumn dampness that chilled our bones. We went first to Miss Bagly's quarters, where Simon Ark inquired as to the girls' condition.

"It's not good, Mr. Ark," she told him. "Nearly all the girls in the college are sick in one way or another now. For some it's probably all in the mind, but I'm really worried about a few of them. I do wish Dr. Lampton would allow us to call in outside help."

"That has all been taken care of, Miss Bagly," he told her. "There will be doctors here within a few hours. But first I must discover the cause of the evil that lurks within your walls."

"I heard that the witch . . . Mother Fortune . . . was dead. Will that help the girls?"

"In a way it will, Miss Bagly. But I fear we'll be unable to completely save the good name of your school." She started to say something else, but he held up his hand to silence her. "Are you certain, Miss Bagly, that none of your faculty has been affected by this sickness?"

"Oh, yes, Mr. Ark. Just the girls have been stricken. Except, of course, for our swimming instructor, who's not really a . . ."

But she never had a chance to finish her sentence. Simon Ark was already out of the room and hurrying down the steps. I ran after him, and I heard him mumble, "Of course! The swimming pool. Of course. . . ."

And we ran through the night, toward the shadowy building that resembled the old Roman baths. Inside, all was darkness, and even the glistening waters of the pool itself were black. We were alone, and Simon Ark drew me into the deeper shadows.

We waited, for what I did not know, and as we waited Simon Ark talked, in a voice so low it hardly reached my ears.

"Suppose," he began, "suppose you were an agent of a foreign power, or even of some private enterprise. Suppose you stole a quantity of radioactive mineral—cobalt or something similar—to use for your own illegal purposes. Suppose you found it necessary to hide it, safely, for a period of several weeks. Where . . . where could you safely hide a supply of illegal radioactive mineral for several weeks? Where would it be far enough away from people so as not to harm anyone with its dangerous rays?"

And I answered him. "In the middle of a college campus closed for the summer vacation. With no one but an occasional watchman to be exposed briefly to its rays."

The darkness was very dark then, and the evil of the unknown hung heavy around us. "Exactly," Simon Ark continued. "And when the school reopened for the fall before you could get rid of the deadly metal, then what would you do? What would you do to explain the radioactivity that would begin to strike down the girls?"

"You mean. . . ?"

"I mean that this building is full of low, but dangerous, amounts of radioactivity. That's what's wrong with those girls, and any doctor who'd been active in recent years would probably have recognized the symptoms. Unfortunately, Doctor Lampton did not, and his pride kept him from calling in assistance. I knew it almost from the beginning, which is why I suggested the blood tests. But I didn't know until tonight just where the source of the dangerous rays was. It had to be some place that the girls used, but not the teachers. I never thought of the swimming pool until now."

"Then the witch business was all a blind!" I said. "The person who hid the uranium or cobalt found out about Mother Fortune's past life and used it as an excuse for the radioactive sickness."

"Correct. A clever but devilish plot. Of course he couldn't depend on the assistance of a crazed old woman forever, so he had to arrange for her death when he feared she might talk."

"But whom. . . ?"

The question was answered for me by a sudden movement on the far side of the black pool. We were no longer alone in the building.

Simon Ark stepped out of the shadows and shouted across the width of the pool. "All right, Professor Westwood. We know all about your murderous activities. . . ."

Professor Hugh Westwood looked at them from across the pool, and he might have been a demon conjured up by Satan himself. Even in the darkness I could feel the evil that seemed now to radiate from him, just as another evil radiated from a rock hidden somewhere in this building.

"It's too late to escape, Professor Westwood. I've already talked to Washington, and they confirmed the theft of the radioactive minerals from a testing lab in New York two months ago. There are doctors and F.B.I. agents on their way here right now. Of course your friends have already been arrested, which is why they never came for the rocks. Where is it, Professor? In the pool itself? In the drain pipe, possibly?"

But Westwood let out a cry of rage, and a tongue of fire seemed to leap from his fingers into the pool. Instantly a wall of flame shot up between Westwood and ourselves. I had just a second to realize that the water in the swimming pool was somehow on fire, and then everything was a nightmare. . . .

Of course we found out later that, in anticipation of danger, Westwood had poured oil on the waters of the pool and then thrown a match into it; but in that instant with the flames all around me it seemed as though the very gates of hell had opened to receive us.

I'll never forget those final seconds, as Simon Ark and Professor Westwood stalked each other around the blazing pool, with the flames leaping high and beating at the skylight until at last the glass burst and showered down upon us.

This was hell, and here at last was Simon Ark, stalking a modern-day version of the devil himself, while the flames waited to consume them both. And then, finally, in a sudden clash of good and evil, their two bodies met and locked in deadly combat, and toppled together into the waiting flames. . . .

The fire died as quickly as it had started, leaving only the steaming water beneath. The oil fire had burnt itself out just in time, for I doubt if even a man such as Simon Ark could have survived another minute in the heated water under those flames. As it was, we were too late to save Professor Westwood. He was already dead when we pulled him from the water.

Later, much later, after the doctors and the police and the F.B.I., after the finding of the thin tube of radioactive cobalt in the swimming pool drain, after everybody had talked and listened and asked . . .

"But how did he kill the woman, Simon? How did he kill Mother Fortune?"

He looked at me with eyes that seemed tired, and he replied. "Remember yesterday in his office, when he tore a sheet from his pad. Remember a Latin phrase that was written on that sheet? It said *'tunica molesta,'* and that told me the answer even before the crime was committed. *'Tunica molesta'* was a name given to one of Nero's particularly horrible devices for killing early Christians. It was a tunic or mantle embroidered with the finest gold. Early Christians and criminals were brought into public arenas dressed in these garments, which were made of a highly combustible cloth that burst into flames when touched with the slightest spark."

I remember the robe that had been hanging in Mother Fortune's trailer. "You mean Westwood made one of these things and gave it to her?"

"Exactly. He no doubt told her it was a reward for her part in the scheme, though I doubt if she ever realized the true nature of his plot to cover up the cache of radioactive cobalt. She was just a confused old woman who jumped at an opportunity of revenging herself upon the school that had once expelled her."

"But you said this garment needed a spark or something to ignite it. How did he get into the trailer to set the robe on fire?"

"He didn't. Once he'd given it to her, he didn't have to worry about the outcome. Remember those cigarette burns we noticed on the sleeves of her old robe? He knew that sooner or later she would smoke a cigarette while wearing the *'tunica molesta.'* And he knew that in her clumsy manner, she'd let a single deadly spark fall onto her robe."

"And you knew this all the time?"

"I suspected it. As a murder method it isn't as strange as you might think, considering the fact that the killer was a professor of ancient history at a school that specialized in the early Roman Empire. The term *'tunica molesta'* came easily to his mind, and his only mistake was in jotting it down on his pad one day. I knew, though, that once Mother Fortune was dead he'd have to get rid of the cobalt, or the whole idea of the hex would be exploded as a fake, and Doctor Lampton would start looking for some medical reason for the girls' illness."

"It still seems so fantastic," I said.

"Life itself is fantastic, and death even more so. There are men in this world far more evil and far more clever than Professor Westwood, and as long as these men live the fantastic will be commonplace."

He left me then, walking out through the night as suddenly as he'd come, but this time I was sure I'd not heard the last of Simon Ark.

Witches' Hollow

H. P. LOVECRAFT
and AUGUST DERLETH

Here is one of the less familiar crypto-science-fiction tales of H. P.
LOVECRAFT *(1890–1937), who most of his life was a resident of Providence, Rhode Island, and was best known for the many weird poems, essays,
and stories he wrote for* Weird Tales *magazine, including "The Rats in
the Walls," "The Dunwich Horror," "The Colour Out of Space," "He"
(in* Weird Tales: The Magazine That Never Dies, Doubleday, *1988),
and many other popular works of shivery fiction. "Witches' Hollow" was
one of several unfinished Lovecraft manuscripts completed by* AUGUST
DERLETH *(1909–1971), who launched the publishing company Arkham
House in Sauk City, Wisconsin, with two large collections of Lovecraft's
prose, the now-rare volumes* The Outsider *and* Beyond the Wall of
Sleep.

District School Number Seven stood on the very edge of that wild
country which lies west of Arkham. It stood in a little grove of
trees, chiefly oaks and elms with one or two maples; in one direction the road led to Arkham, in the other it dwindled away into the
wild, wooded country which always looms darkly on that western
horizon. It presented a warmly attractive appearance to me when
first I saw it on my arrival as the new teacher early in September,

1920, though it had no distinguishing architectural feature and was in every respect the replica of thousands of country schools scattered throughout New England, a compact, conservative building painted white, so that it shone forth from among the trees in the midst of which it stood.

It was an old building at that time, and no doubt has since been abandoned or torn down. The school district has now been consolidated, but at that time it supported this school in somewhat niggardly a manner, skimping and saving on every necessity. Its standard readers, when I came there to teach, were still *McGuffey's Eclectic Readers,* in editions published before the turn of the century. My charges added up to twenty-seven. There were Allens and Whateleys and Perkinses, Dunlocks and Abbotts and Talbots—and there was Andrew Potter.

I cannot now recall the precise circumstances of my especial notice of Andrew Potter. He was a large boy for his age, very dark of mien, with haunting eyes and a shock of touseled black hair. His eyes brooded upon me with a kind of different quality which at first challenged me but ultimately left me strangely uneasy. He was in the fifth grade, and it did not take me long to discover that he could very easily advance into the seventh or eighth, but made no effort to do so. He seemed to have only a casual tolerance for his schoolmates, and for their part, they respected him, but not out of affection so much as what struck me soon as fear. Very soon thereafter, I began to understand that this strange lad held for me the same kind of amused tolerance that he held for his schoolmates.

Perhaps it was inevitable that the challenge of this pupil should lead me to watch him as surreptitiously as I could, and as the circumstances of teaching a one-room school permitted. As a result, I became aware of a vaguely disquieting fact; from time to time, Andrew Potter responded to some stimulus beyond the apprehension of my senses, reacting precisely as if someone had called to him, sitting up, growing alert, and wearing the air of someone listening to sounds beyond my own hearing, in the same attitude assumed by animals hearing sounds beyond the pitch-levels of the human ear.

My curiosity quickened by this time, I took the first opportunity to ask about him. One of the eighth-grade boys, Wilbur Dunlock, was in the habit on occasion of staying after school and helping with the cursory cleaning that the room needed.

"Wilbur," I said to him late one afternoon, "I notice you don't seem to pay much attention to Andrew Potter, none of you. Why?"

He looked at me, a little distrustfully, and pondered his answer before he shrugged and replied, "He's not like us."

"In what way?"

He shook his head. "He don't care if we let him play with us or not. He don't want to."

He seemed reluctant to talk, but by dint of repeated questions I drew from him certain spare information. The Potters lived deep in the hills to the west along an all but abandoned branch of the main road that led through the hills. Their farm stood in a little valley locally known as Witches' Hollow which Wilbur described as "a bad place." There were only four of them—Andrew, an older sister, and their parents. They did not "mix" with other people of the district, not even with the Dunlocks, who were their nearest neighbors, living but half a mile from the school itself, and thus, perhaps, four miles from Witches' Hollow, with woods separating the two farms.

More than this he could not—or would not—say.

About a week later, I asked Andrew Potter to remain after school. He offered no objection, appearing to take my request as a matter of course. As soon as the other children had gone, he came up to my desk and stood there waiting, his dark eyes fixed expectantly on me, and just the shadow of a smile on his full lips.

"I've been studying your grades, Andrew," I said, "and it seems to me that with only a little effort you could skip into the sixth— perhaps even the seventh—grade. Wouldn't you like to make that effort?"

He shrugged.

"What do you intend to do when you get out of school?"

He shrugged again.

"Are you going to high school in Arkham?"

He considered me with eyes that seemed suddenly piercing in their keenness, all lethargy gone. "Mr. Williams, I'm here because there's a law says I have to be," he answered. "There's no law says I have to go to high school."

"But aren't you interested?" I pressed him.

"What I'm interested in doesn't matter. It's what my folks want that counts."

"Well, I'm going to talk to them," I decided on the moment. "Come along. I'll take you home."

For a moment something like alarm sprang into his expression, but in seconds it diminished and gave way to that air of watchful lethargy so typical of him. He shrugged and stood waiting while I slipped my books and papers into the schoolbag I habitually carried. Then he walked docilely to the car with me and got in, looking at me with a smile that could only be described as superior.

We rode through the woods in silence, which suited the mood that came upon me as soon as we had entered the hills, for the trees pressed close upon the road, and the deeper we went, the darker grew the wood, perhaps as much because of the lateness of that October day as because of the thickening of the trees. From relatively open glades, we plunged into an ancient wood, and when at last we turned down the sideroad—little more than a lane—to which Andrew silently pointed, I found that I was driving through a growth of very old and strangely deformed trees. I had to proceed with caution; the road was so little used that underbrush crowded upon it from both sides, and, oddly, I recognized little of it, for all my studies in botany, though once I thought I saw saxifrage, curiously mutated. I drove abruptly, without warning, into the yard before the Potter house.

The sun was now lost behind the wall of trees, and the house stood in a kind of twilight. Beyond it stretched a few fields, strung out up the valley; in one, there were corn-shocks, in another stubble, in yet another pumpkins. The house itself was forbidding, low to the ground, with half a second storey, gambrel-roofed, with shuttered windows, and the outbuildings stood gaunt and stark, looking as if they had never been used. The entire farm looked deserted; the only sign of life was in a few chickens that scratched at the earth behind the house.

Had it not been that the lane along which we had travelled ended here, I would have doubted that we had reached the Potter house. Andrew flashed a glance at me, as if he sought some expression on my face to convey to him what I thought. Then he jumped lightly from the car, leaving me to follow.

He went into the house ahead of me. I heard him announce me.

"Brought the teacher. Mr. Williams."

There was no answer.

Then abruptly I was in the room, lit only by an old-fashioned kerosene lamp, and there were the other three Potters—the father, a tall, stoop-shouldered man, grizzled and greying, who could not have been more than forty but looked much, much older, not so much physically as psychically—the mother, an almost obscenely fat woman—and the girl, slender, tall, and with that same air of watchful waiting that I had noticed in Andrew.

Andrew made the brief introductions, and the four of them stood or sat, waiting upon what I had to say, and somewhat uncomfortably suggesting in their attitudes that I say it and get out.

"I wanted to talk to you about Andrew," I said. "He shows great promise, and he could be moved up a grade or two if he'd study a little more."

My words were not welcomed.

"I believe he's smart enough for eighth grade," I went on, and stopped.

"If he 'uz in eighth grade," said his father, "he'd be havin' to go to high school 'fore he 'uz old enough to git outa goin' to school. That's the law. They told me."

I could not help thinking of what Wilbur Dunlock had told me of the reclusiveness of the Potters, and as I listened to the elder Potter, and thought of what I had heard, I was suddenly aware of a kind of tension among them, and a subtle alteration in their attitude. The moment the father stopped talking, there was a singular harmony of attitude—all four of them seemed to be listening to some inner voice, and I doubt that they heard my protest at all.

"You can't expect a boy as smart as Andrew just to come back here," I said.

"Here's good enough," said old Potter. "Besides, he's ours. And don't ye go talkin' 'bout us now, Mr. Williams."

He spoke with so latently menacing an undercurrent in his voice that I was taken aback. At the same time I was increasingly aware of a miasma of hostility, not proceeding so much from any one or all four of them, as from the house and its setting themselves.

"Thank you," I said. "I'll be going."

I turned and went out, Andrew at my heels.

Outside, Andrew said softly, "You shouldn't be talking about us,

Mr. Williams. Pa gets mad when he finds out. You talked to Wilbur Dunlock."

I was arrested at getting into the car. With one foot on the running board, I turned. "Did he say so?" I asked.

He shook his head. "You did, Mr. Williams," he said, and backed away. "It's not what he thinks, but what he might do."

Before I could speak again, he had darted into the house.

For a moment I stood undecided. But my decision was made for me. Suddenly, in the twilight, the house seemed to burgeon with menace, and all the surrounding woods seemed to stand waiting but to bend upon me. Indeed, I was aware of a rustling, like the whispering of wind, in all the wood, though no wind stirred, and from the house itself came a malevolence like the blow of a fist. I got into the car and drove away, with that impression of malignance at my back like the hot breath of a ravaging pursuer.

I reached my room in Arkham at last, badly shaken. Seen in retrospect, I had undergone an unsettling psychic experience; there was no other explanation for it. I had the unavoidable conviction that, however blindly, I had thrust myself in far deeper waters than I knew, and the very unexpectedness of the experience made it the more chilling. I could not eat for the wonder of what went on in that house in Witches' Hollow, of what it was that bound the family together, chaining them to that place, preventing a promising lad like Andrew Potter even from the most fleeting wish to leave that dark valley and go out into a brighter world.

I lay for most of that night, sleepless, filled with a nameless dread for which all explanation eluded me, and when I slept at last my sleep was filled with hideously disturbing dreams, in which beings far beyond my mundane imagination held the stage, and cataclysmic events of the utmost terror and horror took place. And when I rose next morning, I felt that somehow I had touched upon a world totally alien to my kind.

I reached the school early that morning, but Wilbur Dunlock was there before me. His eyes met mine with sad reproach. I could not imagine what had happened to disturb this usually friendly pupil.

"You shouldn't a told Andrew Potter we talked about him," he said with a kind of unhappy resignation.

"I didn't, Wilbur."

"I know I didn't. So you must have," he said. And then, "Six of our cows got killed last night, and the shed where they were was crushed down on 'em.''

I was momentarily too startled to reply. "A sudden windstorm," I began, but he cut me off.

"Weren't no wind last night, Mr. Williams. And the cows were *smashed.*"

"You surely cannot think that Potters had anything to do with this, Wilbur," I cried.

He gave me a weary look—the look of one who *knows,* meeting the glance of one who should know but cannot understand, and said nothing more.

This was even more upsetting than my experience of the previous evening. He at least was convinced that there was a connection between our conversation about the Potter family and the Dunlocks' loss of half a dozen cows. And he was convinced with so deep a conviction that I knew without trying that nothing I could say would shake it.

When Andrew Potter came in, I looked in vain for any sign that anything out of the ordinary had taken place since last I had seen him.

Somehow I got through that day. Immediately after the close of the school session, I hastened into Arkham and went to the office of the Arkham *Gazette,* the editor of which had been kind enough, as a member of the local District Board of Education, to find my room for me. He was an elderly man, almost seventy, and might presumably know what I wanted to find out.

My appearance must have conveyed something of my agitation, for when I walked into his office, his eyebrows lifted, and he said, "What's got your dander up, Mr. Williams?"

I made some attempt to dissemble, since I could put my hand upon nothing tangible, and, viewed in the cold light of day, what I might have said would have sounded almost hysterical to an impartial listener. I said only, "I'd like to know something about a Potter family that lives in Witches' Hollow, west of the school."

He gave me an enigmatic glance. "Never heard of old Wizard Potter?" he asked. And, before I could answer, he went on, "No, of course, you're from Brattleboro. We could hardly expect Vermonters to know about what goes on in the Massachusetts back country. He lived there first. An old man when I first knew him.

And these Potters were distant relatives, lived in Upper Michigan, inherited the property and came to live there when Wizard Potter died."

"But what do you know about them?" I persisted.

"Nothing but what everybody else knows," he said. "When they came, they were nice friendly people. Now they talk to nobody, seldom come out—and there's all that talk about missing animals from the farms in the district. The people tie that all up."

Thus begun, I questioned him at length.

I listened to a bewildering enigma of half-told tales, hints, legends and lore utterly beyond my comprehension. What seemed to be incontrovertible was a distant cousinship between Wizard Potter and one Wizard Whately of nearby Dunwich—"a bad lot," the editor called him; the solitary way of life of old Wizard Potter, and the incredible length of time he had lived; the fact that people generally shunned Witches' Hollow. What seemed to be sheer fantasy was the superstitious lore—that Wizard Potter had "called something down from the sky, and it lived with him or in him until he died";—that a late traveller, found in a dying state along the main road, had gasped out something about "that thing with the feelers—slimy, rubbery thing with the suckers on its feelers" that came out of the woods and attacked him—and a good deal more of the same kind of lore.

When he finished, the editor scribbled a note to the librarian at Miskatonic University in Arkham, and handed it to me. "Tell him to let you look at that book. You may learn something." He shrugged. "And you may not. Young people now-days take the world with a lot of salt."

I went supperless to pursue my search for the special knowledge I felt I needed, if I were to save Andrew Potter for a better life. For it was this rather than the satisfaction of my curiosity that impelled me. I made my way to the library of Miskatonic University, looked up the librarian, and handed him the editor's note.

The old man gave me a sharp look, said, "Wait here, Mr. Williams," and went off with a ring of keys. So the book, whatever it was, was kept under lock and key.

I waited for what seemed an interminable time. I was now beginning to feel some hunger, and to question my unseemly haste—and yet I felt that there was little time to be lost, though I could not define the catastrophe I hoped to avert. Finally the librarian came, bearing an ancient tome, and brought it around and to a table within his range of vision. The book's title was in Latin—*Necronomicon*—though its author was evidently an Arabian, *Abdul Alhazred,* and its text was in somewhat archaic English.

I began to read with interest which soon turned to complete bewilderment. The book evidently concerned ancient, alien races, invaders of earth, great mythical beings called Ancient Ones and Elder Gods, with outlandish names like Cthulhu and Hastur, Shub-Niggurath and Azathoth, Dagon and Ithaqua and Wendigo and Cthugha, all involved in some kind of plan to dominate earth and served by some of its peoples—the Tcho-Tcho, and the Deep Ones, and the like. It was a book filled with cabalistic lore, incantations, and what purported to be an account of a great interplanetary battle between the Elder Gods and the Ancient Ones and of the survival of cults and servitors in isolated and remote places on our planet as well as on sister planets. What this rigmarole had to do with my immediate problem, with the ingrown and strange Potter family and their longing for solitude and their anti-social way of life, was completely beyond me.

How long I would have gone on reading, I do not know. I was interrupted presently by the awareness of being studied by a stranger, who stood not far from me with his eyes moving from the book I was busy reading to me. Having caught my eye, he made so bold as to come over to my side.

"Forgive me," he said, "but what in this book interests a country school teacher?"

"I wonder now myself," I said.

He introduced himself as Professor Martin Keane. "I may say, sir," he added, "that I know this book practically by heart."

"A farrago of superstition."

"Do you think so?"

"Emphatically."

"You have lost the quality of wonder, Mr. Williams. Tell me, if you will, what brought you to this book?"

I hesitated, but Professor Keane's personality was persuasive and inspired confidence.

"Let us walk, if you don't mind," I said.

He nodded.

I returned the book to the librarian, and joined my new-found friend. Haltingly, as clearly as I could, I told him about Andrew Potter, the house in Witches' Hollow, my strange psychic experience,—even the curious coincidence of Dunlocks' cows. To all this he listened without interruption, indeed, with a singular absorption. I explained at last that my motive in looking into the background of Witches' Hollow was solely to do something for my pupil.

"A little research," he said, "would have informed you that many strange events have taken place in such remote places as Dunwich and Innsmouth—even Arkham and Witches' Hollow," he said when I had finished. "Look around you at these ancient houses with their shuttered rooms and ill-lit fanlights. How many strange events have taken place under those gambrel roofs! We shall never know. But let us put aside the question of belief! One may not need to see the embodiment of evil to believe in it, Mr. Williams. I should like to be of some small service to the boy in this matter. May I?"

"By all means!"

"It may be perilous—to you as well as to him."

"I am not concerned about myself."

"But I assure you, it cannot be any more perilous to the boy than his present position. Even death for him is less perilous."

"You speak in riddles, Professor."

"Let it be better so, Mr. Williams. But come—we are at my residence. Pray come in."

We went into one of those ancient houses of which Professor Keane had spoken. I walked into the musty past, for the rooms were filled with books and all manner of antiquities. My host took me into what was evidently his sitting room, swept a chair clear of books, and invited me to wait while he busied himself on the second floor.

He was not, however, gone very long—not even long enough for me to assimilate the curious atmosphere of the room in which I waited. When he came back he carried what I saw at once were objects of stone, roughly in the shape of five-pointed stars. He put five of them into my hands.

"Tomorrow after school—if the Potter boy is there—you must contrive to touch him with one of these, and keep it fixed upon him," said my host. "There are two other conditions. You must keep one of these at least on your person at all times, and you must keep all thought of the stone and what you are about to do out of your mind. These beings have a telepathic sense—an ability to read your thoughts."

Startled, I recalled Andrew's charging me with having talked about them with Wilbur Dunlock.

"Should I not know what these are?" I asked.

"If you can abate your doubts for the time being," my host answered with a grim smile. "These stones are among the thousands bearing the Seal of R'lyeh which closed the prisons of the Ancient Ones. They are the seals of the Elder Gods."

"Professor Keane, the age of superstition is past," I protested.

"Mr. Williams—the wonder of life and its mysteries is never past," he retorted. "If the stone has no meaning, it has no power. If it has no power, it cannot affect young Potter. And it cannot protect you."

"From what?"

"From the power behind the malignance you felt at the house in Witches' Hollow," he answered. "Or was this too superstition?" He smiled. "You need not answer. I know your answer. If something happens when you put the stone upon the boy, he cannot be allowed to go back home. You must bring him here to me. Are you agreed?"

"Agreed," I answered.

That next day was interminable, not only because of the imminence of crisis, but because it was extremely difficult to keep my mind blank before the inquiring gaze of Andrew Potter. Moreover, I was conscious as never before of the wall of pulsing malignance at my back, emanating from the wild country there, a tangible menace hidden in a pocket of the dark hills. But the hours passed, however slowly, and just before dismissal I asked Andrew Potter to wait after the others had gone.

And again he assented with that casual air tantamount almost to insolence, so that I was compelled to ask myself whether he were worth "saving" as I thought of saving him in the depths of my mind.

But I persevered. I had hidden the stone in my car, and, once the others were gone, I asked Andrew to step outside with me.

At this point I felt both helpless and absurd. I, a college graduate, about to attempt what for me seemed inevitably the kind of mumbo-jumbo that belonged to the African wilderness. And for a few moments, as I walked stiffly from the school house toward the car I almost flagged, almost simply invited Andrew to get into the car to be driven home.

But I did not. I reached the car with Andrew at my heels, reached in, seized a stone to slip into my own pocket, seized another, and turned with lightning rapidity to press the stone to Andrew's forehead.

Whatever I expected to happen, it was not what took place.

For, at the touch of the stone, an expression of the utmost horror shone in Andrew Potter's eyes; in a trice, this gave way to poignant anguish; a great cry of terror burst from his lips. He flung his arms wide, scattering his books, wheeled as far as he could with my hold upon him, shuddered, and would have fallen, had I not caught him and lowered him, foaming at the mouth, to the ground. And then I was conscious of a great, cold wind which whirled about us and was gone, bending the grasses and the flowers, rippling the edge of the wood, and tearing away the leaves at the outer band of trees.

Driven by my own terror, I lifted Andrew Potter into the car, laid the stone on his chest, and drove as fast as I could into Arkham, seven miles away. Professor Keane was waiting, no whit surprised at my coming. And he had expected that I would bring Andrew Potter, for he had made a bed ready for him, and together we put him into it, after which Keane administered a sedative.

Then he turned to me. "Now then, there's no time to be lost. They'll come to look for him—the girl probably first. We must get back to the school house at once."

But now the full meaning and horror of what had happened to Andrew Potter had dawned upon me, and I was so shaken that it was necessary for Keane to push me from the room and half drag me out of the house. And again, as I set down these words so long after the terrible events of that night, I find myself trembling with that apprehension and fear which seize hold of a man who comes for the first time face to face with the vast unknown and knows how puny and meaningless he is against that cosmic immensity. I knew in that moment that what I had read in that forbidden book at the Miskatonic Library was not a farrago of superstition, but the key to a hitherto unsuspected revelation perhaps far, far older than mankind in the universe. I did not dare to think of what Wizard Potter had called down from the sky.

I hardly heard Professor Keane's words as he urged me to discard my emotional reaction and think of what had happened in scientific, more clinical fashion. After all, I had now accomplished my objective—Andrew Potter was saved. But to insure it, he must be made free of the others, who would surely follow him and find him. I thought only of what waiting horror that quartet of country people from Michigan had walked into when they came to take up possession of the solitary farm in Witches' Hollow.

I drove blindly back to the school. There, at Professor Keane's behest, I put on the lights and sat with the door open to the warm night, while he concealed himself behind the building to wait upon their coming. I had to steel myself in order to blank out my mind and take up that vigil.

On the edge of night, the girl came. . . .

And after she had undergone the same experience as her brother, and lay beside the desk, the star-shaped stone on her breast, their father showed up in the doorway. All was darkness now, and he carried a gun. He had no need to ask what had happened; he *knew.* He stood wordless, pointed to his daughter and the stone on her breast, and raised his gun. His inference was plain—if I did not remove the stone, he meant to shoot. Evidently this was the contingency the professor expected, for he came upon Potter from the rear and touched him with the stone.

Afterwards we waited for two hours—in vain, for Mrs. Potter.

"She isn't coming," said Professor Keane at last. "She harbors the seat of its intelligence—I had thought it would be the man. Very well—we have no choice—we must go to Witches' Hollow. These two can be left here."

We drove through the darkness, making no attempt at secrecy, for the professor said the "thing" in the house in the Hollow "knew" we were coming but could not reach us past the talisman of the stone. We went through that close pressing forest, down the narrow lane where the queer undergrowth seemed to reach out toward us in the glow of the headlights, into the Potter yard.

The house stood dark save for a wan glow of lamplight in one room.

Professor Keane leaped from the car with his little bag of star-shaped stones, and went around sealing the house—with a stone at each of the two doors, and one at each of the windows, through one of which we could see the woman sitting at the kitchen table—stolid, watchful, *aware*, no longer dissembling, looking unlike that tittering woman I had seen in this house not long ago, but rather like some great sentient beast at bay.

When he had finished, my companion went around to the front and, by means of brush collected from the yard and piled against the door, set fire to the house heedless of my protests.

Then he went back to the window to watch the woman, explaining that only fire could destroy the elemental force, but that he hoped, still, to save Mrs. Potter. "Perhaps you'd better not watch, Williams."

I did not heed him. Would that I had—and so spared myself the dreams that invade my sleep even yet! I stood at the window behind him and watched what went on in that room—for the smell of smoke was now permeating the house. Mrs. Potter—or what animated her gross body—started up, went awkwardly to the back door, retreated, to the window, retreated from it, and came back to the center of the room, between the table and the wood stove, not yet fired against the coming cold. There she fell to the floor, heaving and writhing.

The room filled slowly with smoke, hazing about the yellow lamp, making the room indistinct—but not indistinct enough to conceal completely what went on in the course of that terrible struggle on the floor, where Mrs. Potter threshed about as if in mortal convulsion and slowly, half visibly, something or other took shape—an incredible amorphous mass, only half glimpsed in the smoke, tentacled, shimmering, with a cold intelligence and a physical coldness that I could feel through the window. The thing rose like a cloud above the now motionless body of Mrs. Potter, and then fell upon the stove and drained into it like vapor!

"The stove!" cried Professor Keane, and fell back.

Above us, out of the chimney, came a spreading blackness, like smoke, gathering itself briefly there. Then it hurtled like a lightning bolt aloft, into the stars, in the direction of the Hyades, back to that place from which old Wizard Potter had called it into himself, away from where it had lain in wait for the Potters to come from Upper Michigan and afford it new host on the face of earth.

We managed to get Mrs. Potter out of the house, much shrunken now, but alive.

On the remainder of that night's events there is no need to dwell —how the professor waited until fire had consumed the house to collect his store of star-shaped stones, of the reuniting of the Potter family—freed from the curse of Witches' Hollow and determined never to return to that haunted valley—of Andrew, who, when we came to waken him, was talking in his sleep of "great winds that fought and tore" and a "place by the Lake of Hali where they live in glory forever."

What it was that old Wizard Potter had called down from the stars, I lacked the courage to ask, but I knew that it touched upon secrets better left unknown to the races of men, secrets I would never have become aware of had I not chanced to take District School Number Seven, and had among my pupils the strange boy who was Andrew Potter.

The Song
of the Morrow

ROBERT LOUIS
STEVENSON

ROBERT LOUIS STEVENSON *(1850–1894), the renowned Scottish author whom the Samoans called "Tusitala" (teller of tales), wrote such popular adventures as* Treasure Island, The Strange Case of Dr. Jekyll and Mr. Hyde, Kidnapped, The Master of Ballantrae, *and the entertaining interconnected short stories that he called* New Arabian Nights. *One of his least familiar fantasies is "The Song of the Morrow," the strange cyclical tale of a prophesying witch and the daughter of a king.*

The King of Duntrine had a daughter when he was old, and she was the fairest king's daughter between two seas. Her hair was like spun gold, and her eyes like pools in a river. The King gave her a castle upon the sea beach, with a terrace and a court of hewn stone and four towers at the four corners. Here she dwelt and grew up, and had no care for the morrow, and no power upon the hour, after the manner of simple men.

It befell that she walked one day by the beach of the sea when it was autumn, and the wind blew from the place of rains. Upon the one hand of her the sea beat, and upon the other the dead leaves ran. This was the loneliest beach between two seas, and strange things had been done there in ancient ages.

Now the King's daughter was aware of a crone that sat upon the beach. The sea foam ran to her feet, and the dead leaves swarmed about her back, and the rags blew about her face in the blowing of the wind.

"Now," said the King's daughter as she named a holy name, "this is the most unhappy old crone between two seas."

"Daughter of a King," said the crone, "you dwell in a stone house, and your hair is like spun gold, but what is your profit? Life is not long, nor lives strong. You live after the way of simple men and have no thought for the morrow, and no power upon the hour."

"Though for the morrow, that I have," said the King's daughter. "But power upon the hour, that I have not." And she mused within herself.

Then the crone smote her lean hands one within the other and laughed like a seagull. "Home!" cried she, "O daughter of a King, home to your stone house! Now the longing is come upon you, nor can you live any more after the manner of simple men. Home, and toil and suffer till the gift come that will make you bare, and till the man come that will bring you care."

The King's daughter made no more ado, but turned about and went home to her house in silence. And when she was come into her chamber, she called for her nurse.

"Nurse," said the King's daughter, "thought is come upon me for the morrow, so that I can live no more after the manner of simple men. Tell me what I must do that I may have power upon the hour."

Then the nurse moaned like a snow wind. "Alas," said she, "that this thing should be! The thought is gone into your marrow, nor is there any cure against the thought. Be it so, then, even as you will. Though power is less than weakness, power shall you have; and though the thought is colder than winter, yet shall you think it to an end."

So the King's daughter sat in her vaulted chamber in the masoned house, and she thought upon her thought. Nine years she sat as the sea beat upon the terrace and the gulls cried about the turrets and the wind crooned in the chimneys of the house. Nine years she came not abroad, nor tasted the clean air, nor saw God's sky. Nine years she sat and looked neither to the right nor to the left, nor heard speech of any one, but thought upon the thought of the morrow. And her nurse fed her in silence. The King's daughter took of the food with her left hand, and ate it without grace.

Now when the nine years were out, it fell dusk in the autumn; and there came a sound in the wind like a sound of piping. At that, the nurse lifted up her finger in the vaulted house.

"I hear a sound in the wind," said she, "that is like the sound of piping."

"It is but a little sound," said the King's daughter, "but yet it is sound enough for me."

So they went down in the dusk to the doors of the house, and along the beach of the sea. Upon the one hand of them the sea beat, and upon the other the dead leaves ran. Above them the clouds raced in the sky, and the gulls flew widdershins. And when they came to that part of the beach where strange things had been done in ancient ages, lo! there was the crone, and she was dancing widdershins.

"Old crone," said the King's daughter, "what makes you dance widdershins here upon the bleak beach, between the waves and the dead leaves?"

"I hear a sound in the wind that is like a sound of piping," quoth she, "and it is for that that I dance widdershins. For the gift comes that will make you bare, and the man comes that must bring you care. But for me, the morrow is come that I have thought upon, and the hour of my power."

"How comes it, old crone," marveled the King's daughter, "that you waver like a rag, and pale like a dead leaf, before my eyes?"

"Because the morrow has come that I have thought upon, and the hour of my power," said the crone. With that she fell on the beach, and lo! she was but stalks of the sea tangle and the dust of the sea sand, and the sand lice hopped upon the place of her.

"This is the strangest thing that ever befell between two seas," said the King's daughter of Duntrine. But the nurse broke out and moaned like an autumn gale. "I am weary of the wind," quoth she, and bewailed her day.

Then the King's daughter was aware of a man upon the beach who went hooded that none might perceive his face, and a bagpipe was underneath his arm. The sound of his pipe was like singing wasps, and like the wind that sings in windelstraw. It took hold upon men's ears like the crying of gulls.

"Are you the comer?" quoth the King's daughter of Duntrine.

"I am the comer," said he, "and these are the pipes that a man may hear; for I have power upon the hour, and this is the song of the morrow." Then he piped the song of the morrow. It was as long as years, and nurse wept out aloud at the hearing of it.

"It is true," said the King's daughter, "that you pipe the song of the morrow; but that ye have power upon the hour—how may I know that? Show me a marvel here upon the beach, between the waves and the dead leaves."

And the man said, "Upon whom?"

"Here is my nurse," quoth the King's daughter. "She is weary of the wind. Show me a good marvel upon her."

And lo! the nurse fell upon the beach as it were two handfuls of dead leaves, and the wind whirled them widdershins, and the sand lice hopped upon the place of her.

"It is true," said the King's daughter of Duntrine. "You are the comer, and you have power upon the hour. Come with me to my stone house."

So they went by the sea margin as the man piped the song of the morrow, and the leaves followed behind them as they went. Then they sat down together as the sea beat upon the terrace and the gulls cried about the turrets and the wind crooned in the chimneys of the house. Nine years they sat; and every year when it fell autumn, the man said, "This is the hour, and I have power in it." But the daughter of the King said, "Nay, but pipe me the song of the morrow." And he piped it, and it was as long as years.

Now when the nine years were gone, the King's daughter of Duntrine got to her feet like one that remembers, and she looked about her in the masoned house. All her servants were gone; only the man that piped sat upon the terrace with the hood upon his face, and as he piped, the leaves ran about the terrace and the sea beat along the wall.

Then she cried to him with a great voice, "This is the hour; let me see the power in it." And with that, the wind blew off the hood from the man's face, and lo! there was no man there—only the clothes and the hood. The pipes tumbled one upon another in a corner of the terrace, and the dead leaves ran over them.

Then the King's daughter of Duntrine got her to that part of the beach where strange things had been done in ancient ages, and there she sat her down. The sea foam ran to her feet, and the dead leaves swarmed about her back, and the veil blew about her face in the blowing of the wind. And when she lifted up her eyes, there was the daughter of a king come walking on the beach. Her hair was like spun gold, and her eyes like pools in a river. She had no thought for the morrow and no power upon the hour, after the manner of simple men.

Little Old
Miss Macbeth

FRITZ LEIBER, JR.

To call the protagonist of the next story a witch is more definition than the author provides, but there is certainly a sense of dark power invested in "Little Old Miss Macbeth." This unusual post-holocaust tale by FRITZ LEIBER, JR.*—the award-winning author of the thrice-filmed* Conjure Wife *as well as* The Green Millenium, Night's Black Agents, *and the sometimes tongue-in-cheek Fafhrd–Grey Mouser swords-and-sorcery series— first appeared in the December 1958 issue of* The Magazine of Fantasy and Science Fiction.

The sphere of dim light from the electric candle on the orange crate was enough to show the cot, a little bare wall behind it and concrete floor beneath it, a shrouded birdcage on the other side of the cot, and nothing more. Spent batteries and their empty boxes overflowed the top of the orange crate and made a little mound. Three fresh batteries remained in a box by the candle.

The little old woman turned and tossed in her sleep under the blankets. Her face was troubled and her mouth pursed in a thin line that turned downward at the corners—a tragic mask scaled down for a little old lady. At times, without waking, she'd creep her hands up from under the blanket and touch her ears, as though they were assaulted by noise—though the silence was profound.

At last, as if she could bear it no longer, she slowly sat up. Her eyes opened, though she did not wake, staring out with the fixity of unconscious seeing. She put her feet into snug felt slippers with a hole in the left toe. She took a woolly bathrobe from the foot of the cot and pulled it around her. Without looking, still sitting on the edge of the cot, she reached for the electric candle. Then she got up and crossed the floor to a door, carrying the candle, which made on the ceiling a circle of light that followed her. At no time was the full size of the room revealed. Her face was still a prim little tragic mask, eyes open, fast asleep.

Outside the door she went down one flight of an iron stairway, which sounded from its faint deep ringing under her light tread as if there were many more flights above. She went through another door, a heavy, softly moaning one like the stage door of a theater, and closed it behind her and stood still.

If you'd been there outside, you'd have seen her holding the electric candle, and a small semicircle of brick wall and iron door behind her and another semicircle of sidewalk under her feet, and nothing more, no other side to the street, no nothing—the feeble light went no further. Then after a while you'd have noticed a ribbon of faint stars overhead—a narrow ribbon, too narrow to show constellations, as if the unseen buildings here were very high. And if you'd have looked up a second time, you'd have wondered if a few of the stars hadn't moved or changed color, or if there weren't extra stars now or missing ones, and it would have worried you.

The little old lady didn't wait long. She started down the street in the dim globe of light from her electric candle, keeping close to the curb, so that even the wall on her side of the street was almost lost in darkness. Her felt slippers scuffed softly. Otherwise the city, for that was what it seemed to be, was absolutely quiet. Except that after a couple of blocks a very faint angry buzzing became audible. And the corner at the next cross street was outlined now by an extremely faint red glow, the exact color of neon signs.

The old lady turned the corner into a block that was crawling with luminous worms, about forty or fifty of them, as thick as your thumb and long as your arm, though some were shorter. They weren't bright enough to show anything but themselves. They were all colors, but neon red was commonest. They moved like caterpillars but a little faster. They looked like old neon tubes come alive and crawled down out of signs, but blackened and dimmed by ages of ions. They crawled in sine curves on the sidewalks and street, a few of them on ledges a little way up the walls, and one or two along what must have been wires hanging overhead. As they moved they buzzed and the wires sang.

They seemed to be aware of the little old lady, for two or three came and circled her, keeping outside her dim globe of light. When she turned at the next corner a mercury-violet one followed her a little way, lifting its head to buzz and crackle angrily, exactly like a defective neon sign.

This block was black again with just the ribbon of elusive stars. But although the little old lady still kept close to the curb, the sidewalk was narrower and the electric candle showed wrecked display windows with jagged edges and occasional stretches of almost unbroken, thick glass. The old lady's eyes, seeing in her sleep, didn't waver to either side, but if you'd have been there you'd have dimly seen dummies behind the broken windows, the men in zoot suits and wide-brimmed hats, the women in tight skirts and glimmering blouses, and although they stood very stiff you'd have wondered if their eyes didn't follow the little old lady as she passed, and there'd have been no way for you to know, as soon as her globe of light was gone, that they didn't step out carefully between the glass razors and follow.

In the next block a ghost light swirled across a flatness that began about a story up in the dark. It seemed to be something moving through the ten thousand bulbs of an old theater marquee, barely quickening for an instant their brittle old filaments—a patchy, restless shimmer. Across the street, but rather higher, there appeared, on the very threshold of vision, a number of large rectangular signs, their murky colors irregularly revealed and concealed—giant bats crawling across almost completely faded luminescent billboards would have given the effect. While at least twenty stories up, at the edge of the dubious starlight, one small window spilled yellow light.

Halfway down the next block the little old lady turned in from the curb to a fence of iron pickets. She leaned against a gate, giving

a querulous little moan, the only sound she'd uttered, and it swung
in, crunching against the gravel.

She pressed it shut behind her and walked ahead, her slippers
crushing dead leaves, her thin nostrils wrinkling mindlessly at the
smell of weeds and dust. Directly overhead a small square of stars
projected from the ribbon. She went up wooden steps and across a
porch and through a six-paneled door that creaked as she opened
and shut it.

The halls of the house were bare and its stairs uncarpeted and its
woodwork tritely ornate. When she reached the third floor with
her dim globe of light there was the faintest crunch from below and
a little later a creaking. She took hold of a rope that hung from
above and added some of her weight to it, swaying a little, and a
ladder swung out of the ceiling and bumped against the floor.

She mounted the ladder, stooping, breathing just a little heavily,
into a low attic. Her candle showed boxes and trunks and boxes,
piles of folded draperies, a metal-ribbed dressmaker's dummy and
the horn of an old phonograph.

Then you would have heard it: *pling!*—four seconds, six, seven—
another *pling!*—another seven seconds—*pling!* again——*pling!*——
pling!——*pling!*

The torment in her sleeping face deepened. She crossed between
the piles to a sink against the wall. On the lip of the single
verdigrised faucet a drop slowly formed as she approached and just
as she got there it fell—*pling!*—and a quick spasm crossed her face.

She put down the electric candle on the drainboard and took the
handle of the faucet in both hands and leaned against it, not looking
at it. There was one more *pling!* but then no more. She touched the
lip of the faucet with a finger and it came away barely wet. She
waited but no new drop formed.

Then her face smoothed out into a small mask of dispassion, the
mouth thin and straight, and she took up her candle and started
back. On the ladder and stairs and out on the walk and the street
she was no longer alone. Presences thronged around her, angry
and menacing, just beyond the candle's glow, and leaves crackled
under other feet than her own. The light from the high window by
the stars pulsed poisonously green, the winged shapes crawled
more restlessly across the spent luminescence of the billboards, and

all the witch-light in the theater marquee drained down into the lowest bulbs, the ones nearest her as she passed.

The wrecked display windows in the Block of the Babes and Zoot-Suiters were all empty.

In the Street of the Neon Worms the colored crawlers all came swiftly toward her, buzzing loudly and angrily, more cracklingly than bees, swarming close to her feet in ribbons of rainbow fire and following her around the corner for half a block.

But none of these things, nor the perceptible dimming of her electric candle, ruffled for one instant her expression of calm security.

She mounted the iron stairs, crossed the boundless room, sat down on the cot and put the electric candle on the orange crate among the heaped dead batteries.

One of them rolled off and hit the floor with a little *tump!* She started, quivered her head and blinked her eyes. Wakefulness had at last come into them. She sat motionless for a while, remembering. She sighed once and smiled a little smile, then she sat up straighter and her thin silvery eyebrows drew together in a frown of determination. She found a fountain pen and a small pad of onionskin paper among the batteries. She tucked a scrap of carbon paper under the top sheet and wrote rapidly for a minute. She tore off the top sheet, folded it and rolled it up tightly, then tucked it into an aluminum cylinder hardly bigger than a paper match.

She got up and went around the cot. She took the cover off the birdcage, opened the small door, and took out a black pigeon. Moaning to it affectionately, she wired the cylinder to one foot. Then she kissed its beak and threw it into the darkness. There was a flapping which grew steadily fainter, then suddenly broke off, as if the bird had winged through a window.

The dim globe of light had shrunk to half its original size, but it was still enough to show the little old lady's face as she got into bed and pulled up the blankets. Her eyes were closed now. She sighed once more and the corners of her lips lifted in another little smile. She became still, the blankets rising and falling almost imperceptibly over her chest, and the smile stayed.

The light was also enough to show the carbon of her note, which read:

Dear Evangeline,

I was overjoyed to receive your note and discover that you too at last have a city of your own and of course your own things. How is Louisville since the Destruction? Quiet, I trust. Pittsburgh is so noisy. I am thinking of moving to Cincinnati. Do you know if it has a tenant?

Yours very truly,
Miss Macbeth

The Mainz Psalter

JEAN RAY

No biographical data are available concerning JEAN RAY *other than the fact that a group of his grisly short stories,* Ghouls in My Grave, *was translated by Lowell Bair and published by Berkley Books in 1965. From that collection was drawn "The Last Traveler" (in* Ghosts, Doubleday, *1981) and "The Mainz Psalter," a harrowing tale of black magic on the high seas that I consider a masterpiece of dark fantasy.*

A man who is about to die is not likely to be very elegant in his last words: being in a hurry to sum up his whole life, he tends to make them rigorously concise.

But it was different with Ballister as he lay dying in the forecastle of the trawler *North Caper,* from Grimsby.

We had tried in vain to stop the flow of blood that was draining his life away. He had no fever; his speech was steady and rapid. He did not seem to see the bandages or the bloody basin: his eyes were following remote and formidable images.

Reines, the radio man, was taking notes.

Reines spends all his spare time writing stories and essays for short-lived literary magazines. As soon as one of them is born in Paternoster Row, his name is sure to appear on the list of contributors. Do not be surprised, therefore, by the rather special style given to this final monologue of a mortally wounded sailor. The blame must fall on Reines, a literary man without glory, who transcribed it. But I can testify that the facts it contains are the same as those reported before four members of the crew of the *North Caper:* Benjamin Cormon, the captain; yours truly John Copeland, first mate; Ephraim Rose, engineer; and the aforementioned Archibald Reines.

Thus spoke Ballister:

It was in the Merry Heart Tavern that I first met the schoolmaster, and it was there that we struck our bargain and he gave me his orders.

The Merry Heart is more of a meeting-place for bargemen than for sailors. Its dilapidated façade is reflected in the water of one of Liverpool's back docks, where barges from the inland waterways are moored.

I looked at the well-drawn plan of a small schooner.

"She's almost a yacht," I said. "In heavy weather, she must be able to sail close to the wind, and that broad stern will make it possible for us to maneuver well when there's a head wind."

"There's an auxiliary engine, too," he said.

I frowned, having always loved sailing.

"Built by Hallet & Hallet, Glasgow, 1909," I said. "She's very well rigged. With her sixty tons and a crew of six, she'll take to the sea better than a transatlantic liner."

His face took on a look of satisfaction, and he ordered a round of expensive drinks.

"Why are you changing her name from the *Hen-Parrot?*" I asked. "It's a nice name. I've always liked parrots."

He hesitated slightly.

"It's a matter of . . . sentiment, or of gratitude, if you prefer."

"So the ship will be called the *Mainz Psalter.* . . . It's odd, but I suppose it's original."

Alcohol had made him a little loquacious.

"That's not the reason," he said. "A year ago a grand-uncle of mine died and left me a trunk full of old books."

"So?"

"Wait! I was looking through them without enthusiasm when one of them caught my attention. It was an incunabulum. . . ."

"A what?"

"An incunabulum," he said with a slight air of superiority, "is a book published shortly after the invention of the printing press. And I was amazed to recognize the almost heraldic mark of Fust and Schaeffer! Those names probably mean nothing to you. Fust and Schaeffer were partners of Gutenberg, the inventor of the printing press. The book I had in my hands was nothing less than a rare and splendid copy of the famous *Mainz Psalter,* published toward the end of the fifteenth century."

I gave him a look of polite attention and false understanding.

"What will impress you more, Mr. Ballister," he said, "is that a Mainz Psalter is worth a fortune."

"Ah!" I said, suddenly interested.

"Yes, it's worth a fine bundle of banknotes big enough to buy the former *Hen-Parrot* and pay ample wages to a crew of six men for the cruise I want to make. Now do you understand why I want to give such an unmaritime name to our little ship?"

I understood it perfectly, and I congratulated him on his greatness of soul.

"And yet it would seem more logical to me," I said, "to name the ship after that dear uncle who left you the book."

He burst into loud, disagreeable laughter. I was disconcerted by such coarseness on the part of an educated man.

"You'll leave from Glasgow," he said, "and sail the ship through the North Minch to Cape Wrath."

"Those are hellish waters," I said.

"I chose you precisely because you know them, Mr. Ballister."

No finer praise can be given a sailor than to say that he knows the horrible corridor of water that is the Minch Channel. My heart swelled with pride.

"That's true," I said. "In fact, I was once nearly killed between Chicken and Tiumpan Head."

"South of Cape Wrath," he went on, "there's a sheltered little bay that's known only to a few bold sailors, by a name that doesn't appear on the map: Big Toe Bay."

I looked at him in surprised admiration.

"Do you know Big Toe?" I said. "That's something that would make you respected by Customs, and would probably get you stabbed by certain men of the coast."

He made a gesture of indifference.

"I'll rejoin the ship at Big Toe Bay."

"And from there?"

He indicated a precise westerly direction.

"Hm, that's a nasty place," I said, "a real desert of water strewn with sharp rocks. We won't see many trails of smoke on the horizon."

"You're quite right," he said.

I winked at him, thinking I understood.

"As long as you pay the way you've said," I replied, "I don't care what you do."

"I think you're mistaken about my plans, Mr. Ballister. They're of a rather . . . scientific nature, but I don't want to have a discovery stolen from me by some envious rival. In any case, it doesn't matter, because I'll pay as I said."

We spent a few minutes drinking. Then, just as we were about to discuss the question of the crew, our conversation veered off strangely.

"I'm not a sailor," he said brusquely, "so don't count on me to help with handling the ship. Let me be specific: I'm a schoolmaster."

"I respect learning," I said, "and I'm not entirely lacking in it myself. A schoolmaster? Good, good!"

"Yes, in Yorkshire."

"Let's go over the crew now," I said. "First of all there's Turnip. It's an odd name, but he's a good man and a good sailor. There's . . . a prison term in his recent past. Is that a drawback?"

"Not in the least."

"Good. You can have him for reasonable wages, especially if you take a little rum on board. It can be cheap rum: he's not particular about quality as long as the quantity is there. And then there's Steevens, a Fleming. He never talks, but he can break a mooring chain as easily as you can bite through the stem of a clay pipe."

"And I suppose he also has a prison term in his past?"

"It's not unlikely."

"I'll take him. What did you say his name was again?"

"Steevens."

"Steevens. . . . Is he expensive?"

"Not at all. He makes up for his low pay by eating vast amounts of bacon and biscuits. And currant jam, if you buy any."

"We'll take half a ton of it on board if you like."

"He'll be your slave. . . . I might suggest Walker to you now, but he's very ugly."

"Are you joking?"

"No. His face lacks half a nose, part of a chin, and a whole ear, so it's not pleasant to look at for someone who's not used to Madame Tussaud's museum of horrors, especially since the operation was sloppily performed by some Italian sailors who were in a bit of a hurry."

"And who else?"

"Two excellent men: Jellewyn and Friar Tuck. Friar Tuck—I don't know him by any other name—is a cook, among other things, a seagoing Jack-of-all-trades. He and Jellewyn are always together. If you see one, you see the other, and if you hire one, you must hire the other. They're rather mysterious. It's said that Jellewyn has royal blood in his veins and that Friar Tuck is a devoted servant who has stayed with him in adversity."

"And their price is in keeping with their mystery?"

"Precisely. The fallen prince must have driven a car in the past, so he'll be the one to take care of your auxiliary engine."

It was then that an incident took place that has little bearing on the events of this story, but that I remember with a certain uneasiness.

A poor devil had just been blown into the bar by the gusty night wind. He was a kind of emaciated, rain-soaked clown, faded by all the miseries of the sea and the waterfront.

He ordered a glass of gin and greedily raised it to his lips. Suddenly I heard the sound of breaking glass and saw the derelict throw up his hands, stare at the schoolmaster with unspeakable terror, then hurry outside into the wind and rain, without picking up his change from the bar. I don't think the schoolmaster noticed the incident, or at least he didn't seem to: but I still dare not imagine the formidable reason that drove that poor wretch to drop his gin on the floor, abandon his money, and flee into the icy street when the bar was filled with exquisite warmth.

· · ·

On one of the first days of a very mild spring, the North Minch opened before us as though for a brotherly embrace. A few angry currents were still moving craftily beneath the surface, but we could detect them by their green backs, writhing like segments of mutilated snakes.

One of those curious southeastern breezes that blow only in that region brought us the fragrance of the early Irish lilacs from two hundred miles away and helped the auxiliary engine to take us to Big Toe Bay.

There, things changed radically. Whirlpools dug holes in the water, hissing like steam engines. We avoided them only with great difficulty. The moss-green hull of a sunken ship, raised from the depths of the Atlantic, shot up almost under the bobstay of our bowsprit and was hurled against a rock wall, where it exploded in a dark burst of rotten wood.

A dozen times, the *Mainz Psalter* was in danger of being dismasted as though by a stroke of a giant razor. Fortunately, she was a beautiful sailer and she lay to with the elegance of a true lady of the sea. A few hours of calm enabled us to run the engine at full speed and pass through the narrow channel of Big Toe Bay just as another furious tide came thundering after us in a green spray of tormented water.

"We're in inhospitable waters," I said to my men. "If the coastal scavengers find us here, we'll have to give them an explanation, and since they'll try to chase us away before hearing what we have to say, we'd better have our guns ready."

The scavengers did put in an appearance, but in so doing they met with a disaster that was as disturbing as it was incomprehensible to us.

For a week, we had been lying at anchor in that little bay, which was as calm as a duck pond. Life was pleasant. Our supplies of food and drink were worthy of a royal yacht. By swimming twelve strokes, or rowing seven times, we could reach a little red sand beach and, further on, a stream of icy fresh water.

Turnip caught halibut on a line. Steevens went inland to the deserted moors, and sometimes, if the wind was right, we could hear the boom of his shotgun. He brought back partridges, grouse, occasionally a big-pawed hare, and always some of those delicious heath rabbits with fragrant flesh.

The schoolmaster had not appeared. We did not worry: we had been paid in cash for six weeks in advance, and Turnip had said he would not leave until the last drop of rum was gone.

One morning this serenity was shattered. Steevens had just filled a keg with fresh water when a shrill sound vibrated above him and, a foot away from his face, a rock exploded into dust. He was a phlegmatic man; without haste, he waded into the bay, spotted a puff of blue smoke rising from a cleft in a rock, ignored the angry little slaps that struck the surface of the water beside him, and calmly swam back to the ship. He went into the forecastle, where the crew was waking up, and said, "Someone's shooting at us."

His words were punctuated by three sharp blows against the hull. I took a rifle from the rack and went up on deck. I instinctively ducked at the sound of a whining bullet; an instant later, a handful of wooden splinters leapt into the air, and the bronze rolling-gear of the boom clanged beneath the impact of a lead slug.

I raised my rifle toward the cleft that Steevens pointed out to me. I saw billows of black-powder smoke coming from it. But suddenly the shooting stopped and was replaced by vociferations and shouts of fear.

Something struck the dark red beach with a heavy thud. I started in horror: a man had just fallen three hundred feet from the top of the cliff. His broken body was almost entirely buried in the sand, but I was able to recognize the coarse leather clothing of the wreckers of Cape Wrath.

I had scarcely turned my eyes away from that lifeless mass when Steevens touched me on the shoulder.

"Here comes another one," he said.

An awkward, ridiculous shape was hurtling toward the ground; it was like the loose, ungainly fall of a big bird that has been hit by shotgun pellets at a great height, and, conquered by gravity and betrayed by the air, comes tumbling down without dignity.

For the second time there was a soft, ghastly thud on the sand. This time a villainous face quivered for a few seconds, spewing crimson froth. Steevens slowly pointed to the top of the cliff.

"One more," he said in a slightly faltering voice.

Wild screams rang out from above. Suddenly we saw the bust of a man against the sky, struggling with something invisible. He made a desperate gesture, then flew from the cliff as though propelled by a catapult. His cry was still floating down to us in a slow tailspin of despair when his body was smashed beside the two others.

We stood still.

"It's true they were trying to kill us," said Jellewyn, "but I'd still like to avenge those poor devils. Please give me your rifle, Mr. Ballister. Friar Tuck, come here!"

Friar Tuck's shaved head emerged from the depths of the ship.

"Friar Tuck is as good as a hunting dog," Jellewyn explained with a touch of condescension. "Or rather he's as good as a whole pack of them: he smells the quarry from very far off. He's phenomenal. . . . And what do you think of *this* quarry, old boy?"

Friar Tuck hoisted his round, massive body onto the deck and waddled over to the rail. He scrutinized the mangled corpses and showed deep surprise; then an ashen pallor came over his face.

"Friar," said Jellewyn with a nervous laugh, "you've seen some strong sights in your day, yet you're turning pale like a young chambermaid."

"No, no, it's not that," Friar Tuck replied dully. "There's something ugly behind this. . . . There's. . . . Shoot, Your Grace!" he suddenly shouted. "Up there! Hurry!"

Jellewyn turned on him furiously:

"I've warned you about calling me by that damned name!"

Friar Tuck made no reply. He shook his head, then murmured, "Too late, it's gone."

"What's gone?" I asked.

"Why, the thing that was watching us from the cliff," he said foolishly.

"What was it?"

He gave me a crafty look.

"I don't know. Anyway, it's gone."

I did not pursue my questioning. Two loud whistles came from the top of the cliff, then a shadow moved against the patch of sky behind it.

Jellewyn raised his rifle. I pushed it aside.

"Pay attention to what you're doing!"

The schoolmaster was coming down toward the beach from the cliff, following a path we had not noticed before.

A beautiful cabin in the stern had been reserved for the schoolmaster, and the adjoining room had been made into a bedroom for me, with two bunks.

As soon as he arrived on board, the schoolmaster shut himself up in his cabin and spent his time going through a pile of books. Once or twice a day he went topside, had the sextant brought to him, and carefully took the sun.

We were sailing northwest.

"We're headed for Iceland," I said to Jellewyn.

He attentively looked at a map and wrote down a figure.

"No," he said, "we're headed for Greenland."

"Well, what's the difference?"

We had left Big Toe Bay on a clear morning, leaving the Ross Mountains to warm their humps in the rising sun behind us. That day we passed a ship from the Hebrides manned by a flat-faced* crew whom we insulted lavishly. Toward evening we saw a ketch in full sail just above the horizon.

Next day, the sea was rising. To starboard, we saw a Danish steamer fighting against the waves. She was surrounded by so much smoke that we could not read her name.

That was the last ship we saw, although on the third day there were two trails of smoke to the south that Walker said were from a dispatch boat of the British Navy.

Every evening the schoolmaster invited me to have a drink in his cabin. He himself did not drink; he was no longer the loquacious companion of the Merry Heart Tavern, but he was still a well-bred man, for he never left my glass empty, and while I drank he kept his eyes on his books.

I must admit that I have few memories of those days. Life was monotonous; and yet the crew seemed apprehensive to me, perhaps because of an incident that occurred one evening.

We were all seized with violent nausea at almost the same time, and Turnip shouted that we had been poisoned. I sternly ordered him to be silent. The nausea passed quickly, and a sudden shift of

---

* The inhabitants of the Hebrides have, in general, disagreeable flat faces.

wind forced us to perform a strenuous maneuver that made us forget everything else.

The sun had risen on the eighth day of our voyage.

I found the crew with anxious, sullen faces. I was familiar with such faces; at sea, they are not a good sign. They indicate an uneasy, gregarious, and hostile feeling that groups men and makes them merge in a single fear or hatred; an evil force surrounds them and poisons the atmosphere of the ship. It was Jellewyn who spoke first:

"Mr. Ballister, we want to talk to you, and we want to talk to you as our friend and shipmate, rather than as our captain."

"That's a fine preamble," I said, laughing.

"We're being nice about it because you're our friend," said Walker, and his horrible shapeless face twisted.

"Tell me what's on your mind," I said.

"Something's wrong," said Jellewyn, "and the worst of it is that none of us can explain it."

I cast a dark glance around me, then held out my hand to him.

"It's true, Jellewyn, I feel it the same as you do."

The faces brightened; the men had found an ally in their captain.

"Look at the sea, Mr. Ballister."

"I've seen it too," I said, looking down.

Yes, I had seen it! The water had taken on a strange appearance that I had never seen before in all my twenty years at sea. It had oddly colored streaks, and it sometimes bubbled suddenly and loudly; unknown sounds, something like laughter, would burst from a rapidly approaching wave and make the men look around in alarm.

"Not one bird is following us any more," said Friar Tuck.

It was true.

"Last night," he said in his deep, slow voice, "a little herd of rats that had been living in the storeroom ran topside and all jumped overboard at once. I never saw anything like it."

"Never!" said the other sailors in a somber echo.

"I've sailed in these waters before," said Walker, "and at about this same time of year, too. The air ought to be full of scoter ducks, and schools of porpoises ought to be following us from morning till night. Do you see any?"

"Did you look at the sky last night, Mr. Ballister?" Jellewyn asked me softly.

"No," I admitted, and I must have blushed a little. I had drunk a great deal in the schoolmaster's silent company, and I had not come up on deck, for I had been in the grip of a powerful intoxication that was still pressing my temples with a lingering headache.

"Where is that devil of a man taking us?" asked Turnip.

"Devil, yes," said the taciturn Steevens.

Everyone had had his say.

I made a sudden decision.

"Jellewyn," I said, "listen to me. I'm the captain, it's true, but I'm not ashamed to admit in front of everyone that you're the most intelligent man on board, and I also know that you're not an ordinary sailor."

He smiled sorrowfully.

"You know more about this than the rest of us, don't you?" I asked.

"No," he replied. "But Friar Tuck is a rather . . . curious phenomenon. As I've already told you, he senses certain things without being able to explain them. It's as though he had one more sense than the rest of us: a sense of danger. . . . Speak, Friar Tuck."

"I know very little, almost nothing," said the low voice. "I know only that something is around us, something worse than anything else, worse than death!"

We looked at each other in alarm.

"The schoolmaster," continued Friar Tuck, seeming to choose his words with difficulty, "is not alien to it."

"Jellewyn," I said, "I don't have the courage myself, but I want you to go and tell him."

"Very well," he replied.

He went below. We heard him knock on the door of the schoolmaster's cabin, knock again and again, then finally open the door.

Minutes of silence went by.

Jellewyn came back up on deck. He was pale.

"He's not there," he said. "Search the whole ship. There's no place where a man can hide for long."

We searched the ship, then went topside one by one, looking at each other uneasily. The schoolmaster had vanished.

• • •

At nightfall, Jellewyn motioned to me to come up on deck. When I was beside him he pointed upward.

I think I fell to my knees.

A strange sky was arched above the roaring sea. The familiar constellations were no longer there; unknown stars in new geometrical groupings were shining dimly in a frighteningly black sidereal abyss.

"Good God!" I exclaimed. "Where are we?"

Heavy clouds were rolling across the sky.

"That's better," Jellewyn said calmly. "The others might have seen it and gone mad. . . . You want to know where we are? How should I know? Let's turn back, Mr. Ballister, even though it's useless, in my opinion. . . ."

I took my head between my hands.

"The compass has been inert for two days," I murmured.

"I know," said Jellewyn.

"But where are we? Where are we?"

"Be calm, Mr. Ballister," he said rather ironically. "You're the captain, don't forget that. I don't know where we are. I might make a hypothesis, to use an erudite word that sometimes covers an imagination that's too daring."

"Even so," I replied, "I'd rather hear stories of witches and demons than that demoralizing 'I don't know.' "

"We're probably on another plane of existence. You have some mathematical knowledge; it will help you to understand. Our three-dimensional world is probably lost to us, and I'll define this one as the world of the Nth dimension, which is very vague. If, by some inconceivable magic or some monstrous science, we were transported to Mars or Jupiter, or even to Aldebaran, it wouldn't prevent us from seeing the same constellations we see from earth."

"But the sun. . . ."

"A similarity, a coincidence of the infinite, a kind of equivalent star, perhaps. Anyway, these are only suppositions, words; and since, I believe, we'll be permitted to die in this strange world the same as in our own, I feel that we can remain calm."

"Die?" I said. "I'll defend myself!"

"Against whom?" he asked sarcastically.

"It's true that Friar Tuck talked about things worse than death. If there's anyone's opinion that shouldn't be ignored in time of danger, it's his." I returned to what he called his hypothesis: "What do you mean by the *N*th dimension?"

"For the love of heaven," he said nervously, "don't give my idea such real importance! There's no proof that existence is possible outside of our three ordinary dimensions. Just as we've never discovered any two-dimensional beings from the world of surfaces, or one-dimensional beings from the linear world, we must be indiscernible to beings, if there are any, who live in worlds having more dimensions than ours. I'm in no mood to give you a lesson in hypergeometry, Mr. Ballister, but I'm sure of one thing: there are spaces different from ours. The space we're aware of in our dreams, for example, which presents the past, the present, and perhaps the future, on a single plane; and then there's the world of atoms and electrons, and relative and immense spaces with mysterious kinds of life. . . ." He made a gesture of lassitude. "What was that enigmatic schoolmaster's purpose in bringing us to this devilish region? How, and especially why, did he disappear?"

I suddenly clapped my hand to my forehead. I had just remembered Friar Tuck's expression of fear, and that of the poor derelict in the Merry Heart Tavern.

I related the incident to Jellewyn. He slowly nodded.

"I mustn't exaggerate Friar Tuck's clairvoyant powers," he said. "When he first saw the schoolmaster, he said to me, 'That man makes me think of an unscalable wall behind which something immense and terrible is taking place.' I didn't question him because it would have been useless: that was all he knew. His occult perceptions take the form of images, and he's incapable of analyzing them. In this case, his apprehension goes back even further. As soon as he heard the name of our schooner, he seemed upset and said there was great malice behind it. . . ."

"How shall we sail?" I asked, abandoning nearly all authority.

"We're on the starboard tack," he said. "The wind seems very steady."

"Shall we heave to?"

"Why? Let's go on making headway. I don't see any sign of a storm, but I think we'd better reef our sails a little just the same."

"Walker will take the helm to begin with," I said. "All he'll have to do is watch for patches of white water. If we hit a submerged rock. . . ."

"It might be the best solution for all of us," said Jellewyn.

I could not have agreed with him more.

While a known danger strengthens a leader's authority, the unknown brings him closer to the level of his men.

That evening the forecastle was deserted and everyone crowded into the narrow room that served as my cabin. Jellewyn gave us two demijohns of excellent rum from his personal provisions, and we used it to make a gigantic bowl of punch.

Turnip was soon in an amiable mood. He began an endless story about two cats, a young lady, and a house in Ipswich, a story in which he had played a favorable part.

Steevens had made some fantastic sandwiches of hardtack and corned beef.

Heavy tobacco smoke made a dense fog around the kerosene lamp hanging motionlessly from its gimbals.

The atmosphere was pleasant and friendly. With the help of the punch, I was on the verge of smiling at the fairy tales Jellewyn had told me earlier.

Walker took his share of warm punch in a thermos bottle, picked up a lighted lantern, bade us good night, and went up to take the helm.

My clock slowly struck nine.

An accentuated movement of the ship told us that the sea was growing rougher.

"We don't have much sail set," said Jellewyn.

I silently nodded.

Turnip's voice droned on, addressed to Steevens, who listened as he ground hardtack between the admirable millstones of his teeth.

I emptied my glass and handed it to Friar Tuck to fill. Then I saw the wild expression on his face. His hand was squeezing Jellewyn's, and they both seemed to be listening to something.

"What . . . ," I began.

Just then we heard loud imprecations overhead, followed by the sound of bare feet running rapidly toward the deckhouse, and then a terrible cry.

We looked at each other, horrified. A high-pitched call, a kind of yodel, came from far away.

We all rushed up on deck at once, jostling each other in the
darkness.

Everything was calm. The sails were purring happily; near the
helm, the lantern was burning brightly, illuminating the squat shape
of the abandoned thermos bottle.

But there was no one at the helm.

"Walker! Walker!" we shouted frantically.

Faraway, from the horizon blurred by the night mists, the mysterious yodel answered us.

The great silent night had swallowed up our poor Walker forever.

A sinister dawn, purple like the swift twilight of tropical savan-
nahs, followed that funereal night.

The men, dulled by anguished insomnia, watched the choppy
waves. The bowsprit frenziedly pecked at the foam of the crests.

A big hole had appeared in our crossjack. Steevens opened the
sail-locker to replace it. Friar Tuck took out his metal palm and
prepared to do a conscientious repair job.

Everyone's movements were instinctive, mechanical, and morose. Now and then I turned the helm and murmured to myself,
"What's the use? What's the use?"

Without having been ordered to, Turnip began climbing up the
mainmast. I watched him distractedly until he reached the main
yard, then the sails hid him from sight.

Suddenly we heard his frenzied shout:

"Hurry! Come up, there's someone on the mast!"

There was a fantastic sound of aerial struggle, then a howl of
agony, and at the same time a whirling shape shot upward, and then
fell into the waves a great distance away from the ship.

Jellewyn swore vehemently and began climbing up the mast, followed by Friar Tuck.

Steevens and I leapt toward the only lifeboat on board. The
Fleming's formidable arms were sliding it toward the water when
we were rooted to the deck by astonishment and terror. Something
gray, shiny, and indistinct, like glass, suddenly surrounded the lifeboat, the chains snapped, an unknown force tilted the schooner to
port, and a wave broke over the deck and poured into the open sail-
locker. An instant later, the lifeboat had vanished without a trace.

Jellewyn and Friar Tuck came down from the mast. They had seen no one.

Jellewyn took a rag and wiped his hands, shuddering. He had found the sail and the rigging splattered with warm blood.

In a faltering voice, I recited the prayer for the dead, interspersing the holy words with curses against the ocean and its mystery.

It was late when Jellewyn and I went topside, having decided to spend the night at the helm together.

At one moment I began to weep and he patted me affectionately on the shoulder. I became a little calmer and lit my pipe.

We had nothing to say to each other. He seemed to have fallen asleep at the helm. I stared into the darkness.

I leaned over the port rail and was suddenly petrified by an unearthly sight. I straightened up, uttering a muffled exclamation.

"Have you seen it, Jellewyn, or are my eyes playing tricks on me?"

"You're not mistaken," he said softly, "but for the love of Christ don't say anything about it to the others. Their minds are already close enough to madness."

I had to make a great effort to go back to the rail. Jellewyn stood beside me.

The bottom of the sea was aflame with a vast bloody glow that spread beneath the schooner; the light slid under the keel and illuminated the sails and rigging from below. It was as though we were on a boat in the Drury Lane Theatre, lighted by an invisible row of flares.

"Phosphorescence?" I ventured.

"Look," whispered Jellewyn.

The water had become as transparent as glass. At an enormous depth, we saw great dark masses with unreal shapes: there were manors with immense towers, gigantic domes, horribly straight streets lined with frenzied houses. We appeared to be flying over a furiously busy city at an incredible height.

"There seems to be movement," I said.

"Yes."

We could see a swarming crowd of amorphous beings engaged in some sort of feverish and infernal activity.

"Get back!" Jellewyn shouted, pulling me violently by the belt.

One of those beings was rising toward us with astounding speed. In less than a second its immense bulk had hidden the undersea city from us; it was as though a flood of ink had instantaneously spread around us.

The keel received a tremendous blow. In the crimson light, we saw three enormous tentacles, three times as high as the mainmast, hideously writhing in the air. A formidable face composed of black shadows and two eyes of liquid amber rose above the port side of the ship and gave us a terrifying look.

This lasted less than two seconds. A heavy swell was headed for us broadside.

"Helm hard to starboard!" shouted Jellewyn.

The lines holding the boom snapped, and it cut through the air like an ax. The mainmast bent almost to the breaking-point. Taut halyards broke with a sound like that of harp strings.

The awesome vision became vague. The water was foaming. To starboard, the glow ran like a burning fringe across the high, galloping crests, then abruptly vanished.

"Poor Walker, poor Turnip," said Jellewyn.

The bell rang in the forecastle: the midnight watch was beginning.

An uneventful morning followed. The sky was covered with thick, motionless clouds of a dirty, yellowish color. The air was chilly.

Toward noon, shining feebly through the mist, I saw a spot of light that might have been the sun. I decided to determine its position, despite Jellewyn's opinion that it would be meaningless.

The sea was rough. I tried to hold the horizon, but a wave would always invade my field of vision, and the horizon would leap up into the sky. Finally I succeeded. But as I was looking for the reflection of the spot of light in the mirror of the sextant, I saw a kind of white streamer quivering in front of it at a great height.

Something indefinable rushed toward me. The sextant flew into the air, I received a jarring blow on the head, and then I heard shouts, sounds of struggle, and more shouts.

I was not exactly unconscious. I was sprawled against the deckhouse. Bells were ringing endlessly in my ears; I even seemed to hear the solemn booming of Big Ben. Mingled with these pleasant sounds were clamors that were more alarming, but also further away.

I was about to make an effort to stand up when I felt myself seized and lifted. I began howling and kicking with all my returning strength.

"Thank God!" said Jellewyn. "He's not dead!"

I managed to open my eyelids, which felt as though they were made of lead. A patch of yellow sky was cut by diagonal ropes. I saw Jellewyn staggering as though he were drunk.

"For the love of God, what's happened to us?" I asked dolefully, for Jellewyn's face was streaming with tears.

Without answering, he led me to my cabin.

I saw that one of the two bunks was occupied by a motionless mass.

At this point, I completely regained my senses. I put my hands over my heart. I had just recognized Steevens' hideously swollen face.

Jellewyn gave me a drink.

"This is the end," I heard him say.

"The end," I repeated stupidly, trying to understand.

He put cold compresses on Steevens' face.

"Where's Friar Tuck?" I asked.

Jellewyn sobbed aloud.

"Like . . . the others. . . . We'll never see him again!"

He told me, in a tear-choked voice, the little he knew.

It had happened with incredible swiftness, like all the successive tragedies that now formed our existence. Jellewyn had been below, checking the oilcups, when he heard shouts of distress from above. He hurried topside and saw Steevens furiously struggling inside a kind of silvery bubble. A moment later, Steevens collapsed and lay still. Friar Tuck was gone; his metal palms and sail-needles were scattered around the mainmast. Fresh blood was dripping from the starboard rail. I was lying unconscious against the deckhouse. He knew nothing more.

"When Steevens comes to, he'll give us more information," I said weakly.

"When he comes to!" Jellewyn exclaimed bitterly. "His body is nothing but a horrible bag filled with broken bones and crushed organs. Because of his Herculean constitution he's still breathing, but for all practical purposes he's dead, dead like the others."

We let the *Mainz Psalter* sail as she pleased. She had little canvas spread, and she drifted sideways almost as much as she moved forward.

"Everything seems to show that the danger is mainly on deck," said Jellewyn, as though talking to himself.

We were still in my cabin when evening came.

Steevens' breathing was labored and painful to hear. We had to keep wiping away the bloody froth that ran from his mouth.

"I won't sleep," I said.

"Neither will I," replied Jellewyn.

We had closed the portholes despite the stuffy atmosphere. The ship was rolling a little.

Toward two in the morning, when an invincible torpor was dulling my thoughts and I was sinking into a half-sleep already packed with nightmares, I suddenly started.

Jellewyn was wide awake. He was looking up in terror at the gleaming wooden ceiling.

"Someone's walking on deck," he said softly.

I seized the rifle.

"That's useless. Let's stay where we are. . . . Ah, they're making themselves at home now!"

We heard rapid footsteps on the deck. It sounded as though a busy crowd were moving around.

"I thought so," said Jellewyn. He laughed. "We're gentlemen of leisure now: we have others working for us."

The sounds had become more precise. The helm creaked; an arduous maneuver was being carried out in the head wind.

"They're unfurling the sails!"

"Of course."

The ship pitched heavily, then listed to starboard.

"A starboard tack, in this wind," Jellewyn said approvingly. "They're monsters, brutes drunk with blood and murder, but they're sailors. The most skillful yachtsman in England, sailing a racer built last year, wouldn't dare to sail so close to the wind. And what does it prove?"

No longer understanding anything, I made a gesture of discouragement.

He answered his own question: "It proves that we have a fixed destination, and that they want us to arrive somewhere."

After reflecting for a moment I said, "It also proves that they're neither demons nor ghosts, but beings like us."

"Oh, that's saying a lot!"

"I'm expressing myself badly. What I mean is that they're material beings, with only natural forces at their command."

"I've never doubted that," Jellewyn said calmly.

Toward five in the morning, another maneuver was carried out, making the schooner roll heavily. Jellewyn opened a porthole. A dirty dawn was filtering through compact clouds.

We cautiously ventured up on deck. It was tidy and deserted.

The ship was hove to.

Two calm days went by.

The nocturnal maneuvers had not been resumed, but Jellewyn pointed out that a very swift current was taking us in what should have been a northwesterly direction.

Steevens was still breathing, but more feebly. Jellewyn had brought a portable medicine chest in his baggage, and from time to time he gave the dying man an injection. We spoke little. I think we had even stopped thinking. For my part, I was stupefied by alcohol, for I was drinking whisky by the pint.

One day, when I was drunkenly cursing the schoolmaster and promising to smash his face into a thousand pieces, I happened to mention the books he had brought on board.

Jellewyn leapt forward and shook me vigorously.

"Careful, I'm the captain," I said gently.

"To hell with captains like you! What did you say? Books?"

"Yes, in his cabin. There's a trunk full of them. I saw them myself. They're written in Latin; I don't know that pharmacist's jargon."

"Well *I* know it. Why didn't you tell me about those books?"

"What difference would it have made?" I muttered thickly. "Anyway, I'm the captain. . . . You . . . you ought to . . . respect me."

"You damned drunk!" he said angrily, going off toward the schoolmaster's cabin. I heard him step inside and close the door behind him.

The inert and pitiful Steevens was my companion during the hours of drinking that followed.

"I'm the captain of this ship," I mumbled, "and I'll. . . . I'll complain to the authorities. . . . He called me a . . . a damned drunk. . . . I'm the master after God on my ship. . . . Isn't that right, Steevens? You're a witness. . . . He insulted me basely. . . . I'll put him in irons. . . ."

Then I slept a little.

When Jellewyn came in to swallow a hasty meal of hardtack and corned beef, his cheeks were flushed and his eyes were glittering.

"Mr. Ballister," he said, "did the schoolmaster ever tell you about a crystal object, a box, perhaps?"

"He didn't confide in me," I grunted, still remembering his rudeness.

"Ah, if only I'd had those books before all these things began happening!"

"Have you found anything?" I asked.

"I'm getting a few glimmers. . . . A path is opening up. It's probably senseless, but in any case it's amazing, more amazing than you can possibly imagine!"

He was terribly excited. I was unable to get anything more out of him. He hurried back to the schoolmaster's cabin, and I left him alone.

I did not see him again until the beginning of evening, and then only for a few minutes. He came in to fill a kerosene lamp and did not say a word.

I slept until late the next morning. As soon as I woke up, I went to the schoolmaster's cabin.

Jellewyn was not there.

Seized with painful anxiety, I called him. There was no answer. I ran all over the ship shouting his name, even forgetting prudence to the point of going up on deck. Finally I threw myself on the floor, weeping and invoking the name of God.

I was alone on board the accursed schooner, alone with the dying Steevens.

Alone, horribly alone.

. . .

It was not until noon that I went back to the schoolmaster's cabin. My attention was immediately caught by a sheet of paper pinned to the wall. I read these words in Jellewyn's handwriting:

Mr. Ballister, I am going to the top of the mainmast. I must see something. Perhaps I shall never return. If so, forgive me for my death, which will leave you all alone, because Steevens is doomed, as you know. But quickly do what I tell you: Burn all these books; do it on the stern, far from the mainmast, and do not go near the edge of the ship. I think an effort will be made to prevent you from burning the books. Everything inclines me to believe it. But burn them, burn them quickly, even at the risk of setting fire to the ship. Will it save you? I dare not hope so. Perhaps Providence will give you a chance. May God have mercy on you, Mr. Ballister, and on all of us!

Duke ——,* known as Jellewyn.

When I returned to my cabin, shaken by that extraordinary farewell and cursing the shameful drunkenness that had probably prevented my valiant companion from awakening me, I no longer heard Steevens' irregular breathing. I leaned over his poor, contorted face. He, too, was gone.

I took two cans of gasoline from the little engine room, and, moved by some sort of providential instinct, I started the engine and turned it up to full speed.

I went back to the helm, piled the books on the deck, and poured gasoline on them.

A high, pale flame arose.

At that moment, there was a cry from the sea, and I heard someone call my name. Then I, too, cried out, in surprise and fear: in the wake of the *Mainz Psalter*, a hundred feet back, swam the schoolmaster.

The flames crackled; the books were rapidly being transformed into ashes.

The infernal swimmer shouted curses and supplications.

"Ballister! I'll make you rich, richer than all men on earth put

---

* Here appears a name that we shall not reveal, in order not to rekindle the sorrow of a great and noble reigning family. Jellewyn bore a heavy weight of guilt, but his death brilliantly redeemed him.

together! I'll make you die, you imbecile, in horrible tortures that are unknown on your accursed planet! I'll make you a king, Ballister, king of a formidable kingdom! Ah, you swine, hell would be sweeter to you than what I have in store for you!"

He swam desperately, but made little progress in overtaking the ship.

Suddenly the schooner made a few strange movements and was shaken by dull blows. I saw the water rising toward me: the ship was being pulled toward the bottom of the sea.

"Ballister, listen to me!" howled the schoolmaster.

He was quickly drawing closer. His face was horribly impassive, but his eyes were burning with unbearable brightness.

Then, in the middle of a mass of hot ashes, I saw a piece of parchment curl up and reveal a sparkling object. I remembered Jellewyn's words. The specially constructed book had been hiding the crystal box he had mentioned to me.

"The crystal box!" I exclaimed.

The schoolmaster heard me. He shrieked like a madman, and I saw an incredible sight: he stood on the water with his hands outstretched like threatening claws.

"It's knowledge, the greatest knowledge of all, that you're about to destroy, you damned fool!" he roared.

Shrill yodels were now coming toward me from all points of the horizon.

The first waves broke over the deck.

I leapt into the flames and smashed the crystal box with my heel.

I had a feeling of collapse, and terrible nausea. Sky and water blended in a flashing chaos, an immense clamor shook the air. I began a frightful fall into darkness. . . .

And here I am. I've told you everything now. I woke up on your ship. I'm going to die. Have I been dreaming? I wish I could believe it.

But I'm going to die among men, on my own earth. Ah, how happy I am!

It was Briggs, the cabin boy of the *North Caper,* who had first sighted Ballister. The boy had just stolen an apple from the galley and was about to eat it, huddled among some coils of cable, when he saw Ballister swimming sluggishly a few yards from the ship.

Briggs began shouting at the top of his lungs, for he saw that the swimmer was about to be drawn into the wash of the propeller.

Ballister was pulled out of the water. He was unconscious: his swimming movements had been automatic, as sometimes happens with very strong swimmers.

There was no ship in sight and no trace of wreckage on the water. But the cabin boy said that he had seen a ship as transparent as glass—those are his own words—rise up off the port beam, then sink below the surface. This earned him a slap from Captain Cormon, to teach him not to tell such wild stories.

We managed to pour a little whisky down Ballister's throat. Rose, the engineer, gave him his bunk, and we covered him warmly.

He soon passed from unconsciousness into deep, feverish sleep. We were waiting, with curiosity, for him to awaken when a terrible incident took place.

This is now being told by John Copeland, first mate of the *North Caper*. It was I, who, with Seaman Jolks, saw the mystery and terror that came out of the night.

The last bearing taken during the day had located the *North Caper* at longitude 22° west and latitude 60° north.

I took the helm myself, having decided to spend the night on deck, because the night before we had seen long ice floes glittering in the moonlight on the northwest horizon.

Jolks hung up the running lights, and since he had a violent toothache that was made worse by the warmth of the forecastle, he came to smoke his pipe beside me. I was glad, because a lonely watch can be terribly monotonous when it lasts all night.

I must tell you that, while the *North Caper* is a good, sturdy ship, she is not a trawler of the latest model, even though she has been equipped with radio. The spirit of fifty years ago still weighs down on her, leaving her with sails that supplement the limited power of her steam engine. She does not have the tall, enclosed ungainly cabin that is perched in the middle of the deck on most modern trawlers like a ludicrous little cottage. Her helm is still on the stern, facing the sea, the wind, and the spray.

I am giving you this description so that you will know that we witness the incomprehensible scene not from a glassed-in observation post, but from the deck itself. Without this explanation, my story would not seem believable to those familiar with the design of steam trawlers.

There was no moonlight because the sky was too overcast; only the diffused glow of the clouds and the phosphorescence of the wave crests made it possible to see anything.

It was somewhere around ten o'clock. The men were sunk deep in their first sleep. Jolks, absorbed in his toothache, was softly moaning and swearing. The binnacle light made his tense face stand out from the surrounding darkness.

Suddenly I saw his grimace of pain change to an expression of astonishment, then of genuine terror. His pipe fell from his open mouth. This struck me as so comical that I made a mocking remark to him. His only reply was to point to the starboard light.

My pipe joined his when I saw what he was pointing to: clutching the shrouds a few inches below the light, two wet hands were emerging from the darkness.

Suddenly the hands let go and a dark form leapt onto the deck. Jolks quickly stepped aside, and the binnacle light shone on the intruder's face. To our indescribable amazement, we saw a kind of clergyman, wearing a black tail-coat and streaming with sea water. He had a small head with eyes like glowing coals that were staring straight at us.

Jolks made a move to take out his fishing knife, but he did not have time: the apparition leapt on him and knocked him down. At the same time, the binnacle light was shattered. A few moments later there was a shrill cry from the forecastle, where the cabin boy had been sitting up with Ballister:

"He's killing him! Help!"

Ever since I had had to stop some serious brawls among members of the crew, I had made it a habit to carry my revolver at night. It was a powerful weapon, and I shot well with it. I cocked it.

The ship was filled with a confused clamor.

A short time after this series of events, a gust of wind ripped a gash in the clouds and a beam of moonlight followed the ship like a spotlight.

I could already hear the captain's swearing above Briggs's cries of alarm when to my right I heard soft footsteps and saw the clergyman leap over the side and into the water.

I saw his small head rise on the crest of a wave. I calmly aimed at it and fired. He uttered a strange howl, and the wave carried him toward the side of the ship.

Jolks appeared beside me. Although he was still a little dazed, he was wielding a grappling iron. The body was now floating alongside the ship, bumping against it. The grappling iron bit into the clothes and pulled up its prey with surprising ease.

Jolks dropped a shapeless wet bundle on the deck, saying that it felt as light as a feather. Captain Cormon came out of the forecastle, holding a lighted lantern.

"Someone tried to kill our shipwreck victim!" he said.

"We've got the bandit," I said. "He came out of the sea . . ."

"You're crazy, Copeland!"

"Look at him, captain. I shot him and. . . ."

We leaned over the pitiful remains, but we immediately straightened up again, shouting like madmen.

The clothes were empty; two artificial hands and a wax head were attached to them. My bullet had gone through the wig and broken the nose.

You already know Ballister's story. He told it to us when he woke up toward the end of that infernal night. He spoke serenely, with a kind of happiness.

We took devoted care of him. There were two holes in his left shoulder, as though he had been stabbed twice, but we would have saved him if we had been able to stop his bleeding, because no essential organs had been damaged.

After having talked so much, he lapsed into a coma. When he came out of it later, he asked how he had been injured. Briggs was the only one with him at the time. Glad to have a chance to make himself interesting, he replied that in the middle of the night he had seen a dark shape rush into the forecastle and strike Ballister. He then told him about the shot and showed him the grotesque remains.

At this sight, Ballister cried out in terror.

"The schoolmaster! The schoolmaster!"

He fell into a painful fever and did not regain consciousness until six days later, in the maritime hospital in Galway, where he kissed the image of Christ and died.

. . .

The tragic mannequin was taken to Reverend Leemans, a worthy ecclesiastic who has been all over the world and knows many of the secrets of savage lands and the sea.

He examined it for a long time.

"What can have been inside it?" asked Archie Reines. "There surely was *something* in it. It was alive."

"Yes, it was alive all right, I can tell you that," grumbled Jolks, rubbing his red, swollen neck.

Reverend Leemans sniffed the thing like a dog, then cast it aside with disgust.

"I thought so," he said.

We also sniffed it.

"It smells of formic acid," I said.

"And phosphorus," added Reines.

Captain Cormon reflected for a moment, then his lips quivered a little when he said, "It smells like an octopus."

Leemans stared at him.

"On the last day of Creation," he said, "it is from the sea that God will cause the Blasphemous Beast to appear. Let us not try to anticipate destiny with impious inquiries."

"But . . . ," began Reines.

" *'Who is this that darkeneth counsel by words without knowledge?'* "

Before the Holy Word, we bowed our heads and gave up trying to understand.

Appendix I

The Two Witchcrafts

Throughout history, society's attitude toward those steeped in arcane knowledge has varied greatly. Nowadays we generally regard sorcerers and "wise women" with suspicion, but in ancient Egypt a politically powerful brotherhood of priests utilized the techniques of magic illusionry to maintain the belief quotient of their congregants (a system stylistically reminiscent of O. Z. Diggs, that canny carnival trickster better known as the Wizard of Oz).

But during the Middle Ages, both church and state opposed the practice of Wicca, often called "the old religion." It is from this period of repression that were born the paraphernalia of Satanism, black magic, and that witchcraft which nowadays is exclusively associated with evil.

"The old religion" is an apt name for old-style witchcraft. Anthropologists have traced its practice at least as far back as paleolithic and neolithic times. In our science-fiction novel, *The Masters of Solitude,* Parke Godwin and I referred to the Wiccan religion as "circle worship," a referent that reflects its structural origin when primitive hunters and farmers sat about a bonfire honoring the slaughtered stag they fed upon. The head of the tribe wore its antlers and, in his guise as the Horned God, led his people in ecstatic song and dance that celebrated the beast's speed and strength, which, through ingestion, they inherited. The rationales of cannibalism and lycanthropy are tacitly implied in this occult rite, but ironically, so is transubstantiation.

Fair enough. Many Christian traditions derive from pagan myths, a fact that anthropologist Margaret Murray indicates was a sign of early church (and state) compromise in order to promulgate conversion. It is probable that most peasants accommodated the new religion by practicing it in tandem with the old faith. Murray maintains that the simple peasant girl known as Joan of Arc was in fact both a Wiccan and a Christian.

Circle worship's transubstantiation myth makes sense anthropologically, but reverence of the beast that sustains life, rooted as it is in the material (i.e., fleshly) sphere, is a concept that the church fathers perceived as antithetical to the spiritual state. (In *The Genealogy of Morals,* Friedrich Nietzsche contends that the Old Testament distinguishes between good and bad, but in the New Testament bad gives way to what the philosopher regards as the noxious concept of evil.) In this fashion, the conceptual groundwork was laid for the medieval persecutions of the Wiccans, many of whom rebelled from that repression which the church came to symbolize. The black mass, with its parody of the sacrament of communion, sprang into being and the antlered circle god metamorphosed into the Devil, complete with tails and horns. (Satan himself is a cultural Johnny-come-lately; the Roman Catholic Church did not officially admit his existence till the Council of Toledo in A.D. 447.)

Thus it is that historian Pennethorne Hughes accurately (and presumably pejoratively) describes the diabolical mode of modern witchcraft as "the degeneration of one of the earliest stages of religious belief and practice."

Appendix II

Notes

The Traveler (pages 49–62)   *Dark Carnival*, Ray Bradbury's first volume of collected tales (Arkham House, 1947), contains in addition to "The Traveler" two other stories about Cecy's bizarre family of vampires and witches: "Uncle Einar" and "The Homecoming," both of which were reprinted in *The October Country*. Cecy, an important subsidiary character in "The Homecoming," is also the protagonist of "The April Witch," a story that may be found in another Bradbury collection, *The Golden Apples of the Sun.*

Sanguinarius (pages 160–93)   Ray Russell appends an author's note to his tale: "Without exception, every person and place named in this story existed. The main lineaments of the narrative are reconstructed from events that did, in fact, occur. Elisabeth Bathory died, as close as can be determined, on August 21, 1614, in a walled-up apartment of Castle Csejthe, county of Nyitra, northwestern Hungary. After her death, the village priest testified that he had been savagely attacked by a multitude of cats which, after biting and scratching him severely, vanished like mist."

Vasilisa and the Witch (pages 194–200)   The witch Baba Yaga and her strange hut on fowl's legs is perhaps best remembered today as the indirect inspiration for the "programme" of the penultimate movement of Modeste Moussorgsky's series of musical portraits, *Pictures at an Exhibition*. One of the oddest aspects of the Baba Yaga legend is that questions are dangerous to her because she ages a year every time she answers one—a detail that figured importantly in the plot of my comic novel *The Amorous Umbrella* (Doubleday, 1981). But in the versions of the Vasilisa tale that I consulted, the beautiful child boldly asks Baba about the mysterious horsemen she saw in the woods and the witch readily replies with impunity. I have revised the latter portion of the tale so that it conforms with customary Baba Yaga myth.

The Tiger's Eye (pages 211–19) If L. Frank Baum intended this story to be published as one of the "Animal Fairy Tales" that ran in *The Delineator* in 1905, it is conceivable that the magazine rejected it because, compared with the other stories in the series, it is frighteningly intense. It is possible, though, that he wrote it later. When the manuscript was first discovered in 1960 in the files of Reilly & Lee, Baum's publisher, it was accompanied by a letter from the author stating that he planned to include it in the book edition of his animal stories, but this never happened. "The Tiger's Eye" first saw print in December 1962, in a special issue of *The American Book Collector* devoted to Baum, and subsequently appeared in the Spring 1979 edition of *The Baum Bugle*.

A Smell of Sulphur (pages 220–24) A pastiche is a composition in conscious imitation of another author's themes and style and does not necessarily imply parody. But in "A Smell of Sulphur" I attempted to graft a contemporary sense of spiritual ennui onto L. Frank Baum's Wicked Witch of the East, a character already dead when her feet are first seen by Dorothy Gale in *The Wizard of Oz*. And though the title refers to a throwaway line of dialogue spoken by Glinda (Billie Burke) in the famous MGM film, the tone of the tale is neither Hollywood nor Baum but runs at a tangent to both. For those unfamiliar with the Oz history developed in the many sequels to "The Wizard," the princess Ozma, rightful ruler of Oz, was kidnapped and magically transformed into a boy named Tip. The Red Witch is Glinda. In the books, Glinda is not the Good Witch of the North, but a mighty sorceress who rules in the Quadling Country, the southernmost state in the land of Oz. Just as the Munchkins' favorite color is blue and the Emerald City naturally favors green, the Quadlings prefer red.

The Up-to-Date Sorcerer (pages 357–71) *The Sorcerer,* Gilbert and Sullivan's third collaborative operetta, was premiered on November 17, 1877, at the Opéra Comique, London. The comedy is set outside the Elizabethan mansion of Sir Marmaduke Pointdextre, an elderly baronet whose son Alexis is about to be wed to Aline Sangazure, a lady of ancient lineage. Most of the villagers busily rejoice at the impending nuptials, but Constance Partlet is melancholy because of her unexpressed love for the vicar, Dr. Daly, who privately regards Constance as desirable but too young to consider as a marital candidate. Meanwhile, Sir Marmaduke and Aline's mother, Lady Sangazure, also are engaged in repressing their affection for one another. An elderly notary appears and produces the marriage contract, which the couple sign. As soon as they are alone, Alexis reveals a surprising scheme to his betrothed. Believing that the world cannot be saved until love conquers all, he has hired John Wellington Wells, of "J. W. Wells & Co., the old-established Family Sorcerers," to concoct a love potion which Alexis intends to pour into the tea at the wedding feast. Aline has grave doubts concerning the wisdom of her fiancé's plan but goes along with it like a dutiful wife-to-be. Mr. Wells conjures up a host of evil spirits to bewitch the tea, and at the end of the first act, everyone but Alexis, Aline, and Mr. Wells swallow the elixir and fall into an enchanted sleep.

The second act begins twelve hours later at midnight. As the villagers wake up, each falls in love with the first person he or she sees. This produces unexpected results: Sir Marmaduke wants to marry Constance's mother, while Constance now has her heart set upon the old, deaf notary, of whom she observes, "You're everything that I detest, but still I love you dearly!" Meanwhile, Lady Sangazure has conceived a passion for none other than Mr. Wells, the sorcerer. To make matters worse, Alexis insists that Aline prove her love to him by also swigging the elixir. She does so dutifully enough, but then falls in love with the first man she sees, Dr. Daly, the vicar, who by now has somehow divined (pun intended) the nature of the problem. When asked to remove the spell, the sorcerer says there is only one way this may be accomplished: "Or you [meaning Alexis] or I must yield up his life to

Ahrimanes. I would rather it were you. I should have no hesitation in sacrificing my own life to spare yours, but we take stock
next week, and it would not be fair on the Co." Aline objects, so
the sorcerer leaves it up to the villagers, who unanimously declare that Wells must die. As he resigns himself to his fate, the
effects of the elixir dissipate and in the midst of a general dance,
"Mr. Wells sinks through trap, amid red fire."

The problem with this ending is its unfairness. Mr. Wells com-
ports himself throughout the whole business like the reputable
tradesperson he is; it is Alexis who, in true Gilbertian fashion,
behaves stupidly and selfishly, and yet Gilbert hardly could consign his hero to the fires of hell. In my novel *The Incredible Umbrella* (Doubleday, 1979), my dimension-traveling protagonist J.
Adrian Fillmore (Gad, what a name!) tried to warn John Wellington Wells of the danger of treating an entire village with love
philtre, but Wells replied with a laugh, "That happened to me
some time ago. I made up that whole silly business of sacrificing
myself! Fact is, it was an easy spell to remove—but I didn't want
to get involved in any lawsuits."

Dr. Asimov's solution to the problem strikes me as ingenious
and quite plausible, though it was the great G&S comedian Mar-
tyn Green who may have devised the most amusing method for
making Wells's damnation palatable. As the cast took its curtain
call at the close of a revival production of *The Sorcerer,* Green
reappeared with a sign: "Come down and see me sometime!"

Ever the Faith Endures (pages 420–30) Manly Wade Wellman
wrote the following afterword to this tale: "This story is in some
degree a love letter to England, where I've been happy on a
number of visits. I think the stuff about Celtic pagan beliefs is
authentic. One person who read it questioned Matthew
Hopkins's witch-finding in 1643, saying he's not on record until
1645; but since 1645 was the year he found his most witches, I
figure he was at the job before that. I like 1643, since that was
the year my own first Wellman ancestor came to Jamestown in
Virginia—and he had to take a special oath of allegiance, too,
and I've always wondered why.

"Not that I'm Wofford Belson in this story. As to Anne Belstone, she may resemble a personable Englishwoman I know,
who is very much up on folk things there."

Doctor Faustus Journeys to Hell (pages 442–45) This episode, comprising the fifteenth chapter, appears in the second section of the *Faustbuch*. The anonymous author's declaration that Faustus was correct in presuming the adventure a dream is more than a moralistic aside. An internal consistency supports the claim, most especially the surprising detail that some of the damned, at least, are allowed to slake their infernal thirst and bathe in the cool waters of the stream surrounding Hell, a notion so at variance with other depictions of the Pit that one concludes it was included solely to delude Faustus into thinking that, after all, damnation is not untempered with mercy.

Appendix III

Suggestions for Further Reading and Viewing

Below is a list of thirteen works of fiction and a like number of films about black magic, sorcery, and witchcraft that I think worth recommending. I have not striven for completeness but have merely been idiosyncratic. If something obvious appears to be missing, it is either because I am not a fan of it or else the work is so well known that it hardly needs my sanction—as, for instance, *Lord of the Rings, The Wizard of Oz,* or *Snow White and the Seven Dwarfs.*

FICTION

BRADBURY, RAY, *Something Wicked This Way Comes.* Though I feel the Walt Disney film of Bradbury's novel deserved a better fate than it got, it cannot begin to compare to the eerie original, which tells of a shivery traveling carnival run by Messrs. Cooger and Dark —the very dark carnival that lent its name to Bradbury's first collection of short stories.

CARR, JOHN DICKSON, *The Burning Court.* This once controversial murder mystery by the master of the impossible crime and locked-room novel is an atmospheric tale of evil that may or may not be the result of witchcraft.

CODY, C. S., *The Witching Night,* is a nightmarish page-turner that begins with murder caused by modern witchcraft and culminates with a race against time as the hero tries to save himself from the same terrifying fate.

EDDISON, E. R., *The Worm Ouroborous*. Long before *Lord of the Rings* achieved its then overdue, well-deserved popularity, many fantasy fans championed this mammoth novel of sorcerous warfare. Readers patient enough to tolerate Eddison's quasi-Biblical language and pacing will be rewarded by epic characters engaged in sweeping adventure. This is not Hollywood hyperbolization. See, for instance, Eddison's dizzying mountain-climbing sequence complete with a battle-to-the-death with one of the most vividly nauseating trolls you're ever likely to encounter in all of fantasy literature.

GARNER, ALAN, *The Weirdstone of Brisingamen*. Though obviously influenced by J. R. R. Tolkien's *Lord of the Rings,* this suspenseful fantasy novel has its own undeniable power. Warring warlocks, a very nasty witch, and terrifying gigantic creatures known as the Mara terrorize the English countryside, but a hardy band of adventurers led by two plucky youngsters combats the forces of darkness. The sequence where the heroes must crawl underground to save their skins is a tour de force of claustrophobic horror.

HUGHES, PENNETHORNE, *Witchcraft,* is an authoritative and eminently readable history and evaluation of the beliefs of the Wiccans. (See Appendix I, pages 518–19.)

MANVELL, ROGER, *The Dreamers*. In this little-known but effective horror novel, an aboriginal witch doctor plans murder by the unusual device of a recurring nightmare that grows progressively more frightening each time it is dreamed.

MERRITT, ABRAHAM, *Burn Witch Burn*. Merritt is best remembered as a "lost-lands" fantasist, but his penultimate novel, set in contemporary America, is an eerie tale of gangsters, witchcraft, and animated, murderous figurines. It was filmed as "The Devil-Doll" (see page 528).

MOORCOCK, MICHAEL, the "Elric" series. Black magicians abound in the numerous interconnected fantasies of the contemporary British novelist Michael Moorcock, who rewrote and expanded two Elric books into six (to my mind somewhat attenuating their power). They are diverting escape reading that culminates in a huge climax of Götterdämmerungian proportions. In sequence, the

Elric books are *Elric of Melnibone*, *The Sailor on the Seas of Fate*, *Weird of the White Wolf*, *The Sleeping Sorceress*, *Bane of the Black Sword*, and *Stormbringer*. Elric also makes guest appearances in other Moorcock works.

MURRAY, MARGARET, *The God of the Witches*, is a fascinating study of European witchcraft from its paleolithic roots to the medieval period. (See Appendix I, pages 518–19.)

VOLSKY, PAULA, *The Luck of Relian Kru*. This author's witty and beautifully wrought fantasy novels include *Curse of the Witch Queen*, *The Sorcerer's Lady*, *The Sorcerer's Heir*, and *King of Darkness*. My personal favorite, *The Luck of Relian Kru*, is the wildly imaginative tale of a luckless young gentleman who, while being followed by a suave assassin, becomes embroiled in a titanic feud between an icily remote witch and a sybaritic warlock.

WHARTON, EDITH, "Bewitched," is a powerful short story of rural American witchcraft, one of several first-rate ghost stories by the renowned author of *Ethan Frome*, *The House of Mirth*, and *The Age of Innocence*.

WHITE, T. H., *The Once and Future King* and *The Book of Merlyn*, are the best-selling novels that are intimately associated with the Alan Jay Lerner–Frederick Loewe musical *Camelot*, but when the author prepared "King" for publication, he greatly rewrote and chopped up three earlier books, which I, as a completist and purist, recommend to those hearty collectors who can find copies. They are, in sequence, *The Sword in the Stone*, *The Witch of the Wood*, and *The Ill-Made Knight*. Once read, they may be followed by "Candle in the Wind" (the final section of *The Once and Future King)* and then by *The Book of Merlyn*. In the latter volume, critics noted the reappearance of the same "ant episode" that White employed in the opening section of "King," but this chapter does not occur in *The Sword in the Stone*, which features a wholly different magical adventure in its place.

FILMS

Bedknobs and Broomsticks (1971) is a Walt Disney extravaganza that, despite echoes of *Mary Poppins*, is an engaging fantasy on its own merits. Angela Lansbury is a resourceful witch who saves England from invasion via some eye-popping special effects. Avoid the cut rerelease; the original runs 117 minutes.

Black Sunday (1961, Italy) is an uneven but frequently chilling tale of a dead witch (Barbara Steele) who returns to wreak vengeance on the descendants of those who killed her.

Burn, Witch, Burn (1962, British), a gruesomely effective chiller about witchcraft in academia, is not based on the Abraham Merritt novel of that title, but on Fritz Leiber, Jr.'s *Conjure Wife*, which was filmed before as *Weird Woman* (1944) and later as *Witches' Brew* (1980). This is generally regarded as the best version.

Day of Wrath (1943, Danish), one of the handful of films made by the great Danish director Carl Dreyer, is a grim drama of a condemned witch and the curse she hurls on her persecutor.

The Devil-Doll (1936), loosely based on Abraham Merritt's *Burn Witch Burn* (see above), is the eerie tale of an escapee from Devil's Island who seeks revenge through voodoo. Its highlight: an uncampy performance by Lionel Barrymore in drag.

I Married a Witch (1942) is a delightful comedy-fantasy directed by René Clair and starring Fredric March, Susan Hayward, Robert Benchley, Cecil Kellaway, and Veronica Lake as the Salem sorceress who returns to earth to haunt the descendants of her Puritan persecutors. Based on *The Passionate Witch*, Thorne Smith's final novel (completed by Norman Matson), this is the movie that many claim inspired the Elizabeth Montgomery TV sitcom *Bewitched*.

Isle of the Dead (1945) is not so much about witchcraft as the fear of witchcraft, but this Val Lewton film starring Boris Karloff is effectively eerie and laden with menace.

Jack the Giant Killer (1962), originally pitched to young audiences, is a rousing fantasy-adventure with marvelously horrifying special effects and a ripsnorting performance by Torin Thatcher as one of the most evil magicians who ever skuldugged! (He plays a similar villain in *The Seventh Voyage of Sindbad*, a film that has much in common with *Jack the Giant Killer*.) Avoid the horrendous rerelease, which dubs terrible songs over the dialogue.

Night of the Demon (1958) is an effective updating of M. R. James's esteemed occult tale "Casting the Runes." This story about sorcerous conjuration boasts an excellent cast (Dana Andrews, Niall McGinnis, Peggy Cummings, Athene Seyler, Maurice Denham) and a distinguished director, Jacques Tourneur (who directed the original version of *The Cat People).* The demon that actually appears is a letdown but reportedly the studio grafted on this visual without Tourneur's knowledge or consent. Normally, I do not support censorship, but this is an exception. I hope that when the film is released for home viewing, the distributor will excise that repulsively ineffectual shot.

The Raven (1963) is one of Roger Corman's spoofs of the horror genre, and is fairly amusing. The opening gag is a howl and the hilarious climax features a three-way sorcerous duel between Boris Karloff, Peter Lorre, and Vincent Prince. Jack Nicholson's in it, too, but that fact doesn't hurt the proceedings overmuch.

Return to Oz (1985) is the underappreciated nonmusical sequel to *The Wizard of Oz* that Walt Disney Studios launched and then decided to scuttle (in terms of promotion) in favor of its next release, an inferior version of Lloyd Alexander's *The Black Cauldron. Return to Oz* was never meant to copy the style of the MGM classic, but instead is closer to that of the original L. Frank Baum books. Jean Marsh plays Mombi, a witch with a weakness for stealing and wearing other women's heads. The scene when her headless trunk gropes menacingly for Dorothy is truly horrifying.

Sunset Boulevard (1950) may seem a whimsical addendum to this list, but I mention it in earnest. The unsavory hold that faded silent star Norma Desmond (Gloria Swanson) has over her unsuccessful screenwriter-lover (William Holden) strikes me as a form of unholy possession. For that matter, I might also make a case for including in this list Mercedes McCambridge's frighteningly witchlike performance in Nicholas Ray's offbeat western, *Johnny Guitar.*

The Thief of Bagdad (1940, British) is chock-full of dazzling color, special effects, a gigantic genie (Rex Ingram), the heroic "elephant boy" Sabu, and perhaps the screen's quintessential evil sorcerer (Conrad Veidt) in a wonderful Arabian Nights extravaganza.